W9-CMN-984

TRACE
&AURA

ALSO BY PATRICK BOUCHERON

France in the World
(editor)

Machiavelli:
The Art of Teaching People What to Fear

The Power of Images:
Siena, 1338

TRACE
&AURA

The Recurring Lives of
St. Ambrose of Milan

PATRICK BOUCHERON

TRANSLATED FROM THE FRENCH BY

LARA VERGNAUD
& WILLARD WOOD

OTHER PRESS | NEW YORK

Originally published in French as *La trace et l'aura: Vies posthumes d'Ambroise de Milan (IVᵉ–XVIᵉ siècle)* in 2019 by Éditions du Seuil, Paris.
Copyright © Éditions du Seuil, 2019
English translation copyright © Lara Vergnaud and Willard Wood, 2022

Juan José Saer epigraph from *The Witness* translated by Margaret Jull Costa (London: Serpent's Tail, 2009).

Production editor: Yvonne E. Cárdenas
Text designer: Julie Fry
This book was set in Empirica and Legacy.

10 9 8 7 6 5 4 3 2 1

All rights reserved. No part of this publication may be reproduced or transmitted in any form or by any means, electronic or mechanical, including photocopying, recording, or by any information storage and retrieval system, without written permission from Other Press LLC, except in the case of brief quotations in reviews for inclusion in a magazine, newspaper, or broadcast. Printed in the United States of America on acid-free paper. For information write to Other Press LLC, 267 Fifth Avenue, 6th Floor, New York, NY 10016. Or visit our Web site: www.otherpress.com

Library of Congress Cataloging-in-Publication Data
Names: Boucheron, Patrick, author. | Wood, Willard, translator. | Vergnaud, Lara, translator.
Title: Trace and aura : the recurring lives of St. Ambrose of Milan / Patrick Boucheron ; translated from the French by Lara Vergnaud and Willard Wood.
Other titles: Trace et l'aura. English
Description: New York : Other Press, [2022] | "Originally published in French as La trace et l'aura : vies posthumes d'Ambroise de Milan (IVᵉ - XVIᵉ siècle) in 2019 by Éditions du Seuil, Paris." | Includes bibliographical references and index.
Identifiers: LCCN 2021031270 (print) | LCCN 2021031271 (ebook) | ISBN 9781635420067 (hardcover) | ISBN 9781635420074 (ebook)
Subjects: LCSH: Ambrose, Saint, Bishop of Milan, -397—Influence. | Bishops—Italy—Milan—Biography. | Church history—Primitive and early church, ca. 30-600. | Christianity and politics—Italy—Milan—History—To 1500.
Classification: LCC BR1720.A5 B6813 2022 (print) | LCC BR1720.A5 (ebook) | DDC 270.2092 [B]—dc23
LC record available at https://lccn.loc.gov/2021031270
LC ebook record available at https://lccn.loc.gov/2021031271

Non vacant tempora nec otiose volvuntur per sensus nostros: faciunt in animo mira opera.

— AUGUSTINE, *Confessions*

They're gonna find him spewed all over Milan in bits and pieces, jigsaw style. Anybody pushes me too far, I don't correct them anymore. I dynamite them, atomize them, ventilate them.

— after MICHEL AUDIARD, *Monsieur Gangster*

In the depths of memory, the sky. Remains.
Remains of light we don't know what to do with.

— HENRI MICHAUX, *Coups d'arrêt*

But it is not easy. These assiduous memories cannot always be grasped; at times they seem clear, austere, precise, all of a piece; but as soon as I make a move to take hold of them and fix them, they start to unfold and expand, and details which, seen from a distance, had been obscured by the whole, then multiply, proliferate and take on an importance they hitherto lacked. There comes a point when I grow dizzy and find it difficult to establish a hierarchy amongst all these presences competing for my attention.

— JUAN JOSÉ SAER, *The Witness*

CONTENTS

PART FOUR

AMBROSE'S FOOT SOLDIERS
(Fourth to Fifteenth Century)

WHAT BRINGS AMBROSE TO LIFE

233

PART FIVE

AMBROSIAN ANAMNESIS
(Fifteenth to Fourth Century)

BECAUSE IT ALWAYS STARTS BEFORE THE BEGINNING
(AND SOMETHING'S ALWAYS MISSING IN THE END)

321

To access the bibliography, please visit
https://otherpress.com/ambrose/

TRACE
&AURA

That Which Returns
to the Same Place

A child cries out.

In Milan, in 374, a child cries out his name.

Ambrose hears it. He understands where it comes from, this cry that cuts through the crowd, shaking it, establishing it. For from the moment the child cried out *Ambrosius episcopus*, the small, unruly flock of Milan's Christians became a people, his people, and Ambrose their bishop. A few seconds earlier, it was still just a crowd agitated by a thousand quarrels that, "in the greatest of turmoil," did not know to which religious leader they should turn. It sufficed for a cry to ring out, it sufficed for the child to say the name of this young patrician, Aurelius Ambrosius – Ambrose of the *gens Aurelia*, a giant of Rome, born to govern – and suddenly all the Christians of Milan torn between rival factions and opposing faiths "agreed on his name alone in shocking and incredible unanimity."

But no, he doesn't want this. They say that on this day in 374, Ambrose slipped away, they say that he resorted to ruses to discourage his followers. He brought prostitutes into his home, he tortured a man under the guise of justice, and, because making blood flow and succumbing to sex wasn't enough to make it clear that he was rejecting the weight of the ecclesiastical charge being foisted upon him – and since nobody had understood that his first maneuver, his decision "to embrace the profession of philosopher," was also a provocation – he fled.

For centuries, every detail of this episode of the *Vita Ambrosii* written by Ambrose's secretary and biographer Paulinus of Milan has been painstakingly scrutinized, passionately questioned, and tirelessly commented on. It contains one of the most influential hagiographic themes in political life: a show of renouncing power as the foundation of power. But before coming to this episode in our turn, and since we are on the brink of a book of history, but one that also intends to penetrate into the thickness of time, before leaping in, fully equipped with all the apparatuses that such expeditions of learning demand, let's paddle for a few more moments in the shallows, skimming the surface of the fiction recounted by Paulinus – here's what comes next.

Wanting to escape his fate, Ambrose "decided to flee." One night, in secret, he left the city. He was alone and trying to reach Pavia, called Ticinum in antiquity after the river crossing it, the Ticino. But though he thought he was walking toward his destination, "they found him in the morning at the so-called Roman Gate of the city of Milan... For God, who was setting up the bulwark of his Catholic Church... prevented his flight." The people took him in safe custody, waiting for the prefect Probus and the emperor Valentinian, the clement, to confirm the election of the new bishop. Ambrose would not get away.

Is Paulinus of Milan writing an account of a failed escape or is he describing the results of disorientation? Ambrose doesn't realize that his steps are taking him back to his starting point, undoubtedly because he doesn't want to believe that every road leads to the *porta Romana,* the equivalent of Paris's *voie triomphale* in the imperial capital that was Milan in the fourth century. But all paths converge: Ambrose is unable to leave the city. He is obstinately brought back. By whom? God, of course. So here we have the history of a man who cannot escape the force of his name or the place that force assigns him. Ambrose will be bishop of Milan, Milan will become Ambrose's city, and the people of Milan, still today, will call themselves Ambrosians.

For nearly fifteen years, I have obsessively explored the history of the memorative gravitation of a name around a city, of a city around a name, murmuring lines from Baudelaire: "I have more memories than if I'd lived a thousand years."[1] What a strange idea, when you think about it, to take an interest in these old refrains and, more seriously, to pretend they could be of interest to anyone else. Yet here's the thing: you can think, or dream really, all you want, but we don't choose the ghosts that haunt us. Menacing or mocking, they remain the faithful companions of our obsessions. And so, here, once again, we will read a ghost story for consenting adults.

Milan was made for this kind of bullheadedness. I chose it nearly thirty years ago precisely because it was a cold city. At the time, it was a question of selecting, heart steeled, a "terrain" for my thesis. At least that's what I naively believed, thinking it unreasonable to grow overly attached. Except, well, it didn't work out that way. Perhaps because the gentle spells cast by the Lombard capital, all the more insidious because they remain discreet, always come as a surprise. Alberto Savinio wrote it better than anyone in 1944 in *Ascolto il tuo cuore, città* (City, I listen to your heart), noting that the fiercest opponents of Stendhalian pleasure, once in Milan, convert to Stendhalism "with the same ease as one tans at the seaside."

That Which Returns to the Same Place

And so I returned to Milan, carefree, reveling in reunions, somewhat regretting the time lost and the missed opportunities – regretting them, yes, without a doubt, but not all that much – and discovered, moved, that my memories weren't that stale or faded, but that they regained form in rhythm with my steps. I returned to Milan and gave myself the gift, surreptitiously – feigning the appropriately hesitant manner of a man out for a stroll, with the vague look of a dreamer, eyes half-closed, willingly letting my feet follow ancient tracks, finding those traces I thought I'd forgotten for good – and so, once again, I gave myself the gift of the unexpected and profuse generosity of a city that imperceptibly brought me as close as possible to its heart. For Milan, whose intractable rotundity was already being lauded by Bonvesin da la Riva at the end of the thirteenth century, is one of those enveloping cities that revolves on itself like a wheel around its hub to lead you, no matter what, to its center.

Is this the metaphor represented by the return of Ambrose, incapable of loosening the city's grip, as if denied all possibility of a narrow escape? It's more than that. Ambrose can't get away from Milan for the same reason that we can't extricate ourselves from the hold of our own names. For what is a proper name, properly speaking, if not the bass line of a rhapsody, its primordial rhythm reminding every individual of the unrelenting invariability of his or her possible futures? A little like *jokari*, an old French children's game: a ball is linked by a string to a small weighted platform; and regardless of the elasticity of the string, and regardless of how hard you hit the ball with your paddle, the twirling foam sphere, whipping the air in complicated spirals, is always drawn back to the center, to the base that anchors it.

But we still need to settle on what Ambrose means to those who, in the Middle Ages, spoke and acted in his name. If, for example, we situate ourselves, as we soon will, in the mid-fifteenth century, Ambrose represents nothing more or less than the memory of a bishop, born in Treves in 339 or 340, who died in Milan in 397, hero of late Roman times, champion of the freedom of the Church, patron saint of the city, and celestial protector of its civic conscience. He is one of those patched-together rememberings through which a society invents a common past, picking out the traces of what remains available. Not every trace: this legacy is, by nature, selective. And so they patiently chose – but who and when, how, why, and under what constraints? That is, as we've seen, the point of this project – scraps of the past useful in supporting the invention of a collective identity.

The Ambrosian tradition isn't the whole of Ambrose, but nor is it a diminished Ambrose, reduced to those parts that serve. I would argue to the contrary that it is a sort of augmented reality, in which the collective memory of Ambrose grows richer and more complex and is clouded by all the other memories that, through resemblance, contiguity, or related ideas, coagulate there – that is to say, before his lifetime, the benevolent cohort of his more or less mythical predecessors, but also and especially after, all those who, among his successors, permitted themselves to use his name to pass for new Ambroses, from the Carolingian bishops of the ninth century to Carlo Borromeo in the sixteenth century. And they are, as a result, *nove sed non nova*. They are not the renewed memory of Ambrose but Ambrose himself, acting, again – a phantom in a way, who returned to Milan, like the recalcitrant bishop after his long night walking in circles.

This work of generative rememoration is anything but spontaneous: it results from an at times conscious and often contentious practice by curators of memory that we will need to identify. For the past divides as much as it unites, representing a discursive resource for any collective mobilization. Which is why we can't solely rely on the notion of civic religion to explore and understand the identification of a political conscience with the patron of the city of Milan, if only because Ambrose, one of the four Latin Doctors of the universal Church, continues to resist any local reduction of a strictly situated memory – and that is undoubtedly also what is prophesized by the fable told by Paulinus of Milan, which is in this sense a political fiction, meaning that it acts as a thought experiment putting the politics to come in written words.

What is one of the most fundamental worries of our day? It resides no doubt in what Jacques Derrida called, back in 1994, the "grave question of the name":[2] when one starts to act *in the name* of a value, allegiance, or religion, and when one no longer recognizes oneself therein, what should be done politically with this thing in the name of which one is acting? We should in no case ever "treat as an accident the force of the name in what happens,"[3] just as we should always take seriously those who claim to speak *in place* of another. Here, we are undoubtedly right up against the venomous heart of the task that will busy us in the pages that follow: to dispel the aura of a proper name that envelops the places it beleaguers in a fog so thick as to render their lineaments indistinct, and, by consequence, teach ourselves to no longer be governed by elusive fictions.

What do they call "Ambrosian" in Milan? The particularity of its liturgy or the pride of its clergy? The *libertas* demanded by its Church or the civic rights of which its government boasts? All this at once, no doubt, from the moment this distant connection is made a cause of pride. The name Ambrose designates nothing other than this vagueness – a halo of uncertain meaning that creeps in and takes us over. Today still, with two soccer clubs from the Lombard capital playing in Italy's top league, when Inter's *nerazzuri* face off against AC Milan's *rossoneri*, it suffices for one of the two teams to win for it to become, as the sports journalists write, that of the valiant *ambrosiani*.

Everything in Milan is Ambrosian – or more precisely, everything has become so, the result of a slow and jerky history whose outlines we will need to redefine. Again in *Ascolto il tuo cuore, città*, Alberto Savinio said it in his way: "Milan shines and reverberates in the glory of its saint...But as the brightness of a lamp dissipates in a blinding light, so does the precise image of the saint dissipate in the midst of such glory." Is it the preciseness of that image that we are chasing here? Perhaps, but we should also clarify the true intentions of the person claiming to lead the hunt. As I was toiling away in an attempt to understand something of the liturgical particularity of the Ambrosian Rite – which I will professorially explain to you in a few hundred pages – I stumbled upon the following remark by one of this subject's most eminent specialists: only the *studiosi ambrosiani* can grasp the deep meaning of these venerable institutions that reach so far into the past, he claims, for, being there in the flesh, it's only natural that they "breathe the air" of the *mysterium*.

Let's be clear: in order to breathe in this very distinctive air, it is without a doubt not enough, according to our liturgist, to roam the streets of Milan; you have to be familiar with its churches. And here, once again, we're confronted by the nebulous density of the term *ambrosianità*: the *studiosi ambrosiani* are not only Milanese, but obviously Catholic as well, and undoubtedly a certain kind of Catholic. It was therefore in the certainty, not in itself particularly blameworthy, of not being Ambrosian that I embarked on this search that is in no way a quest for a personal genealogy, or an attempt to distance myself from any possible attachment to a given place, name, or image, but rather the archaeology of the liturgical foundations of Western government.

And so this history will be far from instinctual. I say this thinking of the first page of Fernand Braudel's *The Identity of France*: "For the historian can really be on an equal footing only with the history of his own country; he understands almost instinctively its twists and turns, its complexities, its originalities and its weaknesses."[4] I don't deny the existence of instinctual understanding, I simply assert that it isn't historical. A historian's work should consist of challenging all that is assumed or accepted as fact, troubling the waters in the way that we might trouble the surface of a mirror by breathing on it. By opting for cold detachment for once, by conceding without fear that we have no affective link to our subject, at the least we are spared from having to battle against all the emotions of belonging. A comfortable choice, no doubt – but it allows us to assess dispassionately the conditions in which were formed, over the long term, in an intermittent, contradictory, and contentious way, collective identities and, perhaps especially, political beliefs.

The discomfort comes from elsewhere. It comes from the always risky adventure that a deep incursion into a very ancient past represents for the historian. Not in relation to the present in which he or she moves, like everyone else, among everyone else, without ever claiming this or that privilege of lucidity, but in relation to what we could simply call their preferred period, or their favored observatory – meaning, more honestly, that province of time that the historian patiently learned to domesticate, tame, and coax, in order to feel like less of a stranger there. For me, the past that is my "present day," that exudes the troubling strangeness of a displaced familiarity, is without a doubt situated in the fifteenth century. That's where I saw the shadowy silhouette of Ambrose for the first time, in the blurry form of an ancient memory, worn out, fatigued, and perhaps unrecognizable from so much handling. It came from so far – over one thousand years of history away, further than the time separating us from the obscure and already legendary fifteenth century. It came from so far, and I could only see it furtively, through a breach created in the order of time by a revolutionary event – the eruption in 1447 of an "Ambrosian Republic."

This shadow had to be met head-on, albeit by fumbling backwards – by nature, historians proceed in reverse, their knowledge of the past limited to what its recent upwellings trap or secrete. This approach was necessary, as compiling a spasmodic chronicle of the political vagaries of the memory of the founder would not have sufficed. Does every era invent a Saint Ambrose at its convenience, gazing at itself in the flattering reflection that it projects into the past? And so what if they do? We know quite well that in the Middle Ages, *auctoritas* had the "waxen nose" evoked by Alain de Lille, a nose that could be twisted any which way to point in any direction. But we also know that the authority of the past has more weight, that something will always resist its coarsest manipulations, and that while there may exist situated forms of what I call the social availability of memory, it obeys a set of rules necessarily constrained by its successive appropriations.

That's why, rather than submitting to being tossed around the raging sea that is the continuous transformation of imaginary Ambroses, I'd like to be able to cast anchors – memories – that prevent this collective memory from drifting too far from the past as it was. These anchors attach simultaneously to urban memory, textual memory, and liturgical memory, configuring the places therein. Monuments and structures are arranged, transforming Milan into a *machina memorialis* in which things remembered latch onto edifices, forming a legendary topography of Ambrosian memory. Then textual terrains form: Ambrose's collected writing was one of the first to be reassembled in the twelfth century in an opera omnia. And finally these locales should be understood, in the liturgical sense, as loci: a specific way of singing hymns established the tradition of the Ambrosian Rite in the ideal of a continual past.

So it was a matter of advancing, as much as needed, into the oblique veins of memory, to move away from the historian's favored terrain toward regions where the foundations are less stable, the surroundings are crumbling, and the ground is slippery – and I ask for the reader's indulgence in advance if I venture into domains in which my expertise as a medievalist weakens, able only to attempt to understand and transmit bits of knowledge molded by others (this is notably the case for the most technical liturgical, philological, and archaeological questions), and certainly not to produce them myself. But I had to keep climbing, as far as possible, without presupposing my strengths and ignorant of my means, not deciding beforehand that there would be impassable thresholds. That the journey would lead us all the way to Ambrose himself was certainly not anticipated from the start. And yet I couldn't exclude it on principle, at the risk of giving this story a lazily Pirandellian moral: to each his or her own Ambrose.

The story had to, quite rightly, attempt to avoid this easy way out through the very movement of its narration. The archaeology of a disputed memory targets the remnant or remainder standing in its way, an abutment that also marks the end of the anachronism fundamental to the historiographical operation. Is this what I've just called "Ambrose himself"? What part of the "real," or the historical truth, will transport us to him? As I write these lines, I finally realize what attracts and repels me in the image of an Ambrose blind to his trek, a myopic Ulysses unaware he's returning home, brought back to Milan against his will. It's that there is something both comic and moving about incessantly colliding with the same obstacles, about returning to the source of your doubts, as if drawn like a magnet to your own failings. How can we write the obligatorily regressive history of a memory while rendering it comprehensible and accurate? How can we avoid the inevitabilities of time without forgetting the aim of historical discourse – truth? How can we tell a story that is vibrant at times but that hides nothing of the unrelenting slowness and the minutiae of the processes of producing knowledge about an era so distant from our own? For a long time I thought that this was a truly insurmountable narrative challenge. I'm finally jumping in, without claiming to have found the solution, but confident in the alluring prospect, in that dream on the horizon, to which, despite everything, whether we want to or not, we all return in the dawn hours.

So Ambrose is indeed that obstinate name that always returns to its place(s) – never acting as diversion and thwarting every effort at symbolization. This name can be interpreted, commemorated, reinvented, reincarnated, anything you want, but it will never be completely liquidated or emptied of its existence. For there remains something irreducible of the experience – the remnant that can't be assimilated and that always blocks the most excessive of manipulations. And we won't call this remnant the true Ambrose, but rather the "real," remembering that according to Lacan, the real is "that which always returns to the same place."[5] Nothing to do with reality, which is merely the "grimace" of the real, meaning the projected shadow of the symbolic. No, the real holds itself apart from any symbolization, and, because it doesn't move, it endures, like trauma – if not inaccessible, at least the ultimate aim of any project of knowledge, at the limit of what can be known.

View of the Basilica of Sant'Ambrogio from the narthex
(*Mondadori Portfolio/Electa/Sergio Anelli/Bridgeman Images*)

ONE

The Archaeology of
a Proper Name
(1447)

There is a place in Milan entirely devoted to Ambrose's name, a place where each stone, image, and shadow seems imprinted with this most ancient memory. Everything appears haloed in his power. That place is the Basilica of Sant'Ambrogio.[1] It was built during the sainted bishop's lifetime, in one of the largest funerary zones in the city's western suburbs, the Ad Martyres necropolis. From this cemetery, vestiges emerged – sculpted marbles, jewels, inscriptions, the bodies of saints – as though working against the accretions of time, which invariably bury the treasures of the past ever deeper.

And there was one treasure in particular: the presence, constantly rejuvenated, of one man's memory, invigorated by the energy of his words. Here, Ambrose said one day, "Dig!" And they found the strong bodies of martyrs, waiting patiently in the ground to be summoned to the city's defense, their saintliness forming a rampart around it. Another day, he said, "Sing!" And the basilica was filled with the sonic aura of those songs of vigilance known as hymns, and they too were identified with Ambrose. On the last day of his life, he made an offering of his own body to the church's high altar, asking to be deposited alongside the saintly bodies he had exhumed in consecrating the church building.

But he had spoken so much and written so extensively. How could we think that his tomb would remain forever silent after his death? There were the cries of joy, surprise, or anger of all those who touched his relics expecting a miracle. There were long silences too, the result of forgetting and indifference. Mostly there was the rustling of dead skins in the crackling fire of manuscripts, the murmuring of copyists, the continued conversation of the written oeuvre, Ambrose's body of doctrinal and literary works. All of it was gathered compactly at the basilica before its dispersal across the world. For it was here, in the Basilica of Sant'Ambrogio in Milan, in the second third of the twelfth century, that the complete works of Ambrose of Milan were compiled and conserved, a task performed by Martino Corbo, custodian of the basilica's treasure.

LOOKING TO THE PRESENT:
THE EVIDENCE OF HISTORY AND THE SUDDENNESS OF EVENTS

Bodies, hymns, texts. Everything took place, in situ, as part of a memory so tenacious that it anchors the recollection of Ambrose, stops it drifting too far from the past that is folded into the basilica itself, so obstinate that it crumples time to blur its tracks, reusing the vestiges of the past to enlarge its influence outward in a nimbus of uncertain borders. Everything, then, starts here, with the force of evidence. One would have to visit this basilica to see, to explain, to unpack – we'd need to take it slowly, patiently noting the signs, intent on dispelling the aura surrounding the great name of Ambrose.

For you see, this place still exists, it persists, seemingly impervious to the cruelty of time. In 1843, Verdi used it as the setting for the first act of his opera *I Lombardi alla prima crociata* (The Lombards on the First Crusade), and one hundred years later, on the night of August 15 to 16, 1943, the basilica collapsed under American bombardment. But it was raised again, and today we can still cross the narthex into the monumental atrium that divides the sober, solemn Roman church from the city that encircles it, still penetrate this pocket of silence, startled by its sudden authority, still lift our eyes to the twelfth-century capitals, where other tightly coiled dramas take place – lions under attack, snakes, and crosses – still leave to our right the carved Greek epitaph that proudly adorns the sarcophagus of a certain humanist of the quattrocento, before we enter the basilica proper and are engulfed in its deep shade. We advance between the majestic columns that mark the basilica's three naves, acknowledge with a glance the lord of the house, who shoots his wasp eyes at us from the ciborium and the mosaics in the choir, slip past the ambo, which is perched above a sarcophagus and is claimed to be the pulpit from which he spoke, allow ourselves to be drawn to the reflections of the golden altar which rises above his tomb, know that we could linger at each of the scenes from his life on the back side of the monumental reliquary, but pass it on the right to wend our way toward his treasure (see color plate 1).

And if you're in the mood, if you have the proper authorizations and have correctly remembered the hours of operation, you can continue on toward the campanile that flanks the small sanctuary, behind the chapel of San Vittore in Ciel d'Oro, where the supposed first portrait of Ambrose can be seen, standing straight and immovable between the martyrs Gervasius and Protasius. You climb the stairs to the top floor, and there, in the small room that houses the capitular archives of the Basilica of Sant'Ambrogio, once its treasure room, you can pull open the cupboards holding the papers, parchments, and papyruses that document the lives of the monks and canons who acted here as the valiant and scrupulous curators of Ambrose's memory. You can also leaf through the volumes of his complete works, still here, in their ancient bindings, laid flat as they should be in this cabinet of medieval codices, deposited like the beautiful corpses of saints just waiting to be raised so they can start performing miracles, once the words have been found to speak their names and tell their stories. Everything is there, defying time, in situ.

The story could well begin here. But it can't start now, like this, in this register, without some acknowledgment at the outset of the solemnities of this long tradition. Let's start again. We are well and truly in the Basilica of Sant'Ambrogio, a monument that seeks to arrest time, we are there, yes, but in 1447, when time is racing, welling up, returning. All through the Middle Ages, the Basilica of Sant'Ambrogio was the site of royal coronations and ceremonial displays of power, political gatherings and partisan mobilizations, expressions of religious fervor and civic identity. It's the black box that recorded all the jolts in Milan's political history, especially during the communal, signorial, and princely periods from the twelfth to the fifteenth century, when the vestiges of the Ambrosian tradition were reused constantly to form new ideological constructs.

What was happening in 1447? A prince had died, a most terrible and redoubted prince, in the Machiavellian sense, who had shut himself away in the stronghold of his fortress, the sinister *castello*, where he was assailed by nightmares and caught in a trap by the very fear he had inspired. That prince was the duke of Milan, Filippo Maria Visconti, last of his line. Between the time of his death, on August 13, 1447, and the triumphal entry into Milan of another prince, his son-in-law the condottiere Francesco Sforza, on February 26, 1450 – a dynastic renewal that rescued the city's tradition as a principality – there was a three-year revolutionary period, a republican interregnum, during which the urban elites, in concert with others, summoned up the city's communal past to declare, calmly and forcefully, that they had no need of a prince. For Milan had been Italy's great free city long before Florence. It was Milan that championed the civic values of the commune, it was Milan that brought together the Lombard League and blunted the power of Emperor Frederick I, defeating his cavalry at Legnano on May 29, 1176, with the city's communal militiamen massed around their standard-bearing chariot, the *carroccio*. The Milanese had called at that time on the memory of Ambrose, bishop of Milan, who in his own day had dealt a telling blow to the pride of Emperor Theodosius – for when it came to battling imperial encroachments on the *libertas* of the Church and the Milanese commune, it was well known that Ambrose brought help.

This "time of holy freedom" – as contemporaries called the fervent period they were living through – is known by modern historians as the Ambrosian Republic, because the reestablished commune embarked on a frenzy of remembering Ambrose, which intensified as the government grew more radical. Ambrose's name was invoked almost obsessively, saturating the public sphere and even precipitating the expression of something like a political belief. In any case, Ambrose's name returned – and with it all the energy of the societal appropriation of a disputed memory. And so we find ourselves in Milan, before the Basilica of Sant'Ambrogio, in the year 1447, in the month of May. And while political battles are raging, the educated and highborn youth of Milan have gathered *in divi Ambrosii celeberrimo templo*, and in all likelihood before the narthex of the Basilica of Sant'Ambrogio – because they have decided to pay attention to the language of stones, speaking at the gates of paradise.[2]

Angelo Decembrio was among those youths: he is the story's narrator. He belonged to one of Milan's great humanist families and to an intellectual tradition long overlooked by historians, who have had eyes only for the Florentines, those great champions of self-promotion, who were then waging a fierce war of words with the Milanese.[3] Angelo was the son of Uberto Decembrio, a disciple of the Byzantine Hellenist Manuel Chrysoloras and a translator of Plato's *Republic*, who died in 1427 and was buried in the Basilica of Sant'Ambrogio – it was Uberto's tomb that we saw earlier, walled into the reverse side of the facade, its alternating Greek and Latin inscriptions exalting the humanist's authority.[4] Next to it we find the funerary monument of Pier Candido Decembrio, Angelo's brother, who was at home in the house of Ambrose.[5] He was the secretary and biographer of Filippo Maria Visconti, whom he described in his unvarnished Suetonian style as a tyrant driven by demons, assailed by night terrors. Pier Candido took part in the war of letters that pitted the Lombard capital against Florence, and his *De laudibus Mediolanensium Urbis* of 1436 was a rejoinder to Leonardo Bruni's elegy of Florence. On Visconti's death, he enlisted heart and soul in the cause of the new republic. His name appears, for instance, among the experts enlisted by the Fabbrica del Duomo, the corporation charged with financing and building the Cathedral of Milan, to design the iconography of the new Ambrosian banner for the young republic's *carroccio*.[6] And he is thought to have written a life of Ambrose in 1467, now lost.

Mausoleum of Pier Candido Decembrio, atrium facade,
Basilica of Sant'Ambrogio (*Patrick Boucheron*)

LOOKING TO THE PAST: REUSING, CONVERTING, REPLACING

Angelo Decembrio, the son of Uberto and brother of Pier Candido, was a brilliant humanist in his own right, having studied at the school of Gasparino Barzizza. But unlike his father and brother, he endured setbacks in his political career, from which his writings and legacy would suffer. It was he, nonetheless, whose pen recorded the present scene, in a short treatise entitled *De supplicationibus maiis.*[7] Let's listen, then, to the family fool, the one whose tomb doesn't appear on the basilica's facade because his poor political choices caused him to stumble on the steep slopes that a man must scale if he would cheat oblivion. The young humanist and his fellow students are standing in front of the ancient basilica, discussing what they see. What they are engaged in is archaeology, in the nineteenth-century sense – when archaeology consisted of confronting the heroic deeds of history with recovered elements of actual life, of everyday practices and customs.[8] Faced with objects from the past, our humanist archaeologists grapple with time, whose salient feature for them is reuse.

On this May day in 1447, as the commune is being reborn and christened with Ambrose's name, a group of young Milanese humanists has assembled in the very place where his memory collects to discuss the consistency of the past – a past so ancient its depths are unfathomable, though it is still liable to resurface abruptly.

This bas-relief for instance. A Bacchic scene is in progress. One of the erudite young men identifies it and voices his surprise.[9] Why does a pagan celebration turn up in a Christian shrine? It isn't Bacchus, the narrator explains learnedly, but Hercules, and he launches into a scholarly lecture on mythology. All the feasts in the Ambrosian liturgy, he explains, and particularly those of the *supplicationes triduanae*, which the greater public now celebrates, have pagan origins.[10] This was Ambrose's genius. He did with time the very thing that others, in this very place and to honor him with the cult he deserved, would do with stones: replace, reuse, and convert – to distinguish what stays from what is lost, what lasts from what passes away, what is transmitted from what is transformed.

The politics and poetics of reuse thus provide us an avenue to explore, in the Middle Ages, the availability[11] of the past to multiple and sometimes contradictory appropriations, by means of which its remains are made to support new edifices of memory. Among the numerous ancient elements that are reused in the architecture of the basilica, some are described in Decembrio's text and can be readily identified. One is "the serpent of Moses," a Hellenistic sculpture perched on a column in the central nave, apparently brought back from Constantinople by Archbishop Arnoldo II in 1002.[12] Others, by contrast, are harder to recognize, such as the bas-relief mentioned in Angelo Decembrio's *De supplicationibus maiis*. But in the end it doesn't matter: his essential point is that the question of reuse in medieval civilization, the way that the uses of *spoliae* or vestiges from the past are redirected, also raises the question of conversion. What does it mean to convert? This is in fact a crucial question, one that arose as soon as the ecclesiastical authorities started to theorize about their missionary efforts. The subject is addressed vigorously in the famous letter Pope Gregory I sent to Mellitus in July 601 about bringing the Gospel to the Anglo-Saxons.[13] The pope had been asked what should be done with the old pagan temples.[14] His answer was unambiguous: when they were well built (*bene constructa*), and once they had been purified of their idols, they were to be used again in service to the Christian God (*in obsequio veri Dei debeant commutari*). The conversion of the natives was also a reuse. Gregory justified it with the precedent of the children of Israel: "Thus, as their hearts were changing, they were losing one thing in sacrifice while preserving another."[15] Losing in order to preserve, forgetting in order to remember: that, in a deep sense, is the logic of reuse. It always entails sacrifice. Since not everything can pass the test of time, since loss has to be allowed, whoever would reemploy the remains of the past must be prepared to sort through its legacy.

To account for this dialectical movement, Jean-Claude Bonne has suggested using the notion of *relève*, or "relief."[16] This term was proposed by Jacques Derrida to translate Hegel's *Aufhebung*, the dialectical movement by which the Mind, in its successive configurations, always progresses toward greater reason.[17] Each stage of this movement sees the abandonment of the preceding moment and its reassumption, but refined by the exposure of a truth that had been present but buried. This is precisely what happens in conversion – and this also applies to Ambrose, whose writings convert the Roman tradition. Thus his *De officiis* can be read as the relief of Cicero's treatise of the same name. Ambrose presents the virtues of the cleric as a transfiguration of the duties of the citizen, at the cost of reusing the notion of *fides* ("good faith," in Cicero, recast simply as "faith" by Ambrose).[18] But if the process of reuse entails some loss, it also brings with it a remainder. In the same letter to Mellitus, the pope hedges on the effectiveness of his evangelical method. "With hard hearts, it is absolutely impossible to cut away [*abscidere*] everything at once." And in fact the laity are like stones – as John of Genoa suggested in his etymological dictionary, deriving *laïcus* from *lapis*. This hard-as-stone remainder, inassimilable and resistant to conversion, always threatens to make its return.

While it's true that the historian's natural bias is to understand the practice of reuse primarily as a way to manipulate the past, so that its recuperation of the past is considered just a by-product and not a way of safeguarding it – for the simple reason that this course more readily provides the materials to construct and support a narrative[19] – it's possible to resist this bias, choose not to hurtle down this slope but find stops along the way, ledges, accidents, discontinuities. The moment that we see it as an act of controlled literary creation, reuse becomes an expression of fidelity and an "active search for interstices" in the fissured surface of a tradition. There, into this cleft, the identity of the person using the practice may insert itself. And when a commentator uses a quote from a Church Father like Ambrose, or more precisely when he inserts a quotation into the setting of his own words, is he not reusing the authority of the patristic past? As Guy Lobrichon has said, "To root oneself in a continuous tradition with perfect orthodoxy and to avoid being constrained, these are the two goals that authors seek to achieve with reuse."[20]

Have these too-general considerations led us away from the Basilica of Sant'Ambrogio? Not really. For in proposing an anthropology of religious belief, Angelo Decembrio's *De supplicationibus maiis* starts with the reuse of the basilica's vestiges. And in the course of the young humanists' erudite and freewheeling discussion of architecture, a different conception of time emerges. That conception still coincides, at least in part, with our own. When Lorenzo Valla composed his implacable *De falso credita et ementita Constantini donatione* (On the false and untruthful donation of Constantine), he adopted the rhetoric characteristic of the great oratory of the humanists of the quattrocento, but with learned critical methods comparable to those we still use today. Let's remember that during the Middle Ages, the papacy based its claims to the exercise of temporal power on a false document, which we now know to have been written in or near the papal chancery in the mid-eighth century. The document claimed to be the "decree" (*constitutum Constantini*) by which Emperor Constantine gave Pope Sylvester a third of his empire, out of gratitude for his conversion.[21] Lorenzo Valla's debunking, as it turns out, relies on a methodical inventory of the linguistic anachronisms in the document, followed by a demonstration – using what today we would call internal criticism – that the text could not possibly have been written in the fourth century. As Carlo Ginzburg remarked, "Valla's sensitivity to linguistic anachronisms stemmed from the humanistic yearning to revive classical Latin as a purified language, free of barbarisms. The attempt to resurrect a lost language, which in a sense had never existed, created the conditions for seeing Latin as a language that had undergone different historical stages."[22]

This paradox very much belongs to the 1440s, when the humanists, who dreamt of stopping time in favor of a perpetual present, sought to liberate the expressions of beauty buried in antiquity and revive the possibility of rejuvenating the world. But in doing so, they invented antiquity as the past. It was no longer a living and unstable material that could be reused, converted, and revived. It became an energetic resource for meanings, values, and problems to be questioned – and questioned according to a method that would then become a critical method. Does that mean we moderns walk in step with the young men of 1447 as they look at the Basilica of Sant'Ambrogio? In many respects, yes, but not entirely. And in this lies the conceptual difficulty of an intellectual history of humanism, which constantly has to resist the propensity of its early promoters, even in the quattrocento, to propagandize tirelessly for a heroic vision of the genesis of modernity.[23] To examine its archaeology, today, would be to practice the discipline as Michel Foucault understood it: as an investigation into our most recent past, the past still acting on us through its latest upwellings, so close and already so available, the past in which we might almost recognize and find ourselves, unless we were to decide on the contrary to use it to measure the distance that separates this "nearly us" from what we have become today.

For now let's merely note that in 1447, Ambrose was both very young and very old. He was young because his name was being bandied in the streets, where the Milanese, drunk with freedom, had eagerly seized on it to propel their political future in an Ambrosian direction. He was old because these same Milanese looked at him as they did at the unfathomable riddle of time's layered thickness. Perhaps, if we wanted to dramatize this story, we could even contrast the two sons of Uberto Decembrio. For Angelo's subsequent life was marked by a literary rivalry with his brother, from which he would emerge as the loser. In 1450 he left Milan, where Pier Candido Decembrio was engaging ever more actively with the new republic. In Ferrara, in the court of Leonello d'Este, Angelo joined the learned circle of Guarino Guarini's disciples. He would produce his most important work for Guarino – the seven books of his *De politia litteraria*, in which he sketches out, again in the form of a dialogue, a humanist theory of intellectual power.[24] Three years later, Angelo was in Naples and seeking a protector. At that point, he returned to his little Milanese treatise, remodeling it thoroughly and giving it a new name: *De religionibus et caerimoniis*. The text is more temperate, and the references to Saint Ambrose have become scarcer. It is now 1453, and we may take it that the saint's name has been compromised by its fervent use at the hands of the proponents of "holy freedom." In fact, the Sforzas sought for a time, if not to forget Ambrose, at least to dampen or neutralize the political charge that his bothersome memory carried. Thus, between 1447 and 1453, between one manuscript and the other, with the rewriting of a brief treatise on the comparative anthropology of ancient and Christian cults, in the space left by the writer's repentance (or at least by his prudent walking back of his position), we can see in negative, as it were, the energy carried by Ambrose's name.

LOOKING AT TIME: THE INDIVISIBLE SOLIDITY OF A NAME

What does Ambrose's name consist of? It is not one of those "names of history" around which the philosopher Jacques Rancière might hope to fashion a poetics,[25] but nor is it a "semi-proper noun" that brings together a cohort of individuals under the collective banner of a category,[26] nor even one of those symptomatic designations that makes a person's patronymic into a conceptual space for a generalized notion.[27] But it might be one of those "indistinct names" under whose political authority, according to linguist Jean-Claude Milner, alienated groups may gather.[28] The inquiry into the memory traces left by Ambrose's name – in texts, but also in the calendar and liturgy, the organization of social life, and the structuring of urban space – is inevitably archaeological in character: the question here is to understand just how a political identity is constructed. And if this archaeology is to have any chance of "stripping the real of its makeup" by profaning the aura of this great name, it will be by revealing what this glorious memory is hiding in the way of mnemonic artifices.[29]

Between "tales of memory" and silences of forgetting,[30] the Ambrosian *memoria* forms as a collective memory through the slow work of "generative rememoration."[31] It all starts, obviously, with the memory of the "historical" bishop, a man of late Roman times, who makes his appearance as a protector and defender of the city in a prayer inserted into the liturgy in the mid-fifth century to celebrate the anniversary of his ordination on December 7.[32] More even than civic rituals, monuments, or speeches, the liturgical *memoria* supports the memory of the *defensor civitatis*: the hymns composed by the bishop of Milan define the specific nature of the Ambrosian Rite, which voices the Church of Milan's desire for independence from Rome. For the Milanese to identify as intensely and as durably with the memory of a fourth-century bishop is more remarkable than a somewhat loose conception of the nature of "civic religion" might suggest. First, because while it is true that the cult of bishop-saints quickly made a widescale appearance in Gaul during the early Middle Ages, it occurred much later in the episcopal cities of northern Italy, the great majority of which "offered no cult to any of their bishops."[33] Second, because Saint Ambrose's universal dimension from the end of the thirteenth century onward as one of the four Latin Doctors of the Church would have made his appropriation by a particular locality a delicate matter.

Yet Milan's claim to Ambrose proceeded triumphantly starting in the year 1000, as the foundational works of Hans Conrad Peyer rigorously demonstrate.[34] In the eleventh century, Landulf Senior named Ambrose as the father of all the ecclesiastic institutions in Milan – already a daring foreshortening of history at that time. Three hundred years later, Galvano Fiamma boldly made Milan's *advocatus* the founder of its communal institutions.[35] And although Augustine referred to Ambrose as "Italy's bishop," the "Milanness" of his memory was soon so clearly established that it became exclusive: the rapid and widespread diffusion of the lexical item *ambrosianus* attests to it. First used to describe a hymn-singing style, the term "Ambrosian" was applied by the seventh century to the liturgy as a whole.[36] Two centuries later, in 881, Pope John VIII referred to an embassy of Milanese citizens as *legatio ambrosianae ecclesiae*.[37] The expression *ecclesia Ambrosiana* gained currency in the twelfth century: Landulf Senior used it often, and Peter Damian, who came to Milan as papal legate, also made use of it, while insisting on the prerogatives of Rome: *ut ecclesia Romana mater, Ambrosiana sit filia*.[38] In 1288, the term completed its evolution with the composition of Bonvesin da la Riva's *De magnalibus urbis Mediolani*. In this monument to the glory of civic virtues, everything that is Milanese has become Ambrosian. The term embodies three main ideas. First, the defense of orthodoxy: Ambrose is a champion in the struggle against heresy but also, as we'll see, and in a more veiled way, a champion of intolerance toward the enemies of Christianity. Next, the promotion of the Church's *libertas*: his fight against the Arians was also a fight to counter imperial intervention in questions of dogma. And finally, the glorification of communal freedoms, which derive from the *libertas* of the Church, since both the Church and the commune hold the emperor in common enmity.

It is the tireless work of time that gives Ambrose's name its stifling density. If the past forms a block, it is because the ages weigh down upon it, the more heavily as they accumulate. Archaeologists are well aware of this compression, but they also know that the slowly sedimented stretches that result are sometimes cut across with strange faults, abrupt intrusions, surprising inversions.[39] In 1447, a breach appeared in the thick wall that had arisen between antiquity, which was being reused, and the present, which was being reinvented. Ambrose's memory, it came to be seen, was more disputed than might have been thought.[40] There would be many ways to tell this story, borrowing from the narrative motifs of montage,[41] palimpsests,[42] reuse,[43] remorse,[44] repetition,[45] anachronism,[46] dread,[47] and reminiscence.[48] But if the story one has to tell is about the discordance between eras, it is essential to take the measure of how deep that discordance is. And that depth is never experienced in the succession of various periods, but in how they make their return.

PART ONE

A LIFE AND NOTHING ELSE

(Fourth to Fifth Century)

The Life of Ambrose by Pier Candido Decembrio, though quite certainly written in 1467, left no direct trace – we know it only by report.[1] When the first Milanese printing presses went into production, what appeared, in 1474, was the *Vita Ambrosii* by Paulinus of Milan. The emerging printing technology almost immediately took possession of Ambrose's memory. A treatise by Ambrose, *De officiis* (On duties), was also published in 1474, and editions of his missal and breviary began to appear that same year as well.[2] A new edition of the *Vita* was published in 1477, and another in 1488, followed by a translation into Lombard in 1492.[3] When it comes to the *volgarizzamento* of the lives of Ambrose, their translation into the vulgar tongue, the numbers are again very limited:[4] the few Italian-language versions of the hagiographic texts in circulation at the end of the Middle Ages relied heavily on Jacobus de Voragine's well-known *Golden Legend* (compiled between 1261 and 1266).[5] This is also true of Nicolò Malermi's 1474 translation into the Venetian-Tuscan language. For his part, Jacobus de Voragine drew heavily on Paulinus of Milan, whose narrative he followed closely, only departing from it to embroider on the supposed etymology of Ambrose's name, which is derived from the Greek. *Ambrosius* is the amber (*ambra*) of God (*syos*), the delicious savor and perfume of the food of the angels; and it is simultaneously *ambrosia*, the food of the angels, and *ambrosium*, celestial honeycomb.[6]

It is a mystery why things are sometimes simple and straight-forward when they should be complicated. The fact puzzles historians, whom simplicity baffles. Yet the hagiographic material on Ambrose is unusually simple: there is the *Vita Ambrosii* and that's it, or very nearly.[7] The *Vita*, as we will see, was composed a few years after the saint's death by his secretary, Paulinus of Milan. It drew on Paulinus's personal memories, but also no doubt on an initial textual and liturgical memory that solidified at the beginning of the fifth century. It was the first Christian biography of an Italian bishop; and until the Counter-Reformation, it remained the robust and massive textual basis for the collective memory of Ambrose. Its manuscript history is continuous and unbroken, both in its chronological and geographic distribution – we find 174 manuscript mentions in catalogs published by the Bollandists. The oldest manuscript was most likely copied in Fulda, Germany, in the first third of the ninth century, in a collection of sermons that included those of John Chrysostom and Augustine of Hippo.[8] But if Paulinus of Milan's *Vita Ambrosii* was widely circulated, it also traveled in the form of quotations, extracts, and fragments, creating the usual cloud of medieval *memoria*, more a peppering of words and sayings than an established text.[9] This textual scattering should be described as a kind of dissemination, in the sense intended by Jacques Derrida: a proliferation of signs that overflows meaning, that exists only through movement, that derives value only from the places it touches and exceeds, since dissemination designates both the scattering of seed and excess.[10]

Still, these shards all come from the same block. The textual stability of Ambrose's Latin lives stands in contrast to the corpus in Greek, which is paradoxically much more ample. As early as the fifth century, three Byzantine historians – Socrates of Constantinople, Sozomen, and Theodorus of Cyrene – composed

historical portraits of Ambrose in their respective ecclesiastical histories.[11] Much later, from the eighth to the tenth century,
Greek authors (most notably Symeon Metaphrastes) wrote further lives of Ambrose.[12] This has allowed historians specializing
in hagiographies to indulge in their favorite game of dissecting a
textual foundation shaken by successive rewritings and prey to
the quirks of memory, or rather, to the interests that the curators of memory had in adapting it to the political ends of their
own times.[13] Nothing conveys this more clearly than Thomas of
Celano's grumblings when asked to write once again about Francis of Assisi, having already produced three successive versions of
his *Vita*, and also to compose, in 1250, his *Tractatus de miraculis san
Francisci*, which flattened the saint's memory a little more: "We
cannot forge something new every day, nor square circles, nor
bring to agreement the innumerable variety of times and wishes
that we received in a single block."[14] Of course, the "block" that
Thomas of Celano was referring to came from the recent past.
Francis of Assisi was the great figure of his lifetime, who had
affected him like a gut punch, and Thomas wanted to keep his
sharp corners from being rounded off.

But the distant past can also form a block, and it does not
erode as easily as one might think—just like those refractory and
tenacious reuses, which, despite their successive conversions,
remain unassimilated. Our aim must therefore be to work our
way toward this solidified memory, looking for what has fissured
it, for the traces of ancient fractures that compromise its obstinate solidity, until it can appear to us as the aura of memory
must, in its diffracted shards. The point is not to find Ambrose
himself behind Ambrosian memory—as those pursuing the so-
called Franciscan question attempt to do, hoping to free the
purportedly authentic Francis from the dross of memory that
imprisons, strangles, and abstracts him from view. Our approach

will be more modest and more secular: to identify the early inventors of the Ambrosian tradition. They were, in successive order: Ambrose, Augustine, and Paulinus of Milan.

TWO

Ambrose as
Self-Inventor
(374)

We would hardly be going out on a limb to say that the first artisan to fashion Ambrose's memory was Ambrose himself – in his doctrinal work, but also and more particularly in his correspondence, which he may have composed, as we'll see later, as an epistolary collection to parallel and clarify his theoretical writings. In this category are the letters addressed to his sister, Marcellina, regarding his treatise *De virginibus*, which he composed in the third year of his episcopate, in 376-77. The letters and treatise together developed a theology of virginity that broke with the Roman theory of continence, as Michel Foucault well understood, since it posited that only the most resolute among the Christian elect were capable of following the rule: "Virginity is for the few, and marriage is for all."[1] Not simply the submission to a particular prohibition, Ambrosian virginity was an activity – in the sense that it was both an art and a way of knowledge – which allows us to understand the birth of sexual subjects in Christianity as the "considered and practical implementation of the relation to self."[2] Virginity provided Ambrose the occasion for a new definition of courage as flight from the world – in this case, flight from the Roman world. While Marcellina had received the veil of consecrated virginity from Pope Liberius, Ambrose's brother, Satyrus, who was following a civil career in politics, had also decided to remain celibate, out of loyalty to the Christian faith.

Satyrus is thought to have died in 378. The two funeral orations that Ambrose delivered – the first at Satyrus's funeral, the second at his graveside several weeks later – are without doubt the most sincere autobiographical testimony Ambrose left us, as he never wrote an autobiography. The first speech is a funeral lamentation in full conformity with the Roman tradition. As in the works of Propertius, Ovid, and Statius, but also as in Virgil's *Aeneid*, with its farewell to the fallen Pallas, Ambrose reacts like a Roman, with an explosion of grief. But his second speech looks toward Seneca and converts his philosophical suffering into Christian consolation.[3] We see that what is most intimate in Ambrose the man is what the events of his time – late antiquity, which was marked by a great shift in epochs – stir up in him. Strong winds were sweeping through history, and through Ambrose himself. For on August 9 of that same year, 378, on the plains of Adrianople, a large part of the Eastern Army of the Roman Empire, overrun by the Goths, perished alongside Emperor Valens. The reverberations of this battle in the distant Balkans terrorized the Roman Empire, whose every member understood they were entering a new phase of crisis. Ambrose, for his part, had his church's gold and silver plate melted down to pay ransom for the disaster victims.[4]

Let's remember that in the two cases mentioned here, virginity and consolation, what is at issue is Ambrose's relation to the pagan past of the Greco-Roman Empire. For Aurelius Ambrosius was born in Trier, most likely in 339/340,[5] into an illustrious Roman family of the *gens Aurelia* that prided itself on its descent from the Greeks. At the time, Trier was one of the four capitals of the Roman Empire (with Rome, Milan, and Constantinople), standing as a bulwark against the barbarians. Although a powerful town, it had nothing of a besieged citadel about it. Constantine II lived there: he had had the offices of the imperial government installed in the vast public baths, the largest in the empire, built by Constantine the Great. Thanks to this showy act of reuse, the building complex became, in the words of Peter Brown, "the Pentagon of the West";[6] the emperor also gave Ambrose's father one of the highest posts in his administration, that of prefect of the Gauls. Ambrose says almost nothing about his father. What we know is that he died fairly young, which forced Ambrose's mother to return to Rome with her three children. Does Ambrose's silence hide some family secret or tale of betrayal? In a recent and somewhat bold hypothesis, Ambrose's father has been identified as a certain Marcellino, an official in the imperial treasury, who threw his support to Magnentius in the latter's bid to usurp the imperial crown. Magnentius's defeat at the Battle of Mursa in 351 would explain the father's disappearance from view and the *damnatio* surrounding his memory.[7]

Ambrose nonetheless received the education of a well-born patrician in Rome, taking courses in grammar and rhetoric, studying the works of the major Greek and Latin authors – a stern Palladius would later reproach the bishop of Milan for "favoring the fables of the poets over the faith of the apostles."[8] In particular, he studied Cicero, whom he read as a master of eloquence, but also, less common at the time, as the author of a political treatise on the loyalty that the elites owed their community–these were the duties of those who governed by virtue of the *officium*. In writing his own *De officiis*–much later, in 388, when he was fifty years old–Ambrose gave a Christian baptism to Cicero's *On Duties*, defining Christian office in its political and liturgical dimensions as the inclusion of the Roman res publica in the bishop's sphere of concern. Ambrose's *De officiis*, though it can also be read as an apologetic for his pastoral practice, represents the spiritualization of the political principles of the Roman government. While Cicero wrote to his son Marcus, Ambrose addressed his "spiritual sons," the priests of Milan and all the bishops of Italy who were ready to follow him in his social project. In this major work, Ambrose "wanted to ask the Scriptures for their teachings on man's duties."[9]

AMBROSIUS EPISCOPUS: PRIEST, DOCTOR, AND JUDGE

The story of Ambrose of Milan is therefore the story of a Christian who became engaged in political activity and undertook to Christianize politics. Working with his brother, Satyrus, he began his career as a lawyer in Sirmium (today's Sremska Mitrovica, in Serbia). The city in which the emperor lived, Sirmium was also the seat of an important bishopric and the capital of Pannonia Secunda. Ambrose and Satyrus were then living with Probus, a family friend and the praetorian prefect of Italy, Illyricum, and Africa, who was already engaged in his struggle with the Arian heresy that would occupy a great portion of his political life. Was it Probus who sent Ambrose to Milan? Paulinus of Milan says so, claiming that the prefect encouraged Ambrose with this prescient advice: "Go, and act not as a judge but as a bishop."[10] The truth of this account is debatable. But whatever the afterthoughts of the participants in an event that may have been painted as fortuitous and improvised only to support the hagiographic theme of Ambrose's election in spite of himself (a child cried out, he called out Ambrose's name, and by the power of that cry, Aurelius Ambrosius became *Ambrosius episcopus*), the election of Ambrose as bishop of Milan in 374 was, if not a surprise, at least, says Peter Brown, "an unforeseen event whose impact on the Christian churches of the West was both a symptom and a cause of changes in the texture of Christianity that were more decisive, in the long run, than had been the conversion of Constantine in 312 A.D."[11]

What were those changes? Two of them were essential and paradoxically connected, as has been well set forth in the work of Neil McLynn and Santo Mazzarino.[12] The first is the enhanced power of bishops, both from the social and the political perspective. Ambrose was rich; he was able to use his personal fortune to build churches and distribute alms to the poor. The dalmatic that he wore on great occasions was a cloak of precious damask silk embroidered with scenes of a lion hunt, comparable in every way to those in fashion among the senators of the day.[13] This was a complete break with the ordinary sociology of contemporary Italian bishops, which inclined more toward *mediocritas* and a low-profile Christianity.[14] But the increased social power of bishops also depended – and this is the second change – on the discovery of a new power base, which Ambrose found in the people of Milan. This importantly led, as we'll see later, to a new discussion within the Church about its relationship to wealth.[15] Historians have tried to work out the sociology of "Ambrose's people": Neil McLynn has described Milan as a cosmopolitan city with few local aristocrats but many passing strangers, bureaucrats, and provision merchants to the imperial court, without an invasive plebeian element as in Rome, Antioch, and Alexandria.[16]

"How strongly I strove to resist ordination!"[17] The story of the ruses Ambrose employed in trying to escape his destiny, despite the heavenly decree, conforms in every way with the hagiographic theme of a first refusal that is seen after the fact to support and validate a true calling. Ambrose, although a Christian, had not been baptized – at the time this was not an unusual occurrence. He most likely received the sacrament of baptism on November 24, though the event is celebrated on November 30 in the Ambrosian liturgical calendar. He was consecrated on December 1 and ordained bishop on December 7, 374. Here again, though the accelerated process ran counter to the second canon of the Council of Nicaea and to the provisions of the *Codex Theodosianus* meant to prevent the flight of Roman officials toward the clergy,[18] it was not unprecedented.[19] One thing is certain: Ambrose was in no way prepared to perform his episcopal duties, the very ones implicitly revealed, in negative, by the tale of his evasions.[20] He was, he writes in *De officiis*, "torn [*raptus*] from the magistracy and the robes of public office to enter the priesthood."[21] The situation could be described in another way: the position of bishop was well within the program of the administrative elites of the Roman Empire, who found bishoprics a way to maintain their dominant position. But in order to attain it, they had to demonstrate a novel virtue, the pillar of Christian *nobilitas*: humility. Achieving one's social ambition, therefore, required one to feign a refusal. This is how Paulinus's account should be read – antithetically. By running away from his responsibility, Ambrose was defining it.[22]

Bishops were priests, doctors, and judges. By inviting prostitutes under his roof, Ambrose was declaring himself unworthy of the continence necessary to the accomplishment of his liturgical duties, including the Sunday celebration of the "divine mysteries" in the presence of the assembled community – which Ambrose was apparently the first to call a Mass (*missa*).[23] But at certain times of the year, the liturgy assumed particular solemnity, and the bishop had to assume the role of doctor and instruct the faithful through sermons. This is no doubt the reason, though the point is contested, that Ambrose pretended in Paulinus's account to refuse the office of bishop by embarking on the trade of philosopher – in the Neoplatonic school, as we shall see – and accepting the benefits of a philosophical life (*philosophium profiteri voluit*) unencumbered by the pastoral duties of the bishop's office.[24] For those duties, in the end, would require the bishop to dispense justice – explaining why Ambrose tortured a man, to compromise in advance the legitimacy of his episcopal court.[25]

But there was nothing for it. The people wanted him; he fled Milan, returned, became bishop. It's as a bishop and not otherwise that Milan would remember Ambrose. When he appears for the first time in the Milanese liturgical memory as the city's protector and defender, it was in the middle of the fifth century, in a prayer for the feast day of his ordination, December 7.[26] Ever since, and to the present day, the Feast of Saint Ambrose has been celebrated on December 7, although the day of his baptism (November 30) and the day of his death (April 5) have gradually been added to the Ambrosian calendar as secondary feast days.[27] What is a saint, if not the chance agreement of a name, a date, and a place? All this came together for Ambrose, in spite of himself, in Milan in 374. Henceforth, he would be no other than what he had pretended to refuse to become, deciding like Jean-Paul Sartre's Saint Genet to be what others wanted him to be, *Ambrosius episcopus*: "Since he cannot escape fatality, he will be his own fatality."[28]

"Abruptly transferred from the courts of law and robes of office to the responsibilities of a bishop, I began to teach you what I had not yet learned…Therefore I must learn and teach at the same time, as I had no leisure to learn before."[29] He would consequently need to improvise, or do research, since, as Roland Barthes has said, "teach[ing] what we do not know; this is called *research*."[30] Therein lies the paradox: by inventing himself as a bishop, Ambrose reinvented the episcopal function, and even – as Peter Brown is right to say, though his statement might at first seem peremptory – the whole of the system of powers in the Christian West. This is unquestionably the block, the all, of Ambrose.

THREE

"But the whole was myself":
Ambrose and Augustine
(384–86)

THE MAN WHO SHAPED HIMSELF BY REMEMBERING

Augustine most certainly began to write *Confessions* in 397, the year of Ambrose's death. His admiring account of the man who would precipitate his conversion in 386 is the first way in which the Christian West would remember the bishop of Milan, conflating him with the solemn, majestic, and erratic figure that so impressed the young rhetorician (Augustine was born in 354 in Tagaste, today's Souk Ahras in Algeria, meaning Ambrose was fourteen years his senior). At this stage it's worth recalling the brilliant passages Peter Brown devotes to him in his biography *Augustine of Hippo*: in Carthage, Augustine was a child bathed in blazing rays, engulfed by an African sun that he celebrated over and over in prose acutely sensitive to the vibrations of light, constantly distracted from his studies by the tangible world. But he was also the incarnation of "a momentous casualty of the Late Roman educational system: he will become the only Latin philosopher in antiquity to be virtually ignorant of Greek."[1] He fumbled his way along, learning by reading excerpts. This slight linguistic baggage made him into "a cosmopolitan *manqué*," who as a result was never entirely integrated into "an international Christian culture"[2] – in short, the opposite of Ambrose, who was fully a man of the Greco-Roman Empire, Greek in culture and Latin in administration.[3]

This also explains why Augustine was attracted, almost magnetically, to Ambrose's eloquence. They were both avid readers of Cicero, but the intriguing bit comes from what Ambrose did with those texts. His words were less lighthearted than those of the rhetoricians Augustine was in the habit of hearing in Rome; they were more serious, more scholarly, but also just as enticing – and indeed, they would entice Augustine, quite far from what he believed himself to be. Ambrose attracted by withdrawing: this is one of the meanings of the *tacite legens*, a scene in which Augustine sees his teacher reading a book with lips shut, and finds himself, self-admittedly "hung on his words,"[4] captive to Ambrose's silence.

Tolle, lege. Tolle, lege. "Take up and read. Take up and read!"[5] It was in a garden in Milan, in October 386, and the man writing his *Confessions* no longer remembers if this ghostly voice emerging behind him came from a little boy or a little girl. But this small, unknown voice was commanding, it chanted and repeated, like in a children's game, "Take up and read" – a game as old as extracting omens from a book opened at random. He takes the book, opens it, and reads it. He falls, literally, upon Paul's Letter to the Romans: "No reveling or drunkenness, no debauchery or vice, no quarrels or jealousies! Let Christ Jesus himself be the armour that you wear; give no more thought to satisfying the bodily appetites."[6] *Nec ultra volui legere nec opus erat*: "No further wished I to read." No need, in fact: Augustine has donned the armor of Christ, he is converted, and his *confessio* is, in itself, the Christian conversion of the admission. In telling his faults, he states the truth of his heart; by inverting the *confiteor*, once a judicial debasement, so that it becomes praise for God, he invents the interior man who shapes himself by remembering.

PAGANS AND CHRISTIANS: POSSIBLE FUTURES

While historians today know perfectly well that Augustine's conversion was a slow process prompted in reality by continued reading of Paul's epistles, they can't help but note the effectiveness, in terms of collective memory, of the Augustinian dramatization on the very notion of conversion as a sudden revelation.[7] Though this one did occur in Milan, in the shadow of an already iconified Ambrose, for Augustine clearly says in his *Confessions* that two years earlier, in 384, he came to Milan to throw himself at the feet of his bishop Ambrose: *Et veni Mediolanum ad Ambrosium episcopum.*[8] The energy of the Latin language in this lexical tightening produces a double interlocking of the man to his function (*Ambrosium episcopum*) and to the place where it is exercised (*Mediolanum ad Ambrosium episcopum*).

Ambrose's memory thus found itself along for the ride with the formidable posterity enjoyed by Augustine, whose works (notably *Confessions*) were of course among the most read, if not the most read, during all of the Middle Ages – and even far beyond. Outside of Milan, the memory of Ambrose was often strictly dependent on that posterity: while there was a specific Ambrosian iconography in Lombardy, for example, and undoubtedly for Italy generally speaking, elsewhere in Europe it was most often incorporated into the representation of the four Doctors of the Church (Ambrose, Augustine, Jerome, and Gregory the Great) honored by Pope Boniface VIII in 1295.[9] Ambrose otherwise appears in illustrations of his major encounters with Augustine, where he is most often represented for having baptized Augustine or instructed his mother, Monica.[10]

But why did Augustine come to Milan in 384, and more importantly under what circumstances? The account he provides in *Confessions* is very brief: he merely notes that the prefect of the city of Rome, Symmachus, who admired his eloquence, sent him to the imperial court of Milan as a "teacher of rhetoric," and more specifically to read the official panegyrics of the emperor and that year's consuls.[11] Remember that it was the crowning of Julian in Milan in 355 that made the capital of northern Italy into the site for the transmission of imperial power in the western part of the empire. Nonetheless, Milan would only benefit from the continuing presence of the imperial residence under the reigns of Gratian, Valentinian II, and Theodosius, or from 378 to 393 – which corresponds to the bulk of Ambrose's episcopate. It is therefore logical that memory would later associate his name with this period of political grandeur.[12]

The first thing awaiting Augustine in the imperial capital was the momentous matter of the "Altar of Victory."[13] In 382, the young emperor Gratian, whose trust Ambrose had succeeded in gaining, made three decisions of import: he abandoned the title of *pontifex maximus*, curbed the fiscal privileges granted the vestal virgins in Rome, and ordered the removal of the statue of winged Victory, which Augustus had brought from Taranto, and on the altar of which senators had to place their offerings before opening their sessions.[14] The nobleman Symmachus then took up the defense, albeit in vain, of ancient religions, citing the long past that connected Rome to its gods, and also, especially, fidelity to the future – for how could they ensure the grandeur of conquering Rome if they abandoned its mission as Virgil had celebrated it in the *Aeneid*? The pagans' main fear was that by failing to honor the victory-granting goddess, Rome would doom itself to an unending defeat. This wouldn't happen, or at least not until much later, with Alaric's arrival in Rome in 410, forcing Augustine to enter the fray to parry the pagan argument: his response would be *The City of God*.

But for the time being, Gratian's death on August 25, 383, gave Symmachus the opportunity to once again defend his cause: he sent a *relatio* to Gratian's successor Valentinian II, who was then just a thirteen-year-old boy, and whose Milanese court was said to be populated by pagan militants led by the *magister militum* Bauto. From Rome, Pope Damasus then called on Ambrose to defend the Christian position before the emperor – this being an admission that the future of the Roman Empire was being decided in Milan. It played out in the form of a dispute, at the most elite level, between Symmachus and Ambrose, who knew and for that matter respected one another, via interposed texts. These texts still exist, as does an adroit dramatization of the controversy created twenty years later by the Spanish poet Prudentius in *Against Symmachus*. For the memorandum from the prefect of Rome was rejected, to the benefit of Ambrose's intellectual and doctrinal prestige, but also to the benefit of the emperor's authority, which was proven to depend on neither ancient religions nor the ancient nobility of Rome's senators. And Victory, being the emperor's companion, was not relegated to Rome but flourished everywhere he was to be found.[15]

"In this matter of the Altar of Victory, pagans and Christians clashed, defending the best part of themselves, their most sacred reasons for living," writes Maurice Testard, somewhat emphatically.[16] Ambrose had succeeded in convincing his audience that Christianity was imposing a new direction on history: "Rather, what is true rightfully carried the day after the opinion that previously prevailed had been rejected."[17] But Symmachus, up against this one-track theology, allowed for stops and forks in the road, maintaining the possibility of a truth that advanced in a number of ways, *non uno itinere*, not by a single path: "Each person has his own customs, each person his own religious observance…We gaze upon the same stars, the sky is common to all, the same world envelops us. What difference does it make by what judgement a person searches out the truth? So great a mystery cannot be arrived at by one path."[18]

It's difficult nowadays not to read this stirring plea as a call for tolerance. And yet we must resist that anachronism, just as we must refuse to see Symmachus as the last pagan.[19] For that would mean essentially accepting Ambrose's victory; Symmachus is only the last pagan for those who think that the world is denominationally divided between pagans and Christians. He saw it otherwise – a very old and diverse world of magnificent landscapes, which could be roamed in every direction. That is the reason that Symmachus continued to write letters in the ever-so-demanding Roman style, to connect his contemporaries through *religio amicitiae*, the religion of friendship, of the kind that gathers some men and excludes others. Christians like Ambrose of Milan or the young poet Ausonius of Bordeaux were entirely welcome here, but their young religion could not purport to re-create a universe as vast as that of the great Roman nobility, a universe that this nobility intended to continue to enjoy. We must also understand, as Peter Brown does, that Symmachus represents less the witness of a past world than the defender of another of its possible futures.[20]

A SINGLE WORLD: I AM A BATTLE

It is precisely in relation to the lofty figure of Symmachus that we should understand Ambrose – and in particular the way that Ambrose appeared to Augustine in 384 – but less as the heroized symbol of the triumphant Christian opposing the resistant pagan than as the inventor of a new, perceptible world that claimed to reconfigure the entire universe. It's not just that Ambrose, by deliberately exaggerating the significance of Gratian's measures, was able to skillfully dramatize the controversy over the Altar of Victory by presenting it as the decisive showdown that would decide the survival of paganism; it's not even that he successfully established himself as the guardian of Valentinian II's Catholic conscience in the city of Milan, where the fate of the Christianized Roman Empire was playing out. It's that he made a certain vision of the world obvious, tangible, and effective, a world in which those who believed in Christ and those who didn't would henceforth live apart. "You beg peace for your gods from the emperors; we ask for peace for the emperors themselves from Christ. You adore the works of your own hands; we consider it an insult that anything that can be made be thought of as a god. God does not want to be worshipped in stones. Even your own philosophers have mocked these things."[21]

Here we find ourselves back amid the stones, faced with this cumbersome legacy of ancient beliefs as heavy as stones; here we are with Angelo Decembrio and his companions in 1447, discussing the reuses of the narthex of the Basilica of Sant'Ambrogio, incredulous and fearful before the density of such a past. For the world that Ambrose brought forth to counter Symmachus, a single world, animated by a directed history, but always working toward its own division – between us and you, between us of today and they of yesteryear or elsewhere – is still the world of the humanists in 1447, and still threatens to be ours today.

But who exactly are these philosophers – "your philosophers" – to whom Ambrose referred? He was undoubtedly targeting the largest possible corpus of Greco-Roman philosophy. But he didn't simply plagiarize Cicero or allow Virgilian reminiscences to electrify his prose; he actually broke from the trademark materialism of Roman philosophy in order to extol a kind of inverted Platonism. From this point of view, Ambrose's reading of the works of Philo of Alexandria, a hellenized Jewish philosopher from the first century of our era, was decisive: as shown by Hervé Savon, Ambrose read Philo to censor and ultimately Christianize him. He relied on his method of allegorical exegesis to rid, for example, the motif of a banquet (in *Proverbs* and especially the *Song of Songs*) of its secular implications: the wedding supper of a husband and wife thus becomes the Eucharistic banquet. This was less a question of confronting Philo's Judaism than his adherence to Alexandrian Neoplatonism, allowing Ambrose to reverse the Platonic relationship between reality and idea, which in his mind was nothing more than a simulacrum.[22]

Now it's easier to understand why Augustine remained so impressed in 384 before Ambrose, an intangible block of authority – and why that impression has been passed down all the way to us, through the genius of *Confessions* itself. For Ambrose introduced Augustine to a world of "totally new ideas," notably by radically deflecting him from the "physical world"[23] of his youth. He taught him that the body was merely a "tattered garment"[24] that we wear. He taught him that all of a man can be found within the folds of his soul. This is what made up the substance of Augustine's conversion – a conversion within, the discovery of the unity of man. When he arrived in Milan in 384, Augustine still thought that the "me" was a glimmer from the kingdom of light, imprisoned in the kingdom of darkness. For him – and in this sense he remained Manichaean – the great battle placed the "me" literally outside of oneself: man is just one stage of the cosmic struggle.

But when he heard Ambrose, he discovered that what sinned inside him was himself: "I still thought that it is not we who sin, but some alien nature which sins in us...I liked to excuse myself and to accuse some unidentifiable power which was with me and yet not I. But the whole was myself and what divided me against myself was my impiety." And later, in the eighth book: "So I was in conflict with myself and was dissociated from myself."[25] This is the grand and terrible discovery he confessed – and therefore rendered manifest. In one swoop, he grasped the unity of "me" and what divided it, mirroring the world that Ambrose transformed by saying it was so.

FOUR

Paulinus of Milan: A First Crisis
in the Memory of Ambrose
(397–430)

We are drawing close to the fractured block that is Ambrose's memory, trying to understand what can break a life into pieces, making shards of existence sparkle in the light of memory. But we are also approaching the *Vita Ambrosii*, the initial and practically sole source for Ambrose's life. What are its opening words? *Hortaris, venerabilis pater Augustinis...* "Venerable Father Augustine, you urge me [also] to set in writing the life of the most blessed Ambrose, bishop of the church of Milan."[1] This is more exhortation than invitation: Augustine's name precedes the text, of which he is also the dedicatee and commissioning agent, and toward whom this life of Ambrose advances. What's more, a prayer to Augustine closes the text: "I also beseech your blessedness, Father Augustine, to deign to pray for me, the most lowly and sinful Paulinus."[2] In a complete inversion of their respective positions, and signaling how rapid was the differential erosion of their memories, Augustine is father to the text; it is from him that the life of Ambrose proceeds.

A BANQUET IN CARTHAGE, OR MEMORY PULLED DOWNWARD

Just who is this *humillimo peccatore Paulino*? Ecclesiastic literature of the fifth century cites two figures named Paulinus: *Paulinus episcopus* and *Paulinus diaconus*. The first is known as Paulinus of Nola. Originally from Aquitaine and a friend of Sulpicius Severus, he settled in Campania, where he became bishop. Clearly this is the wrong Paulinus, even if medieval tradition sometimes confused the two (as did, notably, Jacobus de Voragine),[3] and even if, for an archaeologist of Ambrose's memory in the Middle Ages, it would make historical sense to read Paulinus of Nola and Paulinus of Milan as though they were one and the same author. This almost seems a medievalist take on the contemporary "novelistic criticism" of Pierre Bayard, whose practice of fictionalizing fiction may seem a postmodern game but is entirely in keeping with the premodern variability in attributions.[4]

Let's stick with the second Paulinus, *Paulinus diaconus*. We know that he played a role in the condemnation of Pelagius, beginning in Carthage in 411. This would explain how he might have met Augustine, who became bishop of Hippo in 395, a position he would retain until his death in 430. In a text dated 418, Augustine mentions a Deacon Paulinus who helped him in opposing the Pelagian heresy.[5] This is quite surely the individual we are looking for.

So Paulinus, like Augustine, was an African – that is, from a prosperous and pacified region that was in step with the latest developments in the Roman world. As to when he wrote, the dating of his *Vita* has long oscillated between 412 and 422, hinging on the correct date of a letter by Augustine (29, in the modern numbering system); the great majority of specialists lean today toward 422.[6] And to whom did he write? To Augustine, as we've said, but in the name of posterity, because it was Augustine who had asked him to "also" write the life of Ambrose. *Etiam ego*, the qualification is intriguing – it suggests that there were perhaps other lives of Ambrose, or other commissions, or other attempts to write the life of Milan's bishop. And finally, why did he write? To save from oblivion a life that was already starting to seem damaged, or at least diminished.

At this point in Paulinus's account comes a decisive scene.[7] He was in Carthage, at the house of the deacon Fortunatus, who was giving a banquet. Fortunatus was the brother of the bishop of Carthage, Aurelius, a friend of Augustine. Some among the guests began to slander the bishop of Milan: namely Donatus, a Milanese priest of African origin, and Muranus, bishop of Bolita, who was then passing through Carthage. Both, it goes without saying, were struck down by the vengeance of God. But this was not enough: the calumnies had to be stopped. Then began the work of remembrance, in order that nothing further be taken from the venerable bishop's memory. The Latin word, which is repeated several times, is *detraheret*: *detraheret memoriae Sacerdotis*.[8] It means "to remove" or "peel off," but in the sense of a garment that is pulled downward – from which it derives its secondary sense of "stripping merit" and "diminishing value." Thus *detrahendi causa* can be used by Cicero to mean "in a denigrating spirit."

That is the sense here: all who speak too lightly about the man who was bishop of Milan chip away at his image and pull it downward. This, then, was the initiating incident, though it is only revealed at the end of the *Vita*. Yet it alone can justify the memorializing enterprise, already a question of repairing memory, and the emphasis on truth-telling, which is hammered home in the text: "Nor will I drape the truth in fancy words" (*nec verborum fucis veritatem obducam*).[9] To speak the whole truth and nothing but the truth. "Hence I shall start this narrative with the day of [Ambrose's] birth, so that the man's grace, which was present from the cradle, may be recognized."[10] Ambrose would then be tracked to the grave, so that nothing might be taken from him, documenting a "complete trajectory."[11]

WHO IS CHRISTIAN? IDENTITY PUT TO THE TEST IN THE FIFTH CENTURY

For context on this first threat to Ambrose's memory, it's worth noting, following Peter Brown, the speed and depth of the social and political changes that came over the Roman Empire after Ambrose's death in 397. In this altered world, which was the world of a new generation represented by Augustine, Jerome, and Paulinus of Nola, and particularly after the sack of Rome by Alaric in 410, "many of Ambrose's works became out-of-date with surprising speed."[12] If the years from 380 to 430 represent an important turning point, it's also because they precipitated and dramatized a movement that had long been in the making. The institutionalization of Christianity as the state religion in the Greco-Roman Empire was the upshot of a slow process that extended over a good part of the fourth century – it did not, as a stubborn myth would have it, appear fully formed after Constantine's conversion. Rather than a triumph of Christianity, this emergence of a state religion should be interpreted as the slow political evolution of the system of powers in late antiquity. As Yvon Thébert has argued energetically, "Christianity did not conquer the society of the Later Roman Empire, it was secreted by it."[13]

The new religion gradually took over the pagan realm – notably by Christianizing time and space – and through its practices the ancient Judaic sect was converted into a universalist religion.[14] What philosophers see as having already happened with Saint Paul in the first century and describe as a revolution, historians do not observe until much later, following a long process of secularization and desecularization – the very same process, in fact, that Angelo Decembrio and his companions were seeing in 1447, when they noted that time sometimes glides over and sometimes fastens onto the remains of a very ancient past. This tempo of reuse is in harmony with the "Christianity on a gentle slope"[15] that Ambrose advocated, which made the triumph of the new faith inevitable: "All of this, having prevailed through reason or been brought about through an arrangement, that the cross of Christ may more readily be accepted, will create a slope such that, unable to renounce their own history, they will yet acquiesce to ours."[16]

But what may be described as a gradual reform of Roman society is experienced as a revolution by Christians. In this sense, the Pauline detonation remained explosive for all its readers, again starting with Augustine. Robert Markus describes the encounter with Saint Paul as a painful and dramatic crisis of identity. *Quid sid christianum est?* "What is it to be a Christian?" That is the question put, notably, by the Pelagian heresy, "an onslaught on the languid, second-rate Christianity which blurred the line between a conventional Christian and the ordinary, pagan Roman." Pelagius advocated a sternly ascetic way of life that would allow a small number of people to achieve salvation – an aristocratism, in short, opposed in every way to the *mediocritas* proposed by Augustine.[17] One of the Pelagian treatises, *De vita christiana*, is punctuated by the slogan *non nomine sed opere*: "A Christian is one who is so not in name only, but in action."[18]

Today it is possible to reconstruct the whole of the Pelagian episode, thanks largely to the work of Elena Zocca:[19] after the sack of Rome by Alaric's Visigoths in 410, Pelagius sailed to Africa with his disciples, went to Hippo, and tried to win over Augustine. But Augustine taught what Robert Markus calls "Christian mediocrity." In 418, Pope Zosimus condemned Pelagius as a heretic. Pelagius set off for Jerusalem, then perhaps sought shelter in Egypt, where he died in 420. His disciple Caelestius remained in Africa, but later returned to Italy, where he organized a league of eighteen bishops around Julian of Eclanum. This group, refusing to submit to Zosimus's decree, created the Pelagian schism. What we know from Paulinus of Milan is that in 417, he wrote a letter to Pope Zosimus denouncing Caelestius's errors. From this, we can identify those who wanted to damage Ambrose's memory, namely the faction that disagreed with his handling of the Pelagian crisis, but we can also identify what was primarily at stake in the controversy: the very definition of Christian identity.

EPISCOPAL GOVERNMENT: FROM MARTYRDOM TO MINISTRY

This is no doubt the crux of the story, as the question of Christian identity is also at play in the very genre of the *Vita Ambrosii*. As Stéphane Gioanni has demonstrated, the *Vita* is the first biography of an Italian bishop that departs from the genre of martyrology.[20] Prevailing until Carolingian times, this genre proposed a dominant model of sainthood–although violent martyrdom was gradually replaced, as the Church imposed peace, by what Pope Gregory the Great called "hidden martyrdom," which is to say asceticism. These lives of martyr saints, or ascetics (monks, for the most part), fueled the genre of the *Passiones*, which were mostly anonymous. But that's not what we have here, when Paulinus of Milan took up his pen, in his own name and that of the text's commissioner. Did Paulinus admit to his influences? Yes, he did, as we see by returning to the *incipit* cited earlier: "Venerable Father Augustine, you urge me [also] to set in writing the life of the most blessed Ambrose, bishop of the church of Milan, just as the blessed men Athanasius the bishop and Jerome the priest set in writing the lives of the holy Paul and Anthony, who lived in the desert, and just as the servant of God Severus put into writing the life of the venerable Martin, bishop of the church of Tours."[21]

Filiation from the texts of these authors is claimed – Sulpicius Severus, one of the "fountains of eloquence," Jerome, Athanasius. Their *Vitae* join the resurgence of the ascetic genre. Paulinus of Milan does not mention the *Vita et passio Cypriani*, written in 258 by the deacon Pontius, secretary to Cyprian, bishop of Carthage. That would be because this precursor – still quite close to the martyr's tale, whence its double-barreled title – had little influence. Yet modern scholarship stresses the relation between the lives of Cyprian, Ambrose, and Augustine, who was also portrayed by his secretary, friend, and disciple Possidius.[22] To this lineage, the *Vita Epiphanii* should be added. Written by Ennodius of Pavia shortly after the death of Bishop Epiphanius in 496, it too exalts the saintliness of the bishop's role.[23]

This, in fact, is the dominant trait of these *Vitae*. Paulinus of Milan offers a portrait of the "most blessed bishop of the church of Milan," starting with his ordination in 374. Milan quite rightly figures as the first setting for Ambrose's activities. But his horizons expanded: Ambrose was at the head of a network of Italian bishops, a network that his correspondence identified and formed. Following the Council of Aquileia (late 381 or early 382), he addressed letters to Emperor Theodosius in the name of the Church of Italy: "Ambrose and the bishops of Italy."[24] Subsequently, Ambrose received the embassy of "two very powerful and wise Persian men,"[25] writes Paulinus, and "the holy man was [famous] even among the barbarians,"[26] maintaining contacts among the Franks. Paulinus of Milan stresses the world fame of his hero, the doctrinal importance of his work, and the saintliness of his character, which shows itself mainly in his pastoral activities; but he neglects to mention Ambrose's literary production and does not disclose even the name of his brother, Satyrus.

In confrontations with the crowd, with opponents of the Church, with heretics, with the emperor himself, Ambrose is the one who stands tall, who resists, who fights. Sometimes he backs out – twice he leaves Milan when he is unable to obtain satisfaction, once to Aquileia and another time to Bologna and Florence, but this is another way of applying pressure. He appears in the palace, in court, in the hippodrome, in the basilicas – all the places of power. But most often, he plays the city against the palace, the people against the court. A cry always goes up. A child in the crowd shouts *Ambrosius episcopus*, and he is made bishop. Later, a man "suddenly seized by an unclean spirit"[27] gives voice to his torment, and Ambrose is in danger. This possessed man is one of the fanatical figures who appear so frequently in Paulinus's tale and in those of his contemporaries. Proclaiming on church grounds their allegiance to the devil, they embody a transitional figure, or rather, a figure in crisis, between paganism and conversion.[28] When the risk of demonic contagion reaches even higher levels, Ambrose assembles his people in the basilica, transforms their cries of fear into songs of hope, and in so doing invents hymns. He presides from the height of his cathedra, at the center of what is called the "tribunal," but which is nothing other than the raised portion of the apse. He dominates, he presides – occasionally he negotiates, at times he concedes, at times he remains inflexible, but always he menaces. When all of this is not enough, he cries, but again it is to mobilize political emotions.

In short, this no longer has anything to do with martyrdom – the *Vita Ambrosii* is from start to finish a treatise on episcopal government. Well, perhaps "treatise" is an exaggeration: it is a tale, the juxtaposition of brief episodes that, while hardly eloquent, nonetheless invite reading – *tamen brevitas ad legendem provocet*.[29] These brief, detachable bits – borrowed by preachers, absorbed into the iconography, recycled in other narratives – would have a life of their own. In the end, it is the rustic character of Paulinus's style and narrative method that has given his text its plasticity and, in consequence, its success.

The literary dimension of Paulinus's account would seem to distance it from the historical genre. His goal was "not to write a work of history but to gather in one place all the available memories."[30] Paulinus of Milan gives hardly any dates, for which he was long held in contempt by historians, who found in Ambrose's letters a more stable point of reference. Paulinus also leaves unmentioned a number of essential stages in Ambrose's political life – his relations with the Eastern Churches, the Council of Aquileia in 381, and the Council of Rome the following year. On the other hand, he organizes the episodes of Ambrose's life in chronological order: twelve of the fifty-six chapters start with the same formula, *per idem tempus*, "around the same time." On several occasions, Paulinus goes back in time, *ut retro redeam*[31] and *superioribus diebus* ("a few days before").[32] Jean-Rémy Palanque has taken an inventory of all the sources cited by Paulinus – letters, witnesses, and informants are all presented in support of the account's veracity.[33] The author starts to appear in his own tale as a direct witness in 394, when Ambrose returns to Milan following his trip to Florence, which Paulinus describes in such detail that one can't help wondering whether this is when he met Ambrose, becoming his secretary only at this late date.[34] At any rate, he was thenceforth integrated into the group around Ambrose. Paulinus traveled with the great man, saw what he saw, and felt what he felt: "we have seen the martyr's blood" (*vidimus*), "we have also been filled with an odor," "we at once went over to pray...in the same garden."[35] He was there for Ambrose's final moments, at the death of the man who had declared himself unafraid of death. This last scene, on April 4, 397, would appear to echo one final time the scene that had so impressed Augustine: "We saw his lips moving but did not hear his voice."[36]

Although Paulinus most often says "we," he uses the pronoun "I" eight times. When the miracle of transfiguration occurs, for example, Ambrose's face "became like snow," and a flame "in the shape of a shield" came down over his head. Paulinus then describes the physical effect it had on him: "When this happened I was transfixed and could not write down the things that he was saying until after the vision had passed away."[37] Wonders, miracles, exorcisms, apparitions: the fabulous invaded the genre of biography in the fourth century, especially with the lives of monks. Paulinus embraces the fabulous, but he also contains it, essentially limiting it to miraculous cures. "No celestial visions or demonic apparitions, no mythical animals or extraordinary feats of asceticism, as in the *Life of Anthony*, where the heavens constantly open before the saint…"[38] In the *Vita Ambrosii*, although the dikes start to give way a little at the end, when Ambrose's worn body generates miracle after miracle, the marvelous is systematically introduced only with descriptions of episcopal duties, which is to say, in exaltation of *Ambrosius episcopus*. There is no doubt that the ultimate purpose of writing the *Vita Ambrosii* was a spiritual one: "Hence I exhort and beg each person who reads this book to imitate the life of the holy man."[39] The point is not merely to remember but to make this memory a *magistra vita* – one that will govern our lives, guide our behavior, inspire and strengthen us.

One question remains. By reaffirming the place of the miraculous and the significance of the marvelous in this story of a life, by underlining its pastoral and exemplary value in a militant defense of the bishop's government (all the more militant for being threatened by a competing and detracting memory), are we distancing the *Vita Ambrosii* from the ancient secular tradition of Christian biography, which borrows from the funeral orations and eulogies of the classical Greco-Roman world, and more generally from narrative biography? Not really, if we acknowledge the important work of Glen Bowersock,[40] which has shown that the Greco-Roman Empire at the time of Nero was invaded by the fictional genre, angering the intellectual elite that had trained in the ancient *paidea* (education). This was a true narrative revolution in the fictional order, affecting Christian authors as much as others.

Biographical selectivity, therefore, is not a Christian invention – Plutarch distinguished between what is useful and edifying in a man's past and what is not. But one of the characteristics of classical biography is that it was plural: whole galleries of portraits were written, rafts of parallel lives, collections of the lives of famous men. The Christian exception was to produce plural biographies of a single person, as was obviously the case with Jesus Christ. From this practice came a particular power, which is the power to select and put in order the multiple accounts, an activity that never ends, because the choices constantly need to be glossed.[41] For Christianity was well and truly the product of a normative revolution. Yet how was the normative to be understood once it was no longer just the codification of laws but had been embodied in a story that suggested no direct application to the practical sphere, but concerned the totality of a person's life?

Correspondingly, what does narration become once brought within a normative framework, not to elicit an aesthetic response nor to effect cognitive ends, but to project a norm, that is, to fashion a social body?[42] These are the questions that drive any reflection that seeks to establish, starting from the archaeology of a proper name, an inventory of its traditions, its variations, its identifications, its stubborn obstinacies and clear evasions.

Telling the sequential story of someone's life is "an obscenity," wrote Roland Barthes in *Sade, Fourier, Loyola*. And in any case it's a sham, since "any biography is a novel which dares not speak its name."[43] In the biography that she nonetheless devotes to Barthes, Tiphaine Samoyault tries to honor the way that, while refusing to write another's life, Barthes makes the names of certain authors a locus of assembly and a description of unity. "If I were a writer, and dead, how I would love it if my life, through the pains of some friendly and detached biographer, were to reduce itself to a few details, a few preferences, a few inflections, let us say: to 'biographemes' whose distinction and mobility might go beyond any fate and come to touch, like Epicurean atoms, some future body, destined to the same dispersion."[44]

"Biographemes," then, are shards of life, shards that diffract the particularity of a person's existence, dispersed like ashes in the wind after death, and coming to rest here and there, or being carried elsewhere along with others. To collect and gather biographemes is not just an ethics of biography but an art of memory. The account of a life then becomes an anamnesis, or, as formulated in *Roland Barthes by Roland Barthes*, a "countermarch." What we need to do now is to follow the dissemination of Ambrose's biographemes, shards propelled from the one block, a life and nothing else, but which found ways to connect to certain places, in this city of Milan whose destiny is henceforth indissociable from Ambrose's.

In this sense, his death differed profoundly from Augustine's. Ambrose departed this world in the early hours of Easter Saturday on April 4, 397. The crowd accompanied his body into the basilica, where children were being baptized. "When many

of the baptized children were returning from the font they saw
him: some said that he was sitting in his chair in the tribunal,
while others pointed him out, walking, to their parents."[45] Jacobus de Voragine later added, for good measure, "still others told
how they had seen a star above his body."[46] The lovely image is
already expanding, running through the streets, stretching and
scattering all over the city. Augustine, by contrast, died alone, in
Hippo, with the city under siege from the Vandals, certain that
he was witnessing the collapse of Roman Africa. The date was
August 28, 430. At a moment when Ambrose's memory was flick-
ering and fluctuating, Augustine was trying to gather together
all the various fragments of his own life. At night he read his earlier works, trying to recapitulate everything, and he composed
his *Retractationes*, in which he recalled each of his texts one by
one, criticizing them, sometimes taking them to task, correcting
them, but mostly reordering them into a list of titles, where each
text would henceforth take its place. After his death, his secretary, Possidius, compiled the whole list into a complete catalog,
which he appended to his *Life of Augustine* as a "little directory" or
index, wondering all along if ever the day would come when even
a single human would be capable of reading and understanding
the whole of it.[47]

PART TWO

OCCUPYING THE LAND

(Fourth to Ninth Century)

On Wednesday, June 17, 386, Ambrose felt "at once a kind of prophetic ardour." That's how he described this decisive moment, a few days later, in a letter addressed to his sister Marcellina.[1] Emperor Valentinian II was demanding that he relinquish one of Milan's basilicas for Arian worship. They had reached the crux of the showdown: how to structure the holy space of a city whose *defensor civitatis* the bishop had announced himself to be, not only by becoming the defender of all things holy, but by using them to enlarge the aura of holiness enveloping all society. Ambrose had done in Milan what Constantine did in Rome: cover old burial grounds with basilicas, those citadels of faith.[2] So it was out of the question to hand them over to the heretics. The preacher was ready to resist, supported by a fervent and disciplined flock assembling in large churches, ardently singing the hymns he had just composed.

But the best defenders of the faith were the bodies of saints, relics whose power sufficed to lastingly protect Milan's basilicas from the threat of imperial usurpation – or heretical corruption, as, in the case of Arianism, Ambrose maintained that it was the same thing. On May 9, 386, Ambrose placed apostolic relics from the East in the *basilica apostolorum*.[3] But in the southeastern basilica, which would become the *basilica martyrum*, on this Wednesday in June, Ambrose found himself empty-handed. Hence his "prophetic ardour": there was no doubt that martyrs were waiting beneath the Lombard city to come to the aid of the servants of God – but where?

Native saints were even more effective than imported martyrs, who brought their miracles with them. Before the chancel screen of the saints Felix and Nabor, the only martyrs whose bodies Milan could boast of possessing at the time – they are, he writes, *martryes nostri*, "our martyrs"[4] – Ambrose, suddenly inspired, ordered that the earth be scraped up. In the same letter to his sister, he continues his account: "We found two men of marvellous stature, such as those of ancient days. All the bones were perfect, and there was much blood."[5] In his *Confessions*, Augustine, like an echo, mentions these same bodies that "[lay] hidden away in your secret treasury, out of which at the right moment you produced them to restrain the fury of a woman, indeed a lady of the royal family,"[6] meaning Justina.

Bodies, calm and watchful, from a past greater than ourselves, bodies placed somewhere, waiting to receive their names, and to which, once named, stories would cling: this was the invention of relics, in a world on the cusp of medievaldom. Soon the two saviors, who became the church's divinities, would be given names and a history: Gervasius and Protasius.[7] Two days after their invention, on June 19, the martyrs' bodies were solemnly transferred to the new, soon-to-be-consecrated basilica. Placed beneath the altar, they anchored the edifice in Catholic orthodoxy[8] while also establishing it as a holy place.[9] Ambrose's act, as we know quite well today, had a tremendous impact: beyond this new association between altar and relic, whose influence was recently reevaluated,[10] what played out here was nothing less than the definition of the ritual of the consecration of the church in the medieval West, a ritual through which the division between the secular space and the holy space was established.[11]

Gervasius and Protasius prompted Milan's first burial *ad sanctos*, meaning near the tombs of saints: that of Ambrose himself, who decided that same year, 386, that he would join the martyrs in death, marking with his body the very location of the Eucharistic sacrifice.[12] "For it is fitting that the priest should rest there where he has been wont to offer," he wrote to his sister Marcellina. In 397, Ambrose's body took its place beneath the high altar of the basilica, flanking the twins' altar ("I yield the right hand portion to the sacred victims"[13]). The *basilica martyrum* would henceforth bear his name: *basilica Ambrosiana*, as he named it in advance in his letter from 386. The configuration of Ambrosian monuments, spreading through all of Milan and beyond, had found its central pivot.

FIVE

The First Showdown: Ambrose and the Basilicas (386)

To understand the spectacular rearrangement of memory effected by Ambrose in configuring Milan's monuments, we have to look back at the impact and sequence of events, the latter quite theatrical, of what historiography generically refers to as the "battle of the basilicas."[1] Apart from a few eyewitness accounts or indirect sources, it is primarily documented by Ambrosian texts: two letters from Ambrose, spirited but chronologically muddled, one to his sister Marcellina and the other to the Emperor Valentinian II, and a sermon, *Against Auxentius*, "on the giving up of the basilicas," which an ancient manuscript tradition, perhaps dating back to Ambrose himself, links to his letter to the emperor.[2] So we're missing, and this is crucial, the point of view of Ambrose's opponents. Who were they? Everyone who defended the Arian religion at the imperial court under the patronage of Justina, widow of Emperor Valentinian I and guardian of their son Valentinian II. The leader of what Ambrose presents as an Arian party was Auxentius of Durostorum, also known as Mercurinus, whom historians call "the second Auxentius"[3] because he adopted the name of Ambrose's predecessor, the bishop Auxentius, a moderate Arian who died in 374.[4]

AMBROSE AND THE "HOMOIAN WOLVES":

HERESY, BARBARISM, EMPIRE

But was there really an "Arian party" in Milan? And what is a "moderate Arian" anyway? Arianism in the 380s was certainly no longer the doctrine of the Alexandrian priest Arius, declared a heretic at the Council of Nicaea in 325.[5] This doctrine had attempted to settle the Christological quarrel, advocating a clear subordination of the Son to the Father in the Trinity, following nature. Emperor Constance II had suggested, during synods held in Rimini and Seleucia in 359, a formulation that was more subtle, and likely to garner consensus among scholars: the Son was in fact equal to the Father in nature, in full conformity with the Nicene Creed, but there was a difference of intensity between them that allowed it to be said that the Son was "of the same substance" as the Father (*homoiousios*) and not strictly "consubstantial" (*homoousios*). Between the Homoians and the Nicaeans, there remained, literally, just one iota.[6]

Heresy is always an indicator, as we well know, of contradictions of dogma. Christological heresies, which in their delicious and incomprehensible variety practically exhausted all the logical possibilities of resolving the Trinitarian problem, are no obstacle to that odd rule that dictates that the Church will always choose, from within this range of possibilities, the doctrinal solution that is the hardest to believe – by virtue of a system that will be theorized much later by masters of scholastic

thought and which Catherine König-Pralong calls the "orthodoxy of the unbelievable":[7] in Christian anthropology, this difficulty of belief ultimately reinforces the formula of obedience.

The Homoian doctrine was entirely political; it temporarily
became the official religion of the empire, by way of the general
Council of Constantinople in 360. But for fourth-century Catholic polemicists – and a good part of historiography, always quick
to follow suit – the "Homoian wolves," to borrow Ambrose's term,
were none other than Arians in disguise, prowling around the
sheepfold. Hence why the bishop of Milan directed his attacks
against Auxentius, echoing Juvenal as he mocked this barbarian
from the fringes of Scythia: "outside a sheep, inside a wolf; he
is the one... who wanders around by night, limbs stiffened by
the Scythian frost, and mouth bloodied. He circles, looking for
someone to devour."[8] Ambrose, clearly not one for subtlety, continued in this satirical vein, pretending to wonder why the Goth
soldiers were demanding a basilica in which to pray when a simple chariot would suffice to celebrate their religion, in keeping
with the ancient customs of this nomadic people.[9]

By deliberately conflating Arians and Homoians, Ambrose
was able to link the categories of heresy and barbarism, pushing
back any rejection of Catholic orthodoxy, if not to the geographical limits of the empire, at least far from the cultural values and
spiritual virtues that formed the *mos maiorum* of ancient Rome.[10]
Even today, many historians struggle to break away from this
powerful categorization. Sometimes, for example, one still hears
"Germanic Arianism" used to refer to the Homoian doctrine,
insofar as the bishop Ulfilas had participated in the Council of
Constantinople and, adhering to this new creed, spread it among
the Danube Goths.[11] The Gothic elite adopted this new faith with
all the more enthusiasm as it was also that of Emperor Valens.
His death during the disaster of Adrianople on August 9, 378, was

consequently perceived by many followers of the Nicaean faith as a sign from God: Ambrose himself, in dedicating his tract *De fide* to Gratian, Valens's successor, adopted this providential explanation.[12]

In 380, Emperor Theodosius I promulgated the Edict of Thessalonica, whose main impact was to reestablish the Nicene profession of faith throughout the empire. After this, the Homoian doctrine remained only as the foundation of the ethnogenesis of the Goths, allowing them to emerge as a people, in relation to the neighboring barbarians and confronted with the Nicaeans. It became an ethnic religion among the Goths, with a specific liturgy and alphabet, but was difficult to maintain as an identity basis for a group in power and on the path to acculturation. And it is precisely because their ethnic identity was far from assured that the Lombards appropriated the Homoian faith in the seventh century to cope with pressure from Byzantium, the Franks, and the papacy – until the reign of Aripert I (653–61).[13]

IN THE BESIEGED BASILICA: THE INSTITUTION OF HYMNS (AKA SONGS OF VIGILANCE)

But we're not there quite yet, in Milan in 386. Restored to its true proportions, the battle of the basilicas was merely the conflict, voluntarily dramatized by both sides, between the last followers of a Homoian doctrine threatened by the defeat of Adrianople and their ultra-Nicaean rivals resolved not to cede anything more.[14] Nowadays historiography is better able to describe, day by day, sometimes hour by hour, these "alternating periods of tension and moments of respite,"[15] starting from the imperial law of January 23, 386, that, presented as a law of religious tolerance favorable to those faithful to the dogma of Rimini, ordered that they be given the suburban basilica called Portiana[16] until

Palm Sunday (March 27, if this is indeed 386).[17] In a somewhat desperate overreach, the imperial court then demanded a more important place of worship, the *basilica nova*, part of a complex of cathedrals in the heart of the city.

Now begins the true showdown. During this Holy Week, "persecution rages," writes Ambrose – he uses *persecutio*, though it has a primarily legal meaning here.[18] On March 31, Goth soldiers from the imperial court surround the basilica in which the bishop of Milan has gathered his followers. He writes of the following day, Wednesday, April 1, 386: "when, before dawn, I passed out over the threshold, I found the Basilica surrounded and occupied by soldiers"[19] (*circumfuso milite occupatur basilica*). Ambrose always employs the same verb, *occupare*, but we are undoubtedly meant to understand it more as a taking of control than of possession: the company of soldiers is deployed around the cathedral, applies pressure, besieges it.[20] This is when the bishop, while fully assuming his pastoral duties – he hasn't once failed to give Mass during this Holy Week, diligently comment on the day's evangelical readings, or instruct candidates for baptism – announces he is ready for martyrdom. For he fears, or pretends to fear, that "blood might be shed which would tend to bring destruction on the whole city. I prayed that if so great a city or even all Italy were to perish I might not survive."[21]

This Christian spectacle opens with a dramatic scene: a people in prayer resisting the force of arms. From Friday, March 27, to Maundy Thursday, April 2, 386, needing to give themselves courage and stave off boredom, they launched in unison, inside Milan's basilicas, into a new kind of song, current in the Christian East but not then practiced in the West, at least not in public. What they sang were hymns, the most lasting and most universal testimonies to the memory of Ambrose, essentially the conversion to a Christian setting of imperial acclamations.[22]

The bishop of Milan used liturgical innovation like a political weapon, gathering his supporters in a visible community, mobilizing their energy by teaching them a simple, easily memorized poetic form – eight stanzas formed of four iambic dimeters, short verses most often composed of eight syllables – which represents the first introduction of non-biblical elements into Western liturgy. Most importantly, Ambrose made of these hymns, which posterity would attach to his name, a song of resistance. Milan's distinctive liturgy was inaugurated here, during a long and trying wait on the eve of battle, with members of the clergy and the laity, men and women, children and adults gathered around a new song, which was rhythmical, lively, and enchanting.[23]

So enchanting that some in the imperial court whispered that Ambrose had bewitched his people, having dared in his churches to lead a mixed and indistinct crowd in hymns suspected of some incantatory power. In his sermon *Against Auxentius*,[24] Ambrose is almost boastful of this accusation: "They declare also that the people have been led astray by the strains of my hymns. I certainly do not deny it. That is a lofty strain, and there is nothing more powerful than it. For what has more power than the confession of the Trinity which is daily celebrated by the mouth of the whole people? All eagerly vie one with the other in confessing the faith, and know how to praise in verse the Father, Son, and Holy Spirit. So they all have become teachers, who scarcely could be disciples."[25]

Playing off the old polysemy of the word *carmen* (poem and incantatory spell), Ambrose evokes the magic of a hymn that, declaring the three figures of the Trinity to be equal (the crux of the theological controversy pitting Homoians against Nicaeans), brings all those singing it into the bosom of orthodoxy, the people thus becoming their own catechists. This declaration of faith in the efficacy of the rite, but also in its social capacity to gather all the people in a choral song (*fratrum concinentium voci-bus et cordibus*) can also be seen in an exceptional account – that of Augustine, who, describing in his *Confessions* the day in April 387 when he was baptized in Milan by Ambrose's own hands, exalts the "consolation and exhortation" of Ambrosian hymns. At the time he was writing these lines, the bishop of Hippo was weep-ing for his son Adeodatus, who had been baptized with him.[26] He recalls the emotive power of his teacher Ambrose's "celestial chants," remembering the dramatic circumstances in which they were instituted, one year before his baptism:

> How I wept during your hymns and songs! I was deeply moved by the music of the sweet chants of your Church. The sounds flowed into my ears and the truth was distilled into my heart. This caused the feelings of devotion to overflow. Tears ran, and it was good for me to have that experience. The Church at Milan had begun only a short time before to employ this method of mutual comfort and exhortation. The brothers used to sing together with both heart and voice in a state of high enthusiasm. Only a year or a little more had passed since Justina, mother of the young king Valentinian, was persecuting your servant Ambrose in the interest of her heresy. She had been led into error by the Arians. The devout congregation kept continual guard in the Church, ready to die with their bishop, your servant. There my mother, your handmaid, was a leader in keeping anxious watch and lived in prayer. We were still cold, untouched by the warmth of your Spirit, but were excited by the tension and dis-turbed atmosphere in the city. That was the time when the decision was taken to introduce hymns and psalms sung after the custom of the Eastern Churches, to prevent the people from succumbing to depression and exhaustion. From that time to this day the practice has been retained and many, indeed almost all your flocks, in other parts of the world have imitated it.[27]

As with Ambrose, prayer is as much praise or request as it is encouragement and exhortation. However, the insistence on the sensory dimension of the experience is more Augustinian than Ambrosian: as Peter Brown rightly notes, the bishop of Milan was a theologian of the purity of the soul, more than of the torments of the flesh.[28] Augustine, on the other hand, imitating Christ, was the figure who converted ancient tears into Christian ones: in this passage, like so many others in his writing, they flow like grace, the "sacrificial tears of a crushed heart" giving God the liquid gift of a shared sensitivity running through the bodies of the assembled followers and lifting them up in one sweeping motion.[29] Thus was formed a community of emotions heard like a "melodious concert" of harmonious voices and hearts, which not only spread to "an entire city" but imprinted itself onto its memory, continuing beyond to circulate "among us."[30] We would be hard pressed to better describe the threefold efficacy – emotional, communal, and memorial – of the liturgical act.

But for now the most important thing is to note that the author of *Confessions*, subtly playing on the opposition between hot and cold, clearly situates the liturgical innovation represented by Ambrosian hymns in the heat of political action. Or more precisely – if we follow Jacques Fontaine in his correct interpretation of the Augustinian *institutum est* (when he writes that hymns were instituted by Ambrose) – not the literary invention of a specific genre of liturgical poetry, but its social institution, "what we would call today the success of their institutional introduction into Milanese liturgy, rapidly followed by the adoption of this novelty by the large majority of churches in the West."[31] And indeed, all while confirming the Eastern origin of Ambrosian hymnody, Augustine attests to its circulation in Western churches, ten years later (Book 9 of *Confessions* was written between 397 and 400).

Paulinus of Milan's *Vita Ambrosii*, which constitutes, along with the accounts by Ambrose and Augustine, the third confirmation that the introduction of Ambrosian hymns can be viewed as a political event related to the "battle of the basilicas" of 386, also insists on this geographical expansion of a liturgical custom previously limited to the East, from the city of Milan to the entirety of the Western provinces: "On this occasion, antiphons, hymns, and vigils first began to be practiced in the church at Milan. And the devotion to this custom remains even to this very day, not only in the church, but through almost all the provinces of the West."[32]

While the expression *celebrari coeperunt* appears to confirm the fact that Augustine's *institutum* does indeed designate a political moment of liturgical crystallization more than a literary invention, the sequence *antiphonae, hymni et vigiliae* is harder to interpret, as it connects three words, in an elliptical trilogy, that designate realities of different types.[33] The first, *antiphona*, refers to a mode of choral singing (the act of two voices alternating); the second comes from the literary genre of a religious song; the third references a liturgical moment of time (the service of vigils). If we take the risk of combining these three heterogeneous elements, the semantic effect is thus: by leading all those assembled in the singing of hymns in alternating demi-choirs, Ambrose instituted in Milan a song of vigilance.

AFTER THE HOLY WEEK OF 386
(OR THE MEANING OF THE CHRISTIAN SPECTACLE)

On Thursday, April 2, the imperial court capitulated. Alternately employing the *vehemens et pugnax* tone of Ciceronian harangues and the nuances of biblical glosses[34] in his sermon *Against Auxentius*, Ambrose, a skillful orchestrator of political emotions continually playing the people against the court, succeeded in transforming the circumstances into a litmus test for his new conception of a bishop's power. A sociologist today would admire, apart from his sense of dramatization, the art of the "rise in generality" visible in the shift from a controversy to an affair, and from an affair to a cause.[35] For Ambrose was not only able to conflate Homoian doctrine with heresy and heresy with barbarism, he also transformed the fight against this barbaric heresy into the great cause of a church defending the inviolability of the "domain of God" from imperial intrusions.[36] "The Church is God's, and must not be given up to Caesar," he writes in the letter to his sister Marcellina in which he describes these decisive days.[37] His struggle then became getting the emperor to admit that he was neither above the Church, nor even at its summit, but the "son of the Church," and as such subject to the authority of its father, the bishop.

One modern historian exclaimed: Ambrose "sounds the death knell of the ancient world";[38] another enthused that Ambrose had forced Justina, "the Catherine de Medici of the Arians," to yield.[39] It would no doubt be uncharitable to list other examples of this historiographical enthusiasm, which merely shows us the power of persuasion wielded by Ambrose of Milan, snaring from the start historians in his own account, if only by making them believe in the robustness and airtightness of the categories of heresy and orthodoxy that he reinvented for the occasion. Granted, today there are many specialists dismantling the mechanisms therein, restoring the events of 386 to more reasonable proportions. This is the case, notably, in work by Christoph Markschies defining Ambrose's attitude as "neo-Nicaean"[40] as well as the more recent analysis by Michael Stuart Williams, which gives a sense of Ambrose's rhetorical power and his ability to name an enemy in order to define a community.[41] But this useful *ridimensionamento* has no place when attempting, as we are, to assemble the history of Ambrose's memory. All that matters is the block passed down through Ambrose's writing and Paulinus of Milan's *Vita*. What will then be remembered is an Ambrose who steadfastly confronted the Arian camp, obstinately defending the Church.

In the *Vita Ambrosii*, the election of 374 is almost immediately followed by the confrontation with "the woman's [Justina's] fury [and] the insane Arians' madness."[42] Historians' subtle distinctions are of little concern here, showing for example that Ambrose's election was likely the result of a compromise between Milan's different political-religious factions – which explains Paulinus's amazement when he realized that everyone had agreed on Ambrose's name in incredible unanimity (*repente in hunc mirabili et incredibili concordia consenserunt*).[43] This would also explain why the first years of his episcopate were likely the most conciliatory with the Homoians of Milan. And yet all that remains in memory is the overwhelming interdependence between heresy and barbarism that made the bishop the first defender, including against the emperor, of a Roman Empire assimilated with Christianity.[44]

If further convincing is needed, it suffices to look back at the account in *The Golden Legend* which, let's not forget, was one of the primary vectors of Ambrose's memory beginning in the thirteenth century, using narrative motifs strictly dependent on Paulinus of Milan's *Vita*. When Jacobus de Voragine reviewed all the ways in which Ambrose "set an example," he connected them, in six of eight cases, to the battle of wills between bishop and empire: his generosity ("when the emperor demanded that he surrender his basilica..."), his firmness in his faith ("when the emperor demanded the basilica..."), the desire for martyrdom ("in his letter *De basilica non tradenda*, we read..."), his perseverance in prayer (citing *Ecclesiastical History*, XI, 16, by Eusebius of

Caesarea: "Ambrose defended himself against the queen's fury not with his hand but with fasting and continuous vigils; with his prayers at the foot of the altar he gained God as defender for himself and for the Church"), the abundance of his tears (citing *Against Auxentius*, 2: "Against the Gothic troops my weapons are my tears"), and finally his unwavering courage ("Thus when the emperor wanted to take possession of a certain basilica…").[45]

During this week in the year 386, defending the Christian faith meant defending the city's holy places, that is, those places that Ambrose was at the same time anchoring in the sacredness of their relics. The emperor referred to the bishop as *tyrannus*,[46] accusing him of being a usurper who refused the legitimate right of *religio licita* to use places of worship, thanks to their status as *aedes sacrae*.[47] Ambrose was then forced to oppose the troops of Goth soldiers before him with other *milites*, a personal guard in essence, similar to the emperor's, though these were more like shock troops enlisted from heaven.[48] "Let all be well aware what kind of champions I desire, such as are wont to be protectors [*propugnatores*] not assailants. Such are they, O holy people, whom I have obtained for you, a benefit to all, and a hurt to none. These are the defenders whom I desire, these are my soldiers, not the world's soldiers, but Christ's. I fear no odium on account of these; their patronage is safe in proportion to its power. Nay, I desire their protection [*patrocinia*] for the very men who grudge them to me. Let them come then and see my body-guard [*stipatores*]: I deny not that I am surrounded by such weapons as these."[49] These men would be Ambrose's *defensores* of the city, joining the glorious cohort of its patron saints, and the impact of the discovery of their bodies, in 386, would be a discovery of "benefit to all" (*qui prosint omnibus*). "About the same time," writes Paulinus of Milan, *per idem tempus*, "the holy martyrs Protasius and Gervasius revealed themselves [*revelaverunt*] to the bishop."[50]

SIX

The Legendary Topography
of Ambrose's Memory in Milan
(Fifth to Sixteenth Century)

We are back, then, with the martyrs, at the time of Ambrose's "prophetic ardor," back with his "triumphal victims," who would soon be "exposed to the heavens like trophies." And we now have a better understanding of the context in which to place the dedications of the *basilica apostolorum* (also known as the *basilica Romana*, present-day San Nazaro, in the city's southeast) on May 9, 386, and the *basilica martyrum* (present-day Sant'Ambrogio, in the city's southwest) on June 16, 386. These were two new buildings whose construction must have started in 379 or 380, during Ambrose's episcopacy.[1] This explains, incidentally, why the imperial government, on learning that two new basilicas were about to be presented to the Nicaean Christians, requested that one of Milan's older basilicas be given to the Homoian sect.

The choice of the *basilica Portiana* on the outskirts of Milan seemed logical: first, for historical reasons, because it had most likely been built by Ambrose's predecessor, Auxentius, who had looked kindly on the Homoian faith; second, for liturgical reasons, because it had a baptistery;[2] and third and most important, for geographical reasons. The church of Portius (in Milan, as in Rome, religious buildings in the fourth century were known by the name of their founder or their site's property owner)[3] was destroyed at an unknown date, leaving no trace – at least as far as is known today. Archaeologists have long hesitated over its location. Known to be outside the city walls, it was first identified as the Church of San Lorenzo, south of the city, until recent work on that church's foundations moved the likely date of its construction to the beginning of the fifth century.[4] Consequently, the *basilica Portiana* is now identified with the Church of San Vittore al Corpo, in the city's western *suburbium*, a site known to have had a structure prior to the founding of San Vittore.[5] Siting the basilica there would also conform with the medieval memory of its location. From the *Libellus de citu civitatis*, probably written around the year 1000,[6] to the thirteenth-century *Liber notitiae Sanctorum Mediolani*,[7] tradition associates the former Basilica of Portius with the area around the "rotunda of Saint Gregory," referring to the ancient imperial mausoleum.[8]

IN THE CITY'S HEART: BASILICAS AND A BAPTISTERY

At this point we can reconstruct, in spatial terms, the showdown that occurred during Holy Week in 386. Though historians still hesitate to assign specific identities to the buildings mentioned in Ambrose's correspondence – in the heat of the moment, he identifies them only using such vague and uncertain terms as *basilica, ecclesia, baptisterii basilica*, and *ecclesiae basilica*[9] – the most likely hypothesis is also the simplest: for the duration of the crisis, the bishop almost certainly stayed in the *basilica vetus*, the old church adjoining his palace where he ordinarily celebrated Mass. Ambrose therefore did not venture out into the disputed areas. He went neither to the *Portiana*, though, as we learn from his account, he received running reports from that basilica as developments unfolded, nor to the nearby *basilica nova*, which, let's remember, the emperor also claimed at one point.

The cluster of episcopal buildings in the heart of the city marked the epicenter of the Ambrosian presence, which is to say the active presence of the bishop performing his pastoral duties in the midst of his flock. The archaeological excavations conducted in 2009 in today's Piazza Duomo sector of Milan, whose results are still partially unpublished, have revealed a relatively dense residential zone there in the fourth century, along with much older traces of Roman habitation.[10] The area was said, in medieval times, to have corresponded to the site of a temple dedicated to the Capitoline Triad. The recent discovery of a threshold stone under the central nave of the former Basilica di Santa Tecla, made from an ancient monolith and bearing a very worn inscription to Minerva, gives credence to this hypothesis.[11]

If we concede that, as seems most likely, the *basilica maior* in fact corresponds to the *basilica vetus*, and the *basilica minor* to the *basilica nova*, then the *vetus* is identifiable as the paleo-Christian church that existed on the site prior to Santa Maria Maggiore's construction in Carolingian times. Santa Maria Maggiore was itself superseded by the Milan Cathedral, or Duomo, in 1387.[12] All that is left today of the original church is the octagonal font of the baptistery of Santo Stefano alle Fonti, in which Ambrose was probably baptized in 374.[13] As to the *basilica nova*, which was likely still under construction in Ambrose's time, and whose founding is dated to the mid-fourth century, it corresponds to Santa Tecla, which was entirely destroyed in 1548, aside from a few architectural remains, to which we will return.[14] If Santa Tecla is known today at all, it is only because of the archaeological excavations undertaken in the 1960s by Mario Mirabella Roberti during the tunneling for the M1 subway line and the Duomo station.[15] Before the start of construction on the Duomo in 1387, and throughout the construction period that extended into the fifteenth century, the question of whether or not to keep the double cathedral structure – a feature that still baffles liturgical and archaeological understanding[16] – was an item of contention among those tending Ambrose's memory.

Finally, to complete this picture of the arrangement of monuments in the center of town, we should add the *domus Ambrosii*, or bishop's residence, to the episcopal complex.[17] It was most likely located between today's Piazza Fontana and Santo Stefano in Brolo,[18] not far from the two basilicas, but it probably had no architectural features that stood out in the urban landscape. In Paulinus of Milan's *Vita*, it is referred to simply as "the house where the bishop lived" (*domus in qua manebat episcopus*),[19] and there are no known examples in Italy before the sixth century of a bishop's residence organically integrated into the episcopal complex.[20] In Milan, the increase in size and importance of the bishop's manse coincided, as elsewhere in Italy, with a change in designation. By 863, it was known as the *domus sancte ecclesie*, and by 1137 as the *palatium*.[21]

The very first place designed to carry Ambrose's memory was therefore this network of buildings of worship. Yet if Ambrose chose to build, it was not so much to heighten his power as to widen it, spreading it across the whole city in an articulated structure of prestige that both displayed a constellation of memories and held them fast. This memory trap ordered space in such a way as to make it a *machina memorialis* capable of endlessly reactivating the recollection of Ambrose's undertakings and struggles, thus converting earthly power to heavenly glory, reusing the empire's grandeur to heighten the influence of the Church. Ambrose's only municipal addition to the central area of the episcopal complex – at least the only one to be archaeologically and historically attested – might seem slight, but it is nonetheless ideologically suggestive. The building in question is the Baptistery of San Giovanni alle Fonti, probably built in the central years of his episcopacy, going by the archaeological and numismatic material unearthed during the last cycle of excavations. The baptistery was destroyed toward the end of the fourteenth century or the start of the fifteenth.[22] One of its inscriptions, transcribed in a collection of epigraphs (the Lorsch Abbey sylloge), is attributed to Ambrose, echoing the theology of baptism he articulated in his treatises *De sacramentis* and *De mysteris* between 386 and 390.[23] It allows us to juxtapose Ambrose's liturgical innovations and their architectural expression, making San Giovanni alle Fonti the prototype of octagonal baptisteries in northern Italy and Gaul.[24]

Note that its plan – an octagon flanked by alternately quadrangular and semicircular niches – distinctly echoed the formal typology of imperial mausoleums, and notably Milan's own San Vittore al Corpo. The baptistery therefore signaled its ties to a beyond-the-walls neighborhood – the western *suburbium*, where the big Ad Martyres cemetery adjoined the hippodrome, the palace, and the ancient imperial mausoleum, and therefore, where the clash of powers visibly played out. Ambrose's strategy was clear: the bishop intended to flank Milan the political capital with Milan the Christian city, reordering space in this second Rome so as to reassign the remaining traces of the pagan past to the contemporary glorification of God, in a city that, let's remember, was the primary seat of imperial power in the western *orbis Romanus* during much of the second half of the fourth century.[25]

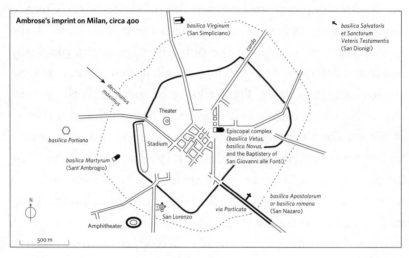

Ambrose's imprint on Milan, circa 400
basilica Virginum
(San Simpliciano)
cardo
basilica Salvatoris
et Sanctorum
Veteris Testamentis
(San Dionigi)
decumanus maximus
Theater
basilica Portiana
Stadium
basilica Martyrum
(Sant'Ambrogio)
Episcopal complex
(basilica Vetus,
basilica Novus,
and the Baptistery of
San Giovanni alle Fonti)
N
basilica Apostolorum
or basilica romana
(San Nazaro)
via Porticata
San Lorenzo
Amphitheater
500 m

(*PAO Seuil*)

ON THE CITY'S MARGINS: APOSTLES AND MARTYRS

And so, through his use of relics – moving the bodies of martyrs, and the stories that attached to them – Ambrose redrew
Milan's public space. To the southeast was the *basilica apostolorum* or *basilica Romana* (known since the seventh century as San
Nazaro); to the southwest the *basilica martyrum*, today's Sant'Ambrogio; to the north the *basilica virginum* (today called San Simpliciano); and to the northeast the *basilica salvatoris et sanctorum
veteris testamentis*. Destroyed in 1549 during the construction of
the advanced bastions of Milan's city walls, the *basilica salvatoris* was dedicated in the ninth century to the memory of Bishop
Dionysius, exiled by Emperor Constance II in 355, presumably to
Cappadocia, where he died a few years later. A late legend, collected or invented by Florus of Lyon in the first third of the ninth
century, relates that it was Ambrose who induced Bishop Basil
of Caesarea to send Dionysius's body to Milan, and that he conferred the title *confessor* on his illustrious predecessor, who had

also stood up to the emperor.[26] Exiled with Dionysius by the Council of Milan in 355, Bishop Eusebius of Vercelli survived long enough to benefit from Emperor Julius's amnesty and was able to resume his episcopal position until his death in 371. According to a late biographical account (the *Vita antiqua S. Eusebii*, which is dated no earlier than the ninth century), Eusebius was buried in a basilica he had built to house the remains of a martyr, the mysterious Theognistus.[27]

Ambrose of Milan in fact had a precursor in Bishop Eusebius of Vercelli.[28] Yet it was Ambrose's actions that struck posterity as foundational. In the 380s, northern Italy received a somewhat inexplicable influx of apostolic remains. Ambrose took advantage of this, turning the basilica that received the bodies of Thomas, John, and Andrew (or else the Roman relics of Peter and Paul—the eleventh-century tradition wavers on this point)[29] into a *basilica apostolorum*. Milan undoubtedly created the prototype here. During the final years of the fourth century, the bishops Bassianus in Lodi, Sabinus in Piacenza, and Gaudentius in Brescia copied Ambrose and consecrated apostolic basilicas at the gates of their cities, importing Eastern relics by a method still unknown to us today.[30] This proliferation of *basilicae apostolorum* in Lombardy was soon followed by another vogue for *basilicae martyrum*, after the discovery of the remains of Gervasius and Protasius. The trend first appeared in the region under Ambrose's metropolitan authority, then spread far beyond those bounds. During his trip to Florence in 393, Ambrose brought with him from Bologna the bodies of the martyrs Vitalis and Agricola.[31] In sees from Nola to Hippo and including, in Gaul, Rouen, Tours, and Vienna, bishops placed the relics of martyrs on the approaches to their towns to form a rampart of their glorious bodies.[32] They marked out the *limina sanctorum* that Magnus Felix Ennodius, bishop of Pavia, described in his *Itinerarium Brigantionis castelli*, a travel poem written in 502, in which the towns Ennodius visited bear the names of the saints surrounding them.[33]

The establishment of these martyrological cults revived the memory of Christian persecution in towns where that memory had long been fading – this was certainly the case in Milan. In 397, the year of Ambrose's death, three missionaries from Cappadocia (Martirius, Sisinnius, and Alexander) were slain in the Tyrol by the inhabitants of the Val di Non, who were defending their pagan rites.[34] The story was widely circulated. Bishop Vigilius of Trent sent his account to John Chrysostomos in Constantinople, and also to Simplicianus, Ambrose's spiritual father, who succeeded him in 397, dying in 400.[35] These victims of paganism arrived at just the right time to endow the *basilica virginum* with their saintly remains, an initiative attributed since the thirteenth century to Ambrose. In fact, it was his successor, Simplicianus, who accepted the remains of the Val di Non martyrs.[36] The *virginum* was the only one of the so-called Ambrosian basilicas not to be located in a funerary precinct,[37] as all the others were in the extensive cemeterial areas situated along the main access routes to the city. This meant that the basilica was part of a broader integration of the *suburbium* into the urban core, in an authentically Christian topography.

CONDUCTIVE BODIES:

AMBROSE AND THE INVENTION OF THE CHRISTIAN CITY

In moving sacred remains, Ambrose was not just rearranging the territory of the Christian city. He was making it into a polarized space. From saintly persons to sacred precincts, the ecclesiastical authority's territorialization created a diverse space with locations of differing intensities.[38] And Ambrose, organizing and disciplining the diffuse sacredness of the classical space, limiting the familial excesses of a cult of the dead he held in deep suspicion, and focusing the power of miracles more sharply, increased sacral efficiency.[39] Peter Brown says no less when he writes that Ambrose "was like an electrician who rewires an antiquated wiring system: more power could pass through stronger, better-insulated wires toward the bishop as leader of the community."[40] He was the inspired expert on conductive bodies, delivering God's power, and everything therefore led back to him. The mechanism would be completed at his death, once his remains were deposited under the main altar of the basilica that would later bear his name, next to the martyrs whom he would accompany, "those triumphant victims [who will] be brought to the place where Christ is the victim," as he wrote his sister Marcellina.[41]

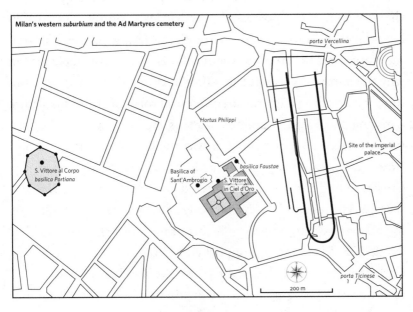

(*PAO Seuil*)

The Legendary Topograpy of Ambrose's Memory in Milan

It's no doubt clearer now why Ambrose, in the same letter, relates that scenes of demoniac possession accompanied the miracles of Gervasius and Protasius: "You have heard the evil spirits cry out, confessing to the martyrs that they are unable to support the tortures that the martyrs inflicted on them." The presence of saints and the demonically possessed, whose scandal shredded the ordinary experience of social life, introduced a transcendence that made God's sphere a distinct domain of activity and communication.[42] In a recent book comparing Ambrose's actions in Milan after the battle of the basilicas to those of John Chrysostomos in Antioch and Cyril in Jerusalem, the U.S. historian Dayna S. Kalleres interprets his policy of distributing sacred relics around the city and polarizing the public space by founding new basilicas in terms of exorcism and charismatic power – Ambrose's aim was to rid polytheistic Milan of its demons. That's why Paulinus of Milan put so much emphasis on the exorcism of the possessed – the Nicaean community bonded over the exclusion of pagans, Arians, and Jews, projecting a common opprobrium on all of them. It's also the most likely reason why the baptistery was at the center of this arrangement of monuments, bringing back the architectural form of the mausoleum, a resting place for the famous dead, as the locus where all Christians received a second birth. It was the visible manifestation of three corporeal envelopes, embedded one inside the other: the Christian body of the newly baptized person, the body of the consecrated church, and the urban body of the entire city.[43] Ambrose, for his part, arranging to be incorporated into the basilica that would bear his name, accomplished what another U.S. historian, Catherine M. Chin, has called "an extrabodily embodiment," meaning the bringing together of his two bodies, the material and the spiritual – material insofar as he was a man, and spiritual insofar as he was invested by sacramental transaction with the power of God – into one place where the invisible was made visible.[44]

In Ambrose's Milan, just as in Pope Damasus's Rome, the invention of the Christian city consisted very much of occupying the land so as to impose on it a particular topography and form of power.[45] The bishop placed himself, says Georges Duby, "right at the point where heaven and earth were joined, between the visible and the invisible. His words were addressed sometimes toward the one and sometimes toward the other."[46] His were the hands that distributed the sacred, with precision and generosity. Did Ambrose overlay a sign of the cross on Milan, placing sanctuaries at each of its cardinal points, as though he were baptizing a Roman city? The hypothesis has been suggested.[47] It might be attributing too much symbolic coherence to the actions of this architect bishop, however. For all his claims to being a *sapiens architectus*, he could only graft the network of basilicas onto the existing system of roads that had linked Milan, a city in the plains, to its surrounding territory since pre-Roman times.[48]

Nonetheless, thanks to the triumph of Christian hermeneutics, this symbolic interpretation of the cruciform layout would prevail, in the same way that the floor plan of transepted basilicas could only be seen as the projected shadow of Christ's cross. Yet the archaeological digs conducted by Yvon Thébert in the House of the Hunt in Bulla Regia have shown that the basilic plan stemmed from the political vocabulary of Roman private architecture: carving out a perpendicular transept in front of the apse made it easier to parade clients in front of the *dominus*. In transitioning from a place of power to a place of worship, the basilica gave the shape not so much a new function as a new meaning. In other words, "a Christian interpretation was slapped onto an architectural trope originally devoid of any meaning of the kind."[49] When, around 380, Gregory of Nazianzus described the Constantinian Church of the Holy Apostles, he compared it to a cross, the symbol of Christ's victory over death, the holy cross of a religion that was then developing very rapidly. But he was the first to do so: fifty years earlier, Eusebius had described the same building without making this connection.

The *basilica apostolorum* that Bishop Ambrose began to build in Milan in 382 replicated – and it was the first in the West to do so – the plan in the shape of a Greek cross of the Apostoleion (as the Church of the Holy Apostles was also known) in Constantinople.[50] The basilica was grafted onto the middle portion of a column-lined monumental avenue that, prolonging the *decumanus maximus* (main thoroughfare) beyond the ramparts, went from the *porta Romana* toward the southwest of the city, like the Church of the Holy Sepulchre in Jerusalem.[51] Archaeological excavations have shown the great disruption this vast construction project brought to the neighborhood, even as it completed in a spectacular way this string of monuments embellishing the Roman city and offering emperors the sumptuous framework of a 2,000-foot-long *via Porticata* for their *adventus* (processional approach).[52] The construction site was still very recent when Ambrose decided to build his new basilica there: the triumphal arch at the head of the avenue was probably raised in 375. It wasn't just that the bishop managed to co-opt the system of monuments in an imperial city to augment the power of the Church, but that he was able to effect this symbolic reassignment *in real time*, impacting historical developments as they were happening.[53]

THE CITY AS MEMORY MACHINE

So what needs to be written here, then, is very much a history of memory, of memory reinventing the meaning of places through its use of time. It didn't simply add thickness or distance to time through the slow sedimentation of accumulated segments; it also revealed time to itself by betraying it. For if memory has a history, it is one with sudden swerves and accelerations. This is true of the 380s, a spasmodic decade with spectacular and historic swings, and it therefore makes good sense to cast the story of the invention of the Christian city as a long-term event. I say event because there was always something violent and sudden in Ambrose's actions – the energy, boldness, and insolence of a military strike, as if he could bend the world to his will with the force of his rhetoric. But more importantly, he had the power to inaugurate, which is why his effectiveness must be measured by the longevity of what he brought about. Milan would long retain the memorializing configuration of monuments imposed upon the city by its bishop. And so Ambrose represents here not so much the origin as the first act in an endeavor of re-remembering. There is no beginning. It's always, already, the reiteration of an older rebeginning.

Ambrose's network of basilicas produced one of Milan's deepest and most significant archives – a "text of the city," and a durable and restrictive configuration of prestige that structured the city's ceremonial and political space.[54] Not long after Ambrose's death, the Basilica of San Lorenzo was erected to complete the set of monuments, though historians and archaeologists are still debating its exact date and purpose.[55] The first bishop to be buried there was Eusebius, a few years after the sack of Milan by Attila in 452, but Eusebius could not have built San Lorenzo.[56] Reusing stones from the amphitheater south of the city, not far from the former imperial palace and near the road leading to Pavia (the *via Ticinensis*), San Lorenzo is arguably the most impressive of Milan's paleo-Christian basilicas. The central-plan building consists of a quadrangle whose arcaded porticos open onto a cloister surmounted by raised galleries and a monumental propylaeum at whose center rises a triumphal arch.[57] The arch is at the head of a major axis along which runs today's *via Torino*, used since at least the thirteenth century for civic processions, but also for political rituals and ceremonies heading toward the heart of the city.[58] The furrow had been deeply and durably traced.

So Ambrose enveloped the city of Milan in the aura of his name, and he did so once and for all. Transforming the Lombard capital into a prototype of the Christian city, he brought its urban development into alignment with the active memory of its own past. Do you remember the telling episode in the *Vita Ambrosii* when the young Ambrose, thinking to escape his calling as a bishop, tries to flee Milan by night, only to find himself at dawn caught in the city's gravitational field and pulled back into it?[59] The Milanese were to relive the experience of this impossible flight over and over; they would never shake it off. For the circular city is very much as Alberto Savinio described it: a wheel that, turning on its central hub, draws the Milanese inward and propels others outward, by turns generating centripetal and centrifugal forces.[60]

Milan's structure, with its roads radiating from the center but concentrically linked to each other, was fixed at an early date by Ambrose's occupation of its land, and the tempo of its urban development was marked by the periodic enlargement of its surrounding walls.[61] The *corpi santi*, which garrisoned Milan's basilicas like sentinels watching over the city, initially formed an advance defense of the urban body beyond its walled perimeter. But the walls in question were Maximian's, built at the end of the third century and enlarging the republican walls to the northeast of the imperial capital to enclose an area of approximately 100 hectares (247 acres). When the walls of the commune were constructed starting in 1156, the enclosed area more than doubled. At over 240 hectares (600 acres), Milan was one of the largest cities in the medieval West. The basilicas built by Ambrose were now no longer in Milan's suburbs but had been swallowed up by the new enclosure and overrun by the expanding town, which spread outward in the thirteenth century, or rather radiated out along the feeder canals bringing water to the circular channel at the foot of the walls. It was to defend these new industrial outskirts that the Redefosso was dug in the fourteenth century, an outer canal that entirely surrounded, though at a considerable distance, the commune walls. The bastions of the Spanish walls built between 1546 and 1560 by Ferrante Gonzaga, who governed Milan in the name of the Spanish Habsburgs, followed the line traced by the old Redefosso. These walls set off an area of 825 hectares (2,040 acres), marking Milan's maximum expansion prior to the industrial era. When the Spanish walls were subsequently destroyed by Napoleon, their imprint remained in the form of a circular avenue.[62]

As Milan's urban geography was extended outward from its initial core, what became of the designation *corpi santi*? It shifted as well. When the bodies of the saints anchored basilicas that were within the city limits, the expression *corpi santi* had to apply to more than just the dead in order for them to project their sacred aura beyond the city gates. By the fourteenth century, *corpi santi* referred to the suburban outskirts that were *extra redefossa Mediolani*, that is, beyond the Redefosso, and these areas benefited from a distinct system of laws, land use, and taxation.[63] Passing into the administrative language of town management, the term *corpi santi* came to apply even farther from the town center in 1783, when it was used to designate the communes outside the city whose farmsteads (*cascine*) provided the manpower and food supply for the populous industrial urban center of Milan. This lasted until 1873, when the *corpi santi* were annexed, ending their judicial autonomy.[64] Fifteen hundred years after

Ambrose, nothing remained of the saints' bodies but a term, a fiction that could be transferred on a whim, and yet the bodies continued, in the area beyond the city, to provide obstinately for its defense.

Here, then, is the configuration of monuments that I propose to call "the legendary topography of Ambrosian memory." It made Milan into a machine for remembering – or rather, re-remembering. In his *Topographie légendaire des évangiles en Terre sainte* (Legendary topography of the Gospels in the Holy Land), a sumptuous and puzzling work, the sociologist Maurice Halbwachs retraces the footsteps of a pilgrim from Bordeaux whose journey in the first quarter of the fourth century provides the earliest such itinerary on record. A journey's beauty is often determined by one's choice of guide. So here we have him traveling, describing, inventing – our pilgrim locates the biblical memory of the city at the moment when that memory is starting to blanket over Jewish memory. And Halbwachs follows him, looking for the shifts that signal the construction of memory, trying to understand how memories owe less to remnants from the past than to present needs. What he finds along the way is what he calls "the resistance of things," their stubborn and resonant obstinacy. It is worth citing Halbwachs at length:

> In their effort to adapt, people encounter the resistance of things, sometimes of rites, of mechanical or material formulas, of ancient commemorations fixed in the stones of churches or monuments, where the beliefs and the testimony once took the form of solid and durable objects. It is true that these objects themselves, as they appear to us, were the result of an earlier adaptation of beliefs inherited from the past to the beliefs of the present; at the same time, they were the result of adaptation of the latter to the material vestiges of ancient beliefs. This is how one traces the course of time.

Whatever epoch is examined, attention is not directed toward the first events, or perhaps the origin of these events, but rather toward the group of believers and their commemorative work.[65]

This is Halbwachs's lesson, establishing memory as a social fact. In brief, a memory is a reconstruction of the past, the recomposing of an old image. Even when remembering individually, a person does so in function of the representational system that is in vigor at the time of remembering, and this system of representations is that of a given society at a given moment. This is what can be called the social framework of memory, in which language itself plays an important role, for this summoning of the past into the present "accords, in each epoch, with the predominant thoughts of the society."[66] Yet at the same time, Halbwachs's lesson is all about the bias of things. In his *Topographie légendaire*, he describes irregular landscape features – slopes, crags, and declivities. Memory attaches to these and is not easily altered afterward. Rocks are like obstacles in the current of a stream. Memories traveling separately and from different sources can flow into one another, braid their waters (as in the legends that surround Mount Zion); others, on the contrary, may on encountering rocks divide and slow down, spreading out over a surface on which a strongly rhythmic narration is mirrored (as with the Holy Sepulchre). But in any case, there is no memorative locus, because the monument itself is no more than the desiccated solidification of a memory. All that exists are patterns of flow, networks, correspondences, which Maurice Halbwachs describes in retrograde, up to the point where all trace of what originated the memory fades away.[67]

A city's past is therefore always a version of the present, hovering beneath the interplay of opposing memories.[68] "Only the image of space, because of its stability, creates for us the illusion that we never change as time passes and that we recapture the past in the present; but this is indeed how one can define memory; and space alone is stable enough to endure without aging or losing any part of itself."[69] Cities, in brief, are like living organisms in not being stable so much as stationary. As time passes, constant modifications are called for, which progress through three phases: reinvestment (to remember is always to repossess a given place); transaction (one has to reach an agreement with the competing interpretations of the place); and consolidation. That is how a tradition is transmitted, and how a memory persists – not despite its transformations but because of them.[70]

Constantly varying but always active, the Ambrosian *machina memorialis* made Milan into an engine for remembering its saints, or more accurately for remembering the saints as Ambrose invented them, by continuously organizing and reorganizing stories about space around a linked set of memories. What is meant here by *machina memorialis* is the mnemonic architecture of monasticism, of which the Christian city can be seen as an amplified form. It does not aim solely at sheltering Christian meditation in a glorious setting but at enabling it, concretely, and guiding its course. As Mary Carruthers writes, "[The buildings'] function is not primarily commemorative or 'symbolic': it is to act as engines channeling and focusing the restless power of the ever-turning wheel that is the human mind."[71] It therefore fell on all the "new Ambroses," that is, all who felt authorized to act in Ambrose's name, to reactivate this memory machine. Many of Milan's bishops did so, including the most illustrious among them, Carlo Borromeo, who was the city's archbishop from 1564 until his death in 1584 and who in many respects represents the endpoint of our quest.

Yes, Ambrose existed, but what we can say about his actual life comes down to the shards of existence, the fragments of a fault-ridden block that I have proposed calling, echoing Roland Barthes, biographemes – moments, details, or scenes in which the particularity of a life is diffracted and which, once they are dispersed, become affixed to other persons, other objects, other places and thus, in the proper sense, make memory. Fastening biographemes to a mnemonic topography, thus making the city into a fictional space – this was the work of the curators of Ambrose's memory in Milan.

SEVEN

A Life in Pieces:
The Golden Altar and the Carolingian
Crystallization of Ambrosian Memory
(Ninth Century)

But where the hell did they put the keys? When, as a measure of penitence, he set out to re-remember the Ambrosian city through the moving and exposition of relics – in more technical terms, translation and ostension – Archbishop Carlo Borromeo of course wanted to begin with the most prestigious of holy bodies: those of the martyrs Gervasius and Protasius, reunited in death by Ambrose, who later joined them beneath the altar of the basilica that carries his name. And so on March 5, 1578, the archbishop tasked Giovanni Francesco Bascapè with identifying and authenticating these venerable remains. A young Milanese noble who had entered Carlo Borromeo's service as a cathedral canon, Bascapè had composed two years earlier, on the occasion of the Jubilee of Milan of 1576, a *Libro d'alcune chiese di Milano* – a practical guide to the city's holy bodies, listing altar by altar the prayers due them.[1] It also included Italian translations of passages from Paulinus of Milan's *Vita Ambrosii*, as well as from Augustine's *Confessions* and Ambrose's letters recounting the invention, or discovery, of relics in his time. He was therefore indisputably the man for the job, which was to find a way to open the locks on the golden altar so that "the paternal and divine examples that [Saint Ambrose] once gave his people"[2] could again be followed.

And yet the prelate was very quickly confronted with the ancestral rivalry of two religious communities fighting over who was to handle saint worship. The guardians of the Sant'Ambrogio sanctuary were the official priests of the basilica; their canonical chapter dated back to at least 1029 and served the church of the same name. But the monks living in the adjacent monastery also served the basilica and contested the chapter's jurisdiction over the abbey. There were therefore two communities at Sant'Ambrogio, the monks and the canons, whose relationship only worsened in the twelfth century. The basilica was a battlefield, sometimes literally – sources make frequent mention of the *effusione sacerdotalis sanguinis* in the second half of the twelfth century.[3] The conflict centered notably on the division of offerings made to the golden altar, which is why the monks and canons each had a key to the precious reliquary that granted access to the holy bodies. Impassioned letters to the Vatican, threats, legal proceedings: nothing doing. Bascapè had to give up on opening the golden altar. Archbishop Carlo Borromeo would never be able to see the holy bodies of Gervasius, Protasius, and Ambrose, and identify them according to the new post-Tridentine protocol requirements for the authentication of relics.[4]

Realizing his failure, his only choice was to rely on a "constant tradition," which "reports that the holy bodies of the martyrs Gervasius and Protasius, and of Ambrose, archbishop of Milan and Doctor of the Church, are found beneath the main altar of the aforesaid church, built long ago on the orders of Angilbertus, archbishop of Milan, constructed of gold and silver, adorned with gems: as is also seen in the images themselves and the letters sculpted on this altar."[5] The sepulchre was not reexamined until 1864 (see color plate 4). That event was momentous, simultaneously prompting an initial campaign of archaeological surveys[6] and a volley of pastoral letters from Lombard bishops enlisting Ambrose in the political battles of their own day. Another ten years later, in 1874, during the solemn celebration that accompanied the translation of the urn holding the remains of the three saints, which were replaced beneath the altar, the bishop of Lodi, Lucido Maria Parocchi, urged the Catholics of the world to share "the Lombards' joy" and remember that Ambrose, champion of the battle against heretics, could support the fight against modern paganism.[7]

ANGILBERT: FRANKISH BISHOP AND *QUASI SANCTUS AMBROSIUS*

In 1578, Bascapè was unable to open the reliquary of the golden altar of the Basilica of Sant'Ambrogio. But he knew enough about it to state the basics: the reliquary had been built on the orders of the archbishop of Milan, Angilbertus; "constructed of gold and silver, adorned with gems"; the fact that it gathered the bodies of the martyrs Gervasius and Protasius and of the holy bishop Ambrose was "also seen in the images themselves and the letters sculpted on this altar." This description suggests an analytical process that we can today follow step-by-step. Let's begin with the reference to the commission and to the man who made it. Angilbert II, archbishop of Milan from 824 to 859, did in fact reunite the bodies of Ambrose and the martyrs Gervasius and Protasius in a single sarcophagus of porphyry.[8] The purple color of the urn likely earmarked it for a member of the imperial family. Local lore turned it into the sarcophagus of Valentinian II, which is unlikely but cleaves nicely to the political aspect of the undertaking. This legend was collected in the second half of the nineteenth century by a priest at the basilica, Francesco Maria Rossi, who left behind a precious chronicle of the archaeological excavations he had undertaken there.[9] Note that the making of a Carolingian monument by Angilbert II features reuse and thereby anchors the Ambrosian gesture more firmly to the imperial ambitions of the enterprise.

Arranged perpendicularly to the two original sepulchres, the sarcophagus was tucked inside the large golden altar, a masterpiece of Carolingian goldsmithery, which then became the *arca*, or reliquary. The *fenestella confessionis* of the rear side of the monument opened directly onto the holy bodies, Roman style–until readjustments made around 972–73, prompted by crypt renovations, reoriented the sepulchres and made them disappear into the base.[10] Above the altar was placed a ciborium, whose stuccos were redone in the Ottonian era, but which from the start had porphyry columns, in all likelihood reusing the same ancient materials as the sarcophagus, adding a touch of solemnity to the staging of its relics (see color plate 5).[11]

Art historians are hesitant about the precise dating of this monumental work, given the questionable authenticity of the episcopal *preceptum* (injunction) of March 1, 835, that mentions it.[12] But it is highly likely that we are somewhere in the 840s, when Angilbert II ordered a major restructuration of the apsidal area of the basilica.[13] Between the earthquake of 1191 and the bombings of 1943, the apse mosaic has endured a fair amount of damage and several restorations, which complicates its interpretation. As seen today, it represents an eloquent political manifesto for the episcopal monarchy and the principle of ecclesial hierarchy, and includes a rather rare representation of the theory of the suffragans,[14] in the form of the orderly group of Lombard bishops who were dependent on the archbishop of Milan – remember that the diocese of Milan was elevated to the rank of archdiocese in the eighth century, its bishops having been called archbishops since Theodore II (732-46) because they oversaw the metropolitan province of the suffragan dioceses of Milan. The model here was clearly Roman, perhaps with even a nod to the primitive mosaics of the apse of St. Peter's in the Vatican.[15] Generally speaking, while Angilbert II's monumental endeavor recalled recent precedents – the translation of the relics of Augustine to Pavia or Mark to Venice (829-36)[16] – it primarily evoked the tomb of Saint Peter in Rome, where the founder's sepulchre and the altar at which his successors officiate were similarly connected.[17]

In the thirteenth century, the *Liber notitiae sanctorum Mediolani*, an inventory of the saints and sanctuaries of the diocese of Milan compiled by Gotofredo da Bussero, again closely linked the golden altar to the person who ordered it, as we can read: *Angelbertus qui fecit deaudari altare sancti Ambroxii*.[18] On the rear side of the altar, the classic scene of dedication to the saint (Angilbert kneeling before Ambrose to offer him the altar) is split: the first image is mirrored by the symmetrical depiction of the goldsmith, also prostrating himself before the patron saint to present him with his work (see color plate 3).[19] The patron and the artist are both being crowned by the bishop-saint; the figure of Volvinus appears surrounded, haloed almost, by an unusual inscription – VOLVINUS MAGIST(ER) PHABER – in which the Hellenistic writing (*phaber* for *faber*) perhaps adds emphasis to this demonstration of "authorship."[20] Note in passing that this "artist signature" from the Carolingian era would complicate in particular the traditional chronology of the progressive affirmation of the "sovereignty of the artist" in the Middle Ages,[21] unless it were to arouse our undoubtedly healthy suspicion of the assumption that an artist's signature invariably meant the work was the product of their individual creativity.[22] The work of art would then appear as a work in the fully religious sense of the word, representing an element of exchange in the general economy of salvation.[23]

What's important to remember here is that Angilbert, very likely of Frankish origin, was a Carolingian par excellence; his project to exalt Ambrose's memory through monuments helped to bind Milan to the imperial and monastic order that governed Charlemagne's *renovatio imperii*.[24] The Benedictine monastery adjoining the Basilica of Sant'Ambrogio was founded in 784, ten years after the Carolingians conquered the city, by Archbishop Peter.[25] Peter was a Frank who played an important role in the Carolingian reforms, notably during the Council of Frankfurt in 794, establishing, among other important disciplinary and doctrinal decisions, the Western position on the Iconoclastic Controversy in the Byzantine Empire.[26] Returning from Rome in 781, Charlemagne had come through Milan – according to the Frankish scholar and Charlemagne biographer Eginhard, he had his daughter Gisela baptized there by Bishop Thomas.[27] He himself confirmed the establishment of the *monasterium sancti Ambrosii* in an April 790 diploma that insisted on the protocols for electing a new abbot in strict conformance with the "Rule of Saint Benedict" so that monks' prayers would ensure the salvation of the empire.[28]

The Milan monastery was the first cisalpine Benedictine institution. However, it's worth noting, as Jean-Charles Picard does, that while this connection between a suburban basilica and a monastic foundation meant to serve it may appear banal in Frankish Gaul, it was unusual in Italy.[29] The same can be said about the figure of a bishop as patron saint of the city, which appeared quite late in northern Italy.[30] As a result, the Milanese crystallization of Ambrosian devotion in the ninth century clearly appears to be a Carolingian moment. It's best understood through the ideological efforts of a line of Frankish bishops intent on reusing the vestiges of Ambrose's memory to construct the glorious edifice of Milan's imperial renaissance under the aegis of Charlemagne and his successors.[31]

Excluding Anselm's support for Bernard's revolt against his uncle Louis the Pious in 817-18, the archbishops of Milan were always unfailingly loyal to the Italian kings of the Carolingian line, who were often crowned and buried in the Basilica of Sant'Ambrogio.[32] During his long episcopate (which, remember, lasted from 824 to his death in 859), Angilbert II of Milan played an important role in Lothar I's government (840-55), inspiring several capitularies, or collections of ordinances, concerning political reform. He was named *missus* (the emperor's envoy) in 844, a year during which he traveled to Rome to attend the crowning of Lothar's son, Louis II of Italy (850-75). However, within the *regnum*, Angilbert II was equally concerned with ensuring the autonomy and standing of his episcopal seat, establishing his scriptorium, which would attract Frankish and Irish monks, and continuing Ambrose's project to occupy Lombard territory with the relics of saints (hence the translations of the body of Calogero di Albenga to the monastery of San Pietro di Civate, on the Lake of Lecco, and of the relics of Primo and Feliciano from Leggiuno, on Lake Maggiore).[33]

Telling from this point of view is an episode recounted by Andreas of Bergamo in which we see Lothar greet Angilbert flatteringly as a *quasi sanctus Ambrosius*, to which the archbishop responds: *nec ego sanctus Ambrosius, nec tu dominus Deus* – "I am no more Saint Ambrose than you are the Lord God."[34] The emperor's greeting betrays the political intention behind the reuse of Ambrose's memory in the Carolingian project: the bishop and the emperor find themselves jointly exalted. But we also hear, in Angilbert II's response, the slight grating produced by this tweaking of the remains of the past: if the archbishop of Milan was the new Ambrose, what was to be done with the memory of his anti-imperial combat? Could this element, crucial as it was, be removed from the story? If so, wouldn't its remainders threaten to come back around, like a past that won't fade and that weakens the edifice of memory being built?

THE ALTAR, THE TOMB, AND THE ARK OF THE COVENANT: POETRY IN THE SHIMMER

To answer this question, we need to patiently resume our inventory of borrowings and successions: What was being reused in Saint Ambrose's golden altar? Consider the object in its materiality[35] – for it is that materiality that, during the early Middle Ages, indicated the highest level of spirituality.[36] This very costly object was in all likelihood paid for with the bishop's personal wealth, recently augmented by a fiscal reform affecting the redistribution of revenues from tax on income from secular properties in Milan.[37] It is composed of a wooden core covered with embossed plaques of gold and silver, which are ornamented with precious gems and enamels. The altar's front facade, gold, presents twelve scenes from the life of Christ, while the reverse side, silver, also displays twelve scenes, from the life of Ambrose (see color plate 2). The craftsmanship of the former appears more dynamic and more clearly inspired by antiquity than that of the latter, which is more static, and is deemed by specialists to be the likely work of an artist or studio other than the one subsequently referred to as "Volvinus." The ensemble presents several characteristics of the Constantinopolitan visual tradition, in all likelihood brought to Lombardy through illuminated works, as the narrativity as a whole is clearly inspired by manuscript art.[38] But before characterizing its legibility, let's first examine its visibility:[39] all that was visible to the believers looking at the golden altar from the nave was the bejeweled cross in the composition's central panel, the narrative scenes around it disappearing into a dazzling shimmer of jewels, etchings, and gemstones.[40]

The long inscription on the rear side of the altar provides an expert explanation for this overall impression, already highly significant in itself. The reliquary's blinding brightness is that of the interior virtue of the souls it protects, made visible on the outside through the shine of gold, as well as of enamels and gems.[41] Metals and gemstones contribute to the altar's ornamental power, which provides additional sacrality or, more precisely, augments the object's sacral efficacy. This is where the dazzle effect takes on an entirely political meaning.[42] Such is the *ornamentum*: a capacity for abstraction – this word should be understood in its full meaning, both in terms of extraction and spiritualization – that goes hand in hand with the act of reuse, thanks to its "power of general orchestration powerful enough to modulate its consonances and its dissonances on multiple registers."[43]

Following the restoration efforts led by Carlo Capponi in 1996 and the concurrent scientific study of the gems, we have a clear understanding of the thirteen cut stones, five cameos, and eight etchings irregularly scattered throughout the altar, primarily on its southern face and western side.[44] All date from antiquity, some bearing pagan motifs: heads of Medusa, profiles of women, and – undoubtedly among the most ancient, likely dating to the first century BCE – a stone carved with the name of its owner, VOTURIA.C.F.[45] It is mounted backward (legible side toward the wall), like many of the recycled *gemmae litteratae*, in order not to create false legibility. Stones and cameos come from antiquity-era jewels, rings, or signet rings. In the case of seals, some are reuses of reuses: Charlemagne himself used etchings of Roman origin as a signet ring, until 813.[46]

Some of these reused materials may have been gifts, but others came directly from ancient necropolises: let's not forget that the Basilica of Sant'Ambrogio was situated atop one of the largest cemeteries in Milan's western district – the Ad Martyres necropolis.[47] This may have served as a gold mine of *spoliae*, not just gems, but also marble, carved stones, inscriptions, sarcophagi: we can therefore assume, in the case of the Ambrosian basilica, that vestiges were "updated" in situ, reused as they resurfaced, in a way inverting the fatality of sedimentation. Note in passing that this extraordinary wealth caused serious problems in terms of the altar's security, and that sources (notably in the thirteenth century) are full of accounts of thefts, sometimes committed by the basilica's guardians themselves: for example, we see Giacomo Descatius, *custos* of the chapter, admitting fault, give up a house located in the parish S. Pietro al Dosso on May 8, 1235, "in restitution for the gold he pilfered from the altar of the aforesaid church."[48] This situation forced Archbishop Ottone Visconti to recommend in 1292 the installation of a metallic barrier isolating the main altar.[49]

The golden altar was also the site of other Ambrosian reuses, nonphysical but highly significant: those of hagiographic motifs. To understand these, we should consider the narrative register of the represented scenes.[50] Facing the nave, the golden altar's front facade displays twelve episodes from the life of Christ in embossed gold, in two columns and three rows that are read bottom to top.[51] On the other side, a response in the form of twelve scenes from the life of Ambrose, following the same rhythmical sequence – three rows on both sides of the central panel of the *fenestella confessionis* on which appears the double dedication of the church and the saint's altar – which are read in the same way, bottom to top and two by two. This parallelism between the two biographical cycles, one depicted in gold, the other in silver, turns Ambrose into an *alter Christus* whose existence is likewise captured by three major moments: birth and life before the calling, the performance of miracles and the governing of souls, and the story of the Passion. In both cases, the Eucharistic sacrifice is at the heart of the narrative.

This bestowed upon the golden altar a very specific liturgical signification adroitly elucidated by the eight-hexameter epigraph running along its sides. Exalting both *sanctus Ambrosius* and *dominus Angilbertus*, using Roman poetic forms (originating notably from the Santa Prassede church), this masterpiece of episcopal monumental epigraphy makes clear, as previously underlined, the theological signification behind the dazzling exterior of the object, which consequently appears like an altar and a tomb, but also like the Ark of the Covenant. A recent hypothesis posits that this analogy may have been made clear in liturgy, since according to the Ambrosian Manual, the processions of December 7 assimilate Ambrose to Moses – which would make Volvinius, the exaltation of whom now makes more sense, a new Bezalel, the architect of the Tabernacle in Exodus.[52]

STORIES IN IMAGES: REMAKE, REUSE, REMORSE

Let's turn to the scenes represented on the rear facade. In succession, on the lower row, we see the miracle of bees and Ambrose's flight as he tries to escape his calling; Ambrose's return to Milan, caught by the hand of God; and his baptism. In the center row, Ambrose is crowned with a halo: his consecration as bishop and the celebration of a Mass are depicted, as is his miraculous presence at the funeral of Martin of Tours and his sermon, inspired by an angel, which prompts the conversion of an Arian. Then, on the upper row, comes a miracle produced by inadvertence (Ambrose heals an invalid, Nicetus, by stepping on his foot) and a premonitory dream (Christ announcing to him his imminent death), followed by the revelation of his death to the bishop Honoratus of Vercelli, who was summoned to bring him communion, and finally the transport of the saint's soul to heaven.

STRUCTURE OF THE GOLDEN ALTAR OF SANT'AMBROGIO

a. Ambrose's original sarcophagus
b. Gervasius and Protasius's original sarcophagus
c. Porphyry sarcophagus in which Angilbert had the bodies
    of Ambrose, Gervasius, and Protasius transferred

THE GOLDEN ALTAR OF SANT'AMBROGIO, REAR SIDE

CENTRAL PANEL OF THE *FENESTELLA CONFESSIONIS*

A. Ambrose crowning Angilbert (*Sanctus Ambrosius/Dominus Angilbertus*)
B. Ambrose crowning Volvinius (*Sanctus Ambrosius/Wolvinius magister phaber*)
C. Saint Michael
D. Saint Gabriel

SCENES FROM THE LIFE OF AMBROSE

1. The miracle of the bees
2. Ambrose's flight
3. Return to Milan
4. Ambrose's baptism
5. Episcopal consecration
6. Celebration of a Mass
7. Presence at the funeral services of Saint Martin of Tours
8. Sermon inspired by an angel and conversion of an Arian
9. Miraculous healing of an invalid
10. Ambrose's premonitory dream
11. Revelation of Ambrose's death to Bishop Honoratus of Vercelli
12. Ambrose's death and the transport of his soul

(*PAO Seuil*)

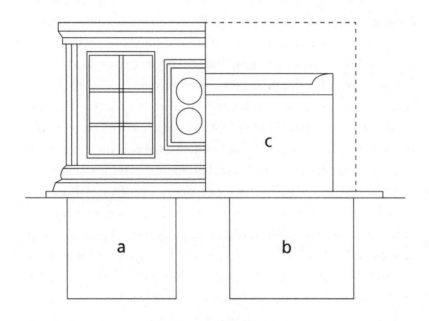

From crib to grave, in twelve images – a half second if we were at the movies. All quite banal: Ambrose is born, speaks, sleeps, dreams, acts, tries to flee, struggles, performs miracles, then he dies. What is a man's life made of, all the same – or perhaps not a life, but in any case everything that will begin to be told about it, a few years after his death, fragments of existence that only endure because they are literary tales as well, and as such, remain readily available to those believers who make the effort to remember them. After all, if the twelve biographemes of this life in pieces are so easily recognized, it's because their identification is made plain in *tituli* that, in ten of twelve cases, are quotes from Paulinus of Milan's *Vita Ambrosii*, which is, as we now know, the primary – and quasi sole – source of Ambrosian hagiography. There are similarities and subtle echoes between the two cycles, which crucial research by Pierre Courcelle has largely contributed to deciphering.[53] But let's content ourselves with two examples here.

The first scene is the miracle of the bees.[54] Paulinus of Milan describes this portent during which a swarm of bees emerges from the mouth of the child Ambrose, rising so high in the sky that it can no longer be seen.[55] His father marvels at this and understands the fate intended for Ambrose. Thus comes to pass the promise of scripture: "Pleasant words are like honey" (Proverbs 16:24).[56] This theme of sacred eloquence was borrowed from the Lives of Plato, Pindar, and Virgil, but it originates in a metaphor from Horace that compares the poet to the bee, making his honey from readings and experiences – as does the bishop, his writings on the care of souls bringing him closer to poetic power. Incidentally, it's worth noting that, in reading Paulinus of Milan, we are still very close to the central stem discussed by Marc van Uytfanghe, from which the accounts of lives written by pagans branch out in the imperial era (for example, the lives of philosophers), the Jewish tradition (the lives of patriarchs by Philo of

Alexandria), and the Christian tradition (the Apocryphal Acts of the Apostles).⁵⁷

The miracle of the bees, the golden altar of the Basilica
of Sant'Ambrogio, rear side (detail) (*Sandro Scarioni*)

The inscription VBI EXAMEN APVM PVERI COMPLEVIT AMBROSI corresponds to the passage *examen apum adveniens faciem eius atque ora complevit* in the *Vita Ambrosii*, when, Ambrose having been placed in his crib and sleeping with his mouth open, "all at once...a swarm of bees came and covered his face."⁵⁸ But in Paulinus of Milan's version, Ambrose is an *infans*, then an *infantulus*. In the *titulus* that accompanies the scene on the golden altar, he is described as *puer*, which incidentally corresponds to the way in which he is depicted, as a child rather than a baby – the ancient *infans* could correspond to the *puer* of the early Middle Ages, designating the child who doesn't speak, or to whom one doesn't listen.[59] For that matter, we can follow the chain of this hagiographic echo, for the reuse doesn't stop here: starting with the lives of philosophers, and including Ambrose, it continues until Charlemagne himself. According to the *Gesta Karoli Magni imperatoris* of Notker the Stammerer (886–87), Charles reportedly hailed the birth of his son Louis with the words *Si vixerit puerulus iste, aliquid magni erit* ("If this child should live, he will become a man of greatness").[60] This is an obvious reuse of Paulinus of Milan's *Vita Ambrosii*, in which Ambrose's father exclaims during the miracle of bees: *Si vixerit infantulus iste, aliquid magni erit.* The *infans* has once again become *puer*: here, we are at the first level of reuse via textual citation, whose typology Umberto Eco cheerily described while taking inspiration from sewing practices, outlining the range that goes from rejuvenation by hemming to radical transformation by patchwork, with, in the middle, invisible mending, patching, and darning – here we're simply in the hemming stage, which consists of adjusting the detached piece to the size of whoever is going to wear it.[61]

The second scene I propose we linger on is the seventh in the narrative sequence of the altar's Ambrosian cycle. It depicts Ambrose attending the funeral of Saint Martin of Tours, the ascetic from Pannonia (current-day Hungary) who became patron saint of the Gauls.[62] Here, the iconography digresses from its main textual source: Paulinus doesn't mention this strange episode, which is highly improbable given that it calls into question the chronology of the deaths of the two saints.[63] It was Gregory of Tours, one of Saint Martin's most illustrious successors in the episcopal see of Tours – he claimed to have been healed by Saint Martin's relics – who invented the story during which Ambrose learns, in a dream, of the imminent death of the patron saint of the Franks and miraculously transports himself to Tours for his funeral.[64] The scene is also depicted on the apse mosaics – whose most ancient components are perhaps contemporaneous with the golden altar,[65] unless they date from the episcopate of one of Angilbert II's successors, Anspert (868–81)[66] – even more pompously, with Ambrose himself appearing to officiate the funeral.[67] As for the figure of Saint Martin, he joins the group of Milanese saints depicted on one of the sides of the altar.[68]

Saint Martin's funeral, the golden altar of the Basilica of Sant'Ambrogio, rear side (detail) (*Sandro Scarioni*)

This linkage is largely political: Saint Martin was at the time the holy protector of the Franks; Gregory of Tours's *Histories* had been exalting his role as the evangelizer of Gaul since the end of the sixth century. But it was Carolingian spirituality that truly established the saint's memory, consecrating numerous churches dedicated to Martin, the primary initiator of monastic life in the West, making his cloak ("the *cappa*," which is most likely the blanket covering his tomb, and which Charlemagne conserved in his private chapel in Aachen) the most illustrious of the treasury's relics, symbolizing the alliance between the Church and Frankish royalty.[69] Making Saint Martin into Ambrose's spiritual brother expressed, in essence, the Milanese Church's unflagging attachment to the Carolingian order.

In fact, this was precisely Angilbert II's cultural and political plan for the city of Milan in general, and for the Ambrosian basilica in particular, which he planned to integrate into a relay of prayers (*laus perennis*) meant to ensure the emperor, his family, and his state were praised in perpetuity.[70] What's more, Martin was the "hammer of heretics": his presence both discreetly evoked Ambrose's fight against Arianism and downplayed it.[71] The holy bishop's stubborn resistance to imperial authorities, for all that it serves as the main dramatic twist of Paulinus's *Vita*, is completely hidden. Saint Martin therefore enables the antiheretical fight to be evoked, while prudently distinguishing it from the desire to thwart imperial intervention in matters of dogma – a desire mixed, in Ambrose, with the defense of orthodoxy, but that obviously was not prudent to mention in the ninth century. The reuse of a hagiographical motif foreign to the Milanese tradition produces here, as previously suggested, some loss and a remainder. It essentially serves to mask anything in the Ambrosian tradition that cannot be transformed in Angilbert II's monastical and imperial discourse.

At this point, it makes sense to examine the final stage of this reuse: a hagiographical smoothing out, stretching traditions to fit from edge to edge, eliminating the bumps, to make the seams invisible. An example can perhaps be seen in the Carolingian *Vita* of Saint Ambrose (*De vita et meritis Ambrosii*), which integrated the Saint Martin episode into a narrative account essentially dependent on Paulinus of Milan.[72] Did I lie to the reader in claiming up until now that when it came to our hagiographic sources "there is the *Vita Ambrosii* and that's it, or very nearly"? Everything was in the "very nearly": in 1964, Angelo Parodi discovered something in manuscript 569 at the library of the Abbey of Saint Gall – an unpublished text that he rapidly identified as an anonymous life of Ambrose, recopied in the last third of the ninth century. This text, clearly written in a Milanese scriptorium, was never circulated. Its discovery therefore is not a shocking scoop, in the sense that it in no way changes the overall structure of the transmission of Ambrose's memory. But it does raise two (symmetrical and connected) questions of historical interpretation: Why, during the Carolingian era, did it appear to some that Paulinus of Milan's *Vita Ambrosii* was no longer sufficient, and why did the hagiographical solution they then devised to solve this problem last so long?

It is particularly difficult to pin a date on this anonymous life; the sole witness manuscript dates from Anspert's episcopate (868–81). According to Paolo Tomea, who recently applied his considerable expertise to close analysis of the text, the most likely period is certainly Angilbert II's episcopate, probably toward the end.[73] If we situate ourselves in the 850s, we find ourselves in a period slightly after the (supposed) date of the commission for the golden altar. At this time, Paulinus of Milan's impassioned accounts of the battle of the basilicas – which we know to be entirely absent from the twelve chosen scenes of the saint's life – as well as the portrait he paints of Ambrose as the energetic defender of episcopal power and an unrelenting opponent of imperial attempts to define orthodoxy, might have appeared embarrassing to supporters of the Carolingian order.

This is probably why it was thought necessary, in all likelihood within the circles of Milan's Frankish bishops, to write a new life of Ambrose. In any event, the *De vita et meritis Ambrosii*, written anonymously in the Carolingian era, borrows heavily from the *Vita Martini*, notably when describing Ambrose's intellectual merits and the intensity of his battle against heresy and Judaism.[74] It therefore constitutes, to quote Paolo Tomea, "a kind of consecration of the link between Martin and Ambrose,"[75] which allows the bishop's energy to be praised while his opposition to the emperor is minimized. But doesn't this consecration first appear in the dazzling images of the golden altar, in a much more striking and doubtlessly longer-lasting way than in this hagiographical rewrite? These images show us, on two occasions, Ambrose valiantly astride a steed, depicted in the energetic and virile manner of the *missi dominici*, the imperial administrators who counted Angilbert II as a member.[76]

This representation of Ambrose as a horse-riding hero will see other evolutions, avatars, and metamorphoses in Ambrosian iconography. Such is the power of images, which oftentimes prove uncontrollable. Rather than considering these images as illustrations of invariably preexisting texts, we could ask if, at times, those texts might be iconographical narratives put into writing. In the present case, the contrast between the golden altar's resounding longevity and the tenuousness of the manuscript tradition of the Carolingian *Vita* is so dramatic that we're entitled to at least raise the question: What if the image here was the source of the text, and what if the *De vita et meritis Ambrosii* merely smoothed out, in the writing, the hagiographic reuse of Martin by way of Ambrose, as shown by the golden altar?

Return to Milan, the golden altar of the Basilica
of Sant'Ambrogio, rear side (detail) (*Sandro Scarioni*)

This would allow us to better understand why the Carolingian *Vita* didn't live on, or if it did, only by indirectly influencing the writing of the lives of Satyrus and Marcellina, Ambrose's brother and sister. Devotion to the latter was narrowly linked to the Ambrosian basilica, and the writing of the *Vita Marcellinae* may have occurred at the same time as the translation of Saint

Marcellina's body initiated by Anselm II and Landulf I, meaning in the last decade of the ninth century.[77] In his will (the first conserved for a bishop of Milan), their predecessor Anspert entrusted the salvation of his soul to the prayers of monks serving a *xenodochium*, a pious foundation for foreigners, that was attached to Ambrose's basilica and dedicated to the memory of his brother Satyrus.[78] But as for relations between Milan's archbishops and the Carolingian Empire, they were rapidly deteriorating even as the Ambrosian memorializing apparatus was being completed.[79] So much so that any political necessity for a memorial reconciliation between imperial grandeur and Ambrose's memory, which the *De vita et meritis Ambrosii* had attempted to put in writing, was eliminated.

RESTORING AMBROSE'S MEMORY:
THE PRELUDE (SIXTH TO NINTH CENTURY)

In 1964, Jacques Le Goff wrote that "Rome both fed [the Medieval West] and paralyzed it."[80] The reason the Carolingian Empire looks like a false start, in the history of the powers of Western Europe, is that political society, beginning in the twelfth century and following the church reform that historiography still refers to as the "Gregorian Reform," was no longer rooted in the glorious and nostalgic foundations of the *renovatio imperii*.[81] Monastic and imperial Christianity yielded to another anthropological system, prompting the rise of other values, beliefs, and social relationships – indeed it would be more useful for historical analysis to consider that system as another religion.[82] The ongoing historiographical reevaluation of the break that occurred during the Gregorian papacy, viewed as a global reshuffling of the world order, has precipitated the internal reperiodization of the medieval era.[83]

For one, the Carolingian false start isn't a flash in the pan, but an event of long duration. Though fleeting, it left a profound imprint on political memory. We see it here, and we'll see it at multiple stages of this archaeological trek aiming to dispel the aura of Ambrose's name by finding traces of his memory: the anamnesis always, or nearly, stumbles at the ninth century. This is where the historian's countermarch meets a threshold difficult to cross, where memory risks losing its footing. This is true of monumental history, but it will also apply once we are dealing with philology, manuscripts or codices (and how they interconnect), and liturgy. We will again collide with this Carolingian sill where a memory over three centuries old crystallizes.

Just think: as much time passed between Ambrose and Charlemagne as has between the death of Louis XIV and today. Granted, the comparison is absurd, assuming as it does that the history of memory crosses time periods of the same texture. The stitches here are much looser: we can't claim to fly through the linear history of centuries that are, if not obscure, at the least obscured by the rarity of written sources. All that remains of the period from the fifth to the eighth century, as you get closer, are a few archaeological vestiges, liturgical recollections, slight textual traces, and the shadow cast by a few borrowings, making it impossible to re-create all the stages of a tradition that dives so deeply into the past. The historian fumbles along, making out in the mist a few beacons that are the waypoints of Ambrose's memory. And the history of the bishop-saint, discontinuous as it is, alternates so forcefully between moments of concealment and remembering that his memory is not so much transmitted as reinvented.

The effort to reconstruct that memory was launched all the more vigorously in the Carolingian era as it came on the heels of a relative eclipsing of Ambrose's memory in the sixth century, at least in certain controversial contexts. References to Ambrose disappeared from theological and doctrinal debates, notably during the Three Chapters Controversy, as it was called, that roiled the Churches of Milan and Aquileia under Justinian's reign, from 544 to 553.[84] But it was primarily the Lombard conquest of Milan in 568 that broke the thread of the Ambrosian tradition.[85] The Lombard kings of the early seventh century (notably Rothari, who reigned from 636 to 652) moved the royal court to Pavia, which became the capital of the Lombard kingdom, supplanting Ravenna and Milan. At that time, the Ambrosian rememoration appeared troublesome, and in any case undesirable: it was hardly appropriate to exalt the champion of Nicaean orthodoxy when the Lombard ethnogenesis was based in large part – and admittedly in a much more complex and ambiguous way than was long believed – on the Arian identity.[86] In any event, it's clear that when Frankish bishops later referenced Ambrose's fight against the Arians, as it is depicted on the golden altar, they were taking aim at the Lombard Arians defeated in 774.[87]

When the Lombards invaded, Milan's archbishop and the cathedral's clergy fled to Genoa to establish a church dedicated to Saint Ambrose. For one century, from 569 to 659, Milan, in terms of church government, was no longer in Milan.[88] And it was its archbishop in exile, named Deusdedit,[89] that Pope Gregory the Great addressed as *vicarius sancti Ambrosii* in a letter dated October 600.[90] This phrase expressed, for the first time in our sources, the assimilation of the Ambrosian tradition into the Milanese identity.[91] The fact that it came from Rome, when the alliance between Milan and Ambrose was temporarily weakening, is only paradoxical in appearance. At war with the Lombard kingdom, Gregory exalted the figure of Ambrose as the founder of an episcopal tradition in order to anchor the Church of Milan in the pontifical orbit.[92] In any case, Ambrose was no longer in

Milan, and, during this time, Milan forgot Ambrose. This was still true during the reign of King Liutprand (712-44), during which, as Jean-Charles Picard writes, Milan experienced "a kind of idyll with the Lombard monarchy."[93] During this period, in 739 specifically, an urban panegyric entitled *Versum de Mediolano civitate* was written. It only mentioned the holy bishop sparingly and with distance: "O how happy and blessed is the city of Milan, that it should merit to have so many saintly defenders through whose prayers it remains unconquered and abundant."[94] Though it boasts of the city's eight martyrs and six holy bishops, the text does not distinguish Ambrose among the latter – he is referred to with the nearly neutral title of *magnus praesul*.

The Carolingian rememoration therefore had to break through this nearly two-century-long wall of forgetting – a relative lacuna, no doubt, but one that was voluntary. Would the Carolingians succeed in boring through entirely, reaching the time of Ambrose himself? Doubtful. Any scraps of memory that they may have grabbed would have been transformed by the fifth century, or more precisely reinvented. To better understand this reinvention, let's begin one final time at Ambrose's tomb. Nothing indicates that it aroused any particular devotion from the start: though the Basilica of Sant'Ambrogio may be the sanctuary, among all those in Milan, that hosts the most bishop tombs, its importance only really rose in the late seventh century. By the tenth century, it was supplanted by the cathedral. No graves belonging to the laity have been located before the eighth century, which is a clear indication that burial *ad sanctos* only belatedly came to center around Ambrose's body.[95] Paulinus of Milan's writing of the *Vita Ambrosii* – which, remember, followed the first period of mnemonic latency, twenty or so years after Ambrose's death – made the bishop into a universal saint of the *orbis christianus*. As a result, and despite his energetic policy of occupying the land, the history of which I attempt to untangle here, the anchoring of Ambrose's memory to Milan struggled to produce any effects. The first archaeological traces of his tomb being explicitly recognized date back to the episcopate of Lawrence (around 489–510/512), an emulator of the eponymous martyr and an admirer of Ambrose, or more than a century after his death. Archaeological excavations in the second half of the nineteenth century uncovered pieces of damask silk and golden thread, various remains, and a few coins, which allowed those traces to be more precisely dated.[96]

It is possible that Lawrence's episcopate corresponds to an initial structuring of Ambrose's tomb as a monument,[97] in conjunction with erecting the impressive ciborium,[98] and more generally, to a revival of the saint's memory. At this time, Ambrose was being exalted in the poetic writing of Ennodius of Pavia, whose role in the reestablishment of the Ambrosian tradition has rightly been reevaluated by Stéphane Gioanni.[99] Born in Arles in 473/474, Magnus Felix Ennodius lived in northern Italy beginning in early childhood and became the secretary of Bishop Epiphanius of Pavia, whose *Vita* he wrote several years after his death in 496. In it, he develops a model for the sanctity of the bishop's role and an ideal of governance very close to Paulinus of Milan's *Vita Ambrosii*; these works notably extol the same balance between the mastery of eloquence, the excellence of virtue, and political courage.[100] In 497, Ennodius found a new employer in the bishop of Milan, Lawrence, and served as a deacon from 501 to 513, all while remaining an influential member of the pontifical chancery. We are now in the era of the Ostrogoth kingdom led by Theodoric the Great (493–526), whose panegyric was written by Ennodius, in all likelihood in 507.[101]

And yet Ennodius's story is that of a relative political failure: he dreamt of becoming the bishop of Milan – he only became the bishop of Pavia, from 512 to his death in 521, though this did give him the see of a very important city, which would later become the capital of the Lombard kingdom. Hence his active role in the rememoration of the man he calls *Ambrosius noster* in his correspondence.[102] That activism was above all literary – Ennodius was a writer and poet with a considerable body of work, whose "sinuous writing"[103] may have bewildered some of his medieval readers, impressed or discouraged by the "inextricable knot" created by his ornate language, as it was described by Arnulf of Lisieux in the twelfth century, playing off the *nodus* (knot) inscribed in the author's name.[104] This poeticism manifests notably in the hymns Ennodius of Pavia wrote in the Ambrosian style – and which can, as a result, be legitimately qualified as Ambrosian hymns, if only in terms of their manuscript transmission, even if this did not ensure them a place in the Milanese liturgical tradition.[105] This is notably the case for the *Hymnus sancti Ambrosii* dedicated to the figure of the bishop, who, under the cantor's pen, appears as the founder of and source of glory for the Church of Milan, fighting heretics with authority and power, holding strong at the Church's helm.[106]

In his *Institutions*, Cassiodorus, Ennodius's great contemporary in Ostrogothic Italy, also depicted Ambrose as a preacher and orator – this was undoubtedly all that remained of Ambrose's memory in the time of Theodoric's reign – but he did not situate this memory in the tradition of the see of Milan. Ennodius, on the contrary, knotted these two memories (a man and an institution) together to forge the identity of the Church of Milan. This identity is expressed literarily in Ennodius's *carmina*, thirteen poems in the form of epitaphs dedicated to Milan's bishops, from Ambrose (considered the founder) to Lawrence. This "poetic *Liber ecclesiae* of the see of Milan"[107] pretends that Ambrose is the first bishop – in fact, he wasn't, and the episcopal lists comprehensively studied by Jean-Charles Picard[108] identify (or invent) as many as eleven predecessors to Ambrose. These include legendary figures (the proto-bishop Saint Anathalon,[109] first on the list beginning with the *Libellus de siti civitatis mediolanensis*, an anonymous list likely dating from the very end of the tenth century and constituting the authentic *Liber pontificalis* of the Church of Milan[110]), deposed or usurper bishops (Auxentius), and others such as Eustorgius I, whose burial (at the Basilica of Sant'Eustorgio) was already structuring the monumental configuration of the city of Milan.[111]

In short, in Ennodius of Pavia's writing, Ambrose rebuilds the Church of Milan. But if we adopt the historian's perspective, it was Ennodius of Pavia who, in the era of Bishop Lawrence, rebuilt the very idea that there could be an Ambrosian foundation to the Milanese identity. Ambrose isn't the first in an episcopal succession, but he is its essential principle. However, this Milanese grandeur in no way exempts him from the pontifical authority ardently defended by Ennodius, among others: Ambrose was now the name that designated the rebuilding of the Milanese Church as one of the foundations of the universal Church dominated by Rome. In the epitaph to Ambrose in Ennodius of Pavia's *carmina*, the poet writes of the "purple of supreme power" (*regifico murice*) that dazzles (*fulsit*) emerging moistly from the husk of language (*roscida lingua*): *Roscida regifico cui fulsit murice lingua*.[112] In the administrative rhetoric of the Ostrogoth, Burgundian, and Frankish kingdoms, and in particular Theodorian eloquence, the "purple tongue" is the dialect of power, building the authority of bishops and kings upon a great ceremonial language.[113] More than just rhetorical virtuosity, Ennodius of Pavia's stylistic affectation pushed Ambrose's beautiful and grand ornate style – the principal legacy of the writing of the Italian Church Fathers on court language – to the limits of intelligibility. The result: its obscure expressiveness became the paradoxical condition for its prestige. We need to take the "purple tongue" metaphor quite literally here: by expressing the dazzle and the purple sheen of Ambrose's language, by making the authority behind its blinding glimmers tangible, by setting his resounding expressions within the antiquity-esque convolutions of an ornate style, the cantor of Milan voiced the poetic equivalent of Bishop Lawrence's monumental endeavor made visible by the golden altar,[114] providing the *ornamentum*, in the full sense of the term, to the assemblage of a life in pieces.

PART THREE

GHOSTS

(Fourth to Twelfth Century)

As death approached, Socrates wasn't afraid – he was going to join the kingdom of the gods. But the soul, he confided to his friend Cebes, is sometimes held back on this side of the world when the end comes. This is because it feels "fear of the invisible" (*Phaedo*, 81c). This dialogue by Plato, in which he advanced his theory of ideas for the first time, was well known to Latin authors, and notably to Cicero. And it was primarily through Cicero (and also Plutarch and Pliny the Younger) that medieval thought developed its conception of spirits.[1] That said, Pierre Courcelle has demonstrated that Ambrose was familiar with this *Phaedo* passage about ghosts (*idôlon*): in his *Commentary on St. Luke*, he contrasts the Gospel "whatever you bind on earth will be bound in heaven" (Matthew 16:19) with the *vetus sententia* that affirms that the soul, even after death, can remain bound to the body.[2] The world is therefore haunted by the unfinished souls of these specters. "They're elsewhere, we're here, tomorrow it will be the reverse. What does it matter?"[3] This world is our world because it is populated by images, and because those images know the way to survive.[4]

Here then are the ghosts prowling around tombs, whispering like regrets, or rather like insistent traces of a past that won't fade. No need to believe in them: if you're at all afraid of them, you'll see them appear.[5] One could say these ghosts are failed reuses, never able to entirely transform the past: they leave sprinkled behind them, like obstinate, sonorous remains, shavings of memory that can't be assimilated, converted, or repaired, and which, as I've mentioned, always threaten to come back around. "But what is a specter made of?" asks Giorgio Agamben: "Signs, or, more precisely, signatures, meaning the signs, numbers, or monograms marked on things by time. A specter always carries a date with it, meaning that it's an intimately historic being."[6] Thus the only history that can be written is a spectral one. Jacques Derrida suggested we call this *hauntology*, not for the sake of making up a new word, but to appreciate the capacity of a historical event to be both repetition and first instance.[7]

When exploring the reuses in a given place, as we've just done by lingering in the Basilica of Sant'Ambrogio, there's always the risk of getting caught up in its aura, which creates an illusion of eternity that paralyzes time. But Ambrose isn't alive – he's a memory that returns over and over, different each time. The form of these returns can be called spectral, for Milan's history is haunted by the specters of Ambrose. They always return, sometimes as a name, sometimes a dream, adapting their form and appearance to the crisis of the time. We will see them appear, menacingly, before Emperor Conrad II, in 1037, to take up the defense of one of their many avatars, Ariberto of Intimiano, the new Ambrose of the day; then again in 1161 on the bas-reliefs of the *porta Romana*; and again in 1338. I propose that we track a few of those posthumous lives here, in a necessarily discontinuous history, riddled as it is with apparitions. These specters are the nightmares of emperors and tyrants; they are the hopes of defenders of the Church, of freedom, and of the commune. They give courage to the combatants of memory, for whom remembering is a battle.

EIGHT

Seeing Ambrose: Ghostly Tales
(Tenth to Eleventh Century)

Once they were draped in shrouds, in fourteenth-century medieval iconography, ghosts began to take on the familiar and simplistic appearance that we associate with them today.[1] But long before that, sanctuaries had been filled with pieces of cloth that became imbued with the *virtus* of saints by having been wrapped around their bodies or simply having touched their tombs.[2] The treasury of the Basilica of Sant'Ambrogio contains fragments of a red silk dalmatic, sewn with yellow lining and covered with a cloth on which one can make out Kufic characters evoking a prince from the Marwanid dynasty.[3] A fourteenth-century inventory conserved in the capitular archives attributes it to Ambrose,[4] but this association is much older. A long ribbon with an inscription in blue letters identifies the dalmatic as belonging to Ambrose, and the *pallio* protecting it as a gift from Archbishop Ariberto of Intimiano: "Under this cloth is conserved the dalmatic of Saint Ambrose. The Archbishop Ariberto protected the aforesaid dalmatic beneath this cloth."[5] Of course, this history hangs by a thread – one that, patching two memories together, protects the venerable relic, making the kind of preservative selection that is common practice among seamstresses, and that can metaphorically describe, as we've seen, the medieval culture of reuse when it patches texts together rather than repurposing stone.

Notwithstanding the technical issues surrounding this ancient piece of cloth,[6] currently under debate, what concerns us here is the chronological gap separating the two edges – Ambrose and Ariberto – of this reuse.[7] Ariberto of Intimiano, the archbishop of Milan from 1018 to 1054, was the great church reformer of the Lombard capital, and his active patronage policy (we owe him the art commission, among others, of the famous and luxurious cathedral evangelistary, or book of the Gospels) was part of a broad plan to rebuild episcopal authority.[8] An energetic proponent of the autonomy, power, and supremacy of the Church, he was considered, as shown by Cinzio Violante, to be an authentic successor to Ambrose.[9] His battle against the heretics of Monforte, near Asti in 1027, as recounted by the chronicler Landulf Senior, made a particularly lasting impression.[10]

ARIBERTO OF INTIMIANO (1018–45)
AND THE PATCHING OF MEMORIES

To understand this political sequence, we need to situate it within a broader context: the history of the emergence of feudal society in northern Italy. Following the extinction of the Carolingian dynasty in 888, the kingdom of Italy was contested by two noble families – those of Spoleto and Ivrea. The kings of Italy resided in Pavia and had delegated their power in Milan to a count. Otto I's rise to power in 950 did not change the situation: whether they called themselves kings or emperors, Italy's sovereigns living in Pavia were "only masters of Milan if the archbishop favor[ed] them," as Yves Renouard wrote.[11] For in Milan, like elsewhere in Italy, but also in much of Europe, the tenth century marked the strengthening of episcopal powers through the devolution of the rights of counts.[12] This general redistribution of powers came hand in hand with the stranglehold of large regional families on the *episcopatus*, which precipitated the feudalization of Lombard society. When Walpert, the archbishop of Milan, received "a great many royal fortresses" in 962, he hastened in return to allot religious rights, rural estates, and communal powers to *milites* (cavalry soldiers) whose loyalty he wished to ensure.[13] Because of their need for knights to protect them in a climate of tremendous social tension – notably against the first demands made by increasingly rich and numerous city dwellers – bishops began to distribute their fiefs en masse, fully integrating themselves into the new feudal organization of political society.[14]

This episcopal clientele bolstered the ruling class, which would profit the most from the economic growth of the tenth century. Though slow and almost imperceptible, that growth was much more sustained than was long believed by historians, who have been overwhelmed by the complexity of sparse sources casting faint rays of light onto a dense tangle of muddled events.[15] Situated along routes that, crossing the Alps, led from Provence to Bavaria and opened a southward path to the vast trade of the Mediterranean, Milan quickly benefited from this economic boom, which was characterized by increased monetary circulation, as well as by an exacerbation of political, and soon-to-be religious, tensions, due to the intensity of social differentiation.[16] This led to the turmoil of the "century of iron," during which causes of growth can be found in the violence of a predatory aristocracy practicing ostentatious consumption. Whence too the establishment of a new social class system, which arose from a necessity to calm and order that growth.[17] Following the 1035 revolt of a group of Milanese bishops' vassals demanding formal recognition of their hereditary right to the fiefs granted them, Emperor Conrad II enacted a law on May 28, 1037, that, settling the question of the devolution of benefices, stabilized the feudal hierarchy of this new society (studied notably by Hagen Keller).[18]

At the top were the *capitanei*, direct vassals of bishops and large monasteries, who were granted, as benefices, entire *plebs*, meaning churches and their districts (which were much larger in Italy than parishes elsewhere in Europe) and associated rights. These captains in turn surrounded themselves with their own vassals, the *valvassores*, who became their lord bishop or abbot's secondary vassals and whose inheritance of fiefs was recognized by the law of 1037. Captains and subvassals formed an aristocracy whose social preeminence was based on their ability to avoid ordinary justice, being judged instead by their peers. Eleventh-century Milanese sources would soon call this aristocracy the *ordo militum*: it combined all the *milites* that would share in the governing of the city of Milan and its richest citizens, the *cives*. The latter were also free, and consequently answerable to the law in public courts, as opposed to the *rustici*, who, in rural areas, were subject to the ban, or call to war, of their lord. This was the Milanese model of social stratification. Does it constitute a society of rigid social orders? Debatable.[19] Nonetheless, its three-way split – captains/subvassals/citizens – would remain the foundation of sociopolitical life in the Lombard capital until at least the thirteenth century.[20]

Ariberto of Intimiano belonged to one of the powerful *capitanei* families that had seized episcopal office in the tenth century. This high-ranking lord had properties in Milan, as well as in Como, Bergamo, Cremona, Lodi, and in the region of Varese, where he acquired a number of signorial rights,[21] leaning notably on his favored canonical chapter, Sant'Ambrogio.[22] He appears for the first time in our sources in 998 as the subdeacon of the Church of Milan and quickly becomes a major figure, playing a decisive political role within it. When he reached the episcopacy on March 28, 1018, he did so with the support of the emperor and the city's most influential citizens (*maiores civitatis*), writes Arnulf of Milan sixty years later in his *Liber gestorum recentium*, which remains our primary source for this period.[23] This chronicle of "recent deeds" was composed by a cleric, a partisan convinced of the need for Church reforms and a fervent supporter of the social hegemony of the *capitanei* elite; it attests to the construction of Ariberto's memory within the religious (notably canonical) communities that he helped reform by promoting the communal life of the clergy.[24] Arnulf of Milan devoted the second book in his chronicle to exalting his subject's political image[25] – an image shaped by the bishop himself during his lifetime through his highly ambitious policy of commissioning art,[26] as well as by his deeply innovative effort to produce monuments substantiating the written documents he produced.[27]

And indeed, Ariberto was a very credible new Ambrose, thanks notably to his concern with reconstructing the Church's legacy and moral authority, combined with an energetic desire to establish his own power. The most eloquent expression of this Ambrosian imitation is the second founding of the *basilica salvatoris et sanctorum veteris testamentis*. This became the Basilica of San Dionigio, in northeast Milan, the final link in the circuit of basilicas surrounding and protecting the city.[28] You may recall that this church, destroyed in the sixteenth century, had been dedicated only in the ninth century to the memory of Bishop Dionysius, thanks to a legend very likely invented for the occasion, which portrayed Ambrose of Milan himself demanding that Bishop Basil of Caesarea move the body to Milan. By performing this action a second time, Ariberto of Intimiano clinched the story's

legitimacy, the holiness of the basilica site, and his own authority; by reinforcing one of the weak links of Ambrose's memory,
or, if you prefer the textile metaphor, patching his memory at
the very spot where the thread was the most frayed, Ariberto presented himself as its restorer.

But the same holds for memory as for patched cloth, and
notably for Ambrose's dalmatic, which was protected by being
covered over. So much so that Ambrosian liturgy would retain
the date of February 19, 1023, to commemorate Dionysius's translation to the basilica to mark its consecration – the date of Ariberto's reenactment of the initial event "covering over" that of
the admittedly more fragile event itself.[29] By establishing a Benedictine monastery adjacent to the church,[30] and by making provisions in his will to be buried there in a tomb laid out in a way
that unambiguously evoked that of his illustrious predecessor
in the Basilica of Sant'Ambrogio,[31] Ariberto of Intimiano was
not imitating Ambrose, acting like him or in his name, he was
another Ambrose. Or more precisely: he embodied the return of
Ambrose as he was transmitted and transformed by Carolingian
memory, and he did this so successfully that this second founding of the Basilica of San Dionigio could also be understood as
an inaugural act.

The solemn and imperialesque diploma issued by Archbishop
Ariberto in March 1026 to create the Benedictine monastery
attached to the church "for the salvation of his soul and that
of the great and august emperor Henry" – referring to Henry II,
dead two years prior – innovated with Ariberto's titulature, presenting him as the "archbishop of the Ambrosian Church": *Ego
Aribertous infinita omnipotentis Dei misericordia Ambrosianae ecclesiae archiepiscopus.*[32] We know, based on the work of Cesare Alzati,
preeminent scholar of the Ambrosian Rite, that the expression
Ambrosiana ecclesia, which appears for the first time in our sources

in a letter from Pope John VIII to Archbishop Anspert dated February 881, began to truly circulate in the early tenth century.[33] This was the moment when the name Ambrose was casting its benevolent shadow over the Church's properties and its calendar: the bishop's palace was called *domus sancti Ambrosii* and certain dues he demanded were to be paid on Saint Ambrose Day, December 7.[34] Even his knights were referred to, by the early eleventh century, as *miles sancti Ambrosii*.[35]

WHEN AMBROSE'S VICAR CROWNED ITALIAN KINGS AND BATTLED HERESY

Ambrose's memory was a centerpiece in the battle waged by Milan's archbishops to impose the supremacy of their metropolitan see over all the bishops of the *regnum Italicarum*. It notably allowed them to counter the claims made by the city of Pavia, the royal capital since the Lombards, which they were fighting for the privilege of bestowing upon emperors the iron crown of the king of Italy.[36] It was in the Basilica of Sant'Ambrogio that Lothar II was crowned in 950; Liutprand of Cremona describes him, cheered by the magnates, as "prostrate before the cross in the church of Ambrose's blessed martyrs and confessors, Gervase and Protase."[37] The ritual should be taken seriously, both in terms of its performative force and its ceremonial splendor: here, it is clearly the memory of the saint that makes the king.[38] The emperors of the Ottonian dynasty would henceforth regularly sojourn in Milan, where they were sometimes crowned, and even buried – as was, for that matter, the case for Lothar II.[39] We have already seen that the ciborium framing the golden altar bears traces of the restorations these emperors undertook. So it was, logically enough, by playing the post-Carolingian card of imperial fidelity that Ariberto of Intimiano intended to make Milan,

because it was Ambrose's city, the new *sedes regni* and, by consequence, the great rival to the *ecclesia Romana*.

Was it he who crowned Conrad II, successor to Emperor Henry
II, in Milan in March 1026? A single source claims so – the chronicle of Arnulf of Milan, who maintains that his hero, Archbishop
Ariberto of Intimiano, acted at that time "in keeping with custom"[40] – though scholars continue to debate the event's historicity.[41] In any case, one thing is certain: Conrad II did find himself
in Milan on March 23, 1026, to receive the diploma establishing
the San Dionigio monastery, seemingly a decisive junction in the
construction of Ambrose's memory; the emperor, coming from
Verona, was headed to Rome, accompanied by Ariberto of Intimiano, who would also help him besiege rebelling Pavia.[42] This is in
all likelihood the same period in which the archbishop refitted
Ambrose's tomb, not only by protecting his dalmatic but also
by restoring the golden altar – which would have been perfectly
consistent with the ideological project of exalting the Church of
Milan and its Ambrosian identity in preparation for the imperial
coronation at the Basilica of Sant'Ambrogio.[43]

Specialists believe that the two new enamel medallions added
to the rear side of the altar at this time came from the same
workshop that produced the golden plate for Ariberto's evangelistary, which is today conserved in the Museum of the Milan
Cathedral.[44] These two masterpieces of European goldsmithery –
Angilbert II's golden altar in the ninth century and Ariberto's
evangelistary in the eleventh – are not only technically and stylistically reminiscent of each other; they represent two mirroring
expressions of Ambrose's affirmation of Milan's primacy before
the empire. While the first plate of the evangelistary's gilded and
embossed silver cover likely dates from early in Ariberto's episcopate, the second was undoubtedly commissioned during the decisive period circa 1026.[45] A remarkable cycle of enamels encircles a

golden crucifix, forming the largest example of cloisonné enamel in Western art. Ambrose and his brother Satyrus appear at the base of the cross, where we see the inscription *Lux mundi*, echoing the phrase on the book brandished by Christ in the apse mosaic of the Basilica of Sant'Ambrogio: *Ego sum lux mundi*.[46] The bishop is anointed by the Lord, and his hands distribute all that is sacred. And so the book shining in his hands is the reflection on earth of the one that sparkles in heaven.

We can see that the archbishop of Milan, Ariberto of Intimiano, worked hard to build his memory as a maker of kings, as Ambrose's vicar, and as the protector of the saint's relics. But he was also a warrior bishop, dramatically incarnating the episcopacy's integration into the militant aristocracy of feudal society—here again, Ambrose's memory served him as a powerful source of legitimization. The first to suffer the consequences were the heretics of Monforte, in Piedmont, burned in 1028 like those of Orléans six years earlier. (As Robert Moore aptly notes, this was the first time since the end of the Roman Empire that heretics had been executed in Western Europe.[47]) In the heat of the moment, these two events were linked by Rodulfus Glaber, the legendary chronicler of the year 1000, in his *Histories*, which he composed in Burgundy; this allowed him to develop a demonic view of heretics as evil and terrifying figures given over to strange satanic rites.[48] Though belated, and, as we will soon see, biased by its author's involvement in the later unrest of the Pataria, the chronicle by Landulf Senior is much more precise.[49] It no doubt relies in part on the minutes conserved by the archiepiscopal curia of the interrogation, by Ariberto of Intimiano, of the individual then presented as the instigator of the heretics, Gerard of Monforte.[50] His followers considered themselves to be "good priests" but had nothing but distrust for the ecclesiastical hierarchy; they professed deviant ideas that Landulf reduces to *falsa rudimenta*, but in which historians of heresy today recognize the spiritual aspirations of cultivated lay communities, inspired notably by the Neoplatonism taught in schools.[51]

But the most important point for us to note in Landulf's account is the energetic portrait of a bishop in combat. We have Ariberto at the head of an army of peace, surrounded by his loyal priests and his valiant *milites*, determined to use his pastoral power to bring lost lambs back to the flock. Discovering the existence of a heretical sect during one of his pastoral visits to the suffragan diocese of Turin, he "sent a large troop of soldiers to Monforte and had all those he could find imprisoned. Among those taken was the countess of the castle." And though he may have preferred not to spill blood, he let himself be convinced by the *maiores laici* of Milan – meaning the elite of the *capitanei* – of the need for a spectacular public execution.[52] When he accompanied Emperor Conrad II on his victorious campaign against the Burgundian rebels in 1036,[53] or when he ordered his *milites* to attack recalcitrant castles in Lombardy, he carried the banner of the triumphant Church: *Fuit enim christiane signifer milicie*: "He was the *signifer* of the Christian armies," claimed Benzo, the bishop of Alba, who assembled Ariberto's writings, perhaps in Milan around 1085, to reaffirm his imperial loyalty, not without some controversy.[54] For the word *signifer*, which originally designated the carrier of a Roman army's flag (*signum*), was first used in imperial armies. Its reappearance in a Milanese episcopal context was characteristic of the symbolic fight then being waged around the sacralization of war and its liturgy.[55]

AMBROSE RETURNS: FROM ARIBERTO OF INTIMIANO'S POLITICAL DREAM TO THE LITURGY OF THE HOLY WAR

The participation of Lombard knights in the First Crusade was without a doubt the major event mobilizing the rituality and symbolism of the *militia Christi*.[56] Invocations to a God of victories and devotion to Saint Victor and military saints were already on dramatic display in the prayer book belonging to Arnulf II, Ariberto's predecessor, who was archbishop of Milan from 998 to 1018.[57] Landulf Senior still remembered that Archbishop Walpert had placed the holy spear that pierced the side of Christ, along with a nail from the True Cross, on the altar of the Basilica of Sant'Ambrogio during the coronation ceremonies for Emperor Otto I in 961.[58] And it was this very lance that Ambrose, the "glorious horseman," armed himself with when the Christian people were in danger. Hence why, according to Guibert of Nogent's chronicle of the First Crusade, "in the army there was an archbishop of Milan [in reality Anselm IV of Bovisio],[59] who had brought with him the cope, that is, the chasuble and alb (I don't know if he brought anything else) of Saint Ambrose. It was adorned with gold and gems so precious that nowhere on earth could anyone find its equal. The Turks took it and carried it off, and thus the foolish clerk was punished for having been insane enough to bring so sacred an object to barbarian lands."[60] It was undoubtedly deemed more prudent thereafter to bring to the Holy Land a relic presented as the arm of Ambrose, and which blessed the armed pilgrims who came to liberate the tomb of Christ.[61] At least that is what the German chronicler Albert of Aix claimed. He also recounted how, during the long and terrible siege of Antioch in 1098, amid a proliferation of miracles and visions, Ambrose appeared to a Lombard priest in his sleep. He came dressed as a pilgrim, through the door of dreams, to give the man courage. Jerusalem, he said, would be delivered.[62]

This revenant was not a phantom, in the medieval sense of *fantasmata*, illusions produced by the excesses of the body and inspired by the devil. Rather, it was an image of a dead man returning, thanks to the power of the *imaginatio*, and returning to the world to leave his imprint—sometimes a physical trace, but always a message of caution, advice, or warning that allowed the individual seeing it to conduct himself virtuously.[63] For the dreamer didn't lose himself in deceptive reverie: while asleep, or half-asleep, he would open himself up to what Augustine called a *visio spiritualis*, in which the image that appears in the dream (*somnium*) is the vehicle of self-understanding.[64] In other words, when Ambrose emerged from the past to intrude on the present, it was to tell the Milanese people who they truly were.

But who were the Milanese to call themselves Ambrosians, and what course of action did it justify? Ariberto of Intimiano's political dream, at the moment it begins to disintegrate, offers a glimpse. The last decade of his episcopate was marked by a spectacular reversal of alliances. The 1035 revolt of Milanese vassals forced Emperor Conrad II, as we've seen, to codify the hereditary possession of fiefs by promulgating the *Constitutio de feudis* during the Diet of Pavia on May 28, 1036. He used this occasion to diminish the power of the archbishop of Milan, accused of being responsible for the social unrest, and imprisoned in a castle near Piacenza. The city of Milan then revolted against the emperor, with the *capitanei* taking up the cause of Ariberto of Intimiano, who managed to escape as Conrad II laid siege to the Lombard capital. New riots erupted in 1040, this time against the nobles. Landulf Senior described this as a true social war: the people, hardened by their combat against Conrad II, turned against the military aristocracy overseeing them. Ariberto of Intimiano returned to his city in 1045 only to die there; the great social upheaval that would lead to the unrest of the Pataria and then the advent of the commune had begun.[65]

What would Ambrose do? Return, of course, to defend his people and admonish the prideful. On May 29, 1037, as Conrad II laid siege to the episcopal *castrum* of Corbetta, a violent storm raged over the imperial camp, leaving many victims. This was when "a man named Bertulfus, the king's secretary,[66] claimed to have seen Saint Ambrose rise in indignation at the king's wrongful deeds." This apparition is described by an anonymous cleric writing, between 1051 and 1054 for the portion that concerns us, a chronicle commissioned by Gerard, the bishop of two dioceses, Arras and Cambrai, from 1012 to 1051. Which prompts the question: What is this Milanese episode doing in the chronicle by a bishop from northern France? The same bishop painted by Georges Duby as one of the inventors of the three orders, and who firmly intended to use all the means at his disposal to brandish the two swords of *auctoritas* and *potestas*, or sacred authority and secular power.[67] Gerard of Cambrai was very hesitant toward the Peace of God movement,[68] and his account of Emperor Conrad II's descent on Italy to fight those who had resorted to arms only makes sense in this context of conflicting opinions.[69]

Milanese sources, which depict the warrior bishop valiantly defended by his *milites* entrenched in their castle, only retain one thing from this Pentecost of 1037: the providential and deadly storm that strikes their imperial besiegers. This is notably the case in accounts by Arnulf of Milan[70] and Landulf Senior, in which the ire of God punishes an emperor guilty of having confused "divine things and human things."[71] The episode in which the specter of a wrathful Ambrose appears was transmitted through another narrative channel, closer to the imperial camp. It is revisited in the *Vita Chunradi Salici Imperatoris* written by Wipo, the chaplain of emperors Conrad I and Henri III, and in which the patron saint appears "sword unsheathed,"[72] and then by Sigebert of Gembloux and Vincent of Beauvais, both of whom embellished the story.[73] When we find Ambrose back in Milan, he has been transformed by this progressive militarization of his memory. Then, in the fourteenth century, Galvano Fiamma dramatized the scene, as was his wont, evoking an Ambrose armed with a broadsword and threatening death to the emperor with "terrible eyes."[74] Of course, this Dominican chronicler, a zealous flatterer of the Viscontis, was, as we will later see, one of the artisans of the signorial appropriation of Ambrose's memory; when he attributed a passion for war to Ariberto of Intimiano (whom he described as *bellorum amator*),[75] he was merely projecting the obsessive fears of his time onto the past – a past that for him was already quite ancient.

But let's be patient. We're not there yet, here in the eleventh century. So what remains of these furtive apparitions? Perhaps a local tradition, making of Corbetta a fragile *lieu de mémoire*: as Miriam Rita Tessera notes, a parchment from the San Vittore church in Corbetta recorded the gift, by an Arnolfo Donini di Porta Vercellina, of *pro remedio animae* relics that included a "robe of Saint Ambrose."[76] But one image in particular persists, one beautiful and powerful image that was destined to travel far from the time and place from which it emerged. Lore has Ariberto of Intimiano as the inventor of the *carroccio*, the standard-bearing chariot of Milan's militias and symbol of the city's civic identity and political unity.[77] We are in 1039 now, during the siege of Milan, which marked the definitive rupture between Conrad II on one side, and Milan and the papacy on the other.[78] Whereas the Paduan *carroccio* had been named Bertha after the wife of Emperor Henry IV, who had granted it to the *cives* and their bishop Milon, the Milanese chariot was the emblem of the anti-imperial struggle.[79] It would remain the active symbol of that combat until the thirteenth century – a protective and mobile monument, ideal for disseminating the liturgy of the holy war everywhere the political necessity for it was felt.[80]

Arnulf of Milan's description of the *carroccio* is vague: a standard (*signum*) perched on the "mast of a ship...raised on high, having been set in a strong wagon" transporting a large crucifix and preceded by men in arms.[81] By the twelfth century, the *carroccio* appears to have acquired its permanent appearance: a parade chariot drawn by several pairs of oxen, bearing the *vexillum sancti Ambrosii*, the white-and-red standard of the commune of Milan with the effigy of Ambrose.[82] Here we find another piece of cloth, not the shroud or the dalmatic, but a banner that would henceforth flap in the wind of the great battles to come. It was logical that lore attributed this to Ariberto, who was the *signifer* of the Ambrosian militias, their standard-bearer. Ariberto of Intimiano was undoubtedly one among many "new Ambroses," but more importantly, he was the one who patched up Ambrose's memory, knotting together its three essential, and politically useful, threads: resistance to imperial aggression, defense of the city's integrity and civic values, and the fight against heresy.

THE PATARIA, OR THE FANATICS OF REFORM (1057–75)

The above history was, as we have seen, in large part dependent on narrative sources that came a good half century later, at least for authors from Milan: Arnulf of Milan's *Book of Recent Deeds* was likely written around 1077, and Landulf Senior's *History of the People of Milan* around 1085.[83] At this moment, everything had changed in Milan, or rather everything was on the cusp of a radical shift. The death of Archbishop Ariberto of Intimiano in 1045 inaugurated a period of political-religious upset referred to as the Pataria, which shook the city of Milan from approximately 1057 to 1075, but whose reverberations spread throughout the entire eleventh century.[84] "If the same Saint Ambrose returned today," lamented Landulf, "he would recognize neither the clergy nor the citizens of the city of which he was bishop."[85] How should we understand this seemingly obvious and deceptively insignificant remark? Milan after the year 1000 was certainly no longer the capital of the Christian Roman Empire that it had been seven centuries earlier. But the disillusioned chronicler is likely referring here to a more rapid change, which had rendered Ariberto's city, insofar as it could have been confused for his political dream of a continuous Ambrosian state, unrecognizable one generation later. Unrecognizable because the relationship between the clergy and laity was being redefined – hence the importance of the precision *nec clerum nec civitatem* ("neither the clergy nor the citizens"). Ambrose himself (*ipse*) or the new Ambroses acting in his name could again haunt the city – for when Landulf spoke of Ambrose like a possible revenant, he was in fact talking about his body returning (*superveniret corpore*).

Indeed, this is how the unrest of the Pataria began: with the moving of holy bodies.[86] It was May 10, 1057, and the Ambrosian liturgy for the translation of the relics of Nazaro was being performed by a solemn procession leading from the Church of San Celso to the *basilica apostolorum*. A cleric then took the floor to excoriate the corruption of the Church of Milan. His name was Arialdo. He energetically and vehemently accused Ariberto of Intimiano's successor, Archbishop Guido da Velate, of being an illiterate simoniac living in concubinage, and denounced a debauched clergy that scooped up offices like they "might have bought a cow."[87] Milan, which had been benefiting for several decades from an economic boom that was strengthening the foundations of feudal society, was without contest the capital of simoniac heresy. (Simony refers here to church offices and property in the redistributive cycle that financially benefited the aristocracy, an inclusion that appeared scandalous only to those who believed in an evangelical purity intended to restore the virtues of the original Church.)[88] Arialdo's impassioned sermon stirred the crowd, which turned on the priests and forced them to take oaths of celibacy. In a city where married priests were particularly numerous,[89] this initial episode triggered a wave of violence that led the Patarenes, if not to seize power, at least to continuously intrude on political and religious life in Milan, until the assassination of Erlembaldo Cotta in 1075. The Patarene troops were in a state of permanent mobilization, a feverish communion whose capacity for action is described in our sources as an emotional contagion.[90]

Who were Arialdo's followers? Their enemies referred to them as flea-ridden – "they called them *paterinos*, meaning 'dressed in rags,' criticizing their poverty," wrote Bonizo of Sutri[91] – and Landulf, likely a married priest himself, presented the Pataria as a social combat between the rich and the poor. This was clearly a way to discredit the enemy: the author of *Historia Mediolanensis*, very hostile to the Patarenes, no doubt exaggerated the poverty of those aiming to reform clerical mores. His description of the heresy in Monforte in 1038, and his exaltation of the role played by Ariberto as the warrior bishop who suppressed it, was in large part provoked by his dread that the recent past would repeat itself: we should always fear, he said, the religious enthusiasm of those who are fanatical about the purity of origins.[92] In reality, we find many rich citizens among the laity involved in the Pataria movement, such as Benedetto Rozzo, the founder of the church that became the Patarenes' headquarters, and the brothers Landolfo and Erlembaldo Cotta, the latter of whom would go on to play a critical role after Arialdo's assassination in 1067. These rich laymen intended to lead an apostolic life, forming a "textual community" gathered around the reading and interpretation of rare texts that they, quite intensely, made their own.[93] This became the Canonica, a site of communal living that trained an alternative clergy openly defying the archbishop's authority by going into churches to preach and contest the validity of oaths taken by nonreformist priests.

After all, the Patarenes were able to rely on powerful support within the Church: when Arialdo and Landolfo Cotta were excommunicated by the archbishop in 1057, they called for arbitration by the pope, who sent to Milan Cardinal Hildebrand, a fervent supporter of Church reforms, and Anselmo da Baggio, who had been edged out by Archbishop Guido da Velate for the same reasons. We know that Anselmo da Baggio became pope under the name Alexander II in 1062, making Erlembaldo his personal representative in Milan, and that Cardinal Hildebrand succeeded him on Saint Peter's throne in 1073 under the name Gregory VII. The Patarenes were therefore radical reformers whom the papacy (or at least a specific Roman group around Hildebrand) managed to exploit for a while in order to assimilate simony and Nicolaitanism (meaning the marriage of priests) with heresy. This continued until they became uncontrollable and were themselves savagely suppressed, even if they were never officially condemned as heretics. It was only much later that the term "Patarene" became the most common designation for heresy in Italy,[94] as the very result of its semantic vagueness: in 1179, the third Lateran Council targeted heretics "that some call the Cathars, others the Patarenes, others the Publicani, and others by different names."[95]

Historiography today is reconsidering the importance of the Church reform incorrectly dubbed Gregorian, after Pope Gregory VII (1073–85), who incarnated its most radical period.[96] Beyond its disciplinary dimension (the fight against priests marrying and the trafficking of church offices and property), and even beyond its political implications (the investiture quarrel between the pope and the emperor), this reform was a wholesale social phenomenon that precipitated the transition from one "world arrangement" to another.[97] Radically dividing Christian society between the order of the clergy, based on celibacy, and the order of the laity, based on marriage, increasing the importance of the sacrament to make the Eucharist the heart of the act of salvation, protecting the Church's property as "spiritual things" (*spiritualia* versus *temporalia*), the Gregorian break brought a new society into being. As Florian Mazel writes, "if Gregorian ecclesiology primarily appears to be an ecclesiology of the institution, we could say, paraphrasing Pierre Legendre, that the principle of separation is what establishes the institution."[98]

But the paradox is that any far-reaching impacts of the Gregorian Reform, notably in terms of the societal and infrastructural change it engendered, stem from its failure to concentrate all power in the hands of the pope, the proponent of the plan to have Christian society entirely subsumed by the *ecclesia*.[99] Theocratic domination was a project dead on arrival, and the distribution of powers in Western Europe was born from the ashes of this political dream. The commune in Italy was nothing other than the urban form of the establishment of a new feudal order.[100] For political systems always first take hold outside the realm of politics. In Milan, the Pataria is generally considered by historians, since at least the work of Cinzio Violante, as the key moment of the precommunal ferment.[101] The final eruptions of religious unrest documented in Lombardy were recorded in 1096, and the first written confirmation of the Milanese commune dates to 1097: *consules* intervened in the election of Archbishop Anselmo IV da Bovisio, who founded a market the following year and granted a toll exemption with "the common counsel of the whole city" (*comuni conscilio totius civitatis*).[102] The term *comune* is here still just an adjective, and consuls were merely men who deliberated. For the Italian commune was not established as a political system; it always appears in our sources surreptitiously, just as we realize that it has been there all along, in deeds. It was the manifestation of a new power dynamic based on representation and deliberation, practiced by the men of this era before they theorized it, like the political experiment of a new world invented, as suggests Chris Wickham, by sleepwalkers.

This was more than just coincidence, for the commune took up the banner of reform insofar as it fundamentally aspired to order and justice.[103] Countering the *superbia* of the secular and ecclesiastical aristocracy, and in order to protect themselves from the arbitrariness of the powerful, the *cives* intended to defend their *libertas*: at least that is the sense that emerges from Landulf's account. Andrea da Strumi, who wrote the life of Arialdo after his martyrdom, however, used new terms, or at least terms that took on new meaning from the moment they designated an aspiration for public order and social peace: *caritas, unanimitas, dilectio, paternitas*.[104] In 1067, in Milan, all those who had not taken the Peace of God oath, or who had betrayed it, were expulsed from the civic community. This practice of *juramentum commune* was the foundation of communal institutions: conjuration – meaning, in its original sense, the act of collectively making a vow (*jurare*) – established the collective on the basis of voluntary adhesion to a cause, bringing together political followers. It was therefore through the Pataria movement that the Gregorian Reform resulted in a new public institution, the commune, situated a good distance from the papacy and the empire, but also from the episcopal power that was in fact its genesis. In this same year, 1067, Arialdo was killed by agents of a niece of Guido da Velate. His body, atrociously mutilated, was thrown in Lake Como, before his followers could piously gather his remains. The Pataria had its martyr; Erlembaldo left for Rome to have Pope Alexander II beatify Arialdo, which occurred the following year. But in the meantime, his body had been carried to Milan in a solemn procession on May 17, 1067, to be laid out in the Basilica of Sant'Ambrogio. Ten years after the sermon that had roused the

Patarines, Arialdo's story finished as it had begun, with a transfer of relics, in the shadow of Ambrose, the great divider.

AMBROSE VERSUS AMBROSE, ROME WITH MILAN

In writing a *Passion of the Blessed Martyr Saint of Milan, Arialdo*, at Vallombrosa Abbey in 1075, Andrea da Strumi launched into a combative hagiography, intended to defend the cause of the revolutionary movement in which he had participated.[105] Indeed, the Pataria is distinctive for being well documented: contrary to most of the dissident religious movements of the Middle Ages, which are only known to us through the malevolent perspectives of their persecutors, forcing historians to construct plausible figures through a technique combining unanimously but varyingly hostile accounts,[106] the radical reformers of the second half of the eleventh century left a positive memory in Milan, which we can compare to that of their adversaries. Two camps faced off, each sufficiently established to polarize the political landscape. "In these days," writes Andrea da Strumi, "if you were to walk through the city, you would scarcely hear anything but debate on this matter," adding: "Some excused the simoniacal heresy, others condemned it constantly." Was it a question of two unflinching sides? Yes and no, for "one house was faithful, another completely unfaithful, in a third the mother and one son were believers, while the father and another son were unbelieving. And the entire city was permeated and filled with confusion and contention…"[107]

Examining the available Pataria-related sources[108] allows for an understanding of how references to Ambrose were equally distributed on both sides, all while helping to divide his memory from the inside. In texts by authors favorable to the Pataria, Ambrose quite logically appears as a merciless critic fighting against simony. For example, in his *Passio Arialdi*, Andrea da Strumi cited "what the blessed Ambrose, our patron, thinks" to support his denunciations. He did not present him as an active and engaged bishop, but as a contemplative, describing the sanctuary of Nemus as a "place where the saint liked to retreat alone when he wanted to flee the confusion of the world and write books" and where Arialdo came to pray in turn.[109] The Patarene leader imitated Ambrose by reoccupying the land: Arialdo visited Ambrose's tomb for contemplation, in the basilica where his martyred body would later be displayed.[110]

But the crux of the dispute over memory concerned the relationship between the Ambrosian identity of the Church of Milan and the preeminence of the Roman papacy. Andrea da Strumi placed a diatribe in the mouth of his adversary Archbishop Guido da Velate against the Patarenes, who, the fictionalized da Velate claimed, insulted Ambrose's memory by implying that Milan was subject to Rome.[111] We find the same imputation in the anonymous *Passio* of Arialdo, likely written in the second half of the twelfth century: we must, says Arialdo's enemy Archbishop Guido, rid the earth of those who deprive Milan of that ancient glory of never having obeyed Rome.[112] Another Pataria supporter, Bonizo of Sutri, also evoked Ambrose's authority in his *Liber ad amicum*, written around 1085–86 to defend the pontifical cause and restore the tarnished memory of Gregory VII.[113] For him, this meant retracing the "history of Milan's submission to Rome,"[114] which was rejected by simoniac bishops when they "addressed the people, falsely denying what Ambrose had often said in his writings, namely that he who avoids, even partially, the jurisdiction of the Church of Rome was a heretic."[115]

When Peter Damian, papal legate to Milan in 1059-60, traveled there to cautiously defend the Augustinian position that the validity of the sacrament was guaranteed by the grace of

God and not by the virtue of the priest – a stance taken during the crisis of the Donatist heresy – he defended the distinctness of the *ecclesia Ambrosiana* all while of course underlining the prerogatives of Rome: *ut ecclesia Romana mater, Ambrosiana sit filia*.[116] In other words, the name of Ambrose – "your very holy Ambrose," as Pope Urban II (1088-99) wrote in an undated letter to the clergy and people of Milan in which he compared him to the "candelabrum of Christ"[117] – allowed the Gregorians to order the Milanese people to respect their duty of filial obedience to their mother Church in Rome.[118] Canonical collections attribute to Ambrose a sentence affirming that every person in disagreement with Rome may be considered a heretic (*Ambrosius: Hereticum esse constat, qui a Romana ecclesia discordat*). Fabrice Delivré has suggested a textual archaeology of this maxim of considerable reach, given that it transformed any disobedience to the Roman Church into a case of heresy: in all likelihood, it dates back to the early 1080s, and again came from this same circle of Roman reformers.[119]

So the Patarenes' enemies were not ready to relinquish their references to Ambrose. He is "our patron" or "our master Ambrose" in Arnulf of Milan's *Liber gestorum recentium*,[120] and the people of Milan were quite foolish not to follow his path, claiming to see the apostle behind the patron saint. The chronicler warned, "these things were not written in the annals of Rome without reason. Indeed, it shall be said in [the] future that Milan is subject to Rome."[121] Which did not stop Arnulf from decreeing, still citing Ambrose, that anyone who disobeyed the Roman Church was not Catholic.[122] As for Landulf Senior, he presented Ambrose as the father of all of Milan's ecclesiastical institutions.[123] Whereas Arnulf exalted the Milanese Church as *honor sancti Ambrosii*, Landulf completed the identification of the city with its patron by using the expression *civitas Ambrosiana*.[124] Under his pen, Milan and its diocese appear like an aristocratic household, "the household of Saint Ambrose, since the regalia of power now belonged to the saint's successor, the archbishop of Milan." By distributing food and clothes to the people, protecting them from famine – Landulf described Ariberto of Intimiano as ordering that 8,000 loaves of bread be kneaded and eight large measures of broad beans boiled each day to feed the starving – the bishop entered Ambrose's *domus*, the effect being "to incorporate all the people thus fed into the prince's private household," according to the analysis by Georges Duby.[125]

Above all, Landulf explicitly accused the reform-bent fanatics that were the Patarenes of "deforming" Ambrose's teachings by having him say things that he did not say.[126] The charge is aggressive and looks a lot like an act of denial, for Landulf himself did not hesitate to enlist Ambrose into the anti-Patarene argument, painting the protest movement as an attack against Ambrosian liturgy: *quam ob misterium Ambrosianum quod ultra fas et nefas, oderat.*[127] Even less scrupulously, he claimed to find justification for priests marrying in Ambrose's teachings – whereas the bishop of Milan always very clearly supported priestly celibacy.[128] The apologetic discourse developed by the anti-reformist Milanese clergy to counter the Patarenes' arguments dug a few useful sentences out of the *scientia Ambrosiana* taught in cathedral schools. But as shown by Cesare Alzati, these *sententiae* were always trimmed to fit with other sentences, from different patristic sources, for which the main objective was less to discover their specific meaning than to ensure their compatibility within an ensemble that was, if not coherent, at least harmonious.[129]

According to Landulf, during a dispute between the two sides, Archdeacon Guibert became involved in the Patarenes' decision to exclude "all Ambrosian sayings."[130] But how could they deprive themselves of such a source of legitimization and mobilization? During the turmoil of the Pataria, the specter of

Ambrose returned but did not choose a side. The enemy camps fought over his memory, but neither was able to definitively compromise it. For now, let's keep the following in mind: the Ambrosian past, confronted with this smoldering present and its thwarted demands for reform, simultaneously aroused competing uses and reciprocal accusations of misuse. It remained in any case fully available for other political appropriations.

By Bernard of Clairvaux, for example, who made use of the Ambrosian past, in the 1130s, during the schism of Anacletus (supported by the Norman king Roger II of Sicily and a majority of Romans, against Pope Innocent II).[131] This prompted Geoffroy of Auxerre, abbot of Clairvaux, the great compiler of Bernard's writings, to compare him to Ambrose in a sermon given on August 20, 1163 (ten years after Bernard's death), that was haunted by Ambrose's presence. Bernard, said Geoffroy, rooted out the schism like the bishop of Milan did Arian heresy; he was not only a new Ambrose in the sense that he was inspired by the saint's doctrine and actions, was encouraged by his example, and claimed to act in the name of what he believed to be fidelity to Ambrose's memory. No, he was *Ambrosius redivivus*, an Ambrose come back to life – so much so that, explained the preacher, if someone were to open his tomb, he would find it empty.[132]

NINE

Reading Ambrose: Textual Tales (Fourth to Twelfth Century)

A king, barefoot in the snow, shivers at the gates of a castle. It is Henry IV, the Holy Roman Emperor. He has been excommunicated by the pope, Gregory VII, after unilaterally declaring the pontiff deposed. Their quarrel was over the appointment of bishops and abbots, but in fact hinged on one of the major questions of the reorganization of power in the West, namely the competition between two players who each claimed universality. The year was 1077, and what historians would much later call the Investiture Controversy was underway. Henry, buckling to pressure from the princes of the Roman Empire, has been forced to seek out Gregory and beg his forgiveness. Knowing that the pope was a guest at the castle of Margravine Matilda of Tuscany in Canossa, in the Apennines,[1] Henry decided to cross the Alps in the dead of winter by the Mont-Cenis Pass, as Charlemagne had done in his day. In his *Annales*, the monk and chronicler

Lambert of Hersfeld describes the royal army hauling itself painfully up the steep slopes, "now scrambling on their hands and feet, now leaning on the shoulders of their guides,"[2] dragging the king along on a cowhide. On January 25, 1077, they arrived at Canossa and stood before the gates of the castle, which, on the pope's orders, had been shut against them. For three days, Henry stood in the deep snow, fasting and in tears, until Pope Gregory relented and welcomed the penitent back into the fold.[3]

"We will not go to Canossa" was Otto von Bismarck's message to the Reichstag on May 14, 1872, following Pope Pius IX's refusal to accredit Germany's ambassador. The leader of the newly formed German Empire then embarked on the Kulturkampf that was intended to secure a new relationship between the Catholic Church and the European states. In a famous book, Harald Zimmermann examined the historical uses of the penitence at Canossa. In the nineteenth century it became an emblem of the submission of secular power to Church authority, but it had an older significance, since the Reformation, symbolizing *Sonderweg*, the special destiny of the German people.[4] This has given rise to virulent historiographical debates, including recently with the work of Johannes Fried, who, building on his deconstruction of the narrative sequence of this "German myth" through close analysis of available sources, has proposed a general theory of the phenomena of memory inversion by those most insistent on textual transmission.[5]

Did the king really suffer humiliation at Canossa? After all, he emerged from the contest stronger than before, whereas the pope had found himself dutybound to give absolution. The scene looks more like the ritualized accomplishment of a prearranged negotiation than a capitulation. It suggests a kind of rationalization of political action that can be interpreted, in the context of a rearticulated relationship between spiritual and secular power, as a form of disenchantment.[6] Everything had occurred according to the implacable order of a ritual: a three-day penance and a pope whose heart softened at the entreaties of three kindly souls (his stepmother Adelaïde, the margravine Matilda, and the abbot Hugh of Cluny, Henry IV's godfather). Each stayed within the boundaries of his role.[7] Even the choice of date (September 25, the Feast of the Conversion of Saint Paul, which also lasted three days) made perfect sense. Through this ritual of public humiliation, Henry restored a Davidian kingship, based on penitence. Through penitence, he acceded to the Christian triumph of humility, just like Emperor Honorius, who, in 403 or 404, had laid his diadem before the altar (*memoria*) of Saint Peter, confessed his sins, and, as Augustine writes in one of his rediscovered sermons, "struck his breast where the sinner's heart resides. He pondered Peter's merits, believed in the saint's victory, hoped to come to God through him, felt and found himself to have been helped by his prayers."[8]

A question still remains: What historical precedent might the contemporaries of this memorable event call on to grasp its import and manage its consequences? For the chronicler Berthold of Reichenau, there was no doubt – the Humiliation at Canossa was directly comparable to the penitence that Ambrose imposed on Emperor Theodosius after the massacre in Thessalonica.[9] The face-off between Ambrose and Theodosius had become one of the founding types of kingly penitence.[10] As Fabrice Delivré writes, "in the last quarter of the eleventh century, the conflict between the two universal powers transformed [Ambrose's showdown with Theodosius] into a commonplace for the superiority of priests over kings."[11] Let's return briefly to the facts: in the spring of 390, a riot broke out in Thessalonica, capital of the imperial province of Thessaly and Achaia, residence of the *magister militum* who commanded the armies of Illyricum, and a key site for Theodosius's eastern strategy.[12] What caused the riot is unclear, but it seems that the arrest of a circus charioteer, one of the *aurigae* of the great chariot races that were both important popular celebrations and highly political spectacles, triggered the anger of the people.[13] The governor, Butheric, tried to intercede and was killed by the crowd. Theodosius was based in Milan when the news reached him; he flew into a rage of the sort that Ambrose, who had known him since 388 when he defeated Maximus, described as a common occurrence.[14] The emperor ordered the execution of the Thessalonicans, and neither Ambrose's call for clemency nor the advice of Flavius Rufinus, his chief of staff, moderated the emperor's resolve. The crowd was herded into a stadium, where soldiers massacred them over the course of three hours. Seven thousand died, according to fifth-century sources, although later sources cite ever-larger numbers of victims.

The news from Thessalonica reached every corner of the empire. Ambrose, who was then organizing a synod of Gaulish bishops in Milan, wrote a letter to Theodosius exhorting him to penitence, urging him to repent publicly. "An act has been committed in the city of Thessalonica, the like of which has never been recorded…I am grieved that you who were an example of singular piety, who stood so high for clemency, who would not suffer even single offenders to be put in jeopardy, should not mourn over the death of so many innocent persons."[15] It was the first time, Peter Brown tells us, that a bishop had dared to raise his voice against an emperor. He expressed himself frankly, speaking truth (*parrhesia*) to a man who had shown himself unworthy of his education (*paidea*), holding up to him the way of just government.[16] He did so with moderation, finding examples in the Book of Kings and in Psalms to show that penitence would in no way diminish the emperor. In fact, a humble acceptance of the frailty of the human condition could paradoxically open a triumphant path to greatness for a Christian ruler. What is at play here is nothing less than the early formulation of the "Gelasian" doctrine of the two kinds of power, *potestas* and *auctoritas*, which would be explicitly set forth at the end of the fifth century, drawing on a compilation of judicial documents signed by Pope Gelasius I (*Decretum Gelasianum*). Relying on numerous writings of the Church Fathers, notably Ambrose, it rests in part on the existing policies toward anathema and excommunication.[17]

Theodosius made plaintive noises for eight months, then gave in. He agreed to repent the enormity of his crime publicly only because, according to Paulinus of Milan in the *Vita Ambrosii*, he became aware of the political power of a David-like kingship. "The emperor defended himself by observing that David had committed both adultery and murder. But the response was immediate: 'If you have followed him in his sin, then follow him also in his amendment.' When the most clement emperor heard this, he was so moved that he did not shrink from public penance, and the improvement that resulted from his amendment won for him a second victory."[18] The subtle play on *clementissimus* (an ordinary element in the emperor's titles, which here takes on a moral connotation, as in Ambrose's letter to Theodosius) shows the extent to which the hagiographer is dramatizing a political exchange that would leave the emperor in an improved situation. This is also the case in Augustine's telling in the fifth book of his *City of God*, written in 415, where "the sight of [Theodosius's] imperial loftiness prostrated made the people who were interceding for him weep more than the consciousness of offense had made them fear it when enraged."[19] That is why, in dedicating his *Apology for David* to Theodosius, Ambrose does not simply invite the emperor to cry out, as did the guilty king, "he who accuses himself is just." He composed "a sort of 'Policy Drawn from the Holy Scriptures' that would serve as a model for Carolingian bishops when they set out to compose a portrait of the perfect prince based on Biblical models," as Pierre Hadot has written.[20]

If the Ambrosian memory of Theodosius's penance was available to authors of the eleventh and twelfth centuries, such as Berthold of Reichenau, when they needed to find a historical precedent to make sense of the episode at Canossa, it's worth noting that it reached them after having passed through the filter of Carolingian memory. The two acts of public contrition made by Louis the Pious during his reign – the first at Attigny in 822 and the second at Soissons in 833 – turned the royal office toward expiation, after which admonishment was elevated to a form of governance. Actually, the reference to Ambrose was already explicit in the Carolingian accounts of the penitential acts of Charlemagne's son.[21] The *Utrecht Psaulter*, an illuminated manuscript dating from 822 to 823, provides an image of this royal penitence inspired by King David, drawn from Ambrose's *Apology for David*. In the Gregorian iteration, things obviously changed: there was no question of Gregory VII presenting himself as the spiritual – or philosophical – guide to the Christian emperor Henry IV, the role that Ambrose assumed with respect to Theodosius. The point at issue was instead to mark the separation between the two powers.

From this perspective, Henry's posture of waiting at the gates of a castle "protected by a triple wall" before being finally admitted on the fourth day, stripped of his royal garb and presented to the pope "inside the second enclosure," echoes the famous scene where Theodosius was stopped at the threshold of the church by the bishop Ambrose.[22] Though this encounter became, as we will see later, one of the great popular subjects of Baroque performance during the Counter-Reformation, it appears nowhere in Western sources.[23] Paulinus of Milan went no further than to say that Ambrose "did not allow the emperor to enter the church, and he judged him unworthy of the assembly of the Church and of participation in the sacraments until he did public penance"[24] – which we should read as meaning simply that he threatened the emperor with excommunication.

It was probably in the *Historia ecclesiastica tripartita* that Berthold of Reichenau found the account of the confrontation of Theodosius and Ambrose at the doors of the sanctuary.[25] The work continues the Latin translation of Eusebius of Caesaria's *Historia ecclesiastica*, completed by Rufinus of Aquileia in 402-3. This was the first history of Christianity from Christ to the reign of Constantine, and it was to have considerable influence in the West – if only because it gave currency to the legend, still alive today, of Constantine's conversion in 312.[26] Its translator, Rufinus, extended the history to the reign of Theodosius.[27] In the second half of the sixth century, Cassiodorus undertook to have the great tradition of Greek Church history translated into Latin, working from the Vivarium monastery that he had founded in Calabria.[28] He first recruited Theodorus Lector,[29] then the monk Epiphanius, to bring the work of Eusebius's continuators to the Latin West. The *Historia ecclesiastica tripartita* devotes twelve chapters to the events of 324 to 439, compiling the writings of three Greek historians: Socrates of Constantinople (also known as Socrates Scholasticum), Sozomen, and Theodoret of Cyrus. Condemned by Pope Gregory I in 597, the work only started to circulate in the eighth and ninth centuries, when it gained widespread popularity.[30] As Bernard Guenée has commented, "Cassiodorus's choice marked the West's historical culture for a thousand years."[31]

All three of the Greek authors – Socrates, Sozomen, and Theodoret – would invoke Ambrose in the course of writing their ecclesiastic histories in the mid-fifth century, thus nurturing in the East a memory of the Italian bishop that was independent of Paulinus of Milan's *Vita Ambrosii*. So lasting was Ambrose's fame in the Byzantine Empire that three Greek hagiographies were written in the eighth to tenth centuries – the most notable by Symeon the Metaphrast – which would set the posthumous life of Ambrose of Milan on an idiosyncratic course in the Byzantine Empire, a fact still awaiting its historian.[32] Meanwhile, as the translated *Historia ecclesiastica tripartita* gained traction in the Latin West, a new Ambrose, as seen by the Greeks, was making his comeback there, which was decisive for the reconstructed memory of Theodosius's penance. Although Socrates does not mention the incident,[33] Sozomen and especially Theodoret amplify and dramatize it, to the point of inventing the episode in which Ambrose stops Theodosius on the threshold of the church:[34] "And when the time came to place the gifts on the holy table, [Theodosius] rose to his feet, still in tears, and entered the sanctuary. And after laying down his gifts, he remained, as was his custom, inside the chancel. But once again the great Ambrose did not remain silent. He gave him a lesson by teaching him to distinguish places."[35]

Taught him to distinguish places: this refers to the dividing line between the areas open to laymen and those reserved for clergy. The emperor was not to penetrate into the sanctuary, a space accessible only to priests. Theodosius received the instruction "most gladly," according to the text. He had learned his behavior in Constantinople, but he now understood that it was inappropriate for a Christian emperor. When he returned to Constantinople, we read in Theodoret of Cyrus's history, he would remember the lesson he had learned in Milan, for in Ambrose he had found a "teacher of truth" who "taught him the difference between an emperor and a priest." It is easy to see how this instructional story might have been used in Constantinople: Ambrose's life served, as Gilbert Dagron has ably shown, to uphold the priestly idea of a separation between the two powers, contradicting imperial claims to a sacerdotal royalty. This question was particularly germane in the tenth century, in the era of Constantine VII Porphyrogennetos (913 to 959). What was then available "to oppose the absolute power of the emperor? Neither rights nor ideas. Only an accumulation of memories, whether true or invented, and images."[36] And at Canossa, in 1077, Theodosius's ghost returned, but was dated as all ghosts are – having traveled from Byzantium and the East, it came with a history that had not yet finished haunting Western Europe.

AUCTOR, ACTOR, AUCTORITAS:
WAS AMBROSE THE AUTHOR OF HIS CORRESPONDENCE?

If any hardy readers consulted the endnotes at the mention, several pages back, of the letter Ambrose addressed to Emperor Theodosius on learning of the massacre in Thessalonica (probably in May or June 390),[37] they may have noticed that the letter in question was cited as *Epist. extra coll. 11*. This means that it was the eleventh of Ambrose's separately transmitted letters, distinct from the collected correspondence. A simple nomenclatural detail? Not really. Starting here, we can tug on a thread dangling from quite the tangled ball, which hides an all-important question: What was Ambrose's part in shaping his textual memory? To what extent was its transmission in manuscript form dependent on what we might call his authorial decisions? Put another way, by paying due attention to irregularities in the texture of time, can we hear the voice of an absent person?

The answer to this question can only come from philology, the historical study of the development of language, or codicology, the comparative study of manuscripts, and must consequently depend on the patient effort to produce indirect evidence. To understand the structure of Ambrose's collected letters, we need first to understand the material circumstances of their transmission.[38] The two oldest manuscripts – one preserved in the Vatican Library and copied in Vercelli or Milan, originally the property of the monastery of Sant'Ambrogio, and the other preserved in Berlin and probably copied in northeastern Gaul – date to the middle or second half of the ninth century.[39] From this first branch are derived more than sixty manuscripts dating from the tenth to the fifteenth century. A second branch, also very productive, takes its origin in three witness manuscripts that were copied in Milan in the eleventh century.[40] All five very likely descend from an archetype dating back to late antiquity with the following structure: seventy-seven letters divided into ten books, the third of which has been lost, organized with a seeming disorderliness that has long confounded scholars.[41]

Fifteen other letters have been transmitted *extra collectionem*, in two groups.[42] The first and largest collects ten letters to the emperors Valentinian and Theodosius and opens with a letter from Ambrose to his sister Marcellina. This corpus was known to Paulinus of Milan – he may in fact have been responsible for its publication and distribution. The second group, consisting of five letters – including the letter to Theodosius – was unknown to Paulinus and does not figure in his account. The first group, which we could call "Paulinian," therefore has an overall coherence in its organization, suggesting an overarching design and allowing for its homogeneous manuscript transmission; the second, which is more disparate, probably goes back to a manuscript that is today lost, a final gathering of the letters that had been left uncollected.[43] Other letters are known by other means, because they were quoted or because they were mentioned by an author or an addressee – these have become separated out from the corpus or lost. Finally, some letters (like Ambrose's famous Letter 77 to his sister Marcellina on the discovery of the remains of Gervasius and Protasius, alluded to more than once above) were transmitted independently.[44]

In short, what is labeled "Correspondence" does not cover the totality of Ambrose's letters. It refers to a collection, almost a work in itself, which the author probably shaped in the last years of his life. He says so unambiguously to one of his correspondents, Sabinus, bishop of Piacenza, apparently asking him to be one of his proofreaders: "These preliminary remarks I am sending you, and I will insert them, if you please, in the book of our letters (*libros nostrarum epistularum*) and place them among their number so that they may be promoted by the inclusion of your name."[45]

The remark is significant, because it shows that the name of the person addressed is, as it were, a dedication. In other words, Ambrose, insofar as he is the author of his correspondence, has dedicatees rather than correspondents. This is one of the first organizing principles of his correspondence: it memorializes a network of friendships and influences, intending not so much to display that network's full extent as to prune back its structure.[46] The addressee with the most appearances is a Milanese clerk by the name of Irenaeus, no doubt a close collaborator of Ambrose, to whom thirteen letters are addressed – or dedicated.[47] Another is the priest Simplicianus, who would succeed Ambrose as bishop and about whom Augustine wrote in the eighth book of his *Confessions* that Ambrose loved him with a father's love.[48] And of course there are the letters to his sister Marcellina. Other names have disappeared: those of emperors, for example, and of great personages (Ambrose's replies to the letters of Symmachus have not been preserved), as well as dates, situations, and references.

This edit exasperates historians, who always hate to be reminded that the people of the past took an interest in different things than we do, or at least in a different way and in a different order. Yet this decontextualization serves the purpose of the correspondence. To add texts that he deemed necessary, or themes not represented in his epistolary, Ambrose would insert fictive letters – or letters that *we* would call fictive, as the distinction was not entirely pertinent in the world of late antiquity. When Augustine, at the end of his life, was revising "two books entitled *In Answer to the Inquiries of Januarius*[, which] contain many discussions of the mysteries," he asked himself about their genre. His answer was: "Of the two books, the first is a letter, for at the start it bears the name of the writer and of the person to whom it is addressed."[49] In other words, as soon as the formal criterion *quis ad quem scribat* (who writes to whom) is fulfilled, it counts as a letter. What accounts for the epistolary nature of a text is therefore its symmetry of address, rather than the reality of the exchange.

One thing is certain: just as Augustine wrote long letter-treatises that were as important for their contents as for their form of address,[50] Ambrose conceived his correspondence in close relation to his treatises, notably as summaries of the main points of dogma and exegesis in his work. In the midst of his correspondence, for instance, a group of "exegetical matters" can be identified, such as the one commenting on the epistles to the Galatians and Romans and Mosaic law.[51] To explain the division of the collection into ten books, an organizational structure that seems haphazard and misleading, some scholars have suggested that Ambrose left the collection unfinished and that the textual evidence therefore represents, though with inevitable alterations, a kind of work in progress. A composite manuscript, copied in the sixth century, containing texts by Ambrose and four of his letters, might be the remains of a separate edition, shaped by the bishop of Milan and forming the prototype of an intended collection.[52] Did Ambrose want his correspondence to resemble models from antiquity, notably the correspondence of Pliny the Younger? This hypothesis has been supported by a variety of arguments.[53] But the literary principle of the *varietas* was not applied in any rigorous way. In fact, Ambrose probably took his inspiration loosely from a kind of Theodosian mannerism then in vogue, applying it in a general fashion to the art of letter writing, which was a literary and political genre in its own right.[54]

Examples of epistolary art date back to antiquity and the early Christian era – it suffices to name Paul's epistles. Ambrose explicitly acknowledges this in one of his letters: "I should cite the example of our elders, who by means of their letters spread the faith into the minds of distant peoples and who wrote entire small but closely-reasoned books, affirming that they were present in their writings despite their absence, as for instance the Apostle saying he was absent in body but present in spirit." This refers to a quote from First Corinthians (I Cor. 5:3), on which Ambrose commented thus: "For a letter from Paul was the image of his presence and the form of his action."[55] In other words, a letter is "a presence between two who are absent."[56] This Ciceronian idea (a letter, as we learn in *Philippics* 2.4, is "a conversation between absent friends" – *amicorum colloquia absentium*), was revived by Ambrose and would gain currency throughout Latin Europe.[57] It therefore makes sense that a letter should document an epistolary ritual, a counterpart to visiting an episcopal see, which Ambrose also practiced. Both are ceremonies of power – Ambrose used them to defend his position as chief bishop in northern Italy, at the head of a network.[58] This is why a number of his letters are written giving explicit directions, and why he expects those to whom they are dedicated to be, as Neil McLynn wrote in his biography of Ambrose, essentially his followers.[59]

Consequently, in dealing with the structure of Ambrose's books of correspondence, we should approach them in their political dimension, as acts of government,[60] remembering that

epistolary efficacy increased during the period of Gregorian turmoil, when the power of letters was sharpened to the point they
became weapons of war.[61] The dissemination of Ambrose's correspondence continued to revive, until deep into the Middle Ages,
the techniques of political persuasion particular to Roman func-
tionaries, blending the facade of authoritarianism with a perpetual negotiation with the elites.[62] Let's look at the last book, the
tenth, by far the longest in the *collectio*, comprising a third of all
the letters.[63] It differs from the other books in the collection by its
break in tone: its eleven texts don't deal with exegeses or the spiritual life but with Ambrose's political-religious struggles. It was
this final emphasis on the bishop's public life that has prompted
the editor of his correspondence to compare its structure to the
correspondence of Pliny the Younger, which also ends with references to his dealings with Trajan.[64] But this final book of his correspondence doesn't solely address Ambrose's relations with the
emperors Valentinian II and Theodosius, since the earlier letters
in it are addressed to bishops. Furthermore, what makes the *collectio* original is that it inserts three documents among the eleven
texts that are not letters at all: the *relatio* (report) of Symmachus,
the sermon *Against Auxentius*, and Ambrose's funeral oration on
the death of Theodosius, placed at the end of the book between
two letters to Marcellina. (These two letters, as it happens,
address the conflict in 386 over the basilicas, which I've discussed
at length above.) The insertion of the funeral oration, delivered
forty days after the death of Theodosius on January 17, 395, therefore provides an interruption to the succession of events in 386.
The inevitable inference is that the textual order of the tenth
book of Ambrose's correspondence is governed by an organizing
principle other than chronology.

The best way to grasp the book's logic is to describe it piece
by piece. The first two letters are communications sent following

a synod: the first was written to Theophilus, bishop of Alexandria, after the Council of Capua; the second was addressed to the bishops of Macedonia and concerned the synod held in Milan in the spring of 393. The backdrop in both cases is doctrinal and relates to the defense of orthodoxy: against the dissenters favorable to the Antioch schism in the first and against the Jovinian doctrine denying the perpetual virginity of Mary in the second.[65] Then comes a section on the controversy between Ambrose and Symmachus over the Altar of Victory (which puts us in the summer of 384); bookending the *relatio* by Symmachus in defense of his point of view are two of Ambrose's letters to Emperor Valentinian II.[66] Next comes a letter Ambrose sent to Emperor Theodosius in the autumn of 388 appealing to him to stop the retribution against the Christians who set fire to the synagogue in Callinicum, on the edges of the Persian Empire.[67] We'll return to this crucial and dramatic event, but I'll simply note here that its place is at the center of the book, and that it already constitutes an energetic remonstrance to the emperor, a prelude to the penitence Ambrose would impose on him after the massacre in Thessalonica. The book ends with an examination of the battle of the basilicas: a letter to Valentinian, the sermon *Against Auxentius*, and the two letters from Holy Week 386 sent by Ambrose to his sister Marcellina, separated as we have seen by his funeral oration for Theodosius.[68]

The book's overall structure reflects a subtle set of symmetries and correspondences, highlighted by Gérard Nauroy in support of his thesis that Ambrose himself created the arrangement of texts. The book functions as a whole, its detailed attention to sequence not precluding a powerful buildup of momentum. The first two letters illustrate, in a minor key, Ambrose's conciliatory authority in the internal affairs of the Church. From there, the subject moves to the three great struggles of Ambrose's political career, which concern, respectively, the pagans (the matter of the Altar of Victory); the Jews (the destruction of the synagogue of Callinicum); and the Arians (the basilicas). The order in which these are presented is highly significant, since it progresses from outside the Church to inside it, raising once more the big and serious question of the separation of powers. The keystone of the entire arc is the funeral oration that Ambrose composed in memory of Theodosius, the dedicatee of his *Apology for David* and an exemplary Christian emperor who, "freed from the muzzle of perfidy, has taken the bit of faith and devotion between his teeth."[69] Truly a political sermon, it reveals the intention of the text shaped from Ambrose's correspondence – to construct a new doctrine of the relations between Church and State.[70]

This leaves an obvious question: Why doesn't the book end here? Because, building in crescendo toward Ambrose's triumph, it finds his apotheosis elsewhere – in the occupation of the soil of Milan, in fact. The invention, or discovery, of the remains of Gervasius and Protasius represents not simply "the happy outcome of *one* episode in the bishop's struggle against Arianism in Milan, but an emphatic justification, through a kind of divine approbation of Ambrose's *entire religious policy*."[71] His invention of the saints' remains gave visible form to his protection by divine grace. And it explains the strategic bearing of what might otherwise seem a diversion in the eulogy of the penitent emperor: the passage where Ambrose brings up the fact that seventy years earlier, Helen, the mother of Constantine, found the holy cross and the nails of the cross.[72] It is only a digression if we look at the letter as a textual unit in and of itself, but the text here is the book that is building – along with the entire correspondence – toward the glorious parallel between Christ's Passion and the sufferings of the martyrs.[73] This unity becomes more apparent when we realize all that has been omitted here, in particular the other letters to Theodosius, one of which appears in Book Five, another in Book Six, while several others have come down to us *extra collectionem*, because they did not fit within this textual arrangement.

Among the letters omitted is the one written by the bishop of Milan "in his own hand," that the ruler might read it alone in the privacy of his own conscience, the letter that exhorts the emperor to penitence after the massacre in Thessalonica, the famous *Epist. extra coll. 11* that first aroused our curiosity.[74] It never found a spot within the *collectio* of Ambrose's correspondence, which could end only with the apotheosis of a grandiose reconciliation. Yet the letter survived, a detached fragment of the great and fracture-riddled block of Ambrosian memory, properly delivered, or rather liberated, since it escaped the careful ordering of the text while remaining available to be otherwise transmitted, otherwise appropriated, otherwise disseminated. In 860, Hincmar, archbishop of Reims from 845 to 882, who searched the work of Ambrose of Milan for material to support his concept of a bishop's political role in the Carolingian Empire,[75] seized on this letter and gave it new currency, quoting parts of it in his treatise on the divorce of Lothar (*De divortio Lotharii e Tebergae*).[76] And so it started all over again: Theodosius's penitence was granted a new life, first in the snows of Canossa, and later in the gilded setting of the Baroque theater. Which goes to show that the order of books can never retain the whole memory of the words that have been spoken.

FROM ANCIENT SARCOPHAGUS TO LITERARY TOMB

Sometimes dictated, often read aloud, a letter is nonetheless always written down, and this defines it as a letter. *Littera, epistola, cartula, carta,* and *pagina*: all the words in the epistolary realm refer us back to written materiality–the oral aspect of a letter is always secondary.[77] We all know from experience that it's easier to write things that we have trouble saying directly. Cicero expresses this basic truth in a letter to his friend Lucius Lucceius (*Epistulae ad familiares*, 5, 12, 1) using just three words: *epistula non erubescit*, "a letter doesn't blush." Ambrose picks up the phrase in his *De virginibus* (1, 1, 1), and it is in losing its author's name that it becomes a proverb, circulating freely, like a detached piece of the collective wisdom. For every quote drags its author along, but the second it becomes anonymous, its burden is lifted; it can circulate unchecked, jumping boundaries, hopping from language to language. This Latin phrase can therefore be found in a number of vernacular languages, including French, where a proverb enshrines it: *Le papier souffre tout et ne rougit de rien* (paper suffers all and blushes at nothing).[78]

As another expression says, *verba volant, scripta manent* (words take flight, writings stay put). But we probably understand this phrase in the opposite sense of how it was meant in medieval times, because we read it as affirming the permanence of the written in contrast to the volatility of the spoken word. To inscribe a thing is to install it securely in time, which explains why the powerful have always tried to maintain a monopoly over written memory. But the proverb can be understood quite differently: *verba volant*, the spoken word flies toward heaven, whereas the written word remains on the ground, stuck in the mud of reality, *scripta manent*.[79] How did words take flight in a church? It all depended on how they were addressed, on *quis ad quem scribat* (who is writing to whom), which defines, as we've seen, even the possibility of an epistolary relation. Because they contained words that the community addressed to God, epistles were read by a subdeacon, from his place in the choir, and therefore with his back to the congregation. But with the Gospels, it was a case of God speaking to man, or, at least, of His having once spoken to him. The Gospels were therefore read from the altar, or from the pulpit that jutted out toward the nave to carry God's Word, a pulpit known as the ambo. But these passages were read in the past tense, preceded by a few words that expressed the disjunction: *in illo tempore*, "in those days…"[80]

We've strayed away from the Basilica of Sant'Ambrogio. Let's return, moving in reverse as always, backing away from the golden altar and into the nave. We now see Saint Ambrose's ambo. As one faces the apse and the altar, this pulpit is on the left. This place for speech, or rather, for the Word, is perched above a tomb, in the same way that Ambrose's sarcophagus is encased within the golden altar. The temporal boundaries between the reused element (a sarcophagus from classical antiquity, whose sculpted scenes evoke Ambrose's preaching, at least for some) and the monument that reuses it are once more far apart: the Romanesque pulpit takes over from the classical sarcophagus and converts it. Wrapping it around with visual commentary, the pulpit redirects the gaze trained on the sarcophagus's ornament, producing an effect of retrospective visual connotation, a capture of the past through reuse.

The inscription visible on the pulpit's shorter side credits the work of a certain Guglielmo da Pomo.[81] This refers not to the initial commission of the work but to its restoration in 1201, after a partial collapse of the vault in 1196. Most of the sculptures and the plan of the whole very likely date back more than a half century earlier. Specialists have determined that the design of the ambo can be linked to the years 1130–40.[82] A study of the magnificent sculpted capitals of the vestibule of the narthex allows us to integrate this date with the chronological sequence of the Romanesque reconstruction of the basilica, from the destructive fire of March 25, 1103, to the construction of the bell tower, which is still referred to in a document dated 1143 as *clocharium sive novum*. Between these two dates, the work of reconstruction progressed from west to east, from the facade and the narthex (1110-20) to the loggia and the bell tower (1125-30), after which the decoration of the church with monuments was carried out, a process that certainly included building the ambo.[83]

Ambo of the Basilica of Sant'Ambrogio: west and south sides, c. 1130-40
(*Sandro Scarioni*)

This time frame also coincides with a period of political confrontation between the monks and canons of Sant'Ambrogio, whose relationship grew ever more bitter during the course of the twelfth century. The basilica was a place where the two communities clashed, particularly in the years 1143-44, 1189-91, and 1198-1201 – key moments in the construction and restoration of the ambo.[84] In 1254, the canons and monks were again at loggerheads over how to divide the costs of further restorations to the ambo;[85] and in 1401, the archbishop even ordered the church to be separated into two parts: the monks would have charge of the right side facing the altar, and the canons would have charge of the left. The ambo therefore lay within the canons' half of the basilica, and the stipulation was made that the monks were not allowed to build another ambo on their side.[86] The conflicts of the commune swept over the Ambrosian basilica, leaving their physical mark, at the same time cleaving Ambrose's memory into two politically antagonistic halves.

It's in this context that the political message of Saint Ambrose's ambo takes on meaning, precisely because it exemplifies reuse. Everything about the structure is unusual: the pulpit rests upon an antique sarcophagus, to which it forms a crown – a design without equivalent elsewhere. The reused sarcophagus is one of the largest known in all of paleo-Christian Lombardy. The decorative plan of the majestic arches that envelop it offers a rich catalog of Romanesque sculpture, and the decorative bronze elements (the eagle and the angel of Saint Matthew) are equally remarkable. The overall impression is striking, as the reuse of the ancient monument plays on echoes and consonances between classical art and Romanesque sculpture. The reprise can be ornamental, as with the ambo's capitals, which reimagine the classical Corinthian model, but it can also be figurative, as in the sculpted lunettes. Here, the Romanesque sculpture envelops and comments on the narrative of the sarcophagus, in just the way that the marginal gloss in a medieval manuscript might encircle a classical text.

The earliest extant description of the ambo, written by Giovanni Battista Villa in 1627, is revealing in this context. Moved and filled with wonder, the canon of Santa Babila discovered strange sculptures, *fatto all'antica*, and found himself disoriented by this assemblage of time frames, where the reprise of the classical is enveloped by a pastiche that makes reuse invisible.[87] This temporal confusion must be kept in mind when trying to understand the aesthetic reception of this instance of reuse and the particular emotion that it was capable of eliciting. The medieval eye, addressing these temporal compilations – whether visual or textual – did not have the same framework and points of reference that we have today to distinguish the antique from the modern. The medieval viewer saw in the same way that he read, rhythmically and harmonically, and not as we do today in our learned editions, with our attention constantly arrested by the typographic devices intended to separate the text from its supposed borrowings.

And what is truly known about the reused sarcophagus? Since the eighteenth century, tradition has identified it as the sarcophagus of Stilicho, from the name of a *magister militium* and consul under Emperor Honorius. The sarcophagus has been in place since the end of the fourth century, as proven by its orientation, which is aligned with the altar but offset with respect to the new axis laid out during the basilica's various reconstructions. Nothing precise is known about the sarcophagus from the end of the fourth century to the twelfth, but we can at least draw the hypothesis that, if it stayed in place (as seems to be the case) and remained intact, it must have been redeployed for other funerary uses. Reassignment therefore preceded reuse, meaning that a new function was first given to the object after its initial use was lost.[88] This reassignment is anything but improbable in the new funerary context of the Basilica of Sant'Ambrogio, which welcomed, as we have seen, the graves of kings and bishops, but also of abbots. Some of these are large monuments and reprise in part the visual design of the ambo. A case in point is the funerary monument of the abbot Guglielmo Costa, deceased in 1267, who is portrayed with Saints Benedict and Ambrose and whose funerary inscription is engraved on the reverse of a reused stone from classical antiquity.[89]

The sculpted bas-reliefs on the sarcophagus are therefore virtually contemporaneous with Ambrose himself and perhaps depict the conversion of the Roman elites to his theology. Art historians have identified the iconographic plan as being clearly influenced by Ambrose's theology, in particular his *Commentary on the Psalms*, which lays out the history of the Church from its prefiguration in classical times to the New Jerusalem as so many stages in man's gradual salvation.[90] And that is precisely what is depicted here, in an ostensibly urban context – the sarcophagus belongs to a type known as "city gates" sarcophagi, in which the city as an architectural presence is rendered and magnified on all four panels. The echoes that arise between the sarcophagus and the monument reusing it form such a dense and harmonious network that the theological discourse expressed by the Romanesque sculpture converts the gaze one trains on the Roman ornamentation. It is therefore not surprising to learn that a stubborn tradition has insisted on recognizing one of the sculpted figures on the west side of Stilicho's sarcophagus as a portrait of Ambrose himself, as though the Ambrosian commentary on the ancient material had ended up by converting it and actually making it Ambrosian. Such is the power of reuse: it rejuvenates what it retrieves, harmonizing it with its own contemporaneity in a majestic synthesis that stops time.

Similarly, the sculpture of Ambrose's ambo has to be seen in context with the making of a monument of a different kind that was its strict contemporary: Martino Corbo's labors, between 1135 and 1152, to gather all of Ambrose's available writings – meaning all those then attributed to Ambrose. Martino Corbo makes his appearance in February 1123 in the basilica's capitular archives as a canon and priest of Sant'Ambrogio, becoming the *custos* or guardian of its treasury and golden altar in December 1126.[91] The treasure at that time comprised a jumbled amalgam of the basilica's jewels, saintly remains, books, and archives.[92] Martino Corbo's activities, as documented by his correspondence,[93] involved managing the church's material goods, but also its spiritual assets. We see him promising sacred relics of Gervasius, Protasius, and Victor to his friend Atto, a monk in Vallombrosa and later the bishop of Pistoia, who had asked for holy relics to consecrate several churches; and he wrote in answer to the canons of Ratisbon, Paul and Gebhard, who wanted a relic of Saint Marcellina to complete their Ambrosian collection – their church apparently owned several excellent relics of Gervasius, Protasius, and Satyrus already. Corbo's letters also reflect his political-religious engagements. During the dual papal election of 1130 following the death of Honorius II, when one faction of cardinals (many of them French) elected Innocent II and their opponents (many of them Romans) elected Anacletus II, Corbo and the canons of Sant'Ambrogio seemed to side with Pope Innocent II, which put them in opposition to the archbishop of Milan, Anselm V, and most of the clergy, who favored the antipope Anacletus II.[94] Ten years later, Corbo adopted a more pro-Roman position faithful to the papacy, at a time when the pope's position had been made more precarious by the preaching of Arnold of Brescia and the restoration of the Roman senate in 1144. These political choices tally with the growing conflict between the monks and canons of Sant'Ambrogio. In calling on Cardinal Goizone to defend these choices with an "impregnable fortress" (*inexpugnabile munimentum*), Martino Corbo was quoting an expression from Seneca's *De clementia* (1.19.6), putting his high culture in service to political battles.[95]

By assembling Ambrose's authentic writings in Milan, Martino Corbo was continuing his pursuit of this political struggle, attempting to anchor the particularity of the Milanese Church in its loyalty to Rome. A scrupulous philologist, he tracked down manuscripts in order to establish the best possible texts, supplementing his privileged access to the Milanese manuscript tradition with outreach to his more far-flung correspondents when the resources of Lombardy failed him. So with Paul and Gebhard in Ratisbon: in exchange for the missals and antiphonaries of the Ambrosian church that the Bavarian canons requested, Corbo prevailed on them to search through libraries, including the library of the Verona chapter of canons, where they found a copy of *De obitu Gratiani*.[96] Through his efforts, Corbo hoped to attach his own memory to Ambrose's: in a miniature illustrating the treatise *In Psalmum*, he had himself depicted prostrate at the saint's feet. This motif was repeated in another manuscript (M31), with the inscription *Martinus presbiter ac prepositus huius ecclesie*. The ornamentation of these manuscripts can be likened to the iconographic motifs of the ambo. But what is truly important, beyond the formal correspondences, is Corbo's overall plan to gather in the *armarium* of the basilica the entire Ambrosian *memoria*, in an authoritative text corresponding to what we would call today an author's collected works. It certainly appears as such in the inventories of the capitular archives from 1247 on, and Petrarch, when he settled in Milan in 1353, made use of this opera omnia.[97] It was originally compiled in four thick volumes, but these were later dismembered into more manageable codices, five of which are still in the cupboards of the Basilica of Sant'Ambrogio.[98]

Martino Corbo prostrates himself before Saint Ambrose,
Archivio Capitolare di Sant'Ambrogio,
manuscript M14, folio 3 recto, c. 1140 (*Akg*)

Thus was the identification of the saint's body with his literary corpus brought about, and the whole memorialized at the site of his death. The Basilica of Sant'Ambrogio, wrote Petrarch, is "where a good portion of the writings of Ambrose lies" (*ubi scriptorum Ambrosii bona pars est*).[99] It's hard to imagine a more spectacular undertaking to solidify a person's memory in a particular place. Ambrose's memory is stowed in the very heart of the basilica that bears his name and to which he made the Eucharistic offering of his body; his remains and his texts are brought together in a locus that holds his memory fast, preventing it from drifting away. But for how long can that locus prevent drift? Ambrose's texts also received an early "canonization," in Jack Goody's sense of the term—the institutionalization of a textual corpus so as to give it authority and constrain the ways it can be transmitted. Goody, an anthropologist who investigated the power of the written word, contrasts the process of oral transmission, in which religious pronouncements are continually re-created in the course of being repeated, with the fixing of a written canon that is intended to limit the amount of variation. But we must keep in mind the explicit lesson of his study, which opens a decisive perspective on the social history of writing: "That is the paradox of formation and transmission: One can have a fixed text only with the aid of a medium that in other contexts invites decanonization."[100] It is to these other contexts that we now turn.

DISSEMINATING AMBROSE: GATHERING AND DISPERSING THE BODY OF THE TEXT

When we say that a writer has been consecrated or talk about the consecration of a particular work of literature, we are using the language of sacrament—loosely, no doubt, yet the symbolic effect derives from this very vagueness and lack of definition. When a written corpus becomes a canon, in the sense of a set of authoritative norms—meaning that one can draw authority from these writings for one's own declarations—then the question arises of the relationship between *auctor* and *auctoritas*, author and authority.[101] Does Ambrose of Milan have *auctoritas* of his own, given that his authority is combined with the chorus of voices from all the Church Fathers? We will even see that between the words *auctor* and *auctoritas* there comes to be interposed the idea of the *actor*, for the issue here is, once again, the question of the proper name and its possible masks, engaging the contradictory movement of canonization and decanonization, of gathering and dispersion. We are back with ghost stories – note that "ghosts" is a term used in modern libraries to refer to the slip inserted between two catalog cards to indicate a book that has gone missing. The ghost bears the name of the book's last borrower, and it is when that borrower himself disappears that the book is declared lost for good.[102]

This moment when Martino Corbo engineered a recapitulation of Ambrose's memory in the mid-twelfth century allows us to take a first X-ray of the history of the manuscript transmission of the texts attributed to Ambrose.[103] The first phase is very fragmentary: only twenty-four witnesses of manuscripts prior to the eighth century have been found to date, most of them heavily damaged. The majority came from northern Italy, and Milan was naturally the primary keeper of Ambrose's memory, along with Novara, Ivrea, and Vercelli. (These towns likely owe their relatively prominent role to the fire that damaged the Milan Cathedral's buildings in 1075, destroying a good portion of the books kept there, according to Arnulf of Milan.[104]) The second phase drew on a wider geographic area: fourteen manuscripts have been identified from the eighth century alone, most of them from the scriptoria of Corbie Abbey, but also from the abbeys of Luxeuil and Lorsch, and to a lesser extent from Monza, Verona, and Bobbio. A bridgehead of Irish monasticism in the Po Valley, Bobbio Abbey was an important crossroads for the diffusion of

Ambrose's works into France and Europe.[105] It is therefore unsurprising that Carolingian lands feature as prominent hosts in the revival of written culture, with such expediters as Bishop Claudius of Turin, who broadcast Ambrose's exegetical works widely,[106] along with a selection of his other works, including *De fide*, *De officiis*, and *In Lucam* (a treatise on the Gospel of Luke), which was the work by Ambrose most frequently represented in the manuscript tradition.

But in the ninth century, there is an observable leap in quantity. This was the point in the Carolingian era when the memory of Ambrose crystallized, and sixty-two manuscripts have been identified from this period, of which only thirteen came from Italy. Hincmar, archbishop of Reims, who relied greatly on the patristic authorities (Jerome and Augustine primarily, but increasingly on Ambrose during the 850s, and again after 870), quoted twenty-two works by Ambrose and directly ordered the copying of *Apology for David* and *On the Sacraments*.[107] It was to the library of Reims Cathedral, in fact, that the canons Paul and Gebhard traveled on behalf of Martino Corbo to find the few surviving fragments of Ambrose's commentary on Isaiah, for which Cassiodorus in the sixth century had searched in vain.[108]

Martino Corbo's labors therefore corresponded to a period during which Ambrose's textual memory was being given its monument. Although his works were disseminated throughout European centers of learning – including Cluny Abbey, which became an important relay point for their diffusion – they were still essentially gathered in a few large collections.[109] Let's take the case of *De fuga saeculi* (Flight from the world), a spiritual meditation written by Ambrose at the very end of his life, gathering a number of his sermons on the soul's aspiration to rise toward God in flight from the corruption of this world. The historian

Camille Gerzaguet has reconstructed the manuscript tradition of *De fuga* to establish the text for the critical edition.[110] In all, eighty-eight witnesses of the complete text have been discovered, of which six belong to the ninth and tenth century, and forty-six to the eleventh and twelfth. The diffusion of the work was assisted by the growing trend toward a moral and theological literature exalting *contemptus mundi*, "contempt of the world," and justifying the practice of monastic isolation, though Ambrose's flight from the world was a more generalized spiritual desire for detachment from earthly riches.[111] This chronological distribution is very comparable to what we see for other of Ambrose's works, such as his *De Iacob et vita beata* (a treatise on mastering one's passions, starting from a commentary on the Jacob cycle in Genesis)[112] and his *De bono mortis* (an exhortation to mortification as a consolation for death).[113]

Working our way up the genealogical tree of source manuscripts for *De fuga saecularis* (what in textual criticism is termed the *stemma codicum*), we find two distinctly separate branches. The first is clustered around a family of manuscripts originating in northeastern France and western Germany; the second comes from Milan and northern Italy.[114] These two branches point back to two earlier source texts, both lost, the first dating probably to the Carolingian period and the second somewhat earlier. These two sub-archetypes derive from a common archetype that, probably shortly after Ambrose's death, gathered together a collection of four treatises on the patriarchs (*De Isaac vel anima, De bono mortis, De fuga saeculi,* and *De Iacob et vita beata*), which have recently been identified as forming a tetralogy.[115] Present are the three essential characteristics for the transmission of Ambrose's texts before the great expansion of the twelfth century: an initial grouping of texts reflecting an authorial plan (whether Ambrose's own, Paulinus of Milan's, or a near contemporary, working while the bishop's memory was crystallizing); a repository in Milan for this memory; and its Carolingian revival.

In thus describing the transmission of Ambrose's memory through manuscripts and subsequently locating the texts in Milanese libraries, all of whose contents have been minutely inventoried,[116] it is interesting to note how the texts are designated – by the name of the work or the collection, by a material description of composite manuscripts including the *incipites*, or opening lines, and, much more rarely, by the author's name. In the latter case, all the texts attributed to Ambrose must obviously be recorded. This was the practice followed by Cécile Lanéry, for example, when she showed that "the hagiographic reputation of the Milanese bishop" owes as much, and perhaps more, to certain pseudepigraphic works by forgers passing themselves off as Ambrose (the Passions of Gervasius and Protasius, for instance, and the Passion of Saint Agnes, whose attribution to Ambrose started in the fifteenth century) as it does to certain of his authentic hagiographies.[117]

For example, one of the most widely disseminated works by Ambrose in the Middle Ages was an exegetical treatise commenting on the thirteen epistles of Paul.[118] Yet this text has been known since the sixteenth century to have been falsely attributed to Ambrose, even if the story of how this attribution was retracted is itself haunted by ghosts. The credit for refuting Ambrose's authorship of the *Commentarii in epistolas B. Pauli* was given to Erasmus, although specialists have combed his work in vain for any refutation of the text's authenticity. A Jesuit by the name of Franciscus Turrianus, writing in 1572, voiced the first doubts about assigning the commentaries to Ambrose. A finding issued by the learned Benedictines of Saint Maur in 1686 named the author of this text as Ambrosiaster, or pseudo-Ambrose. This finding was acknowledged in Jacques Paul Migne's *Patrologia latina* in 1866, but Migne's phraseology was vague and alluded to Erasmus. His ambiguous sentence started the erroneous tradition that it was Erasmus who identified Ambrosiaster.[119]

It would seem to follow that, adopting a historical rather than a philological approach, an investigation into Ambrose's memory in the Middle Ages would incorporate this work, believed at the time to be Ambrose's. How should this ancient text – probably written during the papacy of Damasus I, who died in 384 – be described, given that it has been taken from Ambrose while its true author remains anonymous? By assigning him the borrowed name Ambrosiaster, philologists and catalog authors (who abhor anonymity as nature abhors a vacuum) have invented a category, that of "Anonymous Author." It functions as a ghost for the author's name, complete with capital letter – somewhat in the way that "the Master of…" is used in art history, designating a painter who is unknown but who gathers substance gradually as further paintings are added to his catalog.[120] The same applies to Ambrosiaster, who has been treated as an author by modern critics. They have studied his doctrine[121] and attributed further texts to him – including the *Questions on the Old and New Testaments*, which medieval manuscripts attributed to Augustine.[122]

As a general matter, historians should look more closely at the question of "the surprising success of pseudo-Augustinian writings in the Middle Ages."[123] Why, for example, are there 113 manuscript copies of the authentic *Soliloquia*, while the *Soliloquiorum animae ad Deum*, a pseudepigraphic compilation of the twelfth to thirteenth century, perhaps authored by Alcher of Clairvaux, survives in more than twice as many copies, with 276 manuscripts currently identified? Chance can't explain it all. In reality, imitators – the skillful ones – can produce texts "in the manner of" that are better adapted to the needs of the readership. It's therefore perfectly understandable that readers would prefer this truer-than-nature Augustine to the authentic one, whom time has placed at a remove from their own animating preoccupations. The truth is that, even if we like to believe the contrary, we often prefer the imitation to the original, which is why fakes have greater currency than real works.

Whenever a text or fragment of text has been attributed to an author for several generations, that attribution acquires an almost unshakable authority. This means that we can keep using it in good conscience, even when we know it to be apocryphal. During the controversy between Catholics and Protestants in the sixteenth century, the question of attribution was a constant source of dispute. An Anglican theologian named Lancelot Andrewes, bishop of Ely, argued against the intercession of saints by pointing to Ambrosiaster's commentary, which he attributed to Ambrose. Cardinal Jacques du Perron took exception to this: how was it possible that this "elegant spirit, so deeply versed in literature, and so deeply committed to the task of criticism, should allow himself to be so completely eclipsed and robbed of his nature in the interest of his cause as not to know what every learned man of whatever party knows, namely that Saint Ambrose's commentary on the Epistle to the Romans is not on any account by Saint Ambrose, nor does it answer in the least to his style and ideas."[124] To which Andrewes replied that the commentary had been accredited as authentic in the opera omnia, published in Rome, and that the Roman Catholics invoked it constantly in support of the pope's authority. Let them stop invoking the text, and he would renounce his attribution.

We have already seen that opponents on both sides of many of the great religious controversies – from the Pelagian heresy to the Pataria – claimed Ambrose's authority equally. But during the twelfth century, scholastic dispute underwent a partial change in rules. Patristic arguments were used less to show a faithful adherence to the doctrine of a Church Father than to bring out the "harmony of discordancies," which was at the heart of scholastic thought. In other words, "the search for intellectual incoherencies" between the different authorized voices in the corpus became the mainspring for the construction of truth.[125] Like all the other Church Fathers, Ambrose saw his literary authorship dispersed within a doctrinal authority that surpassed and survived him: that of the patristic canon.[126]

Of course this presupposed that the Fathers of the Church were a confirmed category.[127] Starting in the sixth century, notably with the *Decretum* by the Pseudo-Gelasius, the Church Fathers designated the corpus of orthodox authors on whom one might legitimately rely, particularly when arguing theological controversies.[128] Briefly, it was a list of authorized readings that guaranteed the authority of the past over the historical future. Ambrose had a privileged place in this patristic canon. The canon was recognized in 1295 by Pope Boniface VIII, who distinguished four Doctors of the Latin Church (Ambrose, Augustine, Jerome, and Gregory) in his decretal *Gloriosus Deus*, thereby consecrating the doctors' exceptional authority in matters of faith and doctrine.[129] In 1378, Gregory XI further reinforced the veneration of the faithful for the Fathers by introducing the reading of the Nicene Creed into the liturgy of the Doctors of the Church. Subsequently, Pope Pius V added four Fathers of the Greek Church to Boniface's list, who were soon joined by Thomas Aquinas. This was an affirmation, in the face of the Protestant Reform and the doctrine of *Sola scriptura*, that there in fact existed two sources of revelation: scripture and tradition. And that is why the fourth session of the Council of Trent in 1546 forbade interpreting the scriptures "in opposition to the unanimous consent of the Church Fathers."[130]

What was important, clearly, was less their opinions than the harmony between these opinions. Whence the need to arrange their confrontation in what François Dolbeau has called "a sort of virtual council of authors said to be orthodox," which is one of the principal foundations of Christian doctrine and the establishing of the Church.[131] When it came to texts, it was the collections of the Church Fathers' writings that organized this concordance, this harmony of authorized voices, according to an authorial consensus that Augustine sought and believed to provide the only guarantee against error and neglect.[132] The collections were of two kinds: "pure" anthologies and "mixed" anthologies. The first comprised extracts by a single author and were the chief means of preserving and transmitting textual memory, as well as being a tool for scholastic thought. Of these, the most widely used at the end of the Middle Ages was the *Milleloquium Ambrosianum*, commissioned in the late 1340s by Pope Clement VI from the bishop of Urbino, Bartolomeo Carusi (who had already compiled the *Milleloquium veritatis Augustini*).[133] Mixed anthologies, for their part, juxtaposed extracts from the scriptures with quotations from the Church Fathers. One such was the *Liber Scintillarum*, compiled by Defensor, member of an abbey at Ligugé toward the year 700, which brought together "sparks" from the Bible and "glimmerings" from the Fathers.

A well-known example of these mixed anthologies is the *Collectio ex dictis XII patrum* (Collection of the twelve fathers), by the deacon Florus of Lyon, which appeared in the mid-ninth century.[134] Following the order of Paul's epistles, the author assembled extracts by Ambrose along with other Fathers of the Latin Church (Cyprian of Carthage, Hilary of Poitiers) and the Greek Church (Gregory of Nazianzus) and conciliating texts. Four hundred eleven passages by Ambrose were included, making him by far the most-quoted Church Father. Florus could quote only from the texts at his disposal, which numbered about fifteen of the forty that are today considered authentic. Examining them by title, the *Expositio de psalmo* CXVIII (an exegesis of Psalm 118) leads with 144 extracts, far outstripping the second-most-quoted work, *De fuga saeculi*, with eighteen extracts – but those eighteen extracts comprise a quarter of this relatively brief text, as it was available in the ninth century. There were two manuscript traditions for Ambrose's work, as we've discussed, and Florus consulted both, seeking to draw out the best lesson for each quoted passage. This philological exigency on the part of the compiler – which perhaps led him to correct one of the two copies in consequence[135] – demonstrates that correction was his authorial mark, we might even say his signature. It makes him an author through arrangement.[136]

We shouldn't let ourselves be fooled, therefore, by the false compactness of the proper name "Ambrose." As an author, he was above all available in extracts, meted out in snippets in anthologized literature – puzzle style. So how are we to find our way through the complex tangle of Ambrosian texts and their dissemination? Painstakingly, by bits and pieces, like the historians and philologists who have gathered his fragments in the canonic collections. Take, for example, the *Collectio canonum* compiled by Anselm of Lucca toward 1081 to 1083. Anselm, an intransigent reformer in the entourage of Pope Gregory VII and the bishop of Lucca, had been exiled to the court of Matilda of Tuscany.[137] His compilation contains forty-six texts by Ambrose, spread over nineteen chapters. From there we can see them disperse: to the *Decretum Gratiani*, a foundational textbook for the instruction of canon law in the Latin West, with numerous quotations from Augustine and the Church Fathers; and to Peter Lombard's *Sentences*, also written in the 1140s from a compilation of patristic references, and a work that would become the fundamental tool of scholastic reasoning.[138]

Have we no choice but to see Ambrose erased as an *auctor*, replaced by others who, on the pretext of quoting him, take him over? The historian of philosophy Alain de Libera defines medieval thought as the form of knowledge that radically overthrows the logic of family names or patronymics that organizes our modern idea of literary and philosophical transmission. In contrast to this "relationship of conceptual orders between signatures," medieval thought can be better described as anonymous, a vast collaborative workshop where what counts is less the origin than the pursuit of rewriting through the constant interplay of quotations and glosses. The hope was less to maintain ownership of a work and more that others would soon seize on the pronouncements made therein, take them as their own, and free them from the obligation of attribution; the medieval writer was less inclined to claim paternity for works of which he was, in fact, the progeny than the honor of "being the retailer of words without subject."[139]

If today we feel this medieval situation to be unsettling, it is no doubt related to what Freud called "the uncanny" (*Das Unheimliche*), which is the feeling that something is strangely familiar. "Not only is the *Unheimlich* familiar, but it causes anxiety *for having been so*."[140] Another ghost? What's perfectly clear, at any rate, is that the "author function" – that practice, so pivotal to the modern book-based order, of assigning a proper name to every statement – is nowadays being widely destabilized and that this is making the medieval past resurface in a new way.[141] Hence the many discussions of "the new Middle Ages," which the digital dissemination of the written word now makes intelligible, and the temptation felt by many medievalists, themselves buffeted in their research by the revolutions in computing, to profit sanctimoniously from this unexpected recrudescence of public interest. Yet something can have existed even if it didn't exist the way we normally think of it: there were of course authors in the Middle Ages, and their works bore the imprimatur of their names, even if these did not prevent their works from being pried away from them. When we discuss Ambrose's textual memory, therefore, it's always in terms of gathering and dispersal.

After all, the word *auctor* comes from *augeo*, to augment.[142] The consecration of the author makes him august, like King Philip, known as "Philip Augustus" because he had augmented his kingdom. But what does it mean when a person enlarges the written corpus? Does it simply imply an augmentation in the number of books or is the world itself enlarged? The medieval question of the *auctor* again has an unexpected resonance in the modern world. In a general way, anyone who produces is an *auctor*. But for orthographic reasons, scribes often confused the word with *actor*, which comes from *ago* in the broadest sense, meaning "he who acts" – and who can act, like the theater actor, under cover. To differentiate the two, *auctor* took on a meaning related to *auctoritas*, which contains the idea of origin. Hence an *auctor* is someone at the origin of an action. From there comes his authority and his authenticity, which is also to say his dignity. In Ambrose's case, as we've seen, this recognition took the form of canonization, a great act of gathering together, immediately paired with the opposite motion, churned by the great engine of commentating: decanonization, which dispersed the traces of his statements like a mist, no longer held together by the aura of his name. And so, Ambrose still acts, never ceases to act, long after his death, ghostlike.

TEN

Seeing Ambrose Again: Visual Tales (Twelfth Century)

On June 11, 1991, Umberto Bossi, leader of the Northern League (Lega Nord per l'indipendenza della Padania, referred to as the Lega since the March 2018 elections), summoned his followers to the small town of Pontida, in Bergamo province. Created two years earlier as a confederation of ethno-regionalist and separatist movements, Bossi's xenophobic and populist party, which would increasingly ingratiate itself into Italian politics, was beginning to reap its first electoral wins. The league's militants were scheduled to meet in Pontida's "sacred field," on this day in 1991 to take the same sacred oath reportedly sworn by emissaries from the Lombard city-states allied against Frederick Barbarossa's "centralism" on April 4, 1167, in the Ambrosian-Rite Benedictine abbey. This neo-Guelphism, which deliberately evoked the Middle Ages, manipulating all the symbols of Lombard identity – Pontida's *calcio*, the communal militias' *carroccio*, Ariberto of Intimiano's cross, and obviously Saint Ambrose's banner – clearly identified its enemy: the foreign invasion from the Mezzogiorno, or southern Italy. Since then, the ceremony has taken place every year, and for Italians, Pontida has become the uncontested symbol of *leghismo*.

And yet, as shown by Lynda Dematteo's political anthropology research, Umberto Bossi in fact inverted a unifying, patriotic symbol of the Risorgimento.[1] When Giuseppe Verdi staged his grand opera *La Bataglia di Legnano* in Rome's Teatro Argentina, he appropriated the medieval memory of the Battle of Legnano, in which Emperor Frederick Barbarossa's armies were routed by the communal militias of the first Lombard League, which assembled the sixteen communes of the Po Valley into one *societas* (that's how twelfth-century sources refer to the alliance of cities) dominated by Milan.[2] But Verdi approached this memory as history had transformed it: on the glorious day of battle, May 29, 1176, the Italian communes paved the way for the recognition of their right to rule and the legitimacy of their mode of consular government, conceded by the emperor at the Peace of Constance seven years later (June 25, 1183). In the communal memory, this event would become ever more legendary, notably thanks to the invention – probably in the thirteenth century, though there is no confirmed mention of it before Galvanno Fiamma's *Cronica Galvagnana* in the 1330s – of the figure of Alberto da Giussano, standard-bearer for the Lombard League and valiant captain of the "company of death" that heroically resisted the attacks of the imperial cavalry.[3]

Invented traditions always reference a past that is more recent than we think: the *calcio* of Pontida passes itself off as medieval, but like many such horse races in Italy, is a Fascist reinvention (it dates from 1932 and its creation was directly encouraged by Mussolini). The same goes for the oath of Pontida, which allowed the Battle of Legnano to be celebrated as the foundation not of communal autonomy but of Italy, "the first among all nations." In fact, the expression comes from an exiled romantic poet named Giovanni Berchet, who published the "Giuramento di Pontida" (Oath of Pontida) in Paris in 1829. The last verse, fierce and bellicose, exalts the harmony rediscovered at the same time as national liberation: "What a joyous sight! The Lombards / reconciled, united in one league / The foreigner will give the color of his blood to the league's flag."[4] This explains why Italians today, when they burst into their national hymn "Fratelli d'Italia" (a song dating from 1847), express their unity *Dall' Alpi a Sicilia / Dovunque è Legnano* ("From the Alps to Sicily / Legnano is everywhere").

While Pontida may be a powerful collective memory woven into Italy's fabric, it is a false one – pure literary invention.[5] By reversing an old patriotic symbol – here, the *patria* is Catholic, remobilized by the neo-Guelphism of Italy's Christian Democrats – the Northern League inverted the xenophobic divide: the Romans are the new barbarians, for the danger now comes from the South. Which means that Alberto da Giussano can still, in our day, proudly sport the coat of arms of Matteo Salvini's Northern League. All this is a bit farcical – but that's the point. This political system is constantly playing with carnivalesque inversion, making confusion (*imbroglio*) its main modus operandi.[6] We know today that the most ridiculous ways of exercising power are far from the least dangerous, given how they preemptively disarm any vague desire to subvert through caricature. But can the past, and in this case the past of the commune, be confused to such an extent? That violence to symbols is a key question in the pages that follow.

FOUNDATION IN DESTRUCTION, IDENTITY IN MISFORTUNE

"What is founding?" In 1956, a young professor of philosophy submitted this quintessentially classical subject to the wisdom of his high school literature students. Since this young philosopher was named Gilles Deleuze, and since he later developed a school of thought that can be considered a radical critique of the necessity of laying foundations, his words were religiously gathered by his students, like the class notes conserved in the archives of certain medieval universities. You can find the *reportationes* by the students in this 1956 university prep course on the Internet, that intimately Deleuzian place where everything is interwoven but nothing is founded, or grounded. (These notes are also available in an English-language translation as *What Is Grounding?*) And this is what they will tell you: in philosophical tradition, the idea of "founding" has three primary characteristics: the fact of having a more profound origin than a simple beginning; the fact of being subject to repetition; and finally the fact that the thing assumes a worldly dimension. Founding not only renders something possible, but necessary. And from there we get the crux of Deleuze's text: the operation of founding "consists in rendering necessary the submission of the thing to what it is not."[7]

The medievalist historian should feel quite at home with this philosophical definition, as it overlaps in part with the polysemy of the term *fundamentum* in medieval Latin, which we can translate as "foundation," and notably its ecclesiastical and theological uses. The ritual of consecrating a church links the spiritual and material meanings of the idea of foundation. It first incorporates, in a very concrete way, the foundation of an edifice, not only in the sense of the designation of property (*in fundamento*) but also the deep anchoring of the construction *ad fundamenta*. But in the Christian gift economy, a deep foundation is also a happy foundation, *felicia fundamenta*, building obviously also being understood in a personal and moral sense. So much so that the ritual of leaving precious objects in the foundations of a structure takes on all its significance here.[8]

An origin rather than a beginning; the repetition of the rite; the submission of the thing to that which surpasses it: here we have the triple Deleuzian dimension of the act of founding. To found and refound: in this stammer, this rhythmicity, there is undoubtedly something more than the temporary possibility of redoing what's been undone, of fixing what's been destroyed. Beyond the farcical reenactment of an event and its simulacrum, this duplicity of founding and refounding contains another, more essential, tension, of religious origin: creation versus destruction. As if you can only truly found what has been previously destroyed, and as if the foundation stories of medieval cities, those romances of origin, beyond their pleasant and fantastical overtones that quickly turned into folklore, secretly expressed an anxiety as to the violence of foundations.

In March 1171, the consuls of Milan commissioned bas-reliefs intended to extol the moral strength of a political community that had been able to lift itself from its ruins. These commemorative sculptures were affixed to the *porta Romana*, which, by its very architecture, glorified the founding of the city as a new Rome – and thus a founding that was, once again, a refounding. Noting its secular subject, historians have pegged it as the first known example of communal art.[9] For the truly monumental design of the *porta Romana* was intended to bear the memory of a recent and admittedly bitter event: the city's destruction by Emperor Frederick Barbarossa in 1162, before the creation of the Lombard League headed by Milan, and the return, finally, of the Milanese people to their city, reconquered on April 27, 1167. In the span of a few years, Milan was destroyed and rebuilt, reinvented more than it was restored. And so we see, on the bas-reliefs of the *porta Romana*, the Milanese people who had been expulsed from their city make their triumphant return, led by their bishop. But this joyful scene is mirrored by a more troubling episode: on another bas-relief, we see heretics (or Jews?) being expulsed from the city. And the figure chasing them out is clearly designated by his *titulus*: Ambrose.

To understand this clash of time periods and visual oppositions, let's first remember the extent to which the city's destruction by Barbarossa was foundational to Milan's civic consciousness.[10] It was integrated into a chronological sequence decisive to the history of communal government. In a famous description of the country of cities that Italy had become in 1157, Otto, the bishop of Freising, marvels at and is outraged by the economic power and political insolence of communes now governing themselves, imitating "the wisdom of the ancient Romans…they are so desirous of liberty that, avoiding the insolence of power, they are governed by the will of consuls rather than rulers." These elected consuls deliberated and meted out justice, disdainful of the emperor's rights over Italy: "For they scarcely if ever respect the prince to whom they should display the voluntary deference of obedience or willingly perform that which they have sworn by the integrity of their laws." But among these recalcitrant communes, "Milan now holds chief place…not only because of its size and abundance of brave men," but also from its audacity in "molesting its neighbors…standing in no awe of [the prince's] majesty."[11]

This majestic prince was Frederick Barbarossa, Otto of Freising's uncle and the subject of his *Gesta Frederici*, and he had decided to reclaim his sovereign rights over the imperial land of Italy. The following year, in 1158, Frederick crossed the Alps, laid siege to Milan, which capitulated in September, and convoked the Diet of Roncaglia on November 11, 1158, during which he reaffirmed his sovereignty. This marked the debut of the great military confrontation with the first Lombard League, which in turn prompted the intensification of a conflict with the papacy, complicated by a schism beginning in 1164.[12] The break in loyalty was complete: in the public acts of the commune of Milan, Frederick, previously designated as *dominus*, became *Theutonicus* in the early 1160s.[13] The showdown would ultimately result, as we have seen, in the victory of Legnano on May 29, 1176. But the first wins belonged to the empire, with Milan paying for its aggression toward its rival communes (notably Cremona), which joined forces against their powerful neighbor; following another siege of the city, the emperor ordered its destruction and the expulsion of its inhabitants, on March 10, 1162.[14]

As surprising as it might appear, this expulsion actually occurred. The people of Milan left the city to settle in its peripheral neighborhoods, an exile documented by notarial archives that indicate that citizens did not lose legal claim to their property in town.[15] However, public archives reveal a very distinct documentary lacuna between October 1161 and March 1167, which could prove, if not the extinction of public life, at least an interruption of consular government.[16] The will and testament of a priest named Aliprando, notarized at the end of December 1166, illuminates this rather unusual situation.[17] The document tells us that he moved to the neighborhood of San Siro ad Vesprum because it was the location to which Archbishop Enrico di Liegi, acting as the emperor's *podestà*, or chief magistrate, to Milan, had assigned all the residents excluded from the *porta Vercellina* zone. Everything indicates that, following the expulsion order, the Milanese were forced to move to outlying suburbs based on their original neighborhoods (which were called *sestieri* in Milan, since the six gates to the city oversaw six urban districts). Aliprando's will provides information about concrete living conditions – his nephew built him his house – and the functioning of an unstable economy as these exiles were preparing to move back inside the walls of their city. We don't know if Aliprando died before this return in 1167. In any case he chose to follow his flock and carry out his pastoral duties, which was not true for all of Milan's clergymen: political events had once again divided the Basilica of Sant'Ambrogio's two religious communities, with the modest *decumani* following citizens to the surrounding countryside of San Siro, while the richest canons obtained the right to remain at the basilica by pledging allegiance to the emperor.

The expulsion of the Milanese people was a reality, but what about the destruction of Milan? Searching for archaeological evidence of the city's physical ruin within its walls would be a fruitless endeavor. Imperial destruction in this case did not imply urbicidal fury: the object of annihilation was not an urban space but the political ambition expressed therein through the signs of its sovereignty. Attacking that ambition therefore did not consist solely of inflicting a symbolic wound, in keeping with a rhetoric of urban retribution well established since antiquity,[18] but of symbolically disarming it, by removing its sacred power. Whence no doubt the targeted strategy of desecrating altars and stealing relics, the most painful theft for the Milanese people being the transfer of the relics of the Magi to Cologne in 1164.[19] In leveling the walls of Milan and decapitating its gates, the emperor made a sovereign and adroitly staged gesture – a public ritual of humiliation that forced an ultimate insult into the city's collective memory.[20] Accordingly, each gate was delivered to the vengeance of the inhabitants of the city-state for which it was named: the Pavesans brought down the *porta Ticinese*, the *porta Comacina* was attacked by the Comasques, and the residents of other once-allied city-states of the Lombard metropolis similarly converged on their gates.[21]

It was to exorcise their painful memory of this formative scene – Milan ensnared by the same radial and concentric logic it had applied to both its city planning and its territory – that

Milanese narrative sources celebrated the reconstruction of the city walls, in the very same year that the Lombard League was established (1167), as an act of refoundation. The very progress of the Battle of Legnano symbolically reenacts the reparation, by inversion, of the original affront. Both Italian sources (notably the anonymous *Annales Mediolanensis*) and imperial sources (such as the *Annals of Magdeburg* and Godfrey of Viterbo's *Carmen De Gestis Frederici*) describe Frederick Barbarossa's cavalry besieging the Milanese and Piacenzan foot soldiers massed around their *carroccio* before the cavalrymen of Brescia come to relieve them, attacking the imperial forces from the rear.[22] Once again, it was Galvano Fiamma who embellished the story: the valiant Lombards had formed a circle around their chariot, "those of the *porta Romana* behind their red emblem, those of the *porta Ticinese* behind their white emblem, those of the *porta Comacina* behind their red and white emblem..." thus re-creating the circular enclosure of Milan on the battlefield.[23]

AMBIGUITIES OF THE FOUNDATION STORY
(OR THE VIOLENCE OF THE FOUNDER)

The ritualized destruction of the city walls by Emperor Frederick Barbarossa, as much as their rebuilding, founded the Milanese commune's political identity in the awareness of its misfortune. It might seem paradoxical to maintain the foundational value of an act of destruction, but this paradox appears frequently in accounts of how Italian city-states were founded. These star the figure of an ambiguous founding hero, often a traitor or exile, sometimes a tyrannicide or a man seeking vengeance, whose heroism always consists of assuming his duty to commit violence: violence to the city he founds or violence that he inflicts on himself while founding the city. "At the beginning of the city-state," notes Renaud Villard, "is an act of violence, as if the city's troubled destiny arose from this original sin."[24] This fundamental anthropological trait no doubt explains the profound ambivalence of the foundation story of the Milanese city-state.[25]

Since at least the thirteenth century, the civic memory of Milan has claimed the Gauls as the city's founders. The point of departure is Titus Livius, aka Livy, specifically the fifth book of his *Ab urbe condita libri*, in which he describes "the Gauls' passage to Italy," led by King Bellovesus: after "rout[ing] the Tuscans in battle, not far from the river Ticinus; and, hearing that the district in which they had posted themselves was called Insubria, the same name by which one of the cantons of the Insubrian Æduans was distinguished, they embraced the omen which the place presented, and founded there a city which they called Mediolanum."[26] For authors of the communal era, whom historians have gotten into the habit of referring to as "pre-humanist" and who are defined by their focus on antiquity, the Livian account represented the unsurpassable horizon of truth. So they borrowed from it—*ut dicit Titus Livius*. But another tradition, which Paul the Deacon's *History of the Lombards* unearthed notably in the writing of Justinus, who abridged Pompeius Trogus's *Philippic Histories*, cast Brenno as the founder of the city of Milan.

The majority of Milanese authors in the communal era—notably Benzo d'Alessandria and Giovanni da Cermenate[27]—attempted to reconcile these two traditions, even if they were not of equal value in their eyes. It was only later, in the fourteenth and especially fifteenth century, when the Visconti dynasty made claims of belonging to the Lombard (and therefore anti-Carolingian) line, that the question of the compatibility of civic memory with Paul the Deacon's account became more decisive. This was when authors began to say that the city of Milan had been founded and refounded, first by Bellovesus, then by Brenno.

However, in the 1340s, the Dominican Galvano Fiamma violently broke with this reconciliatory tradition by dramatizing an episode that he invented from beginning to end. This is not the first and especially not the last time that we will come across this complex, prolific, and inventive author, whose importance to the political construction of Milanese collective memory, as well as to the intellectual history of humanist innovation, is still being reevaluated.[28] Born in 1283 to a well-off Milanese family, in 1298 Galvano Fiamma entered the Dominican monastery of Sant'Eustorgio, whose church has conserved since 1164 the empty tomb of the Magi taken to Cologne with Emperor Barbarossa, and where he taught theology. In all likelihood forced into exile by the ban placed on Milan by Pope John XXII in 1321, he returned in 1330 as the rector of Sant'Eustorgio and a confidant of the signor of Milan, Azzone Visconti, for whom he became, as we will see later, an ardent propagandist.[29]

In his *Manipulus florum*, a chronicle of the history of Milan from its beginnings to 1336, Fiamma invented a distinction of nationality between Bellovesus and Brenno. The former is king of the Gauls, while the second is referred to as *rex Suevorum*, attributing to him a German identity unfavorable in the eyes of the Milanese citizens of the fourteenth century, who, following the wars waged by the "Teutonic" Frederick Barbarossa, had lived through the *furor Theutonicorum* of his grandson Frederick II.[30] Fiamma imagines that Brenno, drawn away from Suevia by greed for Milan's riches, takes on Bellovesus's grandson, Brunisendus. The latter tries to resist, heroically but in vain: the city is taken and destroyed. Then Brenno, dreaming of conquering Rome and aware that he needs a support base to do so, refounds the city, renaming it Alba. The refounding of Milan is here an attempt at symbolic destruction achieved through the erasure of the city's very name.[31] In the third act, which can also be interpreted as a refounding (positive this time), the Romans are able to repel the Teutons' attacks (this is the famous episode of the Capitoline geese), expulse the Suevians and Gauls from Italy, and honor Milan with prestigious buildings. This network of Roman-style monuments is akin to a new birth – a rebirth, strictly speaking – that unites the Milanese and the Romans as one people, under the same banner: *et facti sunt Romani et Mediolanenses unus populus; et sub uno vexillo militat utraque gens.*[32]

Everything is ambivalent in this drama, essentially a founding in three acts, the second of which is certainly the most troubling, given its structural ambiguity toward what we could call the "violence of foundations." Perhaps this ambiguity corresponds to Galvano Fiamma's political stance: as a Dominican, he logically would have been an obstinate defender of pontifical prerogatives against imperial ambitions, at a time when this fundamental tension was growing amid the conflict between John XXII and Ludwig of Bavaria; but as a zealous supporter of the Viscontis, he was obliged to consider the political alliance Azzone Visconti had established with the emperor. That is Patrick Gilli's interpretation, which situates – therein lies the strength of his argument – Galvano Fiamma's reconstruction of memory within the coherence of a broader dynamic: the Gallic origins of the Lombard city-state were an essential political playing card in the symbolic battle and ideological confrontation pitting Milan against Florence, where humanists gleefully poked fun at the barbarism of Milan's founders.[33] By reorienting Milan's foundation story toward the Roman Empire and culture, Fiamma accomplished, in short, an act of memorial realpolitik.

Without challenging this general interpretation, we can also hypothesize that this strange account is merely the projection, onto the shaky horizon of the myth of origins, of the original scene of destruction/reconstruction of the city of Milan in the

1160s, during the decisive confrontation between the commune and the emperor, recounted in the epic style in Fiamma's *Manipulus florum*.[34] This narrative expresses the fundamental anxiety of foundational violence, a feeling that is essentially political as it has to do with acute awareness of the fact that institutional constructions can only be grounded in discord. This anxiety is reflected by the ambivalent figure of a founding hero (here split between Bellovesus/Brenno) who welcomes and who expulses, who builds and who destroys. But isn't this also what we see in the *porta Romana*, against a monumental backdrop that solemnly expressed the renaissance – that term understood here, of course, in its twelfth-century meaning – of a Milan asserting itself as the new Rome through the pacifying conciliation of a collective memory (of Ambrose of course) that brought together ancient enemies from the time of the Pataria?[35]

From this perspective, we could argue that, beyond nitpicking over the city's origins in antiquity, and humanists' various narrative configurations, which endlessly muddled Milan's origin story by inventing an obscure cohort of founding heroes who created and destroyed the city at the whim of a lurching, spasmodic account, the Milanese people only truly recognized a single founder in the Middle Ages: their patron, Saint Ambrose. It was in the shadow of his name, and his alone, that they deigned to live. Any foundation is also an occupation of land, the taking of a political and polemical stance, nearly a military act – like the lances of the Gallic soldiers fighting for Brenno who, recounts Antonio Astesano, gave their name to the city they founded (Asti comes from *hastae*, spears).[36] But Ambrose's memory did not merely anchor itself in the city's past: it imposed itself by spreading, settled in by expanding – in other words, to borrow a famous expression from Gilles Deleuze, the great thinker of rhythm and ritornello, it did not take root but formed rhizomes.

But we would be mistaken to oppose the pacifying power of this authority figure with the violence inherent to politics. Ambrose assumed the violence of the founder, and added an even more essential type of violence – belief itself – which is expressed by the ghosts of the *porta Romana*.

THE REVENANTS OF THE *PORTA ROMANA* (1171)

To understand the *porta Romana*, we must first re-create the architectural layout of this gate in the southwestern part of the city, which was razed in 1793. An engraving from the Bertarelli collection, made several years prior to the gate's destruction, gives us some idea of its general appearance as seen from outside the city. Flanked by two high towers, the gate had twin entryways, and we can see that, at the time, the Western arch was walled in. The architecture of these double-arched, fortified gates clearly evoked the Roman model, a vestige of which no doubt could still be seen in Milan in one of the gates of the Maximian enclosure (now the *porta Ticinese*). Likely intended to be plastered with polychromatic marble, the gates standing at the threshold to the city represented a rediscovered Roman culture – which, in the context of Milan in the last third of the twelfth century, simultaneously expressed the pontifical alliance, the appropriation of a sovereignty abandoned by the empire, and, in a more local though no less decisive way, revenge on the great rival that for a long time was Pavia.[37] Furthermore, the *porta Romana* was at the end of the most solemn of imperial Milan's prestigious arteries: lined by glorious Roman porticos, the *via Porticata* was dominated by a triumphal arch destroyed during the construction of the communal enclosure in the twelfth century; it is tempting to see in the layout of the *porta Romana* a reminder of that triumphal arch, whose memory, or so it would seem, had not been lost.[38]

View of the *porta Romana* (around 1790), Civica Raccolta
delle Stampe Achille Bertarelli, P.V. 52-102

In the pendentive separating the two arches, a plaque is
clearly visible, which was likely not placed there originally: it
bears a commemorative inscription explaining that the consuls
of Milan ordered this work in March 1171 as they were rebuilding
the city enclosure. The names of the ten consuls elected for the
year 1171 are engraved; they are referred to as *consules reipublicae*.
This term rarely appears in public documents of the time, while
the expressions *consules civitatis* and *consules communis* were widely
used. Here, it is a reference to antiquity, intended to evoke the

glory days of Republican Rome.[39] Above the plaque is a bas-relief that is also currently kept in the Museo d'Arte Antica in Milan's Castello Sforzesco: it depicts a bearded figure holding a flowering scepter, and wearing a long coat and a short tunic that partly reveals his crossed legs atop a dragon.

Ignominious sculpture of Emperor Frederick Barbarossa (?),
porta Romana, Castello Sforzesco
(*De Agostini Picture Library/Bridgeman Images*)

Interpretation of this image, which mixes signs of sovereignty with satirical symbols of infamy, is still under debate: is it, as the chronicler Galvano Fiamma claimed, an ambiguous homage to the Byzantine emperor Manuel I Komnenos, who had financially contributed to the rebuilding of the city enclosure, or, as Paolo Grillo recently hypothesized, an evocation of the memory of Emperor Maximian, who built the walls of Milan when it was the capital of the Christian Empire of the West?[40] Another hypothesis, which undoubtedly remains the most likely, is that the sculpture is a representation of Frederick Barbarossa intended to exorcize, through derision, the imperial threat.[41] In this case, we see the reversal of the ritual of public humiliation inflicted on the city by its vanquisher, whose ignominious image is pushed – and at the same time exhibited – outside the city.[42] Milan's sacrality is restored, meaning its ability to repulse evil outside itself.[43]

The bas-reliefs that interest us were placed at eye level (approximately 75 inches from the ground), creating a horizontal bar across the structure's central body. The sculptures on the central pillar, which extended across three sides, and the two sculpted faces of the eastern pillar have been conserved. On the late eighteenth-century engraving, the western pilaster is hidden by a building: even though we have no direct proof, it is difficult not to imagine that it had symmetrically sculpted faces. The scenes on the central pillar are the easiest to interpret. They depict two corteges that, departing from the middle of the pillar, separate to enter the city. They are therefore simultaneously separated and convergent. On the left are the Milanese people taking back possession of their city (see color plate 8). One man is on horseback, the others on foot, and this heterogeneous procession is led by clerics: the figure closing the march (and whom we therefore see first, in the middle of the pillar) is also riding a horse; the

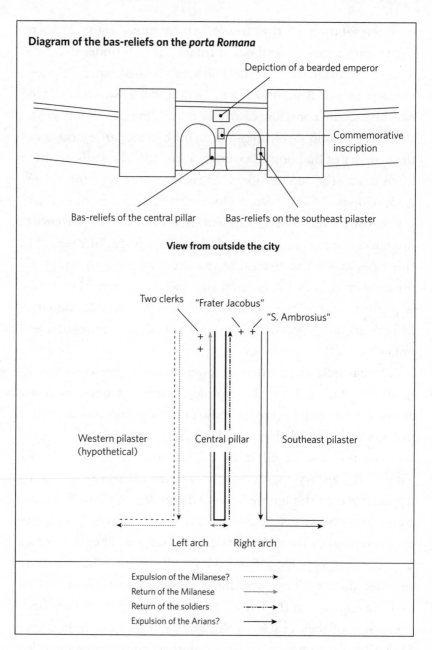

Diagram of the bas-reliefs on the *porta Romana*

Depiction of a bearded emperor

Commemorative inscription

Bas-reliefs of the central pillar   Bas-reliefs on the southeast pilaster

View from outside the city

Two clerks   "Frater Jacobus"

"S. Ambrosius"

Western pilaster   Central pillar   Southeast pilaster
(hypothetical)

Left arch   Right arch

Expulsion of the Milanese?   ┄┄┄➤
Return of the Milanese   ───➤
Return of the soldiers   ┅·┅·➤
Expulsion of the Arians?   ───➤

(PAO Seuil)

figure in the lead brandishes a processional cross and a banner. Two inscriptions commentate on the scene, the first with a very approximate quote from Virgil,[44] the second underlining the religious significance of this moment during which the people, returning to the city, reclaimed their place in its history: "By praising Christ, we have returned to our homes."[45] They advance beneath the volutes' vegetal ornamentation, which are perhaps in this case a symbol of fertility.[46]

Far more orderly is the second cortege, running the length of the internal eastern face of the central pillar: it is made up of Milan's soldiers and their allies, armed with spears, swords, and shields (see color plate 9). Marching beneath crenellations, the cortege is punctuated by images of the city's gates: inscriptions in the middle of the central pillar identify those of Cremona and Brescia, from which foot soldiers emerge; the gate of Bergama is found on the eastern face. This composition depicts the reconciliation of Milan and its territory by symbolically inverting the traumatizing scene of the destruction of the city's gates by subject city-states. This military cortege is also led by a cleric, designated as FRATER JACOBUS: perhaps he is *Jacopus abbas*, an abbot at the Cistercian monastery of Santa Maria in Morimondo, who played an important role as mediator with the imperial powers to allow the Milanese people to return to their city in 1167.[47] He tilts his processional, banner-topped cross before the gate designated as MEDIOLANUM: undoubtedly the *porta Romana* itself, which a visitor passing beneath its right arch would have seen at the very moment he crossed the city's threshold. Unfortunately, the inscriptions here are partially defaced: one praises the name of a second sculptor, Anselmus, compared in his favor to "another Daedalus," while the second appears to allude to the friendship regained during the ordeal and addresses the following prayer to God: "We praise thee in song."[48]

Across from this scene, the carved company advancing across the two faces of the eastern pilaster form somewhat of an inverted reflection: the march of eighteen figures – men, women, and children – carrying bundles, baskets, furniture, and animals in their hands or on their heads (see color plate 10). The group is heterogeneous, but something unites the figures in misfortune: they are all wearing a sort of skirt with vertical bands. They are fleeing the city. More precisely: they are being chased out by two figures. The first is another cleric holding a processional cross. Behind him stands a bishop, who is brandishing a whip at the end of an oversized arm (see color plate 11). An inscription identifies him: SCS AMBROSIUS. Another appears to refer to the crowd of people whose exile he has caused: ARRIANI. But a third inscription complicates the interpretation: "Ambrose the celibate chased the Jews from their houses" (AMBROSIUS CELEBS IUDEIS ABSTULIT EDES).

Before attempting to resolve this seeming contradiction, we should note a few characteristics of the structural organization of the monumental composition as a whole. It clearly plays with symmetry: the three faces of the central pillar are covered by two divergent movements going into the city; the two faces of the eastern pilaster are brimming over with a reverse movement, leaving the city.[49] The question of threshold is therefore at play, undoubtedly inherent to the conception of the urban gate, whose natural mission was to allow passage, open to the comings and goings of those who entered and exited the city. This reflection is less banal than it might seem, since in this case we are dealing with Ambrose and the *porta Romana* – the reader may remember that when he was elected bishop, Ambrose attempted to escape his calling by fleeing the city. At least that is what Paulinus of Milan tells us, conforming to a hagiographical topos already well established: the recalcitrant bishop left the city by the *porta Ticinese* and, after a night of walking, when he believed himself to be in Pavia, he realized that he was before the *porta Romana* in Milan: the Lord had played a trick on him, making him go in a circle to miraculously prevent his escape, "for God...was setting up the bulwark of his Catholic Church against his enemies."[50]

This ancient circular memory associated with the round city might be in play here. But it is less present than a more recent memory: the founding/refounding of the city of Milan, in hardship and reconciliation, expressed both by the exile and the triumphant return of soldiers and citizens. The iconography of the *porta Romana* is remarkable in that it combines a loose narrative form, which Henri Focillon said is specific to the antique frieze, with the tightly coiled action of Roman capitals: "Bound by every limb to the block of stone, and bound by the continuity of the movement to its companions, which are a prolongation and multiplication of itself, it gave rise to compact systems from which the removal of a single element would entail the ruin of the massive unity of the whole. The loose narrative of the frieze-style was succeeded by the complex strength of drama, with its concentrated impact, and its mimicry accentuated by the deformation of the actors." From a strictly formal point of view, the organization of the sculpted faces, which play off angles and contrasts, is reminiscent of both the frieze and the capital.[51]

At this point we can venture a hypothesis: if the western pilaster also included bas-reliefs (and it's hard to see why it wouldn't have), logic would have it that the reliefs opposite those portraying the return of the Milanese people to their city depicted their expulsion by Emperor Barbarossa – seeing as the entirety of this history is being staged by the *porta Romana*. We can clearly distinguish the symmetry between the internal eastern face of the central pillar and the external face of the eastern pilaster: the inscriptions place the houses to which the Milanese people return opposite those the Jews must abandon; the intimidating deployment of military force prompts and justifies the exile of undesirables. However, this contradictory movement, essential to the creation of a political community (one must exclude the other to find oneself), is visibly sanctified by faith – with the inscription "We praise thee in song" across from the depiction of Ambrose. That he was placed before the Milanese army shouldn't be surprising either: Burchard of Worms described, for the first time, the way in which the *carroccio*, the parade chariot behind which the communal troops of Milan confronted Frederick Barbarossa's army, bore the effigy of their patron Ambrose.[52]

Ambrose clearly appears like a warrior saint here, energetically assuming his duty to commit violence that, as mentioned, constitutes the heroism of the (re)founder. His first, never-ending, battle was over the purity of the Church. Hence the inscription referring to him as *Ambrosius celebs*: the matter of priest celibacy had still not been resolved, far from it, when the turmoil of the Pataria came to an end. It resurfaced in force during the pontificate of Alexander III (1159–81), which no doubt justifies the recourse to Ambrose's authority – communal ideology was in this case closely intertwined with the *libertas* of the Church. But the most remarkable resurrection was clearly the battle against Arianism. We have seen at what point this fight, in Ambrose's day, was intertwined with defending the Church's autonomy from imperial attempts to interfere with dogma. The reasoned elaboration of a theory of heresy in the twelfth century – and we now know that the period 1160–80 represents from this point of view a decisive moment – could therefore advantageously reuse the memory of this state-committed heresy, if only to compromise the imperial party.[53] It was in this way that the allusion to the Arians chased from Milan by Ambrose found new political relevance – the first account of Cathar heresy in the Milan area dates from 1167.[54]

At this point we can assert that what is represented on the eastern pilaster of the *porta Romana* is not the vague memory of an ancient past, but the evocation of a contemporary event made righteous by that memory: the banishment of the supporters of Emperor Frederick I Barbarossa and the antipope Pascal II accused of heresy (leaving the city of Milan as the communal forces are taking it back). The representation of religious dissidence then becomes, if not generic, at the least malleable: all the Church's enemies can be conflated, in both the logical and repressive sense, into a single abstract figure accused of heresy, and who here takes on the tattered appearance of the Patarenes.[55] The image of these poor wretches chased from Milan with their meager belongings in tow might strike us as poignant today, but, in the twelfth century, this poverty pointed to their guilt: it made them Patarenes, in the vague and generic sense.

But we still need to consider the calculated ambiguity assimilating both the Arians of the past and Jews with the heretics of today. The inscription placed on the cornice of the impost claims that "Ambrose the celibate chased the Jews from their houses." How should we understand this distortion? The inscription may have been added later (early thirteenth century?), as an epigraphic analysis conducted by Andrea von Hülsen has attempted to prove.[56] But that hypothesis does not explain much; it is more important to grasp how the evocation of Ambrose's memory facilitated the conflation between the antiheretical fight and the persecution of Jews, which incidentally represents a sadly commonplace scenario in the last third of the twelfth century.[57] Here again, the immediate context was undoubtedly imposing a sense of urgency, since the first accounts of forced baptisms, expulsions, and violence against Jews in Milan date precisely from this period during which a persecution society was taking form across the West.[58]

Ambrose, the tireless fighter of the Church's enemies, could quite easily be enlisted in the combats of medieval anti-Judaism.[59] But what textual memory would be solicited? The most readily available in the twelfth century can be found, as previously noted, in the middle of the tenth book of his correspondence: Letter 74, likely dating from December 388, in which Ambrose vehemently contests Emperor Theodosius's decision to order the bishop of Callinicum to rebuild a synagogue burned down by his followers.[60] Let's quickly review the facts: We are in Osroene, on the eastern fringes of the Roman Empire, bordering Sassanian Persia. On the left bank of the Euphrates, Callinicum (today Raqqa, martyr city of Syria) is a strategic intersection of *limes* (limits) in which several communities live side by side. As a procession of monks was traveling to a Maccabean sanctuary on the day of their festival (August 1, 388), it was harried by Valentinians, followers of a gnostic sect. The monks took revenge by burning the Valentinian temple, as well as, for good measure, the neighboring synagogue, carrying out a violent ritual of purification of which Jews were often the victims in the fourth century.[61] Learning of this from Milan, where he was residing, Theodosius decided to apply the law[62] by punishing the troublemakers and forcing the Catholic bishop to rebuild the synagogue at his own expense.[63]

In the letter he addresses to the emperor, writing from Aquileia, Ambrose uses this matter, quite removed from his immediate interests (Callinicum is "a far distant town"), to once again assert his conception of the Christian empire.[64] How could Theodosius place the bishop in the dilemma of becoming a martyr or an apostate? Ambrose declares himself ready to take his place:

"Why order judgment against one who is absent? You have the guilty man present, you hear his confession. I declare that I set fire to the synagogue."[65] Guardian and inheritor of the prophets' plain speaking, Ambrose managed once again to make the emperor yield, but his victory places modern historiography in a stubborn predicament.[66] By maintaining that Jews were perfidious and did not deserve the protection of the law, he gave free rein to the everyday anti-Judaism of the Church, which under his pen took on a particularly aggressive tone. The synagogue is "a home of unbelief, a house of impiety, a receptacle of folly, which God Himself has condemned";[67] several other texts contain passages that assimilate the hatred inspired in Ambrose by heretics with that which he felt for Jews.[68] Paulinus of Milan unambiguously writes as much in his account of the battle of the basilicas: what the Arians said against Ambrose, the Jews could have easily said as well, "given how they resemble one another."[69]

That brutality is expressed in the bas-relief of the *porta Romana* by the whiplash given by Ambrose, emphatically rendered by the sculptor through the exaggeration of a massive arm. Andrea von Hülsen identified this iconographic motif of the whip as emblematic of a violent expulsion in contemporaneous illuminations showing Christ chasing merchants from the temple, notably Matilda of Tuscany's illuminated manuscript of the Gospels.[70] Moreover, according to a common interpretation in the Middle Ages (supported, incidentally, by Ambrose's commentary on John 2:14–15), these merchants are moneychangers, and by consequence Jews.[71] But the most important point to retain is that the bas-relief of the *porta Romana* is one of the first depictions of Ambrose with a whip. This image only truly developed in the twelfth century,[72] but its first appearance may date to the eleventh century, on a bas-relief adorning a pillar in the narthex of the Basilica of Sant'Ambrogio, and which we can date to the episcopate of Ariberto of Intimiano during which, as we saw, the *carroccio* also appeared (see color plate 12).[73] This whip became the saint's iconographic attribute, whether it was menacingly brandished or more calmly worn at his waist, when it was not hung on the wall of the Church Doctor's study: even when the saint's image became more subdued, it almost never lost this attribute (see color plates 13 and 14).[74] For the whip also had a liturgical value: the archbishop of Milan would display Ambrose's *flagellum* in the Basilica of Sant'Ambrogio on the anniversary of the holy bishop's ordination.[75] Its three lashes were an allusion to Trinitarian dogma, and the whip likely represented energetic but dosed violence: when he mentioned the *flagellum* in his sermon *Against Auxentius*, Ambrose noted the contrast between Christ's leniency in chasing the merchants from the temple with a whip and Auxentius's brutality in expulsing Catholics with an ax.[76]

The interpretation suggested here might appear somewhat vague; it relies on the idea that there is more confusion in the bas-reliefs of the *porta Romana* than there is designation, more a concatenation of memory than a specific one. In this sense, the narrative, which both unfolds and coils, is halfway between the story told by a frieze and the drama staged on a capital. It shows us the work of time: not just recent history or the muddled memory of ancient times, but the way in which the past resurfaces in the present, lighting it with the faint glimmer of a beginning. And so we can simultaneously see, being chased from Milan, the Arians of yesterday and those of today, the Jews and the heretics, the enemies of Ambrose and those of the commune: all the undesirables who have to leave so that "we" can rebuild here. We being the Ambrosians. This is the reason that the *titulus* of the eastern pilaster should not be too quickly read as an unequivocal designation. It designates all those who "resemble one another" in the hatred borne for them.

Note for that matter that the clerics are systematically depicted in pairs in each scene – the figure who carries the cross precedes one brandishing the whip – and that this split can be viewed as an expression of the ambivalence of the founder/ refounder who unites and divides, who builds and destroys. *Ambrosius* names the returning specter: Ambrose, he who was, but also all those who act in his name and join the legion of new Ambroses.

Among them is one man, at the time when the consuls were commissioning the sculptures for the gate to Milan, who *appears* to be the new Ambrose – Archbishop Galdino della Sala, champion of the freedom of the Church, the defense of which was confused with that of Milan's political autonomy. Born to the noble Della Sala family, Galdino had a successful career in the entourages of Bishops Pusterla, Robaldo, and finally Oberto da Pirovano, for whom he served as archdeacon. Attributed to him are an essential role in the city's rebuilding, particular attentiveness to public assistance policy, and great firmness in the antiheretical fight: a clear reenactment of Ambrosian themes.[77] Once again, Galdino was not said to conduct himself like Ambrose, but *with him* and *through him*. When sources describe him as a new Ambrose, we should understand that the name of Ambrose was speaking and acting within him – as explicitly shown in liturgy, where their names were brought together in the litany of saints.[78] Galdino della Sala did not act *like* Ambrose, he truly *was* Ambrose. In August 1160, he was on the battlefield of Carcano when Alexander II's pontifical troops and the communal militias confronted the imperial army.[79] When he became archbishop of Milan in 1166 – while remaining a cardinal and pontifical legate in Lombardy – he left the city so as not to live under the imperial yoke.

This means that the sculpted reliefs of the *porta Romana* are also celebrating Galdino della Sala's triumphant return to his liberated city.[80] The archbishop of Milan died on April 18, 1176, one month before the great Battle of Legnano. That battle, a victory for the Lombard League, but also for the Roman Church, marked a new turning point in terms of memory: the Milanese Church could call itself Ambrosian without this claim appearing like an attack against the papacy. There was incidentally a chapel in Legnano dedicated to Ambrose of Milan, established at an unknown date:[81] it is mentioned in the *Notitia Cleri Mediolanensis* of 1398,[82] but it had existed since at least 1257, the year in which the Franciscan archbishop Leone da Perego, who was buried there, died.[83] This church, as it happens, was located in the parish of Parabiago. Of the two new apparitions of Ambrose's ghost awaiting us, one will surface at the turn of the thirteenth century, amid the communal struggles between the *militia* and the *popolo*, while the second, a century later, will emerge at the Battle of Parabiago, where the signorial appropriation of Ambrose's memory will triumph. When these specters appear, we will once again encounter Galdino della Salla, Ambrose's whip, and others...

PART FOUR

AMBROSE'S FOOT SOLDIERS

(Fourth to Fifteenth Century)

If you visit Milan, come see me, you'll have Ambrose for a neighbor. So said Petrarch in 1356 to one of his friends.[1] "Only Ambrose's basilica separates the house I'm living in from the tiny chapel where Augustine was baptized," he had written two years earlier to Giovanni Aghinolfi.[2] Petrarch lived in that house, immediately across from Sant'Ambrogio, from 1353 to 1359.[3] So when he wrote his friend, the grammarian Moggio da Parma, on May 1, 1356, he was justified in saying *vicinus erit Ambrosius*, "you'll have Ambrose for a neighbor." The aura of a name can exert its hold over a place, as we've come to understand: the Basilica of Sant'Ambrogio *was* Saint Ambrose, welcoming the poet to his bosom. Living in the shadow of his memory, Petrarch felt that he was Ambrose's guest. *Ambrosii hospes sum*: this expression often flowed from Petrarch's pen, never to be abandoned, even after his stay in Milan was over. "Blessed Father Ambrose was once upon a time my host," he wrote Francesco Bruni in 1364.[4] And two years earlier, in his long letter to Boccaccio, he had written: "You won't be surprised if I mention this author, as I lived in Milan for almost ten years and was his guest for all of five years."[5]

In reality, Petrarch was the guest of the lord of Milan, Giovanni Visconti, archbishop and *dominus* of his town and his territory, a brilliant patron and a skillful politician.[6] To justify this political friendship, Petrarch worked zealously to defend Visconti's *buon governo*, maintaining that the signory—that is to say the rule of one man – *was* the commune but pursued by other means. In a letter to Francesco Nelli, dated August 23, 1353, Petrarch describes "this great Italian prince who kept me at his side with much affability, showing me marks of honor that I neither expected nor deserved, nor, to speak frankly, desired."[7] Equating Visconti's offering of a place to stay with Ambrose's hospitality was surely a way to offer Visconti a gift in return – an interested gift. Petrarch no doubt wanted to retrace Augustine's course in Milan,[8] and if he imagined an equivalence between his relation to Visconti and Augustine's to Ambrose, it's because the baptism he sought was entirely political, the anointing of his creative sovereignty in the lustral waters of signorial power: "Only Ambrose's basilica separates the house I'm living in from the tiny chapel where Augustine was baptized."

This is exactly what Boccaccio reproached him for. In a letter of July 18, 1353, the author of *The Decameron* voiced his disappointment and indignation at his friend's political insensitivity. Petrarch's father, a notary in Arezzo, had been banished in 1303, two years after Dante, having been caught in the same political trap and similarly forced into exile. How then could Petrarch betray his commitment to the civic ideals of the commune and work on behalf of the rich and powerful, in particular the signor of Milan, a mortal enemy of Florence? Boccaccio denounced Petrarch's betrayal, measuring it against the Dantean past, but perhaps this political betrayal was precisely the cost of the literary adventure we know as humanism.[9] "To live in freedom, lacking for nothing and subject to no one," this is what was required for a literary life, as Petrarch describes it in *On the Solitary Life* (1346). It comes down to "having no other goal than that of kings, though they may attain it by different means."[10] Was there no alternative? Perhaps not, in which case the social aspects of this choice of life had to be reckoned with. Petrarch derived his income from ecclesiastic benefices in Italy – he was a canon of Padua, an honorary archdeacon of the church of Parma – all without any requirement of residency. He obtained the benefices and the dispensation thanks to his position at court, in particular his relations to Pope Clement VI, and also his close ties to the circle of Giovanni Visconti. All of this coincided with an aristocratic conception of his audience, whom he imagined that he was drawing away from the world, like Stendhal writing for the "happy few."[11]

Petrarch spent much of his time with Ambrose the *auctor*, increasingly so as he frequented the library of "the Church of Saint Ambrose of Milan, where a good portion of Ambrose's writings can be found."[12] But theirs was also a sensory and corporal exchange, as Petrarch wrote to Guido Sette, archbishop of Genoa, in 1357: "And so my most sainted host, who affords me much consolation through his bodily presence and, I believe, his spiritual support, also spares me a great deal of strife and bother."[13] The experience of this humanist is unusual in that it responds to the literary consciousness embedded in the city itself, to which Ambrose's memory clings. But it also speaks to an emotional geography that may have been shared at the time by all who lived in Milan and walked its streets, allowing themselves to be guided by the traces of a buried past. Living near the Basilica di Sant'Ambrogio, which oriented the axis of all Milan's religious buildings, Petrarch had the sense of living immediately next to Ambrose's body. Truly his body: he feels his warm, welcoming, reassuring presence – which is ultimately the sensory power of sacred relics. But also the body of his work, meaning Ambrose's written corpus, which the humanist knew well, for the basilica's treasure room gathered in one place all that remained of the saintly man: relics, jewels, archives, and books. All of these spoils were subjected to reuse, and their successive new uses produced different narratives, which are exactly what we're trying to decipher, from those nearest to Ambrose to those farthest away, gradually retreating from Ambrose's body toward the basilica's threshold. Which is where we find ourselves now, looking at Petrarch, as he looks at Ambrose.

What did he see? To know and feel his sense of proximity to this friend who was perfectly visible though he had been dead a long time, it is worth quoting at some length the fine letter Petrarch wrote to Francesco Nelli on August 23, 1353, the eleventh in Book XVI of his *Rerum familiarium libri*:

> I am living in the western outskirts of the city, near the basilica of St. Ambrose. My dwelling is very comfortable, located on the left side of the church, facing its leaden steeple and the two towers at the entrance; in the rear, however, it looks upon the city walls and in the distance fertile fields and the Alps covered with snow, now that summer is passed. Nevertheless, the most beautiful spectacle of all, I would say, is a tomb, which I *know* to be that of a great man, unlike what Seneca says of Africanus, "I believe it to be the grave of a great man." I gaze upward at his statue, standing on the highest walls, which it is said closely resembles him, and often venerate it as though it were alive and breathing. This is not an insignificant reward for coming here, for the great authority of his face, the great dignity of his eyebrows and the great tranquility in his eyes are inexpressible; it lacks only a voice to see the living Ambrose.[14]

This last sentence in particular has a fierce beauty. All that is missing of the man who read with his lips closed is his voice? Others would make it heard, speaking for him or in his name. As we'll see soon, what brought Ambrose to life was the politically charged rejuvenation of his memory, opening the field to successive and conflicting appropriations of the relics from his past. The canons of Sant'Ambrogio undertook to act as curators of memory. They defended the physical place anchoring that memory, to prevent it from drifting wherever interest or ambition might take it. But they, too, were implicated in the politicization of the Ambrosian past, which not only characterized conflicts within the commune but underlay arguments of every political order. This vision of Petrarch's, then, opened the way to Ambrose's foot soldiers, who would go on to reinvent and relaunch his posthumous lives. But it brings much else into view, raising several questions: What does it mean to return and to remember? How do faces and landscapes come down to us from the past?

Here, then, is a man gazing at the figure looking down on him, submitting to the aura of a very ancient past, yet a past that nonetheless appears almost within reach. But what representation is Petrarch actually referring to? This statue on the cusp of breathing (*signa spirantia*) and lacking only a voice (*vox sola deest*) was probably a tondo of polychrome stucco, of uncertain date (but in any case not prior to the twelfth century), and incorporated into what was at the time an exterior wall of the basilica.[15] Ambrose appears as a grave young man dressed in the Roman style, with fine features and a short beard, but haloed, offering a blessing with his right hand and in his other carrying a book on which his name is written, *sanctus ambrosius*. It is he, as it happens, who is featured on the cover of this book. The resemblance is said to be excellent, Petrarch reports. This is intriguing, not least because Petrarch's theory relating the painter's imitation of nature to literary mimesis grew out of his meditation on resemblance and lack of resemblance.[16] How on earth can you say that a portrait is a good resemblance if you aren't familiar with the face of the person depicted? At least it resembles the fifth-century mosaic of San Vittore in Ciel d'Oro, which is claimed to be – though we'll revisit the question – the oldest extant portrait of Ambrose.[17]

For the moment, I'll just note that Petrarch is almost playing in this text with the framing of time. The Milanese landscape is spread out majestically on the horizon above the rooftops. Petrarch doesn't talk about nature's haughty indifference, but rather about men's efforts to take hold of nature (indeed he is *the* poet of this quintessentially political stance). Yet the most beautiful spectacle is a tomb. And what it offers Petrarch is a vision of the living Ambrose. Not in the second-chance survival of reuse, as a *Nachleben* or afterlife, but in life itself, reborn. Petrarch comes so close to this man from Roman times that he believes himself able to trade glances with him, eye to eye, while simultaneously pushing the landscape farther away – the walls of the city, the snow-covered Alps. This intimacy and this distancing reflect the new relation to the world that the humanists would defend, and it is the same relation that Angelo Decembrio and his companions would discuss in this very place, in the narthex of Sant'Ambrogio, in May 1447, where we are about to rejoin them. Petrarch had set out to prune back the dark forest of medieval glossing, converting this civilization of reuse into a society based on quotations: "As Seneca said." The quotation is the opposite of reuse, in the sense that quotation separates, whereas reuse integrates. Petrarch quotes Ambrose, he no longer reuses him. Ambrose is alive, no doubt, but now he lives in the past.

ELEVEN

The Saintly Knight
(Thirteenth to Fourteenth Century)

"The forest has since been cleared. As the place has changed in appearance, only the name is left: 'Ambrose's Wood,' as it is ordinarily called." In *On the Solitary Life* (1346 to 1366), Petrarch sets out to find the isolated places where, far from the bustle of cities, the love of literature can take refuge. But his plan was never to adopt the learned ignorance of hermits permanently: any withdrawal from the world would be temporary. And he looked to classical antiquity for companions who, like himself, occasionally sought solitude. Ambrose was one of these. He was fully engaged in his own century and took part in the political struggles of his era, but "each time that his duties as a bishop allowed him, and that the fraught task he perpetually assumed of driving Arians from the Church gave him a little respite, this saintly man liked to take refuge in a more isolated solitude, for the little time he had to turn to his own occupations." From this humble place, Petrarch continued, "Ambrose scattered those flowers as sweet as honey that are his books, and whose pleasant taste and delicate perfume today pervade all the countries of the Church."[1]

The place Petrarch referred to lay beyond the *porta Comacini*, behind the present-day park of the Castello Sforzesco. It had been the site of a hermitage since at least the eleventh century. In his *Vita sancti Arialdi*, Andrew of Strumi mentions that in 1064 Arialdo, who was one of the leading *patarini* (Patarenes), took refuge in this church "founded by Saint Ambrose."[2] Only in 1375 was a monastery built there, the seat of a new religious order (Ordo Fratrum Sancti Ambrosii ad Nemus), living under the rules of Saint Augustine and officiating according to the Ambrosian Rite, having been recognized by Pope Gregory XI in a papal bull of December 11, 1375.[3] In the fifteenth century, the *fratelli ambrosiani* would attract the favor of the duke of Milan – it was for them that, in 1494, Ludovico Sforza commissioned the famous Pala Sforzesca (Sforzesca Altarpiece), which is today in the collection of the Pinacoteca di Brera (see color plate 16) and shows the duke kneeling at the feet of the Virgin Mary while Ambrose stands behind him, holding his whip in one hand and placing the other on the prince's shoulder. Furthermore, the order's church would prompt many Ambrosian civic processions to venture out of the city.

Indeed, Ambrose's name had traveled far beyond the walls of Milan, judging only from the many churches dedicated to him. That phenomenon shouldn't be interpreted too rigidly – it was likely due more to his universality as a Doctor of the Church than to his saintly patronage of Milan. In the case of other cities in communal Italy, Ambrose's rememoration may have occurred in a political or diplomatic context whose fluctuations merit analysis, but it also rested on the textual bases of local traditions.

In Florence, for example, there is a legend about the spiritual link between Zenobius, who is worshipped as the first bishop of the city, and Ambrose, who is credited with a fundamental role in making Florence Christian.[4] It is now known that in 394 Ambrose spent the Feast of Easter in Florence,[5] where he dedicated the basilica and gave the *Exhortatio virginitatis* (Exhortation to virginity).[6] A later legend has him meeting Zenobius, who was bishop when Paulinus of Milan was writing in the 410s – which gave rise to the hypothesis that Paulinus originally came from Florence and followed Ambrose to Milan after 394.[7] Subsequently, the memory of Ambrose in Florence became enmeshed with the fight against heresy.[8] The Christian community in Florence was even known as "the daughter of Milan." This locution was still used by the chronicler Giovanni Villani[9] but was quietly dropped during the clash with the Viscontis.[10]

The closer one draws to the Lombard capital, the more the glorification of Ambrose's memory takes on a distinctly political dimension of allegiance to the power of Milan. This is particularly clear in the case of the town of Vigevano, which was elevated by the prince's favor to the rank of *civitas*. This promotion was accompanied in the fifteenth century by the architectural development of Vigevano as an ideal city, intended as an echo of the prince's palace,[11] but also by the elevation of the church, which had opportunely been dedicated to Saint Ambrose, to the rank of cathedral.[12] Yet within the diocese of Milan, the number of churches dedicated to Saint Ambrose is not as great as one might think. And it is no easy task to draw up a list of them: the catalog of Milanese saints compiled by Gotofredo da Bussero in the early years of the fourteenth century (probably in 1304 to 1311),[13] known as the *Liber Notitiae Sanctorum Mediolani*, does not inventory the altars and churches dedicated to Ambrose, possibly because he was the focus of a separate list.[14] Re-creating this list by indirect means, with particular reliance on the *Notitia Cleri Mediolanensis de anno 1398*, we reach a total of thirty-one dedications to Ambrose in Milan and its diocese – compared to 289 churches dedicated to the Virgin Mary and 127 to Saint Martin.[15]

But the memory in question here is more sensory, more concrete, than might be suggested by a list of names. It is attached to places, in turn stabilizing an emotional geography, as if registering the mnemonic imprint of a person's passage – that of Ambrose himself. And that is exactly what Petrarch describes – a trace, in the fundamental sense of the indication of a past presence as laid out in Carlo Ginzburg's paradigm: someone has passed this way, let's tell his story.[16] Petrarch describes Ambrose's trace in all its material fragility, but also in its linguistic permanence. The woods are gone, the name persists. Because Ambrose's body found haven in this place, it needs only to be named to be preserved from the vagaries of fate. At the time Petrarch was writing (or rewriting) this passage in *On the Solitary Life* – most likely in 1356 – the death of Matteo II Visconti had unleashed a civil war pitting the brothers Bernabò and Galeazzo II against each other. The citadel that Galeazzo started to build on the bastion of the *porta Giovia* deeply changed the structure of this outlying area of the city, which till then had commemorated the Milanese resistance to Emperor Frederick I.[17] The construction of the signorial citadel, which would become the Castello di porta Giovia, is probably the memorable event that Petrarch alludes to in saying that this once isolated and wooded location "is now part of the last enclosed area that the quick pace of construction has pushed outward."

Sant'Ambrogio ad Nemus was where Ambrose would go to escape the city. Now, the city was catching up with him. No escape, once again; the century always takes its revenge. Reading this passage of Petrarch's, the modern reader has trouble not casting over it the shadow of a Baudelairian nostalgia: "Old Paris is no more (the form of a city / changes faster, alas! than a mortal's heart)."[18] The theme of the expansion of the urbanized area appears again in Petrarch's description of Ambrose's house in the city: "He lived in the most remote quarter of town (according to the extant traces of the walls), where his sainted body lies and where can still be seen the saintly house he built." Like all the basilicas that ringed the city beyond Emperor Maximian's walls, surrounding it with a sacred aura, the Basilica of Sant'Ambrogio had been overrun by the outward movement of the commune's enclosure and swallowed up by Milan's urban space, causing the term *corpi santi* to be transported farther outward, as we've seen.[19] What happened to Ambrose's Wood happened to the saints' bodies as well: a name preserved the memory of a place that had disappeared or been moved.

This is what we turn to now – this expansion that is also a covering up, this displacement that claims to be an extension. Starting in the last third of the thirteenth century in Milan, as in the rest of communitarian Italy, the signory settled in, meaning that it took root and spread. As the establishment of a personal power that would become hereditary, it took root; as the enlargement of a territorial power beyond the walls of the city, it spread. The signory occupied the terrain, in time and space. Historians have long believed that this was a dramatic occurrence, but they have recently discovered that it was gradual, resistible, and reversible.[20] The signorial lords insinuated themselves more than they imposed themselves, sometimes subverting the communal structures abruptly but more often patiently and quietly, causing less a change of regime than a reconfiguring of the commune's government. Note that the signorial experience first took its meaning within the very heart of the long-running conflict in communitarian Italy.

Let's resume our story where we left off, in 1176, on the eve of the Battle of Legnano, the decisive test for communal society, when Galdino della Sala appeared in the bas-reliefs of the *porta Romana* bearing Ambrose's features. This story is certainly laced with apparitions, just as Messianic times are shot through with fragments of the future; here, the Ambrosian past intervened to save the city's future at a perilous moment. Some two decades later, in 1198, what appeared was not a ghost but a name of great power: the Credenza di Sant'Ambrogio, or the Faith of Saint Ambrose. All the chronicles of the time stress this event's importance. The *popolo* of Milan had formed a party under Ambrose's banner to protect all who opposed the Motta. For its part, La Motta included the company of the *capitanei* and *valvassores*. This partition of political society into two groups would henceforth characterize the life of the free commune.[21] Only in 1258 was a peace treaty signed in the Basilica of Sant'Ambrogio between the Societas capitaneorum et valvassorum and the Credenza. This treaty, aptly called the Pace di Sant'Ambrogio, gave the victory to the *popolo*.[22] During the decisive period when the commune's institutions were being consolidated, Ambrose's name therefore designated both a social conflict and its resolution.

This social conflict is inseparable from the formation of the commune as a political system of governance. Historians today distinguish its three stages – the consular, podestal, and popular – less as successive periods than as accumulated experiences.[23] The transition from the first to the second stage resulted from a political experiment in the 1180s that was made necessary by a rapid escalation of conflict in the ranks of the commune's aristocracy, which had immediately seized the levers of consular power.

In consequence, the government of the commune – or at least the power to arbitrate between its consular institutions – was temporarily turned over to a foreign magistrate known as the *podestà*. This professional political actor would impose his political and juridical authority over a city, becoming for a time its *rector* (leader) and *rhetor* (orator).[24] An analysis of the members of this itinerant political caste, whose careers resulted in political experience being shared across the city-states of Italy, shows that Lombardy was the leader in exporting *podestàs* to other regions until the mid-thirteenth century. As the major power in the Lombard League, Milan assumed the "leadership of the world of free communes," in the words of Jean-Claude Maire Vigueur.[25] The city long benefited from this prestige and its reputation for advanced institutions, managing to convince other cities of the political maturity of its mode of government.

This didn't mean that the government ran peacefully and unanimously – far from it. Though the parties' jockeying shouldn't be seen as a conflict between social entities with neatly defined borders, the sociological dividing lines are more apparent in Milan than elsewhere.[26] It seems that the subvassals and captains of the old precommunal order of the eleventh century melded into a single group based on its social rank, its means of support, and its participation in government power: the *militia*. Its members formed an aristocracy of government, characterized primarily by the fact that they fought on horseback. Forming the Motta party, the *milites* organized a strike force in 1201 through a military society known as the Societas Galliardurum (Society of Lads), which was often at the sharp end of street conflicts with the people's faction. The people, for their part, retaliated by forming the Societas Fortium (Society of the Strongmen)[27] – the Lads versus the Strongmen. The former recruited from among young noble horsemen (*ex nobilibus equestris*, according to Galvano

Fiamma), and the latter from members of the *popolo*, who fought on foot (*ex popularibus pedestris*). This was the fundamental dichotomy in Milanese political life, cleaving its ruling class to the point of creating a "seditious bipartisanship" at its heart.[28]

For the *popolo* had gradually infiltrated the workings of the city-state government, thanks to a series of confrontations and compromises. These were once again accelerated by the clash between the Italian free communes and the Holy Roman Emperor, Frederick II, reenacting the epic story of his grandfather Frederick Barbarossa, who had failed to impose his will on what should have been part of his empire – Italy.[29] History seemed to be stuttering: confronted with the aggression of Frederick II, the wonder of the world, the Lombard League had coalesced once more, gaining the support of Pope Honorius III, but it suffered a crushing defeat at Cortenuova on November 27, 1237. The emperor carried the Milanese *carroccio* back to Rome as a trophy and displayed it atop five salvaged columns, hanging from a marble cornice bearing the following inscription: "Behold the illustrious spoils captured in the rout of Milan. May it remind the viewer of the triumphs of Caesar."[30] This triumph was short-lived, but it unified Milan's political society once more in awareness of its misfortune, with Frederick II's chancery reviving the memory of Milan's 1162 destruction using a ceremonial language whose rhetoric electrified all of Europe.[31]

On the death of Frederick II in 1250, at a time of strong economic and demographic growth for Milan, the city's government had attained a high level of politico-social maturity and institutional accomplishment, in matters of municipal, legal, and fiscal management, but also in the production of documents. In other words, the *popolo* not only represented the enlargement of the social base of the city-state government, but its political completion. Milan was then Italy's great city-state, dominant and prosperous, at the heart of Europe's system of exchange, while Europe was at the height of its economic growth.[32] And as it happens, this period from 1198 to 1258, so decisive on the political front, was a key time in the rememoration of Ambrose. The people's commune saw, in 1254, the development of the ritual of making wax offerings to Saint Ambrose on his December 7 feast day, which also coincided with Milan's great market, when bread and wine were distributed to the poor and when, for a time, all activity in the law courts was shut down.[33]

And so it would appear that the past had been mobilized to sanctify the peace—which corresponds nicely to the idea of the all-encompassing virtues of a civic religion, one that is "immutable, unanimist, and peace-promoting," in the words of Cécile Caby.[34] But before it became associated with the peace of 1258, Ambrose's memory in fact served as an identifier to one of the two opposing parties, the *pars populi*. The fact is well-known to historians of the Credenza di Sant'Ambrogio, but it has not generally engaged their attention.[35] In his *Manipulus florum*, Galvano Fiamma gives an explanation for the party's name that most modern historians consider—perhaps wrongly—to be far-fetched. The chronicler claims that the Credenza derived its name from the great credit in which the members of the popular party held the nobility.[36] It's a strange assertion, certainly, but not so absurd from the perspective of political sociology, considering that the Milanese *popolo* was taking direction, as Paolo Grillo has shown, from members of the consular and merchant aristocracy. Furthermore, *credenza* in a general sense refers to the executive session held by consuls when they deliberate, not quite secretly, but away from the public glare of councils.[37] Might the name of the people's party, as Fiamma suggests, be a concession to aristocratic culture or at least to a seemingly communal civic culture that turns out on examination to be directed by the *militia*-dominated ruling group of the city commune? Perhaps not, but Fiamma's claim at least has the benefit of pointing out that the name of the people's party, unremarkable to modern historians, for whom the popular appropriation of civic religion seems a matter of course, was surprising in the fourteenth century, even paradoxical, and needing explanation. In other words, the chronicler's tangled explanation puts us on the track of a disputed memory.

There are other examples among the Italian city-states of popular parties appropriating civic cults to mobilize supporters. One instance is Bologna, where the cult of Saint Petronius was characteristic of this "hagiography of struggle," whose history was strictly tied to the political convulsions of the city commune.[38] Unlike Ambrose, however, Petronius, who was bishop of Bologna from 432 to 450, is a little-known figure. Only in 1141 did his distant successor Henry I dedicate to him a *Sermo de inventione sanctarum reliquiarium*. The cult did not spread beyond the Benedictine monastery of Santo Stefano, where the saint's relics were discovered. Between 1164 and 1180, a monk of the monastery composed a *Vita* of the saint in Latin, which prompted the forgery in 1255 of imperial charters attributed to Emperor Theodosius guaranteeing the autonomy of the university and entered to this effect in the commune's *Registrum Novum*.[39] At that point, the hagiographic project was completed by the *volgarizzamento* of Petronius's *Vita*, probably by a layman, as an expression of love to the city of Bologna.[40] The cult of Saint Petronius, *patronus et defensor civitatis Bononie*, nonetheless met severe competition, for there was also – and there had been since ancient times – the cult of Peter, for whom the cathedral of Bologna was named; and of Procolo, particularly powerful in the thirteenth century, who was championed by the *studium*, the city's powerful university community. No reconciliation between the three was possible, for the struggle was a political one, at a time when the Italian city-states envisaged politics as a zero-sum game: one saint had to win, and the others withdraw.[41]

If Petronius won out in the end, it was thanks to Ambrose's backing. The partisans of the bishop of Bologna's civic cult, clearly linked to the *popolo*, made much of the connection between the two saints, who appear side by side on Bologna's *carroccio*, and also on the city's shield.[42] In the *Vita*, written in the vulgar tongue, Ambrose also appears to lend a hand to Petronius, clearly showing his anti-imperialist solidarity, a sentiment often echoed in the history of mid-thirteenth century Italy. In that *Vita*, there is an episode in which Ambrose helps Petronius rebuild the city that Theodosius had destroyed, marking its neighborhoods with four crosses, which he dedicated to virgins, martyrs, and confessors, consecrating the ground with their relics.[43] For the Bologna city commune, whose councils were long held in the *curia sancti Ambrosi*,[44] invoking Ambrose's backing was politically crucial to gain support for the civic cult of Petronius. Only when the latter was solidly enshrined did references to Ambrose become more problematic than opportune. Mention of Ambrose was dropped from the city-state's statutes in 1378, though they had previously named him as one of the city's patron saints.[45]

If it was possible, in communal Italy at the time of the *popolo*'s victories, to summon Ambrose's memory in aid of civic cults with compatible political leanings, it was no doubt because that memory remained politically available in Milan for such use. The canons of the Basilica of Sant'Ambrogio, whom research by Annamaria Ambrosioni has allowed us to see more clearly,[46] sharply defended their role as guardians of Ambrose's memory. And that memory could not be other than politically oriented: these canons, for the most part minor clerics (*decumani*, as opposed to the *cardinales* in the bishop's circle), played an active role in the formation of the Credenza di Sant'Ambrogio. Paolo Grillo has reconstructed a few of these close-knit family groups with middling political ambitions and moderate economic means, who remained close to the milieu of artisans and notaries to which they were related, and whose ties with the clerical milieu of the *decumani* constituted, in the historian's words, the "political heart of the Ambrosian *popolo*."[47]

Should we go further and look for a "real Ambrose," necessarily of the people, behind the manipulation of his memory at the hands of the feudal lord, then of the prince, who unquestionably distorted things? One might be tempted, because – beyond the civic cult's declared unanimism – each time that only a portion of Milanese political society gave its allegiance to Ambrose, it had always been, since 1258, the *pars populi*. No doubt it was the memory of Ambrose continually and savagely attacking the arrogance and avarice of the wealthy that encouraged the people's party to appropriate him. If Ambrose was "worthy of admiration," wrote Jacobus de Voragine, it was largely for his liberality, "for everything he owned belonged to the poor." In support of this claim, the author of *The Golden Legend* cited Ambrose's response to the emperor who asked him for the use of a basilica: "If he asked me for what belongs to me, that is, my lands, my money, and other goods of that kind, I would not be opposed to it, though everything I own is the property of the poor." And Jacobus de Voragine added, "And this is found in the decree *Convenior* (XXIII, q.8)."[48] Effectively, this quotation from Ambrose's correspondence is picked up in Gratian's *Decretum*.[49] But if such narrative motifs were in wide circulation in urban society, it was less because of quotations from Roman law than from their use as *exempla* in sermons.

Thanks to the work of Silvia Donghi, for example, we know a good deal about the activities of Pietro Maineri, a preacher of the Eremites of Saint Augustine attached to the Convent of San Marco in Milan, where he was active from 1320 to 1350. The site of a *studium* since 1297, San Marco boasted a beautiful and well-stocked library, in which Maineri delved for his sermons, though these remained very dependent on Jacobus de Voragine.[50] In a book of sermons preserved in the Biblioteca Ambrosiana in Milan, we can read the sermon he wrote, for instance, for December 7, the feast day of Saint Ambrose.[51] Maineri hews closely, in the main, to *The Golden Legend*, adapting his argument to his hearers' presumed expectations. For example, he makes a particular case of the confrontation between the Ambrosian and Gregorian rites, lingering over the various fabulous stories (available from Landulf Senior, among others) regarding the books of liturgy. Pietro Maineri supplements his sermon with several instances of miracles, divinations, and other events from Ambrose's life that were drawn from the store of exempla.[52] The most significant—and apparently one of the most widely circulated—is to be found in the *Specchio di vera penitenza* by Jacopo Passavanti (1354).[53] It recounts how Ambrose, spending the night in an inn, heard the proprietor say that he had always lived in prosperity and never suffered a reversal of fortune. Ambrose was not overly sorry to learn that God's wrath had struck the too-fortunate innkeeper the very next day, destroying his house and family.[54] "It is said that a deep ditch appeared on the site, remaining as a testament to this day," says Jacobus de Voragine, who also recorded this legend, which shows the brutal energy that tradition generally assigns to Ambrose in dealing with the rich.[55]

But, if one can reasonably hypothesize an ideological connivance to revive Ambrose's memory on the part of social groups who jointly battled against the *militia*'s political dominance in the thirteenth century, the subversion of communal institutions by the feudal lord in the fourteenth, and, later, the growing absolutism of princely power in the fifteenth, it is not possible to imagine this connivance as an exclusive identification. Rather, it would more closely resemble the "spontaneous sympathy" that sprang up between the *militia* and the Ghibellines (which originally denoted the emperor's faction in Italy), not so much around a body of doctrines as a set of cultural traditions, lifestyles, values, and intentions.[56] Unlike the situation in Bologna, Ambrose's identification with the *popolo* in Milan could not be exclusive – due to the unquestioned universality of the saint that the city had chosen as its patron and protector. What resulted was a dispute over a shared memory, rather than a competition between conflicting memories. Complicating matters was the fact that Ambrose's memory was ballasted by a liturgical tradition, a legacy of texts, and a suite of architectural monuments. It could therefore not be manipulated as easily as the memory of a recent saint like Petronius (recent in the sense of being so ancient that the thread connecting his obscure origins to his recent rediscovery had severed). Hence why, in the Milanese case, self-interested distortions of memory were displaced onto new Ambroses, who could more easily be oriented toward the political needs of the moment. During all of the thirteenth century, as we'll see, a good part of the dispute over Ambrose's legacy was transferred to the contested memory of Galdino della Salla.

Twelve years after his death, this cardinal-archbishop's name appeared in the litany of saints in the Duomo's instructional book, immediately preceding Ambrose's.[57] The *Beroldo Nuovo* of 1269 also mentions him. But the worship of the noble Galdino della Salla appears to have been essentially local, barely extending beyond the cathedral's metropolitan chapter. In the mind of Enrico Cattaneo, there appears little doubt that the Milanese *decumani* obstructed the spread of Galdino's cult.[58] It made little headway until the 1270s, when the archpriest Orrico

Scaccabarozzi collected the cardinal-archbishop's liturgical texts.[59] But he did so in a very specific context: Ottone Visconti's takeover of power in Milan. Visconti had been unexpectedly elected archbishop of Milan in 1262 and had managed to regroup the nobles' faction, weakened by the victory of the Credenza di Sant'Ambrogio in 1258.[60] After his victory in the town of Desio over the rival family of the della Torres, Visconti entered Milan at the head of an army of exiles on the night of January 20–21, 1277. The following day, Ottone Visconti had himself proclaimed signor.[61] He was hardly the first bishop in northern Italy to start a feudal dynasty.[62] Visconti relied on the metropolitan authority conferred on him by his archbishopric to build his territorial state and managed to establish a dynastic power by maintaining the opposing factions in a lasting deadlock.[63] But he also had to find his footing in Milan's history, where a confused relationship had existed between episcopal authority and public power ever since Ariberto of Intimiano, whom Galvano Fiamma described in his *Chronicon maius* as "general monarch, lord over temporal and spiritual."[64]

Back from exile, Ottone Visconti occupied the former palace of another who, like himself, had had to flee the city to protect his freedom: Galdino della Salla. His politics? To preserve the freedom of the Church, stifle religious dissent (vigorously supported by the provincial council of 1287), and provide assistance to the poor.[65] Reviving the memory of Galdino della Salla was very much a way for the new signor of Milan to cautiously take over Ambrose's *memoria* without a head-on confrontation with its associated civic values, thereby cherry-picking Ambrose's legacy, rejecting anything that might get in the way of his personal power.

In the early years of the fifteenth century, Duke Gian Galeazzo Visconti moved Ottone Visconti's funerary monument, originally installed in the Church of Santa Tecla, into the Duomo of Milan, built in 1387, which the prince intended for his dynastic mausoleum.⁶⁶ It was in fact a double sarcophagus, in which Ottone lay next to his successor, the archbishop and signor Giovanni Visconti, according to a funerary practice that recalled the collective tombs of saints – most notably, of course, the tombs of Gervasius and Protasius at Sant'Ambrogio.⁶⁷ The architectural elements included a high window in the apse, finished only after the death of the commissioning duke, whose radial rose window featuring the *razza* of the Viscontis (a star-shaped motif composed of undulating vipers), and which was supported by a sculpted relief of the Annunciation, flanked by two protectors, Ambrose and Galdino della Salla.⁶⁸

With this, the capture of Ambrose's memory by the feudal powers was complete. It had at first been undertaken cautiously and patiently, step by small step, using the memory of Galdino della Salla as a bridge between Ottone Visconti and Ambrose. But the bridge was fragile, and the memory of the cardinal-archbishop was weak and brittle. A trace of this can be found today in a palimpsestic plenary missal from the second half of the fifteenth century, probably copied for use in the Duomo of Milan:⁶⁹ its title makes reference, with an emphasis that was unusual in this type of liturgical manuscript, to Galdino della Salla, whose name was often associated with Ambrose's.⁷⁰ But on the recto of folio 10, a palimpsest can be distinctly seen behind the words *Goterardi episcopi*. Before the *episcopi*, the letters *archi* have been scratched out, and one can make out *aldino* behind *oterardi*. The words *Galdino archiepiscopi* have become *Goterardi episcopi*. One saint has superseded another. At the moment, perhaps, when the missal was on its way to the chapel of the signorial palace of San Gottardo in Palazzo, someone replaced Galdino with Gottardo, whose feast day was added for good measure at the end of the Mass.⁷¹ But

Galdino della Salla could well be forgotten, for by a quiet reversal of signs, followed by a quick strike, Ambrose himself had burst into the political discourse of the lords of Milan.

First, a quiet reversal of signs, followed by a quick strike. One precedes the other, or paves the way for it, but at any rate never prevents it. It is probably a mistake to place in stark opposition two strategies for gaining control over the past, as though they represented different principles between which governments must necessarily choose. In thinking historically about the forms, rhythms, and modes of the signorial subversion of the commune governments, or more generally about the degradation of any kind of government subjected to the stress of democracy, it is important to shield our minds from the fascination with the paroxysmal tipping points toward tyrannical power and to pay attention instead to the gray zone, blurred and uncertain, where convictions gradually slump under the weight of renunciations and doubts, or succumb to the quiet attraction exerted by personal power and the cancellation of public freedoms.[72]

In the specific case of the *insignorimento* ("signorification") of the Milanese commune, any imputation of tyranny is problematic, given how successfully signorial propaganda floated the idea that tyranny could be equitable, therefore acceptable.[73] Furthermore, Ottone Visconti's takeover in 1277 did not signal a definitive Visconti accession to power over the city. The party of the *popolari*, which was allied to the wealthy and prestigious della Torre family, had not put away its arms, and signorial government itself had not achieved a stable form. On the death of Ottone Visconti in 1295, his nephew Matteo had difficulty asserting himself. He was forced into exile in June 1302, prompting the return of Guido della Torre to Milan, along with his supporters in the people's party. Then began an unusual political experiment, in which a people's free commune was reinstated on the one hand and a crypto-signory established on the other, opening a Guelph parenthesis in the history of Milan that lasted until 1311, with the della Torres allied to the "Black Guelphs," who supported Pope Boniface VIII in Italy.[74]

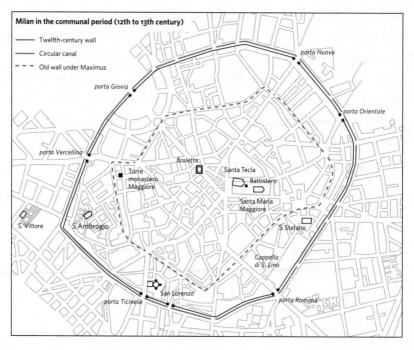

Milan in the communal period (12th to 13th century)

——— Twelfth-century wall
——— Circular canal
– – – Old wall under Maximus

porta Nuova
porta Giovia
porta Orientale
porta Vercellina
Broletto
Torre monastero Maggiore
Santa Tecla
Battistero
Santa Maria Maggiore
S. Vittore
S. Ambrogio
S. Stefano
Cappella di S. Lino
San Lorenzo
porta Ticinese
porta Romana

(PAO Seuil)

When he composed his *De magnalibus urbis Mediolani* in 1288, the friar Bonvesin da la Riva was therefore not wrong in thinking that the march toward a signorial government could still be halted. Nothing was written, all was still possible, and so Bonvesin believed it his duty to mobilize the cultural resources and civic virtues of the commune to rouse his compatriots. Confronted with a reflection of the city's past greatness, they might choose not to sully it by embracing a contemptible government.[75] Hence his famous text, "On the Marvels of the City of Milan," which can be read both as an elegy to the city and a manifesto on communal government for Milan.[76] Bonvesin da la Riva was a teacher of grammar and a member of the Ordigni degli Umiliati, founded in the twelfth century as a religious order of married laymen who chose to embrace poverty and preach penitence. The rule of their order was approved by Pope Innocent III in 1201, after much hesitation on the subject of its orthodoxy. Like all Milanese Umiliati, Bonvesin da la Riva was immersed in the public life of the city, participating in its government but also in its economic activity – the Umiliati were particularly active in textile production.[77]

Bonvesin therefore sang the praises, at a moment of danger, of "the good within things." As Emanuele Coccia has written, "Politics is truly the supreme form of architecture, being the art that allows stones, as well as things, to sing."[78] The city that Bonvesin glorified was protected by its walls, centered on its town square (the Broletto, built in 1228), ennobled by its imposing public and private buildings, and harmoniously integrated into a space where the concept of measure was key. "The plan of this city is round, shaped like a circle, and this marvelous rotundity is a sign of its perfection."[79] What the Umiliati friar held up in opposition to the rampant signorialization of the city's institutions was the city itself, in all its obstinate materiality, as though the urban space could all on its own, which is to say by the political power of its own image, erect a rampart against tyranny. Or again, as though one could use the shape of a city – understood as both the built city and the social customs that gave it meaning – to counter the ambitions of those who would become its masters. As though, the grammarian seems to be saying, power resided in form.[80]

Men and things on one side, ideas on the other: this dichotomy vigorously propels Bonvesin da la Riva's text. The first four chapters praise the city for its site, its buildings, its population, and the abundance of its goods (*ratione situs, ratione habitationis, ratione habitantium, ratione fertilitas et omnium bonorum confluentium*). The next four chapters celebrate Milan as the city of heroes and saints (*ratione fortitutudinis*), the "second Rome" (*ratione constantis fidelitatis*), a bulwark against tyrants (*ratione libertatis*), and finally as the city where emperors are crowned kings of Italy, shining with a dignity unmatched by any other (*ratione dignitatis*). Bonvesin da la Riva is dipping here into the rhetorical repertory of the *laudes civitatum*, but he does bring to his elegy of the city of Milan one major innovation: the introduction of quantitative data as a means of glorification. The author of the *De Magnalibus* provides a census of the churches, evaluates the supply system, details the quantities produced, and measures the distribution area of various merchandises. Bonvesin also extols Milan's spiritual dignity with this attention to numbers: ninety-two bishops, sixty buried saints, and innumerable martyrs. An elegy in figures, an elegy to figures, heralding the appearance in the rhetoric of civic glorification of the "ambience of arithmetic," which, according to Jacques Le Goff, characterizes mercantile culture.[81]

Is this an indication that Ambrose had melted away into the city's numbers? In a sense, yes, but in the same way that a halo might bathe the entire urban body in light. *De Magnalibus urbis Mediolani* was the pinnacle of the movement that, starting in the eighth century, attributed Ambrose's name to all things Milanese: the liturgy, the clergy, the Church, the people, and the city's forms of government.[82] With Bonvesin da la Riva, everything became Ambrosian: churches, bread, people, the earth, the army, windmills, and history.[83] If we analyze his word use, we find that the adjective "Ambrosian" appears thirty-eight times (by comparison, the adjective "Milanese" occurs 106 times). The most common form is evidently *patronus noster beatus Ambroxius* and its variations. *Beatus, beata, beate, beati, beatum* appear thirty-six times in the text, and in a third of those cases (therefore twelve times), it is associated with Ambrose's name.[84] Milan is bathed in his aura.

History proved Bonvesin wrong – in the first place, because the Viscontis captured Milan, and in the second because they took control of the Lombard capital's civic memory, with their municipal policies expressing both this conquest and this substitution. It occurred, notably, during the decisive decade of Azzone Visconti's signory (1329 to 1339).[85] Azzone was the grandson of Matteo Visconti (who was lord of Milan from 1313 to 1322, after the intermediary period of the della Torres's popular but crypto-signorial government), and the son of Beatrice d'Este and Galeazzo Visconti (1322 to 1328). He set out to make good on his grandfather's legacy, where his father before him had failed. Even his first name, Azzone, which was borrowed from the family of the marquis d'Este, speaks to the Viscontis' ambition of establishing a hereditary signory, along the lines of the marquisate of Ferrara.[86] As his grandfather had also done, Azzone first sought to base his political legitimacy on recognition from the emperor. In January 1329, he obtained, in return for 125,000 florins, the title of imperial vicar. Then, in gradual stages, the commune's institutions gave themselves over to their new master. On March 15, 1330, one of the members of the council of 900, a certain Pasio de Mezate, proposed a vote to release Milan to Azzone Visconti *dominus generalis et perpetuus civitatis et districtus Mediolani* – a proclamation that accompanied a rewriting of the city statutes, giving the Viscontis a right of dominium over Milan and the surrounding district.[87] While Matteo Visconti, who had been saddled on the city rather than chosen by it, was able to justify his decisions only as a delegate of imperial power, Azzone found a way to base his power in Milan itself, making the signory the historical endpoint of the commune.[88]

But first the difficult problem of a conflict with the papacy had to be resolved. At the time Azzone Visconti took power, John XXII had placed the city of Milan under interdict and charged Galeazzo's sons with heresy.[89] Azzone's moderation rapidly bore fruit. The pope recognized Azzone's imperial vicariate and lifted the interdict. The new lord of Milan was able to base his power on three separate pillars of authority: delegation from the emperor, the support of the Church, and recognition by the commune's institutions. The Visconti signory at that point took on the aspect of a territorial state. In a relatively fluid diplomatic environment, Azzone Visconti had himself proclaimed lord of Como, then Vercelli, and extended his dominion over Bergamo, Cremona, Novara, Pavia, Piacenza, Lodi – a total of 122 cities, *quasi-città*, and rural communities all told.[90] This policy of territorial unification sometimes took the form of brutal subjugation of subject cities.[91] When it came to imposing his authority on cities considered to be hostile – particularly Monza and Como – Azzone built citadels and fortresses that, in barricading the civic space, arrogantly proclaimed the abridgment of the commune's freedoms.[92]

In Milan, however, Azzone Visconti made a point of avoiding managing-by-intimidation as a style of city management. He tried instead, in his program of large-scale public works, to offer the commune continuity, transforming the civic ideal of the common good into princely magnificence, and depoliticizing the change to some extent by aestheticizing it.[93] A text embracing this transition, by which the city's civic past was reassigned in the present to glorifying the signory, was written by Galvano Fiamma in 1344, his *Opusculum de rebus gestis*.[94] Narrating the "deeds and actions of Azzone, Lucchino, and Giovanni Visconti from 1328 to 1342," the book can be read as a manifesto of government practice during the time of the signory. From this perspective, it was radically different from Bonvesin da la Riva's *De magnalibus*.[95] The city's greatness came from its measure, whereas the prince's came from immeasurable glory. This was emphatically proclaimed by the construction of the prince's palace.[96] This vast dwelling, no longer extant, was the residence of the lords of Milan until Filippo Maria Visconti decided in the 1420s to transfer the court and the city administration to the Castello di porta Giovia, a citadel in the city's northwest along the outer wall.[97] Azzone's palace astonished his contemporaries, being a complete departure from either bishops' residences or civic palaces.[98] In his description, Galvano Fiamma vividly conveys the feeling of "stupefied admiration" the building provoked, with its fountains and water basins, its menagerie, the luxury of its ornamentation, the boldness of its iconographic plan.[99]

Between his palace and the ancient Basilica of Santa Tecla, Azzone Visconti erected a statue of himself as a "hero on horseback,"[100] thereby joining a cavalcade of equestrian statues already existing in Milan to glorify the masters of the city, a custom that started in 1233 when the *podestà* Oldrado di Tresseno had an equestrian image of himself graven onto the facade of the public palace in the Broletto.[101] The campanile that Azzone built next to his palace was also famous for its clock that struck the hour "twenty-four times, to signal the twenty-four hours of day and night," which Fiamma described enthusiastically, and which is the earliest known mention of a public clock designed to mark the hours at even intervals.[102] Dominating all of Lombard art by its height and its influence, the campanile of San Gottardo emphatically expressed Azzone's political ambition. By crowning it with an angel bearing the Visconti banner, by placing it under the patronage of

Saint Gotthard (after the pass that provided a route across the Alps for trade from Lombardy), and by equipping it with his revolutionary clock, Azzone declared his threefold power: dominating the city, controlling the surrounding territory, and mastering time. The chapel of the Corte Ducale was dedicated to the Virgin Mary, attesting to the development of a Marian cult to accompany the Visconti turn toward princely power.[103] Galvano Fiamma describes the sumptuous setting, which shone with the blue of the paintings, the gold of the altar, the precious stones of the ritual furnishings, the porphyry of the liturgical plate – as though, captivated by the dazzling display of ornament, the friar would exhaust himself in the breathless enumeration of its riches.[104]

If magnificence reflects an ethic of spending, it was also for Fiamma a reversal of power signs by which the signor occupied Milan's sites of memory, deploying an architectural strategy of stamping his mark on any place where the city's civic past was liable to further his enterprise of glory. In other words, Azzone Visconti systematically took over the city's monuments and public facilities, which Bonvesin da la Riva had lauded for their grandeur and excellence, with the idea of protecting them from subversion by the signory. In fact, he had inadvertently picked them out as princely targets. They included the cathedral and the grand layout of the thoroughfares, fountains, and public squares, but also the walls of the commune, which Azzone Visconti undertook to raise and reinforce.[105] This renovation was accompanied by such a well-orchestrated propaganda campaign that a belief took hold that Azzone had built the wall from start to finish (or at least cast a persistent doubt on its date of construction).[106] This symbolic appropriation of the city's memory also included commissioning art on a grand scale. Starting in 1335, Azzone ordered the workshop of Giovanni di Balduccio to sculpt a group of five statues for each of the six gates in the perimeter wall – the Virgin

Mary, surrounded by four protective saints identifying the *sestiere* (quarter) to which the gate gave access.[107]

View of the postern of Sant'Ambrogio (*Patrick Boucheron*)

The choice of artist was itself highly significant.[108] Azzone Visconti had Giovanni di Balduccio create the sepulchre for his mother, Beatrice d'Este, in 1334 or 1335.[109] The work, no longer in existence, occupied the *capella della SS. Trinità* in the Church of San Francesco Grande in Milan.[110] It was no doubt inspired by the tomb of Guarnerio degli Antelminelli, who died in 1322 and was the grandson of Castruccio Castracani; Antelminelli's tomb was sculpted by Giovanni di Balduccio at San Francesco in Sarzana. By commissioning an artist whose work for the signor of Lucca had already made him famous, Azzone Visconti was laying claim to a more or less accepted political lineage. Present in Pisa when Castruccio Castracani was named imperial vicar on May 29, 1328, Azzone was burnishing his first political weapons in the entourage of the signor who, much later, would so intrigue Machiavelli.[111] But by commissioning Giovanni di Balduccio, Azzone Visconti was also trying to bring the stylistic vocabulary of Tuscan art to

Milan. While Giotto was painting, probably in fresco, an allegory of Earthly Glory in Azzone's palace during these same years, 1335 to 1336,[112] obliging Ambrogio Lorenzetti two years later to exert himself to the limits of his invention to counter the power and seduction of this signorial propaganda,[113] Azzone was turning the old encircling wall of the commune into a showcase for a new art.

Marble statue of Saint Ambrose from the *porta Ticinese*, workshop of Giovanni di Balduccio, c. 1335-38, Castello Sforzesco (*Civiche Raccolte d'Arte Antica*)

Breaking with the rigid gravitas of Lombard sculpture, these sculptural groups are remarkable for their Tuscan-inspired Gothic naturalism.[114] Surmounting the gates of the city, they refer to Milan's signor as the *populorum patres* (an epithet also used by Galvano Fiamma, Pietro Azario, and the other Lombard chroniclers), making Azzone Visconti the new *defensor civitatis*, endowed with the virtues of clemency, peace, and justice.[115] Note how Ambrose himself enters personally into the matter. His noble silhouette commands the *porta Orientale*, the *porta Vercellina*, and even the *porta Romana*, where the bas-reliefs convey the fraught memory of his eternally fought battles. He kneels, his face serene, to offer the Virgin a model of the city, which ten years earlier had put itself in Azzone's hands. Ambrose will stand at the gate from now on. Sleep well, the master is on duty.

A QUICK STRIKE: THE GHOST OF PARABIAGO
AND THE MILITARIZATION OF AMBROSE'S MEMORY

When the gates to a city are well guarded, it's often through another portal that ghosts come to haunt us – that of dreams. In his *De excessu fratris*, Ambrose recounts his surprise at dreaming of the warm presence of a brother who had died an untimely death, and had come back to console him.[116] But when Ambrose himself intruded on the dreams of others, men who worshipped or feared him, it was either to make threats or spur them to battle.[117] The supporters of Emperor Conrad II, as we've seen, were frightened by his apparition in 1037. Galvano Fiamma turned this political materialization into an epic tale, with Ambrose rolling his terrible eyes and brandishing his sword.[118] Three hundred years later, Ambrose, still armed, appeared directly on the battlefield. The date is February 21, 1339, we are at Parabiago, and Ambrose's ghost has come to drive off the enemies of freedom.

He is dressed all in white, carrying his scourge, and gives the victory to the signor of Milan, Lucchino Visconti.

But what victory was this, and to what effect? It might appear that the warrior-saint had interceded over very little, since the conflict was a local one between the lord of Milan and a junior branch of the Viscontis, led by Lodrisio Visconti. Yet on Lodrisio's side we find Vincenzo Suardi, of Bergamo, and Pietro Tornielli, known as Calcino, who was appointed imperial vicar by Emperor Louis IV in 1327, and also Mastino della Scala, lord of Verona. At a time when the Milanese communal institutions had passed the point of no return in transitioning to a signorial form of government, this coalition wore a distinctly Ghibelline aspect. In other words, as Guido Cariboni has persuasively shown, what had begun as merely a "family affair" had taken a more ominous turn.[119] And it was because its import went well beyond an internal conflict between Milanese factions that the battle's echo resounded outside the circle of Lombard chroniclers. Galvano Fiamma, Bonincontro Morigia, and Pietro Azario[120] told the tale, but so too did Giovanni Villani of Florence and the writer known as Anonimo Romano.[121]

Of all the sources, only two relate Ambrose's miraculous intervention on the field of battle, and once again Galvano Fiamma has to be considered the inventor of the episode, using Ambrose's memory to combine different historical time frames.[122] The archaeological horizon of Fiamma's *Cronica extravagans de antiquitatibus civitatis Mediolani* is the Ambrosian past,[123] an era that reappears in his *Chronica archiepiscoporum* of 1339, in the course of establishing the political and spiritual continuity of the bishops, and then the archbishops, of Milan.[124] Ambrose's conflict with the Arians is repeatedly brought up and reenacted in varying political contexts. For example, it is compared to the conflict between the Guelphs and the Ghibellines in the Braidense

Library's unpublished *Chronica Galvagnana* (composed 1337 to 1338)[125] and in certain passages (not published in the Ceruti edition) of the *Chronicon maius*.[126]

Unlike the other chroniclers, Fiamma does not attribute the victory at Parabiago to the corruption of the enemy troops, but instead insists on the German nationality of Lodrisio Visconti's mercenaries and a conspiracy among them to make Lombardy a German colony. To prevent this, Ambrose appeared visibly (*visibiliter*) on the battlefield, robed in white, scourge in hand, and drove back the enemy as they were on the point of claiming victory.[127] Ambrose's people mobilized because their country was in danger – hence the insistence on Lombard patriotism, which obviously reuses the theme of Ambrose's confrontations with the emperor, reinterpreted to fit the battles that the new Ambroses of the twelfth century (Galdino della Sala chief among them) were waging against the empire. Theodosius assumes the features of Emperor Frederick I, and the ghost of the past intrudes into the present, but it is a distant and long-buried past, unaffected by the recent past.

That this ghost should serve the interests of the signorial power was no surprise. For Fiamma, dynastic loyalty was henceforth inseparably linked to civic conscience. In a passage from *De rebus gestis ab Azone*, he develops the theme of the "love of the Milanese people for their lord," which transcends all other divisions – Guelphs versus Ghibellines, the poor versus the *magnati*, the small versus the great.[128] This unanimous love was clearly founded on a common past and polarized by the sites that concentrate collective memory. Archbishop Giovanni Visconti placed the first stone of the votive church of Sant'Ambrogio della Vittoria, which welcomed annual civic processions.[129] The calendar gained a new event related to Ambrose, a commemorative feast day (February 21), which joined the existing celebrations of the saint's baptism (November 30), his ordination (December 7), and his death (April 5). Yet looking more closely, this memorative undertaking must have been fiercely negotiated. It was the commune, not the Visconti family, that led the initiative to found the "civic temple" that Sant'Ambrogio della Vittoria represents. The *narratio* of the deed notarized on January 8, 1350, stipulates the commune's role in giving the church, which was built with the commune's money, on land belonging to the commune. And the commune reserved the right of *ius patronatus* over it. There is no mention in the deed's preamble of Ambrose's miraculous appearance on the battlefield, and the victory is credited to *dominum et commune Mediolani*.[130]

Nonetheless, in developing a coherent policy of commemorating the Battle of Parabiago, the Viscontis managed to co-opt Ambrose's memory by militarizing it. This was far from an innovation. We've seen how, since the Pataria, Ambrose had become an increasingly explicit resource for collective mobilizations, routinely drafted to strengthen social memberships, fashion political identities, and arm ideological clashes. Ambrose was a militant saint, and those who fought in his memory rallied eagerly to his energy as a combatant whose feats of arms – against heretics and Jews, against the forces of the emperor, and against the enemies of the *libertas* of Church and commune – were constantly retold. Brandishing his whip over his adversaries, Ambrose threatens, punishes, and fights. He is very much the *Sanctissimi Christi confessoris et atletae Ambrosii* referred to in a 1389 decree by Gian Galeazzo Visconti, who was in fact repeating an expression penned by Ambrose himself, in his *De Iacob et vita beata* (1.8.36), when he described the bishop fighting against the heretics "like an athlete full of vigor, who returns blow for blow."[131]

In making military use of the warrior-saint, the signors of Milan were taking part in one of the commune's ongoing traditions. Let's not forget that Ambrose's effigy was painted on the banner that crackled in the wind when the Milanese troops gathered on the battlefield behind their *carroccio*, and it was with Ambrose's shouted name that the priests gave the soldiers courage before an attack.[132] Sometimes even, on great occasions, the saint's relics were displayed, as was the famous "arm of Saint Ambrose" that accompanied the Lombard horsemen on the First Crusade.[133] In 1320, according to the notary and chronicler Pietro Azario, *Ambrogio!* was still the war cry used by the Milanese cavalry.[134] At this point, the signorial appropriation of Ambrose's memory started to transform the iconographic norms that governed his likeness. Although he had long been depicted, notably in the mosaic of San Vittore in Ciel d'Oro and in the polychrome tondo that caught Petrarch's eye, "in the Roman style," as a man in the prime of life with short hair and a close beard, Ambrose had gradually acquired the gravitas and the bushier beard of the Fathers of the Church in medieval representations.[135]

But by making him younger and cutting his beard shorter, the fourteenth century imparted a martial aspect to Ambrosian iconography. Three years after the Battle of Parabiago, in 1342, Archbishop Giovanni Visconti commissioned the sculptor Giovanni di Balduccio to make a funeral monument for the recently deceased Azzone Visconti (see color plate 6).[136] In competition with his brother Lucchino to rule Milan, Giovanni Visconti had every interest in presenting himself as his uncle's worthy successor, copying his policies in municipal management and patronage. This would explain why he paid for the funeral monument, sculpted by Giovanni di Balduccio and his workshop between 1342 and 1346, with his own funds.[137] On Azzone's mausoleum in the Chapel of San Gottardo in Corte, Ambrose's features are more hollowed out and his glance is severe: he is depicted as a war chief on the day following a victory, receiving tribute from the cities he defeated. This new iconography is entirely signorial in that it expresses the personal and authoritative turn that the exercise of power has taken and the territorial expansion it pursued.[138]

Giovanni di Balduccio, Azzone Visconti's mausoleum (detail), 1342–46, Milan, Church of San Gottardo in Corte (© *Studio fotografico Perotti*)

But let's look more closely at the figures surrounding these sculpted scenes on the central and lateral faces of Azzone Visconti's sarcophagus. The city's patron saint is flanked by two smaller male figures, who sit at his feet. On his right is a richly dressed man who carries a purse at his side and grasps with both hands the shaft of the vexillum (flag) also being held by Ambrose. The other figure, more martial looking, carries a globe in his left hand. The object in his right hand, which also continues into the saint's left hand, has disappeared. No doubt a staff or a sword, it was certainly an insignia of rule. Should we read into these two figures an allegory of the commune and Milan, as Peter Seiler has suggested,[139] or rather, as in Evelyn Welch's view, an allegory of the commune and the empire?[140] Closely flanking the imposing figure of the bishop protector, the two smaller men would represent the two pillars supporting the authority of Milan's signor: the popular acclamation of the commune's council (the flag-bearing Milanese citizen on the saint's right) and the imperial vicarate (the emperor or his representative on the saint's left).

I've advanced another hypothesis elsewhere, which develops or corrects those cited above.[141] It seems entirely likely that the richly dressed figure holding the banner of Saint Ambrose represents the civic values of the commune. Everything about his aspect, garb, and iconographic features would seem to confirm this identification. It is more difficult, on the other hand, to confirm the "imperial" character of the second figure, despite his globe and what seems to be his sword. The treatment of the face, the bodily attitude, and the clothes don't conform to the canons of representation for the emperor in Italian art of the trecento. Might it not then represent a social group within Milanese society that saw signorial power as originating with the emperor? In his *Chronicon maius*, Galvano Fiamma held that the partition of Milanese society into the *popolo* and the *militia* coincided with the opposition of the Guelphs and the Ghibellines. The *pars nobilium* remained irreducibly on the side of the imperial party, while the *pars populi* "has always been Guelph, which is to say allied to the Church." In his comments on this passage, Jean-Claude Maire Vigueur has shown that the historians of the medieval commune societies needed to overcome their reluctance toward this seemingly too-simple scheme and admit that, structurally, there existed a cultural rift in the society of the communes: on the one hand, a popular identity linked to the party of the Church, and on the other a *militia* whose values and social practices were upheld by imperial authority.[142] This would explain the imperial globe held by the figure on Ambrose's left. The saint would thus be flanked by two persons embodying not the commune and the empire but the two pillars of Milanese political society, the *popolo* and the *militia*. The tenting held by the angels on either side of the patron saint unites and envelops the two seemingly antagonistic figures, who are joined in civic concord, and who also represent the two foundations of the lord of Milan's authority: the commune and the party of the Church on one hand, and loyalty to the empire on the other. As in 1258, Ambrose here summons conflict and its resolution.

The figures streaming toward the group around Ambrose are the bearers of another political message, which is easier to decipher. Historians have long recognized them to be representations of subject cities under Milan's rule (or their urban elites, which would be consistent with the preceding hypothesis). They arrive, kneeling, to declare allegiance to the patron saint of the ruling city, themselves supported by their patron saints, who stand behind them, hands on their shoulders. A heraldic analysis of the figures' attributes (on their shields and clothing) provides the identity of the subject cities and their saints.[143] The scene clearly alludes to the civic processions that the lords of Milan required of the cities under their power: their representatives were obliged to bring regular and solemn offerings to the sanctuaries belonging to Milan.[144] What is shown here, therefore, is signorial domination over a territory. The selection of cities represented displays the geographic extent of this domination, from Como to Bobbio, and from Brescia to Asti. All of the towns are in the second or third rank in the demographic hierarchy of the Lombard urban network, in which Milan plays a preeminent and outsized role.[145]

The *insignorimento* of Ambrose's memory turned the militant saint into a military saint, who could be depicted as unmistakably aggressive.[146] The culmination of this development was the equestrian representation of Ambrose, an iconographic invention that seems to have no precedent before the second half of the fourteenth century.[147] Coins provide a useful benchmark here. Starting in the thirteenth century, the gold *grosso ambrosino* and the silver *ambrosino* were systematically minted with an image of the city's patron saint on the reverse, giving his blessing, sometimes just from the bust up but usually seated in his cathedra.[148] The obverse generally featured the saints Gervasius and Protasius. Beginning with the coins minted by Galeazzo and Bernabò Visconti (1354 to 1378), Ambrose is shown carrying his whip, but he continues to bless with his right hand. Everything changed with Galeazzo Maria Sforza (1466 to 1476): now the reverse of the eight-sou silver *grosso* features a furious Ambrose on horseback, brandishing his whip, and trampling his enemies underfoot—while a bust of the duke appears on the coin's obverse.[149]

On February 15, 1494, the Milanese printer Filippo Mantegazza published an anonymous short work on Ambrose's miracles at the Battle of Parabiago.[150] The victory-bringing bishop was not only dressed all in white but also, for the first time, riding an equally immaculate charger.[151] That is how he was depicted

Adolfo Wildt, model of bronze statue of Saint Ambrose for the Tempio della
Vittoria di Milano (1924), main courtyard of the Università di Stato, Milan
(*Ospedale Maggiore, Milan, Photo © Mauro Ranzani/Bridgeman Images*)

by the Master of the Sforzesca Altarpiece, on an impressive small panel, preserved today in the Petit-Palais Museum in Avignon, which is generally assigned to the same period, around 1495 (see color plate 17). This image belongs to the great series of equestrian depictions of the masters of Milan, which includes the *gran cavallo* drawn by Leonardo da Vinci for Francesco Sforza's memorial: Ambrose is in the vanguard of the cohort of mounted heroes that form, in this Italy of the quattrocento, a princely cavalcade.[152]

The trend would continue without slackening: Archbishop Carlo Borromeo, styled as the *alter Ambrosius*, expressed his indignation at the ferocity the Milanese gave images of the good pastor.[153] This did not keep the equestrian depictions of Ambrose from evolving, expressing as they did the aspirations of a triumphant Counter-Reformation. Other ghosts of Ambrose will no doubt continue to haunt Milan for a long time, and hardly in an amiable way—on the Piazza del Duomo, for instance, where Arturo Martini's Mussolini-era bas-reliefs decorate the *portici Meridionali* with a disquieting Battle of Parabiago, the identity of whose new Arians one hesitates to guess; and where Adolfo Wildt's sculpture from the same era offers a large and threatening Ambrose.[154] Ambrose's return? If he has returned as a raging horseman, beginning in the second half of the fifteenth century, it's because in the meantime a decisive rupture occurred.

Planche 28

COVPE TRANSVERSALE SVR ABCD
ELEVATION DE LA COVPOLE

S'AMBROISE DE MILAN

1. Cross section of the chancel of the Basilica of Sant'Ambrogio
(*Fernand de Dartein,* Étude sur l'architecture lombarde et sur les origines
de l'architecture romano-byzantine [*Paris: Dunod, 1865–82, plate 28*])

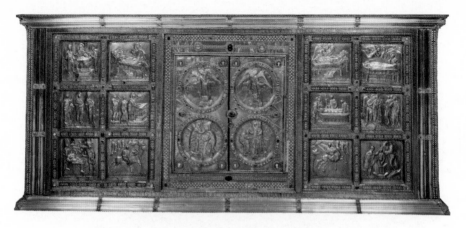

2. Saint Ambrose's golden altar, rear side, Basilica of Sant'Ambrogio
(© *A. Rizzi /De Agostini Picture Library/Bridgeman Images*)

3. Saint Ambrose's golden altar, rear side (detail), the *fenestella confessionis*,
Basilica of Sant'Ambrogio (*Luisa Ricciarini/Bridgeman Images*)

I TRE SEPOLCRI SCOPERTI NELL'ANNO 1864

4. The sepulchres of Ambrose, Gervasius, and Protasius below the golden altar, as reported after the 1864 excavations, *Cenni storici sulla sepoltura ed invenzione dei corpi dei santi Ambrogio vescovo e dottore, Gervaso e Protaso martiri, nella basilica Ambrosiana di Milano* (Milan: 1873)

5. View of the chancel of
the Basilica of Sant'Ambrogio
(© *Mauro Ranzani/Bridgeman Images*)

6. Giovanni di Balduccio, mausoleum
of Azzone Visconti, 1342–44,
Church of San Gottardo in Corte,
Milan (© *Luca Volpi*)

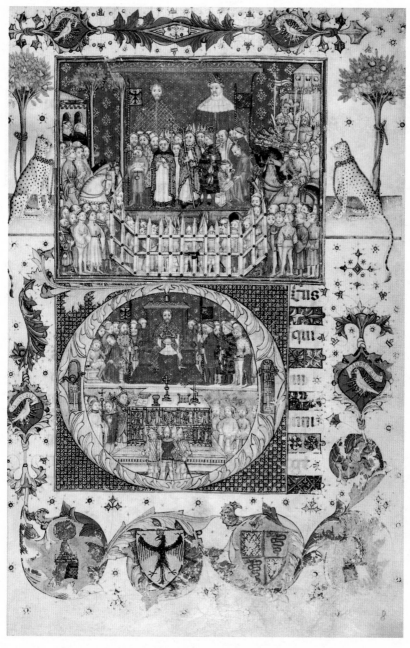

7. Missal depicting the coronation of Gian Galeazzo Visconti, 1395,
Biblioteca Capitolare di Sant'Ambrogio, M6, folio 8 recto
(© *Milano, Basilica di S. Ambrogio, Archivio Capitolare di S. Ambrogio*)

8. *Porta Romana*, central pillar, left face, *The Return of the Milanese People*, Castello Sforzesco, Milan (*De Agostini Picture Library/G. Cigolini/Bridgeman Images*)

9. *Porta Romana*, central pillar, right face, *The Return of the Soldiers*, Castello Sforzesco (*De Agostini Picture Library/G. Cigolini/Bridgeman Images*)

10. *Porta Romana*, southeast pillar, *The Expulsion of the Arians*, Castello Sforzesco (*De Agostini Picture Library/G. Cigolini/Bridgeman Images*)

11. *Porta Romana*, southeast pillar, *The Expulsion of the Arians* (detail),
Ambrose and his whip, Castello Sforzesco
(*De Agostini Picture Library/G. Cigolini/Bridgeman Images*)

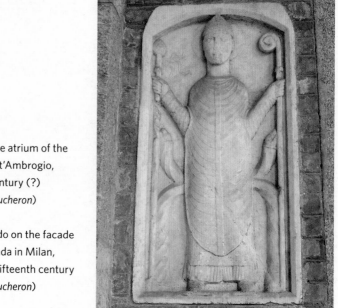

12. Bas-relief in the atrium of the
Basilica of Sant'Ambrogio,
eleventh century (?)
(*Patrick Boucheron*)

13. Terra-cotta tondo on the facade
of the Ca' Granda in Milan,
second half of the fifteenth century
(*Patrick Boucheron*)

14. Master of the *Vitae Imperatorum*,
Saint Ambrose in His Chamber,
c. 1430, watercolor on parchment,
Bologna, Museo Civico Medievale
(© *Istituzione Bologna Musei*)

15. *Cantus ambrosiani, In ordinatione
S. Ambrosii. In Vigilis ad Vesper*, 1386,
Milan, Biblioteca Capitolare di
Sant'Ambrogio, M 24, folio 20 verso
(*Patrick Boucheron*)

16. Pala Sforzesca (Sforzesca Altarpiece), c. 1496–97,
Milan, Pinacoteca di Brera (*Luisa Ricciarini/Bridgeman Images*)

17. Master of the Pala Altarpiece, *Saint Ambrose at the Battle of Parabiago*, c. 1495, Avignon, Petit Palais Museum (*Bridgeman Images*)

18. Bernardo Zenale and Bernardino Butinone, frescoes in the Grifi Chapel,
right wall (detail), 1489–93, Milan, Church of San Pietro in Gessate
(© Mauro Ranzani/Bridgeman Images)

19. Vincenzo Foppa, frescoes in the Portinari Chapel, southwest pendentive, 1462–67, Milan, Basilica of Sant'Eustorgio (*Bridgeman Images*)

20. Giovanni Ambrogio Figino, *Archbishop Ambrose Defeats the Arians*, 1590, Milan, Basilica of Sant'Eustorgio (*Private collection*)

21. Camillo Procaccini, *Ambrose Stops Theodosius from Entering the Basilica,*
1745, sala San Satiro, Basilica of Sant'Ambrogio
(© *Milano, Basilica di S. Ambrogio, Archivio Capitolare di S. Ambrogio*)

22. Saint Ambrose, mosaic in San Vittore
in Ciel d'Oro, fifth century
(*Luisa Ricciarini/Bridgeman Images*)

TWELVE

The Breach

(1447–50)

"The people entered the sanctuary. They lifted the veil that must always cover all that can be said and all that can be believed about the rights of the people and the rights of kings, which are never in greater harmony than when there is silence."[1] Revolutionaries have always been fascinated by this comment by Cardinal De Retz. Even though they know that in reality he was referring to the aristocratic uprising of the First Fronde,[2] in seventeenth-century France, they detect a fleeting and revelatory glimpse into the vacuity of power, whose mysteries are merely hidden misunderstandings.[3] Whence the great silence, sometimes broken by the clamoring of voices. And then the veil is rent, or a breach formed – "breach" in the sense used in the heat of May 1968 by Edgar Morin, Claude Lefort, and Cornelius Castoriadis to describe that eruption amid the bubbling up of a new political speech that cracked the ancient order, rendering obsolete its discourse, dried out as a dead language.[4] A breach can be minuscule. But from the second it fractures and makes brittle something believed to be intangible and firmly entrenched, it never entirely closes.[5] For no power or authority can make us unsee what we make out in the breach. Once it is open, another history rushes out, forcing its way into the narrative, which makes any return to the normal course of things impossible.

THE STATE IS A MORTAL MAN, OR

ADVENTURES IN LIBERTY

This is that history. It is the history of a man who dies. On the night of August 13, 1447, Duke Filippo Maria Visconti, the feared and weakened prince, shut away in his citadel like a prisoner of his own power, died without leaving an heir. The city's notables then decided to do without a prince. They were the Lampugnanis, the Bossis, the Cottas, the Morones, the Trivulzios, and all who counted among the duke's closest counselors. They spoke of Cicero, Livy, the Roman Republic. They warmed and intoxicated themselves at the embers of these great names. In reality, and more prosaically, they only had a single model in mind: the oligarchic republic of Venice, which had managed to preserve its social system with extraordinary stability.[6] On August 14, in the name of *libertas*, the people invaded the Broletto, the former civic palace that the duke had abandoned to hide away in the citadel of the *porta Giovia*. This was of course the staging of a communal renaissance. And in fact the communal organization had never been entirely dissolved in the signorial state, whose institutional structure was still essentially a composite and contractual one.[7] Within that state, communal institutions had been covered up and neutralized by the prince's councils (justice council, privy council, et cetera), which, in the absence of a prince, no longer had a reason to exist. In 1448, communal institutions were quite simply unveiled: twenty-four Capitanei et Defensores Libertatis

(Captains and Defenders of Liberty) were elected; a large council of 900 members, elected on August 17, met on the 18th.

The conspirators of 1447 had no intention of establishing a new regime. They aspired only to re-create the Communitas Libertatis Mediolani, a political abstraction that evoked the ancient days of communal autonomy – and it is of course through this attempt to go backwards that they were truly revolutionaries. For it would be false to say that the commune was embedded in an ancient past: rather it had formed the *communitas* once and for all, which was an ordering of the public sphere that could always be reactivated.[8] This was, perhaps, one of the essential political motors of the history of the quattrocento: though the exercise of power during this period conformed, nearly everywhere in Italy, to a style of government that can be easily qualified as monarchical (in the sense that the monarchy designates the power of a single individual, royalty being just one of its particular modes), the institutional settings in which it developed had no resources for ideological legitimization other than the republican forms inherited from the commune.[9] Signorial domination may have neutralized the commune's political potential but it could not erase its traces, always susceptible to redeployment in a present day reconciled with its history.[10]

There is undoubtedly no better expression of this than the way in which the leaders of 1447 staged the symbolic destruction of the Castello di porta Giovia, the reviled citadel whose stones were carried to the center of town, to be reused at the building site of the Duomo of Milan: on August 30,[11] a decree by the Captains and Defenders of Liberty, anxious to avoid further disruption after the people had broken into the castle and begun to pillage it, organized its destruction in the public interest, with a methodical and solemn procession in which the materials torn from the citadel were used to regenerate the cathedral, the mother of Milan's public spaces.[12] The intention was to restore to Milan's civic history the continuity visibly suggested by the places themselves, and which the princes had transgressed by voluntarily distancing themselves from the urban center of political legitimacy.[13] Here again, the "real" returned to the same place and history repaired itself.

What happened? We left the Viscontis, in the last chapter, as they were patiently infiltrating the high ground of Milan's communal past. The Corte Ducale where they were residing was far from the cathedral, as well as from the Broletto, the civic square, whose general framework of monuments was unchanged after 1228.[14] However Milan's signors occupied this public space as well – albeit symbolically, augmenting it with their presence in the form of monuments: Matteo Visconti's commissioning of the Loggia degli Osii in 1316, Azzone's portico in 1336, the granting of a section of the palace to the notarial college by Gian Galeazzo Visconti in 1399, followed by the gifting of other buildings to the Scuole by his son Giovanni Maria in 1406, et cetera.[15] As a result, the Broletto, a space for political deliberation, became the site of dynastic celebration, increasingly depoliticized as it swelled with monuments. In the fifteenth century, the Corte Ducale gradually lost its function as the main Visconti residence, due to fires (in 1427 and 1433), space lost to the cathedral building site, and in particular, desertion by princes. Filippo Maria Visconti was the first to leave the Corte Ducale for the Castello di porta Giovia. Based on the model of the signorial *rocca*, the citadel straddled the low wall to the northwest of the city, presenting it with a fortified facade viewed by citizens as a threat and an offense.[16]

No wonder – it had been constructed during the civil war that pitted, after 1355, Bernabò Visconti against Galeazzo II Visconti, the two enemy brothers fighting for power in Milan. And so, for the Milanese people, the Castello di porta Giovia was a monument of tyranny.[17] That a weak prince fled the city center to the citadel, fearful of a popular uprising or aristocratic plot, was harped upon by Milan's historiographical tradition, clearly expressing the political impact of an act that had injured the city's communal memory. In his *Vita Philippi Mariae*, the humanist Pier Candido Decembrio described, in the Suetonian style, and with near-clinical precision, the night terrors that beset the prince, tyrannized by the fear he provoked. He had seen his brother Giovanni Maria Visconti die on May 16, 1412, stabbed by conspirators as he was descending the steps of the San Gottardo church in Corte. This is what convinced the duke, they said, to leave the tumultuous heart of Milan. Nonetheless, the fear of assassination did not leave him: he demanded that birds of prey fly through the castle at night to warn him of the slightest movement, but then their penetrating eyes began to terrorize him, spied upon as he was by his own surveillance system.[18] In the political imagination of the Milanese people, the Castello di porta Giovia became the fearful fortress of a feared prince, which Machiavelli would later say displayed too much brutal arrogance to not reveal the weakness of princes.[19] Indeed, as Claude Lefort notes, "the imaginary force materialized in the fortress signals the absence of the Subject—not only the exclusion of the people from power, but the destitution of the prince beneath the apparatus of coercion."[20]

All this shattered in an instant on the night of August 13, 1447. The dying man had no heir. In power since 1412, he was the third duke of Milan, after his brother Giovanni Maria Visconti, who had reigned from 1402 to 1412, succeeding his father Gian Galeazzo Visconti, signor of Milan since 1385. Gian Galeazzo Visconti, the founder of the cathedral, was inarguably the family's most remarkable figure. On September 5, 1395, in the Basilica of Sant'Ambrogio, he had been handed, by Emperor Wenceslas's representative, the insignia that elevated the signorial state to the rank of duchy. An exceptional manuscript documents this apotheosis, which was also an Ambrosian triumph (see color plate 7).[21] Sumptuously illuminated (it notably includes several depictions of Ambrose as well as a very famous representation of the golden altar of the Basilica of Sant'Ambrogio),[22] it records the entire liturgy of the Mass held for Gian Galeazzo Visconti's coronation, and begins with the celebration of the victory of Parabiago[23] and a genealogy of the Visconti family, having them descend from Trojan heroes and evoking the mythical origins of their heraldry – the *guivre*, an undulating serpent spitting out a child.[24]

Confronted with this Milanese power, Florentine humanists sharpened their pens. It was a question of not only standing up to the expansionist ambitions of the duchy of Milan, at the time Italy's greatest territorial power, but also of waging an ideological war against the capital of tyranny.[25] In their tour de force of the early fifteenth century, the Florentines succeeded in universalizing the *florentina libertas* as an "Italian liberty" vital to all and in which the republican ideal of government played an essential role – this is what historians would call, though much later, civic humanism, themselves struggling to resist the seductiveness of this intellectual categorization that claimed to be nothing less than the sole path to liberty.[26] The Florentine merchant and historian Goro Dati described the military conflicts between Florence and Milan as "the history of the long and great war that occurred in Italy in our time between the tyrant of Lombardy, the duke of Milan, and the magnificent Commune of Florence."[27] He saw an essential difference, very reassuring in his eyes, between the commune and the tyrant: "the Commune cannot die [whereas] the duke was only one mortal man whose state would die with him."[28]

Goro Dati was not wrong. On the night of August 13, 1447, a man died, but more importantly, the true weakness of his power was revealed to all. The ducal state was a mortal man. For the past decade or so, Milanese historiography has been edging away from its single-minded fascination with the Visconti state, insisting on its composite, heterogeneous, and discontinuous nature.[29] Factional jockeying, autonomous rural communities, multiple places of power, diverse political languages: none of this disappeared in the reign of princes. Milan's leaders could not simply claim the mantle of Ambrosian greatness to detach themselves from the urban – meaning fundamentally polycentric – origins of power.[30] On the contrary, that urban character repeatedly reasserted itself, forcing the signors to forever renegotiate the bonds of fidelity and obedience that they maintained with their dependents, which was particularly true in the era of Filippo Maria Visconti.[31] It was this underlying political life that brutally erupted in 1447, revealing in one instant the vacuity of grand ideological constructions.

It is clear why the princely state, once it reestablished itself in 1450, was quick to impose a *damnatio memoriae* on the 1447–50 interlude, notably through a document-handling policy aimed at both eliminating archival traces of the Ambrosian Republic[32] and re-creating diplomatic continuity in the chancery's activities,[33] precisely to seal the breach. But it is equally clear why these policies of deliberate forgetting were doomed to failure.[34] From the historiographical perspective as well, the *damnatio memoriae* on the *triennio* of communal resurgence was in force for a long time, but it could not prevent feverish rediscoveries of this period. In Count Pietro Verri's *Storia di Milano* (1783), the communal regime was still viewed with suspicion: he paints it as a weak government, run by "six bad sovereigns" who had no legitimacy.[35] It was only during the Risorgimento that the memory of the Ambrosian Republic became a critical question, in the writings, for example, of the Lombard journalist Aurelio Bianchi Giovini (1799–1862), who translated Pierre-Antoine Daru's *History of the Republic of Venice* and whose abundant historical work was strongly anticlerical. In reaction to this historiography grandiosely celebrating Milan's liberation from the yoke of tyranny,[36] the positivist historians of the twentieth century may have overly minimized its importance.[37] Finally enlightened in regards to the History adroitly wielded by the humanists and those who placed their faith in them, these historians turned to the reality of balances of power and domination: prosopographical analyses now show for example a large continuity in political personnel on both sides of this republican episode.[38] That said, recent studies, in particular one by Marina Spinelli,[39] building on Lauro Martine's ideas,[40] have showed how this political sequence was patterned by an authentically revolutionary tempo. By finding that rhythm, we can work toward repoliticizing this intense moment in Milan's history.

IL TEMPO DE LA SANCTA LIBERTÀ: THE TIME OF RITES AND THE RHYTHM OF POLITICS

The Capitanei et Defensores Libertatis, who governed the political community of Milan from 1447 to 1450, claimed nothing more, as mentioned, than to be carrying on the communal history of the Communitas Libertatis Mediolani. Nor did they deem it necessary to qualify the regime they had established, other than by a few circumlocutions, the most common of which was "the time of sacred liberty." It was the historiography of the Risorgimento that baptized it as the Repubblica Ambrosiana, to reflect the intensity of Ambrosian commemoration during this period. This episode might appear unremarkable: at the time, all of the Milanese duchy's subject city-states were reclaiming their liberty by exalting their communal past, namely by evoking the memory of their patron saints. Pavia established the Repubblica di San Siro, and Como lined up beneath the banner of Sant'Abondio (Abundius, a fifth-century bishop whose body rests in the basilica):[41] each city behind its *defensor civitatis*, one could almost see the sculpted figures on Azzone Visconti's funerary monument coming to life and leaving their tombs. This celestial protection, reassuring and predictable, would appear to support historians' vision of civic religion as a unifying collective memory: in the Middle Ages – this is true during both the quattrocento and the era of Hincmar of Reims – people failed by their princes turned to saints.

Since the 1980s, medievalist historians have indeed gotten into the habit of referring to civic religion as "the appropriation of values inherent to religious life by urban authorities for the purposes of legitimization, celebration and public well-being."[42] Civic religion, both as a historical phenomenon and a historiographical object, therefore sprouts from political transformation – of the balance of ecclesiastical and civil powers, of the exercise of urban government, but also (and perhaps especially) of the very conception that the urban elite have of governmentality: "Everything indicates that divine worship, owing to the very repercussions that it could have on the fate of the city-state, had ended up considered like a public service as vital as the organization of food supplies or defense."[43] There is no doubt that such a shift concerned Italian cities in particular, and Milan first and foremost. And yet I have avoided using the historiographical concept of civic religion up until now, namely because, as its primary proponent André Vauchez admits, it concerns the communal worship of local saints more than it does the "largest cities in Italy," which remained faithful to their traditional patrons: "In the fourteenth century, Milan is still the city of Saint Ambrose, and Venice identifies more than ever with Saint Mark, if not his lion."[44] A historian of sainthood would admit here that civic religion in the thirteenth century, by multiplying intercessors and contributing to the fragmentation of cults, broke the continuity with saintly patronage of classical Roman origin in communal Italy. That was certainly not the case in Milan, where the thread, so thin that it was always on the verge of breaking, remained taut between the past and the present.

But there is another reason I have avoided this concept: the notion of civic religion borrows from the history of Greco-Roman antiquity, notably the link between the city-state and political modes of the organization of worship. Whether we explicitly describe it in Weberian terms as *Sakralgemeinschaft* or settle for the vaguer term *coscienza civica*, we still risk, if we don't pay enough attention, transferring something else along with the notion of civic religion – a utopian Athens, cozily enveloped by a consensual and pacifying cult, like the chorus leader in Aristophanes's *The Frogs* who proclaims civic unanimity in divine worship.[45] When it comes to the late Middle Ages, as we well know, this idealized conception of urban harmony impedes understanding of the future of regional states, and in particular their relationship to religious aspirations for *reformatio;*[46] this conception similarly fails to take into account disputing collective memories that used memorial divergences as arguments to mobilize people for social and political battles.[47]

So then was it to depoliticize the political events underway that the Captains and Defenders of Liberty raised the calming (and supposedly universally agreed upon) figure of Ambrose in Milan in 1447 and particularly in 1448? While such a use of the past may echo certain contemporary aspirations, it in no way corresponds to the medieval context.[48] The idea I would like to defend here is that, on the contrary, recourse to Ambrose's memory served, during this period, to express a radicalization of political aspirations, owing precisely to the ideological connotations discreetly associated with him and with which the historian can only be familiar as a result of this brusque insertion. And so we have political events disrupting religion's tranquil course, creating a breach through which the tensions and conflicts driving the jockeying over Ambrose's memory can be understood. In other words, the rhythm of politics abruptly interrupted the cadence of rituality, which Michel Leiris, a poet and anthropologist (and the author *Phantom Africa*), described as "Rite: strict mimic that rhythms, rules, and ratifies."[49]

With this hypothesis in mind, let's briefly review the chronology of this republic, to better understand how the revival of Ambrose's memory fell into the tempo of these years. In 1448, as we saw, the old nobility and the uppermost fringe of the urban elite were still running the government, which nonetheless developed an ambitious political program: fiscal reform, notably through the establishment of a public debt (the Banco di Sant'Ambrogio),[50] the construction of a general hospital,[51] and the creation of a *studium* meant to shape the republican mindsets of young, freedom-loving patricians. Incidentally, the decree of September 2, 1448, described the *studium* as a restoration, as that university had already existed "in the days of Saint Ambrose, our protector."[52] This first republic was destabilized by war, waged against Milan by Italy's united powers.[53] The turning point came in October 1448: the republic's condottiere, Francesco Sforza, turned traitor for Venice (the Treaty of Rivoltella), which prompted the fall of the council on November 1.[54] Many among Milan's richest notables distanced themselves from the republic and attempted to negotiate with Sforza. Then the government began to radicalize. After elections on January 1, 1449, the social makeup of the new regime changed: men of the law (with the exception of one notary, Giovanni da Appiano) were replaced with artisans (a butcher, a baker, et cetera).[55] The Terror began in February: before the end of May, the jurist Giorgio Lampugnani was decapitated and more than two hundred citizens, accused of being Ghibellines, were sentenced to death and their belongings seized. They included members of the Visconti (the younger branch), Crivelli, Borromei, Dal Verme, Stampa, and Litta families: Milan's grand nobility was under threat. New elections in July: Ghibelline nobles prevailed. Was this Thermidor? No, because a popular riot, on August 31, executed one of the new Captains and Defenders of Liberty. The story ends, classically, with the victory of a jackbooted Caesar, Francesco Sforza, called upon by the noblemen Gasparo da Vimercate and Pietro Cotta to besiege Milan, and who finally took control of the city on February 25, 1450.[56]

During this second phase of the Ambrosian Republic, which we can easily qualify as popular, an intense memorative enterprise developed.[57] This manifested as a ritualized frenzy: not a week went by without processions, advancing behind the new *carroccio della libertà* on which was painted, in November 1448, an imposing effigy of Ambrose surrounded by feminine allegories of virtue.[58] We only know this banner from a seventeenth-century copy, but its conception and fabrication are documented in the archives of the *fabbrica* of the Milan Cathedral.[59] The engineers and painters – notably Giovanni da Vaprio – working on the cathedral building site were mobilized, and ex-*fabbrica* advisors (like the lawyer Antonio Salvatico) and humanists were asked to develop its iconography. Among the latter, we find, once again, Pier Candido Decembrio, at the time very engaged in the political struggle. The renaissance of the *carroccio* of the heroic era of the Lombard commune clearly reflects a humanist view of history, while simultaneously acting as an efficient medium for political communication.

Political messaging also made use of the liturgical calendar of Milan's civic holidays, as can be reconstructed beginning in 1396.[60] At that time, urban statutes (in all likelihood borrowing, in this case, from earlier provisions, and notably those in 1351 modifying the statutes of 1330) noted that all, "regardless of status and circumstance," and under threat of fines, had to participate in the holidays organized in honor of the city's patron saint Ambrose – meaning the anniversary of his ordination on December 7 and the commemoration of Sant'Ambrogio della Vittoria on February 21 – and financially contribute to their organization.[61] Beginning at the city's civic center, the Broletto, the civic procession of December 7 headed toward the Basilica of Sant'Ambrogio, where it would hear Mass. It was led by representatives of communal institutions (the Vicario and the Dodici di Provvisione), followed by the councils and the *podestà*; then came the different trades in orderly fashion, each behind its banner, solemnly carrying its offerings.[62] The essential point here is that, in the signorial state, celebrations of Ambrose remained a civic festival exclusively inspired by and organized like the commune, its role being precisely to manifest this form of political continuity emphasized by the Viscontis. However, those rulers had been working, both generally speaking and particularly in regard to the December 7 holiday, toward a *ridimensionamento* of the role of the arts in civic celebrations.[63]

This is undoubtedly where we can most clearly discern the shift during the revolutionary years of 1447-49. On December 7, 1447, the Captains and Defenders of Liberty called, seemingly using traditional forms, for the festival of the solemn oblation to Ambrose to run smoothly, *in ornamentum et utilitatem ecclesie prelibatis pastoris.*[64] One year later, the tone had changed: town criers in all the city's public places made an announcement, or rather a general mobilization. "Tomorrow, in the early hours, all the artisans will gather, as many as possible, at the Broletto square."[65] Everyone must offer, specifies the text – this time, in Italian – two altar candles "to our protector and patron saint Ambrose." This call, as we can clearly see, served to maintain a political fervor that the republic's leaders hoped was unanimous and popular, and which in any case surpassed the ritual framework of civic celebrations.

The same was true of the *feste delle offerte*, processions of offerings for the cathedral building site intended to demonstrate civic unity,[66] which swelled in scope and dramatization. During the years of the Ambrosian Republic, the cathedral increasingly became the focus of the ritual space; it is hardly surprising to read the deliberation, on February 18, 1449, by which the Captains and Defenders of Liberty decreed that the *offerte* processions for the February 21 celebration would not proceed to the Sant'Ambrogio della Vittoria church, commemorating Ambrose's support for the dynastic consolidation of the Visconti family, but would be rerouted toward the cathedral.[67] In October 1449, a procession organized by the residents of the *porta Romana* during the celebration of Corpus Christi to pay homage to the Captains left San Nazzaro church and headed toward the cathedral: amid chants and hymns, multiple *tableaux vivants* were transported on chariots, evoking Ambrose and other holy bishops as defenders of liberty; there was also an *aurea libertas*, followed by the cardinal virtues, and finally Moses's crossing of the Red Sea.[68] Here, the theatricalization of a civic celebration allowed the threatened regime to emphasize an explicit political message, at a time when it believed itself obliged to constantly relegitimize itself, though its logic was more ceremonial than ritualistic: the people were invited as spectators, whereas, one year earlier, during the "revolutionary days" of December 1448, they had been the principal actors of a political rite in which nothing less than their own strength of mobilization was being staged.

It is on this point that, in my mind, the historiography of revolutionary festivals could serve as a lever. In writing this history – the breach of 1447-50 was my entry point some time ago[69] – I have made very explicit use of revolutionary terminology. "Terror," "Thermidor": are we allowed to talk about the events of the fifteenth century this way? "Controlled anachronism" can sometimes be an easy justification, but we still have to know who controls what.[70] Bringing such analogies to the forefront of one's historical discourse is no doubt a way to show that they are not at play behind the scenes: you objectify them through exposure, and through exposure, you display them while challenging them – in short, you take a risk in showing them. Consider *Festivals and the French Revolution*, an important book published by Mona Ozouf in 1976.[71] It emerged from the festival fervor that enflamed historiography after 1968. Its influence on the study of medieval rituality was also decisive, as seen for example in Richard Trexler's critical work on public rituality in Florence in the late Middle Ages.[72] The view of public rituality not as a representation of social order but as a performative force of regeneration was influenced, as the author himself admitted, by the large anti-Vietnam War demonstrations in the United States.

Mona Ozouf was looking less for a preexisting political order in the revolutionary festival, and more for a founding ritual. But historians retained in particular her conclusion about the revolutionary festival's "transfer of sacrality" from Church to State. For Olivier Ihl, a republican festival is akin to a citizen baptism: "The interlocutors of the celebration are not countable groups of voices but individual entities: the commune, the people, the nation."[73] Nicolas Mariot suggests returning to this idea, taking

Mona Ozouf's book in a contrarian sense, beginning notably with what she refers to as the "stubborn formalism" of the festival: from 1789 to 1799, festivals proceeded identically to one another, "in the customary ways," as they would say in the Middle Ages, and only reacted very gradually to the convulsions of the time.[74] Fanfares, speeches, children, games, a ball, fireworks, and the planting of a tree: the festival repertoire was very limited. In other words, the festival may be revolutionary, but it proceeds in a preestablished framework and is in this sense a social institution. Which means it is perhaps not warranted for the historian to relay the political description of the collective sentiment that he or she finds in their sources. Is the enthusiasm religious or civic? Everything depends on the context in which it is received and expressed – with the understanding that what was documented (in particular in the Middle Ages) were principally the intentions of festival organizers that exist in what Mona Ozouf calls a "timeless present."

It would be similarly imprudent to infer from this inevitably normative documentation the density of a practice, and from that practice the intensity of a belief. Should we consider the acclamatory gesture to be the corporal expression of an engagement or conviction? Not necessarily: it is part of a festive apparatus that gives it meaning and provokes predictable behavior documented by our sources. Therefore civic enthusiasm is nothing more than "enthusiasm manifested in a civic situation recognized as such by the participants, exactly as others, in another context, could evoke 'sacred emotions.'"[75] We can see clearly here how an analogical operation (when it is a true operation and not merely an easy way out) ultimately allows us to limit our interpretations. By comparing the revival of Ambrose's memory and the revolutionary festival, we are not trying to inflame meaning, but on the contrary to subdue it. For when we do so, it becomes clear that the tempo of the period 1447–49 produced neither accelerations nor flare-ups in this "timeless present" of the festival, a social institution. Nor should we exaggerate the evolution between the two identified moments, but on the contrary understand that the civic festival had a political function of cooling the revolution. Those who described it were the ones with festival fever. It is their words that caught fire, and it is on them that we should focus our attention.

THE AMBROSIAN *CRIDA*:
WHAT IS A POLITICAL BELIEF?

This capacity for collective mobilization inherent in the Ambrosian rallying call can be clearly seen in the proclamations, or *crida*, made by the Captains and Defenders of Liberty and gathered in two volumes of the *Registri Panigarola*.[76] Its editor meticulously described the *diplomatica Ambrosiana* therein, combining new recording practices with the old *stilus cancellariae* of the Viscontis. Of the three kinds of acts that make up this register (letters close, letters patent, and *crida*), the third largely dominated the documentary landscape of the *triennio*. Of course there were a few precedents under Bernabò and Galeazzo II (1369), but nothing comparable to this deployment of the *crida* between 1447 and 1449, in different forms (*crida et bando, crida et avisamento, crida et notitia*).[77] These all attest to a politics of proclamation, including the linguistic choice of direct communication in Italian, which likely created an informal public space outside the official observance of power.[78] Marina Spinella has already underlined how the *crida* spoke, day after day, of the rise of perils and political tensions, feverishly amplifying the discourse about a republic in danger, and of the wave of measures taken against blasphemers, sodomites, prostitutes, Jews, those who plot and betray, figures viewed with suspicion and those who had to be unmasked, "those men of poor circumstance who desire nothing more than their own servitude and the ruin of their homeland whom our great patron, our saint Ambrose, will punish as they deserve."[79] The invocation of Ambrose's name became obsessive: the *stato ambrosiano* was fighting for *ambrosiana libertate*, the people had to support the *camera ambrosiana*, itself populated with *megliori ambrosiani*.[80]

This point is all the more significant as expressions of devotion to Saint Ambrose are far from commonplace in these "acts of practice": they are much less frequent than invocations of God's power or the intercession of the Virgin, the latter associated with a discourse exalting liberty.[81] Ambrose's celestial protection sometimes accompanies that of Saint Francis,[82] but he is primarily invoked alongside Saint George, warrior patron and maker of victories: this is notably the case in a call to arms under the command of the captain-general Francesco Sforza on September 3, 1447, in which the expression *stato di libertà* appears for the first time.[83] The rememoration of Ambrose was in fact used frequently to support a discourse of military mobilization. The audience being the "devotees of Saint Ambrose, our patron and protector, and the friends of liberty,"[84] for the faith of "good citizens and true Ambrosians" should show itself through obedience,[85] as well as physical engagement.[86] This discourse of souls and virile bodies inverted the debt inherent in the devotional exchange: the faithful no longer placed themselves under Ambrose's protection, but went to his aid, to protect the celestial protector.

When the invocation of Ambrose is used to justify a financial contribution – which represents its second principal discursive usage, after military mobilization – we can consider it to be another inversion of the debt.[87] Citizens would not be known as *boni ambrosiani, né fidelli al Stato* if they did not pay the tax.[88] This call for fiscal consent borrowed rhetorical motifs that justified, again in the *crida* by the Captains and Defenders of Liberty, the need to contribute to the financing of Ambrosian festivals, *pro oblatione sancti Ambrosii.*[89] Here, we are very close to what Ernst Kantorowicz called the "simultaneously profound and abstruse parallel between *Christus* and *fiscus.*"[90] As we know, monarchical systems relied on the theological-political fiction of the king's two bodies to justify fiscal necessities: "Since the person of the king as the demander of taxes for common property had to distinguish itself from that of the lord, a beneficiary had to be defined that was both legitimate in its person and at the same time transcended that person and the contributing collective: this is none other than the State."[91] But how, in an urban context or a territorial state governed by the simple body of the prince, a mortal man, could taxes be made into a *res quasi sacra* if its beneficiary did not possess the immortality and impartiality of the Crown? It is easy to see here how references to Ambrose were employed to construct a republican transcendence justifying the fiscal levy.

Let's step back one more time to gain some distance from the false evidence before us. What historians of revolutionary festivals recognize in these celebrations is not the expression of a civic religion but rather that of a *civil* religion. So then what is a civil religion? We can consider it to be a modern response to an ancient problem: since at least Machiavelli, the majority of political thinkers have accepted that the State can be neither established nor maintained without religion.[92] Jean-Jacques Rousseau, like many others, was persuaded of this: the only way to convince a people to obey a set of laws based in reality on a convention between men is to make them believe that it came from heaven. Civil religion is nothing other than this pious lie, a generic religion relying on a simplified credo, with a unifying and civic mission. It is therefore no longer a question of reasoning within the imperial framework of a state religion, but within a system of essentially pluralist beliefs. Granted, these distinctions are mainly applicable to the contemporary era.[93] But they nonetheless awaken strange echoes in the medieval world. Alain Boureau noted as much in his genealogy of the theological-political adage *vox populi, vox Dei* from the Carolingian scholar Alcuin to the first words of the United States Constitution of 1787, which endow Law with sacred significance: *We the People of the United States.*[94] Here we more or less have a political cogito: not "I think therefore I am," but "we believe therefore we are."

For that matter, the vocabulary shifts observed in the series of *crida* made by the Captains and Defenders of Liberty, once they are viewed as a literature of political action, led to the sacralization of the political sphere, and therefore to the constitution of a civil religion rather than a civic one. For example, the notion of devotion shifted to that of filiation, which moved the field of belief toward obedience. On February 6, 1449, a *crida* called for the defense of the homeland against the "enraged" enemies who wanted its ruin; the Milanese people therefore had to defend it *virilmente, animosamente et affectionatamente,* successfully convincing themselves they were the "very faithful sons of Saint Ambrose."[95] This rhetoric logically relied on a discourse of filial love. This was the case in another *crida* published the same day, destined for any "friend of our protector and defender Saint Ambrose and the liberty of our commune of Milan."[96] A discourse of community belonging emerged, a declaration of both social unanimity[97] and urban identity.[98] *Vero millanese, overo ambrosiano*: while Ambrose's protection covered all of urban society, it also extended to the entirety of the territory that continued, in the absence of a duke, to be called a duchy, but that is primarily recognized in the expression *terra ambrosiana*.[99]

"Ambrosianness" was therefore a chosen identity – and ultimately, a political value. One could, according to the *crida* of the Captains and Defenders of Liberty, be *veri ambrosiani, buoni ambrosiani*, and even *migliori ambrosiani*.[100] This required something besides devotion: political faith, in the modern sense, meaning adhesion to a system of values and obedience to certain behavioral norms. One should never, for example, speak ill of or "malign the aforesaid holy liberty, the State and its Lords" for, continues this *crida* from March 29, 1449, "no State in the world can do without obedience."[101] This belief of course implied acceptance of the transcendence of an abstract idea: *nostra sancta libertà*.[102] That notion appeared, in 1449, as the political tempo accelerated: now *crida* were calling for the defense of the *conservatione et augmento del Stato*.[103] Faced with the rise of military threats, calls for mobilization multiplied, increasingly inflamed and increasingly affecting. On September 26, 1449, citizens' love for and loyalty to Ambrose, repeatedly invoked by the republic's leaders to mobilize their energies, were transferred to the state that claimed its authority from his name: all able-bodied men were ordered to take up arms and meet the enemy "in order to demonstrate the love and faith we bear for our Ambrosian State [*stato nostro ambrosiano*]."[104] Two days later, the same political justification was employed: Francesco Sforza's troops were approaching the Redefosso, the canal protecting Milan outside the city walls; it was time to "demonstrate the faith, love, devotion, and fervor we bear for Saint Ambrose, the State of sacred liberty, and the love and preservation of the homeland," exhorted the Captains and Defenders of Liberty, who, a few words later, again tightened the formula into a stirring cry to display the "love and devotion one bears for the Ambrosian State."[105]

These were the last cries, or nearly, of this Milanese republic. The rumblings here were nothing less than a political language, in several respects unprecedented, and in any case not reducible to the categories of the different political languages whose polyphony constitutes the dialogic horizon of the Italian states of the quattrocento.[106] Could we say that this political language was ultimately just a manifestation of ordinary humanist republicanism, the discursive vein that silently advances like an underground river through all of Italy's political history, seeking points of resurgence here and there? From a lexical and an ideological perspective (the latter limited to select motifs), of course we could: the commune is that never-ending story which is always ready to contradict the princely epic. But we can clearly see that "Ambrose" did not solely serve here as a name for the eternal return of that institution. The way in which the Milanese people called themselves and became Ambrosian, through ritual or oral proclamation, but always in practice, is a reminder of an essential lesson, applicable to more than just history: there is no identity, there are only intentions of identity; belonging does not exist, only the manifestation of a desire to belong to something or someone. And in this case, to the political belief that took the name Ambrose.

In this sense, a revolution did occur in Milan between 1447 and 1449, for these years were swept up in the acceleration of an authentically revolutionary tempo. Most importantly, they saw the eruption of a new language that spoke of political life and that, like Machiavelli's language later on, was forged in the fire of urgency and necessity. This is the breach. What we see here is in no way an upwelling of memory, ready to storm the bastions of received history. Nor do we see the rivalry of another memory of Ambrose, or its political instrumentalization. No, what reveals itself at a glance is in fact one of Ambrose's profound truths – one that makes the saint, in the eyes of the *popolo*, the resolute adversary of the more powerful. Other than in the breach, we can only guess at its submerged forms. For we know quite well that a political language, when it erupts suddenly, does not come from nowhere. But we also know that what we call power is the force that manages to silence that language – and more than that, tries to erase its tracks.

THIRTEEN

Forgetting,
Then Starting Over
(1450–1550)

He was on horseback when he crossed the cathedral's threshold, and the crowd is said to have been packed so thickly that he
couldn't dismount in front of the altar. It was February 26, 1450,
and Francesco Sforza was making his entry into Milan. He was
to have defended the city; instead he had besieged and starved
it, and now he was claiming possession of it. A son of rural Italy,
his mother an Umbrian peasant, Sforza was forty-nine years old.
He'd been born in the Arno Valley, the bastard son of a condottiere from Romagna named Muzio Attendolo, known as Sforza,
a captain who served Florence during its conquest of Pisa. Francesco too became a mercenary, that is to say a war entrepreneur,
contracting with states to fight on their side, offering his services
to the highest bidder. The condottieri were paid to wage war, but
they were paid even more not to wage it. They spent as much time
negotiating their *condotta* as fighting, carrying with them, in

the dust of their horses' hooves, dreams of the nomad state they longed to establish somewhere.[1]

For Francesco Sforza, that somewhere was Milan. In 1425 Duke Filippo Maria Visconti had armed him to defend the city against the great Venetian captain Francesco Bussone da Carmagnola. Francesco Sforza had just inherited the family business, his father having died in 1424 – and a mercenary army was a business, an *impresa*, a venture company. You didn't increase its value by being loyal. The right move was to betray your employer, which caused your earnings to rise, since whoever hired you had to raise the bid. That's what happened in 1434 when the Venetian pope Eugene IV, from whom Sforza had taken the March of Ancona, managed to turn him. Francesco Sforza then fought on the side of a league against Milan, comprising Florence, Venice, and the pope. The pope promised Sforza the titles of papal vicar and *gonfalonier* of the Church. Milan for its part procured the services of the other great condottiere of the time, Niccolò Piccinino. But Francesco Sforza's victories in the field put him in a position of strength, and Filippo Maria Visconti had to negotiate. What resulted was the Peace of Cremona, in 1441, and the reconciliation between Visconti and Sforza was sealed with a matrimonial alliance: the duke of Milan gave Sforza the hand of his illegitimate daughter Bianca Maria – making the bastard son of an obscure captain from Romagna his son-in-law and heir. Piccinino, logically enough, went over to the pope's side and managed to recapture the Marches from Francesco Sforza.[2]

Are you following all of this? It's not absolutely necessary. The constant reversals of alliance within the tangled skein of intrigues in Italian politics of the quattrocento are at once completely unpredictable and wholly comprehensible. The events are incoherent, but they succeed each other according to a narrative structure that follows a few basic rules.[3] One, for instance, is that a political power always seeks to establish itself in time and space, even when – like that of the condottieri – its very structure is nonterritorial. In consequence, Francesco Sforza, whose home base in the Marches had been taken from him, was inevitably driven – given too the expansionist logic of forward flight – to establish a base for himself in the territories of Milan. The political convulsions of the years 1447 to 1449 provided him the occasion, but he also knew how to be patient. He started as a captain of the Ambrosian Republic and in that role conquered Lodi and Piacenza. When he captured Pavia, he became its lord in his own right, and when he made peace with Venice, he demanded Brescia and Crema in return, taking possession of them before stretching out his hand to Novara and Alessandria. This was the threat whose rumblings we have just heard in the *crida* of the Captains and Defenders of Freedom.

Even as Ambrose's memory was being invoked to strengthen the political resolve of those fighting in his name, the elites had been negotiating Milan's surrender for several months – its capitulation, properly speaking, since Francesco Sforza was acquiring his power through patient negotiation, discussing item by item every article of the *capitoli de dedizione* that he was hammering out with each of the communities, factions, and social groups constituting his state.[4] Behind these negotiations, as we also know, was Francesco Sforza's great ally, to whom he was contracting a deep obligation – a merchant of Florence who became, thanks to his influence and wealth, its hidden prince: Cosimo de' Medici. Francesco Sforza was the primary borrower from the Medici Bank, and the entire diplomatic history of the 1450s in Italy can essentially be traced back to the repayment of this debt. The indissoluble alliance between Cosimo de' Medici and Francesco Sforza was the tent pole supporting the structure of the Peace of Lodi, dated August 30, 1454, whose principle of the balance of powers spread through all of Italy.[5]

All that still lay in the future when, on February 26, 1450, Francesco Sforza and five hundred of his troops entered the town his forces had besieged, distributing bread to feed the population he had been starving. He entered the cathedral, did not dismount, returned to his encampment, and it was there that the delegates of the commune of Milan – not the Captains and Defenders of Freedom but the representatives of the old commune – brought him the surrender agreement. But this was not enough. The condottiere insisted on a ceremony of public acclamation, which was organized for March 11, with all the heads of families gathered on the Piazza dell'Arengo, the old town square. Henceforth, the political legitimacy of Francesco Sforza, duke of Milan, would rest on the triple foundation of military conquest, popular sovereignty, and dynastic continuity. All of this was to be expressed by his triumphal entry, on the Feast of the Annunciation, March 25, 1450.

Giovanni Simonetta, who wrote of the event between 1473 and 1476, well after the death of Francesco Sforza in 1466, and while the brilliant but cruel government of his son Galeazzo Maria Sforza (1466 to 1476) was destabilizing Sforza's political order and sullying his memory, described the condottiere as a virtuoso of political action.[6] Calm and methodical, cold and calculating, he could wait patiently until the Feast of the Annunciation, not because he was hoping for a miracle, but because he wanted to create an effect.[7] The ceremony was at once a military parade – a thousand foot soldiers and a thousand horsemen, all in ceremonial dress – a civic procession (prominent men filing past in close ranks, from representatives of the various trades to ambassadors, while the crowd cheered), and a wedding procession. For Francesco Sforza entered Milan's Duomo a second time, again on horseback, but this time accompanied by his bride, Bianca Maria Visconti. He received the scepter and the keys to the city, and he made his eldest son, Galeazzo Maria Sforza, count of Pavia. All of this was performed according to the prescribed ritual, using the same parade route, rhythms, and actors as for the ceremonial entries of the dukes of Milan in the time of the Viscontis, following time-honored forms in keeping with the perpetual present of ceremonials of power. But one notable person was missing, as you'll have noticed: Ambrose.

A NAME ON THE TIP OF THE TONGUE:
AMBROSE UNDERGROUND

How could he have been forgotten? It was in Ambrose's name that the Milanese had believed they could do away with princes in the first place. But when princes returned – the state under Sforza corresponded to a time when, paradoxically, princely power was intensifying – Ambrose's memory started to become unwelcome.[8] Had his name been compromised by the militant use to which it was put by the partisans of liberty during the Ambrosian *triennio* of 1447 to 1449? And if so, had it been compromised once and for all? It is always worth noting the capacity of those in power to disqualify the values, whether sacred or secular, that motivate their adversaries. "Never treat as an accident the force of the name in what happens," Jacques Derrida warned.[9] From 1447 to 1449, the Milanese had called fervently on Ambrose's memory to rearm their communal past in the fight they were waging against the power of princes. In 1450, they lost this fight. But some among them did not give up, and the moment that the hope of founding a new republic arose once more, Ambrose's name was heard again. On December 26, 1476, the duke of Milan Galeazzo Maria Sforza was assassinated as he was going to Mass at the Church of Santo Stefano.[10] Because they were looking to enact a tyranni-cide and not just wipe out a political rival, hoping to forge anew a broken political pact in the spilled blood of a bad prince, the plotters chose to give their action maximum visibility: in full daylight, in a church, at the end of the Christmas cycle, which was the great princely festival of the Sforza government.[11] The plotters had no chance of escaping. The young patricians, fired up by the humanist ideas of their leader Cola Montano,[12] were immediately arrested, tortured, executed, and made examples of – the vengeance of the princely state continuing to vent itself on their corpses and the memory of their line.[13]

Among them was Giovan Andrea Lampugnani, whose uncle, decapitated in May 1449, had been one of the leaders of the Ambrosian Republic. Lampugnani's companion, Girolamo Olgiati, describes at length, in a confession recorded by the his-torian Bernardino Corio, the highly ritualized preparations of the conspirators. These continued for the entire duration of the Christmas cycle, starting on the Feast of Saint Thomas (December 21). Olgiati tells how the conspirators gathered at dawn at the Basilica of Sant'Ambrogio to recite their oath, and how, before going into action, they prayed before an image of Saint Ambrose.[14] Seven years later, in December 1483, a new con-spiracy took aim at Ludovico Sforza, also known as Ludovico il Moro, who governed the duchy of Milan on behalf of his nephew Giovanni Galeazzo Sforza. The conspirators planned to assassi-nate him in the Basilica of Sant'Ambrogio, on the day of the feast of Ambrose's ordination as a bishop, December 7.[15] At the last moment, they changed their plan. The tyrant was to be struck down in his castle, also on Saint Ambrose's day. The situation was confused, and either an unexpected circumstance made them stand down or the plot was brought to light. The ducal chancery, fearing more extensive machinations, made a point of warning its ambassadors in France, the marquis of Mantua and the duke of Savoy.[16] It was then revealed that persons close to the Duchess Bonne de Savoie were implicated, most likely in league with several Venetian allies. At that point, on February 27, 1484, a courtier by the name of Aloisio Vimercati, who was hiding a dagger under his cloak to assassinate the prince, was arrested. He was drawn and quartered, then decapitated, in front of the Castello di porta Giovia, while his accomplices were arrested, tortured, and imprisoned in the Castle of Sartirana, near Pavia. Every year, on the same day, the conspirators – among whom was another member of the Vimercati family, but also a rich merchant named Pasino – were dropped the length of a rope, twice.[17] And that day was December 7, the Feast of Saint Ambrose, continuing their punishment for the crime they had attempted to commit in the saint's name.

All in all a strange episode, but one that can perhaps be better illuminated by another text, penned by Antonio Averlino, known as Filarete. A Florentine architect in service to Francesco Sforza, Filarete was the author of the *Trattato di architettura*, a treatise on architecture written in 1465 in the Albertian style that offers a disquieting vision of utopia.[18] Filarete describes an ideal city, Sforzinda, which is more a political idealization of the actual city than an urbanized rendering of the ideal life. It contains a prison, called Ergastolon, whose description has horrified commentators.[19] Situated outside the city, Ergastolon has four high towers, each named for a punishment associated with a particular type of crime. When a criminal arrives at the penitentiary, he is hoisted to the top of one of the towers, according to the crime he has committed. There he is executed – or so it's made to seem. In fact the prisoner enters a virtual city of torments, divided into two levels. The first is windowless, and the prisoner is tortured there in great secrecy for four to six years. The unlucky soul then descends through a trapdoor to a second level, where he is put to forced labor.[20] In imagining Ergastolon, Filarete was trying to reconcile three seemingly contradictory political needs. First was to contain the fallout from torture: no one looking on from town would ever know that the prisoners weren't executed at the top of the towers, and thus the punishment would remain irreproachable. But the state also had a legitimate desire for vengeance, which was exacted by the cold monster on the first level, where criminals were tortured in the greatest secrecy. But torture, Filarete believed, cannot on its own satisfy the state. The state needs to make use of every capacity, and even the blackest criminal has a *virtù* that is useful to society. So forced labor was used to complete the prisoner's redemption.[21]

HISTORY SUSPENDED, OR
PRUDENTLY TURNING A MEMORY INTO A MONUMENT

At this point, we can reconstruct a political sequence whose bias against princely power demonstrates the persistence through the fifteenth century of an ideology of republicanism and tyrannicide.[22] And at every step, Ambrose's memory was called into service. We could make an analogous description to the one proposed by Michelle Riot-Sarcey in her underground history of the nineteenth century, where the experience of freedom "can neither be imagined nor developed except as part of a movement to return to the past, whose promises have been left unfulfilled."[23] In confronting this movement, the princely state in the fifteenth century was curiously unperturbed, unlike the signory of the preceding century, believing itself strong enough to shake off its ties to the communal past. Once more, it is the story of the Castello di porta Giovia that expresses this most clearly. During his negotiations with Milan's patricians, Francesco Sforza had been forced to promise not to rebuild or reoccupy the hated citadel.[24] Once in power, he no longer felt bound to his promise. As Giovanni Simonetta wrote, "Not only did he rebuild the *rocca* of Milan, which lay in ruins, but he made it larger and stronger."[25] In fact, it was to work on this very site that Sforza brought Filarete from Florence.

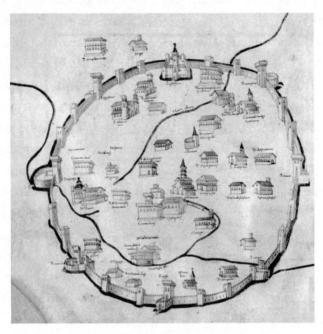

Map of Milan, Pietro del Massaio, c. 1470,
Mediolano con diciture in latino, Biblioteca Apostolica Vaticana,
Rome, Cod. Vaticano Latino 5699, folio 125 verso

Sforza's arrogation of space is visible in the "map" of Milan drawn by Pietro del Massaio for a Florentine translation of Ptolemy's *Geography* in the 1470s, representing the walled town as a two-dimensional surface scattered with perspective drawings of buildings.[26] It differs from the archaeological maps in Galvano Fiamma's *Cronica extravagans,* where the town's present sits weightily on the vestiges of the past, and where the variations in scale and mixing of time frames express the will of signorial power to manipulate time and memory with the same energy it used to extend its control over space. The map by Pietro del Massaio, by contrast, seems to suspend memory.[27] The ground of the city appears as an abstract plane; architectural monuments are set down on it like watchtowers. Whether private or public, secular or religious, they polarize the space, which is at once concrete – the perspectival renderings create a realistic effect – and abstract. The town is abstracted from its history, a blank page on which the builder scrawls his message. And this message is delivered through the buildings and the names associated with them. The prince's residence, for instance, is not labeled a *palazzo* or a *corte*, but a *castello*. A game is in progress – the buildings seem to be placed across the town like pieces on a checkerboard. The pictorial logic is the same as on a heraldic shield: the elements are defined not by their inherent importance but according to their relative position. And the determining factor is the apical position of the castle. The one in question is the citadel of the *porta Giovia*, which is actually northwest of the city. But the round city has pivoted on its axis (and its axis from now on is the Duomo), magnetized by the new site of power. Like a compass finding north, the court now determines the city's orientation and tilts its representation.[28]

Let me ask the question again: Did the princes want to forget Ambrose? It's true that Ambrose was prudently occluded from view during the rule of Francesco Sforza (1450 to 1466), when our bothersome champion of *libertas* withdrew before the conquering hero. Ambrosian iconography went through a period of latency at that time;[29] civic processions were more discreet or avoided the center of town, making their way instead to the Church of Sant'Ambrogio ad Nemus, behind the Castello di porta Giovia, in the isolated neighborhood that inspired nostalgia in Petrarch and gave the Sforzas a useful pretext to divert Ambrosian festivities away from the city.[30] On the coinage, an equestrian portrait of the condottiere replaced the image of the saint on horseback. Only in 1466 did the princely powers start to take back possession of Ambrose's memory, when the new duke of Milan, Galeazzo Maria Sforza, had a fresco of Saint Ambrose painted in the chapel of his castle at the *porta Giovia*,[31] and when the humanist Pier Candido Decembrio wrote, perhaps in 1467, his now lost *Vita Ambrosii*.[32] Altogether, the second half of the fifteenth century was a moment of intense rediscovery by the humanists of Ambrose's legacy.[33] Paulinus of Milan's *Vita* was printed in Latin in 1474, 1477, and 1488, and in Italian in 1492. Other writings by and about Ambrose also came off the presses in Milan,[34] often spreading across Europe through the intercession of humanists in Rome.[35]

The task at hand was not to forget but, on the contrary, to appropriate Milan's key sites and occupy its memorative space. Starting in 1492, the Sforzas took over the stewardship of the Basilica of Sant'Ambrogio as part of their overall plan for the city's monuments. They invested large sums in the construction work, which was directed during the final years of the century by one of their architects – none other than Bramante.[36] Cardinal Ascanio Maria Sforza, no doubt the most brilliant patron among the Sforzas, played a major role in this.[37] The wholesale restructuring of the chapels and cloister undertaken by the Master of Urbino became the architectural prototype for the harmonious articulation between a basilica's core and the cluster of gentilic chapels grafted onto it – chapels intended for the worship of patrician lineages.[38] Similarly, in the Church of San Pietro in Gessate, the former convent of the Umiliati that had been deeded to the Benedictines in 1433 and rebuilt in 1458 by Guiniforte Solari, the funerary appropriation by servants of the prince transformed the ecclesiastic space into a state pantheon.[39] Patronage by the Trivulzio, Rossi, Landriano, and Panigarola families made the Church of San Pietro in Gessate a "veritable art museum," as Luca Beltrami would write.[40]

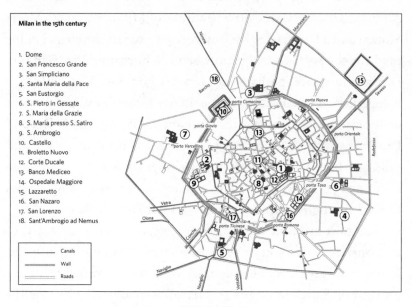

(*PAO Seuil*)

It is there, in the Griffi Chapel, that one finds the most important cycle of fifteenth-century Milanese paintings devoted to Ambrose.[41] Ambrogio Griffi, a physician and ducal counselor, who, as prothonotary apostolic, belonged to the college of notaries for the Roman curia, was a humanist whose fine library is known to us[42] and an important figure in the political history of the Sforza government.[43] Educated at the University of Pavia, he entered the service of Duke Francesco Sforza toward the mid-1450s and became one of the primary physicians to his son, Galeazzo Maria Sforza. He entered religious orders in 1473 without giving up his medical career, moved into the Castello di porta Giovia with the title of ducal archdeacon, and joined the privy council in 1479.[44] According to his will, dated September 4, 1489, he left 760 gold ducats to the monastery of San Pietro in Gessate to decorate and paint the chapel he had founded in Ambrose's honor, build his marble sepulchre, and say Mass on Ambrose's feast days.[45]

The history of the commission and painting of the fresco cycle in the Griffi Chapel, from 1489 to 1493, is relatively well documented. Abandoning a plan to hire Vincenzo Foppa, Ambrogio Griffi entered into a contract with the painter Bernardo Zenale, who would collaborate with Bernardino Butinone to "paint and ornament said chapel with the history of Saint Ambrose, confessor."[46] Because of the poor state of preservation of the frescos, the iconographic plan—which consists of twenty-four panels on two walls—is difficult to interpret. Most of the classic scenes of the Ambrosian cycle are present. On the right-hand wall: the election and acclamation of Ambrose, the baptism of Augustine, the discovery of the relics of saints Gervasius and Protasius, and the miraculous presence of Ambrose at the funeral of Saint Martin. And on the left wall: Ambrose imposing a penance on Theodosius, and the saint's death. Yet the organization of the scenes doesn't correspond to the narrative sequence in Paulinus of Milan's *Vita*, which had influenced all the previous Ambrosian cycles, from the golden altar in the Basilica of Sant'Ambrogio, to the carved stalls of its choir, commissioned in 1469 by Giovanni de San Giorgio di Piacenza.[47] Some have claimed, though without proof, that the cycle took inspiration from the lost *Vita* by Pier Candido Decembrio. What is certain is that the paintings propose a reinterpretation of Ambrose's memory, one that is unconstrained by the canonic narrative sequence and that suggests the tensions and contradictions surrounding Ambrose's memory in the Sforza state.

Two of the panels in particular are remarkable. The first dominates the central lunette with an equestrian depiction of Ambrose, dressed all in white, brandishing his whip. This allusion to the Battle of Parabiago is no doubt the most princely of Ambrosian representations, taking its cue, as we have seen, from the coinage issued by Galeazzo Maria Sforza. But the right wall also displays an impressive scene, which is a long way from the peaceful image of the good pastor and without any iconographic precedent: Ambrose is seated on a platform, while a soldier brings before him a man with his hands tied behind his back (see color plate 18). The assembled crowd calls out, and a *titulus* allows us to hear what it is saying: "Your sin be upon us." This leads us straight to the source of the episode, which is Paulinus of Milan's account of Ambrose's attempts to evade his election as bishop: "When he realized this, he left the church and had a tribunal set up for himself. He who was in fact soon to be bishop mounted it, and then, contrary to his own custom, ordered that individuals be put to torture. But even when he did this, the people cried out, 'Your sin be upon us!' These, however, did not shout as did the people of the Jews, for the latter shed the Lord's blood with their voices when they said: 'His blood be upon us'" (Matthew 27:25).[48]

Beyond the hagiographic motif of the bishop-in-spite-of-himself, beyond even the permeating anti-Judaism of the episode, what we are given to see is an enactment of power. Ambrose judges and condemns. And lest there be any doubt, a person on his right holds a rope that we can trace back to the upper lunette, where it suspends a man who is being tortured. The episode is all the more intriguing for alluding to a practice whose historical veracity we cannot doubt: the episcopal audiences of the fourth century, where the bishop, as the final functionary of the Roman Empire, made arrests and meted out justice.[49] In this context, the scene may also reflect the humanist culture of the patron who commissioned it. But more than anything, it is a forceful representation of sovereign power over life and death. Ambrose sits in judgment here, on the side of the princes who also lay claim to this power, and who at that time laid claim to it unconditionally. Ambrose's image delivers an intimidating message of obedience.

Forget Ambrose? The princes neither could nor would. Paul Ricœur has expressed it strongly: the prevention of memory and the enforcement of forgetting are delusions of power.[50] Traces can never be erased. But you can muddle them, repurpose them to other uses, or make them unavailable for a while. As a result, those in power more often use what Ricœur calls "forgetting due to unavailability."[51] One might also say, more prosaically, that the traces are still there, still preserved, but, as in a computer whose files have been renamed, the paths that would lead you to them no longer serve. Or they lead you elsewhere, to unsuspected places. Substitution, rather than erasure, is the logic of power when faced with a troublesome memory. As Régine Robin has written: "True forgetting is perhaps not blankness but the fact of immediately putting something else in place at a site that was formerly inhabited, whether by an ancient monument, an ancient text, or an ancient name."[52]

That is how Ambrose circulates, in the second half of the fifteenth century, under a number of borrowed names. The Sforzas, for example, promoted the worship of another hero on horseback, Saint George, who afforded them the flattering image of a knightly revival with the court of Milan as one of its main theaters. "This knightly horseman who rescues a princess by combatting a dragon was the paragon of knighthood."[53] Starting in 1475, the year Milan entered into an alliance with Burgundy, the festival of this warrior saint became an occasion for big parades and impressive court festivities.[54] By choosing a dynastic saint with no relation to the patron saints of any of the towns under their dominion, the dukes of Milan clearly asserted the territorial dimension of their power.[55] Others than Ambrose, and other Ambroses: the variation in iconographic models during the second half of the fifteenth century may be symptomatic of the political distancing from a memory that, a century earlier, it had been crucially important to orient and control. While the princely procession of avenging Ambroses rode forth on their steeds, others were assuming the venerable aspect of Doctors of the Church. For example, Vincenzo Foppa, the famous artist who had eluded Ambrogio Griffi, depicted a sage and venerable Ambrose for the Florentine banker Pigello Portinari, who directed the Milan branch of the Medici Bank (see color plate 19).[56] Portinari asked him to paint a fresco in the chapel he had built at Sant'Eustorgio, which became, thanks to his patronage, the bridgehead for new art in Milan.[57] Everything was energetic, powerful, and colorful, meant to hasten the arrival of a new era.[58] From one of the medallions in the lantern, Ambrose looks down from afar. He has aged, his beard is longer, he still carries his whip, but it is tied to his belt while he reads at his desk.

This iconographic ambiguity clearly parallels the history of secular power in Milan in the sixteenth century. The weakness of Ludovico Sforza's government is easily seen in the two sieges that occurred in 1499 and 1500, when – twice – the population rose up and forced the duke to flee before the French. When Louis XII made his royal entry into Milan in 1499, Ambrose welcomed him: the hereditary nobles of Milan had placed a representation of him at the top of the *porta Ticinese*, surrounded by "large, savage and monstrous men, bearing arms," wrote Jean d'Auton in his *Chroniques de Louis XII*. It was Ambrose who, on the commemorative medal struck immediately after the fact, gave the victor the title "duke of Milan."[59] While Ludovico Sforza was dying in France in 1508 in the dungeon of the Château de Loches, his sons tried to retake Milan. Francesco II Sforza succeeded in 1521, becoming the last Sforza to rule the city as its duke, remaining in power until Charles V directly annexed the duchy to his empire in 1535. When Francesco II was besieged in his castle in November 1525 by the imperial troops, he flew a banner with the image of Ambrose, perhaps hoping to revive the Milanese ideal of urban autonomy. But at the same time he was making use of imperial heraldry and the insignias of the Guelph and Ghibelline factions. Financially weakened, in debt to Charles V, he no longer had the means to maintain a sovereign power.[60] Given this context, the Ambrosian reference was probably no more than a clutching at the ideological bric-a-brac of available motifs and memories. It seems as though the cult of Ambrose had become identified with what historians call the calming and consensual aspect of civic religion. Does this mean that civic religion became depoliticized once and for all? If that were the case, our genealogical investigation would end in the sixteenth century. For we would observe memory at that time forming into links, and those links solidifying into a tradition – a tradition that would henceforth have the theological consistency of the Church government.

But we aren't there yet, and in order to reach that point we'd need to perform other anamneses, other feats of recollection. For the moment, let's retain this: starting in the last third of the fifteenth century, Ambrose's memory was caught up in the broad dynamics of the political societies of princely Italy, where power was paradoxically tending toward absolutism. This tendency can be seen in the architecture, where the palaces made an arrogant break with the urban environment – defining their own authentically sacred space;[61] it can be seen in the illumination of manuscripts, where the commissioners of such works abruptly and contemptuously did away with the ornamentation of a continuous past;[62] and it can be seen in the political discourse and practices that cast off the restraints holding them to ancient forms of legitimation.[63]

Governing is always a question of walking in existing tracks or traces, sometimes muddling them a bit, more rarely substituting others for them. But there are historical situations, rarer and more disquieting, when governing means something else: abandoning oneself to the aura of an eternal present that no track or trace binds to the past. Petrarch may have had an intuition of it the day when, looking at Ambrose's face, which stared at him so intently it seemed ready to speak, he believed he was seeing the living saint. Ambrose *was* alive, but from now on he would live in the past, since the humanists had applied themselves to celebrating ancient times so as to no longer have to live in them, inventing antiquity so as to break with the past, and extracting from it a trove of quotations so as to no longer reuse its remains. Petrarch had seen all this, which would only become truly comprehensible a century later. A breach had opened in the current of time. We can call it the Renaissance if we like, as long as what we refer to is not a period but a relationship to time. It's said about the Renaissance that it reflected a desire to re-remember antiquity — which is true. But it is also an era marked by the absolute ambition to renounce times past. The Renaissance was forgetful, and we've forgotten it.

PART FIVE

AMBROSIAN ANAMNESIS

(Fifteenth to Fourth Century)

The reason the breach of 1447 can't be plugged is that it was preceded by earlier tremors. Like on Epiphany 1439. A people's riot targeted the home of Cardinal Branda Castiglione, a powerful prelate who played a major role in the dealings between the duchy of Milan and the pontifical court.[2] He was accused of wanting to suppress the Ambrosian Rite in favor of the Roman liturgy, which, given what we know about his efforts to defend and preserve Ambrosian chant, was not very likely.[3] But ultimately it didn't matter: the rumor had been started. The parishioners of Santa Tecla launched an attack on the cardinal's palace and seized a prized manuscript, a tract about the Holy Spirit attributed to Ambrose, which the prelate, they said, was planning to bring to the Council of Florence in support of efforts to reconcile with the Greek Church.[4] Incidentally, historians have established that in 1437, the archbishop of Milan Francesco Pizolpasso brought the complete works of Ambrose compiled by Martino Corbo to the Council of Basel. So was the manuscript in question two years later Ambrose's tract on Trinitarian theology? It's possible: we know that Andrea Bossi used a lost codex from Santa Tecla to print *De Spiritu Sancto* in 1492.[5] Perhaps this was the manuscript that the rioters of January 6, 1439, wanted to protect.

At the end of the fifteenth century, Bernardino Corio attributed the cardinal's misfortune to the people's attachment to the Ambrosian Rite.[6] Modern historians have long challenged this account, struggling to imagine that obscure liturgical matters could have moved masses.[7] Yet the minutes of the interrogation led by high-ranking members of Milan's archiepiscopal court on January 9–12, 1439, following the riot on Epiphany, largely confirm Corio's interpretation.[8] They include an odd account by the clerics of Santa Tecla, who, subjected to torture, claimed to have seen Ambrose appear on horseback in the cathedral and sing the Mass in keeping with the liturgy that bears his name.[9] The clerics reportedly protested to the bishop in vain, then to the duke, and decided to rouse the people. The social profile of the protagonists is clear – they were nearly all artisans. A grocer, Giovanni Martus Paollayrolus, grabbed the codex and gave it to the draper Galdino de Zurlis, who hid it in his house. The episode is a reenactment, as we will see, of the same eternal scene: the people defending Ambrosian books threatened by the mighty.[10] Ambrose was the patron of the city of Milan – the whole city. But on this day, once again, it was the people who came to his aid, preserving the memory of their patron saint, from whom they expected protection and recognition in return.

The fact that the parishioners of Santa Tecla mobilized in 1439 to defend the Ambrosian *specificum* (meaning the particularity of Catholic liturgy in Milan) was certainly not due to chance. Until the fifteenth century, Santa Tecla was one of Milan's two cathedrals, dubbed *basilica minor* or *nova* by Ambrose, in opposition to the second, older but larger cathedral (*basilica maior* or *vetus*), which would become Santa Maria Maggiore. The two churches each had their baptistery (Santa Tecla's with a *titulus* attributed to Ambrose): these epigrams on Christian edifices, not unlike hymns in terms of their brief format and their metrics, transformed the city into a written corpus.[11] The existence of these twin cathedrals in northern Italy constitutes a

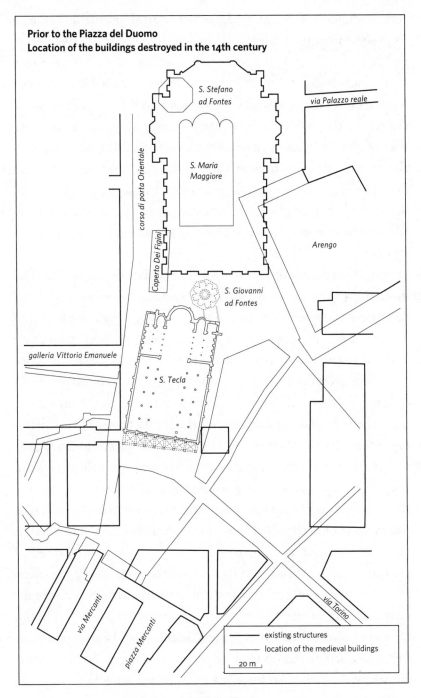

Prior to the Piazza del Duomo
Location of the buildings destroyed in the 14th century

S. Stefano
ad Fontes

via Palazzo reale

corso di porta Orientale

S. Maria
Maggiore

Arengo

Coperto Dei Figini

S. Giovanni
ad Fontes

galleria Vittorio Emanuele

S. Tecla

via Mercanti

piazza Mercanti

via Torino

existing structures
location of the medieval buildings

20 m

(*PAO Seuil*)

very complex historical and archaeological problem.[12] It also imposed a liturgical specificity: in Milan, cathedral services were divided according to the season, before and after Easter. Santa Tecla was the summer church and Santa Maria Maggiore the winter one. The procession to transport holy objects from one church to the other, twice a year, was one of the great ceremonies of the Ambrosian ritual, which reenacted the dedication of the church. But starting in 1387, with the founding of Milan's new cathedral, the Duomo, by Gian Galeazzo Visconti, the old Santa Tecla basilica began to impede the monumental glorification of the Duomo, and in particular the architectural layout of its piazza.[13]

The destruction of the Santa Tecla basilica began in 1461. The duke of Milan's architects (notably Guiniforte Solari) intended to reuse its western nave to construct a long porticoed building hosting a row of shops (the *coperto dei Figini*) to both solemnize and tame the area surrounding the cathedral.[14] But the construction prompted resistance and opposition. The Santa Tecla chapter (which still existed despite the church's demolition) intensified its pleas and protested the injury to Ambrose's memory. More than a place was being lost; with it would disappear a route that had ritually represented the city's identity. Assailed with supplications, some signed by the parishioners themselves, the duke yielded. In 1481, he authorized the construction of a new Santa Tecla church, which however would also be demolished in 1548.[15] Its contradictory history can, once again, be described as that of persistent and popular resistance to princely pressure. For what was progressing here, in tandem with the vast construction site of the Duomo, was devotion to the Virgin Mary, a form of Catholicism which the Viscontis had been promulgating since their accession to the duchy, following a French monarchical model.[16] But Ambrose's *basilica minor*, with the obstinate proof of archaeological fact, of a footprint on the ground that was thought to be expendable but nonetheless remained, clearly shows us what many other histories suggest: the traces of memory cannot be erased.

Finding those traces demands an act of anamnesis. This double negative of a word – *an* + *amnesis* – refers to the effort made *not* to forget, the slow and patient effort of going back in time. So let's begin, moving countercurrent to Ambrose's posthumous lives, from the fifteenth century to the fourth. Historical accounts involve a double negative as well: while any historiographical endeavor that can only reach the past from its most recent upwellings will naturally proceed in reverse, the chronological description of the sedimentation of memories does the opposite. In other words, chronological order is the inversion of the historian's order. If we flip the order again, meaning we proceed antichronologically, we find ourselves practicing the anamnesis that Roland Barthes said should guide the countermarch of historians assembling biographemes to escape the lies of biography. "I call *anamnesis* the action – a mixture of pleasure and effort – performed by the subject in order to recover, without *magnifying or sentimentalizing it*, a tenuity of memory."[17]

And so we'll see, in the pages that follow, that the most tenuous memories are not the least stubborn, and that it's easier to move stones than blur the traces of chants in liturgy. This immaterial power that imposes itself as the aura of memory may be its most vigilant guardian. And indeed, that is precisely what we'll be dealing with from now on. Its modern-day psychoanalytic version notwithstanding, let's not forget that the meaning of anamnesis was originally liturgical, that it designates the very heart of the mystery, that is to say the moment in the Christian celebration when one recalls Christ's last instructions to his disciples – "Do this in remembrance of me" (Luke 22:19) – not to commemorate but to actualize. It is also for that reason that this final journey will be arduous. As we slowly make our way from mystery to ministry, one step at a time, we may glimpse a few glimmers into a discomforting beginning – the liturgical genealogy of modern-day government.

FOURTEEN

Mysterious Beginnings: The Invention of a Liturgical Tradition (Fifteenth to Ninth Century)

Throughout the Middles Ages in Milan, most of the time, and for the greatest number, Ambrose's memory was first and foremost a feeling that came from a specific way of singing hymns and saying Mass. This feeling developed from listening and absorbing, and was shaped by comprehension and incomprehension. In the end, it mattered little whether the faithful were entirely aware of what made the original liturgy of the Ambrosian celebration so particular. It was a fundamental expression of the Milanese identity and undoubtedly the most powerful vector for the socialization of "civic conscience," a concept often evoked by historians but which they struggle to characterize in other than nebulous terms.[1]

But perhaps we can justify approaching Ambrose's memory through liturgy with a more theoretical point of view. Beginning with Gerd Tellenbach, Karl Schmid, and Otto Gerhard Oexle, the *memoria* studied by medieval scholars has had a fundamentally liturgical dimension: *opus Dei,* or God's work, relied on liturgical commemoration, and the memorization of liturgy made medieval clergy into professionals of memory.[2] Rhythmic and by consequence predictable, liturgy obeys the general characteristics of a ritual as defined by structural anthropology. "Thanks to ritual," wrote Claude Lévi-Strauss, "the 'disjoined' past of myth is articulated, on the one hand, with biological and seasonal periodicity, and, on the other, with the 'conjoined' past that unites the dead and the living through the generations."[3] Through the ritualization of *memoria,* the dead find themselves among the living,[4] conjoining the members of a community within a shared past, linked to their origin myth despite its inherent principle of separation. For we know, since Maurice Halbwachs, that religious memory is always eminently contentious, which is why Danièle Hervieu-Léger suggests viewing collective religious memory as "subject to constantly recurring construction" characterized by "the processes of…retrospectively inventing" and an "inseparably creative and normative dynamic function."[5] This reconstruction, which involves selective forgetting and regulation of individual memories, is more performative than prescriptive and occurs within the very structure of the liturgical ritual.

Of course we still need to accept the historicity of liturgy, and recognize its full role in social history. There is no point inventing imaginary enemies easily triumphed over: the fact that the liturgical movement can only be understood through its historical manifestations, and that those manifestations evolved under the constraints of not only religious but political and social contexts, is accepted by the large majority of specialists, including those who claim fidelity to the modern-day Church.[6] If the history of liturgy has meaning for the history of the Middle Ages, it is because "liturgy shaped to a certain extent the constituent forms of society."[7] More precisely, the very fact that the ecclesiastical institution of the city of Milan still makes claim, today, to the irreducible and immemorial specificity of a liturgy-based identity necessarily influences the general direction of research. One could assert, without being reproached for exaggeration, that all the major historians of the Ambrosian liturgy from the eighteenth century to our day mobilized their knowledge for pastoral and regulatory ends, participating in what they view as an ancient combat, which consists of defending the originality, purity, and durability of a liturgical *specificum*.[8]

But that combat is never-ending – and in this respect, the memory of Ambrose's people thrumming in unison to his hymns during the crisis of Easter 386 not only maintains its emotional charge, but its capacity for collective mobilization. After Justina comes Charlemagne, and after him Frederick Barbarossa: the Ambrosian liturgy is first and foremost for Milan's believers. It is a heritage that must be tirelessly preserved, for it is always under threat.[9] The *mysterium ambrosianum* is a basilica under siege. In his entry for the recent *Encyclopedic Dictionary of Liturgy*, Achille Triacca situates the liturgical reforms of the Second Vatican Council within the continuity of a long history: "Once again, the Ambrosian liturgy safeguards its freedom to exist."[10]

For liturgists, history is therefore an auxiliary science to pastoral theology. Even if care is often taken to note the Greek etymology of the term liturgy ("work of the people"),[11] we mustn't forget that this word, unused in medieval times, mainly reflects a contemporary historical reality: the "liturgical movement," a Catholic reform wave that appeared in France in the mid-nineteenth century with the publication of *The Liturgical Year* by Prosper Guéranger, abbot of Solesmes.[12] This explains why Cesare Alzati today prefers to use the Latin expression *mysterium ambrosianum* to refer to what I will, for the sake of convenience, call the Ambrosian liturgical tradition.[13] Incidentally, Alzati has demonstrated the complex usage of *mysterium ambrosianum* in Milanese sources, notably in texts by Landulf Senior, who, as we will see, played a strategic role in this matter.[14]

A BEGINNER'S GUIDE TO THE AMBROSIAN LITURGY:
NOTES IN THE MARGINS OF A MANUSCRIPT

But what exactly is the Ambrosian Rite?[15] One could spend countless hours reading scholarly studies about the Milanese liturgy without getting a clear idea of what exactly distinguishes it from the Roman liturgy: invariably allusive, Milanese scholarship takes maniacal care not to break the enchanted circle of cultish (and cultural) complicity. Take Achille Triacca, who, to explain the uncertainties of his discipline, deplores the fact that catalogs for liturgical books are not always written by *studiosi ambrosiani*: their authors have inevitably never "breathed the air" of *mysterium*.[16] And yet it was a foreign canonist in the fourteenth century, Radulph of Rivo, who penned the clearest and most comprehensive description of the Ambrosian office.[17] Born in Breda, in the province of Brabant, Radulph was the dean of the chapter of Tongeren and spent part of his life in Italy learning Greek; his *De canonum observantia* passes for a highly reliable lesson on the specificities of the Ambrosian liturgy.[18] Far more cursory and incomplete is the information in the *Ordo missae ambrosianae* conserved in the Bibliothèque de l'Arsenal in Paris. That said, this second text has the great merit of revealing what a man of power in fifteenth-century Milan found ideologically useful to distinguish within the Milanese liturgical tradition, notably for purposes of political communication.[19]

Here, in the second half of the 1460s, as the Franco-Milanese alliance was growing stronger, we have Cicco Simonetta, Francesco Sforza's powerful secretary, sending Louis XI an elegant manuscript describing a Mass held in honor of Saint Martin, complete with musical notations.[20] The choice of this diplomatic gift was clearly significant. It expressed the intentions of Milan's rulers to affirm a liturgical identity that was the basis, in a way, of their aspiration to international recognition of the city-state's independence. This choice may have nonetheless appeared strange to the king of France, undoubtedly unfamiliar with such liturgical subtleties – despite the *captatio benevolentiae* visible in the choice to underline the traditional links connecting the memories of Saints Ambrose and Martin. The account of the Mass reminds the reader that Ambrose, while in his wooded retreat, miraculously attended Martin's funeral services, and it notes that Petrarch described the isolated sanctuary of Sant'Ambrogio ad Nemus in his book *On the Solitary Life*.[21] The *Ordo missae ambrosianae* accordingly joined a humanist, and already European, culture of books.[22]

The first notable annotation to Simonetta's document was made by Francesco della Croce (1391–1480), the *primicerio* of the Cathedral of Milan and an archiepiscopal vicar, under whose charge the manuscript was written. A professor at the University of Pavia with a doctorate in canon law, and an astute understanding of the Ambrosian liturgy, Francesco della Croce was one of the main actors of its reform in the fifteenth century.[23] Famous for his love of books[24] and his memory, which was described by Duke Galeazzo Maria Sforza as "marvelous and stupefying,"[25] he was the dedicatee of the now-lost life of Ambrose written by Pier Candido Decembrio in 1467.[26] Francesco della Croce, who also maintained a friendship with Cicco Simonetta, used this marginal note to outline in four points the specificities of a rite he ardently defends.[27]

"Firstly, the office may be called Ambrosian and not Gregorian owing to the hymns, the way of chanting, cantillating, and praying." The fact that the specificity of the Ambrosian chant is immediately emphasized clearly comes as no surprise to us: it was through hymns that the Milanese historically developed a distinct liturgy. But while this digression about sonority (which justified the fact that the manuscript sent to the king of France included neumes, an early form of musical notation) distinguished the Ambrosian ecclesiastical institution from the Gregorian order, the former nonetheless aspired to an eminent position in the universal Church: hence the importance of Francesco della Croce's second notation, which points out that a Mass of this kind was sung publicly during the Council of Constance – in all likelihood by Bartolomeo Capra, archbishop of Milan from 1414 to 1433, who played an important role in the Councils of Constance and Basel alike, participating with his humanist friends in the feverish hunt for manuscripts that characterized that period.[28]

The canonist's third notation concerns the most striking individuating feature of the Ambrosian tradition: "The solemnity of its prefaces during Mass." Recited by the celebrant, the preface comes after the offertory and prepares the Sanctus chant, which is followed by the prayers of the canon.[29] Those recited in Milan were filled with exclamations, anaphora, and "all the pomp of rhetoric."[30] In the Roman missal, only the preface to the Exultet is comparable. These oratory pieces are actually very old: the *Liber notitiae Sanctorum Mediolani*, written in the early fourteenth century, attributes their composition to Bishop Eusebius (449–62).[31] While some researchers question the existence of a collection of prefaces compiled as early as the fifth century[32] and support the idea of a composition staggered over time,[33] the dating of most of these pieces to the mid-fifth century is generally accepted.[34] As shown by Matthieu Smyth, this rich corpus (we currently know of sixty-eight Ambrosian prefaces)[35] conserves the memory of the "creativity of the bishop rhetoricians" of northern Italy – Zeno of Verona, Chromatius of Aquileia, Gaudentius of Brescia, Maximus of Turin, and of course, Ennodius of Pavia – at a time when preaching had become an integral part of the Eucharistic celebration.[36] Even if the Milanese prefaces also attest to the mutual and gradual intermingling of the Ambrosian and Roman traditions, they nonetheless express a singular voice that blends homiletics and euchology, that is to say they combine teaching with prayer.

Francesco della Croce's fourth notation designates the Milanese novelty that was undoubtedly the most disruptive to the Roman desire for liturgical unification, as it related to the calendar, notably how the date for Easter was calculated, which could be different in Rome and in Milan, where the Antioch calculation was used. The period of Lent was shorter in Milan than in Rome; instead of starting on Ash Wednesday, it began on the following Monday, which lengthened the preceding carnival period. As for the fifty days that followed the Easter celebration, in accordance with Ambrose's wishes as expressed in his commentary about Luke, they had to be observed like Sundays: this led to a prolonged Easter during which the faithful did not fast but continued to sing God's praises (the Alleluia was not reserved for Easter day alone, as in the Roman rite). Note in passing that Francesco della Croce was personally involved in an attempted reform of the Ambrosian calendar on behalf of Archbishop Francesco Pizolpasso and was therefore well placed to understand the decisive importance of this matter in the defense of Milan's *specificum*.[37]

This divergence in calendars had other consequences. With the liturgical year beginning on Saint Martin's Day (November 11), the Milanese Advent stretched over six Sundays, instead of four. The Sunday before Christmas, referred to as *Ante nativitatem Domini*, was devoted to the Virgin[38] and inaugurated an entire week dedicated to the Incarnation. At the end of the

Middle Ages, this liturgical calendar had decisive consequences on the rhythm of political life: a period of court festivities stretched from the festival of the Virgin to Epiphany, beginning before Christmas and extending past it, during which the prince, the *alter Christus*, received ambassadors and assembled political society.[39] This explains why the plotters of 1476, in choosing the date of December 26 to kill the tyrant, had committed a particularly resounding act of sacrilege in respect to the liturgical, and therefore political, specificities of the Ambrosian calendar. This also explains why the date of January 6 for the riot of 1439 can't be attributed to chance either.

Cicco Simonetta provides a less expert, but more directly political, reading of the Ambrosian liturgy. In three marginal notes, he directs his royal reader to the points that strike him as worthy of interest. Given the diplomatic significance of sending this manuscript to the king of France, we can imagine that these annotations, which highlight three characteristics of the ordo of the Mass celebrated by what Simonetta calls the "Ambrosians," are about more than the specificities of a technical denomination. So why does Simonetta write in the margins of the introductory liturgy (*ingressa*) that it is called *introitus* in the Roman rite?[40] In all likelihood because he wants to signal a difference that is more than terminological. In the entrance rite that precedes the Milanese Mass, beginning at least in the eighth century, the *ingressa* was more than the equivalent of the Gregorian *introitus*, notably in that it was not an antiphonal chant accompanying access to the altar.[41] More importantly, as Matthieu Smyth notes, "during Lenten Sundays in Milan, after the *ingressa*, the deacon dialogues with the people the litanies *Divinae pacis* and *Dicamus omnes*, adapted from the Greek."[42] These two universal prayers were the object of a book and expert commentary by Paul de Clerck.[43] He identifies numerous traces of their antiquity, notably, in the first prayer, the allusion to the emperor and empress as well as an invocation to peace "between Churches" and to the tranquility of those who carry the memory of ancient doctrinal fights.[44] The second prayer also whispers of an imminent danger from which God must liberate his people and refers to the archbishop as "our pope" (*papa nostro*)[45] – another archaistic trait whose conservation throughout the Middle Ages spread an implicit political message about the ecclesiological preeminence of the see of Milan.

Cicco Simonetta's second notation is a reference to the three triple kyries (the first concluding the Gloria, the second preceding the *dimissio*, the third following the postcommunion).[46] It highlights a custom, described by Ambrose himself,[47] that is also one of the most remarkable legacies of the Ambrosian liturgical tradition.[48] The kyries were sung after the homily and readings, but before the dismissal of the catechumens.[49] These liturgical formulas should have fallen out of use with the disappearance of the adult catechumenate, after which only children were baptized in the Middle Ages. And yet they remained, notably during Lent, when daily instruction was given in the form of the ancient "Mass of the Catechumens," which delivered an "ongoing education" to the faithful in dogma (with a guided reading of Genesis), morality (with that of the Proverbs), and spirituality (based on the chanting of the book of Psalms).[50]

This custom conformed to the requirement formulated by Ambrose in the first lines of *De mysteriis*: "On questions of right conduct we discoursed daily at the time when the lives of the patriarchs or the precepts of the Proverbs were being read, in order that, trained and instructed thereby, you might become accustomed to walk in the paths of our elders..."[51] The Ambrosian Mass therefore had a very pedagogical dimension, which partially justifies Cicco Simonetta's third and final remark, which is more of a value judgment than a liturgical description:[52] *Ambrosiani haec dicunt alte audiente populo. Gregoriani secrete.* "The Ambrosians say these things out loud as the people listen, the Gregorians in private." Did he mean that the Ambrosian liturgy was ultimately characterized by greater accessibility, for the "people," to the *mysterium*? The assertion is abrupt and the opposition schematic – even though the precocity with which the Feast of Corpus Christi became an integral part, beginning in 1327, of the Milanese devotional calendar does attest to this trend of bringing the faithful closer to the Eucharistic presence.[53] At the least, the final note by Cicco Simonetta expresses, with remarkable political clarity, the idea that a man of power in fifteenth-century Milan could have of the individual character of the Ambrosian Rite: powerful, ancient, pedagogical, and popular. It was the expression of a united and combative people, bearing emotions and arms, who never truly left the besieged basilica of 386.

SAVING THE PAST: THE AMBROSIAN RITE
AS ANTI-IMPERIAL RESISTANCE

One could argue that the Ambrosian liturgy therefore observed an accentuated form of Christo-centrism throughout the Middle Ages, starting with anti-Arianism, its supposed "deep matrix."[54] This analysis has the merit of identifying certain remarkable aspects of the Milanese *specificum* – the emphasis on the incarnation of the Word and Mary's virginity – that correspond both to favored themes of Ambrose's theology[55] and salient traits of Milanese spirituality, such as Marian devotion (which we know was put to political use by the signorial and then princely powers beginning in the second half of the fourteenth century).[56] But by directly linking Milan's liturgical distinctiveness to its ancient history, we would be oversimplifying a complex and multilayered history.[57]

Complex namely from a synchronic point of view: even in the city-state of Milan, the Ambrosian Rite was not unanimously accepted, owing to the liturgical pluralism that broadly characterized the history of medieval Christianity. Beginning in the thirteenth century, this pluralism grew, notably because mendicant orders were authorized, after 1247, to follow the *usum Romanae curiae*, the expression of a universal ecclesiology triumphant at that time.[58] This was also the case for the Umiliati. Though Filippo di Lampugnano, the archbishop of Milan from 1196 to 1206, had authorized the order to build the Santa Maria church in Brera on the condition that they adopt the Ambrosian Rite, a decision by Pope Alexander IV dispensed them from this requirement in 1256.[59] Though the Roman curia likely never had the intention, or at least not before the Council of Trent, of attacking the liturgical idiosyncrasies of Milan, the city's archbishops long tried to defend them against ritual pluralism. Largely in vain: Ottone Visconti was unable to force the Ambrosian Rite on the Augustinians, and Giovanni Visconti, in 1342, had to resign himself to allowing the Cistercians of Chiaravalle to officiate "in a private manner," according to the Roman Rite.[60]

Considered from a diachronic perspective, the heterogeneousness of the history of the invention of the Ambrosian liturgical tradition is even more apparent. The debates about the Greek origins of the Ambrosian Rite that long occupied liturgy specialists are now outdated:[61] it is quite clear that the Milanese Church developed "a liturgy that was its own, but [also] essentially Gallican"[62] – "Gallican" meaning nothing more here than "non-Roman Western rite."[63] The Church adopted this liturgy over a very long period of time, burying beneath the thick layer of its historical sediments the "primitive bedrock"[64] that is passionately searched for by liturgists and that remains, despite their efforts, quite far from Ambrose's era. All that counts here is this archaeological approach, and little matter in the end that the history of the Ambrosian Rite is always written, by those ardent specialists refusing to let their research subject grow cold, as the loss of a forgotten tradition, gradually muddled by hybridizations that they can't help but describe in terms of infidelity and contagion. Matthieu Smyth, for example, in showing how the structure of Milanese liturgical books "was upended following Romanizing contamination" beginning in the ninth century, nonetheless concludes that "the archdiocese of Milan conserves, though in a highly adulterated form, the vestiges of the ancient Western rite."[65]

Here's the important part: if we exclude the seventh-century book of sacraments discovered by paleographers under the palimpsest of manuscript 908 of Saint Gall's *Stiftsbibliothek* (it owes its nickname, *rex palimpsestorum*, "king of the palimpsests," to its eleven successive writings),[66] the first written evidence of the Ambrosian liturgy dates to the ninth century, to the episcopate of Odelperto (803-13), likely reformer of the Milanese sacramentary.[67] This concomitance between the conservation of the first "Ambrosian" liturgical books and the Carolingians' desire to unify the liturgy of the Eucharistic celebration according to Roman customs has bothered specialists. Was it the Frankish threat that "made the Ambrosians aware that they were the custodians of a treasure?"[68] A treasure that always had to be defended from attempts, stubbornly repeated from Charlemagne onward, to chip away at its precious uniqueness, for the history of the Ambrosian Rite is a never-ending battle.[69] We can easily circumvent these explanations with a reality that can be described quite simply: stumbling against the Carolingian era as we are trying to trace back in time the written transmission of liturgical sources is no longer surprising – we now know that the crystallization of the Ambrosian Rite in the ninth century is a

fundamental threshold, and one difficult to cross, in the archaeology of the posthumous lives of Ambrose, a figure that is, in
good part, a Carolingian reinvention.

For that matter are we certain that Charlemagne intended to
attack the Milanese *specificum*? Article 80 of the *Admonitio generalis* capitulary (March 23, 789) cites the example of his predecessor
Pepin the Short (*genitor noster Pippinus rex*) "when he suppressed
the Gallican chant with an eye to unity with the apostolic See."[70]
But, in fact, because this desire to Romanize liturgical practices
was entirely political in nature, it was applied pragmatically in
Milan, with whom an alliance was invaluable to the Frankish
rulers. Furthermore, Frankish accounts of the Carolingians' attitude to the specificities of the Ambrosian Rite that could have
impeded their imperial aim of liturgical unification in accordance with the Roman Rite are far from unequivocal. The *Annals
of Lorsch* mention the baptism of one of Charlemagne's daugh-
ters, Gisela, by the archbishop of Milan in 781[71]– he could only
have done so using the Ambrosian Rite. Conversely, an epigram
attributed to Paul the Deacon, conserved in a manuscript in the
Monte Cassino archives, describes a trial by ordeal that reportedly set a "Roman chanter" against an "Ambrosian chanter"
upon the initiative of Paolino, the patriarch of Aquileia.[72] The
Roman chant supposedly emerged victorious from this test,
which convinced Charlemagne to promote its circulation in his
empire, while the Milanese people kept the right to chant per
their custom.[73]

The legend of a Carolingian attack on the Ambrosian liturgy
in reality emerges fully armed from the *Historia Mediolanensis*, the
anonymous chronicle attributed to Landulf Senior, who in all
likelihood finished it in 1085.[74] Chapters 10 to 14 of Book 2 recount
the supposed sermon of the archbishop of Milan, Thomas, who
describes how a mysterious bishop by the name of Eugenius

defended, with many miracles, the *officium Ambrosianum* from Pope Adrian I and Emperor Charles.[75] This account tells us that Charlemagne, against the pious resistance of the Milanese people, ordered the destruction of all Ambrosian books.[76] Here, every word counts: the books are called Ambrosian because they were marked with the *titulus* of Ambrose, whose name qualified (and in this case jeopardized) the liturgical tradition that associated itself with him. The books were surrendered to the Carolingian rulers, willingly or by force, who intended to destroy them by fire or "exile" them to the other side of the mountains. In the eyes of the Milanese people, this separation equated to obliteration. Incidentally the origin of the chronicler's invention of a book burning is clear: the rhetorical amplification of the well-documented phenomenon of the exchange and transfer of liturgical books in the Carolingian era.

The dramatization springs here from the heroic resistance of Bishop Eugenius, who, lovingly defending the *mysterium ambrosianum*, became more than its protector, almost its father; this is all the more striking as he was not the bishop of Milan, but of an unspecified location on the other side of the mountains: *Eugenius transmontanus episcopus, amator et quasi pater Ambrosiani mysterii nec non et protector.*[77] The books themselves attempted to defy the outrage inflicted upon them: those that had been taken, captive, to Rome by the emperor's minions miraculously undid their bonds and rejected the pontifical seal that had been stamped on them, "[giving] forth a great and frightful noise in the hearing of all."[78] But the great miracle occurred in Milan, where the faithful reassembled their dismantled treasure. As they removed a missal faithfully hidden in a cave for six weeks, Bishop Eugenius solicited wise men, "both laymen and clergy," to re-create by memory the handbook of liturgical tradition that was the intended object of destruction and that unlike the single missal could no longer be found in the area at all.[79] It's a good story, which metaphorically describes two strongholds of memory, or more precisely two places that resist forgetting: the physical site (the written trace hiding in the crevices of a rock to await better days) and the mental site (the folds of memory in which the oral traces of a lost tradition come to nestle).[80] These oral traces were gathered by Bishop Eugenius, who re-created, with scraps of individual memories, a unified collective memory. In other words, Eugenius is, in the realm of fiction, the father of the anamnesis of the Ambrosian mystery.

ORDER THROUGH BOOKS: REFORM, PRESERVE, AND GOVERN

Landulf's "fables," wrote Louis Duchesne, the French priest and church historian, "do not merit credibility."[81] Undoubtedly, but they nonetheless became part of the tradition that followed. Milanese chroniclers largely borrowed the episode, all the way to Galvano Fiamma,[82] though he appeared troubled by the ambivalence around the figure of Charlemagne – both "foreign" emperor and hero of the epic tradition – in fourteenth-century Milanese culture.[83] More significantly, the memory of the violent confrontation between the imperial power and the Ambrosian *specificum* was ritualized through the cult of Eugenius, a history of whom was written by Enrico Cattaneo.[84] The foreign bishop was buried in the Basilica of Sant'Eustorgio (which prided itself on having safeguarded the relics of the Magi until Emperor Frederick Barbarossa took them to Cologne in 1164).[85] Milan's large Dominican church, where, remember, Galvano Fiamma was a rector, was also an important site in the transmission of Ambrose's memory.[86] Eugenius was celebrated on the anniversary of his inhumation, on December 30, which meant his festival was incorporated into the long Ambrosian Christmas cycle: the first written account of this festival is found in the Valtravaglia calendar, which slightly preceded Beroldus's great liturgical codification.[87] Presenting himself as *custos et cicendelarius* – guardian of the treasure and responsible for the candelabras of the choir – Beroldus wrote his *Ordo et caeremoniae ecclesiae Ambrosianae Mediolanensis* shortly after the death of Archbishop Olricus in 1126.[88]

The first documentation of Beroldus's large liturgical compilation, contemporaneous with Martino Corbo's textual recapitulation, is found in a famous composite manuscript, likely established in 1139–40, conserved at the Ambrosian Library of Milan.[89] It includes various liturgical texts, including Beroldus's,[90] which immediately precedes the first part of *De situ civitatis Mediolani,*[91] and *De adventu Barabe apostoli,*[92] a short text about Archbishop Anathalon,[93] and *Sermo b. Thomae.*[94] This manuscript was one of the foundational texts of the city of Milan's civic identity: Paolo Tomea has meticulously shown how the legend of Saint Barnabus was the foundation for Milan's attempts to claim an apostolic origin, which is also expressed, quite complexly, in *De situ civitatis Mediolani.*[95] However, this hybrid text (both a *Liber pontificalis* of the bishops of Milan and a *Descriptio* of Milan) was sometimes attributed in the late Middle Ages to Ambrose himself, appearing at the time as *De aedificatione urbis Mediolani*: it was printed with this title in 1478 in Bonino Monbrizio's *Sanctuarium.*[96]

But beyond this codicological proximity, we can hypothesize that Beroldus's *Ordo* and *Sermo b. Thomae archiepiscopi Mediolani* are more tightly connected than one would ordinarily think. This would explain a lexical subtlety worth exploring: the legend of Eugenius claims that he reconstructed the Ambrosian handbook while an unnamed cleric protected the missal in a cave. If we broadly understand "missal" as any liturgical manuscript containing the specific elements of each Mass (sacerdotal expressions, scriptural readings, and chanted portions), then we have to admit that no complete missal of the Ambrosian Rite existed before the fifteenth century.[97] The "handbook" (*manuale* or *liber manualis*), on the other hand, is specific to the Milanese liturgical tradition; it contains all the pieces of the antiphonary; the *incipites* of psalms, hymns, and orisons; as well as, on occasion, certain ritual elements.[98] But the distinction between these two liturgical books didn't truly take on meaning until Beroldus's liturgical compilation, which more clearly defined the roles of two groups of clergy: the *decumani*, the minor clergy; and the *cardinales*, who assisted the archbishop with his celebrations. The missal was reserved for the *cardinales* alone – which no doubt explains the more aristocratic staging of its preservation in the legend of Eugenius. Patrizia Carmassi's important study used this example to show that the liturgical ordo of the Ambrosian Rite was being constructed at the same time as the ordos of the Milanese Church.[99]

This means that Ambrosian liturgical memory was also, and quite logically, structured by books. If we keep going, we will see that this history, at every milestone, bumps into the political history of the communal city-state. In 1269, the rector of the S. Vito church of Milan, Giovanni Boffa, produced a new version of Beroldus's text, which liturgists refer to as *Beroldus novus*.[100] Coinciding with the writings of Bonvesin da la Riva, this initiative likely shared his political aspirations, in line with the new communal age of documentary recording.[101] In the first third of the fourteenth century, as the signorialization of communal institutions was also upsetting the internal hierarchies of the Milanese Church (notably by attenuating the *decumani/cardinales* distinction) and after John XXII placed an interdict on Milan, there emerged a need to write a new compendium of the Eucharistic celebration: Giovanni Bello de Guerciis, in the prologue to his *Liber celebrationis misse ambrosiane*, affirmed once again the necessity to defend the Ambrosian Rite from the threat of being forgotten.[102]

This same desire for preservation drove the reformers of the fifteenth century, such as Archbishop Francesco Pizolpasso and Cardinal Giovanni Arcimboldi. The latter, the great state prelate whose career was built in the shadow of the Sforzas' power and who was archbishop of Milan from 1485 to 1488, understood that the printing press was reigniting the rivalry between the Roman and Ambrosian Rites: after the *Missale romanum* was printed in 1474, a response was needed, and quickly.[103] Beginning in 1475, Arcimboldi also sponsored the publication of the Ambrosian missal and breviary–at the same time as Paulinus of Milan's *Vita* and certain texts by Ambrose were also published (*De officiis* was printed in 1474).[104] Pietro Casola capped off this pastoral and commercial undertaking in 1490 by printing his *Breviarum ambrosianum*, thereby helping to even more firmly establish the liturgical tradition.[105]

So have we finally made it out of the besieged basilica? Most certainly not, for the defenders of the Ambrosian Rite kept inventing adversaries for themselves. The Milanese legend of liturgical books miraculously safeguarded from Carolingian aggression is, in many respects, the foundation of the defensive notion of the Ambrosian *specificum* whose political genealogy I have attempted to trace here. And its genealogy is political–it's easy to see how the Ambrosian Rite could have been interpreted as a resource for collective mobilization against sovereign powers threatening to thwart the long history of Milanese liberties. Indeed, Cicco Simonetta indicates as much in his notes in the margins of the manuscript he sent to the king of France. We should note while the memory of this confrontation is revived time and time again, we are seeing it in a crumpled-up version of sorts: the Eugenius in the legend is the new Ambrose, as

assuredly as the Charlemagne imagined by the Milanese people takes on the role of Theodosius. But when Landulf Senior
incorporated the emperor into his account, he subjected him
to his own preoccupations regarding the precommunal unrest
that erupted after the Gregorian Reform and the confrontation
between the papacy and the empire.[106] One generation after this
notable period of liturgical and ecclesiological organization in
the 1140s – which corresponds to the period in which Martino
Corbo collected Ambrose's works – the shadow of another imperial threat, Frederick Barbarossa, was being cast. So perhaps,
to further smooth out this wrinkled memory, we should linger
a bit longer in Ambrose's company, as the good pastor leads his
besieged flock in singing his hymns. And listen closely to their
far-off echoes, several centuries distant, to hear what they *themselves heard*, or more importantly – *understood*.

FIFTEEN

The Magic of Hymns:
Singing as in Ambrose's Time

Sing an Ambrosian Mass? Not a chance: it might kill him. When Cicco Simonetta sought out Giacomo della Torre, bishop of Pavia, to request that he prepare a Mass in honor of Giovanni Arcimboldi, recently elevated to the cardinal's purple, the prelate was hiding under his blankets, terrified at the prospect of having to sing the service. Because of a troublesome constitution, he ran the risk of fatal suffocation should he even try to voice the first few notes. That, he explained baldly to the ducal counselor on May 20, 1473, was why, as bishop of Pavia, he had prudently avoided celebrating Mass for fourteen years.[1]

Beyond the sharp irony in the report Simonetta made to Galeazzo Maria Sforza, the affair was one of considerable importance. The duke had laid out the matter clearly in a letter to his counselor the previous day, mentioning that his request to Giacomo della Torre had gone unanswered. Arcimboldi, the duke explained, had to be honored with a Mass, and "it is of great importance that this Mass be in the Ambrosian Rite."[2] The new cardinal belonged to the inner circle of Milanese political society (he had been a member of the Privy Council from 1458 to 1464), and it was crucial for political reasons, now that he was transferring to Rome, to remind him of who, in Milan, was his real patron: Ambrose.[3] And the bishop of Pavia's reply was also political, since his diplomatic illness is perhaps best explained, as the last sentence in Simonetta's letter suggests, by the fact that he could see no justification for celebrating an Ambrosian Mass outside the churches of Milan.[4]

Will it in fact prove possible to trace the political genealogy of this identification between a city, a name, and a rite? Anamnesis, as we have seen, is a difficult proposition, because any motion countering the sedimentation of time meets with agglomerations of memory so fiercely resistant as to block one's passage. We have encountered them in retracing the invention of the liturgical tradition, and in unraveling the order of books by which time is compressed into an opaque and perpetual present, always returning to the same historical thresholds: in the eleventh to twelfth century and in Carolingian times, two periods that bookend each other and form an obstacle to accessing an earlier past. Certain pieces of the liturgy, such as the prefaces and the universal prayers, summon echoes from a very ancient time. But Ambrose is still a long way back, so far as to be unrecognizable. The hymns, though, are different. With the hymns, we have a single and possibly last chance to get closer to Ambrose himself and to finally pierce through the layers of time interposed between him and the late Middle Ages in Milan.

WHAT "AMBROSIAN" MEANS: MANUSCRIPT TRANSMISSION, LITERARY ATTRIBUTION

It is the Ambrosian hymns, then, that will allow us to resume our archaeology of a proper name. For when calling Milan's liturgy Ambrosian, we are mostly referring to the hymns sung in Milan's churches.[5] And what distinguishes the hymns is that Ambrose composed them and had them sung. The Ambrosian hymns were in fact a liturgical and textual creation that was quickly stabilized and almost immediately imitated; they had hardly any precedent in the Latin West, and their invention is attributed to Ambrose himself. With these hymns, we find ourselves close to the major turning point of late antiquity associated with Ambrose's name.[6] Taking their meter from the classical lyrics of the Augustan century (verses in iambic dimeter), the hymns owe much of their musicality to Horace's *carmen saeculare*, which had found its full meaning in the context of the public liturgy – but their musicality was also inspired by the qualities of Virgil's narrative.[7] The influence is so unmistakable that it makes the relatively recent practice of pointedly distinguishing between classical and Christian hymns somewhat absurd. It comes down to artificially separating – for what can only be obscurely doctrinal reasons – two traditions that the authors of the early hymns were in fact seeking to link, both through music and meaning.

This clear case of borrowing from the Romans should not obscure the fact that early Christian hymnody was largely drawing on a Hellenistic tradition – and this is what ancient sources meant in citing the hymns' Eastern origin, recalling that Hilary of Poitiers brought the practice of hymn-singing back from Asia Minor in 361. The bishop of Poitiers is credited with composing the Gloria, a morning hymn that has come down to us by virtue of its incorporation into the ordinary of the Roman Mass.[8] Tradition recognizes no other predecessor of Ambrose's in the invention of hymns – and Ambrose was always very forthright in declaring his admiration for Hilary. Both in fact developed their politically committed hymn-singing in the same context of fighting the Arian heresy.

Current scholarship, dominated by the towering figure of Jacques Fontaine, agrees on the authenticity of twelve to fourteen hymns attributed to Ambrose, but at the end of the Middle Ages, at least forty hymns were designated as Ambrosian. What did that mean, exactly? Did it imply that they were considered the personal work of Saint Ambrose, or are we to understand that the term also referred to all the hymns written in Ambrose's style? The ancient authors most likely used the adjective *ambrosianus* sometimes to signal the bishop's authority and sometimes the poet's authorship. This was true of Venerable Bede,[9] and also of Isidore of Seville, who says unambiguously that the Ambrosian hymns were so called "because they started to be sung in the Church of Milan at the time of Ambrose" (*De ecclesiasticis officiis*, 1, 6, 2). It was not a question of noticing what constituted the bishop's personal genius but of describing instead a textual tradition that took its authority from Ambrose's name – a tradition based on metrical and stylistic schemas that could be imitated, reworked, and reused.

Indeed, hymns became common to the Church as a whole upon being incorporated into the liturgical patrimony. In Vannes in 455, Agde in 506, Tours in 567, and Toledo in 633, the councils prescribed the singing of hymns – and in the case of the fourth council of Toledo, explicit reference was made to the hymns of Hilary and Ambrose.[10] The twenty-fourth canon of the second Council of Tours provides an interesting sidelight on the subject: "And it is permitted for us to have Ambrosian [books] in the canon; nevertheless, since there are some of the others, which in form are worthy of singing, we wish freely to embrace besides [those books] the names of whose authors have been written in the margin; since nothing stands in the way of saying those that have accorded with the faith."[11] If we accept the idea that the council fathers were speaking here of a liturgical heritage and not a literary work, it becomes clear that *ambrosianus* refers to the authority of a name, not the name of an author.[12] In other words, contrary to the modern idea of the function of an author, *ambrosius* was already in the seventh century too great a name to be placed at the head of books; instead the name is slipped, more humbly and more gloriously, into the soil of a tradition that it enriches and is transcended by.

Considering what "Ambrosian" might mean also leads us to distinguish more clearly between two questions that, though braided together, are nonetheless distinct in nature: the question of the hymns' attribution and the related one of their manuscript transmission. On the latter point, we can only turn to the work of Marie-Hélène Jullien, who has shown that there is practically no tradition of the hymns as texts independent of their transmission as part of the liturgy.[13] The only exceptions are three school notebooks (the first two copied at Reichenau at the beginning of the eighth century, the third at Saint-Denis in the mid-eighth century)[14] and an anthology of Christian poems of Parisian origin (also dating from the mid-eighth century).[15] All the other surviving witness manuscripts are for liturgical use, and none predates the Carolingian period. The manuscript transmission of Ambrosian hymns, considered as the heritage of the universal Church, cannot be dissociated from the liturgical mutations that affected hymnaries during the early Middle Ages.[16] The preservation, correction, or suppression of one piece or another would in no way have obeyed the logic applicable to literary attribution, but would have followed the vagaries of ecclesiastical decision-making relative to liturgical developments, at least since the Carolingian *reformatio*.

Strictly philological, Marie-Hélène Jullien's undertaking (like Jacques Fontaine's) has consisted of reconstructing the transmission of the fourteen hymns today believed to be authentic, in order to establish their texts. She consequently identifies groups of witnesses, generally on the basis of their place of provenance. A first cluster of Milanese manuscripts can thus be distinguished, consisting of three hymnaries from the last third of the ninth century; the three are nearly identical and are also the only surviving manuscripts to include all fourteen of the Ambrosian hymns.[17] It is reasonable to suppose, therefore, that they recopy an older, presumably pre-Carolingian hymnary. But if there did in fact exist a *hymnarium Ambrosianum*, nothing confirms the prior existence of an Ambrosian *liber hymnorum*, which is to say a collection made during Ambrose's own lifetime, as attested in the case of Hilary of Poitiers by an observation of Jerome's.[18] Consequently, the history of the manuscript tradition relating to Ambrose's hymns differs radically from the tradition relating to his other texts – in particular his correspondence – precisely because his hymns are not considered texts that bear his authorial seal.

The groupings of witnesses allow us to reconstruct the nodes and rhythms of the hymns' transmission in Western liturgy. From Milan, the hymns spread easily toward Italy, France, and Germany, but also toward England; the path they took to reach Spain (where the Ambrosian hymns' manuscript tradition has its own particulars) is much less clear. It seems evident that the "Benedictine family" of monasteries (Bobbio, Reichenau, Saint Gall, Saint-Denis, Canterbury, and Saint Martin of Tours, to mention only the most important) offered relay points for the rapid diffusion of manuscripts. Enjoining monks to sing Ambrosian hymns in his "Rule of Saint Benedict," Benedict of Nursia was already using the term *ambrosianum* as a common noun referring to a liturgical tradition.[19]

One indisputable fact is that, whether the hymns are considered as Ambrose's work or as the patrimony of the Church and drawing authority from his name, they were never included in Ambrose's collected works, which were first compiled, as we know, by Martino Corbo in the 1140s. In citing a hymn, which a preacher might do either implicitly or explicitly, a different way of referencing the text was called for. When, in the second half of the thirteenth century, Federico Visconti, archbishop of Pisa, quoted from a work attributed to Ambrose in one of his sermons (*De officiis ministrorum*, for example, or *De institutione virginis*, to mention only two of his common references), he logically enough would use the formula *ut dicit beatus Ambrosius* (so says Saint Ambrose), yet when he introduced four verses from Hymn 7, *Illuminans altissimus*, it was with the words *unde in ymno dicitur sic* (thus is it said in the hymn).[20]

Yet during the Carolingian period, a certain Walafrid Strabo took issue in his treatise on liturgical history with the great number of hymns attributed to Ambrose: "It seems impossible that he could have made the kind of hymns of which we find so many, pieces that in their very expression betray a lack of culture unusual in Ambrose."[21] But Strabo, who was the tutor to King Louis the Pious's son, was a lonely voice in his century, and even more so in the centuries to follow. If there was indeed a "Carolingian Renaissance," it was no more than a flash in the pan, brilliant but quickly extinguished. Consider, for example, the *Milleloquium Ambrosianum* commissioned by Pope Clement VI from the bishop of Urbino, Bartolomeo Carusi: this anthology contains no hymns because it collects manuscripts of Ambrosian writings, not liturgical manuscripts.[22] Only with the revival of humanism in the fifteenth century would Ambrose's hymns again be read and commented on as literary creations.

The first evidence of any literary attention to the liturgical tradition dates to 1460, with an autograph manuscript by Francesco della Croce, who was, as we've seen, one of the main actors in the fifteenth-century reform of Ambrosian liturgy.

His *Expositio literalis hymnorum sancti Ambrosii Archiepiscopi Mediolani* glosses forty-one hymns that were known as Ambrosian.[23] Beyond the Ambrosian missal and the *Ordo missae*, to which he gave formal definition, Francesco della Croce intended to throw light on the work and doctrine of "our patron saint Ambrose."[24] While his commentaries sometimes dwell on liturgical issues or topographical clarification, it is most often the vocabulary itself that draws the humanist's full attention, but if he sometimes compares a text with other liturgical manuscripts, he never compares it with other works by Ambrose, though he knew them well.[25] In other words, though the project in itself indicates a new interest in Ambrose's hymns, recognizing them as literary texts and separating them out from the anonymous tradition of liturgical books, the means that della Croce uses in his commentary betray the force and pervasiveness of an overall concept of hymnology that is imagined as a component of an original Ambrosian Rite – a paradoxical component, since its widespread diffusion carried far beyond Milan a liturgical tradition whose idiosyncratic aspects continued to be vaunted.

The important point is that in the second half of the fifteenth century, even for an erudite scholar like Francesco della Croce, there existed barely forty hymns that qualified as Ambrosian – with all the nuances that we might attach to the term. This corpus seems to have remained fairly stable all through the Middle Ages, as confirmed by Michel Huglo's study of the catalog.[26] As soon as one tries, as Walafrid Strabo did, to sift through the list so as to keep only those that can reasonably be attributed to Ambrose himself, it melts away like snow under the sun. In the second half of the sixteenth century, only sixteen to eighteen of the hymns were still widely held to be authentic; and in their Paris edition of 1690, the Maurists attributed only twelve hymns to Ambrose – of which another five have since been rejected by more recent scholarship.[27] The Maurists apparently assigned a high degree of credibility to the indirect tradition, that is, the formal attribution, made by contemporaries and later authors thought to be reliable, of certain hymns (or certain of their verses) to Ambrose himself. Since the foundational work of Luigi Biraghi in 1862, modern scholars have generally agreed that authentication by other authors can only become a determining criterion if it coincides with two other criteria: the continued appearance of the hymn in manuscript transcriptions of Milanese liturgy on the one hand, and the consonance of metrical, stylistic, and conceptual particulars with Ambrose's known practices on the other.[28]

But the latter criterion requires having at least a small corpus of unquestioned authenticity. Today, scholars have agreed on four reference hymns.[29] The first is Hymn 1, *Aeterne rerum conditor*, two verses of which are cited by Augustine as "verses of the blessed Ambrose," and which Ambrose himself mentioned in a famous page of his *Hexameron* on the crowing of the cock.[30] The second, also cited by Augustine, is Hymn 3, *Iam surgit hora tertiat*, celebrating the hour when Christ ascended to the cross and offering a meditation on redemption; its liturgical use during the office of terce has been attested to by many authors (Caesarius of Arles, Aurelian, Augustine of Canterbury) and a solid manuscript tradition.[31] The third is Hymn 4, *Deus creator omnium*, an evening hymn that came to be used in the monastic office early on and that had the distinction of being sung every day in Milan. Augustine cites these verses twice, in November 386 in his *De vita beata*, when his mother, Monica, "recognized these words, which were fixed deep in her memory, and, as though awakening into her faith, uttered joyously that verse of our priest," and again in the *Confessions*, where, discussing his distress on the day following his mother's burial, he addresses God, reciting "those true verses of Ambrose" that came back into his memory.[32] The fourth, finally, is Hymn 5, *Intende qui regis Israel*, very likely sung during Advent or Christmas, and whose second strophe was cited by Pope Celestine during the Council of Rome in 430. He attributed it to "Ambrose, of blessed memory," remembering it as if it were a personal memory.[33]

These four hymns share the formal characteristic of being neatly divided into four parts, with a complex interplay of internal correspondences between the four double strophes.[34] Manlio Simonetti has described this as a general stylistic trait that makes of each strophe a symmetrical structure that features both *concinnitas* (symmetrical arrangement) and *variatio* (variation).[35] This structure perhaps reflects the constraints of having to split an antiphonal chant – that is, one sung by two alternating choirs, as opposed to a responsorial chant where the choir responds to a soloist. It allows for considerable flexibility, but probably requires that the syntactical unit accord with the strophic unit. Thus Hymn 9, *Hic est dies uerus dei*, an Easter hymn, was long presumed to be authentic because of its inclusion in the patristic anthology compiled by Caesarius of Arles (not to mention its formal attribution to Ambrose in the fifteenth century by Denys the Carthusian in his *Commentary on the Hymns of the Church*). Today it is generally believed to be apocryphal, for the sole reason that a syntactic break divides the second strophe, with one sentence ending and another starting.[36]

Combining all three criteria identified by Luigi Biraghi as necessary for a presumption of authenticity, Jacques Fontaine has proposed assigning the hymns a place on a graduated scale of "Ambrosianness," divided into four levels: certainly Ambrosian, very probably Ambrosian, possibly Ambrosian, and probably not Ambrosian. Those in the last category are "to be considered as admiring homages, quite ancient ones, to Ambrose's mastery, and not as the impostures of meanly intentioned forgers."[37] If that is the case, an attribution of Ambrosianness points back to an Ambrosian school, contemporary with the bishop or nearly so. The best example of this posthumous life of Ambrosian hymns is the poetic work of Ennodius, bishop of Pavia, at the beginning of the sixth century, which constitutes, as we've already seen, a reactualization rather than an imitation.[38]

THE MEMORY PRINT OF HYMNS

In passing from the meaning of *ambrosianus* in the minds of medieval authors to debates among contemporary scholars on the Ambrosianness of the hymns, we have certainly strayed from the history of the lived memory of Ambrose, which is and remains the purpose of these pages. That memory no doubt vibrated in medieval Milan to the sound of the hymns publicly sung during the various offices, but also in the privacy of individual prayer. Nothing at the time – neither in the liturgical books, nor a fortiori in the hymns' ritual performance – allowed for a distinction between those that were "certainly Ambrosian," "possibly Ambrosian," or "probably Ambrosian." The hymns were all Ambrosian, since Ambrose's memory blanketed the city like a protective cloak, and Ambrose's name stamped the people's proud singing of God's praises, in a manner that had been adopted throughout Christendom, all the while maintaining and celebrating the liturgical specificities that founded their identity, and this with the force of ritual. Proceeding by best practices, the hymns to be considered here should be the forty that were thought to be Ambrosian because transmitted with the complete offices of the Milanese liturgical books.[39] But we lack the sources to recapture the inner vibration felt by Augustine's mother when the still vivid *memoria* of Ambrose's song came unexpectedly to her, or again that felt by her son when the *recordatio* of his dead mother's memory came back to him, and so on along a chain of memory and faith.

Ambrose was incontestably the first to theorize about the emotional effect of hymn-singing on the Christian populace – his *Commentary on the Psalms* (*Explanatio psalmorum XII*) contains a theological meditation on the functions of psalmody.[40] There is no question that hymnody should be considered a continuation of psalmody, which naturally makes Ambrose, exegete of the psalms and author of *De prophetia David*, a new David.[41] The kinship between the two is underlined by the proximity of the psalms and hymns in the liturgy. While it is true that there is nothing in the liturgical sources to indicate exactly when in the service the hymns were to be sung,[42] it is reasonable to follow Antoon Bastiaensen's hypothesis that puts them at the beginning of the service just before the recitation of the psalms, "the normal function of the hymn [being] to introduce the psalmody and inspirit the psalm singers."[43]

Ambrose's gloss on Psalm 118, which develops a theology of the *delectatio* afforded by the musicality of choral song, applies as well to hymns: "The blessed David, in his ardor to taste again and re-create the grace of these eternal and heavenly delights, has made for us, with his gift of psalmody, a model of celestial life."[44] As Cécile Lanéry has shown, this *delectatio*, which provides the listener a sense-derived emotion that leads him or her on the path to conversion, is above all a method of persuasion. And the sublime style plays its part. If Ambrose's poetic prose is characterized by its musical effects (particularly the superposition of the metrical ictus, or stress, on the accented syllable), it stands out for its *suavitas*, which would be better translated by "seduction" rather than "sweetness."[45] Working to establish the kinship between the notions of "glory" and "inactivity," Giorgio Agamben has studied the tradition that emanated from the

Ambrose-inspired hymnic poetry, beyond the Franciscan "Canticle of the Sun," which "constitutes its last great example and also marks its end." In the work of Hölderlin or Rilke, a "clearly hymnic intention" may be expressed in the elegiac form of the lament. By this route, Agamben arrives at the following poetic and intriguing definition: "The hymn is the radical deactivation of meaningful language, speech rendered absolutely without use, and yet preserved as speech in the form of the liturgy."[46]

Song is a gift of God, song is the playing of a child. And through this play, which is an effective tool for teaching the aesthetic perception of Truth, the faithful commune with a gaiety that is the counterpart of the grace bestowed by Christ. Such is the meaning – or one of the meanings – of the first strophe of Hymn 14, *Aeterna Christi munera*, which addresses the martyrs' struggle:[47]

Aeterna Christi munera
et martyrum victorias
laudes ferentes debitas
laetis canamus mentibus.

The eternal games, Christ's gift
and the victories of the martyrs
paying our debts of praise
let us celebrate them joyfully.

The double meaning of *munus* is what gives the hymn its complexity. It's about gifts, and the martyrs are always a gift, either made to Christ or from Christ, as in Hymn 11, which is about the discovery of Gervasius and Protasius:

To thee, Jesus, renewed graces!
Discoverer of a new gift [*noui repertor muneris*],

I sing to thee of having found
The martyrs Protasius and Gervasius.

It's about a gift, but it's also about a game. Christ is both the dedicatee of this game, which the next verse, with its reference to "victory," invites us to identify as the bloody circus games, and its *agonothete* (in ancient Greece, the public official charged with organizing the games). The image crops up often in Ambrose's writing, and he never misses an opportunity to state his aversion to the violent games of the circus: earthly combat is simply the inversion of spiritual combat, where the martyr triumphs by his death over his adversary. And as the verb *canere* in the fourth verse – which often recurs in these hymns – must be understood both in its proper sense (to sing) and figuratively (to celebrate), we gain a better grasp of the sensory and doctrinal import of joy.

Joy is first and foremost the expression of a choir in unison, the strong elation of the irrepressible collectivity singing with one voice. Ambrose has celebrated this force in lively passages of his commentary on the first psalm of David, where he compares the populace raising its voice in song to a lyre vibrating under the breath of the Holy Spirit: "A musician's fingers often play false notes on the few strings of his instrument, but the Holy Spirit playing on the people never strikes a false note."[48] The singing of the congregation reabsorbed the dissension of individual voices in a general *symphonia*, which was at once musical, doctrinal, and social.[49] This inner harmony of the Christian people was just the earthly shadow of the spirit canticles sung by the choirs of angels. But let's travel forward momentarily to the struggles of the communes in the twelfth and thirteenth centuries, when some political thinkers from the *popolo* tried to give a foundation in reason to the idea that the people's authority could lay claim to a kind of infallibility. How can we not think that the liturgical tradition was taken both as an encouragement and an inspiration, and that its social impact was at least as great as the legal adages based on the concept of *vox populi vox Dei*?

We could say the same of the sixth verse of Hymn 13, *Apostolorum supparem*, celebrating the martyrdom of Lawrence, which develops the biblical theme of the poor considered as the Church's treasure. Ordered by his persecutor to turn over the Church's valuables, Lawrence, who was Pope Sixtus's archdeacon, devised a pious ruse, appearing before the praetor with a band of ragged beggars. His words play on the opposition of *inopes* and *opes*:

> *Spectaculum pulcherrimum!*
> *egena cogit agmina*
> *inopesque monstrans praedicat:*
> *"Hi sunt opes ecclesiae."*

> O most glorious of spectacles!
> He gathered up the ranks of the poor,
> showed forth the penniless, and proclaimed,
> "These are the riches of the Church."[50]

There is an account in Ambrose's *De officiis* of a stratagem very comparable to Lawrence's, which ends with the statement *Hi sunt thesauri Ecclesiae*, "Here are the treasures of the Church."[51] This passage occurs within a very specific polemical context, since the bishop was justifying his decision to melt down all the church's valuable plate to ransom the Catholics captured by the Goths after the terrible Battle of Adrianople in 378.[52] The decision, he said, met with a hostile reaction from the court – and presumably from the donors, who saw the proofs of their generosity obliterated.[53] The Lawrence legend allowed Ambrose to equate this criticism with heresy and the barbarity of persecuting rulers.[54] If the true treasure of the Church lay in the poor to whom it brought succor, then the merciful expenditure of material wealth was, in fact, the best way to amass riches.

We saw in the early chapters of this book the social and political context surrounding this episode, and it would be hard to exaggerate the radicalness of Ambrose's social criticism, faced with the very real problems of poverty in the fourth century. Peter Brown has written authoritatively on this subject, stressing the forcefulness of Ambrose's preaching against the greed of the rich, to which he traced all the evils of the day.[55] One of Ambrose's most striking works on this subjects is *De Nabuthae* (*On Naboth*), written between 386 and 390 as a commentary on a chapter in the Book of Kings. This "brutal tale" tells of the greed of King Ahab, who caused the death of a poor, debt-ridden farmer named Naboth in order to take over his vineyard. "The story of Naboth is an ancient tale, but today it is an everyday occurrence," wrote Ambrose at the outset of his book.[56] We should note in passing that modern references to Ambrose are constantly invoked to justify the Church's social doctrine. During the Second Vatican Council, for instance, Pope Paul VI relied largely on the moral authority of the bishop of Milan to support the universal right of the poor to dispose of wealth, basing his encyclical of March 26, 1967, *Populorum progressio*, on a quotation from *On Naboth*: "It is not anything of yours that you are bestowing on the poor; rather, you are giving back something of theirs. For you alone are usurping what was given in common for the use of all. The earth belongs to everyone, not to the rich."[57]

To return to the episode of Lawrence's stratagem, it's worth pointing out that it is often cited in medieval anthologies, which draw heavily on the *De officiis*, for instance Bartolomeo Carusi's *Milleloquium*.[58] But the evocation of the *pauperes* as the army of Christ's soldiers on the march – the usual expression in military vocabulary was *agmen cogere*–has an entirely different social implication when it is sung in chorus in Milan's churches, particularly during the period of the medieval communes. A pure conjecture, no doubt, without any direct evidence to corroborate it, but since Ambrose's name is indissolubly linked to these hymns of vigilance and struggle, it's hard not to see them once again as an indication of the availability of Ambrose's memory for mobilizing the *popolo* at the height of the tensions in Milanese communal society, and then again in the fifteenth century. Part of the historian's task, certainly, is to reconstruct the echoes between a very ancient past and the immediate present–in 1449, for example, when the *crida* of the Captains and Defenders of Freedom proclaimed the country to be in danger.

But to consider Ambrosian hymns as the politically committed song of a people engaged in struggle would be to fall prey to the romance of the origin myth–and the political conversion of the people of God into the *popolo* would only add another layer of naiveté. For the ultimate impact of hymns is not collective emotion but personal edification. Witness the fourth stanza of Hymn 4, *Deus creator omnium*, a song in praise of God at the close of day, sung (as mentioned earlier) in Ambrose's Milan every evening at vespers:

> *Te cordis ima concinant*
> *te uox canora concrepet*
> *te diligat castus amor;*
> *te mens adoret sobria*

> Thee let the secret heart acclaim,
> Thee let our tuneful voices name,
> Round thee our chaste affections cling,
> Thee sober reason own as King.[59]

The first two verses forcefully express the idea of the chorus as a sign of unanimity, by the echo of *concinant* and *concrepet*, which are similar in meaning, form, and placement within the verse, but also by the collective singular *vox canora* (from the same root as *canentes* and *concinant*), which Ambrose and other ancient authors used for the voice and harmony of the lyre's strings (encountered earlier in the commentary on David's first psalm). The hymn's vertical function (praise addressed to God) is obviously inseparable from its horizontal function, the making of the Church, which becomes instituted through the choral singing of its congregation.[60] But this praise of unison leads to an ascetic practice of spiritual innerness. Like an extension into Christianity of the spiritual exercises of late antiquity, whose role in the construction of the self in Western thought Pierre Hadot has shown,[61] the hymns of Ambrose are very much the Church songs used by each congregant to build his "inner temple," where God's true house is found. Such, as is well known, is the founding paradox of Christian individualism: gathering both in the church and in the Church, the faithful hollow out within themselves an interiority that God inhabits and encompasses. Like memory in Augustine's formulation, it is "a place that is not a place."[62]

The *suavitas* of the hymn unquestionably has a disciplinary aim. An effective teaching tool for the aesthetic perception of Truth, it exerts a gentle constraint on the faithful, enlisting their senses to take hold of their bodies. Through the public liturgy of a collective song, a process of incorporation occurs, leading to the *ruminatio* that Ambrose continually praised. This is the hymn's ultimate aim, as it is the psalm's – the interior song of a personal prayer. Its impact is obviously impossible to evaluate, but it captured the attention of classical authors from the time hymns first appeared. Hilary of Poitiers, early on, attributed three functions to hymns: exhortation, affirmation of doctrine, and spiritual

struggle. It's hard not to assign them also a fundamentally political dimension – the inculcation of norms. Jacques Fontaine says
as much in pointing to all that Ambrose's hymns owe to the public liturgy of the Roman state: "solemn gravity, the interiority of a
collective prayer, and the effective expression of a *consensus*."[63]

What is the basis of this consensus? In the beginning, essentially, it was Nicaean orthodoxy, in the troubled context of the
political struggles stemming from the Christological heresies.
This is very clear in the case of Hymn 5, *Intende qui regis Israel*,
which unmistakably carries an echo of the great battles Ambrose
fought against Arianism. "A lyrical and doctrinal prayer on the
birth of the Son," this hymn is sung in celebration of Advent
and Christmas, since it was Ambrose who introduced Milan to
the Roman practice of celebrating the *dies natalis* of Christ on
December 25: they split it from the celebration of the Epiphany
and named the date of the winter solstice as the Feast of the
Invincible Sun (*natalis soli inuicti*).[64] The fullness and equality of
Christ's two natures are clearly stated at the start of the seventh
stanza: *Aequalis aeterno Patri* ("O equal to the eternal Father").
The polemical import of this statement of orthodoxy, against the
backdrop of the doctrinal dispute with Arian subordinationism
(the doctrine that the Son and the Holy Spirit are both inferior
to God the Father), is obvious enough. Yet it would lend itself
to a range of reappropriations and repurposings as the ground
of political struggles shifted.[65] When Pope Celestine quoted the
hymn's second stanza at the Council of Rome in 430, he was targeting other adversaries entirely: the disciples of Nestorius, then
patriarch of Jerusalem, who broke with Nicaean Trinitarianism
by making a clean distinction between Christ's divine nature
and his human nature, assigning priority to the first.[66]

Does this mean that once the Christological debate was
finally settled, the hymn *Intende qui regis Israel* had exhausted its

capacity to be historically updated? Nothing could be less certain, even if we are again reduced to trading in hypotheses. In Ambrose's day, the struggle against Arianism was closely tied to confrontation with imperial power. This gives the hymn a general political cast, starting with the first stanza, which, by reusing the first two verses of Psalm 79,[67] places the Christian people once more in the Messianic expectation of a time when Israel will be restored:

> *Intende, qui regis Israel*
> *super Cherubim qui sedes*
> *appare Ephraem coram, excita*
> *potentiam tuam et ueni.*

> Hearken, you who rule Israel,
> who sit above the Cherubim,
> appear before Ephraim, rouse up
> your power and come.

By shortening the source psalm and eliminating the pastoral metaphor in the second half of the first versicle, the hymn brings the verb *regere* back to its original Latin sense, which is strictly political and relates to the government of people and the world – for we know that the metaphorization of the biblical *rex* is a constant temptation to commentators – and this hardening of the meaning is reinforced by the parallel between *sedes* and *regis*.[68] The Lord presides in majesty, not as Israel's shepherd but as the King and Judge, deploying his *potentia*. The palace is so strongly imagined that it gives rise to an odd metonymy in verse 18, stanza 5: the Virgin's womb is given as *aula regia pudoris*, forcefully expressing Christ's presence in a place that is closed, intact, and in its own right sacred. Ambrose has made the image explicit in his *De institutione uirginis*,[69] but it's hard to deny that it takes on a different connotation when it is sung in the former imperial capital of Milan, where the shadow of the emperors' *palatium* looms in the minds of citizens. And all the more so as the previous stanza develops a suggestive meditation on the "closure of virginity":

Aluus tumescit uirginis,
claustrum pudoris permanet,
uexilla uirtutum micant,
uersatur in templo Deus.

The womb of the Virgin swelled,
while the seal of her modesty stayed,
the banner of virtues glittered,
and God dwells in his temple.[70]

Barriers and banners, temple and *comitatus*: the power of God is in the Virgin's womb, invisible and omnipresent, as once the God of Israel resided in his Temple's Holy of Holies, and as the emperor is now entrenched behind his guard and within his court in his palace in Milan, but also as all those who, long after him, in the fourteenth and fifteenth centuries, would leave the city to shut themselves in their palaces, places made sacred by the very fear they inspired. Jacques Fontaine has aptly shown how Ambrose associated *templum* and *aula* in his writings, the mystery of the Incarnation making the Virgin *admirabile templum Dei et aula caelestis*.[71] In the last verse, Ambrose extends the metaphor: consecrated by the Incarnation, Mary becomes the human residence of the sovereign God. He has chosen to live in her, just as the emperor has chosen to settle his court in one or another of his capitals. And we know that the sovereign's presence in his palace in Milan was indicated by a visible signal: the guard would raise above the *palatium* his banners (*uexilla*). The shining splendor of the banner of Marian virtues has a clearly spiritual quality; nonetheless, the allusion to a military standard gives the hymn a triumphal and imperial connotation that is not undercut by its final verses.

The same could be said of Hymn 10, *Victor, Nabor, Felix pii*, picking up on the literary tradition of Pindar's victory songs and Horace's civic odes and exalting the heroism of the *militia Christi*, Milan's martyrs. Their faith a shield, their death a triumph, the martyrs bring about a true *conversio* of military values. Victor, Nabor, and Felix, African soldiers who were tortured to death in Lodi and whose remains were transferred to Milan, were the only martyrs the Lombard capital could boast of before Ambrose's discovery of the remains of Gervasius and Protasius in June 386. This accounts for their importance in the Milanese liturgy and topography, clearly apparent in this hymn, which, of all those traditionally attributed to Ambrose, is the one most solidly anchored in "our land."[72] The last stanza, in fact, converts the cart used to transfer the martyrs' remains into a quadriga, or chariot drawn by four horses, suggesting a Roman triumph:

Sed reddiderunt hostias;
rapti quadrigis corpora,
reuecti in ora principium
plaustri triomphalis modo.

But they have returned our victims;
Their bodies, borne on chariots,
returned to the gazes of the princes
in the manner of triumphal chariot.[73]

Since the eleventh century, as I've noted, the Milanese raised the effigy of their patron saint Ambrose on another ceremonial chariot: the *carroccio*, which is the symbol of their stubborn resistance against the imperial assault on their civic liberties.[74] During the crucial decade of 1162 to 1176, when the armies of the free commune managed to stand up to Emperor Frederick Barbarossa's troops, and again in 1238, when Frederick II captured his insolent adversaries' standard-bearing *carroccio* and carried it in triumph to Rome, "in place of spoils and booty from the defeated enemy,"[75] there is no question that the hymn held a very specific meaning for the Milanese who sang it. What else can a historian do in trying to apprehend what the Milanese *actually understood* when they heard the name "Ambrose" or when they sang a hymn advertised as Ambrosian but reconstruct these temporal sequences? One has to imagine the echo that a given word, fixed by liturgical tradition and repeated century after century, evokes for a particular person in a particular context. The conflict with the Arians was ancient history, but the struggle against imperial power was a constantly recurring aspect of the past, providing vibrant and energetic access to an effective memory. This is the memory imprint of Ambrose's hymns, which time continued to mold, and which drew their power and presence from a vanished past – the *palatium*, its court, its banners and triumphal processions, but also the unanimous chorus of the people, going back to a time when the poor, so they said, were considered the Church's treasure.

GREGORIAN CHANT VERSUS AMBROSIAN CHANT: JUST WHAT DOES IT MEAN?

In suggesting a few avenues for a historicist reconstruction of the social understanding of the so-called Ambrosian hymns, I am in fact attempting to identify the hidden political message that a liturgical tradition thought to be immutable may carry – a message that will vary, of course, with the historical context. But why then limit ourselves to the words of the hymns, when we now know that the musical forms themselves were an integral part of the medieval system of communication?[76] Yet to go beyond a few general observations would require a technical mastery of musicology that it would be absurd to claim. At least I can sketch out a few avenues for reflection that, going beyond the question of the hymns themselves, concern what tradition has termed "Ambrosian chant," its place in the liturgy, and the ways that certain of its musical forms found their way into secular music in the late Middle Ages.[77]

We always return to the same original scene: in enjoining the faithful in the basilicas of Milan to sing hymns during Holy Week in 386, Ambrose appears to have invented antiphonal singing. This, at least, has been the traditional claim, first made in Paulinus of Milan's *Vita Ambrosii*, even if the references this author makes to *antiphonae* are difficult to interpret.[78] It is worth reviewing a few basic definitions at this stage: responsorial singing belonged to the heritage of the early Church and is known to have existed in the East as well as in the Latin West from the fourth century on, with the singing of the *psalmus responsorius* (a sung psalm with a refrain). In specific terms, this was a psalm chanted by a cleric (the psalmist), whose song is interrupted after every verse by the congregation singing the *responsorium*, in an easily memorized melody. Isidore of Seville distinguishes clearly between this early responsorial system and antiphonal song: "The difference between responsorial song and antiphony is that in the first case, a single person sings each of the psalm's versicles, while in the second, the choirs alternate in singing the versicles."[79]

The introduction of antiphony, that is, the singing of psalms by two alternating choirs, was a gradual process. It eliminated the need for a psalmist (who was replaced by cantors), and the *responsorium* survived only in a vestigial form (for example, Psalm

94 of the Order of Saint Benedict) or became a refrain in the daily office that was revised little by little according to the new Gregorian norms.[80] The Alleluia and the gradual response (in Milan known as the *psalmellus*) therefore derive from early responsorial chants. The text is reduced, but the musical form is amplified and embellished with melismata (a complex ornamentation of simultaneous melodies), as the creation of a *schola cantorum* had occasioned a surge in musical inventiveness. This, then, is the overall scheme – but in what way does the Ambrosian tradition impose a distinctive stamp on it? The use of antiphony must not be conflated with choral singing generally. The hymns had to be sung by alternating half choirs, and this principle of musical performance left its mark on the literary form.[81] The regularity and rigidity of the iambic dimeter harmonized with the principles of tonal music to make memorization easier.[82]

But what of the other moments in the liturgy? As Philippe Bernard has aptly pointed out, "alternate, antiphonal psalm-singing is an art for the learned."[83] It was consistent with the mnemonic practices of monastic communities but was not for the wider congregation of the faithful. What is normally called Ambrosian chant may, therefore, have been nothing more than psalm-singing with a refrain. The question has divided specialists, some of whom doubt whether a genuine antiphonal psalmody existed before the eighth century[84] – despite the fact that Michel Huglo has upheld his contrary position with apparently convincing arguments.[85] In a general way, we should probably follow Olivier Cullin's lead in not making too rigid a distinction between responsorial and antiphonal song, seeing it less as a divergence in genre than in style. Accordingly, antiphony would amount to a "mode of execution" of a piece, whose musical and literary forms could be transmitted separately.[86]

It is nearly impossible to reconstruct this musical evolution over a long period – though the first antiphonaries with neumatic (tonal) notation date to the twelfth century[87] – since it was only in the second half of the fourteenth century and really in the fifteenth that we have choral books in sufficient numbers to give us an overview of Ambrosian chant.[88] But we also find Ambrosian melodies in Italian hymnals that do not follow the Ambrosian Rite, and of the 245 often isolated or fragmentary mentions of Ambrosian chants in manuscripts from the tenth to the twelfth century, more are to be found in Rome than in Milan.[89] The reason is that the process of hybridization, the "Gregorianization of the Ambrosian," operating through borrowings and reworkings, was already well underway by that time.[90]

Historians have long contrasted the staying power of medieval Ambrosian chant with the quasi-disappearance of the Gallican and Hispanic traditions, which seemingly gave ground when the Romano-Gregorian tradition became the norm. But the Milanese Church never faced any political decisions comparable to Pope Alexander II's, in 1065, sanctioning the Hispanic Rite, followed by Pope Gregory VII's imposition of Gregorian chant on the Church of Spain – after 1086, only a few parishes in Toledo were authorized to preserve their old rite.[91] The traditions of Milanese liturgical chant continued to be transmitted and their preservation solidified, so that the distant echoes of classical chant could still be heard at the end of the Middle Ages. In these circumstances, it could reasonably be maintained that Milanese liturgical chant is more Ambrosian than Roman chant is Gregorian.[92] As they gradually adapted their musical tradition to the requirements and seductions of the Romano-Gregorian repertory, Milanese cantors moved the old Ambrosian pieces to less important and less prominent times in the liturgical year. They tucked them away, at the same time preserving them, while other elements of the liturgy (e.g., the responses) continued to be ornamented with ever more complex melismatic phrases. Consequently, the sacred music that one might have heard in Milan in the fifteenth century was most likely a montage of sounds and emotions, some of which echoed the venerable simplicity of a very ancient plainsong, while others displayed the inventiveness of a creative musical avant-garde.

But would these differences have been discernable to the listener? And who – apart from the liturgists and musicologists of today – would actually be capable of "dating" the different strata in the musical flow and distinguishing the various elements in the melodic fusion that makes up the liturgical tradition? Any attempt at reconstructing the felt experience of an Ambrosian Mass in the Middle Ages, based on a few fragmentary and less-than-reliable accounts, would be foolhardy. Two historical accounts are nonetheless worth mentioning, both dating from the very end of the fifteenth century, if only for the contrast they afford. The first is an autograph manuscript by a certain Johanne di Dazii, who in 1490 gathered a collection of *Laudi spirituali, leggende, orazioni* (which is the title of these pious *ricordanze*, written in the vulgate), as uttered in various churches in Milan "to the glory of the most high and mighty God, the Virgin Mary, our patron saint Ambrose, and all the saints and saintesses enjoying life everlasting."[93] In one particularly interesting passage, cited by Enrico Cattaneo,[94] Johanne di Dazii describes for the benefit of a fictional recipient "what you must be thinking when you go to church." Mass is considered both a wedding celebration between Christ and his flock and a ritual of peace between God and the souls of sinners – for the church is both "God's house and the palace of the emperor of life everlasting."[95] Drawn primarily to the political, the layman di Dazii spends little time parsing the liturgical subtleties of the worship service. Yet the sung portions all create a palpable sensation summed up in the idea of joyousness – this is true of "that song of joy, *Gloria in excelsis deo et caetera*" and of the Alleluia, sung by the congregation "as a sign of great joy, and you must conceive of it as the sound of trumpets, violins, zithers, and all the other instruments of the heavenly chorus, reverberating in the hearts of the faithful."[96] The church and the palace, the amplitude of the angelic choir and the intimacy of the hearts of men – it is moving to find that a modest memorialist writing at the end of the fifteenth century should describe the very emotive mobilization that was attributed by Augustine a thousand years earlier to the magic of Ambrose's hymns.

At the other end of the spectrum are the experiences of Johann Burchard, master of ceremonies of the papal chapel from 1483 to 1506, who wrote down in his *Journal* the impressions produced on him by a Mass attended in Milan on August 17, 1496. A professional who knew his liturgy, he obviously noticed all the subtleties, which he scrupulously recorded. What emerges from the account of this church official (Alsatian by birth, but Roman by adoption since 1467) is his surprise at the Ambrosian melodies. Most notable to him was that the celebrant would recite the Paternoster, the Sanctus, and the Agnus Dei in low tones as the cantors sang complex polyphonies. "This practice is unusual to us, but it appears to be customary to Duke Ludovico."[97] If the "us" obviously refers to the Romans – and to all who were accustomed to the Gregorian Rite – the strangeness of the "custom" he has chanced upon is not attributed to a particular locality but to a court practice, that of Ludovico Sforza. Burchard was at that time accompanying the papal legate Bernardino Lopez de Carjaval (named cardinal of Santa Croce in Gerusalemme in July 1496) on a diplomatic mission of the highest importance, which would lead to negotiations with Emperor Maximilian to decide the conditions of his coronation in Rome. The Mass that Burchard attended was therefore in no sense ordinary but intended as political communication. The music was learned, its intricacy literally overlaying the liturgical message, and the whole was intended to impress its audience.[98]

The fact that the music did not simply emphasize the Word but, by its excess of refinement, obscured the import of the liturgy instead was seen as part of an unfortunate trend, on whose account intricate polyphony had long been denounced by the Church. Étienne Anheim, for instance, has shown that Pope John XXII's famous *Docta Sanctorum* decree of 1324 to 1325, which opposed certain ars nova practices that, "under a multitude of notes, obscure the modest ascensions of plainchant," itself derived from a long tradition, drawing on the work of the Church Fathers – and notably on the theology of Ambrose's psalms.[99] But the freeing of learned music from the context of liturgy was part of a larger movement that no theological reaction could stifle, responding as it did to powerful social and political forces. The coupling of the basic liturgical melody with refined polytonal compositions (motets) paralleled the development of court music that borrowed sacred motifs and put them to varied social uses, all political in nature. For there developed in music also, starting in the last third of the fifteenth century, a deliberate policy of making the sacred obscure, which was related to the increasing absoluteness of princely power, a phenomenon I have already noted in the context of architecture, painting, political ideas, and, in a general way, every kind of undertaking referencing memory.

What Burchard heard in Milan in 1496 was not so much an Ambrosian Mass as a ducal chapel Mass, and the liturgical loci that he struggled to identify beneath the mesmerizing stream of subtle polyphonies were all reference points in what musicologists call *motetti missales*.[100] Intended to be sung during the

Elevation of the Sacrament, after the Sanctus, these short polyphonic pieces were first written in the 1470s by such brilliant composers as Josquin des Prez, Loyset Compère, and Gaspar van Weerbeke.[101] Galeazzo Maria Sforza managed to draw these celebrated musicians into his service by his voluntarist cultural policies,[102] and they contributed toward the "paraliturgical ceremonial"[103] of the sound environment for the great princely rituals of the ducal chapel. The motet tradition saw the development of the *sogetto cavato*, where the composer inserted the name of his benefactor in the midst of the liturgical music, making its syllables correspond to the notes of Guido d'Arezzo's hexachord, with the melody thus formed constituting the Mass's cantus firmus. Possibly invented by Josquin des Prez for his famous *Missa Hercules dux Ferrariae*,[104] the technique was notably used by Loyset Compère in his *Missa Galeazescha* of 1474. But it is only truly perceptible in the visual organization of printed sheet music, and it was in 1505 in Venice that Ottaviano Petrucci published his *Motetti libro quarto*, which gathered the cycles of *motetti missales* from Milan.

These had already been compiled between 1490 and 1492 in the *Libroni* of Franchino Gaffurio, who was *maestro di cappella* at the Milan Cathedral from 1484 until his death in 1522.[105] The policy of preserving the musical patrimony of Milan reflected a seamless fidelity to Ambrosian chant. As the deputies of the Fabbrica del Duomo said when they gathered for deliberations on January 21, 1492, everything had to be done *secondo l'ordinem facto per sancto Ambrosio*.[106] Responding to a fear that this choral tradition might be lost—one that has to be called Ambrosian because it seemed a constituent element of Milan's political community—the Milanese designated as their heritage a musical repertory that had been profoundly reconfigured by the learned innovations of the court musicians of the fifteenth century and that had evolved to be far different from the tonal music of Ambrosian chant. This might explain why it was wise on the part of Giacomo della Torre, the bishop of Pavia, to decline the princely invitation to sing an Ambrosian Mass...

To sing as in Ambrose's day? No one can, obviously. Music is the vehicle for an ideally pure transmission of the sensory experience of social harmony: to listen to the hymns bearing Ambrose's name is, for a native of Milan, to vibrate in unison with a melodious choir of similarly attuned hearts. Within the hymns can be heard the distant thunder of ancient battles, still capable of being actualized in songs of political engagement. But beyond the necessary fiction of intact preservation, the music is in a continual state of creation – if only because the historical conditions in which it is being heard are constantly changing. Ambrose's memory, then, must be anchored elsewhere, particularly – we come back to it in the end – to the places in the city that he made sacred with his name, his speech, and his body.

SIXTEEN

Ministry of Glory:
The Last of the New Ambroses

CARLO BORROMEO: A "STORIED NAME"

There came a time when French historian Gérard Labrot wanted to take proper leave of the city he had so loved. He came up with a book – the profound, profuse, and long-misunderstood *The Image of Rome* – and became the "welcoming historian of the beautiful image." For this city isn't just any city, but *the* city – Rome – making it pointless to claim to have ever encountered it with "the dewy-eyed, utterly fresh vision of an absolute first time." That can never be, because an interloper invariably slips in: an image of the city, which always arrives first and transforms "a meeting with a stranger into a rendezvous between two old partners in crime." This intruder can color a visitor's mind, even from a distance, orienting and constraining us, forcing us to see only what we were prepared to see. "For the image is not only the presentation of the city to the World, but the representation of the imitated or real desire that people feel for the city."[1]

This was how the sixteenth-century image of Rome became a "weapon for the Counter-Reformation," allowing the popes to maintain their hold over the city in two dimensions: the "euphoria of the horizontal" and the "gravity of the vertical."[2] The first dimension was that of festivals, processions, and corteges that produced a disciplining of space, notably during grand canonizations. However, the popes attempted a twofold, simultaneous decryption of Rome: across its surface, but also into its depths. For it was the Church, in the sixteenth century, that set out to occupy and excavate underground Rome. It launched a great battle of beginnings, inventing (in the medieval sense) catacombs so as to create an inventory of past persecutions. A thick layer of martyrs – 10,202 martyrs in the baths of Diocletian, they said, very precisely, specificity giving the impression of reality[3] – formed the geological bedrock of a sedimented history. Churches were built on and in temples. The result: a visual schematic that shaped the city during the Counter-Reformation, reflecting the "spatial surgery of Sixtus V": Rome, "that stifled lump in the Tiber loop," needed to unfurl across empty spaces and spread through the open air.[4] It also needed to conquer the skies, dominated by the colossal pillars that were the columns of Trajan and Marcus Aurelius. The idea was to vertically unify the city's sacred space by re-erecting obelisks in key areas. As Labrot writes, "Sixtus V literally built the sky of Rome."[5] This discourse of ascent was also expressed in churches, from catacombs to cupolas: an apotheosis.

Ambrose's Milan was, like Sixtus V's Rome, a weapon for the Counter-Reformation. This tradition has its author, or rather its hero: Carlo Borromeo, who was archbishop of Milan from 1560 to his death in 1584.[6] He was the last of the new Ambroses, leading the episcopal cohort of all those who, from Eugenius to Angilbert, from Ariberto of Intimiano to Galdino della Salla, from

Ottone to Giovanni Visconti, claimed not only to walk in the bishop-saint's footsteps but to share his aura, in order to convert the mystery into ministry. No mysticism here, unless we count the foundations of government. While the lives that circulated after the death of Theresa of Ávila in 1582 narrativized the mystical domain, those that spread throughout Catholic Europe after the death of her contemporary Carlo Borromeo in 1584 disseminated the pastoral program of Tridentine reform, which we could call Borromean as easily as we could Roman. These texts did so with a scale and reach that are difficult to measure: the many Borromean lives represent countless variants of a single account whose power comes from the biographical unit. This is what Michel de Certeau, who dedicated a biting text to Carlo Borromeo, calls a "storied name."[7] Nothing could escape it. The name Borromeo had no remainders or remorse, no erosion or evasion – it assembled, disciplined, and hierarchized.

The narrativization of his legend allows us to grasp the historic importance of this Borromean theater through which the Counter-Reformation chose its hero. Carlo Borromeo was born in 1538 in the family castle of Arona, on the shores of Lake Maggiore. What made his life heroic was its capacity for rupture. The grandeur, richness, and age of his lineage and its clientele were clearly invaluable resources at a time when governing dioceses was a family affair. But while the offices and possessions were accumulating for this man making his fortune as a Roman cardinal – at the time, his household numbered 150 individuals, uniformly dressed in black velvet – the sudden death of his older brother, Federico, violently disrupted the course of his existence. He was expected to replace him in his career in arms and as the head of the family. He did the opposite: on July 17, 1563, Carlo Borromeo was ordained a priest, and on December 7 of that same year, he was consecrated as bishop. (Yes, December 7, the day of the ordination of Ambrose, who was also grieving for his brother, Satyrus.) Borromeo chose Milan as his new home, to defy the power of its governor, appointed by the king of Spain Philip II in 1556.[8] His bishopric would henceforth serve the glory of Milan, in the global context of a Lombard effort to supplant Rome. "Our consecration as bishop placed us on a raised throne,"[9] he said in 1569. And upon that throne, until his death in 1584, Borromeo performed his duties, never again leaving the ecclesiastical province he would roam at length, in the course of his pastoral visits. And thus he became, to his contemporaries, a "quasi-pope," or "another pope."

His was, in fact, a conversion. In the life of Carlo Borromeo written in anticipation of his canonization (1610), Giovanni Pietro Giussani describes the moment when the archbishop removed the paintings in his palace, "emblems of his family, that were painted in different places, with his name," replacing them with pious images of the Virgin and "Saint Ambrose, protector of the city."[10] From a cultural point of view, Carlo Borromeo converted his classic humanist culture into religious reformism. In his youth, he had been an ardent reader of Cicero, Livy, and Virgil; as an adult, he strictly oriented his reading in a pastoral direction, concentrating on the Church Fathers, starting with Cyprian and Ambrose.

This was because he intended to assume the role of the model bishop, by connecting reign and glory, governance and rhetoric, power and persuasion. The archbishop of Milan, Carlo Borromeo, was waging a battle: against rebellions, sects, carnivals, and superstitions, but also against the proud, the corrupt, the unawakened, against the arrogance of the powerful and the lethargy of priests. He tirelessly defended the strict observance of doctrine and the unfailing fidelity of a priestly diocesan corps: "May the text come to life. This was the essential principle inspiring not only an *ars concionandi* but an existence. Bringing forth what had already been said was the archbishop's precise and determined spiritual quest."[11] More than anything else, the Borromean administration was based on preaching, and more than anything else, that preaching was a style. Within it can be glimpsed a haunting, in the literal sense, by the purity of origins, namely by the nostalgic dream of a return to the Church Fathers. This oratory style was the source of Borromeo's power and the popular devotion that prompted his canonization in 1610, shortly after his death. And thus "the episcopal figure became marble and theater," "the legal and narrative instrument of an institution."[12]

Carlo Borromeo was clearly the last of the new Ambroses, not only the last in date but the ultimate figure of his posthumous lives.[13] No one will come after him – his stature was too powerful, imposing, and definitive. Though not to the extent of masking that of Ambrose. Quite the contrary. This is the heart of what Marie Lezowski rightly calls "Ambrosian mimesis."[14] Indeed, in 1576, Carlo Borromeo abandoned his patrician seal, still being used to authenticate archiepiscopal chancery deeds, and adopted a new one depicting Ambrose, at the pulpit, flanked by the martyrs Gervasius and Protasius.[15] With this change, he joined the iconographical line that began with Ottone Visconti's seal, in 1288, followed by Giovanni Visconti's in 1347 (both archbishops became lords of Milan).[16] Carlo Borromeo did add a motto, however, *Tales ambio defensores*, directly evoking Ambrose's famous letter to his sister Marcellina recounting the invention of relics in the summer of 386: "These are the defenders whom I desire, these are my soldiers, not the world's soldiers, but Christ's."[17]

In short, all his preaching bore the Ambrosian seal, to the point that the name of Ambrose became practically indiscernible by dint of its omnipresence.[18] For Carlo Borromeo's administrative and pastoral program had no other aim but to restore – I should say resuscitate – the "holy Ambrosian institutions." In order to do so, he counted on the fidelity and fervor of a militant vanguard, the congregation of oblates of Sant'Ambrogio, established in 1578 in the Church of San Sepolcro, whose virtuous example was intended to permeate the entire city: these professionals at effective remembering were, said their statutes, "fighters under Ambrose's orders" (*Ambrosio Duce militantes*).[19]

Carlo Borromeo's preaching logically painted Ambrose as the ideal model of the priest, as redefined by the Council of Trent: it is in the modern clergy, affirmed the archbishop in his Bellinzona homily on December 7, 1583, that the Ambrose of today, or rather his eternal presence among the living, must be found.[20] But Carlo Borromeo's pastoral ideal wasn't limited by social divisions: beyond the Gregorian break – from one reform to the next, it became a question of healing Christianity's great wound – his proselytizing transcended the split between clergy and laity.[21] He said as much in his sermon on December 7, 1567: "You, magistrates, fathers and mothers, and you all who, in one manner or another, have responsibility for and govern other men; and even all you Christians, all those whom it pleases me, at present, to call preachers, in a fashion, insofar as you are all obliged to aid the good spiritual progress of the souls of those who are in your care."[22]

Everyone, clergy and laity alike, was tasked with the pastoral duty of remembering, for the defense of "holy Ambrosian institutions" was a constant battle. In order for Milan to regain the glory that would become a weapon for the Counter-Reformation, everyone had to remember Ambrose. Two years earlier, in 1565, during that same December 7 sermon, the archbishop exhorted the faithful: "Where has the ancient majesty of our metropolitan Church gone? Where has the august name of Ambrose gone?"[23]

Ambrose was speaking through Carlo Borromeo's lips, but he also spoke through things. And those things, as we now know, were in places, songs, and books.

"But you, Milan, listen to what your preacher Ambrose says: 'Let us do our best to understand, my dearest sons, the great generosity of the Lord toward our Church. Other cities consider themselves happy if they can count on the protection assured by the possession of the relics of a martyr. But here we are a people of martyrs!'" So Carlo Borromeo wrote in a pastoral letter composed on May 8, 1582, on the occasion of the translation of the relics of Saint Simplicianus, Ambrose's first successor.[24] Beginning on the Milanese Jubilee of 1576, during the city's great plague outbreak, Carlo Borromeo had embarked on a vast reconfiguration of its holy bodies, prompting a wave of memorial fervor. Carlo Borromeo repeated Ambrose. He repeated him literally, appropriating in this case what he believed to be one of Ambrose's sermons. In reality, the text he cited, anonymously transmitted by Milanese *legendaria* (collections of saints' lives) since the twelfth century, was only belatedly (and wrongly) attributed to Ambrose, by Erasmus in 1549.[25] For the order created by books was not as immutable as was hoped, disrupted instead by the contradictory currents of making attributions and removing them. In other words, at the same time that an effort to revive the holy bodies of Milan's saints was underway, so was the great metamorphosis of the textual corpus of Saint Ambrose.

During the triumphant Counter-Reformation, Milan's bishops revived the legendary topography of Ambrose's memory by making a penitent city of the Lombard capital. The holy city to come, the one that would wash away its inhabitants' sins, was already there, beneath their feet. This Holy Milan was an archive, left by the city's watchful preacher, waiting to be recognized, heard, inventoried, and in truth rewritten. This was the entreaty Carlo Borromeo tirelessly made to the faithful during his sermons on December 7, the anniversary of Ambrose's episcopal ordination, in the Cathedral of Milan (for under the new archbishop, the Duomo had once again become the locus of Ambrose's memory). By resuming the ritual of the ostentation of relics, Carlo Borromeo was echoing Ambrose's actions, first with the translation of the relics of San Nazaro from the old *basilica Romana* in May 1579, then again in May 1582 with those of San Simpliciano (*basilica virginum*). It was Borromeo who oversaw the recognition of Ambrosian relics in Milan, notably arbitrating an old dispute over the location of Satyrus's body, contested by the Cistercians of Sant'Ambrogio and the Olivetans of San Vittore al Corpo, ruling in favor of the latter in 1576.[26]

The city became a theater of memory, a space crisscrossed with itineraries, shaped by the omnipresent fear of forgetting. From treasure to treasure, the bodies of saints led Milan's inhabitants in devotional exercises that consisted of listening carefully to voices from beyond the grave, where their patron saint's admonishments could still be heard. During the Jubilee of 1576, Carlo Borromeo advocated this active listening, which was quite literally moving, in the sense that it affected and set in motion. That was the pastoral power of Ambrose, whose voice told all who visited these places "Remember." These *ricordi* were "reminders" of the commandments the saint had received from God. Hence why Giovanni Francesco Bascapè's *Libro d'alcune chiese di Milano* recommended that pilgrims place themselves just before the golden altar of Sant'Ambrogio to hear the "paternal and divine reminders that Ambrose once gave his people": "These holy admonitions that our dear preacher and master made to us, so that we never forget them. Why do we not obey him? Why do we not remember these holy reminders at all hours, and especially when we enter his holy church, where his sacred body rests?...Yet he lacks not successors, his imitators, who never cease to make these [reminders] to those willing to hear."[27]

The ostensions of relics organized by Carlo Borromeo were therefore, to quote Marie Lezowski, "a concentrate of Ambrose's memory, combining a rite, holy bodies, and places that appear in the *Vita Ambrosii.*"[28] On August 4, 1568, Carlo Borromeo confirmed the preservation of the Ambrosian Rite as an exception to the universalism of the Roman Rite proclaimed by Pius V in the *Quod a nobis* bull that accompanied the publication of the new pontifical breviary. He did so by drawing on the authority of the past: "As it is evident that the order and model of the Ambrosian office are of the greatest antiquity (a rite that, following its institution by Saint Ambrose, the bishop-saint Eugenius strove to conserve with its doctrine and piety intact); so that it be conserved perpetually, with the accord of the Catholic Church; we, who by the grace of God and the apostolic See administer the Church of Milan, must by all means ensure the maintenance and conservation of this Church's ancient institutions, its ancient rites, particularly those that were instituted by Saint Ambrose."[29] All while situating his pastoral program within a liturgical plurality recognized as legitimate – not all the churches in the diocese of Milan respected the Ambrosian Rite – Carlo Borromeo reaffirmed the specificity of the *mysterium ambrosianum* before the Roman threat of liturgical standardization.[30] He did so in the name of the mythical bishop Eugenius, the first of the new Ambroses, signifying, as we've seen, the Milanese people's stubborn resistance to the Carolingian aggression against the Ambrosian liturgy.

This wasn't a matter of immobilizing history, but, on the contrary, of reforming it to better conserve it: those faithful to the Ambrosian liturgy intended to preserve the individuality of their Church by adapting it to the demands of the time, always in the aim of enabling the Ambrosian Rite to better resist the supposedly implacable logic of the Roman normalization.[31] The reform of Milan's calendar reflected that desire.[32] One of the specificities of the Ambrosian liturgy was, as noted previously, the shortened period of Lent, which began in Milan on the Monday following Ash Wednesday. Even as early as 1288, Bonvesin da la Riva wrote, "As a result we also have a carnival different from foreign carnivals, which contributes to the dignity and glory of the Milanese people," reminding his readers that the tradition came about because one day, the Milanese had piously awaited the return of their bishop Ambrose, delayed by a pilgrimage, before beginning Lent.[33] More than dignity, this particularity allowed the people of Milan to take advantage of four extra days of festivities, notably on the last Sunday of carnival, when celebrations intensified. "No one may be pursued on these days for they are a time of festival in Milan," Francesco Sforza ordered the *podestà* of Lodi in 1451, even specifying "every execution be delayed to Monday morning."[34] Today still, the name Ambrose is associated with this lengthening of the carnival period, contributing to its folkloric appropriation by a farcical vision of controlled subversion. Such as, for example, the one created by the playwright Dario Fo, who repeatedly deployed the insurrectional and jubilatory power of a fantasized Middle Ages:[35] one of his final plays, put on at Milan's Piccolo Teatro in 2009, portrayed Ambrose as a dissenting and unpredictable figure, a "communist before his time" who played the people against the elite and made a virulent denunciation of wealth on stage.[36]

Did Carlo Borromeo decide to reform the calendar and remove the last Sunday of carnival in order to limit the excesses of the people? Historiography today is more distrustful of such an explanation: any possible resistance of the Ambrosian population to Borromeo's reform is not documented, and though the city's Spanish governor, Antonio de Guzmán, marquis of Ayamonte, claimed there was general unrest, it was primarily to defend the urban authorities' ability to control the liturgical calendar from the archbishop of Milan's own attempts.[37] In any event, Carlo Borromeo could not but lean on the Ambrosian past to support his reforms. Hence why his edict of March 1, 1576, claimed to rely on "long and considered study" of different writings by Ambrose of Milan in order to justify, after presenting the most convoluted texts, not only the fact that the Sunday in question would henceforth be the first day of Lent, but that it had always been so in Ambrose's day.[38]

In producing his arguments, Carlo Borromeo set himself up for scholarly refutations: the debate raged until 1580. Ambrose was still a subject of contention. Any claims to master the corpus of Ambrosian writings and references were undoubtedly illusory at this point—printed books were beginning to circulate. At the same time, the first volumes of the complete works of Ambrose of Milan appeared (published 1579–85).[39] But these were printed in Rome, and their chief architect was Felice Peretti, the cardinal of Montalto, who, at the end of this vast scholarly and editorial undertaking, became pope as Sixtus V and embarked upon the grand urban "scenography" studied by Gérard Labrot.[40] Carlo Borromeo's ministers undoubtedly would have liked to be involved in this editorial project of opera omnia, notably the erudite Pietro Galesini, who dreamt of writing a long history of the Church of Milan.[41] In the summer of 1577, he had sent to Rome seventeen unpublished works by Ambrose accompanied by critical notes, drawing primarily from the large Ambrosian collection bequeathed to the Cathedral of Milan by Archbishop Francesco Pizolpasso.[42] But it was likely too late: the editing process had already been completed, essentially on the basis of Roman manuscripts of Ambrose's works. Is that to say that the anchors of memory were giving way? That everything keeping Ambrose's memory in Milan, a point too far from the past as it was, could no longer hold on to him? Ever increasingly authoritarian and emphatic, the Borromean injunction to remember Ambrose was all the more fervently made, as it was meant to echo, like in a Baroque theater, the roar of time so heavy by this point that it was ready to break beneath the weight of being forgotten.

THE CATHEDRAL, THE EMPEROR DRIVEN FROM THE CHOIR, AND AMBROSE'S BEARD

Carlo Borromeo did not write a life of Ambrose, nor did he have one written. He merely controlled, from afar, the text composed in Rome by an Oratorian priest and scholar at the Vatican Library, Cesare Baronio, who compiled Paulinus of Milan's *Vita Ambrosii*, the Greek Lives, and a few medieval legendary amplifications to produce the final volume of the opera omnia.[43] Then again, yes he did: Carlo Borromeo wanted to produce a life of Ambrose, but in images, in the cathedral choir, majestically displaying the episodes of another storied name, with which he would be henceforth confused. Even though the Basilica of Sant'Ambrogio remained the center of the capital of penitence that Milan had become in the sixteenth century, the memory pilgrimages described by Giovanni Francesco Bascapè in his guide for the Jubilee of 1576 steered Ambrose's memory back toward the Duomo, the archbishop's grand church, which little by little was able to reorganize his *memoria*. In this way too, the Borromean period marks the end of our journey, distancing us for good from the Basilica of Sant'Ambrogio, at whose threshold we still found ourselves at the beginning of this book.

The Duomo's dedication to the Virgin had masked its Ambrosian origins. Its treasury was devoid of Ambrose's relics until Carlo Borromeo had a few fragments of his venerable predecessor's dalmatic placed there in 1577.[44] But beyond this Ambrosian reappropriation of the cathedral, the iconographical representation of Ambrose's life in the carved wood of the high-backed stalls of the upper choir reflects a vaster project – the liturgical reorganization of the choir.[45] This essentially consisted of barring access to the laity, confined below to the minor, or senatorial, choir. The new choir, surrounded by a marble balustrade and elevated in relation to the nave level, was reserved for the major chapter, that aristocracy of prayer exalted by the Counter-Reformation. Placed just below a cornice overlooking the *presbyterium* from ten feet up, the seventy-one stalls bearing carvings of Ambrose's life invite us to see – or rather respectfully contemplate, given that we're forced to gaze up at those overlooking us – this apotheosis.

When Carlo Borromeo died on November 3, 1584, not all the stalls were finished – they would be by 1614, during the episcopate of his cousin Francesco, the cardinal-archbishop of Milan from 1595 to 1631. But the project developed by the cathedral's first sculptors, Rizzardo Taurino and Virgilio del Conte, remained the same: dramatically portray Ambrose's life. This energy and vivacity contrast with the doleful succession of Milan's bishop-saints, who obediently line up below, ornamenting the stalls in the minor choir. Intermittent figures in miters, all identical or nearly, they appear to represent the shock wave of Ambrosian mimicry, coming before and especially after the great bishop, whom they anticipated or copied.[46] This sprawl of Ambrosian memory is followed, above, by a sparkling display of memorable and glorious scenes, all theatrically exaggerated. For now, let's look at the center, near the cathedra, the source of the holy preachers' words. Five scenes come in succession, recounting the clash between Emperor Theodosius and the bishop of Milan after the massacre of the people of Thessalonica in 390.

Let's remember that this showdown – which ended with the penitence forced on the Christian emperor by Ambrose as the price of his reintegration into the Eucharistic community – centered on the division of their respective powers. Let's also remember that the account of these events comes from a letter from Ambrose to Theodosius, whose transmission was separate from that of his correspondence, and that Paulinus of Milan's narration on this topic was relatively succinct. And finally, let's remember that it was the Greek lives of Ambrose that developed the striking motif of a Theodosius stopped at the sanctuary threshold, fueling the Carolingian rewriting of sovereign penitence. It was through that filter of Davidian reinterpretation that this great confrontation between emperor and bishop was remembered in the Middle Ages – notably beginning in the sixteenth and seventeenth centuries, when the Gregorian Reform necessitated the revival of the memory of that confrontation during which *potestas* and *auctoritas* felt the limit of their respective spheres by learning, to quote the Greek historian Theodoret of Cyrus, "to distinguish places."[47]

Very specifically, we should be interested in what can be seen in the narrative sequence of the five stalls of the upper choir, the models for which were sketched in Carlo Borromeo's lifetime, between 1582 and 1584.[48] Between Theodosius's excommunication and his absolution are three scenes, detailing three moments during which the Christian emperor cannot take communion – "Ambrose kept him in continual tears and penitence for

Stall in the upper choir of the Cathedral of Milan,
Theodosius Obtains Absolution, late sixteenth century

eight months," Carlo Borromeo somewhat emphatically claimed in one of his sermons.[49] In the second scene, the visit by the emperor's envoy Rufinus is not enough to make Ambrose yield; in the third, Theodosius comes in person before the bishop, who still does not waver; in the fourth, the emperor makes a sign of contrition by delaying the execution of those condemned to death, but the bishop remains unshakable. Then comes the denouement: Theodosius is prostrate at Ambrose's feet, his soldiers lamenting in the background. We understand that Carlo Borromeo wanted to amplify this moment, when the sovereign was kept out of the sanctuary. These scenes are clearly meant to represent the cathedral's inviolability, which is fully consistent with the liturgical and architectural transformation of the cathedral choir, which prevented the laity from mingling with the celebrants. The archbishop of Milan insisted, time and time again: "We must take inspiration from the cathedral where all are seated separate from the clergy, as it should be and as Saint Ambrose teaches us in particular."[50]

Just in case the narrative sequence wasn't clear enough, another stall, to the right of the chorus, offers an epilogue to the story just presented in images.[51] Once again, it depicts Theodosius, who, since admitted into the Eucharistic celebration, is trying to take a seat in the ecclesiastics' choir, whose architecture is easily recognizable: it is clearly the upper choir of the modern cathedral, enclosed by a barrier and elevated, like Carlo Borromeo wanted. Ambrose bars the emperor's path – forcefully. This scene comes, as we've seen, from Theodoret of Cyrus's *Ecclesiastical Histories*. But though known in the Middle Ages, this scene nonetheless had never been the object of any iconographical tradition. Yet here it is, noisily making its entrance into Ambrosian imagery and moving immediately into the forefront. This was where the Counter-Reformation staged its grand political scene, the bravura piece of its Baroque theater.[52] A Bolognese painter working in Milan, Camillo Procaccini (1551–1629), dramatized the episode in a colorful but chaotic muddle (see color plate 21). This undated painting was in all likelihood created for the Church of Sant'Agostino in Cremona: today, it can be found in one of the chapels in the right nave of the Basilica of Sant'Ambrogio. A stern old man with an immaculate beard, Ambrose stands tall at the threshold of his church, rejecting with a disdainful gloved hand an agitated, menacing young emperor, draped in crimson, who is gesturing to the sanctuary from which he is being barred entry.[53] The scene inspired European painting, from the Dutchman Anthony van Dyck circa 1620, who produced a more tormented version, to the Frenchman Pierre Soubleyras, who painted a subdued one around 1745.

All these versions depict a venerable, bearded Ambrose. As do Camillo Procaccini's preparatory sketches for the stalls of the cathedral choir. And yet the stalls show a clean-shaven Ambrose. Did this change occur, as Analisa Albuzzi suggests, following the intervention of the archbishop of Milan, Federico Borromeo, to make Ambrose better reflect the image that his illustrious cousin and predecessor Carlo Borromeo had wanted to give the bishop-saint?[54] By 1565, the Council of Milan was already legislating clerics' beards. At this time, it was less a question of prohibiting the beard itself than excessive attention to its maintenance. But Carlo Borromeo wanted to lead the fight for a beardless clergy: his letter of December 30, 1576, entitled *De barba radenda*, outlined spiritual and ecclesiological reasons to associate pilosity with sinfulness, and in particular the sin of arrogance, a sign of the laity's vain pride. Borromeo held that shaving was a sacrifice to which the man of God must consent. He noted: "By scorning this common facial ornament, we renounce the vain ornaments and prides of men."[55] Here we see the archbishop leading a long-lasting and far-sweeping European wave of clerical legislation: from 1480 to 1670, there were no less than twenty-one provincial councils and seventy-seven synods issuing decrees on the beard, namely in France, Italy, and Spain.[56]

How can we explain the archbishop's aversion to this ostentatious show of masculinity? The renaissance of the beard, in the 1520s, was linked to the virilization of the sovereign power. The association between beards and power explains the spread of this masculine trend in aristocratic, and then bourgeois, circles, until the end of the seventeenth century and the return of clean-shavenness that accompanied the rise of another hair-related, albeit artificial, trend – the wigs of court. The controversy over clergy beards should also be understood in the context of the continuing battle between the ecclesial *auctoritas* and the secular *potestas*, which reenacted the Gregorian break and revived the idea of sacrificing an ornament of pride. The antibeard stance also offered a way to reassert the separation from the Orthodox Church, whose clergy was bearded, as well as from the Jewish and, to a lesser degree, Muslim beard. As a result, beards remained an ambiguous issue in the denominational quarrels of the sixteenth century: they were broadly associated with an anti-papal attitude, but could also be the sign of eremitism and, by extension, of penitence, evoking the monastic or religious orders that encouraged them (for example, the Camaldolese monks or the Cistercian converts referred to as the *fratres barbate*). Pope Clement VII grew a penitential beard after the 1527 sack of Rome, as a sign of mourning, inverting the Levitical directive. The beard became an expression of the melancholy of power, but we know that at this time melancholy was associated with the notion of the genius creator – think about Michelangelo's Moses, sculpted in 1515, fiddling with a long-tormented beard through which are woven action and contemplation, power and knowledge. For the beard was also a divine attribute, evoking ancient wisdom, which is why it is so difficult to imagine a beardless Church Father.

All of which means that Carlo Borromeo was destined to have a hard time giving Ambrose a clean shave. He was up against a long iconographical tradition, like that of equestrian depictions, which the archbishop's learned and faithful minister Pietro Galesini denounced in a 1580 letter regarding the preparation of the breviary: equestrian imagery was, he rightly noted, linked to the 1339 Battle of Parabiago, which represented nothing but the victory of one faction over another; it did not concern the Church, and furthermore, "it is not customary to celebrate the apparitions of saints." This is why Galesini advised against incorporating February 21, the date of the battle, into the liturgical calendar, and undoubtedly why the scene is not included in the iconographical cycle of the cathedral choir. The three matins celebrating the Battle of Parabiago were in fact removed from the Ambrosian breviary in 1582, as was the procession of February 21. Two years later, the provostship was transferred from Parabiago to Legnano, and the former's church fell into ruin. Denouncing the Borromean reforms, the local priest Gerolamo Rafaelli wrote a book in which he not only assembled "the true story of the victory of Azzone Visconti," but also the inventory of all that Parabiago had lost.[57]

If Carlo Borromeo didn't want to see Ambrose astride a horse any more than he did with a beard, it's because the militarization of the bishop-saint's portrayal had come with the signorial appropriation of his memory. That appropriation was not, however, incompatible with the vision of a Christianity in combat, as promoted by the Catholic Reformation. In fact, the equestrian representation of a triumphant Ambrose had a bright future, notably in seventeenth-century painting: from its distant start, the Ambrosian cavalcade kept going. In a large painting made for the Church of Sant'Eustorgio, Giovanni Ambrogio Figino (1548–1608) portrayed a warrior Ambrose astride a white charger with flared nostrils trampling the bodies of the last Arians scattered on the ground (see color plate 20).[58] A violent wind appears to be lifting up the scarlet cape the knight-saint is wearing over his white dalmatic; a golden miter on his head, Ambrose brandishes a whip and holds his cross. Here we have an image of Ambrose as a warrior of the Counter-Reformation that the popes had every reason to highlight. In 1580, the cardinal Felice Peretti, the future Sixtus V, asked Carlo Borromeo to send him, in Rome, a portrait of Ambrose so that his "true effigy" could adorn the frontispiece of the first volume of his complete works, which was then going to press. The cardinal insisted that an equestrian representation be found. The archbishop of Milan resisted: there was no "authentic" representation of Ambrose on horseback.[59] He sent a different one, which Cardinal Peretti judged "true" and "authentic" as he recognized Ambrose's traits "from his lifetime." But what or who does a so-called true-to-life portrait resemble when you've never seen the face of the person it represents?[60]

SEEING HIS REAL FACE AT LAST

The only Milanese contribution to the publication of the opera omnia of the universal Church Father was therefore the "true effigy" of Ambrose sent in 1580 to Cardinal Peretti, which was inserted in the frontispiece of every printed volume.[61] Upon reception, the cardinal wrote to Carlo Borromeo to share his enthusiasm: "It seems to me that Ambrose could not be any other way, a formidable and venerable face, terrifying to Kings and Emperors. I had it showed to many lords, all of whom were quite edified by it, and think there can be no other true effigy but this."[62] In this letter, Peretti perfectly described the image Carlo Borromeo

S. AMBROSII EPISCOPI EFFIGIES EX ANTIQVIS EIVS
IMAGINIBVS MEDIOLANI OLIM DEPICTIS AD VIVVM EXPRESSA.

Frontispiece of the complete works of Ambrose,
Operum sancti Ambrosii Mediolanensis episcopi, tomus primus,
Romae ex typographia, Dominici Basae, 1580

had of Ambrose – an image that, here again, was a weapon for the Counter-Reformation. This effigy was all the more formidable because it was venerable, prompting the edification of the faithful and the terror of the powerful – coming from so far, it was here to stay, face-to-face with the present, firmly decided to vanquish oblivion. So in this sense, yes, the portrait of their patron saint that the Milanese sent to Rome to adorn the printed copies of his complete works did resemble Ambrose as he looked in 1580. And yes, this portrait should be considered as the "true effigy" of his posthumous life. But was there any trace of what had been a man's life eleven centuries prior? This archaeological scruple was likely not a primary concern for Carlo Borromeo, too busy enlarging the aura of this name.

We don't know his reaction when he opened the first volume sent to him one year later. Ambrose was indeed depicted on the frontispiece of his collected works, as firmly entrenched on the title page as he once was at the threshold of his cathedral. Strong nose, sharp face, etched features, and eyes looking straight at the reader. But, lo and behold, he also had a full white beard. Which apparently was not the case for the image sent by Carlo Borromeo – one of his Roman correspondents, the bishop of Novara Cesare Speciano, warned him of the switch in a letter dated September 24, 1581: the pope had appreciated the portrait submitted to him, "but he had not wished that he be printed shaven in this way [così raso], so some beard was added."[63] While the archbishop of Milan had succeeded in eliminating the horse, he failed to impose his clean-shaven Ambrose.

But what was the "true effigy" that he was trying to promote, and what allowed him to claim its authenticity? In one of his previous letters, Carlo Borromeo maintained that his proffered portrait of Ambrose was identical "to an image from antiquity that is in the Church of Sant'Ambrogio, which had always been honored by the people as the veritable image [*vera imagine*] of this glorious saint."[64] There is little doubt what image he is referring to. It can only be the tondo in polychrome stucco that Petrarch contemplated during his stay in Milan: "I gaze upwards at his statue, standing on the highest walls, which it is said closely resembles him, and often venerate it as though it were alive and breathing." This was in 1353. Lifting his gaze to the figure looking at him, Petrarch was overcome by its aura: "This is not an insignificant reward for coming here, for the great authority of his face, the great dignity of his eyebrows and the great tranquility in his eyes are inexpressible; it lacks only a voice for one to see the living Ambrose."[65] Two centuries went by but the image's power remained, though the image was on the move: the tondo seen by Petrarch on one of the basilica's exterior walls, as he took in the landscape stretching into the distance in the same glance, had been brought inside the church, where it would decorate the organ platform.[66] Though the image still couldn't speak, in Borromeo's time, it sang, which is what brought Ambrose to life. But it sang from an era so far away it was called ancient, and it was this unfathomable stretch of time that gave the effigy its veracity.

"It is because the image is true, and not because it is beautiful, that it is convincing."[67] This truth comes not from imitation, but incarnation; what Giorgio Vasari calls the "truth of nature" refers not only to appearance but to the underlying breath of life, something acting with the force of truth and that, buried beneath our modern regime of the aesthetic, is always prone to new, surprising, reincarnations. True image, authentic image, ancient image: historians can attempt to untangle these categories by reconfiguring time. They know, or think they know, what Carlo Borromeo's contemporaries no longer knew, or pretended to no longer know: that this bas-relief in polychromatic stucco measuring a little over three feet in diameter bearing the bust of

Ambrose cannot be a portrait made in his lifetime. Using stylistic criteria (the severe rigidity of traits characteristic of Roman sculpture) and in particular paleographical criteria (based on the legible inscription on the open book held by Ambrose), specialists today agree on a date that is still very approximate: toward the end of the twelfth century.[68] The reason being that the object lacks any documentary, architectural, or iconographical context.

We can link the tondo to a single image only, which, though its age is subject to discussion, we know is in fact the oldest of Ambrose's effigies preserved today: the mosaic of the small sanctuary (*sacellum*) of San Vittore in Ciel d'Oro adjoining the Basilica of Sant'Ambrogio (see color plate 22). We recognize, thanks to their *titulus*, Protasius, Ambrose, and Gervasius on the northern wall, and Felix, Materno, and Nabor on the southern wall: all are shown from head to toe, solemn and erect, dressed in the Roman style, in sandals and without halos, at a time when – we are probably at the end of the fifth century or the very beginning of the sixth century – the burgeoning cult of Ambrose had not yet given him the stature that would allow him to cleanly detach himself from the group of martyrs and confessors of the city-state of Milan.[69] Instead of the toga of the Roman aristocracy, Ambrose is wearing a *casula* beneath a dalmatic with wide sleeves, clasped with a small gold cross and not a fibula. Plump mouth, full face, but with worn features, brown hair and a short beard, a high forehead with thinning hair at his temples, big eyes and a somber gaze, right eye slightly higher than the left: if one was to look at these two effigies of Ambrose today, the late fifth-century mosaic and the late twelfth-century bas-relief, it'd be hard not to notice a family resemblance.

So how could this likeness escape the people of Milan living in the glorious shadow of Carlo Borromeo's government? Why, in the sixteenth century, did the span of time separating these two images – at least six centuries, a truly unfathomable distance – itself appear so far away that it shrunk and blurred in the indistinct cloud of remote antiquity, to the point that the oldest representation of Ambrose seemed to them to be a bas-relief that might have been contemporaneous with those of the *porta Romana*? Couldn't they see that if the tondo looked like something, it was less Ambrose's face than his image shining in mosaic gold? Probably not. In 1576, the fourth provincial Council of Milan had established a catalog of the city's bishops, each name paired with a short physical description: Ambrose, one reads, "was of modest stature, his face serious and handsome, oblong nose, blond hair, large forehead, with one eyebrow higher than the other."[70] All these distinctive traits, apart the blondness, can be found in Ambrose's "true effigy."

This portrait-in-words technique, which was used to establish saint iconography, originated in Elpios the Roman's collection of *eikonismoi*, dating in all likelihood to the sixth century.[71] As shown by Gilbert Dagron, these typologies established a figurative norm for the identification of every saint very early on, before the iconic portrait became its own reference, the icon resembling itself. The iconic portrait was intended to teach the viewer the art of recognizing the saint when he appeared in a dream. When the saint appeared, he began to resemble his own image; the icon authenticated the vision, and not the reverse. Hence the need to write a name – in the case of both the mosaic and the bas-relief, *Ambrosius* – that "transforms the icon itself into a seal and an imprint, that is to say an image authenticated by its model, which acknowledges and names itself."[72] Here it says: "I am Ambrose."

The 1576 *eikonismos* does not have a known textual source: it is therefore, in great likelihood, nothing more than a figurative description that the Milanese had in front of them, and which they took for a look-alike image, made in Ambrose's lifetime, that showed his face. So then why consider the bas-relief seen by Petrarch, and which was subsequently placed on the organ platform, as ancient and a "veritable image of this glorious saint"? It is no doubt impossible to answer that question, which brings us to the edge of the abyss of time. Because art historians tell us we are dealing with a late fifth-century or early sixth-century mosaic, we don't doubt, when looking at Ambrose in the glimmering mosaics of San Vittore in Ciel d'Oro, that we are incomparably closer to the man he was, as compared to the twelfth-century tondo, even when we see Petrarch looking at the bust. But are we sure? If we consider these images as we do time, then we must admit that painting has since the sixteenth century brought on the destruction of mimetic resemblance, and that this dissimilitude troubles the order of time.[73]

We shouldn't say that a mosaic is *from* the fifth century but that it has existed *since* the fifth century: its deceptive shimmer in the present is in fact the last gleam of its successive states – the final burst of brilliance of its posthumous lives. In the small sanctuary of San Vittore in Ciel d'Oro, significant reworking in the nineteenth century erased all traces of previous restorations, which the great specialist Cesare Bertelli nonetheless describes as "tormented."[74] In 1994, historian Martin Raspe believed he could reassemble this history, by retracing what had been erased.[75] He insisted on the importance of restorations undertaken at the end of the sixteenth century, which, he argued, impacted the figure of Ambrose in particular. His conclusions were shocking: it is not impossible, he claimed, that attempts were made to make Ambrose resemble the last of the new Ambroses, modifying the saint's features to make them more similar to those of Carlo Borromeo. That similarity is attested to by other iconographic representations, in which the confusion between Ambrose and Borromeo may have been deliberately orchestrated.[76] So it wasn't merely a matter of shaving the bishop-saint's beard or unseating him from his horse, but of readjusting the past to a likeness of the present. Though it initially aroused incredulity, this hypothesis – unverifiable in any case – currently has some followers.[77] Likely because it has at least the merit of making us imagine another kind of anamnesis, in which Ambrosian mimicry inversed itself, like a retrospective act of reuse.

And yet we were so close to our goal, face-to-face with Ambrose, finally seeing his true visage. We were about to realize our archaeological dream of stopping time, just like Angelo Decembrio and his companions had hoped to, one day in 1447, at the threshold of that large memory machine that is the Basilica of Sant'Ambrogio, where the ages pile up in one imperious and stubborn block of time. We just needed to step back a bit, to find the welcoming shade of the small sanctuary adjoining the basilica where a truth, a presence, was waiting for us, a little bit of life still left, trapped beneath the surface. But alas, the anamnesis reversed itself. We find ourselves, once again, hurtling across the slopes of time, abruptly thrown from the fifth century to the sixteenth century. The lesson learned, albeit a bit late, is that what we call chronology is merely the inversion of time.

The golden altar in 1917, departure for the Vatican (*top*) and arrival at the Vatican galleries (*bottom*), anonymous photographs, Archivio Capitolare di Sant'Ambrogio

AFTERWORD

Although surrounded by a crowd pressing him to act, Ambrose is all alone. He is alone because he is reading silently. And Augustine, observing him, holds back, astonished, on the threshold of Ambrose's silence. As Augustine writes so vividly in his *Confessions*: "When he was reading, his eyes glided over the pages, and his heart searched out the sense, but his voice and tongue were at rest. Ofttimes when we had come (for no man was forbidden to enter, nor was it his wont that any who came should be announced to him), we saw him thus reading to himself, and never otherwise; and [we] long sat silent (for who durst intrude on one so intent?)."[1] Ambrose is close by – accessible even, since he stands in plain sight of all, while around him is the "compact throng" of those who would seek favors from him, or a word of advice, a prayer. But in presenting us the astonishing sight of a person reading in silence, *tacite legens* – the phrase can also be translated as "reading quietly" or "reading in low tones," either way he barely moved his lips – and in thereby expressing his desire to withdraw from the "hubbub of the business of others," Ambrose recedes like a ghost. He is still *in our presence*, but far, far away.

This scene of him reading silently is perhaps what remains most lastingly of Ambrose. Historians have pored over this account for a long time without ever really knowing what to make of it. Is it to be interpreted as the first instance of a cultural muta-tion in the practice of reading? But this would be to subscribe naively to the belief that the historian's highest task is to attach a firm date to great and sudden shifts, when all the evidence indi-cates on the contrary that cultural history – and maybe history in general – belies such a peremptory view of time.[2] Writers may put us on the right track here, because they've tended to see this prac-tice as related to literature.[3] To read silently is a "strange art," says Jorge Luis Borges, writing about Augustine's description, because it leads to "the concept of the book as an end in itself, not as a means to an end."[4] This may be the reason that the contemporary French writer Pascal Quignard makes almost obsessive use of this Ambrosian scene. As the author of *Barque silencieuse* (Silent boat, 2009), *Le vœu de silence* (The vow of silence, 1985), and *Le nom sur le bout de la langue* (The name on the tip of one's tongue, 1993), Quig-nard has written again and again about musicians who have been struck dumb; he is haunted by the silent orality of the writer.[5] In one of his *Petits traités* (Little treatises), he writes: "A book is a piece of silence in the hands of the reader." The interaction between Augustine and Ambrose makes its appearance in several of his texts, which trace "a strange contagion of silence coming from Ambrosian reading."[6]

Augustine has described Ambrose as making the choir of his congregation vibrate in unison with his hymns, which promise the Kingdom of God. Here he describes him as the silent reader who, lips sealed, enters the kingdom of interiority. The aura sur-rounding his *tacite legens* is made of admiration and, perhaps, anxiety. For face-to-face with his book, Ambrose not only with-draws from the company of other men but withdraws from any possibility of exchange with them. He quits the sound-based world of classical dialogue to enter the silent world of reading. Henceforth, he can no longer be argued with on the subject of truth; by reading in silence, Ambrose cuts short all debate. Those who watch him read therefore become mute in turn, particularly Augustine, who "went about things backwards. He wanted to speak when he did not know how to speak."[7] He had been told that a brilliant rhetorician lived in Milan, and he had gone there to see Ambrose bandy speech as if it were a sword, yet what he saw was the gifted speaker being quiet.

And so, this scene should be read backwards, starting from the account of Augustine's conversion. It may be remembered that in his case as well, a child cried. This is in Book 8 of *Confessions*. Augustine is in Milan, in a garden. He is sitting with Alypius and reading a book. But he is overcome with weeping and cries out impatiently: "How long, how long? Tomorrow and tomorrow? Why not now? Why not this very hour?" Full of bitterness, his heart crushed, he flings himself down under a fig tree. There, he hears the voice of a little boy or a little girl, he is not sure which, coming from the neighboring house, singing a little song: *tolle, lege, tolle, lege*. "Take up and read!" says the child. Or, in another translation: "Pick it up, read it."[8] It's like a game, an old game, coming to us from afar. Augustine runs to the place where he'd dropped his book, opens it at random, and silently reads the first passage he sees. "Then, putting my finger or something else for a mark, I shut the book." Augustine is converted, the classical world experiences a shift, turns to a new page, opens to the truth about itself – the way you might open a stray book to the right page.

But if the book opens and offers itself up, we still have to search further, dig down to the heart of the words Augustine uses, as Maria Tasinato invites us to do. In saying of Ambrose that his heart searched out the sense, we are only giving a weak translation to *et cor intellectum rimabatur*. As Augustine uses it, the word *cor* covers a complex set of meanings, in contrast to *vox, lingua, labia,* and generally anything exterior. "*Cor,* in the end, suggests that which in man is separate (from the body or its limbs), something in profound *discordance* with the *attuned* resonance of a chorus of consenting voices."[9] We now understand better why Ambrose's *unheard of* solitude is the exact negative of hymn singing; for Augustine, it tests the very idea of conversion. Tests it, yet paradoxically brings it about. For what Ambrose's *cor* searches for in the text, ferrets out, is the *rima* – a word that among other things means, according to Isidore of Seville, the crack between poorly joined boards. All of this makes perfectly concrete sense when we consider the materiality of the thing Ambrose is looking at: a *scriptio continua,* that is, a compact mass of letters that is interrupted neither by spaces nor punctuation. In consequence, and without the reassuring help of a voice, the active mind must seek out the breaks and divisions, and by this "*sensible* and entirely visual pursuit, arrive at meaning,"[10] which makes reading already a question of interpreting. It is the stylus that cuts into the body of the text, slices it, opens it up. And as this interpretation can only be silent and solitary, Ambrose withdraws from dialogue. He no longer has anything to say; his speech no longer prompts the tuneful choir of consenting voices.

Reading in order to interpret, looking for the cracks to find a way in, trying to understand what it all means. Someone had to try to tell the whole story at least once. Something had to be built, a silent craft that heaved through the sea-foam, even if the planks were poorly joined, to see where the plot would lead us, what consistency its time would have. What's left? A man desperate to show himself, drawing everything toward him even as he fades away. And what's to be made with him if not the work of a historian? "To do the work of the historian does not mean knowing 'how things really happened.' It means seizing upon a memory, just as it arises at the moment of danger."[11]

Trace and aura. The trace is appearance of a nearness, however far removed the thing that left it behind may be. The aura is appearance of a distance, however close the thing that calls it forth. In the trace, we gain possession of the thing; in the aura it takes possession of us.[12]

This passage by Walter Benjamin has long haunted me. I don't feel that I read it – it read me. I thought I should devote a whole book to this brilliant formulation, or nearly, in order to grasp that it was in fact the opposite of a historian's magic key to open all the doors of time.[13] Even if I can hardly imagine how a book of history could be named anything but "trace and aura," the expression keeps short-circuiting in my mind, flooding everything with a sudden glare, but so electrically that it offers no real light. As I was finishing this book, I dreamt of a reader who would be unaffected by all this because unaware of the above fragment from *The Arcades Project* – a chance reader who, inspired by the book's title, would have picked it up, read it in silence, and soon grown irritated to find that the author never bothers to define what "trace and aura" means to him. And this irritated reader would decide on finishing the book to jot down a sentence summing it all up, the way you might scrawl a suddenly remembered quote in the margins of a book, an address, the name of a long-forgotten friend, a longing, or a flash of anger. And I dreamt that the sentence could be none other than the above.

Returning to it, how else could the idea be expressed? The trace and the aura are two apparitions. The trace is the appearance of something near, while the aura is the appearance of something distant. We bend down toward the trace, lying humbly at our feet. We recognize the imprint that time makes in matter, we know that someone passed this way, that we can tell his or her story, and we're off – following the trace, moving against time. *The trace is appearance of a nearness, however far removed the thing that left it behind may be.* With the aura, it's the other way around. It appears and calls to us, but at the same time draws away. Yet it seems so familiar. There it is, within arm's length yet inaccessible, it withdraws while pretending to offer itself, it makes us look up at what's looking at us. *The aura is appearance of a distance, however close the thing that calls it forth.* Have we talked of anything else here? And what do we make of it if not history, which is or should be an emancipating art and therefore takes the trace's side against the aura? *In the trace, we gain possession of the thing; in the aura it takes possession of us.*

By severing the concept of aura from its mystical substrate, Walter Benjamin has relaunched it forward in time to our own day – and I, for one, can no longer look at an old photograph without seeing in it what he called "a peculiar web of space and time."[14] I remember the moment I found photographs in a box labeled "V.B.2 Altare d'oro," from the capitular archives of Sant'Ambrogio, preserved in the basilica's bell tower, where material had been accumulating for ages. And if I didn't remember it, the metadata from the digital snapshots that I took would at least give me the date: February 8, 2007, at 3:32 p.m. That is our current relationship with time, whose elapsed minutes are tracked independently of us. It was once a different story. The folder into which these photographs had been put said: "1918. *Trasporto altare d'oro.*" In fact, it was in fall 1917 that the golden altar was transported away from Milan, out of fear that the German and Austro-Hungarian offensive on the Piave Line, in Friuli, would threaten the Lombard capital. The golden altar was therefore crated and shipped to the Vatican, returning to Milan in 1920.[15] In the first photograph, the holy crate has moved as far as the threshold of the basilica's narthex. The picture shows a little girl in a hat, wearing a white dress and a suspicious expression.

Next to her is a little boy, his coat over his arm, looking incredulous. Another child is turning toward the lens, as often happens in old photographs, where the picture-taking is itself an event. We also see flat caps and straw boaters, a priest's cassock, cigarettes hanging from lips, walrus mustaches. In the second photograph, more of the same, with riding coats and well-tailored outfits. The reliquary, it appears, has now reached its destination. It is in a safe place, a storage room in the Vatican. The second photograph is more composed, more solemn, and also clearer: the danger is past.

The file has other photographs too – workers in shirtsleeves straining to load the heavy crate onto a wagon, then posing in front of it with solemn faces. But we don't see the altar's return to Milan, which apparently wasn't photographed. And why should it have been? The real is what always comes back to the same place, and Ambrose's place was in Milan. I don't know why these photographs move me, as a historian. They teach us nothing, really, except for documenting a minor excursion. But their weakness and poverty, which quietly testify to history's inadequacy, play in their favor. For there are letters painted on the sides of the wooden crate, an ordinary inscription in all its prosaic crudeness. That is history, no more no less, the ability to put a name to things, to stop time and return it to where it belongs. Just two words. *Milano. Ambrogio.*

ACKNOWLEDGMENTS

As I come, at last, to take leave of this troublesome companion, my grateful thoughts go out to those who have made him bearable, if only by suffering me to discuss him. From my oral defense of a research project in November 2009 to my course at the Collège de France in winter 2016, and including along the way the various seminars, conferences, and panel discussions at which I aired my perplexities, there have been many who have helped me with their patience, their willingness to listen, their advice and encouragement, or simply by their pained expression. On that score, Matthieu, Léonie, and Madeleine quite obviously led the pack. But I want to reassure them: the irascible old guy has been shut away in his box once and for all; he won't be back to bother us again.

Thanks to Cesare Alzati, Philippe Artières, Vincent Azoulay, Romain Bertrand, Philippe Buc, Guido Cariboni, Enrico Castelnuovo, Federica Cengarle, Giorgio Chittolini, Élisabeth Crouzet-Pavan, Annick Custot-Peters, Fabrice Delivré, Marco Folin, François Foronda, Laura Gaffuri, Andrea Gamberini, Claude Gauvard, Adrien Genoudet, Marco Gentile, Camille Gerzaguet, Paolo Grillo, Nathaniel Herzberg, Gary Ianziti, Véronique Lamazou-Duplan, Régine Le Jan, Marie Lezowski, Florian Mazel, Neil McLynn, François Menant, Giuliano Milani, Pierre Monnet, Miri Rubin, Jean-Claude Schmitt, Zrinka Stahuljak,

Valérie Theis, Pierre Toubert, and Paolo Ventrone, each of whom, at one point or other, said something to strike a spark.

If I managed in the end to overcome the doubts and discouragement that I experienced in the course of this long journey, I also owe it to the confidence of Jacques Dalarun, the impatience of Jean-Louis Biget, the skepticism of Jean-Philippe Genet, the passionate enthusiasm of Judith Gurewich – and the unshakable friendship of Yann Potin. Since our joint organization of a program of collective research on the memory of the Church Fathers in medieval Italy at the École française de Rome, right up to his generous and attentive reading of this manuscript, Stéphane Gioanni has been my boon companion on this adventure, imparting his meticulous and joyful knowledge. Étienne Arnheim knows and yet doesn't know how important our discussions were in resolving certain narrative dilemmas: it was he, in particular, who convinced me to start the film with Robert de Niro's car exploding. Finally, knowing that Roger Chartier was expecting this book inspired such a sense of pride in me that it could by itself have justified my desire to write it.

As to the book, it wouldn't exist without the steadfastness, energy, and delicacy of Séverine Nikel, who was – and I don't know why it gives me so much pleasure to say so – its editor. The fact is that at my French publishers, the Éditions du Seuil, the confidence I received from Olivier Bétourné and Hughes Jallon, the generous and attentive care from Caroline Pichon, the amused protectiveness from Séverine Roscot, the seriousness and integrity with which each understood his or her professional role has inspired me with more than a sense of gratitude, let's call it a new confidence in the future of intellectual endeavor. And I am grateful to Emmanuelle Portugal for having helped me go over the proofs, the French term for which, as she has pointed out to me, has the well-earned second meaning of "trials."

I could also wish to thank certain landscapes – the one at the Fondation des Treilles, for instance, which in the spring of 2018 afforded me a setting of inexorable solitude, leaving me no choice but to finish my project. Any number of city walks, and not only in Milan, made me understand bits of this story – my companions on those occasions, living and dead, are too numerous to name. Or maybe just those around me on May 14, 2017, when we were carried to the threshold of what can still be said, seen, and lived. It was in Milan, at the Basilica of Sant'Ambrogio, contemplating time at a standstill, before going off to immerse ourselves for a long moment in the Rondanini Pietà, which, finally, twists time and arrests it. They were Evelyn Prawidlo, Serge Renko, and Mathieu Riboulet. And also, it goes without saying, Mélanie Traversier, an irresistible dispeller of ghosts.

NOTES

PROLOGUE:
THAT WHICH RETURNS TO THE SAME PLACE

1. Charles Baudelaire, "Spleen," in *The Flowers of Evil*, trans. William Aggeler (Fresno, CA: Academy Library Guild, 1954).

2. Jacques Derrida, *Acts of Religion*, ed. Gil Anidjar (New York: Routledge, 2002), 46.

3. Derrida, 46.

4. Fernand Braudel, *The Identity of France. Vol. 1: History and Environment*, trans. Sian Reynolds (New York: Harper & Row, 1988), 15.

5. Jacques Lacan, *The Four Fundamental Concepts of Psychoanalysis*, ed. Jacques-Alain Miller, trans. Alan Sheridan (New York: W.W. Norton & Company, Inc., 1978), 280.

CHAPTER ONE:
THE ARCHAEOLOGY OF A PROPER NAME

1. I will cite a considerable number of sources throughout this book, beginning with the following, which provides an overview of the Basilica of Sant'Ambrogio: Maria-Luisa Gatti Perer, ed., *La basilica di S. Ambrogio: il tempio ininterrotto* (Milan: Vita e Pensiero, 1995).

2. Laura Riva, *Alle porte del paradiso. Le sculture del vestibolo di Sant'Ambrogio* (Milan: LED, 2006).

3. Antonio Lanza, *Firenze contro Milano. Gli intellettuali fiorentini nelle guerre con i Visconti (1390–1440)* (Rome: De Rubeis, 1991).

4. Alessandro Rovetta, "Memorie e monumenti funerari in S. Ambrogio tra Medioevo e Rinascimento," in Gatti Perer, *La basilica di S. Ambrogio*, 1:290–91.

5. Mario Borsa, "Pier Candido Decembrio e l'Umanesimo in Lombardia," *Archivio storico lombardo* 10 (1893): 5–75 and 358–441. On their respective deaths in 1458 and 1464, Pier Candido Decembrio also chose to bury his adopted daughter, Costanza, and his wife, Caterina, in the Basilica of Sant'Ambrogio. He himself died on the night of November 12–13, 1477.

6. Evelyn Welch, "The Ambrosian Republic and the Cathedral of Milan," *Arte lombarda* 100 (1992): 24.

7. Franco Gualdoni, "Dal *De supplicationibus maiis* al *De religionibus et caerimoniis*. Vicende di un testo inedito di Angelo Decembrio," *Italia medioevale e umanistica* 41 (2000): 179–241. There are three known manuscript mentions of this treaty in its initial form: manuscript Z 184 sup. in the Biblioteca Ambrosiana in Milan and Lat. 121 in the Biblioteca Estense in Modena, both dating from the second half of the fifteenth century, and a very faithful copy from the sixteenth century conserved in the Biblioteca Trivulziana of Milan (Triv. 756).

8. Zrinka Stahuljak, *Pornographic Archaeology: Medicine, Medievalism, and the Invention of the French Nation* (Philadelphia: University of Pennsylvania Press, 2012), 5.

9. This sculpted backdrop creates more difficult problems of identification: Gualdoni, "Dal *De supplicationibus maiis*," 194–96, n. 63.

10. Enrico Cattaneo, "L'evoluzione delle feste di precetto a Milano dal secolo XIV al XX. Riflessi religiosi e sociali," in *Studi in memoria di mons. Cesare Dotta*, Archivio ambrosiano 9 (Milan: 1956), 71–151.

11. On the disposability of the past, see Reinhardt Koselleck, *Futures Past: On the Semantics of Historical Time*, trans. and with an introduction by Keith Tribe (New York: Columbia University Press, 2004), 192 et seq.

12. Carlo Bertelli, "Percorso tra le testimonianze figurative più antiche," in Gatti Perer, *La basilica di S. Ambrogio*, 2:341–42.

13. The context of Abbot Mellitus's mission to convert England and the connection between Gregory's letter to King Ethelbert (June 22, 601) and the letter to Mellitus (July 18, 601) are explored in Sofia Boesch Gajano, *Grégoire le Grand. Aux origines du Moyen Âge*, trans. Jacqueline Martin-Bagnaudez and Noël Lucas (Paris: Cerf, 2006), 141–43.

14. Note that this question is the object of an exacting analysis in Book 16 of the *Codex Theodosianus*, which benefits from an excellent French translation and commentary: *Les lois religieuses des empereurs romains de Constantin à Théodose II (312–438)*, vol. 1: *Code Théodosien. Livre 16*, Latin text by Theodor Mommsen, translated by Jean Rougé, introduction and notes by Roland Delmaire (with François

Richard), Sources Chrétiennes 497 (Paris: Cerf, 2005). Trans. Clyde Pharr, with Theresa Sherrer Davidson and Mary Pharr, in *The Theodosian Code and Novels, and the Sirmondian Constitutions* (Princeton, NJ: Princeton University Press, 1952).

15. This text is translated with a brief commentary in Bruno Judic, "Grégoire le Grand et son influence sur le haut Moyen Âge occidental," in *Le christianisme en Occident du début du VIIᵉ siècle au milieu du XIᵉ siècle*, ed. François Bougard (Paris: SEDES, 1997), 10–11. Judic reconsidered his analysis of this text, notably in proposing a cautious analysis of the comparison with the "people of Israel": see "Le corbeau et la sauterelle. L'application des instructions de Grégoire le Grand pour la transformation des temples païens en églises," in *Impies et païens entre Antiquité et Moyen Âge*, eds. Lionel Mary and Michel Sot (Paris: Picard, 2002), 97–125. Bruno Dumézil suggests that the method of conversion laid out by Gregory the Great in his letter to Mellitus could truly have been implemented in England: Bruno Dumézil, *Les racines chrétiennes de l'Europe. Conversion et liberté dans les royaumes barbares, Vᵉ–VIIIᵉ siècles* (Paris: Fayard, 2005), 315.

16. Jean-Claude Bonne, "'Relève' de l'ornementation celte païenne dans un Évangile insulaire du VIIᵉ siècle (Les Évangiles de Durrow)," in *Ideologie e pratiche nel riempiego nell'alto Medioevo. Atti della Settimana di studio del Centro italiano di studi sull'alto medioevo (Spoleto, 16–21 aprile 1998)* (Spoleto: Centro italiano di studi sull'alto medioevo [46], 1999), 2: 1018–20.

17. Jacques Derrida, "Le puits et la pyramide. Introduction à la sémiologie de Hegel," in *Marges de la philosophie* (Paris: Minuit, 1972), 79–127. Published in English as "The Pit and the Pyramid: Introduction to Hegel's Semiology," in *Margins of Philosophy*, trans. Alan Bass (Chicago: University of Chicago Press, 1984).

18. Pierre-Emmanuel Dauzat, *Les Pères de leur Mère. Essai sur l'esprit de contradiction des Pères de l'Église* (Paris: Albin Michel, 2001), 146: "Far from being an accident, it follows a logic that allows the reader to pass quietly from a pagan reading to a Christian one."

19. See on this point the illuminating analyses of Salvatore Settis, "Les remplois," in *Patrimoine, temps, espace: Patrimoine en place, patrimoine déplacé*, ed. François Furet, Collection des actes des Entretiens du patrimoine 2 (Paris: Fayard, 1997), 67–86.

20. Guy Lobrichon, "La relecture des Pères chez les commentateurs de la Bible dans l'Occident latin (IXᵉ–XIIᵉ siècle)," in *Ideologie e pratiche*, 1:257.

21. Nicolas Huyghebaert, "Une légende de fondation: le Constitutum Constantini," *Le Moyen Âge* 85 (1979): 173–209.

Notes

421

22. Carlo Ginzburg, "Lorenzo Valla on the 'Donation of Constantine,'" in *History, Rhetoric, and Proof: The Menahem Stern Jerusalem Lectures* (Hanover, NH: University Press of New England, 1999), 54-70, at 64-65.

23. From a large bibliography, see the overview provided in Clémence Revest, "La naissance de l'humanisme comme mouvement au tournant du xve siècle," *Annales. Histoire, Sciences Sociales* 68 (2013): 665-96.

24. See Michael Baxandall, "A Dialogue on Art from the Court of Leonello d'Este: Angelo Decembrio's *De Politia Litterariae* Pars LXVIII," *Journal of the Warburg and Courtauld Institute* 26 (1963): 304-26; and Christopher S. Celenza, "Creating Canons in Fifteenth-Century Ferrara: Angelo Decembrio's *De Politia Litteraria* 1.10," *Renaissance Quarterly* 57 (2004): 43-98. The text is now available in a critical edition: Angelo Camillo Decembrio, *De politia litteraria*, ed. Norbert Witten (Berlin: De Gruyter, 2002).

25. Jacques Rancière, *Les noms de l'histoire. Essai de poétique du savoir* (Paris: Seuil, 1990). Published in English as *The Names of History: On the Poetics of Knowledge*, trans. Hassan Melehy (Minneapolis, MN: University of Minnesota Press, 1994).

26. Jean-Charles Passeron, *Le raisonnement sociologique. L'espace non-poppérien du raisonnement naturel* (Paris: Nathan, 1991), 163 et seq. Published in English as *Sociological Reasoning: A Non-Popperian Space of Argumentation*, trans. Rachel Gomme, ed. and introduced by Derek Robbins, European Studies in Social Theory (Oxford: The Bardwell Press, 2013).

27. Alain Badiou, *De quoi Sarkozy est-il le nom?* (Paris: Lignes, 2007). Published in English as *The Meaning of Sarkozy*, trans. David Fernbach (New York: Verso, 2008).

28. Jean-Claude Milner, *Les noms indistincts* (1983; reprint, Paris: Verdier, 2009).

29. For more on this idea of patched-together memories, see Roger Bastide, "Mémoire collective et sociologie du bricolage," *L'année sociologique* 21 (1970): 65-108.

30. Lucette Valensi, *Fables de la mémoire. La glorieuse bataille des trois rois* (Paris: Seuil, 1992), 278.

31. On this concept, see Jean Pouillon, "Plus c'est la même chose, plus ça change," *Nouvelle revue de psychanalyse* 15 (1977): 203-20.

32. Angelo Paredi, ed., *Sacramentarium Bergomense* (Bergamo: *Monumenta Bergomensia*, 1962), 49, cited in Enrico Cattaneo, "La tradizione e il rito ambrosiani nell'ambiente lombardo-medioevale," in *Ambrosius episcopus. Atti del Congresso internazionale di studi ambrosiani nel XVI centenario della elevazione di Sant'Ambrogio*

alla cattedra episcopale (Milano, dicembre 1974), ed. Giuseppe Lazzati (Milan: Vita e Pensiero, 1976), 2:6, also in Enrico Cattaneo, *La Chiesa di Ambrogio. Studi di storia e di liturgia* (Milan: Vita e Pensiero, 1984), 118.

33. Jean-Charles Picard, *Le souvenir des évêques. Sépultures, listes épiscopales et culte des évêques en Italie du Nord des origines au xe siècle* (Rome: École française de Rome, 1988), 575.

34. Hans-Conrad Peyer, *Stadt und Stadtpatron in Mittelalterliche Italie* (Zurich: Europa Verlag, 1955), 25-45. For an analysis of the historiographical significance of this text, see the introduction to the Italian edition by Anna Benvenuti: *Città e santi patroni nell'Italia medievale* (Florence: Le Lettere, 1998), 7-37.

35. Cattaneo, "La tradizione e il rito," 36-37; reprinted in Cattaneo, *La Chiesa di Ambrogio*, 148-49. This collection of articles is a fundamental reference for the subject of the present book.

36. As shown by the important work by Cesare Alzati, *Ambrosianum mysterium. La Chiesa di Milano e la sua tradizione liturgica* (Milan: NED, 2000).

37. Cited in Cattaneo, "La tradizione e il rito," 15.

38. Cited in Cattaneo, "La tradizione e il rito," 27.

39. Laurent Olivier, *Le sombre abyme du temps. Mémoire et archéologie* (Paris: Seuil, 2008). Published in English as *The Dark Abyss of Time: Archaeology and Memory*, trans. Arthur Greenspan (Lanham, MD: AltaMira Press, 2011).

40. Patrick Boucheron, "La mémoire disputée: le souvenir de saint Ambroise, enjeu des luttes politiques à Milan au xve siècle," in *Memoria, communitas*, ed. Hanno Brandt, Pierre Monnet, and Martial Staub (Paris-Francfort: Thorbecke [Beihefte di Francia], 2003), 201-21.

41. Patrick Boucheron, "Tout est monument. Le mausolée d'Azzone Visconti à *San Gottardo in Corte* de Milan (1342-1346)," in *"Liber largitorius." Études d'histoire médiévale offertes à Pierre Toubert par ses élèves*, ed. Dominique Barthélemy and Jean-Marie Martin (Geneva: Droz, 2003), 303-26.

42. Patrick Boucheron, "Palimpsestes ambrosiens: la commune, la liberté et le saint patron (Milan, xie-xve siècles)," in *Le passé à l'épreuve du présent. Appropriations et usages du passé au Moyen Âge et à la Renaissance*, ed. Pierre Chastang (Paris: PUPS, 2008), 15-37.

43. Patrick Boucheron, "Au cœur de l'espace monumental milanais: les remplois de Sant'Ambrogio (ixe-xiiie siècles)," in *Remploi, citation, plagiat. Conduites et pratiques médiévale (x^e-xiie siècles)*, ed. Pierre Toubert and Pierre Moret (Madrid: Casa de Velázquez, 2009), 161-90.

44. Patrick Boucheron, "Une tradition liturgique et ses messages implicites:

remarques sur l'horizon de réception politique de l'*ambrosianum mysterium* à Milan," *Annali di Storia moderna e contemporanea* 16 (2010): 177–96, reprinted in *Images, cultes, liturgies. Les connotations politiques du message religieux*, eds. Paola Ventrone and Laura Gaffuri (Paris–Rome: Publications de la Sorbonne – Publications de l'École française de Rome, 2014), 73–92.

45. Patrick Boucheron, "La violence du fondateur. Récits de fondation et souvenir ambrosien à Milan (XIIIe–XVe siècles)," in *"Ab urbe condita." Fonder et refonder la ville: récits et représentations (second Moyen Âge – premier XVIe siècle). Actes du colloque international de Pau (14–15–16 mai 2009)*, ed. Véronique Lamazou-Duplan (Pau: Presses universitaires de Pau et des pays de l'Adour, 2011), 127–45.

46. Patrick Boucheron, "Religion civique, religion civile, religion séculière. L'ombre d'un doute," *Revue de synthèse* 134 (2013): 161–83.

47. Patrick Boucheron, "Dissiper l'aura du nom propre," in *Le roman français contemporain face à l'histoire*, ed. Gianfranco Rubino and Dominique Viart (Rome: Quodlibet, 2014), 43–61.

48. Patrick Boucheron, "Les combattants d'Ambroise. Commémorations et luttes politiques à la fin du Moyen Âge," in *La mémoire d'Ambroise de Milan. Usages politiques d'une autorité patristique en Italie (V^e–XVIIIe siècle)*, ed. Patrick Boucheron and Stéphane Gioanni (Paris–Rome: Publications de la Sorbonne – Publications de l'École française de Rome, 2015), 483–98.

PART ONE:

A LIFE AND NOTHING ELSE

1. We know that Francesco della Croce, *primicerio* of the Milan Cathedral and an ardent defender of the Ambrosian liturgy, was the dedicatee of this work: Mirella Ferrari, "Un bibliotecario milanese nel Quattrocento: Francesco della Croce," in *Ricerche storiche sulla Chiesa ambrosiana* 10, Archivio ambrosiano 42 (Milan: NED, 1981), 185–86.

2. Enrico Cattaneo, "Lo studio delle opere di S. Ambrogio a Milano nei sec. XV–XVI," in *Studi storici in memoria di Mons. Angelo Mercati* (Milan: A. Giuffrè, 1956), 147–61. See also Antonio Manfredi, "Vicende umanistiche di codivi vaticani con opere di sant'Ambrogio," in *Aevum* 72 (1998): 559–89.

3. Felice Valsecchi, ed., *La vita di s. Ambrogio nella edizione milanese del 149* (Milan: Allegretti, 1974).

4. According to Jacques Dalarun and Lino Leonardi, eds., *Biblioteca Agiografica Italiana (BAI). Repertorio di testi e manoscritti, secoli XIII–XV* (Florence: Edizioni del Galluzzo, 2003), 2:40–42.

5. Giorgio Varanini and Guido Baldassarri, eds., *Racconti esemplari di predicatori del Due e Trecento* (Rome: Salerno Editrice, 1993), 3–698.

6. Jacobus de Voragine, *The Golden Legend: Readings on the Saints*, trans. William Granger Ryan (Princeton, NJ: Princeton University Press, 2012), 229. Jacobus only strays from Paulinus's account, as we'll see later, in his telling of the penitence imposed on Theodosius.

7. Gabriele Banterle, ed., *Le fonti latine su Sant'Ambrogio*, Opera omnia di sant'Ambrogio, Sussidi 24/2 (Rome: Città Nuova Editrice, 1991).

8. This manuscript, which belonged to the humanist Pierre Pithou (d. 1596), is kept at the Bibliothèque nationale de France (under the number Latin 1771): Pierre-Patrick Verbraken, "Le manuscrit latin 1771 de la Bibliothèque Nationale de Paris et ses sermons augustiniens," *Revue bénédictine* 78 (1968): 67–81.

9. Lellia Cracco Ruggini, "Sulla fortuna della 'Vita Ambrosii,'" *Athenaeum* 51 (1963): 101–2.

10. Jacques Derrida, *La dissémination* (Paris: Seuil, 1972). Published in English as *Dissemination*, trans. and with an introduction and additional notes by Barbara Johnson (1981; reprint, Chicago, IL: University of Chicago Press, 2017).

11. See in particular François van Ortroy, "Les vies grecques de Saint Ambroise et leurs sources," in *Ambrosiana. Scritti vari pubblicati nel XV Centenario della morte di sant'Ambrogio* (Milan: L. F. Cogliati, 1897), 1–37.

12. Cesare Pasini, "La Vita premetafrastica di Sant'Ambrogio," *Analecta Bollandiana* 101 (1983): 101–50.

13. Monique Goullet, *Écriture et réécritures hagiographiques. Essai sur les réécritures de Vies de saints dans l'Occident latin médiéval (VIIIe–XIIIe s.)*, Hagiologia 4 (Turnhout: Brepols, 2005).

14. Jacques Dalarun, *The Misadventure of Francis of Assisi: Toward a Historical Use of the Franciscan Legends*, trans. Edward Hagman (St. Bonaventure, NY: Franciscan Institute Publications, Franciscan Institute, 2002), 173.

CHAPTER TWO:
AMBROSE AS SELF-INVENTOR

1. Ambrose, *De virginibus* 1.7.35, cited in Michel Foucault, *Histoire de la sexualité*, vol. IV: *Les aveux de la chair*, ed. Frédéric Gros (Paris: Gallimard, 2018), 186.

2. Foucault, *Les aveux de la chair*, 202.

3. Yves-Marie Duval, "Formes profanes et formes bibliques dans les oraisons funèbres de saint Ambroise," in *Christianisme et formes littéraires de l'Antiquité tardive en Occident*, Entretiens sur l'Antiquité classique 23 (Geneva: Fondation Hardt,

1997), 235–301. See also Hervé Savon, *Ambroise de Milan* (Paris: Desclée, 1997), 69–70.

4. Ambrose, *De officiis* 2.15.70 and 2.28.136–143b. Using gifts to the Church in this way was understood by Ambrose as *aurum utile*, useful gold. On the event itself, see Alessandro Barbero, *The Day of the Barbarians: The Battle That Led to the Fall of the Roman Empire*, trans. John Cullen (New York: Walker & Company, 2007).

5. The date of Ambrose's birth is still uncertain, and it depends on the interpretation given his *Letter to Severus* (*Letters* 49.3–4), where he describes himself as "exposed to barbarian incursions and the tempests of war" in his fifty-third year. Is the reference to the invasion of Maximus (387) or the usurpation of Eugenius (393–94)? If the first, he would have been born in 333–34, if the second in 339–40. For the reasons leading current scholars toward the second, see Giuseppe Visonà, *Cronologia ambrosiana. Bibliografia ambrosiana (1900–2000)*, Opera omnia di sant'Ambrogio, Sussidi 25/26 (Rome: Città Nuova Editrice, 2004), 15–20.

6. Peter Brown, *Through the Eye of a Needle: Wealth, the Fall of Rome, and the Making of Christianity in the West, 350–550 AD* (Princeton, NJ: Princeton University Press, 2012), 187.

7. Luigi Pizzolato, "L'enigma del padre di Sant'Ambrogio," *Aevum* 88 (2014): 149 et seq.

8. Cited in Savon, *Ambroise de Milan*, 105.

9. Cited in Savon, *Ambroise de Milan*, 249.

10. Paulinus of Milan, *Vita Ambrosii* 8, in *Ambrose*, ed. Boniface Ramsey (New York: Routledge, 1997), 199. See Clementina Corbellini, "Sesto Petronio Probo e l'elezione episcopale di Ambrogio," *Rendiconti dell'Istituto Lombardo. Classe di Lettere e Scienze Morali e Storiche* 109 (1975): 181–89.

11. Brown, *Through the Eye of a Needle*, 120.

12. Neil B. McLynn, *Ambrose of Milan: Church and Court in a Christian Capital* (Berkeley: University of California Press, 1994), 1–52; Santo Mazzarino, *Storia sociale del vescovo Ambrogio* (Rome: L'Erma di Bretschneider, 1989).

13. Hero Granger-Taylor, "The Two Dalmatics of Saint Ambrose," *Bulletin de liaison du Centre international d'études des textiles anciens* 57–58 (1983): 127–73.

14. Claire Sotinel, "Les évêques italiens dans la société de l'Antiquité tardive: l'émergence d'une nouvelle élite?," in *Le trasformazioni delle élites in età tardoantica. Atti del convegno internazionale di Perugia, 15–16 marzo 2004*, ed. Rita Lizzi Testa (Rome: L'Erma di Bretschneider, 2006), 377–404.

15. This happened, we should note, well after Ambrose's death, since only

three percent of Italian bishops in the years from 350 to 450 were of senatorial rank. See Lellia Cracco Ruggini, "Prêtre et fonctionnaire: l'essor d'un modèle épiscopal aux IVᵉ-Vᵉ siècles," *Antiquité tardive* 7 (1999): 175–86.

16. McLynn, *Ambrose of Milan*, 220–25. During the basilica controversy of Holy Week 386, the emperor put pressure on the *mercatores*, whom he threatened with a fine ten times greater than required by the Theodosian Code. See Lellia Cracco Ruggini, *Economia e società nell' "Italia Annonaria." Rapporti fra agricoltura e commercio dal IV al VI secolo d. C.* (Bari: Edipuglia, 1995), 106–9. See also Brown, *Through the Eye of a Needle*, 125.

17. Ambrose, *Epist. extra collectionem* 14 (63 M).65, in *Ambrose of Milan: Political Letters and Speeches*, trans. J. H. W. G. Liebeschuetz with the assistance of Carole Hill (Liverpool: Liverpool University Press, 2005), 318. For a plausible reconstruction of the events of 374, the best account is still Yves-Marie Duval's "Ambroise de son élection à sa consécration," in *Ambrosius episcopus. Atti del Congresso internazionale di studi ambrosiani nel XVI centenario della elevazione di Sant'Ambrogio alla cattedra episcopale (Milano, dicembre 1974)*, ed. Giuseppe Lazzati, Studia patristica mediolanensia 7 (Milan: Vita e Pensiero, 1976), 2:243–83. One should also consult Timothy D. Barnes, "The Election of Ambrose of Milan," in *Episcopal Elections in Late Antiquity*, ed. Johan Leemans et al. (Berlin: De Gruyter, 2011), 39–59.

18. In theory (see *Codex Theodosianus* 8.4.7.361), the judge was supposed to confiscate two-thirds of his fortune, which he would then give to the civil office that the new bishop had just left. See Bruno Dumézil, *Servir l'Etat barbare. Du fonctionnariat antique à la noblesse médiévale* (Paris: Tallandier, 2013), 59.

19. Rita Lizzi Testa, "374 d. C. Da Milano al Mondo," in *Storia mondiale dell'Italia*, ed. Andrea Giardina (Bari-Rome: Laterza, 2017), 172–75.

20. Paulinus of Milan, *Vita Ambrosii* 7. For an analysis of the text, except where I have cited a different bibliographical reference in the pages ahead, I would point the reader to the following recent bilingual critical edition: Paolino di Milano, *Vita di Sant'Ambrogio. La prima biografia del patrono di Milano*, ed. Marco Navoni (Milan: San Paolo, 2016), whose notes record the various interpretations and the debate surrounding them (in this instance, see 80–81n23).

21. Ambrose, *De officiis* 1.1.4.

22. The hagiographic motif of election in spite of oneself is much rarer in the Middle Ages than in late antiquity, or else it appears as a necessary fiction. This is the case in the *Chronicle* by the Franciscan Salimbene de Adam in the thirteenth century, which alludes to Ambrose's flight in the context of a group of prelates seeking to avoid their responsibilities: "As to Ambrose, who was also

chosen by God's will, it is similarly reported that he did everything in his power not to become bishop" (Salimbene de Adam, *The Chronicle of Salimbene de Adam*, trans. Joseph L. Baird, Giuseppe Baglivi and John Robert Kane, *Medieval and Renaissance Texts and Studies* 40 [Binghamton, NY: Center for Medieval and Early Renaissance Studies, University Center at Binghamton, 1986]).

23. Ambrose, *Epist.* 76 (20 M).4.

24. On the subject of the philosopher's profession in Rome, see Goulven Madec, *Saint Ambroise et la philosophie* (Paris: Études augustiniennes, 1974), and related criticism by Hervé Savon, "Saint Ambroise et la philosophie, à propos d'une étude récente," *Revue de l'histoire des religions* 191-92 (1977): 173-96; on Ambrose's supposed adherence to Neoplatonism, see Pierre Courcelle, *Recherches sur Saint Ambroise. "Vies" anciennes, culture, iconographie* (Paris: Études augustiniennes, 1973), 11-15; and the critical views of Luigi Pizzolato, "Ricerche su Sant'Ambrogio. A proposito di un recente libro di P. Courcelle," *Aevum* 48 (1974): 500-505.

25. See in particular the classic study by Giulio Vismara, *Episcopalis audientia. L'attività giurizionale del vescovo per la risoluzione delle controversie private tra laici nel diritto romano e nella storia del diritto italiano fino al secolo nono* (Milan: Vita e Pensiero, 1938), and Giulio Vismara, "Ancora sull'episcopalis audientia (Ambrogio arbitro o giudice?)," *Studia et documenta historiae et iuris* 53 (1987): 55-73. On Ambrose specifically: Olivier Huck, "Oppositions religieuses et querelles d'influence dans les cités de l'Italie tardo-antique. À propos d'une audience épiscopale d'Ambroise de Milan," in *Les cités de l'Italie tardo-antique (IVᵉ–VIᵉ siècle). Institutions, économie, société, culture et religion*, ed. Massimiliano Ghilardi, Christophe J. Goddard, and Pierfrancesco Porena, Collection de l'École française de Rome 369 (Rome: École française de Rome, 2006), 309-24.

26. *Sacramentarium Bergomense*, ed. Angelo Paredi (Bergamo: Monumenta Bergomensia, 1962), 49, cited in Enrico Cattaneo, "La tradizione e il rito ambrosiani nell'ambiente lombardo-medioevale," in Lazzati, *Ambrosius episcopus*, 15, also available in Enrico Cattaneo, *La Chiesa di Ambrogio. Studi di storia e di liturgia* (Milan: Vita e Pensiero, 1984), 127.

27. See on this point the exhaustive study by Enrico Cattaneo, "L'evoluzione delle feste di precetto a Milano dal secolo XIV al XX," in *Studi in memoria di Mons. C. Dotta*, Archivio ambrosiano 9 (Milan: 1956), 69-200.

28. Jean-Paul Sartre, *Saint Genet: Actor and Martyr*, trans. Bernard Frechtman (Minneapolis: University of Minnesota Press, 2012), 49.

29. Ambrose, *De officiis* 1.4.

30. Roland Barthes, "Inaugural Letter, Collège de France," in *A Barthes Reader*, ed. Susan Sontag (New York: Hill and Wang, 1982), 478.

CHAPTER THREE:
"BUT THE WHOLE WAS MYSELF"

1. Peter Brown, *Augustine of Hippo: A Biography* (Berkeley and Los Angeles: University of California Press, 2000), 24.

2. Peter Brown, *Augustine of Hippo*, 268.

3. In the sense, of course, employed in Paul Veyne, *L'empire gréco-romain* (Paris: Seuil, 2005).

4. Augustine, *Confessions*, trans. Henry Chadwick (Oxford: Oxford University Press, 1991), Book 5.

5. Augustine, *Confessions*, Book 8.

6. *The Letter of Paul to the Romans*, ed. Ernest Best (Cambridge: Cambridge University Press, 1967), 151–52.

7. A vast bibliography exists for this subject, rendering any claim of an exhaustive reference ludicrous. Nonetheless, for a complete though somewhat dated overview, see *Agostino a Milano e il Battesimo. Agostino nelle terre di Ambrogio (22–24 aprile 1987)* (Palermo: Ed. Augustinus, 1988).

8. Augustine, *Confessions* 5.13.23.

9. Umberto Betti, "A proposito del conferimento del titolo di Dottore della Chiesa," *Antonianum* 13 (1988): 278–91. On this iconography: Pierre Courcelle, *Recherches sur Saint Ambroise. "Vies" anciennes, culture, iconographie* (Paris: Études augustiniennes, 1973), 156–57.

10. On this subject, see the Museo Diocesano exhibition catalog, Paolo Pasini, ed., *387 d. c.: Ambrogio e Agostino. Le sorgenti dell'Europa* (Milan: Olivares, 2003), 136–41.

11. Augustine, *Confessions* 5.13: "An oration I gave on a prescribed topic was approved by the then prefect Symmachus, who sent me to Milan." This is what Stéphane Ratti calls "Milan's compromise of principles": Stéphane Ratti, *Le premier saint Augustin* (Paris: Belles Lettres, 2016), 153–72.

12. Lellia Cracco Rugini, "Nascita e morte di una capitale," *Quaderni catanesi di studi classici e medievali* 2 (1990): 5–51.

13. Rita Lizzi Testa, "The Famous 'Altar of Victory Controversy' in Rome: The Impact of Christianity at the End of the Fourth Century," in *Contested Monarchy: Integrating the Roman Empire in the Fourth Century AD*, ed. Johannes Wienand (Oxford: Oxford University Press, 2015), 405–19.

Notes

14. Jean-Rémy Palanque saw this as an attempt to wrest away paganism's status as an established religion, and as a policy dictated by Ambroise's influence: Jean-Rémy Palanque, *Saint Ambroise et l'Empire romain. Contribution à l'histoire des rapports de l'Église et de l'État à la fin du quatrième siècle* (Paris: De Boccard, 1933), 119. Modern historiography has a much more measured position; see for example Alan Cameron, *The Last Pagans of Rome* (Oxford: Oxford University Press, 2011), 33–51.

15. See on this point the work of Rita Lizzi Testa, in particular "Christian Emperor, Vestal Virgins and Priestly Colleges: Reconsidering the End of Roman Paganism," *Antiquité tardive* 15 (2007): 251–62, and *Senatori, popolo, papi: il governo di Roma al tempo dei Valentiniani* (Bari: Edipuglia, 2004), 447 et seq.

16. Maurice Testard, "Saint Ambroise de Milan," *Bulletin de l'Association Guillaume Budé* 51 (1992): 384.

17. Ambrose, *Epist.* 73 (18 M).29. Ramsey, *Ambrose*, 191.

18. Symmachus, *Relatio* 3.8. Ramsey, *Ambrose*, 181. See also Domenico Vera, *Commento storico alle "Relationes" di Quinto Aurelio Simmaco* (Pisa: Giaredini, 1981), esp. 12–53.

19. For a fuller picture of this major figure, see Cristiana Sogno, *Q. Aurelius Symmachus: A Political Biography* (Ann Arbor: University of Michigan Press, 2006). See also Brown, *Through the Eye of a Needle*, 93–119.

20. Brown, *Through the Eye of a Needle*, 93: "Rather than standing as a lonely relic of the past, Symmachus represented an ever-present, living alternative to Christian versions of what the Roman empire and its cities should be like."

21. Ambrose, *Epist.* 73 (18 M).8. Ramsey, *Ambrose*, 186.

22. Hervé Savon, *Saint Ambroise devant l'exégèse de Philon le Juif* (Paris: Études augustiniennes, 1977).

23. Brown, *Augustine*, 75–76.

24. Augustine, *Confessions* 5.10.18.

25. Augustine, *Confessions* 8.10.22.

CHAPTER FOUR:
PAULINUS OF MILAN

1. Paulinus of Milan, *Vita Ambrosii* 1.1. Ramsey, *Ambrose*, 196.

2. Paulinus of Milan, *Vita Ambrosii* 56.1. Ramsey, *Ambrose*, 218.

3. Jacobus de Voragine, *The Golden Legend*, 229.

4. Pierre Bayard, *Et si les œuvres changeaient d'auteur?* (Paris: Minuit, 2010).

5. Augustine, *De gratia Christi et de peccato originali* 2.3.8.26 (PL 44, 386–389.397). See on this point Marco Navoni's introduction to Paolino di Milano, *Vita di*

Sant'Ambrogio. La prima biografia del patrono di Milano, ed. Marco Navoni (Milan: San Paolo, 2016), 26.

6. See Emile Lamirande, "La datation de la 'Vita Ambrosii' de Paulin de Milan," *Revue d'études augustiniennes* 27 (1981): 44–55; and for a thorough exposition of the question and a run-through of the various positions, see Elena Zocca, "La 'Vita Ambrosii' alla luce dei rapporti fra Paolino, Agostino e Ambrogio," in *Nec timeo mori. Atti del Congresso internazionale di studi ambrosiani nel XVI centenario della morte di sant'Ambrogio* (Milan: Vita e Pensiero, 1998), 804–10. See also, as for any question of chronology, Visonà, *Cronologia ambrosiana*, 139–40.

7. In this, I follow Stéphane Gioanni, "Augustin, Paulin, Ennode et les origines de la mémoire d'Ambroise (V^e–VIe siècles). Une nouvelle fondation de l'Église de Milan?" in *La mémoire d'Ambroise de Milan. Usages politiques d'une autorité patristique en Italie (V^e–XVIIIe siècle)*, ed. Patrick Boucheron and Stéphane Gioanni (Paris–Rome: Publications de la Sorbonne–Publications de l'École française de Rome, 2015), 235–52.

8. Paulinus of Milan, *Vita Ambrosii* 54.1 (…*tunc Murano episcopo detrahenti sancto viro rettuli*…) and 55.1 (*Unde hortor et obsecro omnem hominem, qui hunc librum legerit, ut imitetur vitam viri, laudet Dei gratiam et declinet detrahentium linguas*…).

9. Paulinus of Milan, *Vita Ambrosii* 1.3. Ramsey, *Ambrose*, 196.

10. Paulinus of Milan, *Vita Ambrosii* 2.2. Ramsey, *Ambrose*, 197.

11. Paulinus of Milan, *Vita Ambrosii* 53.1.

12. Peter Brown, *Through the Eye of a Needle* (Princeton: Princeton University Press, 2012), 146.

13. Yvon Thébert, "A propos du 'triomphe du christianisme,'" *Dialogues d'histoire ancienne* 14 (1988): 325. For an analysis of this historiographic position and its largely arrested subsequent development, see Patrick Boucheron, "Le génie de l'athéisme," *Afrique & histoire* 3 (2005): 103–20.

14. Éric Rebillard and Claire Sotinel, eds., *Les frontières du profane dans l'Antiquité tardive*, Collection de l'École française de Rome 428 (Rome: École française de Rome, 2010).

15. Pierre-Emmanuel Dauzat, *Les Pères de leur Mère. Essai sur l'esprit de contradiction des Pères de l'Église* (Paris: Albin Michel, 2001).

16. Ambrose, *De officiis* 3.36.

17. Jean-Marie Salamito, *Les virtuoses et la multitude. Aspects sociaux de la controverse entre Augustin et les pélagiens* (Grenoble: Jérôme Million, 2005).

18. Robert Markus, *The End of Ancient Christianity* (Cambridge: Cambridge University Press, 1990), 43.

Notes

19. Zocca, "La 'Vita Ambrosii,'" 807–10.

20. See the excellent overview in Stéphane Gioanni, "Les Vies de saints latines composées en Italie de la Paix constantinienne au milieu du VIᵉ siècle," in *Hagiographies* 5, ed. Guy Philippart (Turnhout: Brepols, 2010), 361–436.

21. Paulinus of Milan, *Vita Ambrosii* 1.1. Ramsey, *Ambrose*, 196.

22. Jean-Pierre Mazières and Nadine Plazanet-Siarri, eds., *Trois vies par trois témoins. Cyprien, Ambroise, Augustin par trois témoins* (Paris: Migne, 1994). See also *Vita di Cipriano. Vita di Ambrogio. Vita di Agostino*, ed. Christine Mohrmann (Rome-Milan: Mondadori, 1975).

23. Gioanni, "Les Vies de saints latines," 398–407.

24. Camille Gerzaguet, "Pouvoir épiscopal et luttes d'influence: Ambroise de Milan, le 'parrain' des évêques d'Italie du Nord?," *Revue des études tardo-antiques* 3–1 (2014): 219–40.

25. Paulinus of Milan, *Vita Ambrosii* 25.1. Ramsey, *Ambrose*, 206.

26. Paulinus of Milan, *Vita Ambrosii* 30.2. Ramsey, *Ambrose*, 208.

27. Paulinus of Milan, *Vita Ambrosii* 16.1. Ramsey, *Ambrose*, 202.

28. See Aline Rousselle, *Croire et guérir. La foi en Gaule dans l'Antiquité tardive* (Paris: Fayard, 1990). For a more specific study on the therapeutic aspects of Ambrose's words, see Raffaella Passarella, *Ambrogio e la medicina. Le parole e i concetti* (Milan: LED Edizioni Universitarie, 2009).

29. Paulinus of Milan, *Vita Ambrosii* 1.1.

30. Gioanni, "Augustin, Paulin, Ennode," 241.

31. Paulinus of Milan, *Vita Ambrosii* 35.1.

32. Paulinus of Milan, *Vita Ambrosii* 43.1.

33. Jean-Rémy Palanque, "La 'Vita Ambrosii' de Paulin. Étude critique," *Revue des sciences religieuses* 4 (1924): 26–42 and 401–40.

34. Antoon Bastiaensen, "Paulin de Milan et le culte des martyrs chez saint Ambroise," in *Ambrosius episcopus. Atti del Congresso internazionale di studi ambrosiani nel XVI centenario della elevazione di Sant'Ambrogio alla cattedra episcopale (Milano, dicembre 1974)*, Studia patristica mediolanensia 6, vol. 1 (Milan: Vità e Pensiero, 1976).

35. Paulinus of Milan, *Vita Ambrosii* 33.1. Ramsey, *Ambrose*, 209.

36. Paulinus of Milan, *Vita Ambrosii* 47.1. Ramsey, *Ambrose*, 215.

37. Paulinus of Milan, *Vita Ambrosii* 42.1. Ramsey, *Ambrose*, 213.

38. Palanque, "La 'Vita Ambrosii' de Paulin," 406.

39. Paulinus of Milan, *Vita Ambrosii* 55.1. Ramsey, *Ambrose*, 218.

40. Glen Bowersock, *Fiction as History: Nero to Julian* (Berkeley: University of California Press, 1994).

41. Alain Boureau, *L'événement sans fin. Récit et christianisme au Moyen Âge* (Paris: Belles Lettres, 1993).

42. Emanuele Coccia, "Qu'est-ce que la vérité? (Jean 18, 38). Le christianisme ancien et l'institution de la vérité," in *Aux origines des cultures juridiques européennes. Yan Thomas entre droit et sciences sociales,* ed. Paolo Napoli, CEFR 480 (Rome: École française de Rome, 2013), 207-30.

43. Roland Barthes, "Réponses" (interview with Jean Thibaudeau, *Tel Quel* 47 (Autumn 1971), in Roland Barthes, *Œuvres complètes* 3, *1968–1971,* ed. Éric Marty (Paris: Seuil, 2002), 1023), cited in Tiphaine Samoyault, *Barthes: A Biography,* trans. Andrew Brown (Cambridge: Polity Press. 2017), 16.

44. Roland Barthes, *Sade, Fourier, Loyola,* trans. Richard Miller (New York: Hill and Wang, 1976), 9.

45. Paulinus of Milan, *Vita Ambrosii* 48.1. Ramsey, *Ambrose,* 215.

46. Voragine, *The Golden Legend,* 234.

47. Possidius, *Vita Augustini* 18.9.

PART TWO:

OCCUPYING THE LAND

1. Ambrose, *Epist. 77 (M 22): Epistulae LXX–LXXVII. Epistulae extra collectionem traditae. Gesta Concili Aquileiensis.* English translation: Letter 22, in *Nicene and Post-Nicene Fathers: Second Series, Volume 10,* ed. Philip Schaff and Rev. Henry Wallace (New York: Cosimo Classics, 2007), 437. For clarification on the dating and interpretation of this famous letter, see: Visonà, *Cronologia ambrosiana,* 81, and on the context of March-April 386, 37-43.

2. Marco Sannazaro, "Considerazioni sulla topografia e le origini del cimitero milanese *Ad Martyres,*" *Aevum* 70 (1996): 81-111.

3. Or possibly one or two years prior, though still on May 9 as the date of *Martyrologe hiéronymien (VII Idus Maii)* has been confirmed by Ambrosian calendars since at least the eleventh century. See on this point Jean-Charles Picard, *Le souvenir des évêques. Sépulture, listes épiscopales et culte des évêques en Italie du Nord des origines au xe siècle,* BEFAR 268 (Rome: École française de Rome, 1988), 50-51n108, which remains the fundamental reference on this subject.

4. Ambrose, *In Luc.* 7.178 (PL 15, c.1746).

5. Ambrose, *Epist. 22, Nicene,* 437.

6. Augustine, *Confessions* 9.7.16: *Tunc memorato antistiti tuo per visum aperuisti, quo loco laterent martyrum corpora Protasii et Gervasii, quae per tot annos incorrupta in thesauro secreti tui reconderas, unde oportune promeres ad cohercendam rabiem femineam, sed regiam.* English trans. Henry Chadwick (Oxford: Oxford University Press, 1991). See also Augustine, *De civitate Dei* 22.8.2, when Ambrose's revelation comes to him in a dream.

7. See on this point the analysis of Jean Doignon, "Perspectives ambrosiennes: SS. Gervais et Protais, génies de Milan," *Revue des études augustiniennes* 2 (1956): 313–34.

8. For more on the ideological impact of the *inventio* of the martyrs Gervasius and Protasius in the context of Ambrose's battle against the imperial court and Arianism, see Jesús San Bernardino, "'Sub imperio discordia': l'uomo che voleva essere Eliseo (giugno 386)," in *Nec timeo mori. Atti del Congresso internazionale di studi ambrosiani nel XVI centenario della morte di sant'Ambrogio*, ed. Luigi Pizzolato and Marco Rizzi (Milan: Vita e Pensiero, 1998), 709–37, which refers back to the earlier literature.

9. According to Claire Sotinel, Ambrose's act achieves a symbolic inversion of the holy place and the place of worship, via the "sanctifying element" that is the martyr's body: it's not the church that is built on a holy place, but the holy body that turns the church into a holy place: Claire Sotinel, "Les lieux de culte chrétien et le sacré dans l'Antiquité tardive," *Revue de l'histoire des religions* 222, no. 4 (2005): 411–34 (esp. 422 et seq. for an analysis of the invention of the martyrs Gervasius and Protasius).

10. Anja Kalinowski, *Frühchristliche Reliquiare im Kontext von Kultstrategien, Heilserwartung und sozialer Selbstdarstellung* (Wiesbaden: Reichert, 2011), esp. 13 et seq.

11. Dominique Iogna-Prat, *La Maison Dieu. Une histoire monumentale de l'Église au Moyen Âge* (Paris: Seuil, 2006), 42–43. See also Didier Méhu, ed., *Mises en scène et mémoires de la consécration de l'église dans l'Occident medieval*, Collection d'études médiévales de Nice 7 (Turnhout: Brepols, 2007).

12. See on this point the fundamental work of Yvette Duval, *Auprès des saints, corps et âme. L'inhumation "ad sanctos" dans la chrétienté d'Orient et d'Occident du III͏ᵉ au VI͏ᵉ siècle* (Paris: Études augustiniennes, 1988). For an excellent overview of this polarization of the urban space by holy places, see Gisella Cantino Wataghin, "Les villes et leurs saints, dans l'Antiquité tardive et le haut Moyen Âge. Un regard archéologique sur l'Italie," in *Des dieux civiques aux saints patrons (IV͏ᵉ–VII͏ᵉ siècle)*, ed. Jean-Pierre Caillet et al. (Paris: Picard, 2015), 167–83.

Notes

13. Ambrose, *Epist. 77* (M 22): *Succedant victimae triumphales in locum ubi Christus hostia est.* English translation: Letter 22, *Nicene*, 438.

CHAPTER FIVE:
THE FIRST SHOWDOWN

1. A detailed account built upon rigorous assessment of the sources can be found in Ernst Dassmann, *Ambrosius von Mailand: Leben und Werk* (Stutggart: Kohlhammer, 2004), 92–108.

2. I rely here on the chronology compiled in Gérard Nauroy, "Le fouet et le miel. Le combat d'Ambroise en 386 contre l'arianisme milanais," *Recherches Augustiniennes* 23 (1988): 3–86, included and expanded in Gérard Nauroy, *Ambroise de Milan. Écriture et esthétique d'une exégèse pastorale. Quatorze études*, Recherches en littérature et spiritualité 3 (Bern: Peter Lang, 2003), 33–189, with important updates (see notably 135–149 on the relative chronology of letters 75 and 76 and of *Against Auxentius*).

3. Hervé Savon, *Ambroise de Milan (340–397)* (Paris: Desclée, 1997), 201. The city of Durostorum (today Silistra, on the border between Bulgaria and Romania) was an ancient Roman *castrum* established on the southern bank of the Danube; it was therefore situated within the empire, even though Ambrose casts Auxentius into the fog of barbarian lands.

4. For a reevaluation of the importance of the anti-Nicene circle around Auxentius, see Cesare Alzati, "'Numquam scivi arium.' Contributo per un ripensamento delle presenze antinicene nella Milano della seconda metà del IV secolo," in *Ambrogio e l'arianesimo*, ed. Raffaele Passarella, Studia ambrosiana 7 (Milan: Biblioteca Ambrosiana, 2013), 29–45.

5. Amid an expansive range of sources, see, for a general framework, Jean-Marie Mayeur et al., eds., *Histoire du christianisme, des origines à nos jours*, vol. 2, *Naissance d'une chrétienté (250–430)* (Paris: Desclée, 1995) (where Charles Piétri usefully reevaluates the impact of the battle of the basilicas, demonstrating "the delayed resistance of a small Arian group," 395), as well as, more specific to the Milanese context, Cesare Alzati, "Arianesimo," in *Dizionario della Chiesa ambrosiana*, ed. Angelo Majo (Milan: NED, 1987), 1:255–64.

6. On the Council of Rimini and its aftermath, see in particular Yves-Marie Duval, *L'extirpation de l'Arianisme en Italie du Nord et en Occident* (Aldershot: Variorum, 1998).

7. Catherine König-Pralong, "L'empire de la doctrine. Théologie *versus* sens commun," in *La vérité. Vérité et crédibilité: construire la vérité dans le système de*

communication de l'Occident (xiiie–xviie siècle), ed. Jean-Philippe Genet, CEFR 485/2 (Paris–Rome: Publications de la Sorbonne – Publications de l'École française de Rome, 2016), 95–113, esp. 97 et seq.

8. Ambrose, *In Luc.* 7.52–53. English translation: *Exposition of the Gospel According to Luke* 7.52, in Maura K. Lafferty, "Translating Faith from Greek to Latin: Romanitas and Christianitas in Late Fourth-Century Rome and Milan," *Journal of Early Christian Studies* 11, no. 1 (2003): 59.

9. Ambrose, *Epist.* 76 (M 20).12. See Nauroy, "Le fouet et le miel," 103.

10. Catherine Lheureux-Godbille, "Barbarie et hérésie dans l'œuvre d'Ambroise de Milan," *Le Moyen Âge* 109, no. 3–4 (2003): 481. See esp. Lellia Cracco Ruggini, "L'idea di barbarie nel iv e v secolo. Ammiano Marcellino e i suoi contemporanei," *Annali della Facoltà di Lettere e Filosofia* 29 (2008): 19–34. Note incidentally that Ambrose holds an apocalyptic view of the barbarian rush on the empire, expressed for example in this striking gloss on the Gospel of Luke, which is frequently cited by historians (notably by Jacques Le Goff, *Medieval Civilization: 400–1500*, trans. Julia Barrow [Oxford: Blackwell, 1988], 10): "None are witnesses to the heavenly words more than we, whom the end of the world has found. Indeed, how great the battles and what rumors of battles have we heard! The Huns rose against the Alans, the Alans against the Goths, and the Goths against the Taifals and Sarmatians, and the exile of the Goths made us even in Illyricum exiles from our fatherland and there is not yet an end" (Ambrose, *In Luc.* 21.9, cited in Kristen Jones, "Ambrose and the Aftermath of the Battle of Adrianople," *CERES* 3 [2017]: 48n27.)

11. Bruno Dumézil, "Arianisme germanique," in *Les Barbares*, ed. Bruno Dumézil (Paris: PUF, 2016), 231–35.

12. Giuseppe Visonà, "'Gog iste Gothus est.' L'ombra di Adrianopoli su Ambrogio di Milano," in *Ambrogio e i Barbari*, ed. Isabelle Gualandri and Raffaele Passarella, Studia ambrosiana 5 (Milan: Biblioteca Ambrosiana, 2001), 133–67.

13. Steven Fanning, "Lombard Arianism Reconsidered," *Speculum* 56, no. 2 (1981): 241–58.

14. See on this point Daniel H. Williams, *Ambrose of Milan and the End of the Nicene-Arian Conflicts* (Oxford: Clarendon Press, 1995), esp. 210–15. The author reevaluates the social foundations of the Nicene revival in fourth-century Milan and determines that it was Emperor Theodosius's arrival in the city in 388 that marked the definitive triumph of the Nicene party.

15. Nauroy, "Le fouet et le miel," 87, contra Ernesto Teodoro Moneta Caglio, "Dettagli cronologici su S. Ambrogio," *Ambrosius* 31 (1955): 278–90.

16. *Codex Theodosianus* 16.118–119.

17. Nauroy, "Le fouet et le miel," 55. Gérard Nauroy (who guides us here) provides strong arguments (83–89) for situating all the events recounted in Ambrose's two letters and his sermon *Against Auxentius* in 386.

18. Ambrose, *Epist.* 76 (M 20).7.

19. Ambrose, *Epist.* 11: *Ante lucem ubi pedem limine extuli, circumfuso milite occupatur basilica.* English translation: *The Letters of Saint Ambrose, Bishop of Milan*, trans. H. Walford (Aeterna Press, 2015), 122.

20. Nauroy, "Le fouet et le miel," 98.

21. Ambrose, *Epist.* 76 (M 20).9. English translation: *The Letters of Saint Ambrose, Bishop of Milan*, trans. H. Walford (Aeterna Press, 2015), 122.

22. Michael Stuart Williams, "Hymns as Acclamations: The Case of Ambrose of Milan," *Journal of Late Antiquity* 6, no. 1 (2013): 108–34.

23. For a recent overview of the emotive power of this enchantment, see Brian P. Dunkle, *Enchantment and Creed in the Hymns of Ambrose of Milan* (Oxford: Oxford University Press, 2016).

24. Transmitted with Ambrose's correspondence (it corresponds to *Epistula 75a*), *Sermo contra Auxentium de basilicis tradendis* constitutes both a homily devoted to explaining the biblical reading of the day—Jesus's entry into Jerusalem as recounted in the Gospel of Luke—and a political exhortation to resistance: Maurice Testard, "Observations sur la rhétorique d'une harangue au peuple dans le 'Sermo contra Auxentium' de saint Ambroise," *Revue d'études latines* 63 (1985): 193–209.

25. Ambrose, *Sermo contra Auxentium* 34. English translation: "Sermon Against Auxentius on the Giving Up of the Basilicas," in Brian P. Dunkle, *Enchantment and Creed in the Hymns of Ambrose of Milan* (Oxford: Oxford University Press, 2016), 46. On this passage and, more broadly, the spiritual importance of music in the patristic tradition, see Thédodore Gérold, *Les Pères de l'Église et la musique* (1931; repr., Geneva: Minkoff, 1973), esp. 47 et seq.

26. On this context, see Serge Lancel, *Saint Augustin* (Paris: Fayard, 1999). Published in English as *Saint Augustine*, trans. Antonia Nevill (London: SCM Press, 2002).

27. Augustine, *Confessions* 9.6–7, trans. Henry Chadwick (Oxford: Oxford University Press, 1991), 164.

28. Brown, *Augustine of Hippo*, 104–5. Note that the famous passage in which the bishop of Hippo marvels at Ambrose's silent and contemplative reading ("his eyes ran over the page and his heart perceived the sense, but his voice and

tongue were silent," *Confessions* 6.3.3) takes its meaning from this truly revolutionary reorientation spurred by Ambrose, from the exteriority of the tangible world to the interiority of the world of ideas that is the human soul.

29. Piroska Nagy, *Le don des larmes au Moyen Âge. Un instrument spirituel en quête d'institution (v^e–xiiie siècle)* (Paris: Albin Michel, 2000), 123. See also Christoph Benke, *Die Gabe der Tränen. Zur Tradition und Theologie eines vergessenen Kapitels der Glaubengeschichte*, Studien zur systematischen und spirituellen Theologie 35 (Würzburg: Echter, 2002).

30. On the notion of an emotional community envisaged as a human group in which actors adhere to identical norms of emotional expression at the same time as a corresponding system of values, see Barbara H. Rosenwein, *Emotional Communities in the Early Middle Ages* (Ithaca, NY: Cornell University Press, 2006), and the critical note by Piroska Nagy, "Les émotions et l'historien: De nouveaux paradigmes," *Critique* 716-17: *Émotions médiévales* (2007): 10-22.

31. Jacques Fontaine, "Introduction générale," in *Ambroise de Milan. Hymnes,* ed. Jacques Fontaine (Paris: Cerf, 1992), 20. See also Jacques Fontaine, *Naissance de la poésie dans l'Occident chrétien. Esquisse d'une histoire de la poésie latine chrétienne du IIIe au Ve siècle*, Série Antiquité 85 (Paris: Études augustiniennes, 1981), 127-41.

32. Paulinus of Milan, *Vita Ambrosii* 13.3: *Hoc in tempore primum antiphonae, hymni et vigiliae in ecclesia Mediolanensi celebrari coeperunt; cuius celebritatis devotio usque in hodiernum diem non solum in eadem ecclesia, uerum per omnes pene provincias occidentis manet*, cited in Brian P. Dunkle, *Enchantment and Creed in the Hymns of Ambrose of Milan* (Oxford: Oxford University Press, 2016), 46.

33. Fontaine, "Introduction générale," 21.

34. Maurice Testard, "Observations sur la rhétorique d'une harangue au peuple dans le *Sermo contra Auxentium* de saint Ambroise," *Revue des études latins* 63 (1985): 193-209.

35. In the sociological meaning of "affair," provided by Élisabeth Claverie and Luc Boltanski: Luc Boltanski, Élisabeth Claverie, Nicolas Offenstadt and Stéphane Van Damme, eds., *Affaires, scandales et grandes causes. De Socrate à Pinochet* (Paris: Stock, 2007).

36. Timothy D. Barnes, "Ambrose and the Basilicas of Milan in 385 and 386: The Primary Documents and Their Implications," *Zeitschrift für antikes Christentum* 4 (2000): 282-99.

37. Ambrose, *Epist.* 75A (21A M), *Contra Auxentium.*

38. Michel Meslin, *Les Ariens d'Occident, 335-430*, Patristica Sorbonensia 8 (Paris: Seuil, 1967), 53.

39. Jean-Rémy Palanque, *Saint Ambroise et l'Empire romain. Contribution à l'histoire des rapports de l'Église et de l'État à la fin du quatrième siècle* (Paris: De Boccard, 1933).

40. Christoph Markschies, *Ambrosius von Mailand und die Trinitätstheologie. Kirchen- und theologiegeschichtliche Studien zu Antiarianismus und Neunizänismus bei Ambrosius und im lateinischen* Westen *(364–381 n. Chr.)* (Tübingen: Mohr, 1995).

41. Michael Stuart Williams, *The Politics of Heresy in Ambrose of Milan: Community and Consensus in Late Antique Christianity* (Cambridge: Cambridge University Press, 2017), esp. 289 et seq.

42. Paulinus of Milan, *Vita Ambrosii* 13.1. Ramsey, *Ambrose*, 201. See, on the concatenation of the events of 386 in this account, the long and specific note by Marco Navoni (Paolino di Milano, *Vita di Sant'Ambrogio. La prima biografia del patrono di Milano*, ed. Marco Navoni [Milan: San Paolo, 2016], 92–95n47).

43. Paulinus of Milan, *Vita Ambrosii* 6.1.

44. See on this point the reflections of Arnaldo Momigliano, "The Disadvantages of Monotheism for a Universal State," *Classical Philology* 81 (1986): 285–97.

45. Jacobus de Voragine, *The Golden Legend*, 234–35. Only the second and eighth virtues (respectively, purity and denunciation of vice) are lacking.

46. Ambrose, *Epist.* 22 (M 35): *Si tyrannus es, scire volo, ut sciam quemadmodum me adversus te praeparem* (an imperial notary is addressing Ambrose).

47. Since Constantine's conversion, Christian churches had indeed benefited from the same status as temples, which, as *aedes sacrae*, were protected by law, and therefore under the emperor's authority; Roland Delmaire, *Largesses sacrées et res privata. L'aerarium impérial et son administration du IVe au VIe siècle*, CEFR 121 (Rome: École française de Rome, 1989), esp. 641–45.

48. Bruno Dumézil, *Les racines chrétiennes de l'Europe. Conversion et liberté dans les royaumes barbares, V^e–VIIIe siècle* (Paris: Fayard, 2005), 69.

49. Ambrose, *Epist.* 77 (M 22). English translation: Letter 22, cited in *The Letters of Saint Ambrose, Bishop of Milan*, trans. H. Walford (Aeterna Press, 2015), 146–47. Note that ten years later, when Victricius, bishop of Rouen, received relics for his city, he also described them as "soldiers" sent him by the celestial camp as reinforcements to defend against his enemies: Edina Bozóky, *La politique des reliques de Constantin à Saint Louis* (Paris: Beauchesne, 2007), 35. On this martial vocabulary of the protection afforded by saints, see Bruno Bureau, "*Martinus uir potens et uere apostolicus,*" *Vita Latina* 172 (2005): 106–29.

50. Paulinus of Milan, *Vita Ambrosii* 14.1, cited in Robert Wiśniewski, *The Beginnings of the Cult of Relics* (Oxford: Oxford University Press, 2019), 109.

1. Historiography generally assigns a date of 379 for the *basilica martyrum* and 382 for the *basilica apostolorum*, though these dates are only hypothetical. See Gemma Sena Chiesa and Ermanno Arslan, eds., *Felix temporis reparatio. Atti del Convegno archeologico internazionale "Milano, Capitale dell'impero romano, 286–402 d.C." (Milano, 8–11 aprile 1990)* (Milan: Edizioni ET, 1992), 434 and 119 respectively. For a useful overview of the architectural history of the Ambrosian basilicas, albeit one that does not incorporate the latest archaeological findings, see Mario Mirabella Roberti, "Contributi della ricerca archeologica all'architettura ambrosiana milanese," in Giuseppe Lazzati, ed., *Ambrosius episcopus. Atti del Congresso internazionale di studi ambrosiani nel XVI centenario della elevazione di Sant'Ambrogio alla cattedra episcopale (Milano, dicembre 1974)*, Studia patristica mediolanensia 7 (Milan: Vita e Pensiero, 1976), 1:335–62; and Neil McLynn, *Ambrose of Milan: Church and Court in a Christian Capital* (Berkeley: University of California Press, 1994), 174–79, for the context of Ambrose's (supposed) aedilician authority. A more recent account appears in Silvia Lusuardi Siena, Elisabetta Neri, and Paola Greppi, "Le chiese di Ambrogio e Milano. Ambito topografico ed evoluzione costruttiva dal punto di vista archeologico," in Patrick Boucheron and Stéphane Gioanni, eds., *La Mémoire d'Ambroise de Milan. Usages politiques d'une autorité patristique en Italie (Vᵉ–XVIIIᵉ siècle)* (Paris and Rome: Publications de la Sorbonne and Publications de l'École française de Rome, 2015), 31–86 (esp. 48–67). I am indebted throughout the upcoming pages to this remarkable summary, to which I refer the reader once and for all, while generally sparing him the intermediary bibliographical references cited in the article. It sums up the contributions of this remarkable school of monumental archaeology, which has profoundly renewed our understanding of the structuring of Milan's urban space in late antiquity and Ambrose's role in its reconfiguration.

2. In this I follow Marcia L. Colish, "Why the Portiana? Reflections on the Milanese Basilica Crisis of 386," *Journal of Early Christian Studies* 10, no. 3 (2002): 361–72.

3. Julia Hillner, "Clerics, Property and Patronage: The Case of the Roman Titular Churches," *Antiquité tardive* 14 (2006): 59–68.

4. Elisabetta Neri, Silvia Lusuardi Siena, and Paola Greppi, "Il problema della cronologia del cantiere di S. Lorenzo a Milano. Vecchi e nuovi dati a confronto," in *Il culto di San Lorenzo tra Roma e Milano. Dalle origini al Medioevo*, ed. Raffaele Passarella, Studia ambrosiana 8 (Milan: Biblioteca Ambrosiana, 2015), 1–50. For

construction techniques in early Christian Milan, consult Paolo Greppi, *Cantieri, maestranze e materiali nell'edilizia sacra a Milano dal IV al XII secolo. Analisi di un processo di trasformazione*, Contributi di archeologia medievale 12 (Florence: All'Insegna del Giglio, 2017).

5. Elisabetta Neri, Silvia Lusuardi Siena, "La Basilica Portiana e San Vittore al Corpo: un punto di vista archeologico," in *Ambrogio e l'arianesimo*, ed. Raffaele Passarella, Studia ambrosiana 7 (Milan: Biblioteca Ambrosiana, 2013), 147–92.

6. *Libellus de situ civitatis mediolani, de adventu barnabae apostoli et de vitis piorum pontificum mediolanensium*, RIS 1.11.

7. Gotofredo da Bussero, *Liber notitiae sanctorum Mediolani. Manoscritto della Biblioteca Capitolare di Milano*, ed. Marco Magistretti and Ugo Monneret de Villard (Milan: Allegretti, 1917).

8. Silvia Lusuardi Siena, "Il recinto di San Vittore al Corpo e l'ottagono di San Gregorio," and "Il mausoleo imperiale," in *Milano capitale dell'impero romano, 286–402 d. C.* (Milan: Edizioni ET, 1990), 111–12 and 114–15. In the *Libri indulgentiarum* of the fourteenth century, one still finds mention of *Ecclesia sancti Gregorii et iusta ecclesiam portianam* (Silvia Lusuardi Siena *et al.*, "Le chiese di Ambrogio e Milano," in Boucheron and Gioanni, *La Mémoire d'Ambroise de Milan*, 47, n. 57.

9. Gérard Nauroy, "Le fouet et le miel. Le combat d'Ambroise en 386 contre l'arianisme milanais," *Recherches augustiniennes* 23 (1988): 161–69. See also Silvia Lusuardi Siena, "Il complesso episcopale di Milano: riconsiderazione della testimonianza ambrosiana nella *epistola ad sororem*," *Antiquité tardive* 4 (1996): 124–29; and Giuseppe Visonà, "Topografia del conflitto ariano: Ambrogio e la basilica porziana," in Passarella, *Ambrogio e l'arianesimo*, 113–45.

10. Silvia Lusuardi Siena, ed., *Piazza Duomo prima del Duomo. Piazza Duomo before the Duomo. Apparato didattico del percorso espositivo dell'area archeologica, a cura di S. Lusuardi Siena* (Milano: Edizioni ET, 2009).

11. Antonio Sartori, "Mediolanum nelle sue pietre iscritte: specificità e novità," *Rendiconti. Atti della Pontificia Accademia romana di archeologia* 84 (2011–12): 431–45. For a more general account, see also Dario Daffara, "I basamenti di piazza del Duomo e di via Mercanti in Milano," *LANX. Rivista della Scuola di Specializzazione in Archeologia. Università degli Studi di Milano* 23 (2016): 53–86.

12. Silvia Lusuardi Siena et al., "Le nuove indagini archeologiche nell'area del Duomo," in *La città e la sua memoria. Milano e la tradizione di Sant'Ambrogio*, ed. Marco Rizzi (Milan: Electa, 1997), 40–67.

13. Silvia Lusuardi Siena et al., "*Lettura archeologica e prassi liturgica nei battisteri ambrosiani tra IV e VI secolo*," in *Studia Ambrosiana: annali dell'Accademia di*

Sant'Ambrogio 5 (2011): 89-119. Augustine's place of baptism, on the other hand, is more open to question: Mario Mirabella Roberti, "I battisteri di Sant'Ambrogio," in *Agostino a Milano. Il battesimo. Agostino nelle terre di Ambrogio (22–24 aprile 1987)* (Palermo: Edizioni Augustinus, 1988), 77–83.

14. Ada Grossi, *Santa Tecla nel tardo medioevo. La grande basilica milanese, il Paradisus, i mercati*, Collana di studi di archeologia lombarda 5 (Milan: Edizioni ET, 1997), 131–37; and Marco Rossi, "Le cattedrali perdute: il caso di Milano," in *Medioevo. L'Europa delle cattedrali. Atti del Convegno internazionale di Studi (Parma, 19–23 settembre 2006)* (Parma: Electa, 2007), 228–36.

15. Mario Mirabella Roberti, "La cattedrale antica di Milano e il suo battistero," *Arte lombarda* 8, no. 1 (1963): 77–98.

16. There's an excellent update in Attilio Pracchi, *La cattedrale antica di Milano. Il problema delle chiese doppie tra trada antichità e medioevo* (Rome–Bari: Laterza, 1996).

17. Gisella Cantino Wataghin, "Una nota sui gruppi episcopali paleocristiani di Milano e Aquileia," in *"Orbis romanus christianusque ab Diocletiani aetate usque ad Heraclium": travaux sur l'Antiquité tardive rassemblés autour des recherches de Noël Duval*, ed. François Baratte, Jean-Pierre Caillet, and Catherine Metzger (Paris: De Boccard, 1995), 73–87.

18. Adele Buratti Mazzotta, ed., *Domus Ambrosii. Il complesso monumentale dell'arcivescovado* (Milan: Silvana, 1994).

19. Paulinus of Milan, *Vita Ambrosii*, 20.

20. Yuri A. Marano, *"Domus in Qua Manebat Episcopus*: Episcopal Residences in Northern Italy during Late Antiquity (4th to 6th c. A.D.)," in *Housing in Late Antiquity; From Palaces to Shops*, ed. Luke Lavan, Lale Özgenel, and Alexander Sarantis (Leiden: Brill, 2007), 97–129, esp. 106–11.

21. Maureen Miller, *The Bishop's Palace; Architecture & Authority in Medieval Italy* (Ithaca: Cornell University Press, 2000), 273.

22. Siena et al., "Lettura archeologica e prassi liturgica," 102–17; Greppi, *Cantieri, maestranze e materiali*, 31.

23. *Octacorum sanctos templus surrexit in usus/octagonus fons est munere dignus eos*: Othmar Perler, "L'inscription du baptistère de Sainte-Thècle à Milan et le *De sacramentis* de saint Ambroise," *Rivista di archeologia cristiana* 27 (1951): 147–66. The structure's formal symbolism (its eight sides refer back to the eighth day of the resurrection) has been analyzed in the classic study by Franz Joseph Dölger, "Zur Symbolik des altchristlichen Tauhause," *Antik und Christentum* 4 (1935): 153–87.

24. Jean-Charles Picard, "Ce que les textes nous apprennent sur les équipements et le mobilier liturgique nécessaires pour le baptême dans le Sud de la Gaule et l'Italie du Nord," in *Actes du XIe congrès international d'archéologie chrétienne. Lyon, Vienne, Grenoble, Genève, Aoste, 21–28 septembre 1986*, CEFR 123 (Rome: École française de Rome, 1989), 1451-68.

25. Richard Krautheimer, *Three Christian Capitals; Topography and Politics* (Berkeley: University of California Press, 1983), esp. 111.

26. Elisabeth Paoli, "Les notices sur les évêques de Milan (IVe-VIe siècle)," *Mélanges de l'École française de Rome – Moyen Âge* 100, no. 1 (1988): 216-18. On this very late and doubtful tradition, see Jean-Charles Picard, *Le souvenir des évêques. Sépultures, listes épiscopales et culte des évêques en Italie du Nord, des origins au Xe siècle*, BEFAR 268 (Rome: École française de Rome, 1988), 608-13.

27. Enrico dal Covolo, Renato Uglione, and Gioavanni Maria Vian, eds., *Eusebio di Vercelli e il suo tempo* (Rome: Libreria Ateneo Salesiano), 1997.

28. Picard, *Le souvenir des évêques*, 289-93.

29. Gisella Cantino Wataghin, "Les villes et leurs saints," in *Des dieux civiques aux saints patrons*, ed. Jean-Pierre Caillet et al. (Paris: Picard, 2015), 169-70n15.

30. Picard, *Le souvenir des évêques*, 273.

31. Ernst Dassmann, "Ambrosius und die Märtyrer," *Jahrbuch für Antike und Christentum* 18 (1975), 49-68. Ambrose had left Milan at that point to escape the usurper Eugenius. On this episode, see Neil McLynn, *Ambrose of Milan: Church and Court in a Christian Capital* (Berkeley: University of California Press, 1994), 344-53.

32. Florian Mazel, *L'Évêque et le Territoire. L'invention médiévale de l'espace (V^e–XIIIe siècle)* (Paris: Éd. du Seuil, 2016), 68-69.

33. Wataghin, "Les villes et leurs saints," 178. This is also the case with Venantius Fortunatus's description of his trip from Ravenna to Tours in 565.

34. Rita Lizzi Testa, "Ambrose's Contemporaries and the Christianization of Northern Italy," *Journal of Roman Studies* 80 (1990): 156-73.

35. Enrico Menestò, "Le lettere di s. Vigilio," in *I martiri della Val di Non e la reazione pagana alla fine del IV secolo. Atti del Convegno, Trento 27–28 marzo 1984*, ed. Antonio Quacquarelli and Iginio Rogger, Scienze Religiose 9 (Bologna: EDB, 1985), 151-70. On Simplicianus's bishopric, his memory, and his role in Ambrose's spiritual education, see Cesare Pasini, "Simpliciano e il vescovo Ambrogio," in *Contributi di ricerca su Ambrogio e Simpliciano. Atti del secondo dies academicus, 3–4 aprile 2006*, Studia ambrosiana 1 (Milan: Biblioteca Ambrosiana, 2007), 45-65.

36. Claudio Batistini, "Milano, chiesa di San Simpliciano. La sua evoluzione formale letta e documentata attraverso il rilievo," *Arte lombarda* 52 (1979): 5–20.

37. Mario Sannazaro, "San Simpliciano come complesso funerario: tipologia e testimonianze epigrafiche," in *Contributi di ricerca su Ambrogio e Simpliciano* (Milan: Biblioteca Ambrosiana, 2007), 105–28.

38. Michel Lauwers and Laurent Ripart, "Représentation et gestion de l'espace dans l'Occident médiéval (v^e–xiiie siècle)," in *Rome et l'État moderne européen*, ed. Jean-Philippe Genet, CEFR 377 (Rome: École française de Rome, 2007), 115–71, esp. 133–37.

39. On this point see Jean-Michel Spieser, "Les fondations d'Ambroise à Milan et la question des *martyria*," *Deltion of the Christian Archaeological Society* 20 (1998): 29–34.

40. Peter Brown, *The Cult of the Saints: Its Rise and Function in Latin Christianity* (Chicago, University of Chicago Press, 1981).

41. Ambrose, *Epist.* 77 (M 22). Philip Schaff, *Ambrose: Selected Works and Letters,* Letter 22.

42. Pierre-Henri Ortiz, "Le scandale de la possession démonique à l'épreuve de la *Systemtheorie* de Niklas Luhmann," *Hypothèses* 16 (2013): 159–77.

43. Dayna S. Kalleres, *City of Demons: Violence, Ritual and Christian Power in Late Antiquity* (Berkeley: University of California Press, 2016), 201.

44. Catherine M. Chin, "The Bishop's Two Bodies: Ambrose and the Basilicas of Milan," *Church History* 79, no. 3 (2010): 548.

45. For a comparison between the monuments policies of Ambrose and Damasus, see Markus Löx, *Monumenta sanctorum. Rom und Mailand als Zentren des frühen Christentums. Märtyrerkult und Kirchenbau unter den Bischöfen Damasus und Ambrosius* (Wiesbaden: Reichert, 2013).

46. Georges Duby, *The Three Orders: Feudal Society Imagined*, trans. Arthur Goldhammer (Chicago: University of Chicago Press, 1980), 15.

47. Enrico Villa, "Il vescovo Ambrogio '*sapiens architettus*,'" *Ambrosius* 25 (1949): 115–37.

48. Wataghin, "Les villes et leurs saints," 171–72. For a recent overview, see also Markus Löx, "L''architectus sapiens.' Ambrogio e le chiese di Milano," in *Milano allo specchio. Da Costantino al Barbarossa, l'autopercezione di una capitale*, ed. Ivan Foletti, Irene Quadri, and Marco Rossi (Rome: Viella, 2016), 55–80.

49. Yvon Thébert, "Private Life and Domestic Architecture in Roman Africa," in Georges Duby and Philippe Ariès, general eds., *A History of Private Life*, vol. 1,

From Pagan Rome to Byzantium, ed. Paul Veyne (Cambridge, MA: Belknap Press of Harvard University Press, 1987).

50. Richard Krautheimer, *Three Christian Capitals* (Berkeley: University of California Press, 1983), 125–27.

51. Donatella Caporusso, "La via porticata e l'arco onoraro," in *Milano capitale dell'impero romano 286–402 d. C.* (Milan: Silvana, 1990), 98.

52. Donatella Caporusso, "La zona di corso di porta Romana in età romana et medievale," in Donatella Caporusso, ed., *Scavi MM3. Ricerche di archeologia urbana a Milano durante la costruzione della linea 3 della metropolitana, 1982–1990*, vol. 1, *Gli scavi. Testo* (Milan: Edizioni ET, 1991), 237–61.

53. Marco Sannazaro, "*Ad modum crucis*: la basilica paleocristiana dei SS. Apostoli e Nazaro," in *Contributi di ricerca sulla poesia in Ambrogio. Atti del Terzo dies academicus (26–27 mars 2007)*, Studia ambrosiana 2 (Milan: Biblioteca Ambrosiana, 2008), 135.

54. Thus at any rate did I describe it in a youthful work: Patrick Boucheron, *Le pouvoir de bâtir. Urbanisme et politique édilitaire à Milan (XIVᵉ–XVᵉ siècles)*, CEFR 239 (Rome: École française de Rome, 1998), 87–93.

55. Neri, Lusuardi Siena, and Greppi, "Il problema della cronologia," 1–50 (see note 4). The most likely hypothesis puts the date of the church's founding in the very first years of the fifth century.

56. Picard, *Le souvenir des évêques*, 59–91.

57. Jean-Charles Picard, "Le quadriportique de Saint-Laurent de Milan," *Mélanges de l'École française de Rome: Moyen Âge* 85 (1973): 691–712.

58. Maria Luisa Gatti Perer, "Milano ritrovata, ovvero il Tempio della memoria," in Maria Luisa Gatti Perer, ed., *Milano ritrovata. L'asse via Torino* (Milan: Il Vaglio Cultura Arte, 1986), 31–99.

59. Paulinus of Milan, *Vita Ambrosii* 8.1.

60. Alberto Savinio, *Ville, j'écoute ton cœur* (1944; repr. Paris: Gallimard, 1982).

61. This plan was common to the principal cities of medieval Italy (Rome and Venice excepted). See Étienne Hubert, "La construction de la ville. Sur l'urbanisation dans l'Italie médiévale," *Annales. Histoire, Sciences sociales* 59, no. 1 (2004): 109–39.

62. On all of the foregoing, see Patrick Boucheron, "Water and Power in Milan, c. 1200–1500," *Urban History* 28, no. 2 (2001): 180–93; and Patrick Boucheron, "Milano e i suoi sobborghi: urbanità e pratiche socio-economiche ai confini di uno spazio incerto (1400 ca.–1550 ca.)," *Società e storia* 112 (2006): 235–52.

63. Boucheron, *Le pouvoir de bâtir*, 513–14.

Notes

64. Luca Mocarelli, "I *Corpi santi* di Milano tra XVIII e XIX secolo: trasformazioni istituzionali e assetti economici," *Società e storia* 112, no. 2 (2006): 285–95; and Luca Mocarelli, "The Long-Term Evolution of the Suburbs of Milan," *Popolazione e storia* 1 (2015): 135–56. On the restructuring in 1808 and Milan's urban development in the nineteenth century, see also Olivier Faron, *La ville des destins croisés. Recherches sur la société milanaise du XIXe siècle*, BEFAR 297 (Rome: École française de Rome, 1997).

65. Maurice Halbswachs, *La topographie légendaire des évangiles en Terre sainte. Étude de mémoire collective* (1941; repr. Paris: PUF, 2008), 163, cited in *On Collective Memory*, ed. and trans. Lewis A. Coser (Chicago: University of Chicago Press, 1992), 234–35.

66. Maurice Halbswachs, *Les cadres sociaux de la mémoire* (Paris: F. Alcan, 1925; reissued Albin Michel, 1994), viii.

67. On this point, see the assessment by Dominique Iogna-Prat, "Maurice Halbwachs ou la mnémotopie. 'Textes topographiques' et inscription spatiale de la mémoire," *Annales. Histoire, Sciences Sociales* 66, no. 3 (2011): 821–37.

68. On this point, see Bernard Lepetit, who was one of the earliest and most penetrating commentators on Maurice Halbwachs's contribution to the historical sociology of urban memory: Bernard Lepetit, "Le présent de l'histoire," in his *Carnet de croquis. Sur la connaissance historique* (Paris: Albin Michel, 1999), 273–98, esp. 276.

69. Maurice Halbwachs, *On Collective Memory*, cited in Michel Beaujour, *Poetics of the Literary Self-Portrait* (New York: NYU Press, 1992), 104.

70. I rely here on the interpretation in Éric Brian, "Portée du lexique halbwachsien de la mémoire," in Halbwachs, *La topographie légendaire*, 113–46, esp. 125–30.

71. Mary Carruthers, *The Craft of Thought: Meditation, Rhetoric, and the Making of Images, 400–1200* (Cambridge: Cambridge University Press, 1998), 258.

CHAPTER SEVEN:

A LIFE IN PIECES

1. Marie Lezowski, *L'abrégé du monde. Une histoire sociale de la bibliothèque Ambrosienne (v. 1590 – v. 1660)* (Paris: Classiques Garnier, 2015), and Marie Lezowski, "L'atelier Borromée, L'archevêque de Milan et le gouvernement de l'écrit (1564-1631)," history thesis, Université de Paris-Sorbonne, Denis Crouzet advisor (2013), 163 et seq. Giovanni Francesco Bascapè joined the Barnabites and adopted "Carlo" as his religious name in 1578 as well. It was as Carlo Bascapè that he became bishop

of Novara in 1593, one year after writing a *Vita di San Carlo Borromeo* using an indisputably Ambrosian model.

2. Giovanni Francesco Bascapè, *Libro d'alcune chiese di Milano, fatto nell'occasione del giubileo d'ordine dell'ill. Monsig. Cardinal di Santa Prassede, Arcivescovo di Milano*... (Milan: appresso Pacifico Pontio, 1576, "Della chiesa di S. Ambrosio"), fol. G3v-G4r, cited and translated by Marie Lezowski, "Portraits de Milan par Charles Borromée (1564-1584): la dynamique rigoriste de l'écriture," *Seizième Siècle* 9 (2013): 130.

3. Annamaria Ambrosioni, "L'altare d'oro e le due comunità santambrosiane," in *L'altare d'oro di Sant'Ambrogio*, ed. Carlo Capponi (Milan: Silvana, 1996), 57-127 (included in *Milano, papato e impero in età medievale. Raccolta di studi*, ed. Maria Pia Alberzoni and Alfredo Lucioni (Milan: Vita e Pensiero, 2003), 271). On the continuation of this quarrel into the modern era, see Danilo Zardin, "Profilo storico dal XVI al XIX secolo," in *La basilica di S. Ambrogio: il tempio ininterrotto*, ed. Maria Luisa Gatti Perer (Milan: Vita e Pensiero, 1995), 1:253-67, esp. 261, and also the remarks of Marie Lezowski, "La publication de 'monuments' du Moyen Âge au milieu du XVIIe siècle: Giovanni Pietro Puricelli, entre édition et censure," *Histoire, économie & société* 31, no. 3 (2012): 3-18.

4. Dominique Julia, "L'église post-tridentine et les reliques. Tradition, controverse et critique (XVIe-XVIIIe siècle)," in *Reliques modernes. Cultes et usages chrétiens des corps saints des Réformes aux révolutions*, ed. Philippe Boutry, Pierre-Antoine Fabre, and Dominique Julia (Paris: Ed. de l'EHESS, 2009), 1:69-120.

5. ASCMi, X, *S. Ambrogio*, vol. 21/9, notes, cited and translated by Lezowski, *L'atelier Borromée*, 1:183.

6. The collection can be found in the *Archivio capitolare* of the Basilica of Sant'Ambrogio, classified as VI. A. 1 *Autentiche SS. Reliquie*. See also Luigi Biraghi, *I tre sepolcri santambrosiani scoperti nel gennaio 1864* (Milan: Boniardi-Pogliani, 1864).

7. Xenio Toscani and Maurizio Sangalli, eds., *Lettere pastorali dei vescovi della Lombardia*, Fonti e materiali per la storia della Chiesa italiana in età contemporanea. Lettere pastorali 3 (Rome: Herder, 1998), 270 (Lodi, no. 113, April 30, 1874). See also ibid., 15 (Bergamo, no. 113, May 5, 1874), 50 (Brescia, no. 94, February 2, 1874), 157 (Crema, no. 121, March 15, 1874), 214 (Cremona, no. 120, October 21, 1874), 337 (Milan, no. 108, April 22, 1874), and 390 (Pavia, no. 116, April 26, 1874).

8. Walter Cupperi, *"Regia purpureo marmore crusta tegit"*: il sarcofago reimpiegato per la sepoltura di sant'Ambrogio e la tradizione dell'antico nella Basilica ambrosiana a Milano, Annali della Scuola Normale superiore di Pisa 4, Quaderni 16 (2002): 141-76.

Notes

9. Francesco Maria Rossi, *Cronaca dei restauri e delle scoperte fatte nell'insigne basilica di S. Ambrogio dall'anno 1857 al 1876* (Milan: San Giuseppe, n.d. [1884]), 71. On the importance of this source to understanding the structure, see Giuliana Righetto, "Scavi ottocenteschi in S. Ambrogio. La basilica ambrosiana in età paleocristiana e altomedioevale nella 'Cronaca dei restauri' di mons. Rossi," in *La basilica di S. Ambrogio*, ed. Gatti Perer, 1:127-47.

10. Sible de Blaauw, "Il culto di Sant'Ambrogio e l'altare della basilica Ambrosiana a Milano," in *I luoghi del sacro: il sacro e la città fra Medioevo ed età moderna: atti del convegno, Georgetown University, Center for the study of Italian history and culture, Fiesole, 12–13 giugno 2006*, ed. Fabrizio Ricciardelli (Florence: Edizioni Polistampa, 2008), 43-62. See also Ivan Foletti, "Le tombeau d'Ambroise: cinq siècles de construction identitaire," in *L'évêque, l'image et la mort: Identité et mémoire au Moyen Âge*, ed. Nicolas Bock, Ivan Foletti, and Michele Tomaso (Rome: Viella, 2014), 73-101; and Ivan Foletti, *Oggetti, reliquie, migranti. La basilica ambrosiana e il culto dei suoi santi (386–972)* (Rome: Viella, 2018), 107-60.

11. Carlo Bertelli, "Percorso tra le testimonianze figurative più antiche: dai mosaici di S. Vittore in Ciel d'oro al pulpito della basilica," in *La basilica di S. Ambrogio*, ed. Gatti Perer, 2:339-87, in particular 368-73. See, more recently, Ivan Foletti, "Il ciborio di Sant'Ambrogio tra passato (e futuro). Un monumento perno nella ricezione e nella costruzione dell'identità figurativa milanese," in Foletti, Quadri, and Rossi, *Milano allo specchio*, and included in part in Foletti, *Oggetti, reliquie, migranti*, 181-201.

12. Ambrosioni, "L'altare d'oro," 267-68.

13. Carlo Bertelli, "Sant'Ambrogio da Angilberto II a Gotofredo," in *Il millennio ambrosiano. La città dai Carolingi al Barbarossa*, ed. Carlo Bertelli (Milan: Electa, 1988), 16-81.

14. According to Patrick Demouy, this is actually the sole known example, apart from the high glass windows of the choir of Reims Cathedral: Patrick Demouy, *Genèse d'une cathédrale. Les archevêques de Reims et leur Église aux XIe et XIIe siècles* (Langres: D. Guéniot, 2005), 590n20.

15. Ivan Foletti and Irene Quadri, "L'immagine e la sua memoria. L'abside di Sant'Ambrogio a Milano e quella du San Pietro a Roma nel medioevo," *Zeitschrift für Kunstgeschichte* 76 (2013): 475-92.

16. Cupperi, *"Regia purpureo marmore crusta tegit,"* 152-55.

17. De Blaauw, "Il culto di Sant'Ambrogio," 60.

18. *Liber notiatiae sanctorum Mediolani*, coll. 397 A. For more on this text, see Paolo Tomea, "San Giorgio in Crimea. Per una nuova edizione del *Liber notitiae*

sanctorum mediolani (con una nota sulla papessa Giovanna)," *Aevum* 73 (1999): 423-56.

19. Regarding Volvinius himself, the little that is known about him can be found in Victor Elbern, "Vuolvinio," in *Enciclopedia dell'Arte Medievale*, ed. Maria Angiola Romanini (Rome: Istituto della Enciclopedia italiana, 2000), 750-52.

20. Mirella Ferrari, "Le iscrizioni," in Capponi, *L'altare d'oro di Sant'Ambrogio*, 148.

21. See on this point Daniel Russo, "Le nom de l'artiste, entre appartenance au groupe et écriture personnelle," in *L'individu au Moyen Âge. Individuation et individualisation avant la modernité*, ed. Dominique Iogna-Prat and Brigitte Bedos-Rezak (Paris: Aubier, 2005), 235-46. Other examples in Jacqueline Leclercq-Marx, "Signatures iconiques et graphiques d'orfèvres dans le Haut Moyen Âge: une première approche," *Gazette des beaux-arts* 137 (2001): 1-16.

22. See on this point the recent suggestions of Ivan Foletti, "La firma d'artista, i miti vasariani e *Wolfinus magister phaber*," *Venezia Arti* 26 (2017): 35-48.

23. Pierre-Alain Mariaux, "Quelques hypothèses à propos de l'artiste roman," *Médiévales* 44 (2003): 199-214, and Pierre-Alain Mariaux,"Art, artiste, moine à la période romane: quelques réflexions," in *Cluny. Les moines et la société au premier âge féodal*, ed. Dominique Iogna-Prat et al. (Rennes: Presses universitaires de Rennes, 2013), 181-91.

24. See overview in Chris Wickham, *Early Medieval Italy: Central Power and Local Society, 400-1000* (London: The Macmillan Press, 1981).

25. Gabriella Rossetti, "Il monastero di Sant'Ambrogio nei due primi secoli di vita: i fondamenti patrimoniali e politici della sua fortuna," in *Il monastero di S. Ambrogio nel Medioevo: convegno di studi nel XII centenario: 784-1984 (5-6 novembre 1984)* (Milan: Vita e Pensiero, 1988), 20-34.

26. See Annamaria Ambrosioni, "Pietro († 803c)," in *Dizionario della Chiesa ambrosiana*, ed. Angelo Majo (Milan: NED, 1992), 5:2792-93, as well as Annamaria Ambrosioni, "Per una storia del monastero di S. Ambrogio," in *Ricerche storiche sulla Chiesa ambrosiana* 9, ed. Enrico Cattaneo, Archivio ambrosiano 40 (Milan: NED, 1981), 291-317, included in Alberzoni and Lucioni, *Milano, papato e impero in età medievale*, 175-202.

27. Picard, *Le souvenir des évêques*, 90.

28. On the history of this foundation and its land assets, see Ross Balzaretti, *The Lands of Saint Ambrose: Monks and Society in Early Medieval Milan*, Studies in the Early Middle Ages 44 (Turnhout: Brepols, 2019).

29. Picard, *Le souvenir des évêques*, 624-25: "There's no doubt that S. Ambrose

Notes

enjoyed great prestige among the Franks, and that in return, this 'international' reputation benefited him on a local level."

30. On this point, consult the seminal study by Hans Conrad Peyer, *Stadt und Stadtpatron im Mittelalterlichen Italien* (Zürich: Europa Verlag, 1955), 25-45.

31. Annamaria Ambrosioni, "Gli arcivescovi nella vita di Milano," in *Milano e i Milanesi prima del Mille (VIII–X secolo). Atti del X Congresso internazionale di studi sull'alto medioevo (Milano, 26–30 settembre 1983)* (Spoleto: Centro italiano di studi sull'alto medioevo, 1986), 85-118.

32. This was notably the case for Pepin in 810 and Louis II in 875: Picard, *Le souvenir des évêques*, 95.

33. Margherita Giuliana Bertolini, "Angilberto," in *Dizionario Biografico degli Italiani*, ed. Alberto M. Ghisalberti, vol. 3: *Ammirato-Arcoleo*, 1961, online. http://www.treccani.it/enciclopedia/angilberto_(Dizionario-Biografico).

34. Andreas Bergomatis, *Historia*, ed. Georg Waitz, MGH, SS rer. Langobardicarum (Hanover, 1878), 225.

35. For an overview, see the seminal work by Victor Elbern, *Der karolingische Goldaltar von Mailand* (Bonn: Kunsthistorisches Institute der Universität, 1952) and the analysis of Sandrina Bandera, "L'altare di Sant'Ambrogio: indagine storico-artistica," in Capponi, *L'altare d'oro di Sant'Ambrogio*, 73-111.

36. Erik Thunø, "The Golden Altar of Sant'Ambrogio in Milan: Image and Materiality," in *Decorating the Lord's Table: On the Dynamics between Image and Altar in the Middle Ages*, ed. Søren Kaspersen and Erik Thunø (Copenhagen: Museum Tusculanum Press, 2006), 63-78.

37. Bertelli, "Sant'Ambrogio da Angilberto II a Gotofredo," 17. See also the recent article by Ivan Foletti, "Le fléau des hérétiques. Ambroise de Milan, l'exclusion 'ethnique' et l'autel d'or de la basilique Ambrosiana," *Bulletin monumental* 175, no. 2 (2017): 102, included in part in Foletti, *Oggetti, reliquie, migranti*, esp. 177 et seq.

38. Bandera, "L'altare di Sant'Ambrogio," 79-86.

39. According to a distinction usefully highlighted by Louis Marin, "Visibilité et lisibilité de l'histoire: à propos des dessins de la colonne Trajane," in *Caesar triumphans, Catalogue de l'exposition*, ed. Daniel Arasse (Paris-Florence: Institut français de Florence, 1984), 33-45, included in Louis Marin, *De la représentation*, ed. Daniel Arasse, Alain Cantillon and Giovanni Careri (Paris: Gallimard/Éd. du Seuil, 1994), 219-34. Published in English as "History Made Visible and Readable: On Drawings of Trajan's Column," in *On Representation*, trans. Catherine Porter (Stanford: Stanford University Press, 2002), 219-35.

40. Thunø, "The Golden Altar of Sant'Ambrogio," 66.

41. Ferrari, "Le iscrizioni," 150: ÆMICAT ALMA FORIS RVTILOQUE DECORE VEN-VSTA / ARCA METALLORUM GEMMIS QVAE COMPTA CORUSCAT / THESAVRO TAMEN HAEC CVNCTO POTIORE METALLO / OSSIBVS INTERIVS POLLET DONATA SACRATIS.

42. Geneviève Bührer-Thierry, "Lumière et pouvoir dans le haut Moyen Âge occidental: célébration du pouvoir et métaphores lumineuses," *Mélanges de l'École française de Rome – Moyen Âge* 116 (2004): 521-56; and Marta Cristiani, *Lumières du haut Moyen Âge. Héritage classique et sagesse chrétienne aux tournants de l'histoire* (Florence: Sismel, 2014).

43. Jean-Claude Bonne, "De l'ornemental dans l'art médiéval (viie-xiie siècle). Le modèle insulaire," in *L'image. Fonctions et usages des images dans l'Occident médiéval*, ed. Jérôme Baschet and Jean-Claude Schmitt, Cahiers 5 (Paris: Le Léopard d'Or, 1996), 239. Note also that the golden altar of Sant'Ambrogio is part of a series, and that one could cite other contemporaneous and comparable *antependia* (like the Basel *antependium*, conserved in the Musée de Cluny) which also reused ancient stones. On this point, see recently Jean-Pierre Caillet's article, "De l'antependium' au retable. La contribution des orfèvres et émailleurs d'Occident," *Cahiers de Civilisation Médiévale* 49, no. 193 (2006): 3-20.

44. Margherita Superchi, "Le gemme dell'arca di Volvino," in Capponi, *L'altare d'oro di Sant'Ambrogio*, 185-207. See also Elisabetta Gagetti, "'Cernimus…in gemmis insignibusque lapidibus mira sculptoris arte…formatas imaginesi.' L'altare d'oro di Sant'Ambrogio e il reimpiego glittico nell'alto medioevo," *Archivio storico lombardo* 128 (2002): 11-61.

45. Gem no. 170 in the catalog (Superchi, "Le gemme dell'arca di Volvino," 193): Microcrystalline quartz and incised cornelian agate (first century BCE?). Dimensions: 8.31 × 1147 mm. See also Gagetti, "'Cernimus…in gemmis,'" 31-32.

46. Another example is Charlemagne's primary seal, documented from 772 to 813, and already used by Pepin the Short, which reused a Roman etching of a profile portrait, stylistically similar to certain portraits of Commodus (Percy Ernst Schramm, *Die deutschen Kaiser und Könige in Bildern ihrer Zeit*, I Teil, 751–1152 [Leipzig-Berlin: B. G. Teubner, 1928], fig. 2a). See Gagetti, "'Cernimus…in gemmis,'" 55.

47. Marco Sannazaro, Cristina Cattaneo, and Cristina Ravedoni, "La necropoli rinvenuta nei cortili dell'Università Cattolica," in *La città e la sua memoria. Milano e la tradizione di sant'Ambrogio*, ed. Marco Rizzi (Milan: Electa, 1997), 120-29.

48. The document is edited and commentated by Girolamo Biscaro, "Note e documenti santambrosiani. Seconda serie," *Archivio storico Lombardo* 32 (1905): 91.

49. Ambrosioni, "L'altare d'oro e le due comunità santambrosiane," 277.

50. Cynthia Hahn, "Narrative on the Golden Altar of Sant'Ambrogio in Milan: Presentation and Reception," *Dumbarton Oaks Papers* 53 (1999): 167–87. See also Cynthia Hahn, *Strange Beauty: Issues in the Making and Meaning of Reliquaries, 400–circa 1204* (Philadelphia: Pennsylvania State University Press, 2012).

51. These are, successively, in the bottom row: Annunciation and Nativity, then Presentation in the Temple and Wedding in Cana; in the middle row: Resurrection of the Daughter of Jairus and Transfiguration, then Expulsion of Merchants from the Temple and Miracle Healing of the Blind Man; in the upper row: Crucifixion and Pentecost, then Resurrection and Ascension (these last three panels were redone in the sixteenth century).

52. Marco Petoletti, "'Urbs nostra': Milano nello specchio delle epigrafi 'arcivescovi' dell'alto medioevio (secc. VIII–IX)," in Foletti, Quadri, and Rossi, *Milano allo specchio*, 22–24.

53. Courcelle, *Recherches sur Saint Ambroise, "Vies" anciennes, culture, iconographie* (Paris: Études augustiniennes, 1973).

54. Courcelle 172.

55. Paulinus of Milan, *Vita Ambrosii* 3.1–4.

56. Illona Opelt, "Das Bienenwunder in der Ambrosiusbiographie des Paulinus von Mailand," *Vigiliae Christianae* 22 (1968): 38–44.

57. Marc Van Uyftanghe, "Le remploi dans l'hagiographie: une "loi du genre" qui étouffe l'originalité?," in *Ideologie e pratiche nel riempiego nell'alto Medioevo. Atti della Settimana di studio del Centro italiano di studi sull'alto medioevo (Spoleto, 16–21 aprile 1998)*, Settimate di studio del Centro italiano di studi sull'alto medioevo 46 (Spoleto: Centro italiano di studi sull'alto medioevo, 1999), 1.363. See also from the same author, on the biblical echoes in the *Vita Ambrosii*, "L'empreinte biblique sur la plus ancienne hagiographie occidentale," in *Le monde latin et la Bible*, ed. Jacques Fontaine and Charles Piétri, Bible de tous les temps 2 (Paris: Beauchene, 1985), 565–611, esp. 593–611.

58. Paulinus of Milan, *Vita Ambrosii* 3.1. English translation: Ramsey, 197.

59. See, on the vocabulary of *infantia* and *pueritia* in hagiographic accounts, Didier Lett, *L'enfant des miracles. Enfance et société au Moyen Âge (XIIᵉ–XIIIᵉ siècles)* (Paris: Aubier, 1997).

60. Notkeri Balbuli, *Gesta Karoli Magni imperatoris*, ed. Hans F. Haefele, MGH, SS rer. Germ. NS 12 (Berlin: Weidmann, 1959), 55. See Cattaneo, "La tradizione e il rito ambrosiani nell'ambiente lombardo-medioevale," in *Ambrosius episcopus. Atti del Congresso internazionale di studi ambrosiani nel XVI centenario della elevazione*

di Sant'Ambrogio alla cattedra episcopale (Milano, dicembre 1974), ed. Giuseppe Lazzati, Studia patristica mediolanensia 7 (Milan: Vita e Pensiero, 1976), 2:126.

61. Umberto Eco, "Riflessioni sulle tecniche di citazione nel medioevo," in *Ideologie e pratiche nel riempiego nell'alto Medioevo. Atti della Settimana di studio del Centro italiano di studi sull'alto medioevo (Spoleto, 16–21 aprile 1998)*, Settimane di studio del Centro italiano di studi sull'alto medioevo 46 (Spoleto: Centro italiano di studi sull'alto medioevo, 1999), 1.463. A French translation of this text is available in Umberto Eco, *Écrits sur la pensée au Moyen Âge* (Paris: Grasset, 2016), 1040–59 ("Réflexions sur les techniques de la citation au Moyen Âge").

62. Courcelle, *Recherches sur saint Ambroise*, 175.

63. Historically, Ambrose is believed to have died on April 4, 397, and Martin of Tours on November 8 of the same year: Visonà, *Cronologia ambrosiana*, 56–57.

64. As recounted in a passage in *De virtutibus sancti Martini* 1.5, in Banterle, *Le fonti latine su sant'Ambrogio*, 132–34. On the close links between the churches of Milan and Tours, and how Martin's visit to Milan was remembered, see Luce Piétri, *La ville de Tours du IVᵉ au VIᵉ siècle: naissance d'une cité chrétienne*, CEFR 69 (Rome: École française de Rome, 1980), 487–93.

65. Carlo Bertelli, "Percorso tra le testimonianze figurative più antiche: dai mosaici di S. Vittore in Ciel d'oro al pulpito della basilica," in Gatti Perer, *La basilica di S. Ambrogio*, 2:356–64.

66. Ivan Foletti, "Del vero volto di Ambrogio. Riflessioni sul mosaico absidiale di Sant'Ambrogio a Milano in epoca carolingia," *Arte lombarda* 166 (2012): 5–14.

67. Courcelle, *Recherches sur saint Ambroise*, 180–82. See also Eva Tea, "I cicli iconografici di Sant'Ambrogio in Milano," in *Ambrosiana. Scritti di storia, archeologia ed arte pubblicati nel XVI centenario della nascita di S. Ambrogio CCCXL–MCMXL* (Milan: Biblioteca Ambrosiana, 1942), 290–93.

68. Mirella Ferrari, "Il nome di Mansueto arcivescovo di Milano (c. 672–681)," *Aevum* 132 (2008): 281–91.

69. Stéphane Gioanni, "397. Le saint patron de la Gaule venait d'Europe centrale," in *Histoire mondiale de la France*, ed. Patrick Boucheron (Paris: Seuil, 2017), 76–80. Published in English as "397: St. Martin: Gaul's Hungarian Patron Saint," in *France in the World: A New Global History*, ed. Patrick Boucheron and Stéphane Gerson (New York: Other Press, 2019), 75–80.

70. Ambrosioni, "Gli arcivescovi," 106.

71. Hahn, "Narrative on the Golden Altar," 176.

72. First published by Angelo Paredi in 1964, *De vita e meritis Ambrosii* benefits

from a new edition and specialized commentary in Courcelle, *Recherches sur saint Ambroise* (Paris: Etudes Augustiniennes, 1973), 49–153 (107 for the episode where Ambrose attends Saint Martin's funeral). See also *De vita et meritis Ambrosii*, in Banterle, *Le fonti latine su sant'Ambrogio*, 214.

73. Paolo Tomea, "Ambrogio e i suoi fratelli. Note di agiografia milanese altomedioevale," *Filologia mediolatina* 5 (1998): 154 et seq.

74. Tomea, "Ambrogio e i suoi fratelli," 175 (and 170–72 for a summary chart of borrowings from *Vita Martini* as well as from other Martinian sources).

75. Tomea, "Ambrogio e i suoi fratelli," 169.

76. Foletti, "Le fléau des hérétiques," 109.

77. Tomea, "Ambrogio e i suoi fratelli," 206. It is also possible that Marcellina (and not the Virgin, as is most often believed) is represented on the north face of the ciborium above the altar. For this hypothesis, see Paolo Tomea, *Tradizione apostolica e coscienza cittadina a Milano nel medioevo. La leggenda di san Barnaba* (Milan: Vita e Pensiero, 1993), appendix 10: "Sull' iconografia del ciborio di S. Ambrogio a Milano," 550–79 (in particular 565–66).

78. Picard, *Le souvenir des évêques*, 95–96.

79. Annamaria Ambrosioni, "'Atria vicinas struxit et antes fores.' Note in margine a un' epigrafe del IX secolo," in *Medioevo e latinità in memoria di Ezio Franceschini*, ed. Annamaria Ambrosioni et al. (Milan: Vita e Pensiero, 1993), 35–50 (included in Ambrosioni, *Milano papato e impero in età medievale*, 229–44).

80. Jacques Le Goff, *Medieval Civilization, 400–1500*, trans. Julia Barrow (Oxford: Blackwell, 1988), 3.

81. Florian Mazel, *L'évêque et le territoire. L'invention médiévale de l'espace (Vᵉ–XIIIᵉ siècle)* (Paris: Éd. du Seuil, 2016), 375.

82. As maintained by Jean-Philippe Genet, and expressed notably in his introduction to *Église et État, Église ou État? Les clercs et la genèse de l'État moderne*, ed. Christine Barralis et al., Le pouvoir symbolique en Occident (1300–1640) 10, CEFR 485/10 (Paris-Rome: Publications de la Sorbonne – Publications de l'École française de Rome, 2014), 9–22.

83. Florian Mazel, "Un, deux, trois Moyen Âge…Enjeux et critères des périodisations internes de l'époque médiévale," in "Découper le temps: actualité de la périodisation en histoire," ed. Stéphane Gibert, Jean Le Bihan, and Florian Mazel, special issue, *Atala. Cultures et sciences humaines* 17 (2014): 101–13.

84. Claire Sotinel, "Ne pas se souvenir d'Ambroise. L'effacement de la référence ambrosienne en Italie du Nord au VIᵉ siècle," in Boucheron and Gioanni, *La mémoire d'Ambroise de Milan*, 253–60.

85. Overview in Stefano Gasparri, *Italia longobarda. Il regno, i Franchi, il papato* (Rome–Bari: Laterza, 2011), 3–23.

86. On the disputed question of whether the *gens langobarda* defined themselves by a superficial Arianism, and on the composite Lombard identity, see Walter Pohl, "Deliberate Ambiguity: The Lombards and Christianity," in *Christianizing Peoples and Converting Individuals*, ed. Guyda Armstrong and Ian N. Woods (Turnhout: Brepols, 2000), 47–58, as well as, for a broader, European perspective, Walter Pohl, "Aux origines de l'Europe ethnique. Transformations d'identités entre Antiquité et Moyen Âge," *Annales. Histoire, Sciences Sociales* 60–61 (2005): 183–208. The documentary angle is aptly explored in Bruno Dumézil, "La religion et l'ethnogenèse des Lombards au regard des sources franques. Le dossier épistolaire," in *La fabrique des sociétés médiévales méditerranéennes. Les Moyen Âge de François Menant*, ed. Diane Chamboduc de Saint Pulgent and Marie Dejoux (Paris: Éditions de la Sorbonne, 2018), 25–35.

87. Foletti, "Le fléau des hérétiques," 107–8.

88. Cattaneo, "La tradizione e il rito ambrosiani," 120–22.

89. Cesare Pasini, "Deusdedit († 628)," in *Dizionario della Chiesa ambrosiana*, ed. Angelo Majo (Milan: NED, 1988), 2.1041–44.

90. Gregorio Magno, *Lettere*, ed. Vincenzo Recchia (Rome: Città Nuova, 1999), 28–31.

91. Marco Navoni, "'Comitur Ambrosii meritis urbs Mediolana.' L'identità ambrosiana della Chiesa e della città di Milano nel primo Millenio," in Foletti, Quadri, and Rossi, *Milano allo specchio*, 40.

92. Cesare Alzati, *Ambrosiana ecclesia. Studi su la Chiesa milanese e l'ecumene critisana fra tarda antichità e medioevo*, Archivio ambrosiano 65 (Milan: NED, 1993), 327.

93. Picard, *Le souvenir des évêques*, 86. See also Jean-Charles Picard, "Conscience urbaine et culte des saints. De Milan sous Liutprand à Vérone sous Pépin Ier d'Italie," in *Hagiographie, cultures et sociétés (IVᵉ–XIIᵉ siècles), Actes du Colloque organisé à Nanterre et à Paris, 2–5 mai 1979, Centre de recherches sur l'Antiquité tardive et le haut Moyen Âge, Université de Paris X* (Paris: Études Augustiniennes, 1981), 455–69.

94. Gian-Battista Pighi, ed., *Versus de Verona/Versus de Mediolano civitate* (Bologna: Università degli studi di Bologna, 1960), 146. English translation cited in Paul Oldfield, *Urban Panegyric and the Transformation of the Medieval City, 1100–1300* (Oxford: Oxford University Press, 2019), 84. On this text, see the classic study by Alessandro Colombo, "Il 'Versus de mediolana civitate' dell'anonimo liutprandeo e la importanza della metropoli lombarda nell'alto Medioevo," in

Miscellanea di studi lombardi in onore di Ettore Verga (Milan: Archivio Storico Cittadino, 1931), 69–104.

95. Picard, *Le souvenir des évêques*, 98.

96. Marielle Martiniani-Reber, "Stoffe tardoantiche e medievali nel Tesoro di Sant'Ambrogio," in *Il millenio ambrosiano. Milano, una capitale da Ambrogio ai Carolingi*, ed. Carlo Bertelli (Milan: Electa, 1987), 178–200, and Giuliana Righetto, "Scavi ottocenteschi in S. Ambrogio. La basilica ambrosiana in età paleocristiana e altomedievale nella 'Cronaca dei Restauri' di mons. Rossi," in Gatti Perrer, *La basilica di S. Ambrogio*, 127–47.

97. Foletti, "Le tombeau d'Ambroise," 79–82.

98. Carlo Bertelli, "Il ciborio restaurato," in *Il ciborio della basilica di Sant'Ambrogio a Milano*, ed. Carlo Bertelli, Pinin Brambilla Barcilon, and Antonietta Gallone (Milan: Credito artigiano, 1981), 3–66.

99. Here, I am entirely indebted to these analyses, notably Stéphane Gioanni, "Augustin, Paulin, Ennode et les origines de la mémoire d'Ambroise (v^e–vi^e siècles). Une nouvelle fondation de l'Eglise de Milan?," in Boucheron and Gioanni, *La mémoire d'Ambroise de Milan*, 235–52, and esp. 244–51.

100. Stéphane Gioanni, "Les Vies de saints latines composées en Italie de la Paix constantinienne au milieu du vi^e siècle," in *Hagiographies 5*, ed. Guy Philippart, Corpus Christianorum (Turnhout: Brepols, 2010), 399.

101. Simona Rota, "Introduzione," in *Magnus Felix Ennodius, Panegyricus dictus clementissimo regi Theoderico*, ed. Simona Rota (Rome: Herder, 2002), 22–25.

102. Magnus Felix Ennodius, *Lettres, Livres I et II*, ed. Stéphane Gioanni, Collection des universités de France. Série latine 393 (Paris: Les Belles Lettres, 2006), 50–51 (Epist. 2.1.3).

103. Magnus Felix Ennodius, *Lettres*, Introduction, ciii.

104. Céline Urlacher-Becht, "Les hymnes d'Ennode de Pavie: un 'nœud inextricable'?," in *La traduction du langage religieux*, ed. Muguraş Constantinescu, Elena Brânduşa Steiciuc, and Cristina Drahta (Suceava: Editura Universităţii din Suceava, 2008), 125–36.

105. Céline Urlacher-Becht, "La tradition manuscrite des hymnes d'Ennode de Pavie," *Paideia* 65 (2010): 511–31.

106. On the relationship between these hymns, Milanese liturgy, and the political model of Ambrosian episcopal government, see the analyses by Céline Urlacher-Becht, *Ennode de Pavie, chantre officiel de l'Église de Milan* (Paris: Institut d'études augustiniennes, 2014), in particular 283 et seq.

107. Gioanni, "Augustin, Paulin, Ennode," 247.

Notes

108. Picard, *Le souvenir des évêques*, 442–59.

109. Enrico Cattaneo, "Il culto di S. Anatalone nella Chiesa milanese e bresciana," *Ambrosius* 34 (1958): 247–52.

110. Paolo Tomea, "Le suggestioni dell'antico: qualche riflessione sull'*epistola proemiale* del 'De situ civitatis Mediolani' e sulle sue fonti," *Aevum* 63 (1989): 172–85.

111. Picard, *Le souvenir des évêques*, 41–42.

112. Gioanni, "Augustin, Paulin, Ennode," 248.

113. Stéphane Gioanni, "La langue de 'pourpre' et la rhétorique administrative dans les royaumes ostrogothique, burgonde et franc (VIᵉ-VIIIᵉ siècles)," in *La culture au haut Moyen Âge: une question d'élites? (Cambridge, 6–8 septembre 2007)*, ed. François Bougard, Régine Le Jan, and Rosamond McKitterick (Turnhout: Brepols, 2009), 13–38.

114. Urlacher-Becht, *Ennode de Pavie, chantre officiel*, 156 et seq.

PART THREE:

GHOSTS

1. Jean-Claude Schmitt, *Ghosts in the Middle Ages: The Living and the Dead in Medieval Society*, trans. Teresa Lavender Fagan (Chicago: University of Chicago Press, 1998).

2. Pierre Courcelle, "Ambroise et les spectres," in *Recherches sur saint Ambroise* (Paris: Études augustiniennes, 1973), 35–40.

3. Mathieu Riboulet, *Nous campons sur les rives. Lagrasse, 7–11 août 2017* (Lagrasse: Verdier, 2018), 34.

4. Georges Didi-Huberman, *L'image survivante. Histoire de l'art et temps des fantômes selon Aby Warburg* (Paris: Minuit, 2002).

5. Jean Bazin, "Les fantômes de Mme du Deffand: exercices sur la croyance," *Critique* 529-30 (1991): 492–511; included in Jean Bazin, *Des clous dans la Joconde. L'anthropologie autrement* (Toulouse: Anacharsis, 2008), 381–406.

6. Giorgio Agamben, "De l'utilité et de l'inconvénient de vivre parmi les spectres," in *Nudités* (Paris: Payot-Rivages, 2009), 69. On the concept of signature proposed here, see Giorgio Agamben, "Théorie des signatures," in *Signatura rerum. Sur la méthode* (Paris: Vrin, 2008), 37-91. Signatures are signs that indicate the order to which something originally belonged.

7. Jacques Derrida, *Specters of Marx: The State of the Debt, the Work of Mourning and the New International*, trans. Peggy Kamuf (New York: Routledge, 1994), 10.

Notes

1. Jean-Claude Schmitt, "Figurer et mimer les fantômes au XIVe siècle. La représentation des revenants dans l'iconographie médiévale," Fantômes, *Terrains* 69: 134-51.

2. Catherine Metzger, "Tissus et culte des reliques," *Antiquité tardive* 12 (2004), 183-86.

3. Marielle Martiniani Reber, "Stoffe tardoantiche e medievali nel Tesoro di Sant'Ambrogio," in *Il millennio ambrosiano. Milano, una capitale da Ambrogio ai Carolingi*, ed. Carlo Bertelli (Milan: Electa, 1987), 179. See also Flavia Fiori, "Il Pallio di Ariberto," in *Ariberto da Intimiano. Fede, potere e cultura a Milano nel secolo XI*, ed. Ettore Bianchi et al. (Cinisello Balsami: Silvana, 2009), 156-59.

4. Mirella Ferrari, "'Libri canonicorum sancti Ambrosii,'" in *La basilica di S. Ambrosio: il tempio ininterrotto*, ed. Gatti Perer (Milan: Vita e Pensiero, 1995), 1:326.

5. SUB HOC PALLIO TEGITUR DALMATICA SCI AMBROSII SUB QUO EANDEM DALMATICAM TEXIT DOMNUS HERIBERTUS ARCHIEPISCOPUS: Marco Petoletti, "Voci immobili: le iscrizioni di Ariberto," in Bianchi et al., *Ariberto da Intimiano*, 148-49.

6. The recent restoration of the dalmatic has likely eased certain lingering doubts about the authenticity and dating of this piece. The ongoing analyses are being conducted in the laboratory of Sabine Schrenk at the University of Bonn.

7. On the history of the memory of Ambrose in the tenth and eleventh centuries, and in all that follows, I am indebted to the excellent and richly suggestive summary by Miriam Rita Tessera, "La memoria di Ambrogio a Milano nei secoli X-XI," in Boucheron and Gioanni, *La mémoire d'Ambroise de Milan*, 421-40.

8. Beat Brenk, "La committenza da Ariberto d'Intimiano," in *Il millennio ambrosiano. La città dai Carolingi al Barbarossa*, ed. Carlo Bertelli (Milan: Electa, 1988), 124-55; and Graziano Alfredo Vergani, "Ariberto d'Intimiano: arcivescovo e committente nella Milano dell'XI secolo," in *Evangeliario di Ariberto. Un capolavoro dell'oreficeria medievale lombarda*, ed. Alessandro Tomei (Milan: Silvana, 1999), 23-49. See also Bianchi et al., *Ariberto da Intimiano*.

9. Beat Brenk, *La società milanese nell'età precomunale* (Rome-Bari: Laterza, 1981), 253.

10. Huguette Taviani, "Naissance d'une hérésie en Italie du Nord au XIe siècle," *Annales ESC* 29 (1974): 1224-52.

11. Yves Renouard, *Les villes d'Italie de la fin du Xe siècle au début du XIVe siècle*, ed. Philippe Braunstein (Paris: SEDES, 1969), 2:381.

12. On this point, see the classic study by Girolamo Arnaldi, "Papato, arcivescovi e vescovi nell'età post-carolingia," in *Vescovi e diocesi in Italia nel Medioevo (sec. IX–XIII)*, Italia sacra 5 (Padua: Herder, 1964), 27–53; and, for a wider perspective that includes Europe, see Michel Parisse, "Princes laïques et/ou moines. Les évêques du Xe siècle," in *Il secolo di ferro: mito e realtà del secolo X*, Settimane di studio del Centro italiano di studi sull'Alto Medioevo 38 (Spoleto: Centro italiano di studi sull'alto medioevo, 1991), 1:449–508.

13. François Menant, *Campagnes lombardes au Moyen Âge. L'économie et la société rurales dans la région de Bergame, de Crémone et de Brescia du Xe au XIIIe siècle*, BEFAR 281 (Rome: Collection de l'Ecole française de Rome, 1993), 580–89 (580 for the quote and translation of the privilege of Otto II, MGH, DO II, 256).

14. For an overview, the reader is directed to the luminous pages by Giovanni Tabacco, "Gli orientamenti feudali dell'impero in Italia," in *Structures féodales et féodalisme dans l'Occident méditerranéen (X^e–XIIIe siècles). Bilan et perspectives de recherches (Ecole française de Rome, 10–13 octobre 1978)* (Paris: CNRS, 1980), 219–40.

15. Pierre Toubert, *L'Europe dans sa première croissance. De Charlemagne à l'an mil* (Paris: Fayard, 2004).

16. Cinzio Violante, *La società milanese nell'età precomunale* (Rome-Bari: Laterza, 1953), 137 et seq.

17. It was Georges Duby who brought these general phenomena and their problematic consequences to the attention of historians. See Georges Duby, *The Early Growth of the European Economy; Warriors and Peasants from the Seventh to the Twelfth Century*, trans. Howard B. Clarke (Ithaca, NY: Cornell University Press, 1974) and *The Three Orders: Feudal Society imagined*, trans. Arthur Goldhammer (Chicago, University of Chicago Press, 1980). For an analysis of this historiographic moment, see Mathieu Arnoux, "Duby historien de l'économie et la question de la croissance," in *Georges Duby, portrait de l'historien en ses archives*, ed. Patrick Boucheron and Jacques Dalarun (Paris: Gallimard, 2013), 328–43; and Mathieu Arnoux, *Le temps des laboureurs. Travail, ordre social et croissance en Europe (XIe–XIVe siècle)* (Paris: Albin Michel, 2012), esp. 19–57.

18. Hagen Keller, *Adelsherrschaft und städtische Gesellschaft in Oberitalien (9.–12. Jarhundert)* (Tübingen: Max Niemeyer Verlag, 1979).

19. For a discussion of the robustness of the social taxonomy proposed by Hagen Keller, see François Menant, "La société d'ordres en Lombardie. À propos d'un livre récent," *Cahiers de civilisation médiévale* 26 (1983): 227–37; and François Menant, "La féodalité italienne entre XIe et XIIe siècles," in *Il feudalesimo nell'alto Medioevo*, Settimane di studio del Centro internazionale di studi sull'Alto

Medioevo 47 (Spoleto, Centro italiano di studi sull'alto medioevo, 2000), 1:346–87.

20. Keller, *Adelsherrschaft und städtische Gesellschaft*, 61. This "Milanese" model for creating a militia is discussed and put in perspective in Jean-Claude Maire Vigueur, *Cavaliers & citoyens. Guerre, conflits et société dans l'Italie communale, XIIᵉ–XIIIᵉ siècles* (Paris: EHESS, 2003), 221–29.

21. Martina Basile Weatherill, "Una famiglia 'longobarda' tra primo e secondo millenio: i 'da Intimiano.' I parenti e le proprietà di Ariberto," in Bianchi et al., *Ariberto da Intimiano*, 318–27.

22. Cinzio Violante, "L'arcivescovo Ariberto II (1018–1045) e il monastero di S. Ambrogio di Milano," in *Contributi dell'Istituto di storia medioevale* (Milan: Vita e Pensiero, 1972), 2:608–23.

23. *Arnulf von Mailand. Liber gestorum recentium*, ed. Claudia Zey (Hanover, Hansche Buchhandlung, 1994), 145. On the import of this work (which is in fact a chronicle of the kings of Italy and the bishops of Milan from 925 to 1077), see Claudia Zey, "Una nuova edizione del 'Liber gestorum recentium' di Arnolfo di Milano: un progresso?," in *Le cronache medievali di Milano*, ed. Paolo Chiesa (Milan: Vita e Pensiero, 2001), 11–27. In English: Arnulf of Milan, *The Book of Recent Deeds*, trans. W. L. North (Hanover: Hahnsche Buchhandlung, 1994).

24. Alfredo Lucioni, "L'arcivescovo Ariberto, gli ambienti monastici e le esperienze di vita comune del clero," in Bianchi et al., *Ariberto da Intimiano*, 347–55.

25. Miriam Rita Tessera, "L'imagine rifratta. Ariberto nelle cronache del Medioevo," in Bianchi et al., *Ariberto da Intimiano*, 493–97.

26. On this point, see the brief but thought-provoking recent synthesis by Marco Rossi, "Ariberto da Intimiano e la coscienza episcopale nella tradizione artistica ambrosiana," in Foletti, Quadri, and Rossi, *Milano allo specchio*, 147–68.

27. On this point, the reader is directed to the very valuable critical edition by Martina Basile Weatherill, Miriam Rita Tessera, and Manuela Beretta, eds., *Ariberto da Intimiano. I documenti segni del potere* (Cinisello Balsamo, Silvana, 2009).

28. Gianmarco Cossandi, "Ancora su Ariberto da Intimiano. Qualche riflessione a margine di due recenti volumi," *Archivio storico lombardo* 138 (2012): 201–2.

29. Picard, *Le souvenir des évêques*, 609.

30. Cinzio Violante, "Le origini del monastero di San Dionigi," in *Studi storici in onore di Ottorino Bertolini* (Pisa: Pacini, 1972), 735–809.

31. Walter Cupperi, "La tomba di Ariberto, 'alius Ambrosius,'" in Bianchi et al., *Ariberto da Intimiano*, 462–81. Of this tomb, only Ariberto's sarcophagus, today preserved in Milan's Duomo, is left.

32. Basile Weatherill et al., *Ariberto da Intimiano*, 35–37n2.

33. Cesare Alzati, "Chiesa ambrosiana e tradizione liturgica a Milano fra xi e xii secolo," in *Milano e il suo territorio in età comunale (xi–xii secolo)*. *Atti dell' 11 Congresso Internazionale di studi sull'Alto Medioevo, 26–31 ottobre 1987 (Spoleto, 1989)*, 1:395–423; reprinted in Cesare Alzati, *Ambrosiana ecclesia. Studi su la Chiesa milanese e l'ecumene critisana fra tarda antichità e medioevo*, Archivio ambrosiano 65 (Milan: NED, 1993), 255–80.

34. Tessera, "La memoria di Ambrogio a Milano," 433.

35. Miriam Rita Tessera, "'Christiane signifer milicie.' Chiesa, guerra e simbologia imperiale ai tempi di Ariberto," in Bianchi et al., *Ariberto da Intimiano*, 378–81.

36. Pietro Majocchi, *Pavia città regia. Storia e memoria di una capitale medievale* (Rome: Viella, 2008), esp. 69–80.

37. *Liudprandi Cremonensis Opera omnia*, ed. Paolo Chiesa, *Corpus Christianorum Continuatio Medievalis* 156 (Turnhout: Brepols, 1998), 140 (5.28): *misericordia inclinati Lotharium in ecclesia beatorum confessoris et martyrum Ambrosii, Gervasii et Protasii ante crucem prostratum erigerent regemque sibi constituerent.* For an English-language source, see *The Complete Works of Liudprand of Cremona*, trans. Paolo Squatriti (Washington, D.C.: The Catholic University of America Press, 2007), 191.

38. I direct the reader here to the analyses by Philippe Buc, *Dangereux rituel. De l'histoire médiévale aux sciences sociales* (Paris: PUF, 2003), esp. 19–61, on the concept of the efficacity of rituals in Liudprand of Cremona.

39. Annamaria Ambrosioni, "Gli arcivescovi nella vita di Milano," in *Atti del 10 congresso internazionale di studi sull'Alto Medioevo* (Spoleto, 1986), 110.

40. *Arnulf von Mailand. Liber gestorum*, 147: *Talis fultus remigio veniens Chuonradus Italiam ab eo, ut moris est, coronatur in regno.*

41. Annamaria Ambrosioni, "La Corona Ferrea e le incoronazioni: certezze e ipotesi," in *La corona ferrea nell'Europa degli imperi*, ed. Graziella Buccellati, vol. 1, *La Corona, il Regno e l'Impero: un millennio di storia* (Milan: Mondadori, 1998), xix–xxxvi.

42. Tessera, "La memoria di Ambrogio a Milano," 436–37.

43. Rossi, "Ariberto da Intimiano e la coscienza episcopale," 149.

44. Chiara Maggioni, "*Fulgeat ecclesiae:* le committenze orafe di Ariberto," in Bianchi et al., *Ariberto da Intimiano*, 287.

45. Chiara Maggioni, "Le trésor de l'ancienne cathédrale de Milan: objets liturgiques et mémoire de la *sancta mediolanensis ecclesia*," *Les Cahiers de Saint-Michel de Cuxa* 61 (2010): 225.

46. Sandrina Bandera, "L'Evangeliario di Ariberto. Un messagio salvifico offerto alla sua città," in *Evangeliario di Ariberto. Un capolavoro dell'oreficeria medievale lombarda*, ed. Alessandro Tomei (Milan: Silvana, 1999), 63.

47. R.I. Moore, *The War on Heresy; Faith and Power in Medieval Europe* (London: Profile, 2012).

48. Raoul Glaber, *Histoires*, ed. Mathieu Arnoux (Turnhout: Brepols, 1996), 231-33 (4.2.5). Historiography has followed in his footsteps, linking these two first waves of heresy (see, for instance, Georges Duby in *The Three Orders*).

49. *Landulfi senioris historia mediolanensis*, ed. Ludwig Conrad Bethmann and Wilhelm Wattenbach, MGH, SS rer. Germ. 8 (Hanover, 1848), 67-69.

50. Jörg W. Busch, "*Landulfi Senioris Historia Mediolanensis*. Überlieferung, Datierung und Intention," *Deutsches Archiv* 45 (1989): 1-30.

51. See Moore, *The War on Heresy*.

52. Huguette Taviani, "Naissance d'une hérésie en Italie du Nord au XIᵉ siècle," *Annales ESC* 29, no. 5 (1974): 1227.

53. Giuseppe Sergi, "L'unione delle tre corone teutonica, italica e borgognona e gli effetti sulla valle d'Aosta," *Bollettino storico-bibliografico subalpino* 103 (2005): 5-37.

54. Benzo von Alba, *Ad Heinricum IV. imperatorem libri VII*, ed. Hans Seyffert, MGH, SS rer. Germ. 65 (Hanover: 1996), 384. On this author, see, in addition to the editor's useful introduction, the classic profile by Giovanni Miccoli, "Benzone d'Alba," *Dizionario biografico degli Italiani* 8, 1966, online.

55. Tessera, "Christiane signifer milicie," 375-95.

56. On this point, see the essays gathered in Giancarlo Andenna and Renata Salvarani, eds., *Deus non voluit. I Lombardi alla prima crociata (1100–1101)* (Milan: Vita e Pensiero, 2003).

57. Andenna and Salvarani, eds., *Deus non voluit*, 384-85, for the full-length portrait of Saint Victor (London, British Library, Egerton 3763, fol. 116v). On the subject of this manuscript, see Angelo Paredi, "Il salterio di Arnolfo," in *Studi ambrosiani in onore du mons. Pietro Borella*, ed. Cesare Alzati and Angelo Majo, Archivio ambrosiano 63 (Milan: NED, 1982), 197-203.

58. *Landulfi senioris historia mediolanensis*, 53. On the presence of the nail from the True Cross among the relics preserved in the Duomo's treasury (a fact not reported before 1389), see Gianantonio Borgonovo and Marco Navoni, *Il chiodo di Cristo. Storia di una reliquia del Duomo di Milano* (Milan: Booktime, 2016), esp. 36 et seq.

59. Alfredo Lucioni, *Anselmo IV da Bovisio arcivescovo di Milano (1097–1101)*.

Episcopato e società urbana sul finire dell'xi secolo (Milan: Vita e Pensiero, 2011), esp. 180 et seq.

60. Guibert de Nogent, *The Deeds of God Through the Franks*, trans. Robert Levine (Woodbridge, UK: The Boydell Press, 1997), 148.

61. Albert of Aachen, *Historia Ierosolimitana. History of the Journey to Jerusalem*, ed. Susan B. Edgington (Oxford: Clarendon Press, 2007), 604-7 and 306-9.

62. Jean Flori, *Pierre l'Ermite et la première croisade* (Paris: Fayard, 1999), 367.

63. Jean-Claude Schmitt, *Les revenants. Les vivants et les morts dans la société médiévale* (Paris: Gallimard, 1994), 239-43.

64. Gisèle Besson and Jean-Claude Schmitt, *Rêver de soi. Les songes autobiographiques au Moyen Âge* (Toulouse: Anacharsis, 2017), 14-15.

65. Giovanni Tabacco, *L'Italie médiévale. Hégémonies sociales et structures de pouvoir*, trans. Colette Orsat (Chambéry: Université de Savoie, 2005), 170-72.

66. *Gesta pontificum Cameracensium*, ed. G.H. Pertz, MGH, Scriptores 7 (Hanover: 1846), 487: *Bertulfus etiam quidem secretarius regis sanctum se vidisset dixit Ambrosium, pro his quae rex male gerebat, indignatione commotus.*

67. From an abundant literature, see Laurent Jégou, "L'évêque entre autorité sacrée et exercice du pouvoir. L'exemple de Gérard de Cambrai (1012-1051)," *Cahiers de civilisation médiévale* 47 (2004): 37-56.

68. Dominique Barthélemy, *L'an mil et la paix de Dieu. La France chrétienne et féodale, 980-1060*, (Paris: Fayard, 1999), 439-68.

69. Sam Janssens, "La Paix de Dieu dans les *Gesta episcoporum Cameracensium*," *Revue du Nord* 410 (2015): 313.

70. *Arnulf von Mailand. Liber gestorum recentium*, 163-64.

71. *Landulfi senioris historia mediolanensis*, 62.

72. *Wiponis Gesta Chuonradi II imperatoris*, ed. Harry Breslau, MGH, Scriptores rerum Germanicarum in usum scholarum 61 (Hanover: 1915), 56.

73. On the ambiguity of Ariberto's image in Wipo, see Tessera, "L'imagine rifratta," in Bianchi et al., *Ariberto da Intimiano*, 491-92.

74. This textual tradition is relayed in Giuseppe Calligaris, "Il flagello di sant'Ambrogio e le leggende delle lotte ariane," in *Ambrosiana. Scritti varii pubblicati nel xv centenario della morte di S. Ambrogio* (Milan: 1897), 30 et seq.

75. Galvano Fiamma, *Chronicon maius*, ed. Antonio Ceruti, *Miscellanea di storia italiana* 7 (1869): 605-6.

76. Tessera, "Christiane signifer milicie," 393.

77. Hannelore Zug Tucci, "Il carroccio nella vita comunale italiana," *Quellen und Forschungen aus italienischen Archiven und Bibliotheken* 65 (1985): 19 et seq.

Notes

78. Tessera, "Christiane signifer milicie," 390.

79. Tucci, "Il carroccio nella vita," 97–98; and Gérard Rippe, *Padoue et son contado (X^e–XIIIe siècle). Société et pouvoirs*, BEFAR 317 (Rome: École française de Rome, 2003), 333.

80. Ernst Voltmer, *Il carroccio* (Turin: Einaudi, 1994), esp. 38–44 for the Milanese invention of the *carroccio*. See also Ernst Voltmer, "Nel segno della Croce. Il carroccio come simbolo del potere," in *"Militia Christi" e Crociata nei secoli XI–XIII. Atti della undecima Settimana internazionale di studio, Mendola, 28 agosto–1 settembre 1989* (Milan: Vita et Pensiero, 1992), 193–207; see also, in the same volume, Michael McCormick, "Liturgie et guerre des Carolingiens à la première croisade," 209–38.

81. *Arnulf von Mailand. Liber gestorum recentium*, 161–62; Arnulf of Milan, *The Book of Recent Deeds*, trans. W. L. North (Hanover: Hahnsche Buchhandlung, 1994), 24.

82. Tessera, "Christiane signifer milicie," 389–90. The most detailed description of the *carroccio* appears at a late date, in the fourteenth-century writings of Galvano Fiamma (*Chronicon maius*, 605–6).

83. Jörg W. Busch, *Die Mailänder Geschichtsschreibung zwischen Arnulf und Galvaneus Flamma: Die Beschäftigung mit der Vergangenheit im Umfeld einer oberitalienischen Kommune vom späten 11. bis zum frühen 14. Jahrhundert* (Munich: Wilhelm Fink Verlag, 1997), 38–50.

84. Hagen Keller, "Mailand im 11. Jahrhundert: das Exemplarische an einem Sonderfall," in *Die Frühgeschichte der europäischen Stadt im 11. Jarhundert*, ed. Jörg Jarnut and Peter Johanek (Cologne: Böhlau, 1998), 81–104; trans. into Italian in Hagen Keller, *Il laboratorio politico del Comune medievale* (Naples: Liguori editore, 2014), 229–62.

85. *Landulfi senioris historia mediolanensis*, 69:…*ut si ipse sanctus Ambrosius modo superveniret corpore, nec clerum nec civitatem ipsam testaretur fore, in qua cum adhuc viveret episcopatum rexisset.*

86. It would be best to start here with a classic essay by Giovanni Miccoli, "Per la storia della Pataria milanese," *Bolletino dell'Istituto storico italiano per il Medioevo* 70 (1958): 43–123, revisited and amplified in *Chiesa gregoriana. Ricerche sulla Riforma del secolo XI* (Florence: La nuova Italia, 1966), 101–67; and another by Cinzio Violante, "I laici nel movimento patarino," in *I laici nella "societas christiana" dei secoli XI e XII. Atti della terza Settimana internazionale di studio. Mendola, 21–27 agosto 1965*, ed. Giuseppe Lazzati (Milan: Vita e Pensiero, 1968), 597–687, reprinted in Cinzio Violante, *Studi sulla Cristianità medioevale* (Milan: Vita e Pensiero, 1975), 145–246.

87. These events truly take on significance in the context of the Council of

Fontaneto in 1057: see Alfredo Lucioni, "Gli altri protagonisti del sinodo di Fontaneto: i Patarini milanesi," in *Fontaneto: una storia millenaria. Monastero. Concilio metropolitico. Residenza Viscontea, Atti dei convegni di Fontaneto d'Agogna (settembre 2007, giugno 2008)*, ed. Giancarlo Andenna and Ivana Teruggi (Novare: Interlinea, 2009), 279–313.

88. R. I. Moore, *The War on Heresy* (London: Profile Books, 2012), 77.

89. Gabriella Rossetti, "Il matrimonio del clero nella società altomedievale," in *Il matrimonio nella società altomedievale*, (Spoleto: Centro italiano di studi sull'alto medioevo, 1977), 473–513.

90. On this point, see the ongoing work of Piroska Nagy, "Collective Emotions, History Writing and Change: The Case of the *Pataria* (Milan, Eleventh Century)," *Emotions: History, Culture, Society* 2, no.1 (2018), 132–52. On the concept of the emotional community, see Piroska Nagy and Damien Boquet, *Sensible Moyen Age. Une histoire des émotions dans l'Occident médiéval* (Paris: Seuil, 2015).

91. Bonizonis episcopus Sutriensis, *Liber ad amicum*, ed. Ernst Dümmler, MGH, Libelli de lite imperatorum et pontificum (Hanover, 1891), 1:591.

92. Paolo Golinelli, ed., *La Pataria. Lotte religiose e sociali nella Milano dell'XI secolo* (Bergamo: Europia, 1984), 30–33.

93. Brian Stock, *The Implications of Literacy: Written Language and Models of Interpretation in the Eleventh and Twelfth Centuries*, (Princeton: Princeton University Press, 1983), 151–240, esp. 230–31 for its analysis of the functioning of the Canonica.

94. See, for example, Jacques Dalarun, "Hérésie, commune et inquisition à Rimini (fin XIIIᵉ – début XIVᵉ siècle)," *Studi medievali* 39 (1988): 641–83.

95. Jean-Louis Biget, "'Les albigeois' Remarques sur une dénomination," in *Inventer l'hérésie? Discours polémiques et pouvoirs avant l'Inquisition*, ed. Monique Zerner, Collection du centre d'études médiévales de Nice 2 (Nice: Université de Nice, 1998), 242–43. For an English-language source, see https://www.papalencyclicals.net/councils/ecum11.htm at 27.

96. Pierre Toubert, "Église et État au XIᵉ siècle: la signification du moment grégorien pour la genèse de l'Etat moderne," in *État et Église dans la genèse de l'État moderne. Actes du colloque organisé par le CNRS et la Casa de Velázquez (Madrid, 30 novembre et 1ᵉʳ décembre 1984)*, ed. Jean-Philippe Genet and Bernard Vincent (Madrid: Bibliothèque de la Casa de Velázquez, 1986), 9–22.

97. In the sense of the classic but still fundamental work of Gerd Tellenbach, *Libertas. Kirche und Weltordnung im Zeitalter des Investiturstreites*, Forschungen zur Kirchen- und Geistesgeschichte 7 (Stuttgart: Kohlhammer, 1936).

98. Florian Mazel, "Pour une redéfinition de la réforme 'grégorienne.' Éléments d'introduction," *Cahiers de Fanjeaux* 48 (2013): 22; quotation from Pierre Legendre, *Les enfants du texte. Etude sur les fonctions parentales des Etats. Leçon VI* (Paris: Fayard, 1992), 49.

99. On this point, see Umberto Longo, *Come angeli in terra. Pier Damiani, la santità e la riforma del secolo XI* (Rome: Viella, 2012).

100. Chris Wickham, "The 'Feudal Revolution' and the Origins of Italian City Communes," *Transactions of the Royal Historical Society* 6, no. 24 (2014): 29–55.

101. See Cinzio Violante's classic and still fundamental *La società milanese nell'età precomunale* (Rome-Bari: Laterza, 1953); but also Cinzio Violante, "I movimenti patarini e la Riforma eclesiastica," in *Annuario dell'Università Cattolica del Sacro Cuore 1955–56, 1956–57* (Milan: 1957), 207–23.

102. Chris Wickham, *Sleepwalking into a New World. The emergence of Italian City Communes in the Twelfth Century* (Princeton, NJ: Princeton University Press, 2015), 27.

103. Hagen Keller, "Pataria und Stadtverfassung, Stadtgemeinde und Reform: Mailand im 'Investiturstreit,'" in *Investiturstreit und Reichsverfassung*, ed. Josef Fleckenstein, Vorträge und Forschungen 17 (Sigmaringen: 1973), 321–50.

104. Pierre Racine, "Evêque et cité dans le royaume d'Italie: aux origines des communes italiennes," *Cahiers de civilisation médiévale* 105-6 (1984): 135.

105. Paolo Golinelli, "Une hagiographie de combat dans le contexte de la lutte pour les investitures," in *Hagiographie, idéologie et politique au Moyen Âge en Occident. Actes du colloque international du Centre d'Études supérieures de Civilisation médiévale de Poitiers, 11–14 septembre 2008*, ed. Edina Bozoky (Turnhout: Brepols, 2012), 243–54.

106. In the words of the famous methodological critique by Arsenio Frugoni, *Arnaud de Brescia dans les sources du XIIe siècle*, trans. Alain Boureau (Paris: Les Belles Lettres, 1994), 2.

107. Andrea di Strumi, *Vita sancti Arialdi*, ed. Friedrich Baethgen, MGH, Scriptores rerum Germanicarum Nova series 30 (Leipzig: 1934), 1057. For an English-language version, see Andrea da Strumi, *Passion of Arialdo*, trans. William North, in *Medieval Italy: Texts in Translation*, ed. Katherine L. Jansen, Joanna Dress, and Frances Andrews (Philadelphia, PA: University of Pennsylvania Press, 2009), 346.

108. This investigation has been greatly facilitated by the remarkable work of Paolo Golinelli, ed., *La Pataria. Lotte religiose e sociali nella Milano dell'XI secolo* (Bergamo: Europia, 1984).

109. Andrea di Strumi, *Vita sancti Arialdi*, 1056 and 1061.

110. On this point, see Marco Navoni, "Introduzione," in Andrea da Strumi, *Arialdo. Passione del santo martire milanese*, ed. Marco Navoni (Milan: Jaca Book, 1994), 31–32, n. 73.

111. Andrea di Strumi, *Vita sancti Arialdi*, 1064.

112. *Passione del beato martire Arialdo, sepolto nella chiesa du S. Dionigi (Passio beati Arialdi martyris qui ad sanctum Dionysium tumulatur)*, in Andrea da Strumi, *Arialdo. Passione del santo martire milanese*, 208.

113. Walter Berschin, *Bonizone di Sutri. La vita e le opere* (Spoleto: Centro italiano di studi sull'alto medioevo, 1992).

114. Fabrice Delivré, "Ambroise, le schisme et l'hérésie (xie-xiie siècles)," in Boucheron and Gioanni, *La mémoire d'Ambroise de Milan*, 451.

115. Bonizonis episcopus Sutriensis, *Liber ad amicum*, 591.

116. Pier Damiani, *Opusculum quintum. Actus Mediolani, de privilegio Romanae Ecclesiae*, PL 145, col. 89-98, col. 92. On this point, see Jean-Marie Sansterre, "Le passé et le présent dans l'argumentation d'un réformateur du xie siècle: Pierre Damien," in *L'autorité du passé dans les sociétés médiévales*, ed. Jean-Marie Sansterre, CEFR 333 (Rome: École française de Rome, 2004), 221-35, esp. at 230, for Pierre Damien's use of the Ambrosian reference.

117. Robert Somerville, *Pope Urban II, the Collectio Britannica and the council of Melfi* (Oxford: Clarendon Press, 1996), 62. The letter is preserved in a canonical anthology of the late eleventh century, the *Collectio Britannica* (see Delivré, "Ambroise, le schisme et l'hérésie," 455-57).

118. Giorgio Picasso, "Il ricordo di sant'Ambrogio nelle opere di san Pier Damiani," in *Ricerche storiche sulla Chiesa ambrosiana 4*, Archivio ambrosiano 27 (Milan: 1974), 111-22.

119. Delivré, "Ambroise, le schisme et l'hérésie," 443-46.

120. *Arnulf von Mailand. Liber gestorium recentium*, 190: *cum magister noster dicat Ambrosius*. Arnulf, *The Book of Recent Deeds*, 34.

121. *Arnulf von Mailand. Liber gestorium recentium*, 185: *Certe, certe non absque re scripta sunt hec in Romanis annalibus. Dicetur enim in posterum subiectum Rome Mediolanum*.

122. *von Mailand. Liber gestorium recentium*, 225-26. On this point, see Delivré, "Ambroise, le schisme et l'hérésie," 453.

123. Enrico Cattaneo, "La tradizione e il rito ambrosiani nell'ambiente lombardo-medioevale," in *La Chiesa di Ambrogio. Studi di storia e di liturgia* (Milan: Vita e Pensiero, 1984), esp. 23.

124. Cesare Alzati, "Chiesa ambrosiana e tradizione liturgica a Milano tra XI e XII secolo," in *Milano e il suo territorio in età comunale (XI–XII secolo). Atti dell'11 Congresso Internazionale di studi sull'Alto Medioevo, 26–31 ottobre 1987* (Spoleto: 1989), 1:395–423, reprinted in *Ambrosiana ecclesia. Studi su la Chiesa milanese e l'ecumene critisana fra tarda antichità e medioevo*, Archivio ambrosiano 65 (Milan: NED, 1993), 255–80, esp. at 268.

125. Georges Duby, "Private Power, Public Power," in *Revelations of the Medieval World*, ed. Georges Duby, trans. Arthur Goldhammer, vol. 2 of *A History of Private Life*, ed. Philippe Ariès and Georges Duby (Cambridge, MA: The Belknap Press of the Harvard University Press, 1988), 3–32.

126. *Landulfi senioris historia mediolanensis*, 95–96 (3.30).

127. *Landulfi senioris historia mediolanensis*, 99 (3.32).

128. Roger Gryson, *Le prêtre selon saint Ambroise* (Louvain: Impr. Orientaliste, 1968), 308–11. On the theology of marriage in Ambrose, see Dominique Lhuillier-Martinetti, *L'individu dans la famille à Rome au IVᵉ siècle d'après l'œuvre d'Ambroise de Milan* (Rennes: PUR, 2008).

129. Cesare Alzati, "Parlare con la voce dei Padri. L'apologetica ambrosiana di fronte ai riformatori del secolo XI," in *Leggere i Padri tra passato e presente. Atti del Convegno internazionale di studi (Cremona, 21–22 novembre 2008)*, ed. Mariarosa Cortesi (Florence: SISMEL-Edizioni del Galluzzo, 2010), 9–26.

130. *Landulfi senioris historia mediolanensis*, 89 (3.23). On this question, see Cesare Alzati, "Tradizione e disciplina ecclesiastica nel dibattito tra Ambrosiani e Patarini a Milano nell'età di Gregorio VII," in *La Riforma Gregoriana e l'Europa. Atti del Congresso Internazionale promosso in occasione del IX Centenario della morte di Gregorio VII (1085–1985), Salerno, 20–25 maggio 1985*, Studi Gregoriani 14 (Rome: 1992), 175–94, included in *Ambrosiana ecclesia*, 194.

131. Pietro Zerbi, "I rapporti di s. Bernardo di Chiaravalle con i vescovi e le diocesi d'Italia," in *Vescovi e diocesi in Italia nel medioevo, sec. IX–XIII, Atti del 2 Convegno di storia della Chiesa in Italia, Roma, 5–9 sett. 1961*, Italia sacra. Studi e documenti di storia ecclesiastica 5 (Padua: 1964), 219–313; reprinted in Pietro Zerbi, *Tra Milano e Cluny. Momenti di vita e cultura ecclesiastica nel secolo XII* (Rome: Herder, 1979), 3–109.

132. Jean Leclercq, *Études sur saint Bernard et le texte de ses écrits*, Analecta sacri ordinis Cisterciensis 9, 1–2 (Rome: Piazza del Tempo di Diana, 1953), 151–70, esp. at 163, quoted and discussed by Fabrice Delivré, "Ambroise, le schisme et l'hérésie (XIᵉ–XIIᵉ siècles)," 458–60.

1. For a summary of Italian research on this point, see Eugenio Riversi, "Usi politici delle memorie monastiche del potere di Matilde di Canossa," *Quellen und Forschungen aus italienischen Archiven und Bibliotheken* 92 (2012): 1-32.

2. *Lamperti monachi Hersfeldensis Opera*, MGH, Scriptores rerum Germanicarum in usum scholarum separatim editi (Hanover: 1894), 1-304, esp. 289, trans. G. A. Loud, *The Annals of Lambert of Hersfeld*, Leeds History in Translation Website, Leeds University (2004).

3. For a recent survey of interpretations of this famous episode, see Johannes Fried, *Canossa. Entlarvung einer Legende. Eine Streitschrift* (Berlin: Akademie Verlag, 2012).

4. Harald Zimmermann, *Der Canossagang von 1077. Wirkungen und Wirklichkeit* (Mainz: Steiner, 1975).

5. Johannes Fried, *Canossa. Entlarvung einer Legende. Eine Streitschrift* (Berlin: Akademie Verlag, 2012). For a critical analysis of these interpretations and an overall account of the epistemological and political issues underlying this controversy, see Benoît Grévin, "Polémique de la 'mémorique.' À propos de 'Canossa. Entlarvung einer Legende. Eine Streitschrift,'" *Francia* 42 (2015): 275-89.

6. In the sense proposed by Stefan Weinfurter, *Canossa. Die Entzauberung der Welt* (Munich: C. H. Beck, 2006).

7. On this point, see the now classic works of Gerd Althoff, *Die Macht der Rituale. Symbolik une Herrschaft im Mittelater* (Darmstadt: WBG, 2003); and, more recently, Gerd Althoff, "Das Amtsverständnis Gregors VII. und die neue These vom Friedenspakt in Canossa," *Frühmittelalterliche Studien* 48, no. 1 (2014): 261-76.

8. Augustine, *26 sermons au peuple d'Afrique*, ed. François Dolbeau (Turnhout: Brepols, 2010), 531 (Dolbeau Sermon 25, 26), trans. E. Hill, in *Sermons (Newly Discovered)*, The Works of Saint Augustine: A Translation for the 21st Century (Hyde Park, NY: New City Press, 1997). See Philippe Buc, "Rituel politique et imaginaire politique au haut Moyen Âge," *Revue historique* 620 (2001): 853.

9. *Bertholdi Chronicon, 1054-1080*, in *Die Chroniken Bertholds von Reichenau und Bernolds von Konstanz, 1054-1100*, ed. Ian Stuart Robinson, M.G.H., Scriptores rerum germanicarum, Nova series 14 (Hanover, 2003), 161-381, at 283: *Theodosius imperator a sancto Ambrosio ab introitu ecclesie propellitur et ob scelera sua ad agendam penitentiam octo mensibus in custodiam mittitur*. See Fabrice Delivré, "Ambroise, le schisme et l'hérésie (XIᵉ-XIIᵉ siècles)," in Boucheron and Gioanni *La mémoire d'Ambroise de Milan*, 441.

Notes

10. Rudolf Schieffer, "Von Mailand nach Canossa. Ein Beitrag zur Geschichte der christlicher Herrscherbuße von Theodosius d. Gr. bis zu Heinrich IV," *Deutsches Archiv für Erforschung des Mittelalters* 28 (1972): 333–70.

11. Delivré, "Ambroise, le schisme et l'hérésie," 442.

12. A full account of the episode appears in Neil McLynn, *Ambrose of Milan. Church and Court in a Christian Capital* (Berkeley: University of California Press, 1994), 315–30. For a recent summation of these interpretations, see Rob Meens, *Penance in Medieval Europe, 600–1200* (Cambridge: Cambridge University Press, 2014), 21–25.

13. Gibert Dagron, *L'hippodrome de Constantinople. Jeux, peuple et politique* (Paris: Gallimard, 2011).

14. Ambrose, *De obitu Theodosii* 13, ed. Otto Faller, CSEL 73 (Vienna: Hölder-Pichler-Tempsky, 1955): *cum fuisset commotio maior iracundiae*. See Bertrand Lançon, *Théodose* (Paris: Perrin, 2014), 110.

15. Ambrose, *Epist. extra coll.* 11 (M 51).6 and 11 (M 51).12, trans. Hervé Savon, *Ambroise de Milan (340–397)* (Paris: Desclée, 1997), 271. Translation Tertullian.org, anonymous, from Oxford Movement Library of the Fathers.

16. Peter Brown, *Power and Persuasion in Late Antiquity: Towards a Christian Empire* (Madison, WI: University of Wisconsin Press, 1992).

17. Pierre Toubert, "La doctrine gélasienne des deux pouvoirs. Propositions en vue d'une révision," *Studi in onore di Giosuè Musca* (Bari: 2000), 519–40, reprinted in Pierre Toubert, *L'Europe dans sa première croissance. De Charlemagne à l'an mil* (Paris: Fayard, 2004), 385–417. See also Giovanni Tabacco, *La relazione fra i concetti di potere temporale e di potere spirituale nella tradizione cristiana fino al secolo XIV*, ed. Laura Gaffuri (Florence: Reti Medievali–Firenze University Press, 2010).

18. Paulinus of Milan, *Vita Ambrosii* 24.

19. Augustine, *The City of God* 5.26. See Angelo Paredi, "Ambrogio, Graziano, Teodosio," *Antichità Altoadriatiche* 22 (1982): 1:17–49, at 38. Translation newadvent .org.

20. Pierre Hadot, "Introduction," in Ambroise de Milan, *Apologie de David*, ed. Pierre Hadot and Marius Cordier, Sources chrétiennes 239 (Paris: Éditions du Cerf, 1977), 43.

21. Mayke de Jong, *The Penitential State: Authority and Atonement in the Age of Louis the Pious, 814–840*, (Cambridge: Cambridge University Press, 2009), 122 et seq.

22. *Lamperti monachi Hersfeldensis Opera*, 290.

23. Paolo Cammarosano, "Ambrogio e Teodosio: assenze e affermazioni di temi iconografici nei conflitti tra *regnum* e *sacerdotium*," in *Scritti di storia*

medievale offerti a Maria Consiglia de Matteis, ed. Berardo Pio (Spoleto: Centro italiano di studi sull'alto medioevo, 2011), 81–90.

24. Paulinus of Milan, *Vita Ambrosii* 24.1.

25. *Cassiodori-Epiphanii Historia ecclesiastica tripartita. Historiae ecclesiasticae ex Socrate, Sozomeno et Theodorito in unum collectae et nuper de graeco in latinum translatae libri numero duodecim* 9.30, ed. Walter Jacob and Rudolphe Hanslik, CSEL 71 (Vienna: 1952), 540–46.

26. For an overview of the research on this question, see Marcel Simon and André Benoit, eds., *Le judaïsme et le christianisme antique. D'Antiochus Épiphane à Constantin* (Paris: PUF, 1998), esp. chap. 8, "La 'conversion' de Constantin," 308–34.

27. See the writings of Françoise Thélamon, "Écrire l'histoire de l'Église d'Eusèbe de Césarée à Rufin d'Aquilée," in *L'historiographie de l'Église des premiers siècles*, ed. Yves-Marie Duval and Bernard Pouderon (Paris: Beauchesne, 2001), 207–35; and Françoise Thélamon, "L'*Histoire ecclésiastique* et ses lecteurs occidentaux," in *L'Oriente in Occidente. L'opera di Rufino di Concordia*, ed. Maurizio Girolami, Supplementi Adamantius 4 (Brescia: Morcellania, 2014), 163–78.

28. On this point, see the classic work by Pierre Courcelle, *Les lettres grecques en Occident. De Macrobe à Cassiodore* (Paris: De Boccard, 1943).

29. Pierre Nautin, "Théodore Lecteur et sa 'réunion de différentes Histoires' de l'Église," *Revue des études byzantines* 52 (1994): 213–44.

30. At present, 155 manuscripts have been entered in the database *Fama. Œuvres latines médiévales à succès* of the Institut de recherche et d'histoire des textes (IRHT), http://fama.irht.cnrs.fr

31. Bernard Guenée, *Histoire et culture historique dans l'Occident médiéval* (Paris: Aubier, 1980), 302. For example, in the second version of his *Golden Legend*, Jacobus de Voragine departs from Paulinus of Milan's account to emphasize the episode of the penance of Theodosius, which illustrates Ambrose's virtue of "courageous constance." See Jacobus de Voragine, *The Golden Legend* (Princeton, NJ: Princeton University Press), 229–37. He says, "one reads in the *Tripartite History* and in a chronicle…" The first is the work of Epiphanius, while the second is Sicard of Cremona's *Chronica*, which partly derives from it. See *Sicardi Episcopi Cremonensis Chronica*, ed. O. Holder-Egger, MGH, Scriptores 31 (1903), 128.

32. Although see Giovanni Galbiati, "Della fortuna letteraria e di una gloria orientale di Sant'Ambrogio," in *Ambrosiana. Scritti di storia, archeologia ed arte pubblicati nel XVI centenario della nascita di S. Ambrogio, CCCXL–MCMXL* (Milan: Biblioteca ambrosiana, 1942), 49–95; and, more particularly, *Le fonti greche su*

Sant'Ambrogio, ed. Cesare Pasini, SAEMO 24 (Milan-Rome: Biblioteca Ambrosiana-Città Nuova, 1990).

33. Jean-Rémy Palanque, "Le témoignage de Socrates le Scholastique sur Saint Ambroise," *Revue des études anciennes* 26 (1924): 216–26, at 217.

34. Sozomenus, *The Ecclesiastical History* 7.25.

35. Thedodoret, *The Ecclesiastical History* 5.17, quoted in Gibert Dagron, *Empereur et prêtre. Étude sur le "césaropapisme" byzantin* (Paris: Gallimard, 1996), 127, trans. Jean Birrell, *Emperor and Priest: The Imperial Office in Byzantium* (Cambridge: Cambridge University Press, 2003), 112.

36. Dagron, *Empereur et prêtre*, 129.

37. The date is not exact because doubt still lingers: the letter alludes to "signs in the heavens," which some specialists have identified as a passing comet, visible from August 22 to September 17, 390, which would entail a different dating of Theodosius's penance the following year. See Antonio Vecchio, "La strage di Tessalonica. Nuove ricerche sulla date: 389 o 390?," in *"Humanitas" classica e "sapientia" cristiana: scritti offerti a Roberto Iacoangeli*, ed. Sergio Felici (Rome: LAS, 1992), 115–44.

38. In the following pages, I rely in all important points on the recent summation by Gérard Nauroy, "Édition et organisation du recueil des lettres d'Ambroise de Milan: une architecture cachée ou altérée?," in *La* Correspondance *d'Ambroise de Milan*, ed. Aline Canellis (Saint-Etienne: Publications de l'Université de Saint-Etienne, 2012), 19–73, at 24–26.

39. The manuscripts in question: Vatican, Bibl. Apostolica, Vat. Lat. 286 (*E*); and Berlin, D. Staatsb. Preuss. Kulturbesitz, theol. Lat. 908 (*B*). See Mirella Ferrari, "'Recensiones' milanesi tardo-antiche, carolingie, basso-medievali di opere di S. Ambrogio," in Lazzati, *Ambrosius episcopus*, 41–43 (see chap. 1, n. 32).

40. Lazzati, *Ambrosius episcopus*, 101–2. Two manuscripts – Milan, Ambros. J 71 sup (*A*) and Ambros. B 54 inf. (*M*) – come from the scriptorium of Santa Tecla in Milan; the third – Cologne, Dombibliothek 32 (*K*) – was also copied in Milan.

41. Nauroy, "Édition et organisation du recueil," 31–45.

42. Michaela Zelzer, "Die Biefbücher des hl. Ambrosius und die Briefe *extra collectionem*," *Anzeiger der Akademie der Wissenschaften in Wien* 112 (1975), 7–23.

43. Camille Gerzaguet and Paul Mattei, "Les lettres d'Ambroise *extra collectionem*. Présentation philologique du dossier. Approche historique et doctrinale," *Revue des études tardo-antiques*, suppl. 2 (2014): 67–69.

44. Nauroy, "Edition et organisation du recueil," 26. Another example is the letter to the Church of Vercelli (*Epist. extra coll.* 14), transmitted with a group of texts on the *vita beata caelestis*. See Nauroy, "Vers un nouveau texte critique du *De*

Iacob et vita beata," in *Lire et éditer aujourd'hui Ambroise de Milan* (Bern: Peter Lang, 2007), 68.

45. Ambrose, *Epist.* 32 (M 48).7, trans. J. H. W. G. Liebeschuetz and Carole Hill, *Ambrose of Milan: Political Letters and Speeches* (Liverpool: Liverpool University Press: 2005), quoted 27. See also *Epist.* 37 (M 47).4–5, addressed to the same Sabinus, in which Ambrose confirms that he submits his writings to the critical judgment of his friend.

46. Camille Gerzaguet, "Pouvoir épiscopal et luttes d'influence: Ambroise de Milan, le 'parrain' des évêques d'Italie du Nord?," *Revue des études tardo-antiques* 3, suppl. 1 (2014): 227–28.

47. He is the intended recipient, for example, of six of the seven letters making up Book 4 of Ambrose's correspondence (*Epist.* 11, 12, 13, 14, 15, and 16). See Jean-Pierre Mazières, "Les lettres d'Ambroise de Milan à Irenaeus," *Pallas* 26 (1979): 103–14.

48. Hervé Savon, "Simplicien, père d'Ambroise, *in accipienda grata*," *Studia Ambrosiana* 1 (2007):147–59.

49. Augustine, *Retractiones*, 2.20 (47): *Epistula est, habet quippe in capite quid ad quem scriba.*

50. What we might call, following Pierre Descotes, their "epistolarity." See Pierre Descotes, "L'épistolarité des lettres-traités d'Augustin d'Hippone," in *Epistola 1. Ecriture et genre épistolaires, IVᵉ–XIᵉ siècle,* ed. Thomas Deswarthe, Klaus Herbers, and Hélène Sirantoine (Madrid: Casa de Velázquez, 2018), 195–208.

51. Hervé Savon, "Un dossier sur la loi de Moïse dans le recueil des lettres d'Ambroise," in Canellis, *La Correspondance d'Ambroise,* 75–91.

52. The manuscript is preserved at the municipal library of Boulogne-sur-Mer (Bibliothèque municipale 32). It has recently been described and studied by Gérard Nauroy, "Les lettres du manuscrit de Boulogne-sur-Mer (Bibl. mun. 32) et l'épistolaire d'Ambroise de Milan," *Revue d'études augustiniennes et patristiques* 61 (2015): 111–34.

53. The idea, developed by the scientific editor of the correspondence, Michaela Zelzer, provoked a number of questions (Hervé Savon, "Saint Ambroise a-t-il imité le recueil de lettres de Pline le Jeune?," *Revue des études augustiniennes* 41 (1995): 3–17), to which Zelzer replied, incorporating certain of the criticisms. See now Michaela Zelzer, "*Retractationes* zu Brief und Briefgenos bei Plinius, Ambrosius und Sidonius Apollinaris," in *"Alvarium." Festschrift für Christian Gnilka,* ed. Wihelm Blümer, Jahrbuch für Antike und Christentum 33 (Münster: Aschendorff, 2002), 393–405.

54. Yves-Marie Duval, "Les lettres d'Ambroise de Milan aux empereurs. Les échanges avec Gratien," in *Correspondances. Documents pour l'histoire de l'Antiquité tardive (Actes du colloque international, Lille, 20–22 novembre 2003)*, ed. Roland Delmaire, Janine Desmulliez, and Pierre-Louis Gatier (Lyon: Maison de l'Orient et de la Méditerranée-Jean Pouilloux, 2009), 199–226.

55. Ambrose, *Epist.* 37 (M 47).6.

56. Ambrose, *Epist.* 33 (M 49).1: *inter absentes praesentium sermon est.*

57. Notably through Alcuin's *colloquia absentium*, see Christiane Veyrard Cosme, *Tacitus nuntius. Recherches sur l'écriture des lettres d'Alcuin (730?–804)* (Paris: Institut d'études augustiniennes, 2013), 107.

58. Gerzaguet, "Pouvoir épiscopal et luttes d'influence," 228.

59. McLynn, *Ambrose of Milan*, 282.

60. In this, I draw upon recent developments in medieval epistolography. See, from an abundant literature, Stéphane Gioanni and Paolo Cammarosano, eds., *Les correspondances en Italie II. Formes, styles et fonctions de l'écriture épistolaire dans les chancelleries italiennes (Vᵉ–XVᵉ siècles)*, CEF 475-Atti 06 (Rome-Trieste: École française de Rome–Centro Europeo di Ricerche Medievali, 2013). Also: Bruno Dumézil and Laurent Vissière, eds., *Épistolaire politique I. Gouverner par les lettres* (Paris: Presses de l'université Paris-Sorbonne, 2014).

61. Thomas Deswarthe, "Introduction," in Deswarthe, Herbers, and Sirantoine, *Epistola I*, 1–7.

62. Brown, *Power and Persuasion*. See also Lelia Cracco Ruggini, "Prêtre et fonctionnaire: le modèle ambrosien," *Antiquité tardive* 7 (1999): 178–80; and the comments of J. H. W. G. Liebeschuetz, *Ambrose of Milan. Political Letters and Speeches* (Liverpool: Liverpool University Press, 2010) and, by the same author, *Ambrose and John Chrysostom: Clerics between Desert and Empire* (Oxford: Oxford University Press, 2011).

63. In this, I rely mainly on Gérard Nauroy, "Qui a organisé le Livre X de la Correspondance d'Ambroise de Milan?," *Revue des études tardo-antiques*, suppl. 2 (2014): 13–50.

64. Michaela Zelzer, "Ambrosius von Mailand und das Erbe der klassischen Tradition," *Wiener Studien* 100 (1987): 201–26.

65. Ambrose, *Epist.* 70 (M 56) and 71 (M 56a). The attribution of the second letter to Ambrose is no longer disputed today. See Yves-Marie Duval, *L'affaire Jovinien. D'une crise de la société romaine à une crise de la pensée chrétienne à la fin du IVᵉ et au début du Vᵉ siècle* (Rome: Institutum Patristicum Augustinianum, 2003), esp. 81–95.

66. Ambrose, *Epist.* 72 (M 17), 73 (M 18), and 72a (M 17a). See, from a very abundant literature, Fabrizio Canfora, *Simmaco e Ambrogio o di un'antica controversia sulla tolleranza e sull'intolleranza* (Bari: Adriatica Editrice, 1970).

67. Ambrose, *Epist.* 74 (M 40). On the subject of this letter, see Gérard Nauroy, "Ambroise et la question juive à Milan à la fin du IV⁺ siècle. Une nouvelle lecture de l'*Epistula* 74 (Maur. 40) à Théodose," in *Les chrétiens et leurs adversaires dans l'Occident latin au IV⁺ siècle*, ed. Jean-Michel Poinsotte (Rouen: Publications de l'Université de Rouen, 2001), 37–59, reprinted in Gérard Nauroy, *Ambroise de Milan. Ecriture et esthétique, d'une exégèse pastorale* (Bern: Peter Lang, 2003), 217–44.

68. Ambrose, *Epist.* 75 (M 21), 75a (M 21a) = *Sermo Contra Auxentium*, 76 (M 20), 77 (M 22).

69. Ambrose, *De obitu Theodosii* 8–11. Quoted in Cristiana Sogno, Bradley K. Storin, and Edward J. Watts, eds., *Late Antique Letter Collections; A Critical Introduction and Reference Guide* (Oakland: University of California Press, 2017).

70. Tiphaine Moreau, "Le *De obitu Theodosii* d'Ambroise (395): Une refonte des genres littéraires dans le creuset du sermon politique," in *Shifting Genres in Late Antiquity*, ed. Geoffrey Greatrex and Hugh Elton (London: Ashgate, 2014), 27–40.

71. Nauroy, "Qui a organisé le Livre X?," 27.

72. Ambrose, *De obitu Theodosii* 41–51. See Moreau, "Le *De obitu Theodosii* d'Ambroise," 33–34.

73. Cécile Lanéry, *Ambroise de Milan hagiographe* (Paris: Institut d'études augustiniennes, 2008), 39–40.

74. Ambrose, *Epist. extra coll.*, 11 (M 51).14: *scribo manu mea quod solus legas*.

75. Clémentine Bernard-Valette, "*Talis debet esse, qui consilium alteri dat.* L'évêque conseiller du prince: Ambroise de Milan vu par Hincmar de Reims," in "*Nihil veritas erubescit*": *Mélanges offerts à Paul Mattei par ses élèves, collègues et amis*, ed. Clémentine Bernard-Valette, Jérémy Delmulle, and Camille Gerzaguet (Turnhout: Brepols, 2017), 623–35. For a general treatment of the patristic culture of Hincmar of Reims, see Jean Devisse, *Hincmar, archevêque de Reims* (Geneva: Droz, 1975), esp. 3:1074 et seq.

76. Gerzaguet and Mattei, "Les lettres d'Ambroise *extra collectionem*," 69.

77. On this point, see the discussion in Paul Zumthor, *La lettre et la voix. De la "littérature" médiévale* (Paris: Seuil, 1987).

78. Renzo Tosi, *Dictionnaire des sentences latines et grecques*, trans. Rebecca Lenoir (Grenoble: Jérôme Millon, 2010), 1547 (no. 2156).

79. Here again, we would need to set forth the entire argument of this

Notes

fundamental work: Michael Clanchy, *From Memory to Written Record; England, 1066–1309* (London: Edward Arnold, 1979).

80. Alain Boureau, "La norme épistolaire, une invention médiévale," in *La correspondance. Les usages de la lettre au XIXe siècle*, ed. Roger Chartier (Paris: Fayard, 1991), 131–32.

81. +GVILLEMVS: DE POMO: SVPERSTES: / HV(IUS:) ECCL(ESI)E: HOC: OPUS: MVLTA(QUE): ALLIA: F E C I T. See Bertelli, "Percorso tra le testimonianze," 378 (see chap. 7, n. 65).

82. Serena Colombo, "L'ambone della basilica di Sant'Ambrogio," in *L'ambone di Sant'Ambrogio*, ed. Carlo Capponi (Milan: Silvana, 2000), 34–36.

83. Laura Riva, *Alle porte del paradiso. Le sculture del vestibolo di Sant'Ambrogio* (Milan: Università degli Studi di Milano, 2006), 30–34.

84. Annamaria Ambrosiani, "L'altare d'oro e le due comunità santambro-siane," in *L'altare d'oro di Sant'Ambrogio*, ed. Carlo Capponi (Milan: Silvana, 1996), reprinted in *Milano, papato e impero in età medievale. Raccolta di studi*, ed. Maria Pia Alberzoni and Alfredo Lucioni (Milan: Vita e Pensiero, 2003), 263–79, esp. at 271.

85. Ambrosiani, *Milano, papato e impero*, 274.

86. Colombo, "L'ambone della basilica di Sant'Ambrogio," 28.

87. Giovanni Battista Villa, *Le sette chiese o' siano basiliche stationali della città di Milano, seconda Roma*, (Milan: Carlo Antonio Malatesta, 1627), 39.

88. For other examples of reused sarcophagi, see Mario D'Onofrio, ed., *Rila-vorazione dell'antico nel Medioevo* (Rome: Viella, 2003).

89. Alessandro Rovetta, "Memorie e monumenti funerari in S. Ambrogio tra Medioevo e Rinascimento," in Gatti Perer, *La basilica di S. Ambrogio: il tempio inin-terrotto*, 1:277–79.

90. Colombo, "L'ambone della basilica di Sant'Ambrogio," 44–45.

91. Annamaria Ambrosioni, "Corbo (Corbus, Corvus), Martino," in *Dizion-ario biografico degli Italiani*, vol. 28 (Rome: 1983), 770–74; reprinted in Ambrosiani, *Milano, papato e impero*, 203–12.

92. Lucas Burkart et al., *Le trésor au Moyen Âge. Questions et perspectives de recher-che/Der Schatz im Mittelalter. Fragestellungen und Forschungsperspektiven*, (Neuchâ-tel: Institut d'Histoire de l'art et de Muséologie, 2005).

93. Marco Petoletti and Miriam Rita Tessera, "*Custos thesaurorum Sancti Ambrosii*. Le lettere del preposito Martino Corbo e dei suoi corrispondenti (sec-olo XII)," in Gioanni and Cammarosano, *Les correspondances en Italie II*, 201–37.

94. On the effects of Anacletus's schism, which followed the Diet of Worms (1122) and ended the quarrel over investiture, see Myriam Soria, "La propagande

pontificale et sa réception au temps des schismes (XIᵉ-XIIᵉ siècles). Innocent II, Anaclet II: la mémoire d'une guerre de libelles, lectures et débats," in *Comunicazione e propaganda nei secoli XII e XIII*, ed. Rossana Castano, Fortunata Latella, and Tania Sorrenti (Rome: Viella, 2007), 595-612.

95. Petoletti and Tessera, "*Custos thesaurorum Sancti Ambrosii*," 231.

96. Marco Petoletti, "Le lettere di Martino Corbo 'Ambrosiani saporis amicus.' Vicende politiche e filologia nella Milano del sec. XII," in Boucheron and Gioanni, *La mémoire d'Ambroise*, 392-93.

97. Mirella Ferrari, "Due inventari quattrocenteschi della biblioteca capitolare di S. Ambrogio in Milano," in *Filologia umanistica per Gianvito Resta*, ed. Vincenzo Fera and Giacomo Ferraù (Padua: Antenore, 1997), 775-76.

98. ASA M 31 to 35. Two other manuscripts are still preserved in the Vatican's library: Vat. Lat. 268 and 282. See Giuseppe Billanovich and Mirella Ferrari, "La tradizione milanese delle opere di sant'Ambrogio," in *Ambrosius episcopus*, 5-102, esp. 6-26.

99. Francesco Petrarch, *Rerum senilium libri* 2.4.10., trans. Aldo S. Bernardo, Saul Levin, and Rita A. Bernardo, *Letters of Old Age* (New York: Italica Press, 2014). Written in 1364, the letter was most probably addressed to Giovanni Quatrario.

100. Jack Goody, "Canonization in Oral and Literature Traditions," in *The Power of the Written Tradition* (Washington D. C.: Smithsonian Press, 2000), 131.

101. Michel Zimmermann, ed., *Auctor & auctoritas. Invention et conformisme dans l'écriture médiévale. Actes du colloque de Saint-Quentin-en-Yvelines (14-16 juin 1999)*, Mémoires et documents 59 (Paris: École des Chartes, 2001).

102. Maurice Olender, "Un fantôme dans la bibliothèque," in *L'homme qui lit*, special issue, *Revue de la BnF* 41 (2012): 21-22; reprinted as the eponymous essay in Maurice Olender, *Un fantôme dans la bibliothèque* (Paris: Seuil, 2017), 185-92.

103. I rely here mainly on the excellent summation by Camille Gerzaguet, "La 'mémoire textuelle' d'Ambroise de Milan en Italie: manuscrits, centres de diffusion, voies de transmission (Vᵉ-XIIᵉ siècle)," in Boucheron and Gioanni, *La mémoire d'Ambroise*, 211-33.

104. *Arnulf von Mailand. Liber gestorum recentium*.

105. Mirella Ferrari, "La trasmissione dei testi in Italia nord-occidentale. Centri di trasmissione: Monza, Pavia, Milano, Bobbio," in *La cultura antica nell'Occidente latino dal VII all'XI secolo. Atti della Settimana di studio (Spoleto, 18-24 aprile 1974)* (Spoleto: Centro italiano di studi sull'alto medioevo, 1975), 1:303-20.

106. Michael Gorman, "From Isidore to Claudius of Turin: The Works of

Ambrose on Genesis in the Early Middle Ages," *Revue des études augustiniennes* 45 (1999): 121–38.

107. These two manuscripts are preserved to this day in the Reims municipal library (Mss. 376 and 377). See Devisse, *Hincmar archêvêque de Reims*, 1475–76; and Dominique Alibert, "La transmission des textes patristiques à l'époque carolingienne," *Revue des sciences philosophiques et théologiques* 97 (2007): 13.

108. Roger Gryson and Dominique Szmatula, "Les commentaires patristiques sur Isaïe d'Origène à Jérôme," *Revue des études augustiniennes* 36 (1990): 5–7.

109. Veronika von Büren, "Ambroise de Milan dans la bibliothèque de Cluny," *Scriptorium* 47, (1993): 127–65.

110. Ambroise de Milan, *La fuite du siècle*, ed. and trans. Camille Gerzaguet, Sources chrétiennes 576 (Paris: Cerf, 2015).

111. Ambroise de Milan, *La fuite du siècle*, 145 ("Introduction").

112. Gérard Nauroy, "Vers un nouveau texte critique du *De Jacob et uita beata* d'Ambroise de Milan," in *Lire et éditer aujourd'hui Ambroise de Milan. Actes du colloque de l'Université de Metz (20–21 mai 2005)*, ed. Gérard Nauroy (Bern: Peter Lang, 2007), 37–73.

113. Lama El Horr, "La tradition manuscrite du *De bono mortis* de saint Ambroise," in Nauroy, *Lire et éditer aujourd'hui*, 75–106.

114. Camille Gerzaguet, "Le *De fuga saeculi* d'Ambroise de Milan: transmission, diffusion et circulation de la tradition manuscrite (ixe–xiiᵉ)," *Segno & Testo: International Journal of Manuscripts and Text Transmission* 12 (2014): 83–151.

115. Gérard Nauroy, "Les 'Vies des patriarches' d'Ambroise de Milan: de Cassiodore au débat critique moderne," *Recherches augustiniennes* 54 (2008): 43–61; and Camille Gerzaguet, "Ambroise, Cassiodore et la série dite *De patriarchis*," *Revue d'études augustiniennes et patristiques* 59 (2013): 275–98.

116. Monica Pedralli, *Novo, grande, coverto e ferrato. Gli inventari di biblioteca e la cultura a Milano nel Quattrocento* (Milan: Vita e Pensiero, 2002).

117. Lanéry, *Ambroise de Milan hagiographe*, 520.

118. For a recent assessment of this text, see the essays gathered in Theodore S. de Bruyn, Stephen A. Cooper, and David H. Hunter, eds., *Ambrosiaster's Commentary on the Pauline Epistles: Romans* (Atlanta: Society of Biblical Literature, 2017).

119. René Hoven, "Note sur Erasme et les auteurs anciens," *L'Antiquité tardive* 38 (1969): 169–74.

120. On this point, see the thinking of Etienne Anheim, "Anonyme," in *Mots médiévaux offerts à Ruedi Imbach*, ed. Iñigo Atucha et al., (Porto: FIDEM, 2011), 63–72.

Notes

121. Sophie Lunn-Rockliffe, *Ambrosiaster's Political Theology* (Oxford: Oxford University Press, 2007).

122. Ambrosiaster, *Contre les païens (Question sur l'Ancien et le Nouveau Testament 114) et Sur le destin (Question sur l'Ancien et le Nouveau Testament 115)*, ed. and trans. Marie-Pierre Bussières, Sources chrétiennes 512 (Paris: Cerf, 2007); trans. anonymously as *Questions on the Old and New Testaments by Ambrosiaster*, ed. John Litteral (n.p.: CreateSpace Independent Publishing Platform, 2018).

123. Eligius Dekkers, "Le succès étonnant des écrits pseudo-augustiniens au Moyen Âge," in *Fälschungen im Mittelalter. Internationaler Kongress der Monumenta Germaniae Historica, München, 16.–19. September 1986* (Hanover: Hahn, 1988), 5:361–68.

124. Cited by Jean-Louis Quantin, "L'Augustin du xviie siècle? Questions de corpus et de canon," in *Augustin au xviie siècle. Actes du Colloque organisé par Carlo Ossola a Collège de France les 30 septembre et 1er octobre 2004*, ed. Laurence Devillairs (Florence: Leo S. Olschki Editore, 2007), 56.

125. Alain Boureau, "L'usage des textes patristiques dans les controverses scolastiques," *Revue des sciences philosophiques et théologiques* 91 (2007): 42.

126. This point is argued in Patrick Boucheron and Stéphane Gioanni, "Gouverner, prier et combattre avec les Pères en Italie (ve–xviiie siècle). Pour une histoire politique de la mémoire d'Ambroise," in Boucheron and Gioanni, *La mémoire d'Ambroise de Milan*, 7–27; esp. 9–16.

127. Bernard Meunier, "Genèse de la notion de 'Pères de l'Église' aux ive et ve siècles," *Revue des sciences philosophiques et théologiques* 93 (2009): 315–30.

128. Stéphane Gioanni, "Les listes d'auteurs 'à recevoir' et 'à ne pas recevoir' dans la formation du canon patristique: le *decretum gelasianum* et les origines de la 'censure' ecclésiastique," in *Compétition et sacré au Haut Moyen Âge: entre médiation et exclusion*, ed. Philippe Depreux, François Bougard, and Régine Le Jan (Turnhout: Brepols, 2015), 17–38.

129. The decretal *Gloriosus Deus* was published as part of the bull *Sacrosanctae Romanae ecclesiae* on March 3, 1298, but was preceded by directives "of local authority" on September 20, 1295: *Corpus iuris canonici II*, ed. Emile Friedberg (Lipsiae: 1922), col. 934 et seq. and col. 1059 et seq. See on this point Umberto Betti, "A proposito del conferimento del titolo di Dottore della Chiesa," *Antonianum* 63 (1988): 278–91.

130. Jean-Louis Quantin, *Le catholicisme classique et les Pères de l'Église. Un retour aux sources (1669–1713)* (Paris: Institut d'études augustiniennes, 1999), 31.

131. François Dolbeau, "La formation du Canon des Pères, du ive au vie siècle,"

in *Les réceptions des Pères de l'Eglise au Moyen Age: le devenir de la tradition ecclésiale, Actes du Congrès du Centre Sèvres–Facultés jésuites de Paris (11–14 juin 2008)*, ed. Rainer Berndt and Michel Fédou (Münster: Aschendorff, 2013), 1:29.

132. Éric Rebillard, "Augustin et ses autorités: l'élaboration de l'argument patristique au cours de la controverse pélagienne," *Studia patristica* 38 (2001): 245–63.

133. Bartolomeo Carusi, *Divi Ambrosii milleloquium* (Lyon, 1556). See Etienne Anheim, *Clément VI au travail. Lire, écrire, prêcher au XIVᵉ siècle* (Paris: Publications de la Sorbonne, 2014), 108. Ambrose is strongly represented in the library of Pierre Roger, the future Clement VI: of the 325 titles in a 1314 listing, twenty-eight were by Ambrose, or twice as many as by Jerome, placing him second in the rank of authors, though at a considerable distance behind Augustine, who had 130 titles and accounted for 40 percent of the total collection (ibid., 94). Ambrose is nonetheless cited less frequently than Jerome in the sermons of Pierre Roger/Clement VI (ibid., 142).

134. Pierre Chambert-Protat, Franz Dolvek, and Camille Gerzaguet, eds., *Les douze compilations pauliniennes de Florus de Lyon: un carrefour des traditions patristiques au ixe siècle*, CEFR 524 (Rome: École française de Rome, 2016).

135. According to a hypothesis developed by Camille Gerzaguet, based on the lessons in a twelfth-century manuscript (Dijon, Bibliothèque municipale, 125), which might be drawn from one of the copies in the library of Florus. See Camille Gerzaguet, "La *Collectio* ambrosienne de Florus de Lyon: sources d'une compilation et enjeux d'une méthode de travail," *Mélanges de l'Ecole française de Rome* 123 (2011): 531–43.

136. Guenée, *Histoire et culture historique*, 211–14.

137. Andrey Mitrofanov, *L'ecclésiologie d'Anselme de Lucques (1036–1086) au service de Grégoire VII: Genèse, contenu et impact de sa 'Collection canonique'* (Turnhout: Brepols, 2015).

138. Roberto Bellini, "I frammenti di Ambrogio nelle fonti canonistiche. Nuove prospettive di studio," in Boucheron and Gioanni, *La mémoire d'Ambroise*, 329–65, esp. 331–36.

139. Alain de Libera, *Penser au Moyen Âge* (Paris: Seuil, 1991), 67.

140. Jean-Baptiste Brenet, *Averroès l'inquiétant* (Paris: Les Belles Lettres, 2015), 17.

141. I am obviously referring here to Michel Foucault, "Qu'est-ce qu'un auteur?" in *Dits et écrits. 1954–1988* (Paris: Gallimard, 1994), 1:789–821, trans. Donald F. Bouchard and Sherry Simon, "What Is an Author?" in *Language, Counter-Memory, Practice*, ed. Donald F. Bouchard (Ithaca, NY: Cornell University Press,

1977), 113–38; and the commentary on this famous text in Roger Chartier, *Culture écrite et société. L'ordre des livres (XIVᵉ–XVIIIᵉ siècle)* (Paris: Albin Michel, 1996), 45–80.

142. All that follows draws on the work of Marie-Dominique Chenu, "Auctor, actor, autor," *Archivum latinatis Medii Ævi (Bulletin du Cange)* (1927): 81–86.

CHAPTER TEN:
SEEING AMBROSE AGAIN

1. Lynda Dematteo, "La Lega Nord: entre volonté de subversion et désir de légitimité," *Ethnologie française* 31 (2001): 143–52. See also Lynda Dematteo, *L'idiotie en politique: Subversion et néo-populisme en Italie* (Paris: Éditions de la Maison des sciences de l'homme, 2007), 13 et seq.

2. See, for a French-language point of entry, Pierre Racine, *La bataille de Legnano, 29 mai 1176* (Clermont-Ferrand: Lemme, 2013). But the authoritative work on this is now Paolo Grillo, *Legnano 1176. Una battaglia per la libertà* (Rome-Bari: Laterza, 2011).

3. Grillo, *Legnano 1176*, 154.

4. Dematteo, "La Lega Nord," 144.

5. Piero Brunello, "Pontida," in *I luoghi della memoria. Simboli e miti dell'Italia unita*, ed. Mario Isnenghi (Rome-Bari: Laterza, 1996), 15–28.

6. Lynda Dematteo, "Anthropologie de l'*imbroglio*. Formes de la conflictualité politique dans les régimes de l'apparence," *Vacarme* 55 (2011): 50–53.

7. Gilles Deleuze, "Qu'est-ce que fonder?," a secondary-school course given at the Lycée Louis le Grand in 1956–57, available online at www.webdeleuze.com, trans. Arjen Kleinherenbrink; *What is Grounding?*, from transcribed notes taken by Pierre Lefebvre, ed. Tony Yanick, Jason Adams, and Mohammad Salemy (Grand Rapids, MI: &&& Publishing, the New Centre for Research and Practice, 2015), 175–76. On the Deleuzian criticism of the idea of founding, starting with *Différence et répétition* (1968), trans. Paul Patton, *Difference and Repetition* (New York: Columbia University Press, 1994), see Arnaud Bouaniche, *Gilles Deleuze, une introduction* (Paris: Pocket, 2007), 103 et seq.

8. Dominique Iogna-Prat, *La Maison Dieu. Une histoire monumentale de l'Église au Moyen Âge* (Paris: Seuil, 2006), 542 et seq.

9. I draw here mainly on the classic analyses by Luca Beltrami, "I bassorilievi commemorativi della Lega Lombarda gia esistentei alla antica Porta Romana," *Archivio storico lombardo* 22 (1895): 395–416; and Paolo Mezzanotte, "Degli archi di Porta Romana," *Archivio storico lombardo* 37 (1910): 423–38; updated by the

analyses of Andrea Von Hülsen, "À propos de la *Porta Romana* de Milan: dans quelle mesure la sculpture de l'Italie du Nord reflète-t-elle certains aspects de l'histoire communale?," *Cahiers de civilisation médiévale* 35 (1992): 147-53. For a more thorough analysis of this iconographic program, and for a comparison with that of the Church of San Zeno of Verona, see Andrea Von Hülsen-Esch, *Romanische Skulptur in Oberitalien als Reflex der kommunalen Entwicklung im 12. Jahrhundert. Untersuchungen zu Mailand und Verona*, Artefact 8 (Berlin: Akademie Verlag, 1994); and Andrea Von Hülsen-Esch, "Les saints patrons des villes au service des communes," in *Crises de l'image religieuse/Krisen religiöser Kunst*, ed. Olivier Christin and Dario Gamboni (Paris: Éditions de la Maison des sciences de l'homme, 1999), 75-92. See also the work of Michele C. Ferrari, "Die Porta Romana in Mailand (1171). Bild, Raum und Inschrift," in *Literatur und Wandmalerei I. Erscheinungsformen höfischer Kultur und ihre Träger im Mittelalter*, ed. Eckart Conrad Lutz, Johanna Thali, and René Wetzel (Tübingen: Niemeyer, 2002), 115-51.

10. See the overview presented in Pietro Silanos and Kai-Michel Sprenger, eds., *La distruzione di Milano (1162). Un luogo di memorie* (Milan: Vita e Pensiero, 2015).

11. *Ottonis Episcopi Frisingensis et Rahewini Gesta Frederici seu rectius Cronica* 2.16, ed. Franz-Josef Schmale (Darmstadt, 1974), 312-13. Otto of Freising, *The Deeds of Frederick Barbarossa*, trans. Charles Christopher Mierow (New York: Columbia University Press, 1953), 128-29.

12. From a superabundant literature, I would mention Paolo Grillo, *Le guerre del Barbarossa. I comuni contro l'imperatore* (Rome-Bari: Laterza, 2018).

13. Maria Pia Alberzoni, "La distruzione di Milano nella memoria comunale (secc. XII–XIII)," in Silanos and Sprenger, *La distruzione di Milano*, 43.

14. Holger Berwinkel, *Verwüsten Und Belagern: Friedrich Barbarossas Krieg Gegen Mailand (1158–1162)* (Tübingen: Niemeyer, 2007), esp. 189-217, on the destruction of the city.

15. Gian Piero Bognetti, "La condizione giuridica dei cittadini milanesi dopo la distruzione di Milano (1162-1167)," *Rivista di storia del diritto italiano* 1 (1928): 311-35.

16. Alberzoni, "La distruzione di Milano," 45.

17. The section ahead draws on the edition and commentary of Annamaria Ambrosioni, "Il testamento del prete Ariprando (1166). Note sulla situazione dei Milanesi dopo la distruzione della città," *Ricerche storiche della Chiesa ambrosiana* 2, Archivio ambrosiano 21 (Milan: 1971), 116-31, reprinted in Ambrosioni, *Milano, papato e impero*, 41-56.

18. Patrick Gilli and Jean-Pierre Guilhembet, eds., *Le châtiment des villes dans les espaces méditerranéens (Antiquité, Moyen Âge, Époque moderne)*, Studies in European Urban History (1100–1800) 26 (Turnhout: Brepols, 2012).

19. Patrick. J. Geary, "The Magi and Milan," in *Living with the Dead in the Middle Ages*, (Ithaca, NY: Cornell University Press, 1994), 243–56. See also Richard C. Trexler, *The Journey of the Magi: Meanings in History of a Christian Story* (Princeton, NJ: Princeton University Press, 2016, originally published 1997).

20. About this ritual, see Jean-Marie Moeglin, "*Harmiscara / Harmschar / Hachée*. Le dossier des rituels d'humiliation et de soumission au Moyen Âge," *Archivum latinitatis medii Aevi, Bulletin Du Cange* 64 (1994): 11–65.

21. *Ottonis Morenae et continuatorum Historia Frederici I*, ed. Ferdinand Güterbock, MGH, Scriptores rerum Germanicarum, Nova series 7 (Weimar, 1930), 157: *Precepitque Laudensibus, ut portam Orientalem, que vulgo Arienza dicitur, totam destruerent; Cremonensibus vero portam Romanam demoliendam commisit, Papiensibus portam Ticinensem, Novariensibus portam Vercellinam, Cumensibus portam Cumacinam, illis vero de Seprio ac de Martexana portam Novam.*

22. Racine, *La bataille de Legnano*, 61–66.

23. Galvano Fiamma, *Chronica Mediolani, sive Manipulus florum*, ed. Ludovico Antonio Muratori, *RIS* 11 (Milan, 1729), col. 650–51. It was in another chronicle (the *Chronicon minus*) that our prolix and imaginative Dominican would invent the character of Alberto da Giussano: *Galvanei Fiammae ordinis praedicatorum Chronicon minus*, ed. Andrea Cerutti, *Miscellanea di storia italiana* 7 (Turin, 1869), 718–19.

24. Renaud Villard, "Le héros introuvable; les récits de fondations de cités en Italie: xive–xvie siècles," *Histoire, économie et société* 19, no. 1 (2000), 21.

25. I draw here mainly on Patrick Gilli, *Au miroir de l'humanisme. Les représentations de la France dans la culture savante italienne à la fin du Moyen Âge*, BEFAR 296 (Rome: École française de Rome, 1997), 346 et seq.

26. Titus Livius, *The History of Rome* V: 34: 9, trans. George Baker (New York: 1832). https://oll.libertyfund.org/titles/1754

27. *Il "Chronicon" di Benzo d'Alessandria e i classici latini all'inizio del xiv secolo: edizione critica del libro xxiv "De moribus et vita philosophorum,"* ed. Marco Petoletti (Milan: Vita e Pensiero, 2000); also, Giovanni di Cermenate, *Historia*, ed. L. A. Ferrai (Rome, 1889). See Gilli, *Au miroir de l'humanisme*, 347–49 and 351–52.

28. Paolo Tomea, "Per Galvano Fiamma," *Italia medioevale e umanistica* 39 (1996): 423–36.

29. While Galvano Fiamma is certainly one of the most important historians

of the trecento, the interpretation of his work is hampered by the paucity of critical editions. Most of his works – and they are many and almost always contradictory – have been published badly or not at all. But see this recent edition of *La Cronaca estravagante di Galvano Fiamma*, ed. Sante Ambrogio Céngarle Parisi and Massimilano David (Milan: Casa del Manzoni, 2013), with a copious introduction, 25–196, addressing the manuscript tradition of Fiamma's work.

30. The expression appears in a letter from Luca Grimaldi, *podestà* of Milan, to Gregorio di Montelongo, the papal legate, in 1242: *Gli atti del Comune di Milano nel secolo XIII*, vol. 1, 1217–1250, ed. Maria Franca Baroni (Milan: Capriolo, 1976), 601–2, no. 165. See Alberzoni, "La distruzione di Milano," 53.

31. Fiamma, *Chronica Mediolani, sive Manipulus florum*, col. 550: *ipsam civitatem Albam nominavit et nomen antiquum cilicet Mediolanum, abstulit.*

32. Fiamma, *Chronica Mediolani*, col. 585.

33. Gilli, *Au miroir de l'humanisme*, 350–56.

34. I reprise here briefly the hypothesis more fully developed in Patrick Boucheron, "La violence du fondateur. Récits de fondation et souvenir ambrosien à Milan (XIIIe–XVe siècle)," in *"Ab urbe condita." Fonder et refonder la ville: récits et représentations (second Moyen Âge – premier XVIe siècle). Actes du colloque international de Pau (14–15–16 mai 2009)*, ed. Véronique Lamazou-Duplan (Pau: Presses universitaires de Pau et des pays de l'Adour, 2011), 127–45.

35. On the theme of Milan as a *secunda Roma*, see, in a general way, Chiara Frugoni, *Una lontana città. Sentimenti e immagini nel Medioevo* (Turin: Einaudi, 1985), 61 et seq.

36. Antonio Astesano, *Carmen de varietate fortunae, sive de vita et gestis civium astensium*, ed. Ludovico Antonio Muratori, RIS 14 (Milan, 1729), 1029, quoted by Villard, "Le héros introuvable," 11.

37. Paolo Grillo, "Una politica della memoria: Milano fra Roma antica, Pavia et Federico Barbarossa," in *La politique de l'histoire en Italie. Arts et pratiques du remploi (XIVe–XVIIe siècle)*, ed. Caroline Callard, Elsabeth Crouzet-Pavan, and Alain Tallon (Paris: PUPS, 2014), 19–33.

38. Massimiano David, "'Urbs veneranda nimis.' Urbanistica, epigrafia e religione nella rifondazione di Milano, 1171–1233," *Temporis signa. Archeologia della tarda antichità* 10 (2015): 67–84.

39. Grillo, "Una politica della memoria," 24. An epigraphic and prosopographical study of the inscriptions on the *porta Romana* is forthcoming from Marialuiza Botazzi.

40. Grillo, "Una politica della memoria," 28–29.

41. Von Hülsen, "À propos de la *Porta Romana* de Milan," 149 et seq. See also Jean Wirth, *L'image à l'époque romane* (Paris: Cerf, 1999), 170.

42. This parallel with defamatory painting should not be pushed too far, however, in part because of the formal difference (a sculpted image), but also because the message of infamy projected by the *porta Romana* has no legal standing–it is intended to support a campaign of political messaging and not to limit the emperor's actual powers. See Gherardo Ortalli, *La peinture infamante du XIIIᵉ au XVIᵉ siècle*, trans. Fabienne Pasquet and Daniel Arasse (Paris: Gérard Montfort, 1994), 32-33.

43. Galvano Fiamma claimed that the Roman-era arch of triumph, destroyed to make way for the commune's walls, bore a fierce inscription: QUI VULT MODICO TEMPORE VIVERE MEDIOLANUM INHABITET, UBI VIVES PRO LEGIBUS ET IURA IN OSSIBUS DESCRIBUNTUR ("Whoever would live briefly may live in Milan, where force belongs to the law, and right is written in men's bones"), *Cronaca estravagante*, 298. If this is more than a literary invention (Benzo d'Alessandria quotes almost the same inscription), this warning to the city's enemies would have been replicated on the *porta Romana*. See David, "Urbs veneranda nimis," 67-68).

44. FATA VETANT ULTRA PROCEDERE STABIMUS ERGO / HII MEDIOLANO LAPSO DUM FORTE RESURGIT SUPOSUERE. This nearly repeats a verse from the Aeneid (8.5.398): *nec pater omnipotens Troiaü nec fata vetant stare* (For neither Jove almighty nor the Fates forbade Troy to endure [trans. Robert Fitzgerald, New York: Random House, 1983, 243]), thus linking Milan to the fate of ancient Troy. The inscriptions of the *porta Romana* have been published in *Iscrizioni delle chiese e delle altri edifici di Milano dal secolo VIII ai gioni nostril*, ed. Vincenzo Forcella (Milan: 1892), 10:3-6.

45. REDENTES GRATES CHRISTO SUBEAMUS IN URBEM / ISTUD SCULPSIT OPUS GIRARDUS POLICE DOCTO / CHRISTUM LAUDENTES PATRIAS REMEAMUS IN EDES.

46. Jean-Claude Schmitt, "Le seuil et la porte. A propos de la *Porta Romana* de Milan," in *Marquer la ville. Signes, traces, empreintes du pouvoir (XIIIᵉ–XVIᵉ siècle)*, ed. Patrick Boucheron and Jean-Philippe Genet, Le pouvoir symbolique en Occident (1300-1640) 8 (Paris-Rome: Publications de la Sorbonne–Publications de l'École française de Rome, 2013), 172.

47. Such, at least, is the seductive hypothesis proposed by Marialuisa Bottazzi, "*Frater Jacobus, Jacobus abbas*. Impero, cistercensi e celebrazione monumentale nel conflitto milanese, 1160-1183," *Studi medievali* 48 (2007): 271-306.

48. Top: HOC OPUS ANSELMUS FORMAVIT DEDALUS ALTER. Just above the

soldiers: FACTUM DECLARAT AMICOS / DANS DEUS AUT TOLLENS REDDENS. ESTO BENEDITUS [...] PSALLIMUS ECCE TIBI [...] DEUS URBE RECEPTA.

49. Jean-Claude Schmitt, "Le seuil et la porte," 173.

50. Paulinus of Milan, *Vita Ambrosii* 8.1, Eng. trans. in Boniface Ramsey, *Ambrose: The Early Church Fathers*, ed. Carol Harrison (London and New York: Routledge, 1997), 199.

51. Henri Focillon, *The Art of the West in the Middle Ages*, (Ithaca, NY: Cornell University Press, 1980), 2:107.

52. Ferdinand Güterbock, "Le lettere del notaio imperiale Burcardo intorno alla politica del Barbarossa nello scisma e alla distruzione di Milano," *Bolletino dell'istituto storico italiano per il medioevo* 61 (1949): 63.

53. See, in a general way, Monique Zerner, ed., *Inventer l'hérésie? Discours polémiques et pouvoirs avant l'inquisition*, Collection du centre d'études médiévales de Nice 2 (Nice: Presses Universitaires de Nice, 1998).

54. Von Hülsen-Esch, "Les saints patrons des villes," 90.

55. Alessia Trivellone, *L'hérétique imaginé. Hétérodoxie et iconographie dans l'Occident médiéval, de l'époque carolingienne à l'Inquisition* (Turnhout: Brepols, 2009), 193–202.

56. Von Hülsen-Esch, *Romanische Skulptur in Oberitalien*, 36–118.

57. On this subject, see Dominique Iogna-Prat, *Ordonner et exclure. Cluny et la société chrétienne face à l'hérésie, au judaïsme et à l'islam (1000–1150)* (Paris: Aubier, 1998).

58. See Shlomo Simonsohn, *The Jews in the Duchy of Milan* (Jerusalem: Publications of the Israel Academy of Sciences and Humanities, 1982), 1:XVI; and, for general background, R. I. Moore, *The Formation of a Persecuting Society: Authority and Deviance in Western Europe, 950 to 1250*, 2nd ed. (Malden, Mass.: Blackwell, 2007).

59. Gavin I. Langmuir, "From Ambrose of Milan to Emicho of Leiningen: the transformation of hostility against Jews in northern Christendom," in *Gli Ebrei nell'alto medioevo*, Settimane di studio del Centro italiano di studi sull'alto medioevo 26 (Spoleto: Centro italiano di studi sull'alto medioevo, 1980), 1:327–35.

60. Ambrose, *Epist.* 74 (M40). From the abundant literature on this text and its interpretation, see Gérard Nauroy, "Ambroise et la question juive à Milan à la fin du IVe siècle. Une nouvelle lecture de l'*Epistula* 74 (=40) à Théodose," in *Les Chrétiens face à leurs adversaires dans l'Occident latin au IVe siècle*, ed. Jean-Michel Poinsotte (Rouen: Publications de l'université de Rouen, 2001), 37–89.

61. Pierluigi Lanfranchi, "Des paroles aux actes. La destruction des syna-

gogues et leur transformation en églises," in *Chrétiens persécuteurs. Destructions, exclusions, violences religieuses au IVᵉ siècle*, ed. Marie-Françoise Baslez (Paris: Albin Michel, 2014), 311–35, esp. 317–19.

62. *Codex Theodosianus* 16.8.9: "It is well known that the Jewish sect is not forbidden by any law…Therefore, may your sublime majesty repress with adequate severity the excesses of those who, in the name of the Christian religion,…attempt to destroy and pillage the synagogues."

63. Pierre Maraval, *Théodose le Grand. Le pouvoir et la foi* (Paris: Fayard, 2009), 223–27.

64. McLynn, *Ambrose of Milan*, 298–315.

65. Ambrose, *Epist.* 74 (M40).8.

66. Paul Mattéi, "Ambroise antijuif dans l'affaire de la synagogue de Callinicum? Hésitations et errements de l'historiographie (XVIIᵉ–XXᵉ s.). Essai de mise au point," in *L'antijudaïsme des Pères. Mythe et/ou réalité?*, ed. Jean-Marie Auwers, Régis Burnet, and Didier Luciani (Paris: Beauchesne, 2017), 77–99.

67. Ambrose, *Epist.* 74 (M40).5, trans. H. de Romestin, *Ambrose: Selected Works and Letters*, in Philip Schaff and Henry Wace, eds., *Nicene and Post-Nicene Fathers*, series 2, vol. 10 (Grand Rapids, MI: WM. B. Eerdmans Publishing, n.d.). https://archive.org/stream/St.AmbroseSelectedWorksAndLetters/st_ambrose_selected_works_and_letters_djvu.txt

68. See, for example, *De vita et meritis Ambrosii* 73–74, in *Le fonti latine su Sant'Ambrogio*, ed. Gabriele Banterle (Rome: Città Nuova Editrice, 1991), 210.

69. Paulinus of Milan, *Vita Ambrosii* 15.

70. New York, Pierpont Morgan Library, ms. 492, fol. 84r.

71. Von Hülsen-Esch, "Les saints patrons des villes au service des communes," 90.

72. Giuseppe Calligaris, "Il flagello di sant'Ambrogio e le leggende delle lotte ariane," in *Ambrosiana. Scritti varii pubblicati nel XV centenario della morte di S. Ambrogio* (Milan, 1897), 1–63.

73. Courcelle, *Recherches sur saint Ambroise*, 158–59.

74. Enrico Cattaneo, "Il flagello di sant'Ambrogio. Lo sviluppo di una leggenda," in *Studi storici in onore di Ottorino Bertolini* (Pisa: Pacini, 1972), 1:93–103.

75. Von Hülsen-Esch, *Romanische Skulptur in Oberitalien*, 86–90.

76. Ambrose, *Contra Auxentium* 23 (PL 16, 1014b). See chap. 9n68.

77. All this builds on Enrico Cattaneo, "Galdino della Sala, cardinale arcivescovo di Milano," in *Contributi dell'Istituto di Storia medioevale, II, Raccolta di studi in memoria di Sergio Mochi Onory* (Milan: Pubblicazioni dell'Università Cattolica

del S. Cuore, 1972), 356–83, repr. in Enrico Cattaneo, *La Chiesa di Ambrogio. Studi di storia e di liturgia* (Milan: Vita e Pensiero, 1984), 49–76.

78. *Liber notitiae sanctorum Mediolani. Manoscritto della Biblioteca Capitolare di Milano*, ed. Marco Magistretti and Ugo Monneret de Villard (Milan, 1917), col. 160–61. On this text, see now Paolo Tomea, "San Giorgio in Crimea. Per una nuova edizione del *Liber notitiae sanctorum mediolani* (con una nota sulla papesse Giovanna)," *Aevum* 73, no. 2 (1999): 423–56.

79. Annamaria Ambrosioni, "Alessandro III e la Chiesa ambrosiana," in *Miscellanea Rolando Bandinelli, papo Alessandro III*, ed. Filippo Liotta (Siena: Accademia senese degli Intronati, 1986), 3–41, repr. in Ambrosioni, *Milano, papato e impero*, 428–34.

80. On this point, see Marialuisa Bottazzi, "La porta Romana (1171). Un luogo della memoriae della distruzione della città," in Pietro Silanos and Kai-Michel Sprenger, eds., *La distruzione di Milano (1162). Un luogo di memorie* (Milan: Vita e Pensiero, 2015), 74–76.

81. Italo Allegri, "Luoghi di culto santambrosiani. Le chiese e la devozione," in *Ambrogio vescovo di Milano (397–1997). Atti del Convegno di Cassago Brianza, 29 agosto–7 settembre 1997* (Lecco: Associazione Storico Culturale S. Agostino, 1999), 343.

82. *Notitia Cleri Mediolanensis de anno 1398 circa ipsius immunitatem*, ed. Marco Magistretti, *Archivio storico lombardo* 27 (1900), 9–57 and 257–304, at 259.

83. Reading the acts of Leone da Perego, the first Franciscan to become archbishop of Milan, one can track how the devotions of Francis and Ambrose became enmeshed. See, for example, *Gli atti dell'arcivescovo e della curia arcivescovile di Milano nel sec. XIII. Leone da Perego (1241–1257), sede vacante (1257 ottobre – 1262 luglio)*, ed. Maria Franca Baroni (Milan: Università degli Studi, 2002), the indulgence granted on April 23, 1247, (document 43, p. 50): *Universis et singulis quolibet die lune convenientibus ad eorum preicationem in locum Sancti Francisci vere penitentibus et confessis quadraginta dies ex iniuncta sibi pentitentia auctoritate sancte Mediolanensis ecclesie confisi de omnipotentis Dei clementia et meritis patroni nostri beati Ambrosii misericorditer relaxamus.*

PART FOUR:
AMBROSE'S FOOT SOLDIERS

1. Petrarch, *Rerum familiarium 19.5.9: Unum tibi preterea, quod non in ultimis licet in ultima epystole parte posuerim: vicinus erit Ambrosius. Vale.* See Francesco Petrarch, *Letters on Familiar Matters*, trans. Aldo S. Bernardo (New York: Italica Press, 2005), 3:87.

2. Petrarch, *Rerum familiarium* 17.10.14: *Ambrosii basilica sola est inter domum quam inhabito, et cappellam perexiguam, ubi in archano conflictu dissidentium curarum tandem victor Augustinus, sacro fonte ab eodem Ambrosio viteque prioris solicitudine liberatus est.* Petrarch, *Letters on Familiar Matters*, 3:32.

3. Giuseppe Frasso, Giuseppe Velli, and Maurizio Vitale, *Petrarca e la Lombardia. Atti del Convegno di Studi, 22–23 maggio 2003*, Studi sul Petrarca 31 (Padua: Antenore, 2005).

4. Petrarch, *Rerum senilium* 6.3: *Pro libro autem beatissimi Patris atque hospitis olim mei Ambrosii gratias ago…* See Francesco Petrarch, *Letters of Old Age*, trans. Aldo S. Bernardo, Saul Levin, and Reta A. Bernardo (New York: Italica Press, 2005), 1:194.

5. Petrarch, *Rerum senilium* 1.5.35: *Nec miraberis hoc auctore uti me, qui iam prope decennium mediolanensis totoque quinquennio suus hospes fuerim.* Petrarch, *Letters of Old Age*, 1:21.

6. Alberto Cadili, *Giovanni Visconti arcivescovo di Milano (1342–1354)* (Milan: Edizioni Biblioteca Francescana, 2007); and Alberto Cadili, "Giovanni Visconti committente: un quadro documentario," in *Modernamente antichi. Modelli, identità, tradizione nella Lombardia del Tre e Quaatrocento*, ed. Pier Nicola Pagliara and Serena Romano (Rome: Viella, 2014), 45-70.

7. Petrarch, *Rerum familiarium* 16.11.9: *Unum tibi preterea, quod non in ultimis licet in ultima epystole parte posuerim: vicinus erit Ambrosius. Vale.* Petrarch, *Letters on Familiar Matters*, 2:318.

8. Marcello Simonetta, *Rinascimento segreto. Il mondo del Segretario da Petrarca a Machiavelli* (Milan: FrancoAngeli, 2004), 30-31.

9. On this use of the Dantean past in the controversy between Boccaccio and Petrarch concerning the political nature of the signory, see Karlheinz Stierle, "Le monde de Dante et le monde de Pétrarque," *Po&sie* 160-61 (2017): 205-22.

10. Petrarch, *De vita solitaria* 2.8.2; trans. Jacob Zeitlin, *The Life of Solitude* (n.p.: University of Illinois Press, 1924), 278. On this point, see Etienne Anheim, "Pétrarque: l'écriture comme philosophie," *Revue de synthèse* 129 (2008): 587-609.

11. On this social reading of Petrarch's intellectual adventure, see the writings of Etienne Anheim, "Culture de cour et science de l'État au XIVe siècle," *Actes de la recherche en sciences sociales* 133, *La science de l'État* (2000): 40-47; and Etienne Anheim, "L'individu, l'écriture et la prière. Une lecture de Pétrarque," in *L'individu au Moyen Âge*, ed. Brigitte Bedos-Rezak and Dominique Iogna-Prat (Paris: Flammarion, 2005), 187-209.

12. Petrarch, *Rerum senilium* 2.4: *Ego ipse in magno quodam vetustoque volumine*

quod Ambrosiana mediolanensis habet Ecclesia, ubi scriptorum Ambrosii bona pars est, librum stili alterius Ambrosio datum vidi. Petrarch, *Letters of Old Age*, 1:67. The letter was written in 1364, probably to Giovanni Quatrario.

13. Petrarch, *Rerum familiarium* 19.16.17: *Sic iste sanctissimus hospes meus, ut consolationis plurimum corporali sua presentia atque, ut reor, spirituali etiam prestat auxilio, sic tedii at fastidii multum eripit.* Petrarch, *Letters on Familiar Matters*, 3:109.

14. Petrarch, *Rerum familiarium* 16.11.12–13: *Iocundissimum tamen ex omnibus spectaculum dixerim quod aram, quam non ut de Africano loquens Seneca, "sepulcrum tanti viri fuisse suspicor," sed scio, imaginemque eius summis parietibus extantem, qua milli viro simillimam fama fert, sepe venerabundus in saxo pene vivam spirantemque suspicio. Id michi non leve precium adventus; dici enim non potest quanta frontis autoritas, quanta maiestas supercilii, quanta tranquillitas oculorum; vox sola defuerit vivum ut cernas Ambrosium.* Petrarch, *Letters on Familiar Matters*, 2:319.

15. Carlo Bertelli, "Percorso tra le testimonianze figurative più antiche: dai mosaici di S. Vittore in Ciel d'oro al pulpito della basilica," in Gatti Perer, *La basilica di S. Ambrogio*, (Milan: Vita e Pensiero, 1995), 2:339–87, at 378.

16. Michael Baxandall, *Giotto and the Orators: Humanist Observers of Painting in Italy and the Discovery of Pictorial Composition, 1350–1450* (Oxford: Oxford University Press, 1971).

17. Simone Piazza, "Il volto di Ambrogio. La fortuna del modello paleochristiano e alcune varianti altomedievali," in Boucheron and Gioanni, *La mémoire d'Ambroise de Milan*, 99–102.

CHAPTER ELEVEN:
THE SAINTLY KNIGHT

1. Petrarch, *De vita solitaria* 2.3.2; trans. Jacob Zeitlin, *The Life of Solitude* (n.p.: University of Illinois Press, 1924), 204.

2. Andrea di Strumi, *Vita sancti Arialdi* 1061: *Prandente namque universa urbe ipse sanctam noctem ieiunus cum fratribus aliquibus prestolabatur atque cum eis ad quendam exiebat locum, qui dicitur Nemus, miliario a civitate secessus. Ibi enim adhuc est ecclesia a beato Ambrosio constructa et dedicata, ubi, sicut fertur, isdem, fugiens populi tumultum, solitus erat degere librosque dictare.*

3. Giovanni Turazza, *S. Ambrogio "ad Nemus" in Milano, chiesa o monastero dall'anno 357 al 1895* (Milan: Scuola Tipografica Istituto S. Gaetano, 1914), 39. The order became the Congregatio Fratrum S. Ambrosii ad Nemus Mediolanensis in 1441 (by papal bull of Eugenio IV, dated October 4, 1441) and was dissolved in 1645.

4. See Mario Naldini, ed., *La presenza di sant'Ambrogio a Firenze. Convegno di studi ambrosiani*, (Florence: Il Ventilabro, 1994).

5. Elena Giannarelli, "Ambrogio a Firenze: cronaca di una visita," in *Le radici cristiani di Firenze*, ed. Anna Benvenuti et al. (Florence: Alinea, 1994), 33–43.

6. Luigi Franco Pizzolato, "Ambrogio a Firenze: l'*Exhortatio virginitatis*," in Naldini, *La presenza di sant'Ambrogio*, 7–21. *Exhortatio virginitatis* is preserved in a very elegant fifteenth-century manuscript in the Biblioteca Medicea Laurenziana, along with numerous other works by Ambrose. In the same volume, see also Mario Naldini, "Attività pastorale di S. Ambrogio. Firenze e i codici della biblioteca medicea laurenziana," 24.

7. Carlo Nardi, "'Sanctus Zenobius episcopus' (Paolino, 'Vita Ambr.' 50,1). Sviluppi di una memoria patristica," in *Vescovi e pastori in epoca teodosiana*, Studia Ephemeridis Augustinianum 58 (Rome: Institutum Patristicum Augustinianum, 1997), 2:614.

8. Marta Niccolucci Cortini, "Il flagello di Ambrogio: la memoria dell'ortodossia fiorentina," in Benvenuti et al., *Le radici cristiani di Firenze*, 45–75.

9. Anna Benvenuti, "Le fonti agiografiche nella costruzione della memoria cronistica: il caso di Giovanni Villani," in *Il pubblico dei santi. Forme e livelli di ricezione dei messaggi agiografici*, ed. Paolo Golinelli (Rome: Viella, 2000), 92.

10. Anna Benvenuti, "San Lorenzo: la cattedrale negata," in Benvenuti et al., *Le radici cristiani di Firenze*, 122.

11. Wolfgang Lotz, "La piazza ducale di Vigevano. Un foro principesco del tardo Quattrocento," *Studi bramanteschi* (1974): 205–21.

12. Michele Ansani, "Da chiesa della comunità a chiesa del duca. Il 'vescovato sfortiano,'" in *Metamorfosi di un borgo. Vigevano in età visconteo-sforzesco*, ed. Giorgio Chittolini (Milan: FrancoAngeli, 1992), 117–44. We should point out that if Ludovico Sforza made approaches to the authorities in Rome starting in the 1490s, they came to fruition only in 1532. Note that the ducal chapel of Sant'Ambrogio in Vigevano became, in the sixteenth century, a central point for the preservation of "Ambrosian" musical heritage. See Christine Getz, "The Sforza Restoration and the Founding of the Ducal Chapels at Santa Maria della Scali in Milan and Sant'Ambrogio in Vigevano," *Early Music History* 17 (1998), 109–59.

13. Paolo Tomea, "San Giorgio in Crimea. Per una nuova edizione del *Liber notitiae sanctorum mediolani* (con una nota sulla papesse Giovanna)," *Aevum* 73, no. 2 (1999), 423–56.

14. *Liber notitiae sanctorum Mediolani. Manoscritto della Biblioteca Capitolare di Milano*, ed. Marco Magistretti and Ugo Monneret de Villard (Milan, 1917).

15. Italo Allegri, "Luoghi di culto santambrosiani. Le chiese e la devozione," in *Ambrogio vescovo di Milano (397–1997). Atti del Convegno di Cassago Brianza, 29 agosto–7 settembre 1997* (Lecco: Associazione Storico Culturale S. Agostino, 1999), 190–91.

16. Carlo Ginzburg, "Clues, Roots of an Evidential Paradigm," in *Clues, Myths, and the Historical Method*, trans. John and Anne C. Tedeschi (Baltimore: Johns Hopkins University Press, 1989), 87–113.

17. Alessandro Colombo, "Il 'Campo Marzio' di Milano e il Castello di porta Giovia," *Archivio storico lombardo* 56 (1929): 1–70. On the history of the beginnings of this construction site, see Patrick Boucheron, *Le pouvoir de bâtir. Urbanisme et politique édilitaire à Milan (XIVᵉ–XVᵉ siècles)*, CEFR 239 (Rome: École française de Rome, 1998) 200–202.

18. Charles Baudelaire, *The Flowers of Evil*, trans. Keith Waldrop. (Middletown, CT: Wesleyan University Press, 2008).

19. This question is further addressed in Alessandro Colombo, "Milano e i suoi sobborghi: urbanità e pratiche socio-economiche ai confini di uno spazio incerto (1400 ca.–1550 ca.)," *Società e storia* 112 (2006): 235–52.

20. Recent historiography has searchingly reexamined Italy's urban signory, as shown in these two summaries: Andrea Zorzi, *Le signorie cittadine in Italia (secoli XIII–XV)* (Milan-Turin: Mondadori, 2010); and Riccardo Rao, *Signori di popolo. Signoria cittadina e società comunale nell'Italia nord-occidentale 1275–1350* (Milan: FrancoAngeli, 2011). See also the collective output of the PRIN 2008 research program *Le signorie cittadine in Italia (metà XIII – metà XV secolo*, collected *Signorie cittadine nell'Italia comunale*, ed. Jean-Claude Maire Vigueur [Rome: Viella, 2013], and specifically Giampaolo Francesconi, "I signori, quale potere? Tempi e forme di un esperienza politica 'costituzionale' e 'rivoluzionaria,'" 327–46).

21. François Menant, "La transformation des institutions et de la vie politique milanaises au dernier âge consulaire (1186–1216)," in *Atti del'XI Congresso internazionale di studi sull'alto medioevo (Milano, 1987)* (Spoleto, 1989), 1:113–44.

22. See on this point the foundational work of Paolo Grillo, *Milano in età comunale (1183–1276). Istituzioni, società, economia* (Spoleto: Centro italiano di studi sull'alto medioevo, 2001), esp. 675–89 for profiles of the representatives of both factions.

23. See Giuliano Milani, *I comuni italiani. Secoli XII–XIV* (Rome-Bari: Laterza, 2005). For French-language summaries, see Elisabeth Crouzet-Pavan, *Enfers et paradis. L'Italie de Dante et de Giotto* (Paris: Albin Michel, 2001); Patrick Boucheron, *Les villes d'Italie (vers 1150–vers 1340)* (Paris: Belin, 2004); Patrick Gilli, *Villes*

et sociétés urbaines en Italie: milieu XIIe–milieu XIVe siècle (Paris: Sedes, 2005); and François Menant, *L'Italie des communes (1100–1350)* (Paris: Belin, 2005).

24. Enrico Artifoni, "I podestà professionali e la fondazione retorica della politica comunale," *Quarderni storici* 63 (1983): 687–719.

25. Jean-Claude Maire Vigueur, "Flussi, circuiti e profili," in *I podestà dell'Italia comunale. Parte I, Reclutamento e circolazione degli ufficiali forestieri (fine XII sec–metà XIV sec.)*, ed. Jean-Claude Maire Vigueur (Rome: ISIME and École française de Rome, 2000), 985. On this fundamental question, see Patrick Boucheron, "L'espace politique des podestats dans l'Italie communale (note critique)," *Histoire urbaine* 3 (2001): 181–89.

26. On this point, see John Koenig, *Il "popolo" dell'Italia del Nord nel XIII secolo* (Bologna: Il Mulino, 1986). The book is discussed in Pierre Racine, "Le 'popolo,' groupe social ou groupe de pression?," *Nuova Rivista Storica* (1989): 133–50.

27. Jean-Claude Maire Vigueur, *Cavaliers & citoyens. Guerre, conflits et société dans l'Italie communale, XIIe–XIIIe siècles* (Paris: EHESS, 2003), 137.

28. Roberta Mucciarelli, *Magnati e popolani. Un conflitto nell'Italia del Comuni (secoli XIII–XV)* (Milan-Turin: Mondadori, 2009).

29. From an ample literature, see Pierre Toubert and Agostino Paravicini Bagliani, eds., *Federico II e le città italiane* (Palermo: Selerio, 1994).

30. "Iscrizione del carroccio," in *Federico II e l'Italia. Percorsi, Luoghi, Segni e Strumenti* (Rome: De Luca, 1995), 336–37, quoted by Véronique Rouchon-Mouilleron, in *Villes d'Italie. Textes et documents des XIIe, XIIIe, XIVe siècles*, ed. Jean-Louis Gaulin, Armand Jamme, and Véronique Rouchon Mouilleron (Lyon: PUL, 2005), 66.

31. Benoît Grévin, *Rhétorique du pouvoir médiéval. Les lettres de Pierre de la Vigne et la formation du langage politique européen (XIIIe–XVe siècle)*, BEFAR 339 (Rome: École française de Rome, 2008), 785.

32. On this point, see Alfred Haverkamp, "Das Zentralitätsgefüge Mailands in hohen Mittelalter," in *Zentralität als Problem der mittelalterlichen Stadtgeschichtsforschung*, ed. Emil Meynen (Cologne-Vienna: Böhlau, 1979), 159–78.

33. Archivio Capitolare di Sant'Ambrogio, Milan, parchment no. 175, diploma of the archbishop Leone da Perego (1254). See Annamaria Ambrosioni, "I paratici e sant'Ambrogio," in *Le corporazioni milanesi e Sant'Ambrogio nel Medioevo*, ed. Annamaria Ambrosioni (Milan: Silvana, 1997), 96.

34. Cécile Caby, "Religion urbaine et religion civique en Italie au Moyen Âge. Lieux, acteurs, pratiques," in *Villes de Flandres et d'Italie (XIIIe–XVIe siècle). Les enseignements d'une comparaison*, ed. Élisabeth Crouzet-Pavan and Élodie Lecuppre-Desjardin, Studies in European Urban History (1100–1800) 12 (Turnhout:

Notes

Brepols, 2008), 14. The author goes on to say that "studies of recent cases, by contrast, emphasize the slow accretions, bitter negotiations…and political conflicts that underlie the advancement of one or another sect." In the next chapter, we'll return to a critical view of this notion of civic religion.

35. See the classic work of Isaia Ghiron, "La credenza di Sant'Ambrogio o la lotta dei nobili e del popolo in Milano (1198–1292)," *Archivio storico lombardo* 3 (1876): 583–609; and 4 (1877): 70–123.

36. Fiamma, *Chronica Mediolani, sive Manipulus florum*, col. 679. On this point, see Grillo, *Milano in età comunale*, 475.

37. Lorenzo Tanzini, *A consiglio. La vita politica nell'Italia dei comuni* (Rome-Bari: Laterza, 2014), 25.

38. Antonio Ivan Pini, "Un'agiografia 'militante': San Procolo, San Petronio e il patronato civico di Bologna medievale," in *Città, Chiesa e culti civici in Bologna medievale* (Bologna: Casa editrice CLUEB, 1999), 251–79. See also Paolo Golinelli, *Città e culto dei santi nel Medioevo italiano* (Bologna: Casa editrice CLUEB, 1996), 79 et seq.

39. I draw here on Maria Olba Orselli, "Spirito cittadino e temi politico-culturali nel culto di san Petronio," in *La coscienza cittadina nei Comuni italiani del Duecento Atti del IX Convegno storico internazionale dell'Accademia tudertina, Todi, 11–14 ottobre 1970* (Todi: Accademia tudertina, 1972), 283–343, reprinted in *L'immaginario religioso della città medievale*, ed. Mario Lapucci (Ravenna: Edizioni del Girasole, 1985), 183–241, esp. 206–14. On Theodosius's charter, see Gina Fasoli, "Il privilegio Teodosiano, edizione critica e commento," in *Studi e memorie per la storia dell'Università di Bologna*, Nuova serie vol. 2 (Bologna, 1961), 55–94.

40. *Biblioteca Agiografica Italiana (BAI). Repertorio di testi e manoscritti, secoli XIII–XV*, ed. Jacques Dalarun and Lino Leonardi (Florence: Edizioni del Galluzzo, 2003), 2:585. The debate as to whether this *Vita* in the vernacular tongue might have a Latin core dating back to before the Santo Stefano *Vita* is ongoing.

41. Antonio Ivan Pini, "Santo vince, santo perde: agiografia e politica in Bologna medievale," in *Il pubblico dei santi. Forme e livelli di ricezione dei messaggi agiografici*, ed. Paolo Golinelli (Rome: Viella, 2000), 105–23.

42. Augustine Thompson, *Cities of God. The Religion of the Italian Communes, 1125–1325*, (University Park, PA: Pennsylvania State University Press, 2005), 117.

43. *Vita di san Petronio con un appendice di testi inediti del secoli XIII e XIV*, ed. Maria Corti, Scelta di curiosità letterarie inedite o rare del secolo XIII al XIX 260 (Bologna: Commissione per testa di lingue, 1962), 42–43.

44. Orselli, "Spirito cittadino," 214.

45. Pierre Kerbrat, "Corps des saints et contrôle civique à Bologne du XIIIe siè-cle au début du XVIe siècle," in *La religion civique à l'époque médiévale et moderne (Chrétienté et Islam)*, ed. André Vauchez, CEFR 213 (Rome: École française de Rome, 1995), 165–85.

46. Annamaria Ambrosioni, "Controversie tra il monastero e la canonica di S. Ambrogio alla fine del secolo XII," in *Rendiconti dell'Istituto lombardo–Accademia di sscienze e lettere. Classe di Lettere e Scienze morali e Storiche* 105 (1971): 643–80, reprinted in Ambrosioni, *Milano, papato e impero*, 3–39.

47. Grillo, *Milano in età comunale*, 361.

48. Jacobus de Voragine, *The Golden Legend*, 234 (see chap. 9, n. 31).

49. *Corpus Juris Canonici*, ed. Emil Friedberg (Leipzig, 1879), 1:959 (cause 23 of q. 8, chap. 21). The quote is in Ambrose, *Epist.* 76 (M 20).8.

50. Silvia Donghi, "'*Legitur enim in legenda quadam…*': sulle fonti di un predi-catore milanese del Trecento," *Aevum* 78 (2004): 541–62.

51. Milan, Biblioteca ambrosiana, E 58 *infra*, fol. 10r-15r. This sermon has been published in Silvia Donghi, "Predicare a Milano nel Trecento: l'agostiniano Pietro Maineri," in *Ricerche storiche sulla Chiesa ambrosiana* 22, Archivio ambro-siano (Milan: NED, 2004), 9–69, at 40.

52. Jacques Berlioz, Marie Anne Polo de Beaulieu, and Pascal Colomb, eds., *Thesaurus Exemplorum Medii Aevi* (ThEMA), available online at the GAHOM (EHESS) site: http://gahom.ehess.fr/document.php?id=434

53. See Angelo Monteverdi, "Gli esempi dello specchio di vera penitenza," in *Studi e saggi di Letteratura italiana dei primi secoli* (Milan-Naples: Ricciardini, 1954), 195–96, for an analysis of this exemplum.

54. Giorgio Varanini and Guido Baldassarri, *Racconti esemplari di predicatori del Due e Trecento* (Rome: Salerno, 1993), 2:556–57. The same exemplum can also be found in an essay by Domenico Cavalca (Varanini and Baldassarri, *Racconti esemplari*, 3:84–86).

55. Jacobus da Voragine, *The Golden Legend*, 280.

56. Jean-Claude Maire Vigueur, "Représentation et expression des pouvoirs dans les communes d'Italie centrale (XIIIe–XIVe siècles)," in *Culture et idéologie dans la genèse de l'État moderne. Actes de la table ronde organisée par le CNRS et l'École française de Rome, Rome, 15–17 octobre 1984*, CEFR 82 (Rome: École française de Rome, 1985), 479–89.

57. Biblioteca Ambrosiana, A 189 below. See Robert Amiet, "La tradition man-uscrite du manuel ambrosien," *Scriptorium* 49 (1995): 137.

58. Cattaneo, "Galdino della Sala, cardinale," 377–79 (see chap. 10, n. 77).

Notes

59. Federica Peruzzo, "Orrico Scaccabarozzi: un arciprete poeta nella Milano del XIII secolo," *Aevum* 86, no. 2 (2002): 325-68.

60. Enrico Cattaneo, "Ottone Visconti arcivescovo di Milano," in *Contributi dell'Istituto di Storia medioevale, I, Raccolta di studi in memoria di Giovanni Soranzo* (Milan, 1968), 129-65, reprinted in Cattaneo, *La Chiesa di Ambrogio*, 77-113.

61. On this point, see the important article by Guido Cariboni, "Comunicazione simbolica e identità cittadina a Milano presso i primi Visconti (1277-1354)," *Reti Medievali Rivista* 9 (2008): 1-50, esp. 10-12, for an analysis of the famous fresco cycle in the castle of Angera representing Ottone Visconti's entry into Milan.

62. Gigliola Soldi Rondinini, "Vescovi e signori nel Trecento: i casi di Milano, Como, Brescia," in *Vescovi e diocesi in Italia dal XIV alla metà del XVI secolo atti del VII Convegno di storia della Chiesa in Italia, Brescia, 21-25 settembre 1987*, Italia sacra 42-43 (Rome: Herder, 1990), 2:837-68. See also the essays by Flavia Negro, "I signori vescovi: note sul senso di una categoria," in Maire Vigueur, *Signorie cittadine nell'Italia comunale*, 263-301 (see n. 19); and Flavia Negro, "Vescovi signori e monarchia papale nel Trecento," in *Signorie italiane e modelli monarchici*, ed. Paolo Grillo (Rome: Viella, 2013), 181-204.

63. Francesco Somaini, "Processi costitutivi, dinamiche politiche e strutture istituzionali dello Stato visconteo-sforzesco," in *Comuni e signorie nell'Italia settentrionale: la Lombardia*, ed. Giancarlo Andenna et al., Storia d'Italia VI (Turin: UTET, 1998), 681-786, esp. 690 et seq.

64. Fiamma, *Chronicon maius*, in Antonio Ceruti, ed., *Miscellanea di storia italiana 7* (1869), 604: *Dominus in temporalibus et spiritualibus et monarchus generalis.*

65. On the theme of public assistance and its growing importance in constructing Galdino della Sala's image as a good bishop, see Maureen C. Miller, *The Bishop's Palace: Architecture and Authority in Medieval Italy* (Ithaca, NY: Cornell University Press, 2000), 158 et seq.

66. This story, now well-known, has recently been revisited by Paolo Grillo, *Nascita di una cattedrale. 1386-1418: la fondazione del Duomo di Milano* (Milan: Mondadori, 2017), esp. 69-82.

67. Cariboni, "Comunicazione simbolica," 20-21.

68. Boucheron, *Le pouvoir de bâtir*, 189-92 (see n. 17), along with the relevant references. It is worth pointing out that the duke's project was initially much more ambitious, but it was foiled by the stubborn opposition of the councilors of the Fabbrica del Duomo. On Ambrosian iconography in the sculpture and stained glass of Milan Cathedral, see Angelo Paredi and Anna Maria Brizio,

eds., *Sant'Ambrogio nell'arte del Duomo di Milano* (Milan: Veneranda fabbrica del Duomo di Milano, 1973).

69. Biblioteca del Capitolo Metropolitano de Milan Cod. 2. D. 2. 32, fol. 10r.

70. *Ad honorem Dei omnipotentis necnon beate Marie Virginis atque beati Galdini archiepiscopi incipit liber missarum per totius anni circulum secundum ordinem beatissimi pontificis nostri Ambrosii.* Robert Amiet, "La tradition manuscrite du missel ambrosien," *Scriptorium* 14 (1960): 50.

71. Biblioteca del Capitolo Metropolitano de Milan Cod. 2. D. 2. 32, fol. 229r.

72. I resume here a line of thought started in Patrick Boucheron, *The Power of Images; Siena, 1338,* trans. Andrew Brown (Cambridge: Polity, 2018).

73. Andrea Gamberini, "Orgogliosamente tiranni. I Visconti, la polemica contro i regimi despotici e la risignificazione del termine *tyrannus* alla metà del Trecento," in *Tiranni et titannide nel Trecento italiano,* ed. Andrea Zorzi (Rome: Viella, 2013), 77-93. See also, in another context, Jean-Baptiste Delzant, "Dénoncer le tyran. Eléments sur l'étude du langage politique dans les petits centres urbains (Italie, fin du Moyen Âge)," in *Società e poteri nell'Italia medievale. Studi degli allievi per Jean-Claude Maire Vigueur,* ed. Silvia Diacciati and Lorenzo Tanzini (Rome: Viella, 2014), 115-29.

74. Paolo Grillo, *Milano guelfa (1302-1310)* (Rome: Viella, 2013).

75. On Bonvesin da la Riva, see now the essays collected in Raymund Wilhelm and Stephen Dörr, eds., *Bonvesin da la Riva. Poesia, lingua e storia a Milano nel tardo Medioevo. Atti della giornata di studio, Heidelberg, 29 giugno 2006* (Heidelberg: Winter 2009).

76. Elisa Occhipinti, "Immagini di città. Le *Laudes civitatum* e la rappresentazione dei centri urbani nell'Italia settentrionale," *Società e Storia* 51 (1991): 23-52.

77. Enrico Guidoni, "Gli Umiliati e la cultura urbana lombarda," in *La città dal medioevo al Rinascimento* (Rome-Bari: Laterza, 1989), 159-85.

78. Emanuele Coccia, *Le bien dans les choses* (Paris: Rivages, 2013), 39.

79. Bonvesin da la Riva, *De magnalibus Mediolani,* ed. Paolo Chiesa (Milan: Libri Scheiwiller, 1998), 67 (2.4): *Civitas ipsa orbicularis est ad circuli modum, cuius mirabilis rotonditas perfectionis eius est signum.* On the tenacity of the circle motif in urban elegies to Milan, see Lucio Gambi and Maria Cristina Gozzoli, *Milano,* Le città nella storia d'Italia (Rome-Bari: Laterza, 1982), 5-12.

80. See Boucheron, *Le pouvoir de bâtir,* 72-81, on the *De magnalibus*'s power as a "text of the city" to influence representations of Milan, and also its layout.

81. For a discussion of this question, see Alfred W. Crosby, *The Measure of*

Reality: Quantification and Western Society, 1250–1600 (Cambridge: Cambridge University Press, 1997), which dates the shift from a qualitative understanding of number to the mercantile ideal of quantification to 1275-1325, quoting (p. 70) the fourteenth-century Oxford theologian Walter Burley: "Every saleable item is at the same time a measured item."

82. Cattaneo, "La tradizione e il rito ambrosiani" (see chap. 8, n. 123).

83. Bonvesin da la Riva, *De magnalibus Mediolani*, 7.1 and 8.2 (*in ecclesia beati Ambroxii*); 3.11 (*ambrosiano pane*); 5.16 (*popullus Ambroxianus*); 3.12 (*ambrosiane terre*); 5.13 (*Ambroxianorum exercitus*); 4.14 (*Suprascripta equidem flumina non solum piscium, non solum feni copiam prestant, sed cum suis molendinis, que plura nonagentis sunt numero cum suis rotis, que sunt (ultra tria millia, non solum) tot Ambroxianos*); 5.16 (*ambrosianae historiae*).

84. The others lag far behind: *Mary* appears three times; *Augustine, Lawrence,* and *Barnaby* twice each.

85. For a general understanding of Milan's political history in the time of Azzone Visconti, see the summary, written long ago but still fundamental, by Francesco Cognasso, "L'unificazione della Lombardia sotto Milano," in *Storia di Milano,* vol. 5, *La signoria dei Visconti (1310–1392)* (Milan: Fondazione Treccani degli Alfieri, 1955), 203-84. And for an overall analysis of Azzone's activity as a city magistrate, compared to the practice in other signories, see Patrick Boucheron, "De l'urbanisme communal à l'urbanisme seigneurial. Cités, territoires et édilité publique en Italie du Nord (XIIIᵉ-XVᵉ siècle)," in *Pouvoir et édilité. Les grands chantiers dans l'Italie communale et seigneuriale,* ed. Elisabeth Crouzet-Pavan, CEFR 302 (Rome, Ecole française de Rome, 2003), 41-77.

86. Gian Maria Varanini, "Propaganda dei regimi signorili: le esperienze venete del Trecento," in *Le forme della propaganda politica nel due e nel trecento,* ed. Paolo Cammarosano, CEFR 201 (Rome, Ecole française de Rome, 1994), 311-43. On Ferrara as a "quasiparadigm" for the vitality of first-generation Italian signories, see the comments of Crouzet-Pavan, *Enfers et paradis,* 245-47 (note 22).

87. Federica Cengarle has proposed a revised reading of this political sequence. See, for instance, Federica Cengarle, "La signoria di Azzone Visconti tra prassi, retorica e iconografia (1329-1339)," in *Tecniche di potere nel tardo erdioevo. Regimi comunali e signorie in Italia,* ed. Massimo Vallerani (Rome: Viella, 2010), 89-116.

88. Federica Cengarle, "A proposito di legittimazioni: spunti lombardi," in Maire Vigueur, *Signorie cittadine nell'Italia comunale,* 479-93 (see n. 19).

89. Sylvain Parent, *Dans les abysses de l'infidélité. Les procès contre les ennemis de*

l'Eglise en Italie au temps de Jean XXII (1316–1334), BEFAR 361 (Rome: Ecole française de Rome, 2014), esp. 33-40, for an overall perspective.

90. Pierre Racine, "Les Visconti et les communautés urbaines," in *Les relations entre princes et villes aux 14ᵉ–16ᵉ siècles: aspects politiques, économiques et sociaux (Rencontres de Gand, septembre 1992)*, Jean-Marie Cauchies, ed., Publications du centre européen d'études bourguignonnes 33 (Neuchâtel: Centre européen d'études bourguignonnes, 1993), 187-99. On the concept of the *quasi-città*, see Giorgio Chittolini, "'Quasi-città.' Borghi e terre in aera lombarda nel tardo medioevo," in *Società e storia* 13 (1990): 3-26, reprinted in Giorgio Chittolini, *Città, comunità e feudi negli stati dell'Italia centro-settentrionale (secoli XIV–XVI)* (Milan: Unicopli, 1997), 85-104.

91. Mario Spigaroli, "La piazza in ostaggio. Urbanistica e politica militare nello stato visconteo," *Storia della città* 54 (1990): 33-40.

92. Bonincontro Morigia, *Chronicon Modoetiense*, RIS 12, (Milan, 1728), col. 1163. On this point, see Andrea Zorzi, "Un segno della 'mutazione signorile': l'arrocamento urbano," in Boucheron, *Marquer la ville*, 23-40 (see chap. 10, n. 46).

93. Patrick Boucheron, "Politisation et dépolitisation d'un lieu commun. Remarques sur la notion de 'bien commun' dans les villes d'Italie centro-septentrionale entre commune et seigneurie," in *"De bono communi." Discours et pratiques du Bien Commun dans les villes d'Europe (XIIIᵉ–XVIᵉ s.) / "De bono communi." The Discourse and Practice of the Common Good in the European City (13th–16th c.)*, ed. Élodie Lecuppre-Desjardin and Anne-Laure Van Bruane, Urban History 22 (Turnhout: Brepols, 2010), 237-51.

94. Galvano Fiamma, *Opusculum de rebus gestis ab Azone, Luchino et Johanne Vicecomitibus*, ed. Cesare Castiglione, RIS2 12.4 (Bologna, 1938). On this text, see Louis Green, "Galvano Fiamma, Azzone Visconti and the Revival of the Classical Theory of Magnificence," *Journal of Warburg and Courtauld Institutes* 53 (1990): 98-113.

95. On this point, see the comments of Giuseppe Polimeni, "'*In contrarium est cronica Bonvesini.*' La 'Cronica extravagans' di Galvano Fiamma e la nuova 'commendatio civitatis,'" in Wilhelm and Dörr, *Bonvesin da la Riva*, 81-93 (see n. 74).

96. Luciano Patetta, *L'architettura del Quattrocento a Milano* (Milan: CLUP, 1997), 249-51. For a fresh look at the history of urban development and placement of monuments in this urban zone, see Edoardo Rossetti, "In 'contrata de Vicecomitibus.' Il problema dei palazzi viscontei nel Trecento tra esercizio del potere e occupazione dello spazio urbano," in *Modernamente antichi. Modelli,*

identità, tradizione nella Lombardia del Tre e Quaatrocento, ed. Pier Nicola Pagliara and Serena Romano (Rome: Viella, 2014), 11–43.

97. About this transfer, conceived as an urbanistic divorce between the court and the city, and as a transgressive takeover of communal property by the seignorial power, see Boucheron, *Le pouvoir de bâtir*, 200–217.

98. Miller, *The Bishop's Palace*.

99. Galvano Fiamma, *Opusculum de rebus gestis* 16–17. See Serena Romano, "Palazzi e castelli dipinti. Nuovi dati sulla pittura lombarda attorno alla metà del Trecento," in *Arte di corte in Italia del Nord. Programmi, modelli, artisti (1330–1402 ca.)*, ed. Serena Romano and Denise Zari (Rome: Viella, 2013), 251–74.

100. Georges Duby, *Fondements d'un nouvel humanisme, 1280–1440* (Geneva: Skira, 1966), 135; trans. *Medieval Art: Foundations of a New Humanism, 1280–1440* (Geneva: Skira, 1995).

101. Enrico Guidoni, "Apunti per la storia dell'urbanistica nella Lombardia tardo-medievale," in *La Lombardia. Il territorio, l'ambiente, il paesaggio*, ed. Carlo Pirovano (Milan: Electa, 1981), 1:118.

102. Gerhard Dohrn-van Rossum, *L'histoire de l'heure. L'horlogerie et l'organisation moderne du temps*, trans. Olivier Mannoni (Paris: Editions de la MSH, 1997), 113–14. The author points out that the description of Azzone Visconti's death in the *Annales Mediolanenses Anonymi* as having occurred on August 14, 1339, at the twentieth hour is the first modern mention of time of day in an urban context, see *Annales Mediolanenses Anonymi*, RIS 16 (1730), 710.

103. Federica Cengarle, "I Visconti e il culto della Vergine (XIV secolo): qualche osservazione," in *Images, cultes, liturgies. Les connotations politiques du message religieux*, ed. Paola Ventrone and Laura Gaffuri, Le pouvoir symbolique en Occident (1300–1640) 5 (Paris–Rome: Publications de la Sorbonne – Publications de l'École française de Rome, 2014), 111–24.

104. Galvano Fiamma, *Opusculum de rebus gestis* 16.

105. Alessandro Colombo, "Le mura di Milano comunale e la pretesa cerchia di Azzone Visconti," *Archivio storico lombardo* 50 (1923): 277–334.

106. Galvano Fiamma, *Opusculum de rebus gestis* 26: *Murus civitatis interior fuit completus.*

107. Maria Teresa Fioro, "Uno scultore campionese a Porta Nuova," in *La Porta Nuova delle mura medievali di Milano dai Novelli ad oggi venti secoli di storia milanese* (Milan: ET, 1991), 107–28. Of the thirty statues originally present, most of which were moved and reused elsewhere, twenty-six have now been identified.

See Luca Tosi, "La ricomposizione dei gruppi scultorei delle porte ubiche di Milano: nuove ricerche e proposte," *Arte lombarda* 172 (2014): 13–23.

108. On this point, see the remarks by Serena Romano, "Azzone Visconti: qualche idea per il programma della magna salla, e una precisazione sulla *Crocifissione* di San Gottardo," in *L'artista girovago. Forestieri, avventurieri, emigranti e missionari nell'arte del Trecento in Italia del Nord*, ed. Serena Romano and Damien Cerutti (Rome: Viella, 2012), 135–62.

109. Enzo Carli, "Giovanni di Balduccio a Milano," in *Il millenio ambrosiano. La nuova città dal Comune alla Signoria*, ed. Carlo Bertelli (Milan: Electa, 1989), 75.

110. Patetta, *L'architettura del Quattrocento a Milano*, 75–82. In the fifteenth century, this chapel was one of the burial sites mainly reserved for the ducal family and the major figures of Milanese nobility.

111. Louis Green, *Castruccio Castracani: A Study on the Origins and Character of a Fourteenth-Century Italian Despotism* (Oxford: Clarendon Press, 1986), esp. 104–12. It is even possible that Castracani's urban planning projects in Lucca (building a signorial enclosure, the Augusta, to isolate a portion of the city reserved for the signor and his clients) played an important role in inspiring the repressive urbanism practiced by Azzone in the cities subject to him.

112. Creighton Gilbert, "The Fresco by Giotto in Milan," *Arte lombarda* 47–48 (1977): 31–72.

113. Boucheron, *The Power of Images*, esp. 188–91.

114. Costantino Baroni, *La scultura gotica lombarda* (Milan: Edizioni d'arte Emilio Bestetti, 1944), 78–83.

115. Federica Cengarle, "I gruppi scultorei delle porte milanesi: una forma di comunicazione politica?," *Arte lombarda* 172 (2014): 24–29.

116. Jean-Claude Schmitt, *Ghosts in the Middle Ages: The Living and the Dead in Medieval Society*, trans. Teresa Lavender Fagan (Chicago: University of Chicago Press, 1998), 60.

117. In his *Historia Mediolanensis*, Landulf Senior describes how Ambrose appeared before King Lambert to dissuade him from subjugating Milan (*Landulfi senioris Historia Mediolanensis*, 46 (2.2.24–28). The episode is revisited by Galvano Fiamma in his *Chronicon maius*: see Calligaris, "Il flagello di sant'Ambrogio," 25 (see chap. 10, n. 72).

118. Galvano Fiamma, *Chronicon maius* 612: *Beatus Ambroxius liberavit civitatem de obsidione. Cum autem in die Pentecostes Bruno archiepiscopus Coloniensis in parva ecclexia sancti Michaelis missam celebraret coram imperatore et baronibus, facta sunt tonitrua et coruscationes maiores quam nulla etas recordari potuisset. Beatus Ambroxius*

cum gladio extracto appariut in ecclexia, et terribilibus oculis imperatori comminatus est mortem, nisi de obsidione civitatis recedere.

119. Guido Cariboni, "I Visconti e la nascita del culto di Sant'Ambrogio della Vittoria," *Annali dell'Istituto storico italo-germanico in Trento* 26 (2000): 595-613.

120. Bonincontro Morigia, *Chronicon Modoetiense,* ed. Ludovico Antonio Muratori, RIS 12 (Milan, 1728), col. 1174-75; Pietro Azario, *Liber gestorum in Lombardia,* ed. Francesco Cognasso, RIS 16 (Bologna, 1926-39), 4:33-35.

121. Giovanni Villani, *Nuova Cronica,* ed. Giuseppe Porta (Parma: Guanda, 1990), 3:100-101; Anonimo Romano, *Cronica,* ed. Giuseppe Porta (Milan: Adelphi, 1979), 50-55. See Cariboni, "I Visconti," 600.

122. On this point, see the important remarks by Tomea, "Per Galvano Fiamma," *Italia medioevale e umanistica* 39 (1996): 423-36; and Paolo Chiesa, "Galvano Fiamma fra storiografia e letteratura," in *Courts and Courtly Cultures in Early Modern Italy and Europe. Models and Languages,* ed. Simone Albonico and Serena Romano (Rome: Viella, 2016), 77-92. For an example of a critical analysis of the chronicler in political sociology: Jean-Claude Maire Vigueur, *Cavaliers & citoyens. Guerre, conflits et société dans l'Italie communale, xii*ᵉ*–xiii*ᵉ *siècles* (Paris: EHESS, 2003), 135 et seq.

123. Massimilano David, "Galvano Fiamma et la prima antiquaria," in Parisi and David, *La Cronaca estravagante,* 668-86 (see chap. 10, n. 29)

124. Milan, Biblioteca Ambrosiana, ms. Trotti 109, fol. 48r.

125. Milan, Biblioteca Braidense, ms. AE X 10, fol. 28r-29v. To Fiamma, the Arian heresy provoked the first division in the city (*fuit prima divisio civitatis, quia aliqui erant christiani arriani, aliqui erant christiani ambrosiani*) and was logically resolved by the banishment of the vanquished: *arrianos qui erant ex nobilioribus civibus de Mediolano exbanivit.*

126. Milan, Biblioteca Ambrosiana, ms. A 275 inf, fol. 132r: *Pro tempore erat imperator arianus et papa similiter. Beatus Dyonisius archiepiscopus erat exiil ultra mare. Et civitas mediolanensis erat divisa inter arrianos et catholicos. Et clerici erant eorem molto divisi sicut modo sunt divisiones inter gybilinos et guelfos. Et fiebant in civitate et comitatu rixe, occisiones, quia pater contra filium, et frater insurgebat contra fratrem, unus prelatus contra alium, et unus clericus dimicabat contra alium.* Fiamma then explains that the Arians came from the ranks of the richest and noblest society in Milan.

127. Galvano Fiamma, *Opusculum de rebus gestis* 31: *De miraculo beati Ambroxii quando civitatem liberavit.*

128. Galvano Fiamma, *Opusculum de rebus gestis* 27: *Et hoc similiter signo amoris Azo Vicecomes dominum animarum se esse comprobare potuit.*

129. Maria Luisa Gatti Perer, *La chiesa e il convento di S. Ambrogio della Vittoria a Parabiago* (Milan: La Rete, 1966).

130. ASMi, *Fondo di Religione*, P. A. 2716, notarized deed dated January 8, 1350, naming Giordano da Marliano as the church's administrator (Rog. Francesco de Ariverio de Milano), published in Gatti Perer, *La chiesa e il convento*, 106-7.

131. ASMi, *Registri Panigarola*, Ref. 1, fol. 146r (August 31, 1389).

132. Diana M. Webb, "Cities of God: The Italian Communes at War," in William J. Sheils, *The Church and War*, Ecclesiastical History Society, Studies in Church History 20, (London: Blackwell, 1983), 114.

133. Aldo A. Settia, "L'esercito lombardo alla prima crociata," in *Deus non voluit. I Lombardi alla prima crociata (1100–1101). Dal mito alla ricostruzione della realtà. Atti del Convegnon, Milano 10–11 dicembre 1999*, ed. Giancarlo Andenna and Renata Salvarani (Mila: Vita e Pensiero, 2003), 23.

134. Azario, *Liber gestorum in Lombardia* 22: *Veneruntque Novariam in nomine sanctorum Ambroxii confessoris et Zorzii martiris qui cingulo milicie estiterat decoratus*.

135. On this point I refer the reader to the classic studies of Pierre Courcelle, *Recherches sur Saint Ambroise. "Vies" anciennes, culture, iconographie* (Paris: Études augustiniennes, 1973); and Stefano Zuffi, "Un volto che cambia, una figura che si consolida: l'iconografia ambrosiana dalle origini all'età sforzesca," in *Ambrogio. L'immagine e il volto. Arte dal XIV al XVII secolo* (Venice: Marsilio, 1998), 13-21.

136. For a general overview of the Viscontis' funeral choices, see Piero Majocchi, "'Non iam capitanei, sed reges nominarentur': progetti regi e rivendicazioni politiche nel rituali funerari dei Visconti (secoli XIV)," in Albonico and Romano, *Courts and Courtly Cultures*, 189-205.

137. Patrizia Mainoni, "Un bilancio di Giovanni Visconti, arcivescovo e signore di Milano," in *L'età dei Visconti. Il dominio di Milano fra XIII e XV secolo*, ed. Luisa Chiappa Mauri, Laura De Angelis Cappabianca, and Patrizia Mainoni (Milan: La Storia 1993), 3-26.

138. For a history and an analysis of the monument, see Peter Seiler, "Das Grabmal des Azzo Visconti in San Gottardo in Mailand," in *Skulptur und Grabmal des Spätmittelalters in Rom und Italien. Akten des Kongresses "Scultura e monumento sepolcrale del tardo medioevo a Roma e in Italie" (Rom, 4.–6. Juli 1985)*, ed. Jörg Garms and Angiola Maria Romani (Vienna: Verlag der österreichischen Akademie der Wissenschaften, 1990), 367-92; and Patrick Boucheron, "Tout est monument. Le mausolée d'Azzone Visconti à *San Gottardo in Corte* de Milan (1342-1346)," in *"Liber largitorius." Études d'histoire médiévale offertes à Pierre Toubert par ses élèves*, ed. Dominique Barthélemy and Jean-Marie Martin (Geneva: Droz, 2003), 303-26.

Notes

139. Seiler, "Das Grabmal," 376–85.

140. Evelyn Welch, *Art and Authority in Renaissance Milan* (New Haven: Yale University Press, 1995), 18.

141. Boucheron, "Tout est monument," 316–22.

142. Jean-Claude Maire Vigueur, "Religione e politica nella propaganda pontificia (Italia comunale, prima metà del XIII secolo)," in Cammarosano, *Le forme della propaganda*, 65–83, esp. 80 (see n. 85).

143. Giuseppe Gerola, "Le figurazioni araldiche nel Mausoleo di Azzone Visconti," in *Rendiconti del Reale Istituto lombardo di scienze e lettere* 66 (1928), 99–102. Identifiable, from right to left, are Bobbio and San Colombano; Novara and San Gaudenzio; Bergamo and Sant'Alessandro; Vercelli and Sant'Eusebio; Como and Sant'Abondio; and, to Ambrose's right, Brescia and San Faustino (or San Giovita?); Cremona and Sant'Imerio; Piacenza and Sant'Antonio Martire; Asti and San Secondo Martire; Lodi and San Bassiano.

144. Giorgio Chittolini, "Civic Religion and the Countryside in Late Medieval Italy," in *City and Countryside in Late Medieval and Renaissance Italy. Essays presented to Philip Jones*, ed. Trevor Dean and Chris Wickham (London: Hambledon Press, 1990), 69–80.

145. Maria Ginatempo and Lucia Sandri, *L'Italia delle città. Il popolamento urbano tra Medioevo e Rinascimento (secoli XIII–XVI)* (Florence: Le Lettere, 1990), 252 et seq.

146. Guido Cariboni, "Il codice simbolico tra continuità formale e mutamento degli ideali a Milano presso i primi Visconti," in Ventrone and Gafuri, *Images, cultes, liturgies*, 93–110 (see n. 102); and Guido Cariboni, "L'iconografia ambrosiana in rapporto al sorgere e al primo svilupparsi della signoria viscontea," in Boucheron, *La mémoire d'Ambroise*, 129–53.

147. Excepting, of course, the two medallions from the Carolingian gold altarpiece in Sant'Ambrogio, though they belong in an entirely different iconographic context, representing the young Ambrose, before his baptism, making his way toward Milan; see Courcelle, *Recherches sur saint Ambroise*, 173. Those medallions may also refer, as we've seen, to the administrative rounds of the new Carolingian Ambroses, *missi dominici* such as Angilbert. For a general view, see Enrico Cattaneo, "Dell'effigie equestre di S. Ambrogio," *Ambrosius* 15 (1939): 7–13.

148. Ermanno Arslan, "Ambrogio e la sua moneta," in *Ambrogio. L'immagine e il volto*, 35–44 (see note 134).

149. Carlo Crippa, *Le monete di Milano dai Visconti agli Sforza dal 1329 al 1535* (Milan: Carlo Crippa Editore, 1986), 201, doc. 9.

150. Felice Valsecchi, *Incunaboli dell'Ambrosiana* (Vicenza: Neri Pozza, 1972), 49, no. 83. Only one other copy of this text is known; it is in the Biblioteca Trivulziana in Milan (Inc. C. 209).

151. Milan, Biblioteca Ambrosiana, Inc. 121 (in 8, 28 lines).

152. Patrick Boucheron, "La statue équestre de Francesco Sforza: enquête sur un mémorial politique," *Journal des savants* (1997): 421-99.

153. Cristina Geddo and Silvia Paoli, "I santi Ambrogio e Carlo: una pagina inedita di iconografia ambrosiana," in *La città e la sua memoria. Milano e la tradizione di Sant'Ambrogio* (Milan: Electa, 1997), 298-307.

154. On this point, see the catalog of the Musée d'Orsay exhibition, *Adolfo Wildt: The Last Symbolist* (Geneva: Skira, 2015).

CHAPTER TWELVE:
THE BREACH

1. Jean-François Paul de Gondi, cardinal de Retz, *Mémoires*, in *Œuvres*, Bibliothèque de la Pléiade (Paris: Gallimard, 1984), 202.

2. See Marina Stefanovska, *La politique du cardinal de Retz. Passions et factions* (Rennes: PUR, 2008), 44-45.

3. Jean-Claude Milner, *Relire la Révolution* (Lagrasse: Verdier, 2016), 112: "If the rights of the people and the rights of kings require silence to harmonize, it is because, in fact, the rights of kings do not exist; the people speak all alone; their ears hear nothing but their own voices; when they love those who wear the crown, they only love themselves, as Narcissus did, through a foolish image."

4. Edgar Morin, Claude Lefort, and Jean-Marc Coudray (alias Cornelius Castoriadis), *Mai 68: La Brèche* (Paris: Fayard, 1968).

5. I have tried to develop the idea of this friable, open conception of time in *L'entretemps. Conversations sur l'histoire* (Lagrasse: Verdier, 2012), esp. 95 et seq.

6. Lauro Martines, *Power and Imagination. City-States in Renaissance Italy* (Baltimore: Johns Hopkins University Press, 1979), 141.

7. For a recent overview of the Milanese political system, see Francesco Del Tredici, "Il quadro politico e istituzionale dello Stato visconteo-sforzesco (XIV-XV secolo)," in *Lo Stato del Rinascimento in Italia, 1350-1520*, ed. Andrea Gamberini and Isabella Lazzarini (Rome: Viella, 2014), 149-66, with special attention to its relevant bibliographical references.

8. On the notion of the *communitas* as it influenced the republican experiment in Milan from 1447-50, see the important remarks by Marina Spinelli, "Finanza

pubblica e modalità di 'raccatto del denaro' a Milano durante il triennio della Repubblica ambrosiana (1447-1450)," in *Politiche finanziarie e fiscali nell'Italia settentrionale (secoli XIII–XV)*, ed. Patrizia Mainoni (Milan: Unicopli, 2001), 414-16. And, on a more general note, see Michel Hébert, *La voix du peuple. Une histoire des assemblées au Moyen Âge* (Paris: PUF, 2018), 148-51.

9. See on this point Riccardo Fubini, *Italia quattrocentesca. Politica e diplomazia nell'età di Lorenzo il Magnifico* (Milan: FrancoAngeli, 1994). I worked to develop this idea of an Italy that is monarchichal in its power structure and republican in its thinking in "Les laboratoires politiques de l'Italie," in *Histoire du monde au XVᵉ siècle*, ed. Patrick Boucheron (Paris: Fayard, 2009), 53-73.

10. On this point, see E. Igor Mineo, "Liberté et communauté en Italie (milieu XIIIᵉ-début XVᵉ s.)," in *La république dans tous ses états. Pour une histoire intellectuelle de la république en Europe*, ed. Claudia Moatti and Michèle Riot-Sarcey (Paris: Payot, 2009), 215-50.

11. *Acta Libertatis Mediolani. I Registri n. 5 e n. 6 dell'Archivio dell'Ufficio degli Statuti di Milano (Repubblica Ambrosiana 1447–1450)*, ed. Alfio R. Natale (Milan: Camera di commercio industria artigianato e agricoltura di Milano, 1987), 299, doc. 25 (Reg. 6, fol. 7, August 30, 1447).

12. Patrick Boucheron, "À qui appartient la cathédrale ? La fabrique et la cité dans l'Italie médiévale," in *Religion et société urbaine au Moyen Âge. Études offertes à Jean-Louis Biget par ses élèves*, ed. Patrick Boucheron and Jacques Chiffoleau (Paris: Publications de la Sorbonne, 2000), 95-117 (reprinted in *Les espaces sociaux de l'Italie urbaine, XIIᵉ–XVᵉ siècle*, ed. Patrick Boucheron and Olivier Mattéoni [Paris: Publications de la Sorbonne, 2005], 285-308).

13. Patrick Boucheron, *Le pouvoir de bâtir. Urbanisme et politique édilitaire à Milan (XIVᵉ–XVᵉ siècles)*, CEFR 239 (Rome: École française de Rome, 1998), 208-11.

14. Francesca Bocchi, "Il broletto," in *Milano e la Lombardia in età comunale, secoli XI–XIII* (Milan: Silvana, 1993), 38-42; and Paolo Grillo, "Spazi privati e spazi pubblici nella Milano medievale," *Studi storici* 39 (1998): 277-89.

15. For a floor plan and an analysis of the layout of the Broletto in the fifteenth century, see Boucheron, *Le pouvoir de bâtir*, 543-47.

16. The story of the Castello di porta Giovia is broadly based on the now ancient but still fundamental writings of Luca Beltrami, *Il Castello di porta Giovia sotto il dominio degli Sforza 1450–1535* (Milan: Hoepli, 1885); and Luca Beltrami, *Il Castello di Milano sotto il dominio dei Visconti e degli Sforza, 1368–1535* (Milan: Hoepli, 1894). These two works contain a considerable trove of documents on the building of the castle. See also Evelyn Welch, *Art and Authority in Renaissance Milan*

(New Haven: Yale University Press, 1995), 203–38; and, more recently, Maria Teresa Fiorio, ed., *Il Castello Sforzesco di Milano* (Milan: Skira, 2005).

17. On all this, see also Patrick Boucheron, "Hof, Stadt und öffentlicher Raum. Krieg der Zeichen und Streit um die Orte im Mailand des 15. Jahrhunderts," in *Der Hof und die Stadt. Konfrontation, Koexistenz und Integration im Verhältnis von Hof und Stadt in Spätmittelalter und Früher Neuzeit*, 9, ed. Werner Paravicini and Jörg Wettlaufer, Residenzenforschung 20 (Ostfilden: Thorbecke, 2006), 229–48; and Patrick Boucheron, "L'architettura come linguaggio politico: cenni sul caso lombardo nel secolo xv," in *Linguaggi politici nell'Italia del Rinascimento*, ed. Andrea Gamberini and Giuseppe Petralia (Rome: Viella, 2007), 3–53.

18. Pier Candido Decembrio, *Vita Philippi Mariae tertii Ligurum ducis*, ed. Attilio Butti, Felice Fossati, and Giuseppe Petraglione, RIS 20 (Bologna: Zanichelli, 1925–1958), 379 et seq.: *De pavore nocturno et custodiarum ordine. Solitudinis ac quietis nocturne timidissimus fuit, ita ut nisi aliquo excubante quiesceret...* See Gary Ianziti, "Pier Candido Decembrio and the Suetonian Path to Princely Biography," in *Portraying the Prince in the Renaissance: The Humanist Depiction of Rulers in Historiographical and Biographical Texts*, ed. Patrick Baker et al., (Berlin: De Gruyter, 2016), 237–70. See also this recent critical edition with English translation: Pier Candido Decembrio, *Lives of the Milanese Tyrants*, trans. Gary Ianziti, ed. Massimo Zaggia, I Tatti Renaissance Library (Cambridge: Harvard University Press, 2019).

19. Nicolas Machiavel, *De principatibus / Le Prince*, ed. and trans. Jean-Louis Fournel and Jean-Claude Zancarini (Paris: PUF, 2000), 179 (20.27–29).

20. Claude Lefort, *Machiavelli in the Making*, trans. Michael B. Smith (Evanston, IL: Northwestern University Press, 2012), 311.

21. Milan, Sant'Ambrogio, Archivio capitolare, M6. See Marco Petoletti, "Il messale di Gian Galeazzo Visconti per S. Ambrogio (Milano, Archivio capitolare della basilica di S. Ambrogio, M6)," *Aevum* 83 (2009): 629–64.

22. Four of the seventeen miniatures represent Ambrose: his attendance at Saint Martin of Tours's funeral (fol. 177r); his baptism (fol. 193r); a depiction of him holding his whip (fol. 198v); and his ordination as a bishop (fol. 217r). The missal opens with a full-page illustration of the coronation of Galeazzo Visconti in the basilica (fol. 8r).

23. Fol. 6r-v: *Missa in die victorie de Parabiago, ubi sanctus Ambrosius visus fuit in aere cum scutica in manu 1277* (correction in a later hand, probably from the sixteenth century: 1337) *die XXI februarii, dominante Azone Vicecomite*.

24. Paolo Zaninetta, *Il potere raffigurato. Simbolo, mito e propaganda nell'ascensa della signoria viscontea* (Milan: FrancoAngeli, 2013), 141 et seq.

Notes

25. Antonio Lanza, *Firenze contro Milano. Gli intellettuali fiorentini nelle guerre con i Visconti (1390–1440)* (Rome: De Rubeis, 1991).

26. From an abundant literature, see the recent and insightful essay by Luciano Piffanelli, "De part et d'autre de la *Libertas*. Éléments du discours politique florentin dans les guerres anti-Visconti (XIVe–XVe siècle)," *Medioevo e Rinascimento* 32 (2018): 25-71, and its appended bibliography.

27. Goro Dati, *Istoria di Firenze dall'anno 1380 all'anno 1405* (Florence: Giuseppe Manni, 1735), 1-2. English translation: John M. Najemy, *A History of Florence: 1200–1575* (Malen, MA: Blackwell Publishing, 2006), 203.

28. Dati, *Istoria di Firenze*, 69. English translation: Najemy, *A History of Florence*, 204. See Piffanelli, "De part et d'autre de la *Libertas*," n. 187.

29. On this point, see the writings of Andrea Gamberini, *Lo stato visconteo. Linguaggi politici e dinamiche costituzionali* (Milan: FrancoAngeli, 2005); Andrea Gamberini, *Oltre le città. Assetti territoriali e culture aristocratiche nella Lombardia del tardo medioevo* (Rome: Viella, 2009); and Andrea Gamberini, *La legitimità contesa. Costruzione statale e culture politiche (Lombardia, XII–XV sec.)* (Rome: Viella, 2016).

30. See overview in Andrea Gamberini, ed., *A Companion to Late Medieval and Early Modern Milan: The Distinctive Features of an Italian State* (Leiden-Boston: Brill, 2014).

31. Federica Cengarle, *Immagine di potere e prassi di governo. La politica feudale di Filippo Maria Visconti*, (Rome: Viella, 2006).

32. Alfio Rosario Natale, "Un contributo alla storia dell'Archivio della Repubblica Ambrosiana," *Acme* 34 (1981): 181-220.

33. Alfio Rosario Natale, *Stilus cancellariae. Formulario visconteo-sforzesco*, Acta italica 19 (Milan: Giuffré, 1979), XVI et seq.

34. On this point, see the fundamental writings of Nicole Loraux, *The Divided City: On Memory and Forgetting in Ancient Athens*, trans. Corinne Pache with Jeff Fort (Brooklyn, NY: Zone, 2001).

35. Pietro Verri, *Storia di Milano*, (repr. Florence: Le Monnier, 1851), 2:4.

36. See Alessandro Colombo, "Della vera natura e importanza dell'Aurea Repubblica Ambrosiana," in *Raccolta di scritti in onore del professore G. Romano* (Pavia, 1907), 1-13.

37. This "historiographic cooling" is clearly perceptible in the sober, measured account of Francesco Cognasso, "La Repubblica di Sant'Ambrogio," in *Storia di Milano 6, Il Ducato visconteo e la Repubblica ambrosiana: (1392–1450)* (Milan: Fondazione Treccani degli Alfieri, 1955), 387-450.

38. See, for example, Franca Leverotti, *Diplomazia e governo dello stato. I "famigli cavalcanti" di Franceso Sforza* (Pisa: Gisem, 1992), 57–70.

39. Marina Spinelli, "Ricerche per una nuova storia della Repubblica ambrosiana," *Nuova rivista storica* 70 (1986): 231–52; and 71 (1987): 27–48.

40. Martines, *Power and Imagination*, 140–48.

41. Alessandro Colombo, "Vigevano e la Repubblica Ambrosiana nella lotta contro Francesco Sforza," *Bolletino della società pavese di storia patria* 3 (1903): 315–77.

42. André Vauchez, "Introduction," in *La religion civique à l'époque médiévale et moderne (Chrétienté et Islam)*, ed. André Vauchez, CEFR 213 (Rome: École française de Rome, 1995), 1. Cited, in English translation, in Gabriella Zarri, "The Church, Civic Religion, and Civic Identity," in *A Companion to Medieval and Renaissance Bologna*, ed. Sarah Rubin Blanshei (Leiden and Boston: Brill, 2018), 361.

43. Vauchez, "Introduction," 4.

44. André Vauchez, "Patronage des saints et religion civique dans l'Italie communale à la fin du Moyen Âge," in *Patronage and Public in the Trecento. St. Lambrecht symposium, Abtei St. Lambrecht, Styria 16–19 July 1984*, ed. Vincent Moleta (Florence: Leo S. Olschki, 1987), 59–80, reprinted in André Vauchez, *Les laïcs au Moyen Âge. Pratiques et expériences religieuses* (Paris: Cerf, 1987), 185. See also André Vauchez, "La religione civica," in André Vauchez, *Esperienze religiose nel Medioevo* (Rome: Viella, 2003), 247–52.

45. Louise Bruit Zaidman, "Le religieux et le politique: Démeter et Koré dans la cité athénienne," in *Athènes et le politique. Dans le sillage de Claude Mossé*, ed. Pauline Schmitt Pantel and François de Polignac (Paris: Albin Michel, 2007), 81.

46. Giorgio Chittolini, "Società urbana, Chiesa cittadina e religione in Italia alla fine del Quattrocento," *Società e storia* 87 (2000): 1–17.

47. This analysis, briefly sketched here, is developed in Patrick Boucheron, "Religion civique, religion civile, religion séculière. L'ombre d'un doute," *Revue de synthèse* 134 (2013): 161–83.

48. The glorification of Ambrose's influence over the Milanese Republic of 1447–50 may follow from a current desire on the part of the Church's proponents to legitimize a republic whose origin and inspiration were specifically Christian, inevitably injecting a degree of historical distortion. See, in this vein, *La Repubblica ambrosiana (1447–1450). Sant'Ambrogio patrono e protettore dello stato della libertà*, Quaderni ambrosiani (Milan: Libreria Musicale Italiana, 2009).

49. Michel Leiris, *Langage tangage. Ce que les mots me disent* (Paris: Gallimard,

1985), 54. On the subject of rites and rhythms see, naturally, Jean-Claude Schmitt, *Les rythmes au Moyen Âge* (Paris: Gallimard, 2016).

50. Spinelli, "Finanza pubblica" (see n. 8). On the fiscal and social consequences of a policy vacuum surrounding public debt in Milan, see Anthony Molho, "Lo Stato e la finanza pubblica. Un'ipotesi basata sulla storia tardomedioevale di Firenze," in *Origini dello Stato. Processi di formazione statale in Italia fra medioevo ed età moderna,* ed. Giorgio Chittolini, Anthony Molho, and Pierangelo Schiera, Annali dell'Istituto storico italo-germanico 39 (Bologna: Il Mulino, 1994), 225-80; and Patrizia Mainoni, "Finanza pubblica e fiscalità nell'Italia centro-settentrionale fra XIII e XV secolo," *Studi storici* 2 (1999): 449-70.

51. Franca Leverotti, "Ricerche sulle origini dell'Ospedale Maggiore di Milano," *Archivio storico lombardo* 107 (1984): 83.

52. Quoted by Evelyn Welch, "The Ambrosian Republic and the Cathedral of Milan," *Arte lombarda* 100 (1992): 21.

53. On the political context, see Gigliola Soldi Rondinini, "Milano, il Regno di Napoli e gli aragonesi (secoli XIV-XV)," in *Saggi di storia e storiografia visconteo-sforzesche* (Bologna: Cappelli, 1984), 83-131.

54. On this reversal in alliance and its decisive effect on military history, see Georges Peyronnet, "François Sforza: de condottiere à duc de Milan," in *Gli Sforza a Milano e in Lombardia e i loro rapporti con gli Stati italiani ed europei (1450–1535)* (Milan: Cisalpino-Goliardica, 1982), 7-25.

55. Martines, *Power and Imagination,* 145.

56. Alessandro Colombo, "L'ingresso di Francesco Sforza in Milano e l'inizio di un nuovo principato," *Archivio storico lombardo* 32, no. 1 (1905): 297-344; and 32, no. 2 (1905): 33-101.

57. Spinelli, "Ricerche per una nuova storia," 235 et seq. (see n. 39).

58. *Annali della Fabbrica del Duomo di Milano dall'origine fino al presente,* ed. Cesare Cantù (Milan, 1877-1885), 2:119.

59. Welch, "The Ambrosian Republic," 24.

60. Enrico Cattaneo, "L'evoluzione delle feste di precetto a Milano dal secolo XIV al XX. Riflessi religiosi e sociali," in *Studi in memoria di mons. Cesare Dotta,* Archivio ambrosiano 9 (Milan, 1956): 71-151.

61. *Statuta iurisdictionum Mediolani,* ed. Antonio Ceruti, Historiae patriae monumenta 16, Leges municipales (Turin, 1876), col. 977.

62. Annamaria Ambrosioni, "I paratici e Sant'Ambrogio," in *Le corporazioni milanesi e Sant'Ambrogio nel Medioevo,* ed. Annamaria Ambrosioni (Milan,

Silvana, 1997), 93–102. See also, in the same volume, Anna Maria Rapetti, "Fonti normative e documentarie," 127–57.

63. On this point, see the comparison by Paola Ventrone between the Florentine Feast of Saint John the Baptist and the Milanese Feast of Saint Ambrose, "Feste e rituali civici: città italiane a confronto," in *Aspetti e componenti dell'identità urbana in Italia e in Germania (secoli XIV–XVI)/Aspekte und Komponenten der städtischen Identität in Italien und Deutschland (14.–16. Jahrhundert)*, ed. Giorgio Chittolini and Peter Johanek, Contributi dell'Istituto storico italo-germanico in Trento 12 (Milan-Berlin: Il Mulino-Duncker, 2003), 155–91, esp. 184.

64. *Acta Libertatis Mediolani. I Registri n. 5 e n. 6 dell'Archivio dell'Ufficio degli Statuti di Milano (Repubblica Ambrosiana 1447–1450)*, ed. Alfio R. Natale (Milan: Camera di commercio industria artigianato e agricoltura di Milano, 1987), 277, doc. 103 (Reg. 6, fol. 29, December 5, 1447): *Ad honorem et reverentiam individue Trinitatis et ad exultationem, gaudium et consolationem exhimii et irreprehensibilis doctoris et inconvincibilis protectoris nedum huius nostre felicis Libertatis.*

65. *Acta Libertatis Mediolani*, 472–73, doc. 305 (Reg. 6, fol. 96, December 5, 1448): *che domane, a bona hora, siano tuti li paratici, con più numero che se possano, su la piaza del Broleto, con li payli più belli e più honorevoli che sia possibille, per andare a fare la offerta al glorioso nostro protectore e patrone sancto Ambrosio; et che ciaschaduno paratico voglia portare uno cillostro per offrire. Anchora fi' confortato e carichato zascaduno zentilhomo e citadino che vogliano convenirse con le sue porte e andare, di poi, a la corte de l'Arengho per acompagnare li illustri nostri signori Capitanei etc. a la offerta predicta; e acaduno voglia portare quella quantitate de dinari che ye piacerà per offrire.*

66. They are known to have been held since 1389 (*Annali della Fabbrica del Duomo, Appendici*, 1:105). See Giuliana Ferrari, "Gli spettacoli all'epoca dei Visconti e degli Sforza: dalla festa cittadina alla festa celebrativa," in *La Lombardia delle signorie* (Milan: Electa, 1986), 219–43.

67. Enrico Cattaneo, "Dell'effigie equestre di S. Ambrogio," *Ambrosius* 15 (1939): 8.

68. AFD, Reg. 589, fol. 89v (June 12, 1449), quoted in Welch, "The Ambrosian Republic," 28.

69. Patrick Boucheron, "La mémoire disputée: le souvenir de saint Ambroise, enjeu des luttes politiques à Milan au XVᵉ siècle," in *Memoria, communitas, civitas*, ed. Hanno Brandt, Pierre Monnet, and Martial Staub (Paris-Frankfurt: Thorbecke, Beihefte di Francia, 2003), 201–21. The account that I gave then has been amplified in Patrick Boucheron, "Les combattants d'Ambroise.

Notes

Commémorations et luttes politiques à la fin du Moyen Âge," in Boucheron and Gioanni, *La mémoire d'Ambroise de Milan*, 483–98: it is this version that I revisit critically here.

70. Nicole Loraux, "Eloge de l'anachronisme en histoire," *Le genre humain* 27 (1993): 23–39, reprinted in *La tragédie d'Athènes. La politique entre l'ombre et l'utopie* (Paris: Seuil, 2005), 173–90.

71. Mona Ozouf, *Festivals and the French Revolution*, trans. Alan Sheridan (Cambridge, MA: Harvard University Press, 1988).

72. Richard Trexler, *Public Life in Renaissance Florence* (Ithaca, NY: Cornell University Press, 1980). See, on this moment in historiography, Philippe Braunstein and Christiane Klapisch-Zuber, "Florence et Venise: les rituels publics à l'époque de la Renaissance," *Annales. Économies, Sociétés, Civilisations* 38 (1983): 1110–24.

73. Olivier Ihl, *La fête républicaine* (Paris: Gallimard, 1996), 289.

74. Nicolas Mariot, "Qu'est-ce qu'un 'enthousiasme civique'? Sur l'historiographie des fêtes politiques en France après 1789," *Annales. Histoire, Sciences Sociales* 63 (2008): 113–39.

75. Mariot, "Qu'est-ce qu'un 'enthousiasme civique'?," 138.

76. *Acta Libertatis Mediolani*. The *Registri Panigarola* collects the documents of the Officia Gubernatorum et Statorum, which is charged with overseeing the enactment of municipal statutes. This office of the commune appears in official records for the first time in 1351; it was held by the Panigarola family, whose name the registers bear. See Nicolà Ferorelli, "L'ufficio degli statuti del comune di Milano, detto Panigarola," *Bolletino della Società pavese di Storia Patria* (1929): 1–43, reprinted in *Archivi e archivisti milanesi*, ed. Alfio R. Natale (Milan: Cisalpino-Goliardica, 1975), 1:233–77.

77. *Acta Libertatis Mediolani*, 51. The first recorded *crida* imposes a collective oath on all the gentlemen in the duchy who *debia jurare et havere jurato suxo uno missalle ad li sancti Evangelii de Dio in mane de voi Vicario de la provisione, recevente ad nome de questa illustre Communità: de dovere essere e ch'el serà omni tempore fidelle e liale a la prefata Communità e a la sua Libertà* (21, doc. 10, Reg. 5, fol. 5v-6r, November 24, 1447).

78. On this theme, see Didier Lett and Nicolas Offenstadt, eds., *Haro! Noël! Oyé! Pratiques du cri au Moyen Âge* (Paris: Publications de la Sorbonne, 2003). And on the concept of an informal public space, borrowed from Oskar Negt, see Patrick Boucheron and Nicolas Offenstadt, "Une histoire de l'échange politique au Moyen Âge," in *L'espace public au Moyen Âge. Débats autour de Jürgen Habermas*, ed. Patrick Boucheron and Nicolas Offenstadt (Paris: PUF, 2011), 1–21.

Notes

79. *Acta Libertatis Mediolani*, 586, doc. 440 (Reg. 6, fol. 135v, May 2, 1449): *Siché ogni homo stia de bona voglia et attenda ad far bene et obedire li prefati Signori, como è debito, et non dia audentia ead alchuno susuratore et maldicente, il qualle parlasse in contrario; avisando che questi talli sono sforzeschi et homoni di malla condicione, che non desiderano altro che la servitute et la disfactione de la patria propria, et li qualli affine nostro signore Dio, el bon patrono nostro sancto Ambroso punirà commo meritano.*

80. Spinelli, "Ricerche per una nuova storia," 252n112.

81. *Acta Libertatis Mediolani*, 64–65, doc. 35 (Ref. 5, fol. 26–27, July 23, 1448). Ruling in favor of processions for the Feast of the Assumption, a procession in honor of the Virgin Mary: ...*quello solenne et gloriosissimo giorno de l'assumptione de la sanctissima Virgine Maria, ne la cui vigilia fu recuperata, per divina gratia et summa clementia, questa nostra aurea, justa et amenissima Libertate.*

82. *Acta Libertatis Mediolani*, 75, doc. 43 (Reg. 5, fol. 31v–32r, September 30, 1448): a *crida* on the merits and intercession of Saint Francis, responsible for the "memorable victory" of Caravaggio (September 15).

83. *Acta Libertatis Mediolani*, 212, doc. 28 (Reg. 6, fol. 7v–8r, September 3, 1447): ...*che qualuncha persona de questa inclita città e burghi, chi volle bene a santo Ambrosio e desidera et ama questo Stato di Libertà, apta a portare arme, da qui a martedì, per tuto el dì, se metta in poncto per usire el dì che serà ordinato con lo nome del prefato glorioso santo Ambroso e del victorioso san Georgio et andare ad unirse con lo illustre conte Francescho, nostro capitano generale, er con lo nostro felicito exercito, perché non se dubita, facendo ciaschaduno virilmente como debbe, a questa volta se metterano li inimici, quali fano ogni cossa, pera vollere opprimere questa Libertà nostra...*

84. *Acta Libertatis Mediolani*, 84–85, doc. 53 (Reg. 6, fol. 35v–36r, August 8, 1448): ...*e che è devoto di sancto Ambroso, patrono et protectore nostro, et amatore de questa sancta libertà, vada fora, o manda persone, per sì, che siano apte et bene in puncto et quanto meglio farà tanto più sarà commendato.*

85. *Acta Libertatis Mediolani*, 185–86, doc. 150 (Reg. 5, fol. 86, December 1, 1449). A call to the citizenry to find the traitors Antonio and Ugolino Crivelli and Francesco Botti, who had gone over to Francesco Sforza, in order that they might be punished as an example: *et que sia ad exemplo de bene vivere et dritamente et lialmente, come deve qualunche bono citadino et vero ambrosiano, né lasasse corrumpere per pretio, né per qualuncha altra cossa de la fede et devocione se deve portare a la sua Republica...*

86. *Acta Libertatis Mediolani*, 171, doc. 134 (Reg. 5, fol. 78r, Septembrer 19, 1449): ...*et adesso ogni homo dimostra la fede e l'animo portino a sancto Ambrosio et a questo Stato de Libertà in andare animosamente e bene in puncto.*

Notes

87. I revisit here an idea proposed in Patrick Boucheron, "Fiscalité urbaine et fabriques de cathédrales en Italie (XIIIᵉ-XVᵉ siècles): remarques sur l'acculturation fiscale," in *L'impôt dans les villes de l'Occident méditerranéen. Actes du colloque tenu à Bercy (3, 4 et 5 octobre 2001)* (Paris: Comité pour l'histoire économique et financière de la France, 2005), 543-60.

88. *Acta Libertatis Mediolani*, 726-27, doc. 589 (Reg. 6, fol. 183v, October 1, 1449): *Che ciaschuno, qualle sia bono et vero ambrosiano et desidera l'honore et bene di questo Stato e la conservatione de la libertate, il debia demonstrare in andare a pagare non havendo pagata to la quarta parte de la sua taxa del Thesoro…*

89. *Acta Libertatis Mediolani*, 277, doc. 103 (Reg. 6, fol. 29, December 5, 1447): *Ad honorem et reverentiam individue Trinitatis et ad exultationem, gaudium et consolationem exhimii et irreprehensibilis doctoris et inconvincibilis protectoris nedum huius nostre felicis Libertatis, sed ymo et totius Communitatis et Reipublice huius nostre civitatis Mediolani…*

90. Ernst H. Kantorowicz, "Christus-Fiscus," in *Mourir pour la patrie et autres textes* (Paris: PUF, 1984), 65.

91. Jean-Philippe Genet, "L'État moderne: un modèle opératoire?," in *Genèse de l'État moderne. Bilans et perspectives*, ed. Jean-Philippe Genet (Paris: CNRS, 1990), 264.

92. Sébastien Fath, "Religion civile," in *Dictionnaire des faits religieux*, ed. Régine Azria and Danièle Hervieu-Léger (Paris: PUF, 2010), 1029-36.

93. See Emilio Gentile, *Politics as Religion*, trans. George Staunton (Princeton, NJ: Princeton University Press, 2006); and Olivier Ihl, "Religion civile: la carrière comparée d'un concept France/États-Unis," *Revue internationale de politique comparée* 7, no. 3 (2000): 595-627.

94. Alain Boureau, "Vox populi, vox Dei," in *Dictionnaire du vote*, ed. Pascal Perrineau and Dominique Reynié (Paris: PUF, 2001), 965-67.

95. *Acta Libertatis Mediolani*, 95-96, doc. 64 (Reg. 5, fol. 40, February 6, 1449): *…che ciaschuna persona talle non si dubiti per alchuno modo da essere in simili casi da essi Signori abandonati, ma vadeno come fidellissimi filioli del glorioso sancto Ambrosio, patrone et protectore de la dicta alma città, a combatere contra li perfidi inimici de questa excelsa Communità…*

96. *Acta Libertatis Mediolani*, 518-19, doc. 360 (Reg. 6, fol. 112r, February 6, 1449): *amatrice del nostro protectore et deffensore sancto Ambrosio et de la libertà di questa nostra excelsa Communità de Millano.*

97. *Acta Libertatis Mediolani*, 34, doc. 20a (Reg. 5, fol. 10v-11r, January 15, 1448): *Sia facto crida e publicamente divulgato: che ciascaduna persona de qualunque*

condicione, stato, grado et preheminentia voglia se sia, dal maiore al minore, niuno reservato, o apito, quale sia posta et taxata in lo extimo del Thesoro del gloriosissimo patrone nostro sancto Ambrosio...

98. *Acta Libertatis Mediolani*, 156, doc. 123 (Reg. 5, fol. 70, September 1, 1449): *...ma ciaschuno vero millanexe, overo ambrosiano, atenda a servare li ordeni de questa excelsa Communitate, acciò le cosse nostre prestissimamente se possano adrizare in bonissima forma, con la gratia de l'altissimo Dio et intercessione e adiuto del beatissimo Ambrosio, nostro protectore.*

99. *Acta Libertatis Mediolani*, 139–40, doc. 107 (Reg. 6, fol. 61, June 7, 1449). The *crida* orders the requisitioning of hay *in el dicto Ducato: Item, che tutte le biade, o in grana, o in paglia posseno essere conducte et portate dentro de Millano et li borghi, senza alchuno pagamento de datio, confortando ogni homo le conducha piutosto intra la citate che in veruna altra terra ambrosiana, etiandio murata, et facendone ogni opera et instantia.*

100. *Acta Libertatis Mediolani*, 456, doc. 286 (Reg. 6, fol. 90v–91r, November 10, 1448): Rulings to ensure the town's bread supply; any individual may bake and sell bread, and the loaf must be as large as possible "according to the price of flour," *perché quanto serà più bello et più grosso, tanto ne venderano et guadegnarano più et serano reputati essere migliori ambrosiani et più affectionati et devoti del Stato de la Libertà.*

101. *Acta Libertatis Mediolani*, 99–101, doc. 68 (Reg. 5, fol. 44, March 29, 1449): *...peroché non è Stato alchuno al mondo che senza la debita reverentia et obedientia se serva et digna cossa è che mal dire sia ben punito.*

102. *Acta Libertatis Mediolani*, 160, doc. 126 (Reg. 5, fol. 72, September 6, 1449).

103. *Acta Libertatis Mediolani*, 583, doc. 437 (Reg. 6, fol. 134, April 30, 1449): *Perchè li illustri signori Capitanei et Deffensori de la Libertate de la illustre et excelsa Communità de Millano hanno ordinato per salute di questa illustre Communitate et per conservatione et augmento del Stato de questa gloriosa Libertate de urtare lo inimico nostro et scaciarlo del mondo et metello in rotta e in ruyna, como sono certi farano con la gratia de l'altissimo Dio e del patrono nostro glorioso sancto Ambroso.*

104. *Acta Libertatis Mediolani*, 719–20, doc. 581 (Reg. 6, fol. 181, September 26, 1449).

105. *Acta Libertatis Mediolani*, 724, doc. 586 (Reg. 6, fol. 182v, September 28, 1449): *...et, per obviare a questi incovenienti, li prefati illustri signori Capitanei etc. confortano e carichano de novo qualuncha persona: che, de presente, demonstando la fede, lo amore e devotione e fervente desiderio portano a sancto Ambroso, al Stato di sancta Libertate e a l'amore e a la conservatione de la patria vogliano andare, saltim, uno per*

Notes

*casa de tuti quilli pono portare arme a logiare cadauno in li burgi de le porte ad opposito
de lo inimico e più apo posseno al redefosso e lì stiano dì et nocte: et cadauno, qualle staga e
habia casa in li dicti burgo habia pacientia de lassare dentro esse case alogiare questi talli;
avisando ogni homo che adesso è il tempo che ciascaduno debia monstrare quello amore e
devotione portano al dicto Stato Ambrosiano...*

106. Andrea Gamberini and Giuseppe Petrali, eds., *Linguaggi politici nell'Italia
del Rinascimento* (Rome: Viella, 2007).

CHAPTER THIRTEEN:

FORGETTING, THEN STARTING OVER

1. Maria Nadia Covini, *L'esercito del duca. Organizzazione militare e istituzioni
al tempo degli Sforza (1450–1480)* (Rome: Istituto storico italiano per il medioevo,
1998).

2. For a succinct account of the political developments, see Marco Fossati
and Alessandro Cellerino, "Dai Visconti agli Sforza," in *Comuni e signorie nell'Italia settentrionale: la Lombardia*, ed. Giancarlo Andenna et al., Storia d'Italia 6
(Turin: UTET, 1998), 573-636.

3. For a summary of the new diplomatic history of the Italian states in the
fifteenth century, see Isabella Lazzarini, *Communication and Conflict. Italian Diplomacy and the Early Renaissance, 1350–1520* (Oxford: Oxford University Press, 2015).

4. Giorgio Chittolini, "Il capitoli di dedizione delle comunità lombarde
a Francesco Sforza: motivi di contrasto tra città e contado," in *Felix olim Lombardia. Studi di storia padana dedicati a Giuseppe Martini* (Milan: Instituto di Storia medioevale e moderna della Facoltà di Lettere e Filosofia dell'Universita di
Milano, 1978), 673-98; reprinted in Giorgio Chittolini, *Città, comunità e feudi negli
stati dell'Italia centro-settentrionale (secoli XIV–XVI)* (Milan: Unicopli, 1996), 39-60.

5. Vincent Ilardi, "The Banker-Statesman and the Condottiere-Prince:
Cosimo De' Medici and Francesco Sforza (1450-1464)," in *Florence and Milan:
Comparisons and Relations: Acts of Two Conferences at Villa I Tatti in 1982–1984*, ed.
Craig Hugh Smyth and Gian Carlo Garfagnini (Florence: La Nuova Italia, 1989),
2:217-39; reprinted in Vincent Ilardi, *Studies in Italian Renaissance Diplomatic His-
tory* (London: Variorum reprints, 1986), 1-36.

6. Giovanni Simonetta, *De rebus gestis Francisci Sfortiae commentarii*, ed.
Giovanni Soranzo, RIS2 21.2 (Bologna, 1932-59), 342.

7. Gary Ianziti, *Humanistic Historiography under the Sforzas: Politics and Propaganda in Fifteenth Century Milan* (Oxford: Oxford University Press, 1988), 184-93.

8. Jane Black, *Absolutism in Renaissance Milan: Plenitude of Power under the*

Visconti and the Sforza 1329–1535 (Oxford: Oxford University Press, 2009). The theme of princely power paradoxically becoming more absolutist in the fifteenth century – paradoxically because princely power remained structurally weak – is also developed in Patrick Boucheron, "Les laboratoires politiques de l'Italie," in Boucheron, *Histoire du Monde*, 53–73.

9. Jacques Derrida, *Acts of Religion*, ed. Gil Anidjar (New York: Routledge, 2002), 46.

10. Vincent Ilardi, "The Assassination of Galeazzo Maria Sforza and the Reaction of Italian Diplomacy," in *Violence and Civil Disorder in Italian Cities, 1200–1500*, ed. Lauro Martines (Berkeley: University of California Press, 1972), 72–103.

11. Gregory Lubkin, "Christmas at the Court of Milan: 1466-1476," in Smyth and Garfagnini, *Florence and Milan*, 2:257–70.

12. Renaud Villard, *Du bien commun au mal nécessaire. Tyrannies, assassinats politiques et souveraineté en Italie, vers 1470 – vers 1600*, BEFAR 338 (Rome: École française de Rome, 2008), 154.

13. Lauro Martines, *April Blood: Florence and the Plot Against the Medici* (Oxford: Oxford University Press, 2003), 20–21.

14. Bernardino Corio, *Storia di Milano*, ed. Anna Morisi Guerra (Turin: UTET, 1978), 2:1401-7: *Nostri conjuratores armati circa primam horam noctis post Sanctum Ambrosium in ea via quae duos monasterii ortos dividit denno in sacramentum sanctum devenimus, primum confirmavimus nova juravimus fraternitate bonorum de futuris bonis et malis communem omnem rem parentes, amicos, fratresque nostros diversos simul equaliter unanimiterque tractare multaque reliquia his similia. Dehinc in recessu. Ego ad imaginem Divi Ambrosii oculos elevavi auxilium implorans pro nobis et populo suo; pro quo cera mihi et certa benefaciendi intentio erat; sic ex verbis ab extra socios duos fore dispositos iudicabam* (1405). On the subject of this author, see Stefano Meschini, *Uno storico umanista alla corte sforzesca. Biografia di Bernardino Corio* (Milan: Vita e Pensiero, 1995).

15. Corio, *Storia di Milano*, 2:1454–55.

16. See Nadia Covini, *"La balanza dritta." Pratiche di governo, leggi e ordinamenti nel ducato sforzesco* (Milan: FrancoAngeli, 2007), 302n160 (for the letters to the Milanese ambassadors to the French court dated January 7 and February 3, 1484, and the letter to the duke of Savoy dated January 7); and Villard, *Du bien commun au mal nécessaire*, 326 (for the letter to the marquis of Mantua dated January 5, 1484).

17. Corio, *Storia di Milano*, 1427. See Covini, *"La balanza dritta,"* 302.

18. On Filarete, see the essays collected in "Architettura e Umanesimo: Nuovi

studi su Filarete," special issue, *Arte lombarda* 155 (2009), esp. the contribution by Andreas Tönnesmann, "Il dialogo di Filarete: l'architetto, il principe e il potere," 7-11; and Hubertus Günter, "Ideal und Utopie in Filaretes irrealen Stadtentwürfen," in *Das Mittelalter. Perspektiven mediävistischer Forschung* 18 (2013): 73-97.

19. Robert Klein, for instance, describes it as "a welter of sadistic and schizoid fantasies" in "L'urbanisme utopique de Filarete à Valentin Andreae," in *La forme et l'intelligible* (Paris: Gallimard, 1970), 312. Filarete's writings are all the more striking when we realize that their author was himself probably tortured in Rome. The Ergastolon has done much to discredit Filarete, a tormented soul who, it seems, subjected architecture to torture.

20. Antonio Averlino detto il Filarete, *Trattato di architettura*, 2 vols., ed. Anna Maria Finoli and Liliana Grassi (Milan, Il Polifilo, 1972), Book 20, fol. 164r-166v.

21. The analysis is further developed in Patrick Boucheron, "Fragments d'un dépit amoureux: Filarete, de la ville idéale à l'utopie," *D'ailleurs. Revue de l'école régionale des beaux-arts de Besançon* (2010): 137-53.

22. Élisabeth Crouzet-Pavan, *Renaissances italiennes, 1380–1500* (Paris: Albin Michel, 2007), 177–82.

23. Michelle Riot-Sarcey, *Le procès de la liberté. Une histoire souterraine du XIXe siècle en France* (Paris, La Découverte, 2016), 213.

24. Patrick Boucheron, *Le pouvoir de bâtir. Urbanisme et politique édilitaire à Milan (XIVe–XVe siècles)*, CEFR 239 (Rome: École française de Rome, 1998) 211-13.

25. Giovanni Simonetta, *Compendio de la historia sforzesca*, ed. Giovanni Soranzo, RIS2 21.2 (Bologna, 1932-59), 514.

26. Louis Duval-Arnould, "Les manuscrits de la *Géographie* de Ptolémée issus de l'atelier de Pietro del Massaio (Florence, 1469-vers 1478)," in *Humanisme et culture géographique à l'époque du concile de Constance: autour de Guillaume Fillastre. Actes du colloque de l'Université de Reims, 18–19 novembre 1999*, ed. Didier Marcotte, Terrarum orbis 3 (Turnhout: Brepols, 2002), 227-44.

27. Patrick Boucheron, "La carta di Milano di Galvano Fiamma/Pietro Ghioldi (fine XIV secolo)," in *Rappresentare la città. Topografie urbane nell'Italia di antico regime*, ed. Marco Folin (Reggio Emilia: Diabasis, 2010), 77-98.

28. Patrick Boucheron, "Le passé, mais pas exactement. Mémoire urbaine et miroir princier à Milan au XVe siècle," in *Le miroir et l'espace du prince dans l'art italien de la Renaissance*, ed. Philippe Morel (Rennes-Tours: PUR/PUFR, 2012), 315-38.

29. Stefano Zuffi, "Un volto che cambia, una figura che si consolida: l'iconografia ambrosiana dalle origini all'età sforzesca," in *Ambrogio. L'immagine e il volto. Arte dal XIV al XVII secolo* (Venice: Marsilio, 1998), 18.

Notes

30. ASMi, *Litterarum ducalium*, Reg. 8, fol. 6r (April 7, 1450) and fol. 24v (April 24, 1451). See Caterina Santoro, *I registri delle lettere ducali del periodo sforzesco* (Milan: Castello Sforzesco, 1961), 310 and 317.

31. See on this point Evelyn Welch, "The Image of a Fifteenth-Century Court: Secular Frescoes for the Castello di Porta Giovia Milan," *Journal of the Warburg and Courtauld Institutes* 53 (1990): 163–84.

32. Mirella Ferrari, "Un bibliotecario milanese nel Quattrocento: Francesco della Croce," in *Ricerche storiche sulla Chiesa Ambrosiana* 10, Archivio ambrosiano 42 (Milan: NED, 1981), 185.

33. Enrico Cattaneo, "Lo studio delle opere di S. Ambrogio a Milano nei sec. XV–XVI," in *Studi storici in memoria di Monsignore Angelo Mercati* (Milan, A. Giuffrè, 1956), 147–61.

34. Ambrose's correspondence was published by Giorgio Crivelli and Stefano Dolcino in 1491: See Giuseppe Billanovich and Mirella Ferrari, "La tradizione milanese delle opere di sant'Ambrogio," in *Ambrosius episcopus. Atti del Congresso internazionale di studi ambrosiani nel XVI centenario della elevazione di Sant'Ambrogio alla cattedra episcopale (Milano, dicembre 1974)*, ed. Giuseppe Lazzati, Studia patristica mediolanensia 7 (Milan: Vità e Pensiero, 1976), 1:52.

35. Antonio Manfredi, "Vicende umanistiche di codici vaticani con opere di sant'Ambrogio," *Aevum* 72 (1998): 559–89.

36. Luciano Patetta, "Bramante e la trasformazione della basilica di Sant'Ambrogio," *Bollettino d'arte* 21 (1983): 49–74. See also Luciano Patetta, "Nuove ipotesi su alcuni monumenti del quattrocento milanese," in *Bramante milanese e l'architettura del Rinascimento lombardo*, ed. Christoph L. Frommel, Luisa Giordano, and Richard Schofield (Venice: Marsilio, 2002), 147–63, esp. 159 et seq.

37. Maria Luisa Gatti Perer, "Il Cardinale Ascanio Maria Sforza e il rinnovamento del monastero," in *Dal monastero di S. Ambrogio all'Università Cattolica*, ed. Maria Luisa Gatti Perer (Milan: Vita e Pensiero, 1990), 55–89. For a general view, see Marco Pellegrini, *Ascanio Maria Sforza. La parabola politica di un cardinale-principe del Rinascimento*, 2 vols. (Rome: Istituto Storico Italiano per il medioevo, 2002).

38. Maria Luisa Gatti Perer, "I temi nuovi dell'architettura milanese del Quattrocento e il Lazzaretto," *Arte lombarda* 79 (1986): 75–84.

39. Adriano Frattini, "Documenti per la commitenza nella chiesa di S. Pietro in Gessate," *Arte lombarda* 65 (1983): 133–43.

40. Luca Beltrami, *Notizie e ricordi di opere d'arte del secolo XV nella chiesa di S. Pietro in Gessate di Milano* (Milan: n.p., 1932), 11.

Notes

41. Eva Tea, "I cicli iconografici di Sant'Ambrogio in Milano," in *Ambrosiana. Scritti di storia, archeologia ed arte pubblicati nel XVI centenario della nascita di S. Ambrogio CCCXL–MCMXL* (Milan: Biblioteca Ambrosiana, 1942), 285–308, esp. 297–302.

42. Monica Pedralli, *Novo, grande, coverto e ferrato. Gli inventari di biblioteca e la cultura a Milano nel Quattrocento* (Milan: Vita e Pensiero, 2002), 438–43.

43. Paolo M. Galimberti, "Ambrogio Griffi († 1493)," in *La generosità e la memoria. I luoghi pii elemosinieri di Milano e i loro benefattori attraverso i secoli*, ed. Ivanoe Riboli, Marco G. Bascapè, and Sergio Rebora (Milan: Amministrazione delle II.PP.A.B., 1995), 85–91.

44. Marilyn Nicoud, *Le prince et les médecins. Pensée et pratiques médicales à Milan (1402–1476)*, CEFR 488 (Rome: École française de Rome, 2014), 61–62.

45. Marilyn Nicoud, "Il testamento e la biblioteca di Ambrogio Griffi, medico milanese, protonotario apostolico e consigliere sforzesco," *Aevum* 72 (1998): 447–83.

46. Beltrami, *Notizie e ricordi*, 14: *pingere et ornare predictam capellam ad istoriam Sancti Ambrosii confessoris, et eam istoriam facere et compartiri in XXVIII aut XXX capitulis, aut plus vel minus, prout prefato Rev. dom. Protohonotario videbitur, dummodo dicta capella impleatur picturae seu figuris.* For a complete catalog of the work of Zenale, see Giovanna Carlevaro, ed., "Materiale per lo studio di Bernardo Zenale," special issue, *Arte lombarda* 63 (1982).

47. Tea, "I cicli iconografici," 293; and Maria Luisa Gatti Perer, "La prima riforma cattolica e i suoi influssi sul programma iconografico del coro ligneo. Una testimonianza dello stato della basilica ambrosiana negli anni Settanta del Quattrocento," in Gatti Perer, *La basilica di S. Ambrogio*, 2:66–85.

48. Paulinus of Milan, *Vita Ambrosii* 7.1. Ramsey, *Ambrose*, 198–99.

49. On this topic, consult the recent work of Olivier Huck, "Oppositions religieuses et querelles d'influence dans les cités de l'Italie tardo-antique. À propos d'une audience épiscopale d'Ambroise de Milan," in *Les cités de l'Italie tardo-antique (IV*e*–VI*e* siècle): institutions, économie, société, culture et religion*, CEFR 369 (Rome: École française de Rome, 2006), 309–24.

50. Paul Ricœur, *Memory, History, Forgetting*, trans. Kathleen Blamey and David Pellauer (Chicago: University of Chicago Press, 2004), 574 et seq.

51. Paul Ricœur, "Esquisse d'un parcours de l'oubli," in *Devoir de mémoire, droit à l'oubli?*, ed. Thomas Ferenczi (Brussels: Complexe, 2002), 23. See also the analysis by Jean Greisch, "Trace et oubli: entre la menace de l'effacement et l'insistance de l'ineffaçable," *Diogène* 201 (2003): 82–106.

Notes

52. Régine Robin, *La mémoire saturée* (Paris: Stock, 2003), 91.

53. Colette Beaune, *Naissance de la nation France* (Paris: Gallimard, 1985), 272.

54. Gregory Lubkin, *A Renaissance Court. Milan under Galeazzo Maria Sforza*, (Berkeley: University of California Press, 1994), 215.

55. For other examples of dynastic sainthood, see Jean-Marie Le Gall, "Denis, Georges, Jacques, Antoine, André, Patrick et les autres. Identité nationale et culte des saints (xvᵉ-xviiiᵉ siècle)," in *Comportements, croyances et mémoires. Europe méridionale, xvᵉ-xxᵉ s. Études offertes à Régis Bertrand*, ed. Gilbert Buti and Anne Carol (Aix-en-Provence: Presses universitaires de Provence, 2007), 147-69.

56. Joanne Gitlin Bernstein, "A Florentine Patron in Milan: Pigello and the Portinari Chapel," in Smyth and Garfagnini, *Florence and Milan*, 1:171-200.

57. Marisa Dalai Emiliani, "Il ciclo del Foppa nella cappella Portinari," in *La basilica di sant'Eustorgio in Milano* (Milan: Electa, 1984), 155-71.

58. Joanne Gitlin Bernstein, "Science and Eschatology in the Portinari Chapel," *Arte lombarda* 60 (1981): 33-40.

59. Nicole Hochner, "Le trône vacant du roi Louis XII. Significations politiques de la mise en scène royale en Milanais," in *Louis XII en Milanais*, ed. Philippe Contamine and Jean Guillaume (Paris: Librairie Honoré Champion, 2003), 227-44. On this new staging of power, see Nicole Hochner, *Louis XII. Les dérèglements de l'image royale, 1498-1515* (Seyssel: Champ Vallon, 2006); also Stefano Meschini, *Luigi XII duca di Milano. Gli uomini e le istituzioni del primo dominio francese (1499-1512)* (Milan: FrancoAngeli, 2004); Stefano Meschini, *La Francia del ducato di Milano. La politica di Luigi XII (1499-1512)*, 2 vols. (Milan: FrancoAngeli, 2006); and Stefano Meschini, *La seconda dominazione francese nel ducato di Milano. La politica e gli uomini di Francesco I (1515-1521)* (Varzi: Guardamagna, 2014).

60. On this point, see the work of Séverin Duc, whom I thank for having alerted me to these facts: "Les Milanais face à l'effondrement du duché de Milan (c. 1500 - c. 1560)," in *Etats et crises du xviᵉ au xxiᵉ siècles. Europe et Outre-mer* (Paris: Armand Colin, 2014), 101-11; and Séverin Duc. "Il Prezzo delle guerre lombarde. Rovina dello stato, distruzione della ricchezza e disastro sociale (1515-1535)," *Storia economica* 19 (2016/1): 219-48.

61. Patrick Boucheron, *De l'éloquence architecturale. Milan, Mantoue, Urbino, 1470-1520* (Paris: Éditions B2, 2014); and Patrick Boucheron, "L'architettura come linguaggio politico: cenni sul caso lombardo nel secolo xv," in *Linguaggi politici nell'Italia del Rinascimento*, ed. Andrea Gamberini and Giuseppe Petralia (Rome: Viella, 2007), 3-53.

62. Patrick Boucheron, "La norma y la desviación: modelos políticos y

creatividad artística en la producción de Libros miniados en Francia e Italia a fines de la Edad Media. Algunas observaciones a propósito de los Libros de Horas de los príncipes," in *Modelos culturales y normas sociales al final de la Edad Media*, ed. Patrick Boucheron and Francisco Ruiz Gómez (Cuenca: Casa de Velázquez/Ediciones de la Universidad de Castilla-La Mancha, 2009), 167-201.

63. Patrick Boucheron, "Théories et pratiques du coup d'État dans l'Italie princière du *Quattrocento*," in *Coups d'État à la fin du Moyen Âge? Aux fondements du pouvoir politique en Europe occidentale*, ed. François Foronda, Jean-Philippe Genet, and José Maria Nieto Soria, Collection de la Casa de Velàzquez 91 (Madrid: Casa de Velàzquez, 2005), 19-49.

PART FIVE:
AMBROSIAN ANAMNESIS

1. Mathieu Riboulet, *Entre les deux il n'y a rien* (Lagrasse: Verdier, 2015), 11.

2. For more on this figure, see Gigliola Soldi Rondinini, "Branda Castiglioni nella Lombardia del suo tempo," *Nuova rivista storica* 70 (1986): 147-58.

3. In fact, he founded a school of Ambrosian chant at Castiglione Olona in 1423: Tino Foffano, "La costruzione di Castiglione Olona in un opuscolo inedito di Francesco Pizzolpasso," *Italia medioevale e umanistica* 3 (1960): 153-87.

4. Giuseppe Billanovich and Mirella Ferrari, "La tradizione milanese delle opere di sant'Ambrogio," in *Ambrosius episcopus. Atti del Congresso internazionale di studi ambrosiani nel XVI centenario della elevazione di Sant'Ambrogio alla cattedra episcopale (Milano, dicembre 1974)*, ed. Giuseppe Lazzati, Studia patristica medio-lanensia 7 (Milan: Vita e Pensiero, 1986), 1:33.

5. Mirella Ferrari, "Per la fortuna di s. Ambrogio nel Quattrocento milanese: appunti su umanisti e codici," in *Ricerche storiche sulla Chiesa ambrosiana* 4, ed. Enrico Cattaneo, Archivio Ambrosiano 27 (Milan: NED, 1973-74), 139-41.

6. Bernardino Corio, *Storia di Milano*, ed. Anna Morisi Guerra (Turin: UTET, 1978), 2:1144.

7. See Remigio Sabbadini, "Il Cardinale Branda da Castiglione e il rito romano," *Archivio storico lombardo* 19 (1903): 397-408.

8. ASMi, Archivio Notarile, cart. 342 (Beltramino Capra). The edited and annotated text can be found in Cristina Belloni, *"Donec habuero lignam ego vollo procurare pro offitio Sancti Ambrosii.* Una sommossa populare in difesa del rito ambrosiano a metà del xv secolo," in *L'età dei Visconti. Il dominio di Milano fra XIII e xv secolo*, ed. Luisa Chiappa Mauri, Laura De Angelis Cappabianca, and Patrizia Mainoni (Milan: La Storia 1993), 443-66.

Notes

9. Chiappa Mauri et al., *L'età dei Visconti*, 464: *Interrogatus si scivit de novitate que facta fuit pridie ad monasterium Sancti Celsi, respondet quod non, nisi quod eo die quo occurit dicta novitas obviavit presbitero Beltramolo, rectore Sancti Viti, qui sibi dixit; "Vidi unum miraculum: vidi unum sanctum Ambrosium parum (?) equestrem in Ecclesia Maiori Mediolani et ordinarios Ecclesie Maioris euntes Sancti Celsi cum crucibus ad dicendum missam ambroisianam"et tinc ipse presbiter Andriolus etiam ivit post dictos ordinarios ad dictam ecclesiam Sancti Celsi et ibidem celebravit missam et dicta missa, inde recessit nec aliquam vidit novitatem licet postea senserit de dicta novitate.*

10. Chiappa Mauri et al., *L'età dei Visconti*, 466: *Iste dominus cardinalis non est bene Ambrosianus ad volendum destruere odffitium ambrosianum et exportando istum librum.*

11. Giuseppe Visonà, "I *Tituli* ambrosiani: un riesame," *Studia ambrosiana* 2 (2008): 51–107.

12. A useful update is Attilio Pracchi, *La cattedrale antica di Milano. Il problema delle chiese doppie tra trada antichità e medioevo* (Rome–Bari: Laterza, 1996).

13. Patrick Boucheron, *Le pouvoir de bâtir. Urbanisme et politique édilitaire à Milan (XIVᵉ–XVᵉ siècles)*, CEFR 239 (Rome: École française de Rome, 1998), 552–53.

14. Luciano Patetta, *L'architettura del Quattrocento a Milano* (Milan: CLUP, 1997), 252–59.

15. On this episode, see Ada Grossi, *Santa Tecla nel tardo medioevo. La grande basilica milanese, il Paradisus, i mercati*, Collana di studi di archeologia lombarda 5 (Milan: Edizioni ET, 1997), 131–37.

16. Cengarle, "I Visconti e il culto della Vergine" (see chap. 11, n. 102).

17. Roland Barthes, *Roland Barthes by Roland Barthes*, trans. Richard Howard (New York: Farrar, Straus and Giroux, 1977), 109.

CHAPTER FOURTEEN:
MYSTERIOUS BEGINNINGS

1. The classic work on the concept–vague as it is–of "civic conscience" remains *La coscienza cittadina nei comuni italiani del Duecento. 11–14 ottobre 1970*, Centro di studi sulla spiritualità medievale (Todi: Accademia tudertina, 1972). A reappraisal of this historiographic tradition (essentially based on a reading of the *laudes civitatum*) can be found in Elisa Occhipinti, "Immagini di città. Le *Laudes civitatum* e la rappresentazione dei centri urbani nell'Italia settentrionale," *Società e Storia* 51 (1991): 23–52. See also Jean-Charles Picard, "Conscience urbaine et culte des saints. De Milan sous Liutprand à Vérone sous Pépin Ier d'Italie," in *Hagiographie, cultures et sociétés (IVᵉ–XIIᵉ siècles), actes du colloque organisé*

à *Nanterre et à Paris, 2–5 mai 1979, Centre de recherches sur l'Antiquité tardive et le haut Moyen Âge, Université de Paris X* (Paris: Études Augustiniennes, 1981), 455–69.

2. See Karl Schmid and Joachim Wollasch, eds., *Memoria: der geschichtliche Zeugniswere des liturgischen Gedenkens im Mittelalter* (Munich: Wilhelm Fink Verlag, 1984). For a historiographic overview: Michel Lauwers, "*Memoria*. À propos d'un objet d'histoire en Allemagne," in *Les tendances actuelles de l'histoire du Moyen Âge en France et en Allemagne*, ed. Jean-Claude Schmitt and Otto Gerhard Oexle (Paris: Publications de la Sorbonne, 2002), 105–26. See also the remarks of Patrick Geary, "Mémoire," in *Dictionnaire raisonné de l'Occident médiéval*, ed. Jacques Le Goff and Jean-Claude Schmitt (Paris: Fayard, 1999), 684–98.

3. Claude Lévi-Strauss, *Wild Thought: A New Translation of "La Pensée sauvage*,*"* trans. Jeffrey Mehlman and John Leavitt (Chicago: University of Chicago Press, 2021), 267.

4. Otto Gerhard Oexle, "Di Gegenwart der Toten," in *Death in the Middle Ages*, ed. Hermann Braet and Werner Verbeke (Leuven: Leuven University Press, 1983), 19–77.

5. Danièle Hervieu-Léger, *La religion pour mémoire* (Paris: Cerf, 1993), 179; trans. Simon Lee, *Religion as a Chain of Memory*, (New Brunswick, NJ: Rutgers University Press, 2000), 124–25. For a recent look at this strand of research, see Camille Tarot, *Le symbolique et le sacré. Théories de la religion* (Paris: La Découverte, 2008), esp. 238–42.

6. For a recent appreciation of the historicity of liturgy, see Matthieu Smyth, *"Ante Altaria." Les rites antiques de la messe dominicale en Gaule, en Espagne et en Italie du Nord*, Liturgie 16 (Paris: Cerf, 2007), 8–9. This author, whose work on fresh problems in liturgical analysis will prove essential in the pages ahead, trains his focus on the archaeology of Gallican liturgical practices, which are mostly prior to the Roman normalization of the ninth century, as a way of breaking with "the victors' perspective," at 15.

7. Éric Palazzo, *Liturgie et société au Moyen Âge* (Paris: Aubier, 2000), 214.

8. This is true of Enrico Cattaneo, probably the greatest authority on the subject, but also of many others. See Angelo Majo and Enrico Marco Navoni, eds., *L'attività e gli studi storico-liturgici di mons. Enrico Cattaneo*, Archivio ambrosiano 60 (Milan: NED, 1987).

9. This applies to today as well as yesterday, it goes without saying: see Burkhard Neunheuser, "Riforme della liturgia ambrosiana. Progetti. Iniziative. Realizzazioni. Speranze," in *Studi ambrosiani in onore du mons. Pietro Borella*, ed. Cesare Alzati and Angelo Majo, Archivio ambrosiano 43 (Milan: NED, 1982), 173–90.

10. Achille M. Triacca, "Ambrosienne (liturgie–)," in *Dictionnaire encyclopédique de la liturgie*, ed. Domenico Sartore and Achille M. Triacca (Turnhout: Brepols, 1992), 1:11–38.

11. Palazzo, *Liturgie et société*, 12.

12. In his *Institutions liturgiques*, Guéranger characterizes the particularity of the Ambrosian Rite as a stubborn (obstinate, even) resistance to the Roman effort at unification: "The Milanese have always guarded their rite with zeal and succeeded, mostly, in maintaining its integrity, despite introducing many new saints' days. But their intolerance for other liturgies, including the Roman, surpasses even that of the Apostolic See at its most exclusive. The truth of this may be judged from the following example. In 1837 we were in Rome and had just celebrated the holy mysteries in the Chapel of Saint Peter, when a canon of the Milan Cathedral appeared, accompanied by a Milanese clerk. The latter carried an Ambrosian missal; he placed it on the altar beneath which are the ashes of the Prince of Apostles, venerated by the entire universe. The Milanese canon then embarked on the Mass and concluded it calmly, using the foreign rite. A few months later, we were ourselves in Milan and asked to celebrate the holy offices over the body of Saint Ambrose. Our attention was directed to a solemn injunction forbidding any Mass at this altar but the Ambrosian: no latitude was given even for the Roman Rite. We were forced to sacrifice our pious desire." Prosper Guéranger, *Institutions liturgiques* (Paris-Brussels: Société générale de librairie catholique, 1878), 191.

13. Cesare Alzati, "Appunti di lessico medioevale ambrosiano: *mysterium* nella *historia* di Landolfo seniore," *Civiltà ambrosiana* 6 (1989): 181–85, reprinted in Cesare Alzati, *Ambrosiana ecclesia. Studi su la Chiesa milanese e l'ecumene cristiana fra tarda Antichità e Medioevo*, Archivio ambrosiano 65 (Milan: NED, 1993), 249–53.

14. Cesare Alzati, *Ambrosianum mysterium. La Chiesa di Milano e la sua tradizione liturgica*, Archivio ambrosiano 81 (Milan: NED, 2000), 19–29. See also Achille M. Triacca, "La liturgia ambrosiana," in *Anàmnesis. Introduzione storico-teologica alla Liturgia*, ed. Salvatore Marsili, vol. 2, *La liturgia, panorama storico generale* (Milan: Casale, 2005), 88–185, at 88. Triacca distinguishes between Ambrosian and "Sant-Ambrosian" liturgy, the latter being attributable to Saint Ambrose himself. He further distinguishes a Milanese (or Ambrosio-Milanese) liturgy, distinct from the Ambrosian liturgy of Bergamo, Ticino, or Novara.

15. The word *rite* here designates both a liturgical family, defined by common practices (e.g., the Gallican, Roman, or Ambrosian Rite–*rit* in Middle French), and a particular sacred function (e.g., the rite of baptism or marriage). The word

ritual designates more generally the set of actions, gestures, and attitudes relating to a given rite. See Cyrille Vogel, *Introduction aux sources de l'histoire du culte chrétien au Moyen Âge* (Spoleto: Centro italiano di studi sull'alto medioevo, 1975), 101.

16. Achille M. Triacca, "Libri liturgici ambrosiani," in Marsili, *Anàmnesis*, 2:201–17: "I cataloghi delle fonti ambrosiane sono stati redatti da studiosi non ambrosiani, fatta eccezione per alcuni pochi (Paredi, Borella, Cattaneo, Villa, ecc.). Questo fatto che a prima vista sembrerebbe di minore importanza, all'atto pratico ha una incidenza notevole per la mancanza di una diretta conoscenza di particolarità, usi e notizie che solo 'in loco' si riesce a conoscere, 'respirandole dall'aria' oseremmo dire" (at 203).

17. Lejay, "Ambrosien (rit)" in *Dictionnaire d'archéologie chrétienne et de liturgie*, ed. R. P. dom Fernand Cabrol (Paris, 1907), 1378.

18. *Maxima bibliotheca veterum Patrum* (Lyon: 1677), vol. 26. Another valuable testimony is to be found in the *Expositio missae ambrosianae* of the Bibliothèque universitaire in Montpellier (MS 76, fol. 73–81). See André Wilmart, "Une exposition de la messe ambrosienne," *Jahrbuch für Liturgiewissenschaft* 2 (1922): 46–47.

19. Michel Huglo et al., *Fonti e paleografia del canto ambrosiano*, Archivio ambrosiano 7 (Milan: Rivista "Ambrosius," 1961), 107–10 (no. 216). This manuscript is reproduced in Enrico Cattaneo, "L'esposizione della messa ambrosiana donata da Cicco Simonetta al re di Francia," *Ambrosius* 29 (1953): 180–87.

20. Paris, Bibliothèque de l'Arsenal, MS 221: *Ordo missae ambrosianae quo utitur civitas Mediolani quando celebratur cum diacono e subdiacono*. The following handwritten note appears on fol. 19v: *Cicchus Symonetta ducalis Secretarius, qui hunc librum Christianissimo domino Lodovico Francorum Regi mittit, se Majestati suae humiliter ac plurimum comendat. Manu propria.*

21. At fol. 3r, in the margin of the title *Ordo missae ambrosianae*, appears this note: *Beatus Ambrosius qui fuit tempore S. Martini qui etiam per tempora moram traxit Mediolani in parvo tugurio ubi nunc adest ecclesia sua extra muros civitatis. sepe S. Ambrosius eum devotissime visitabat ut refert F. petrarcha in opusculo suo de vita solitaria. Initium officii sui et missae ponit de Sancto Martino hoc ordine.* As we have seen, Petrarch does in fact describe Saint Ambrose's Wood in his *De Vita solitaria*. See Petrarch, *De vita solitaria* 2.3.2; trans. Jacob Zeitlin, *The Life of Solitude* (n.p.: University of Illinois Press, 1924), 204.

22. The manuscript passed through several hands, from Louis's doctor and counselor Pietro Colier (whose name appears on the flyleaf's ex libris), to Ambrose of Cambrai, chancellor of the University of Paris, who willed it on his death (1496) to one of his nephews, who in turn deeded it to Jean Huet, a

priest at the Church of Saint Paul. The manuscript then resided in the library of the Carmelite convent before entering the Bibliothèque de l'Arsenal, which now houses it. Henry Martin, *Catalogue des manuscrits de la bibliothèque de l'Arsenal* (Paris: Plon-Nourrit, 1885–99), 1:115–16 and 8:451–52.

23. Cristina Belloni, *Francesco della Croce. Contributo alla storia della chiesa ambrosiana nel Quattrocento*, Archivio Ambrosiano 71 (Milan: NED, 1995).

24. On this point, see the list of the manuscripts inventoried by the Fabbrica del Duomo after Francesco della Croce's death: Monica Pedralli, *Novo, grande, coverto e ferrato. Gli inventari di biblioteca e la cultura a Milano nel Quattrocento* (Milan: Vita e Pensiero, 2002), 468–69 (doc. 63c).

25. As the duke says himself in the cover letter for an anthology of the lives of captains and famous men (ASMi, *Autografi*, 124, fasc. 1, April 22, 1474). See Belloni, *Francesco della Croce*, 242.

26. Mirella Ferrari, "Un bibliotecario milanese nel Quattrocento: Francesco della Croce," in *Ricerche storiche sulla Chiesa ambrosiana* 10, Archivio ambrosiano 42 (Milan: NED, 1981), 185–86.

27. Paris, Bibliothèque de l'Arsenal, MS 221, fol. 1v: *Habet nostra inclita Civitas Mediolani haec spiritualia privilegia: primo utitur officio Ambrosiano et non Gregoriano in hymnis, in cantando et psalmis et orationibus: II in ordine missae hic inferius notate, quae fuit semel solemniter cantata in concilio Constantiensi publice et sic ab universali ecclesia comprobata; III In tot solemnibus praefactionibus missae; IIII In speciali Quadragesima ut hic patet.*

28. As is shown by his letter to Leonaredo Bruni dated July 15, 1423; see Pedralli, *Novo, grande, coverto*, 275 (doc. 16a).

29. Jean-Baptiste Lebigue, *Initiation aux manuscrits liturgiques*, available online at the IRHT website, https://irht.hypotheses.org/category/initiation-aux-manuscrits-liturgiques, 121.

30. Lejay, "Ambrosien (rit)," 1413.

31. *Liber notitiae sanctorum Mediolani. Manoscritto della Biblioteca Capitolare di Milano*, ed. Marco Magistretti and Ugo Monneret de Villard (Milan: Allegretti, 1917), 420. See Vogel, *Introduction aux sources*, 28 (see n. 15).

32. See Pietro Borela, *Il rito ambrosiano* (Brescia: Morcelliana, 1964), 68 et seq.

33. Achille M. Triacca, *I prefazi ambrosiani del ciclo "De Tempore" secondo "il sacramentarium Bergomense": avviamento da uno studio critico-teologico* (Rome: Pontificium Athenaeum Anselmianum, 1970), 237–38.

34. For recent thinking on this point, see Cécile Lanéry, *Ambroise de Milan hagiographe* (Paris: Institut d'Études Augustiniennes, 2008), 486.

35. They are published in Angelo Paredi, *I prefazi ambrosiani. Contributo alla storia della liturgia latina* (Milan: Pubblicazioni dell'Università Cattolica del S. Cuore, 1937).

36. Matthieu Smyth, *La liturgie oubliée. La prière eucharistique en Gaule antique et dans l'Occident non romain* (Paris: Cerf, 2003), 236.

37. Belloni, *Francesco della Croce*, 71–72; and Ferrari, "Un bibliotecario milanese," 197–98. See also Enrico Cattaneo, "Un tentativo di riforma del Breviario Ambrosiano ad opera dell'arc. Francesco Piccolpasso," *Ambrosius* 31 (1955): 96–98.

38. Alzati, *Ambrosianum mysterium*, 154 et seq. (see n. 14).

39. Gregory Lubkin, "Christmas at the court of Milan: 1466–1476," in *Florence and Milan: comparisons and relations. Acts of two conferences at Villa I Tatti in 1982–1984* (Florence: Villa I Tatti, 1990), 2:257–70.

40. Paris, Bibliothèque de l'Arsenal, MS 221, fol. 4r (in the margin of the *Ingressa*): *More romano nominatur Introitus.*

41. Alzati, *Ambrosianum mysterium*, 135.

42. Smyth, *"Ante Altaria,"* 58 (see n. 6).

43. Paul de Clerck, *La "prière universelle" dans les liturgies latines anciennes. Témoignages patristiques et textes liturgiques*, Liturgiewissenschaftliche Quellen und Forschungen 62 (Münster: Aschendorff, 1977), 155–65 and 205–14: *Pro pace ecclesiarum, vocatione gentiumet quiete populorumprecamur teDomine miserere.*

44. de Clerck, *La "prière universelle,"* 160.

45. de Clerck, *La "prière universelle,"* 210.

46. Paris, Bibliothèque de l'Arsenal, MS 221, fol. 7r (in the margin of the kyrie): *Nota: in missa romanae ecclesiae in principio Kiriel. Kristeleyson novem vicibus simul dicunt. Ambrosiani dicunt finito Gloria in excelsis ter Kyriel., prius Credo totidem; in fine totidem.*

47. Ambrose, *Epist.* 20 (M77).4–5.

48. Smyth, *"Ante Altaria,"* 64. For a description of the major features of the Ambrosian *specificum* in the ordo of the Mass, see Matthieu Smyth, *La liturgie oubliée*, 99–100: "The *Kyrie* after the *Gloria, preces* during Lent, a system of triple readings, a *Kyrie* and a *post evangelium* antiphon, two pre-anaphoral orisons accompanied by specified diaconal monitions, the recitation of the Symbol just before the *prex*, an *ad confractionem* antiphon (the Fraction remaining in its original place, which is to say before the *Pater*), a postcommunion *Kyrie* and a distinct formula for the dismissal."

49. *Liber notitiae sanctorum Mediolani*, 82 and 90. The formula for the monition may be short (*ne quis catechumenus*) or long.

50. Dom Jean Claire, "Le rituel quadragésimal des catéchumènes à Milan," in *Rituels. Mélanges offerts à Pierre-Marie Gy, o.p.*, ed. Paul de Clerck and Éric Palazzo (Paris: Cerf, 1990), 131–51.

51. Ambrose, *De mysteriis* 1.1: *De moralibus quotidianum sermonem habuimus, cum uel patriarcharum gesta uel Proverbiorum legerentur praecepta, ut his informati atque instituti adsuesceretis maiorum ingredi uias eorumque iter carpere ac diuinis oboedire oraculis, quo renouati per baptismum eius uitae usum teneretis quae ablutos deceret.* This translation: Ambrose, *On the Mysteries and the Treatise on the Sacraments by an Unknown Author*, trans. T. Thompson, B.D. (New York: Macmillan 1919), at https ://oll.libertyfund.org/titles/ambrose-on-the-mysteries-and-the-treatise-on-the -sacraments

52. Paris, Bibliothèque de l'Arsenal, MS 221, fol. 16r (in the margin of the *Libera nos*): *Ambrosiani haec dicunt alte audiente populo. Gregoriani secrete.*

53. Enrico Cattaneo, "Istituzioni ecclesiastiche milanesi," in *Storia di Milano*, vol. 9, *L'epoca di Carlo V (1535–1559)* (Milan: Fondazzione Treccani degli Alfieri, 1961), 507–720, at 546.

54. Triacca, "La liturgia ambrosiana," 92–93 (see note 14).

55. Hervé Savon, "Un modèle de sainteté à la fin du IVᵉ siècle. La virginité dans l'œuvre de saint Ambroise," in *Sainteté et martyre dans les religions du Livre*, ed. Jacques Marx (Brussels: Éditions de l'université de Bruxelles, 1989), 21–31.

56. Cengarle, "I Visconti e il culto della Vergine" (see chap. 11, n. 102).

57. On this point, see the remarks by Patricia Carmassi, "L'eredità ambrosiana nelle fonti liturgiche medievali," in *Ambrogio e la liturgia*, ed. Raffaele Passarella, Studia ambrosiana 6 (Rome-Milan: Biblioteca ambrosiana-Bulzoni editore, 2012), 153–74; and Cesare Alzati, "Genesi e metamorfosi della tradizione ambrosiana," in Boucheron and Gioanni, *La mémoire d'Ambroise*, 367–84.

58. Cesare Alzati, "Clero milanese e *officium ambroxianum* tra riforma e continuità (sec. XI–XIII)," in Alzati, *Ambrosiana ecclesia*, 292 (see n. 13).

59. Cattaneo, "Istituzioni ecclesiastiche milanesi," 555.

60. Alberto Cadili, *Giovanni Visconti arcivescovo di Milano (1342–1354)* (Milan: Edizioni Biblioteca Francescana, 2007).

61. A valuable update is in Triacca, "Ambrosienne (liturgie–)" (see note 10).

62. Smyth, *"Ante Altaria,"* 18 (see n. 6).

63. Vogel, *Introduction aux sources*, 90 (see n. 15).

64. Smyth, *La liturgie oubliée*, 13 (see n. 36).

65. Smyth, *La liturgie oubliée*, 312 and 567.

66. Patrizia Carmassi, *Libri liturgici e istituzioni ecclesiastiche a Milano in età*

Notes

medioevale. Studio sulla formazione del lezionario Ambrosiano, Liturgiewissenschaftliche Quellen und Forschungen 85, Corpus ambrosiano-liturgicum 4 (Münster: Aschendorff, 2001), 106–23.

67. The manuscript, known as the "S. Simpliciano missal," is number 2.D.3.3 in the Biblioteca del Capitolo Metropolitano in Milan and has been reprinted in Judith Frei, *Das ambrosianische Sakramentar D 3–3 aus dem mailändischen Metropolitankapitel: eine textkritische und redaktionsgeschichtliche Untersuchung der mailändischen Sakramentartradition,* Liturgiewissenschaftliche Quellen und Forschungen 56, Corpus ambrosiano-liturgicum 3 (Münster: Aschendorff, 1974).

68. Triacca, "Ambrosienne (liturgie–)," 21.

69. Borella, *Il rito ambrosiano* (Brescia : Morcelliana, 1964), 121–29.

70. MGH Leg. Capitularia regum Francorum, 1(1), 61. See Cyrille Vogel, "La réforme liturgique sous Charlemagne," in *Karl der Grosse,* ed. Bernhard Bischoff, vol. 2, *Das Geistige Leben* (Düsseldorf: L. Schwann, 1965), 218–19: *quando gallicanum [cantum] tulit ob unanimitatem apostolicae sedis.*

71. MGH SS 1: *Annales Laurissenses,* 160.

72. MGH SS 25, 629. See Enrico Cattaneo, "La tradizione e il rito ambrosiani nell'ambiente lombardo-medioevale," in *La Chiesa di Ambrogio. Studi di storia e di liturgia* (Milan: Vita e Pensiero, 1984), 123.

73. Alzati, *Ambrosianum mysterium,* 86–87.

74. On this author, see the discussion in Paolo Tomea, *Tradizione apostolica e coscienza cittadina a Milano nel medioevo. La leggenda di san Barnaba* (Milan: Vita e Pensiero, 1993), 44; see also Jörg W. Busch, "*Landulfi senioris Historia Mediolanensis*–Überlieferung, Datierung und Intention," *Deutsches Archiv für Erforschung des Mittelalters* 45 (1989): 1–30.

75. Landulfus Mediolanensis, *Historia Mediolanensis* 2.10.61–62 (p. 49): *Sermo b. Thomae archiepiscopi Mediolani qualiter officium Ambrosianum per b. Eugenium ab Adriano papa et Karulo imperatore evidentissimis miraculis defensum est* (for complete reference see chap. 8, n. 49).

76. Landulfus, *Historia* 2.10.29–30 (p. 49): *omnes libros ambrosianos, titulo sigillatos, quos vel pretio vel dono vel vi habere potuit alios comburrens, alios trans montes, quasi in exilio secum detulit. Sed religiosi viri, tantos libros videntes, religiose tenuerunt.*

77. Landulfus, *Historia* 2.11.34–35 (p. 49). On the use of the expression *mysterium ambrosianum,* see Alzati, "Appunti di lessico medioevale," 253 (see n. 13).

78. Landulfus, *Historia* 2.12.7–10 (p. 50): *Quo viso cunctis mirantibus valdeque obstupescentibus nimiumque congemescentibus, libri ligaturas per se rumpentes, sonum magnum atque terribilem audientibus universis dederunt, et sese digito Dei*

aperientes, ita ambo aperti sunt, ut aliquis unam illorum foliam non inveniret plus in *unam partem quam in alteram.* English trans.: https://sicutincensum.wordpress .com/2018/09/03/how-the-ambrosian-rite-survived-charlemagne

79. Landulfus, *Historia* 2.12.22-25 (p. 50): *Nichil enim praeter missale remansit, quod quidam bonus atque fidelis sacerdos absconsus in cavernis montium per sex ebdomadas fideliter reservavit. Manualem autem postea astante Eugenio episcopus fidelissimus, sapientes tam sacerdotum quam clericorum, qui multa memoriter tenebant, convenientes in unum, Deo opitulante, ut antea integer fuit invenientes, in posteris traditerunt.*

80. On the question of a "localizing memory" in medieval culture, see Mary Carruthers, *The Craft of Thought: Meditation, Rhetoric, and the Making of Images, 400–1200* (Cambridge: Cambridge University Press, 1998).

81. Louis Duchesne, *Christian Worship: Its Origin and Evolution. A Study of the Latin Liturgy Up to the Time of Charlemagne*, trans. M. L. McClure (London: Society for Promoting Christian Knowledge, 1903), 105.

82. The key reference here is the systematic study by Jörg W. Busch, *Die Mailänder Geschichtsschreibung zwischen Arnulf und Galvaneus Flamma. Die Beschäftigung mit der Vergangenheit im Umfeld einer oberitalienischen Kommune vom späten 11. bis zum frühen 14. Jahrhundert*, Münstersche Mittelalter-Schriften 72 (Munich: Wilhelm Fink Verlag, 1997).

83. Patrick Gilli, *Au miroir de l'humanisme. Les représentations de la France dans la culture savante italienne à la fin du Moyen Âge*, BEFAR 296 (Rome: École française de Rome, 1997), 360-62.

84. Enrico Cattaneo, "Sant Eugenio vescovo e il rito ambrosiano," in *Ricerche storiche sulla Chiesa ambrosiana* I, Archivio ambrosiano 18 (Milan: NED, 1970), 30-43; reprinted in Cattaneo, *La Chiesa di Ambrogio*, 21-43.

85. Patrick. J. Geary, "I Magi e Milano," in *Il millennio ambrosiano. La città del vescovo dai Carolingi al Barbarossa*, ed. Carlo Bertelli (Milan: Electa, 1988), 274-87.

86. Patrick Boucheron, *Le pouvoir de bâtir. Urbanisme et politique édilitaire à Milan (XIVᵉ–XVᵉ siècles)*, CEFR 239 (Rome: École française de Rome, 1998) 94-95.

87. Cattaneo, "Sant Eugenio vescovo," 35; reprinted in Cattaneo, *La Chiesa di Ambrogio*, 26.

88. The text has been published in *Beroldus sive ecclesiae ambrosianae Mediolanensis kalendarium*, ed. Marco Magistretti (Milan, 1894).

89. Milan, Biblioteca ambrosiana, Ambr. I 152 infra, fol. 26r-93r. See Mirella Ferrari, "Valutazione paleografica del codice ambrosiano di Beroldo," in *Il Duomo cuore e simbolo di Milano. IV Centenario della Dedicazione (1577–1977)*, Archivio ambrosiano 32 (Milan: NED, 1977), 302-7. For a description of the

manuscript, see in the same volume Giovanna Forzatti Golia, "Le raccolte di Beroldo," 310-16.

90. Milan, Biblioteca ambrosiana, Ambr. I 152 infra, fol. 26r-93r.

91. Milan, Biblioteca ambrosiana, Ambr. I 152 infra, fol. 94-98r.

92. Milan, Biblioteca ambrosiana, Ambr. I 152 infra, fol. 99r-103r.

93. Milan, Biblioteca ambrosiana, Ambr. I 152 infra, fol. 103r-104v.

94. Milan, Biblioteca ambrosiana, Ambr. I 152 infra, fol. 105r-110v. See Celestina Milani, "Osservazioni linguistiche sul 'Sermo beati Tomae episcopi Mediolani,'" *Aevum* 45 (1971): 87-129.

95. Tomea, *Tradizione apostolica*, 320-440.

96. Tomea, *Tradizione apostolica*, 91n86.

97. Robert Amiet, "La tradition manuscrite du missel ambrosien," *Scriptorium* 14 (1960): 16-60. The first plenary missal being MS E 18 inf. of the Ambrosian Library in Milan, dating to the first half of the fifteenth century, at 45n21.

98. Roberet Amiet, "La tradition manuscrite du manuel ambrosien," *Scriptorium* 19 (1995): 135: "this book is truly a complete *directorium chori*, gathering all the choral elements of the missal and the breviary."

99. Carmassi, *Libri liturgici*, 164-79 (see n. 66).

100. Milan, Biblioteca del Capitolo Metropolitano, 2.D.2.28. See Forzatti Golia, "Le raccolte di Beroldo," 330-60.

101. Carmassi, *Libri liturgici*, 363.

102. Giordano Monzio Compagnoni, "Un trattato rituale trecentesco: il 'Liber celebrationis misse ambrosiane' di Giovanni Bello de Guerciis," in *Ricerche storiche sulla Chiesa ambrosiana* 19, Archivio ambrosiano 86 (Milan: NED, 2001), 73-107.

103. Francesco Somaini, *Un prelato lombardo del XV secolo. Il card. Giovanni Arcimboldi vescovo di Novara, arcivescovo di Milano*, Italia sacra, Studi e documenti di storia ecclesiastica 74 (Rome: Herder, 2003), 3:1201.

104. Enrico Cattaneo, "Lo studio delle opere di S. Ambrogio a Milano nei sec. XV-XVI," in *Studi storici in memoria di Monsignore Angelo Mercati* (Milan: A. Giuffrè, 1956), 147-61. See also Antonio Manfredi, "Vicende umanistiche di codivi vaticani con opere di sant'Ambrogio," *Aevum* 72 (1998): 559-89.

105. Federica Peruzzo, "Pietro Casola editore di libri liturgici ambrosiani nel Quattrocento," *Italia medioevale e umanistica* 46 (2005): 148-206; and "Il *Breviarium ambrosianum* di Pietro Casola (1490)," in *Ricerche storiche sulla Chiesa ambrosiana* 24, Archivio ambrosiano 92 (Milan: NED, 2006), 9-52.

106. Jörg W. Busch, "Die Vereinnahmung eines gegnerischen Textes. Die Verweise auf ein Investiturprivileg in der sogenannten 'Historia Landulfi senioris,'"

Frühmittelalterliche Studien 32 (1998): 146–63. I am very grateful to Pierre Toubert for having brought this article to my attention.

CHAPTER FIFTEEN:

THE MAGIC OF HYMNS

1. ASMi, *Sforzesco*, 913, letter of Cicco Simonetta to the Duke of Milan, May 20, 1473: *Questa nocte hebbe la lettera dela E.V. continente quanto haveva ad dire ad monsignore da Parma circa'l cantare de la messa ambrosiana per lo aviso che la S.V. li haveva dato...Questo matina inanti el dì, lo andai a trovare in lecto, per disturbarlo uno poco, et li dice quanto la S.V. me haveva scripto, elquale me respose subito che tanto ad luy seria possibile, cantare ne messa ambrosiana né romana, quanto che volare, salvo se'l se volesse mettere al pericolo de la morte. Perché como el cantasse, subito li descenderia el cattarro, che forse lo porria suffocare, e per tale casone sonno XIIII anni che non canto messa. Ma che se maravigliaria venendose a Pavia como la S.V. ha ordinato, se dovesse cantare messa ambrosiana in tale arto, laquale non se po celebrare non ma qui un Milano in le chiese ambrosiane.*

2. ASMi, *Missive*, fol. 235r (May 19, 1473): *Noi havimo scripto al lo reverendo vescovo de Parma che la santità del papa gli manda uno breve, ch'ello habbia ad dire la messa in la exhibitione del capello del reverendissimo cardinale de Novara. Et noi lo havimo admonito ad preparase ad dire questa messa, maxime havendo ad essere ambrosiana, del dicto breve nuy non havimo altro se non quanto ne ha scripto Sacramoro, el quale scrive haverlo veduto.* On this incident, see Paul A. Merkley and Lora M. Merkley, *Music and Patronage in the Sforza Court* (Turnhout: Brepols, 1999), 97.

3. For general context, see Giorgio Chittolini, ed., *Gli Sforza, la Chiesa lombarda, la corte di Roma. Strutture e pratiche beneficiarie nel ducato di Milano (1450–1535)* (Pisa-Naples: GISEM, 1989). For the career of Giovanni Arcimboldi, bishop of Novara (1468–84), archbishop of Milan (1485–88), and "the duke's cardinal" in Rome from 1473 on, see Francesco Somaini, *Un prelato lombardo del XV secolo. Il card. Giovanni Arcimboldi vescovo di Novara, arcivescovo di Milano*, Italia sacra, Studi e documenti di storia ecclesiastica 74 (Rome: Herder, 2003), at 1:527 for the quotation. Arcimboldi left instructions on his death that he was to be buried in Milan's Duomo (*in ecclesia sua Mediolanensi*, says his will, dated September 18, 1488: ibid., 1:166, n. 47. This broke with the practice of other cardinals, who customarily chose a Roman church as a burial site. Arcimboldi never forgot Ambrose's city, even distinguishing himself as a defender of its liturgical tradition, as noted earlier (see Chapter 14, "Order Through Books: Reform, Preserve, and Govern").

Notes

4. The ceremony to honor the new orator would eventually be held, but in Milan, at an Ambrosian Mass officiated by the archpriest of the Duomo, as Cicco Simonetta reported in his diary. See Gregory Lubkin, *A Renaissance Court: Milan under Galeazzo Maria Sforza* (Berkeley: Berkeley University Press, 1994), 164.

5. Ernesto Teodoro Moneta-Caglio, "Perché il rito ambrosiano si chiama ambrosiano," *Ambrosius* 50 (1974): 393–400.

6. This perspective is particularly prevalent in recent historiography: see Michael Stuart Williams, "Hymns as Acclamations: The Case of Ambrose of Milan," *Journal of Late Antiquity* 6, no. 1 (2013): 108–34; and Brian P. Dunkle, *Enchantment and Creed in the Hymns of Ambrose of Milan* (Oxford: Oxford University Press, 2016).

7. Jacques Fontaine, "L'apport de la tradition poétique romaine à la formation de l'hymnodie latine chrétienne," *Revue des études latines* 52 (1974): 318–55, reprinted in Jacques Fontaine, *Études sur la poésie latine tardive d'Ausone à Prudence* (Paris: Belles Lettres, 1980), 146–83.

8. On the influence of Hilary's hymns (only three of which have come down to us) on Ambrose, the key reference is still Jacques Fontaine, "Les origines de l'hymnodie chrétienne latine, d'Hilaire de Poitiers à Ambroise de Milan," *Revue de l'Institut catholique de Paris* 14 (1985): 15–51.

9. Bede, *De arte metrica* 21, in *Bedae opera didascalica*, ed. C. W. Jones, CCL 123 A (Turnhout: Brepols, 1975), 135: *Metrum iambicum tetrametrum recipit iambum locis omnibus, spondeum tantum locis inparibus. Quo scriptus est hymnus Sedulii: A solis ortu carmine… Sed et Ambrosiani eo maxime currunt: Deus creator omnium; Iam surgit hora tertia; Splendor paternae gloriae; Aeterne rerum conditor; et caeteri perplures. In quibus pulcherrimo est decore conpositus hymnus beatorum martyrum, cuius loca cuncta inparia spondeum, iambum tenent paria; cuius principium est: Aeterna Christi munera.*

10. These were canon 14 at the Council of Vannes (455); canon 30 at the Council of Agde (506); canon 24 at the second Council of Tours (567); and canon 13 at the fourth Council of Toledo (633). They are cited by Jacques Fontaine, "Introduction générale," in *Ambroise de Milan. Hymnes*, ed. Jacques Fontaine (Paris: Cerf, 1992), 110 and n. 223.

11. *Les canons des conciles mérovingiens (VIe–VIIe siècles)*, ed. and trans. Jean Gaudemet and Brigitte Basdevant, 2 vols., Sources chrétiennes 354–55 (Paris: Cerf, 1989). Council of Tours II (567), canon 24: *Et licet libros Ambrosianos habeamus in canone, tamen quoniam reliquorum sunt aliqui, qui digni sunt forma cantari, uolumos libenter amplectere praeterea, quorum auctorum nomina fuerint in limine prenotata; quoniam, quae fide constiterint, dicendi ratione non obstant.* The translation has been modified

here: the editors follow Baümer in changing *libros* to *hymnos*, which is probably unjustified (Suitbert Baümer, *Histoire du Bréviaire*, trans. Dom Réginald Biron (Paris, 1905), 2.34). English trans. of canon 24, Susan Boynton in "The Theological Role of Office Hymns in a Ninth-Century Trinitarian Controversy," https://www.academia.edu/1364084/THE_THEOLOGICAL_ROLE_OF_OFFICE_HYMNS_IN_A_NINTH-CENTURY_TRINITARIAN_CONTROVERSY

12. On the problematics presented here, see the array of contributions collected in Michel Zimmermann, ed., *Auctor & auctoritas. Invention et conformisme dans l'écriture médiévale. Actes du colloque de Saint-Quentin-en-Yvelines (1416 juin 1999),* Mémoires et documents 59 (Paris: École des Chartes, 2001). See also the recent summation by Pierre Chastang, "L'archéologie du texte médiéval. Autour de travaux récents sur l'écrit au Moyen Âge," *Annales HSS* 63, no. 2 (2008): 245–69. But I draw here particularly on the thoughts of Gérard Leclerc, *Histoire de l'autorité. L'assignation des énoncés culturels et la généalogie de la croyance* (Paris: PUF, 1996). See also the insightful remarks by Paul Gerhard Schmidt, "Peché tanti anonimi nel medioevo? Il problema della personalità dell'autore nella filologia mediolatina," *Filologia mediolatina* 6 (1999): 1–8.

13. Marie-Hélène Jullien, "La tradition manuscrite des quatorze 'Hymnes' attribués à saint Ambroise, jusqu'à la fin du XIᵉ siècle," doctoral thesis, University of Paris 4, Jacques Fontaine advisor. See also Marie-Hélène Jullien, "Les sources de la tradition ancienne des *Hymnes* attribuées à Ambroise de Milan," *Revue d'histoire des textes* 19 (1989): 57–189.

14. Respectively: Karlsruhe, Badische Landesbibliothek, Aug. 195; Sankt Paul im Lavanttal, Stiftsbibliothek, 86 b/1; Paris, Bibliothèque nationale de France, lat. 528.

15. Berne, Stadtbibliothek, 455.

16. Joseph Szövérffy, *Latin hymns*, Typologie des sources du Moyen Âge occidental 55 (Turnhout: Brepols, 1989), 35 et seq.

17. Münich, Bayerische Staatsbibliothek, Cla. 343; Rome, Biblioteca Vaticana, Vat. lat. 82; Rome, Biblioteca Vaticana, Vat. lat. 83. For a table showing the occurrence of Ambrose's *hymnes* in manuscript, see Fontaine, *Ambroise de Milan. Hymnes,* 696–98.

18. Quoted by Walther Bulst, *Hymni latini antiquissimi LXXV, Psalmi III* (Heidelberg: F.H. Kerle, 1956), 31. See also Jacques Fontaine, "Introduction générale," in Fontaine, *Ambroise de Milan. Hymnes,* 13–14, n. 5.

19. For the night office (9.4): *Inde sequatur ambrosianum, deinde sex psalmi cum antiphonas*; for lauds (12.4): *Inde benedictiones et laudes, lectionem de Apocalypsis una*

ex corde, et responsorium, ambrosianum, versu, canticum de Evangelia, litania, et completum est; but also for the end of lauds and for ordinary days (13.11): *Post haec sequantur laudes; deinde lectio una apostoli memoriter recitanda, responsorium, ambrosianum, versu, canticum de Evangelia, litania et completum est;* and for vespers (17.8): *Post quibus psalmis, lectio recitanda est; inde responsorium, ambrosianum, versu, canticum de Evangelia, litania, et oratione dominica fiant missae.*

20. Federico Visconti, *Les sermons et la visite pastorale de Federico Visconti, archevêque de Pise (1253–1277),* ed. Nicole Bériou and Isabelle Le Masne de Chermon, Sources et documents d'histoire du Moyen Âge 3 (Rome: École française de Rome, 2001), 492 and ad indicem.

21. Walafrid Strabo, *Libellus de exordiis et incrementis quarundam in observationibus ecclesiasticis rerum,* PL, vol. 114, 955A: *incredibile enim uidetur illum tales aliquos fecisse quales multi inueniuntur, id est qui…insolitam Ambrosio in ipsis dictionibus rusticitatem demonstrant.*

22. Bartolomeo Carusi, *Divi Ambrosii milleloquium* (Lyon: Senetonii, 1556).

23. Milan, Biblioteca Capitolare Metropolitano, 2.D.2.23. This manuscript, comprising 23 folios, is cited by Enrico Cattaneo, "Lo studio delle opere di S. Ambrogio a Milano dei sec. XV–XVI," in *Studi storici in memoria di Mons. Angelo Mercati, prefetto dell'Archivio vaticano,* Fontes ambrosiani 30 (Milan: Giuffrè, 1956), 147–67; at 151, a listing of the forty-one hymns glossed.

24. Milan, Biblioteca Capitolare Metropolitano, 2.D.2.23, fol. 23v: *Hos hymnos beati Ambrosii quibus sua ecclesia Mediolanensis utitur cum etiam in officio et Missa alius ritus et singularis sit, aliaque observantia, a ceteris omnibus totius orbis christiani ecclesiis decrevi ego Franciscus de lacruce minimus decretorum doctor, Primicerius et ordinarius dictae ecclesiae, pro litteali expositione apud rudiores minusque intelligentes clericos, glosulis explanare. Non ut graves tanti doctoris sententias, altaque misteria videar attigisse, sed ut dumtaxat vocabula, non omnibus nota, et litterae sensus ad omnium cognitionem planiorem reducerem, pro fraterna caritate mea in omnes, pro devocione quoque mea singulari ad hunc sanctum et patrem nostrum Ambrosianum.*

25. As demonstrated by his two wills (August 9, 1464, and March 18, 1474), which mention manuscripts that include texts by Ambrose. See Monica Pedralli, *Novo, grande, coverto et ferrato. Gli inventari di biblioteca e la cultura a Milano nel Quattrocento* (Milan: Vita e Pensiero, 2002). On the commentaries themselves, see Mirella Ferrari, "Un bibliotecario milanese del Quattrocento: Francesco della Croce," in *Ricerche storiche sulla Chiesa ambrosiana* 10, Archivio ambrosiano 42 (Milan: NED, 1981), 182.

26. Michel Huglo et al., *Fonti e paleografia del canto ambrosiano,* Archivio ambro-

siano 7 (Milan: NED, 1961), 85–98 (nos. 160 to 198): approximately forty songs compose the "hymnic block" of the Milanese tradition. The most complete hymnal with musical notation was copied no earlier than 1336 (since it includes, in its correct place in the liturgy, the hymn of the Feast of *Corpus Domini*); its *incipit* unambiguously states the prevailing concept of Ambrose's authorship of the corpus: *In Christi nomine incipit liber hymnorum per totius anni circulum secundum consuetudinem sacratissimi doctorique patris nostri Ambrosii* (Milan, Biblioteca Trivulziana, M32, p. 87, no. 162).

27. These are *Orabo mente Dominum* (attributed to Ambrose by Cassiodorus); *Fit porta Christi praevia* (cited as a work of Ambrose by Ildefonso of Toledo); and three hymns wrongly assigned to Ambrose on the basis of Hincmar's testimony, *Somno refectis artubus*, *Consors paterni liminis*, and *O lux beata Trinitas*. None of these hymns, it's worth noting, figures in the list by Francesco della Croce, as they failed to correspond to the liturgical tradition of the Milanese Church: see *Sancti Ambrosii Mediolanensis episcopi opera…studio et labore monachorum ordinis sancti Benedicti e congregatione Sancti Mauri*, 4 vols. (the hymns constitute a portion of the last volume, c. 1219–24).

28. Luigi Biraghi, *Inni sinceri e carmi di Sant'Ambrogio, vescovo di Milano*, (Milan: 1862). This method, for instance, allowed Biraghi to authenticate Hymn 8, *Agnes beatae virginis*, as Ambrose's, despite the lack of any late-Roman *testimonia*, but on the basis of an analysis of stylistic similarities and manuscript transmission. Today this piece is considered as very probably Ambrosian (see the comment by Gérard Nauroy in Fontaine, *Ambroise de Milan. Hymnes*, 363–74; and Cécile Lanéry, *Ambroise de Milan hagiographe* [Paris: Institut d'Études Augustiniennes, 2008], 238–42). A useful account of Biraghi's method of attribution is in Lugi Pizzolato, "Luigi Biraghi e l'innografia ambrosiana," *Studia ambrosiana. Annali dell'Academia di Sant'Ambrogio* 2 (2008): 197–228.

29. While some scholars have kept the numbering system of Biraghi's eighteen hymns, e.g., Visonà, *Cronologia ambrosiana*, 109–16 (see chap. 2, n. 5), we follow here the practice (also adopted by Jacques Fontaine for his recent edition) defined by Guido Maria Dreves in *Analecta Hymnica*, 50 (*Hymnographi latini. Lateinische Hymnendichter des Mittelalters*), (Leipzig, 1907): 10–21, which numbers the hymns from one to fourteen in the order set by the liturgical year, as they appeared in the first Milanese manuscripts forming the *Hymnarium Ambrosianum*.

30. Augustine, *Retractationes* I.21.1, CCL 57, 62: *In quo dixi quodam loco de apostolo Pietro, quod in illo tamquam in petra fundata sit ecclesia, qui sensus etiam cantatur*

Notes

ore multorum in uersibus beatissimi Ambrosii, ubi de gallo gallinacio ait: "Hoc ipse petra ecclesiae canenete culpam diluit"; Ambrose, *Hexameron* 5.24.88. See the comment by Jacques Fontaine in Fontaine, *Ambroise de Milan. Hymnes*, 143–47.

31. See the comments by Jean-Louis Charlet in Fontaine, *Ambroise de Milan. Hymnes*, 207–8.

32. Augustine, *De beata vita* 35: *Hic mater recognitis uerbis quae suae memoriae penitus inhaerebant et quasi euigilans in fidem suam, uersum illum sacerdotis nostri: "Foue precantes, Trinitas"...* and Augustine, *Confessions*, 9.12.32: *recordatus sum uersus Ambrosii tui: "tu es enim, Deus creator omnium...luctusque soluat anxios."* Note that, from the *memoria* of the mother to the *recordatio* of the son, these two passages nicely illustrate the emotional and mnemonic power of hymns, whose memory brings comfort. On the manuscript tradition, see the comments of Michel Perrin in Fontaine, *Ambroise de Milan. Hymnes*, 231–34. English translation of passage from *De vita beata*: Augustine of Hippo, *Trilogy of Faith and Happiness*, trans. Ronald J. Teske et al., ed. Boniface Ramsey (Hyde Park, NY: New City Press, 2010), 53.

33. *Pontificum Romanorum epistulae genuinae*, PL 53, 289 B: *Recordor beatae memoriae Ambrosium in dies natalis Domini nostri Iesu Christi omnem populum fecisse una uoce Deo canere...* Quoted in the commentary by Jacques Fontaine in Fontaine, *Ambroise de Milan. Hymnes*, 265–67, at 267n5.

34. On the quadripartite division of the hymns, see Jacques Fontaine, "Introduction générale," in Fontaine, *Ambroise de Milan. Hymnes*, 64.

35. Manlio Simonetti, *Studi sull'innologia popolare cristiana dei primi secoli – Atti della Accademia nazionale dei Lincei. Memorie, Classe di Scienze morali, storiche e filologiche* (Rome, 1952), 383.

36. This basis of argument, it should be noted, is open to challenge. A case in point is Hymn 13, *Apostolorum supparem*, devoted to the martyrdom of Saint Lawrence, which is very close to the account given by Ambrose in his *De officiis* but is somewhat idiosyncratic in its partition and symmetry. In his introduction, Jacques Fontaine settles on a label of "doubtful authenticity," directing the reader to the discussion by Jeannine de Montgolfier and Gérard Nauroy, who for their part defend the hymn's probable authenticity (Fontaine, *Ambroise de Milan. Hymnes*, 101 and 549–58), reprising the arguments in Gérard Nauroy, "Le martyre de Laurent dans l'hymnodie et la prédication des IVe et Ve siècles et l'authenticité ambrosienne de l'hymne 'Apostolorum supparem,'" *Revue des études augustiniennes* 35 (1989): 44–82.

37. Jacques Fontaine, "Introduction générale," in Fontaine, *Ambroise de Milan*.

Hymnes, 102. The hymns considered "certainly Ambrosian" are Hymn 1, *Aeterne rerum conditor*; Hymn 3, *Iam surgit hora tertia*; Hymn 4, *Deus creator omnium*; and Hymn 5, *Intende qui regis Israel*. In the "very probably Ambrosian" category are Hymn 2, *Splendor paternae gloriae*; Hymn 8, *Agnes beatae virginis*; Hymn 10, *Victor, Nabor, Felix pii*; and Hymn 11, *Grates tibi, Iesu nouas*. Labeled "possibly Ambrosian" are Hymn 6, *Amore Christi nobilis*; Hymn 12, *Apostolorum passio*; and Hymn 14, *Aeterna Christi munera*. Those considered "probably not Ambrosian" are Hymn 7, *Illuminans altissimus*; Hymn 9, *Hic est dies uerus*; and Hymn 13, *Apostolorum supparem*.

38. Céline Urlacher-Becht, "La tradition manuscrite des hymnes d'Ennode de Pavie," *Paideia* 65 (2010): 511–31. The fact that Ennodius's compendium includes twelve Ambrosian hymns is perhaps an indication that Ambrose was himself the author of twelve hymns, as Stéphane Gioanni has in fact suggested.

39. See for example MS M32 in the Biblioteca Trivulziana in Milan, written after 1336, since the hymn for the Feast of Corpus Christi appears there in its proper liturgical place. It is probably the most complete hymnal with neumatic notation (Huglo, et al., *Fonti e paleografia*, no. 162, p. 87). Its *incipit* gives a good sense of the contemporary concept of a liturgical tradition deriving its authority from Ambrose's patronage: *In Xsti nomine incipit liber hymnorum per totius anni circulum secundum consuetudinem sacratissimi doctorique patris nostri Ambrosii.*

40. The fundamental study on this subject is still Hans Jörg Auf der Maur, *Das Psalmenverständnis des Ambrosius von Mailand. Ein Beitrag zum Deutungshintergrund der Psalmenverwendung im Gottesdienst der Alten Kirche* (Leiden: Brill, 1977). See also (notably for the Ambrosian recasting of Greek authors such as Philo and Origen) Paola Francesca Moretti, *Non harundo sed calamus. Aspetti letterari della "Explanatio psalmorum XII" di Ambrogio*, Il Filarete (Milan: LED, 2000).

41. On this point, see the remarks of Pierre Hadot, "Introduction," in Ambroise de Milan, *Apologie de David*, Sources chrétiennes 239 (Paris: Cerf, 1977), 7–48.

42. For Jacques Fontaine, the exact location is "probably variable." See his "Introduction générale," in Fontaine, *Ambroise de Milan. Hymnes*, 13 (see also p. 45, where he refers to it as an "unresolved problem").

43. Antoon Bastiaensen, "Les hymnes d'Ambroise de Milan: à propos d'une nouvelle édition," *Vigilae Christianae* 48 (1994): 164.

44. Ambrose of Milan, *Expositio psalmi 118*, ed. Michael Petschenig and Michaela Zelzer, CSEL 62 (Vienna: 1999), 1.1: *Unde et David sanctus ... aeternae illius caelestisque delectationis gratiam ... studens reformare psallendi munere caslestis nobis*

instar conversationis instituit. See the comments on this text in Jacques Fontaine, "Prose et poésie: l'interférence des genres et des styles dans la création littéraire d'Ambroise de Milan," in *Ambrosius episcopus. Atti del Congresso internazionale di studi ambrosiani nel XVI centenario della elevazione di sant'Ambrogio alla cattedra episcopale, Milano 2–7 dicembre 1974*, ed. Giuseppe Lazzati (Milan: Vita e Pensiero, 1976), 1:142 et seq.

45. Lanéry, *Ambroise de Milan hagiographe*, 75–77 and 228 et seq.

46. Giorgio Agamben, *The Kingdom and the Glory, Homo Sacer, II, 2*, trans. Lorenzo Chiesa (with Matteo Mandarini) (Stanford, CA: Stanford University Press, 2011), 352 and 354.

47. See the comments of Alain Goulon in Fontaine, *Ambroise de Milan. Hymnes*, 585–94. There are still doubts about the Ambrosianness of this hymn, though it has quantitatively the best manuscript tradition: it features in fifty-eight of the seventy-six witness manuscripts addressed by Marie-Hélène Jullien. On this point, see the recent article by Marco Navoni, "'Hymni ex eius nomine ambrosiani vocatur.' Gli inni di sant'Ambrogio nella liturgia ambrosiana," *Studia ambrosiana. Annali dell'Accademia di sant'Ambrogio* 2 (2008): 229–50.

48. Ambrose, *In psalm.* 1.9: *In paucissimus chordis saepe errant digiti artificis, sed in populo spiritus artifex nescit errare.* And, further along, at 1.11: *quid igitur psalmus nisi uirtutum est organum, quod sancti spiritus plectro pangens propheta uenerabilis caelestis sonitus fecit in terris dulcedinem resultare?*

49. Lanéry, *Ambroise de Milan hagiographe*, 230–31.

50. English trans.: Brian P. Dunkle, *Enchantment and Creed in the Hymns of Ambrose of Milan*, Oxford Early Christian Studies (Oxford: Oxford University Press, 2016)

51. Ambrose, *De officiis* 2.18.140, 71: *Tale aurum sanctus martyr Laurentius Domino reseruauit, a quo cum quaererentur thesauri Ecclesiae, promisit se demonstraturum. Sequenti die pauperes duxit. Interrogatus ubi essent thesauri quos promiserat, ostendit pauperes dicens: Hi sunt thesauri Ecclesiae.*

52. Jesús San Bernardino, "*Sub imperio discordia:* l'uomo che voleva essere Eliseo (giugno 386)," in *Nec timeo mori. Atti del Congresso internazionale di studi ambrosiani nel XVI centenario della morte di sant'Ambrogio*, ed. Luigi Pizzolato and Marco Rizzi (Milan: Vita e Pensiero, 1998), 709–37, esp. 719 et seq.

53. Ambrose, *De officiis* 2.28.136, p. 70: *Melius est enim pro misericordia causas praestare uel inuidiam perpeti quam praetendere inclementiam ut nos aliquando in inuidiam incidimus quod confregerimus uasa mystica ut captivos redimeremus, quod arianis displicere potuerat; nec tam factum displiceret quam ut esset quod in nobis reprehenderetur.*

Notes

54. Lanéry, *Ambroise de Milan hagiographe*, 141–53.

55. Peter Brown, *Through the Eye of a Needle* (Princeton, NJ: Princeton University Press, 2012), 135–47.

56. Ambrose, *De Nabuthae* 1.1, trans. Boniface Ramsey, *Ambrose* (New York: Routledge, 1997), 117.

57. Ambrose, *De Nabuthae* 12.53, Ramsey, *Ambrose*, 135.

58. Bartolomeo Carusi, *Divi Ambrosii milleloquium* (Lyon: Senetonii, 1556), 1467.

59. English trans.: Charles Bigg, *The English Hymnal* (London: Oxford University Press, 1906).

60. This twin function of hymns is suggested by Jacques Fontaine in his "Introduction générale," in Fontaine, *Ambroise de Milan. Hymnes*, 51.

61. Pierre Hadot, *Exercices spirituels et philosophie antique*, (Paris: Albin Michel, 2002), esp. 81 et seq.

62. Augustine, *Sermo 336 in dedicatione ecclesiae*, PL 38, col. 1475, § 6, quoted by Dominique Iogna Prat, *La maison Dieu. Une histoire monumentale de l'Église au Moyen Âge* (Paris: Seuil, 2006), 581.

63. Jacques Fontaine, "Introduction générale," in Fontaine, *Ambroise de Milan. Hymnes*, 25.

64. See the commentary by Jacques Fontaine in Fontaine, *Ambroise de Milan. Hymnes*, 268.

65. All the more so as it is not impossible that Ambrose might have reworked his hymns after the resolution of the conflict of 386 to give them a calmer aspect – such at any rate is the hypothesis developed in Francesco Corsaro, "L'innografia ambrosiana dalla polemica teologica alla liturgia," *Augustinianum* 38 (1998): 371–84. By attenuating the polemical thrust of these songs of resistance, he no doubt made it easier to integrate them into the liturgical order, while opening them to possible reappropriation and reinterpretation for political ends.

66. See Chapter 5: Ambrose and the "Homoian wolves": heresy, barbarism, empire.

67. In the old Roman psalter: *Qui regis Israhel intende, qui deducis uelut ouem Ioseph, qui sedes super Cherubin, appare coram Effrem et Beniamin et Manasse, excita potentiam tuam et ueni, ut saluos facias nos.* Certain scholars (Manlio Simonetti among them) cast doubt on the authenticity of this first stanza, arguing from stylistic criteria (which Jacques Fontaine disputes) and pointing to discrepancies in the manuscript transmission, since only a third of the witness

Notes

manuscripts include it. But those manuscripts, it should be noted, include all the representatives of the Milanese tradition. Eng. trans. from Dunkle, *Enchantment and Creed in the Hymns of Ambrose of Milan*, 224.

68. Philippe Buc, *L'ambiguïté du Livre. Pouvoir et peuple dans les commentaires de la Bible au Moyen Âge* (Paris: Beauchesne, 1994).

69. Ambrose, *De institutione virgines* 12.7: *habitauit in nobis quasi rex sedens in aula regali uteri uirginalis… Aula regalis est uirgo quae non est uiro subdita, sed Deo soli.*

70. Dunkle, *Enchantment and Creed in the Hymns of Ambrose of Milan*, 224.

71. Ambrose, *In psalm.* 45.13. But also: *De institutione virgines* 17.105: *ut habitationi proproae caelestis aulam uirginis dedicaret*; and 7.50 (still referring to Mary): *aula caelestium sacramentorum.* See the commentary by Jacques Fontaine in Fontaine, *Ambroise de Milan. Hymnes*, 287–88.

72. Thus, for example, in the first stanza: *Victor Nabor Felix pii/Mediolani martyres,/solo hospites, Mauri genus/terrisque nostris aduenae.* Giuseppe Lazzati, "L'inno Victor, Nabor, Felixque pii," *Ambrosius* 36 (1960): 69–80.

73. Dunkle, *Enchantment and Creed in the Hymns of Ambrose of Milan.*

74. Hannelore Zug Tucci, "Il carroccio nella vita comunale italiana," *Quellen und Forschungen aus italienischen Archiven und Bibliotheken* 65 (1985).

75. *Historia diplomatica Friderici secundi*, ed. Jean-Louis Alphonse Huillard-Bréholles (Paris, 1852), 1:161–63 (letter from Frederick II to the Roman Senate, sent to accompany his trophy, January 1238), trans. Véronique Rouchon Mouilleron, "Frédéric II et le *carroccio* de Milan," in *Villes d'Italie. Textes et documents des XII*, *XIII* *et XIV* *siècles*, ed. Jean-Louis Gaulin, Armand Jamme, and Véronique Rouchon Mouilleron (Lyon: PUL, 2005), 65.

76. From an abundant literature on the politicization of music at the end of the Middle Ages, see the insightful remarks of David Fiala, "Le prince au miroir des musiques politiques des XIV* et XV* siècles," in *Le Prince au miroir de la littérature politique de l'Antiquité aux Lumières*, ed. Lydwine Scordia and Frédérique Lachaud (Rouen: Publications des Universités de Rouen et du Havre, 2007), 319–50.

77. A first approach in Terence Bailey, "Ambrosian Choral Psalmody: An Introduction," *Rivista internazionale di Musica Sacra* 1 (1980): 82–99.

78. Paulinus of Milan, *Vita Ambrosii* 13.3: *Hoc in tempore primum antiphonae, hymni et vigiliae in ecclesia Mediolanensi celebrari coeperunt.* Ramsey, *Ambrose*, 201.

79. Isidore of Seville, *Etymologiae* 6.19.8, PL 82, col. 252 C: *Inter responsorios autem et antiphonas hoc differt, quod in responsoriis unus versum dicit, in antiphonis autem versibus alternant chori.*

Notes

80. All according to Michel Huglo, "Le Répons-Graduel de la Messe. Évolution de la forme. Permanence de la fonction," *Schweizer Jahrbuch für Muzikwissenschaft Neue Folge* 2 (1982): 53–73, esp. 56; reprinted in Michel Huglo, *Chant grégorien et musique médiévale* (Aldershot and Burlington, VT: Ashgate/Variorum, 2005).

81. See for example Carl P. E. Springer, "Ambrose's 'Veni redemptor gentium': the Aesthetics of Antiphony," *Jahrbuch für Antike und Christentum* 34 (1991): 121–37. At issue is Hymn 5, *Intende qui regis Israel*, the authenticity of whose first stanza is open to question.

82. See Lanéry, *Ambroise de Milan hagiographe*, 233.

83. Philippe Bernard, *Du chant romain au chant grégorien* (Paris: Cerf, 1996), 241.

84. As has Philippe Bernard, "A-t-on connu la psalmodie alternée à deux chœurs en Gaule, avant l'époque carolingienne?," *Revue bénédictine* 114 (2004): 280–325; and 115 (2005): 33–60.

85. Michel Huglo, "Recherches sur la psalmodie alternée à deux-chœurs," *Revue bénédictine* 116 (2006): 352–66.

86. Olivier Cullin, "De la psalmodie sans refrain à la psalmodie responsoriale. Transformation et conservation dans les répertoires liturgiques latins," *Revue de Musicologie* 77, no. 1 (1991): 24: "The Rule of Saint Benedict in fact allows for two possibilities. *Antiphona*, in a somewhat abstract sense, designates a mode of execution: *alternation*, with two traditional choirs in a monastic assembly familiar with the psalms. This style is applicable to a direct, unaltered form, but also to a responsorial form, which is by definition antiphonal. The second sense actually corroborates this point of view. More concrete in meaning, it designates the piece of song, the refrain, that the choirs add to the psalmody (which thus becomes responsorial in its literary form), either adding it after each versicle, or after every two versicles, or else before and after the psalm, according to actual practice."

87. Huglo et al., *Fonti e paleografia*, 39–44 (n. 23), for a description of the main witness manuscript from the twelfth century (no. 50), London, British Museum, Add. 34209.

88. Huglo et al., *Fonti e paleografia*, 66–86, nos. 98 to 122bis. This handsome manuscript, for instance, at 49–50, no. 61, entitled *Cantus ambrosiani* and dated 1386, is an antiphonary for the offices from the Septuagesima to Holy Saturday (Milan, ASA, M 24).

89. Huglo et al., *Fonti e paleografia*, 127.

90. In a phrase used by Bernard, *Du chant romain*, 766.

91. Alejandro Planchart, "Les traditions du chant dans l'Europe occidentale," in *Musiques. Une encyclopédie pour le XXIᵉ siècle*, vol. 4, *Histoire des musiques européenes*, ed. Jean-Jacques Nattiez (Arles: Actes Sud/Cité de la Musique, 2006), 156.

92. Bernard, *Du chant romain*, 762.

93. Milan, Biblioteca Trivulziana, Cod. 92 (H 125): *Questo libro si è de Iohanne di sazii, scripto per sua mane propria, ad honore de l'alto e superno Dio e de la glorioxa Vergene Maria e de Sancto Ambroxio patre nostro z sz tuti li santi e sante de vita eterna, 1490, fornito a dì XI de novembre. E sii noto e manifesto a zeschaduna fedele persona, che legiarà questo libro, voglia dire per sua gratia una Ave Maria per l'anima de colui che à scripto questo libro MCCCCLXXXX.*

94. Milan, Biblioteca Trivulziana, Cod. 92 (H 125), fol. 111v–115r, partially published in Enrico Cattaneo, "Un Milanese a Messa alla fine del Quattrocento," *Ambrosius* 38 (1962): 1–14.

95. Cattaneo, "Un Milanese a Messa," 5: *Dilcho, prima, che tu dì pensare quando tu voy andare a la giexa, e dire a te medesmo unde vay; pensa che ta vay alla chaxa de dio e al palazo de lo imperatore de vita eterna, in lo quale se fa la pace tra dio e l'anima del peccatore e si se ghe fa le noze intra cristo suo fiolo e le anime nostre, che sonon spoxate a luy, cioè quele che sono in stato de gratia et amano luy sopra tute le cose."*

96. Cattaneo, "Un Milanese a Messa," 6–7: *Et quando el dice* chirieleyson, *che se dice nove volte per memoria de novy ordine de angeli che sono in cello, pensa che de zascuno ordine si ne descende alquanti a quela messa per noy adiutare e per movere y core nostri a devotione, aspetando el signore che de venire; e in segno di questo se dice incontinente quelo canto de alegreza, zioè* gloria in escelsis deo *et cetera: lo qual canto se li angeli in quela hora che christo nassete per insegnare a li homini como lo dovesse laudare e rengratiare de tanto beneficio e tu dì guardare e alegrarte de questo angelico canto e dirlo con loro se tu lo say…In continente poy se canta* aleluya *in segno de grandissima alegreza, et tu di alora pensare che queste son le trombe e le violle e le githare con tuti li altri instrumenti che se fa in contra al nostro signore, che vene a alegrete in lo tuo core e fa festa aspetando de vedere el to signore.*

97. Johannes Burckard, *Liber notarum ab anno 1483 ad 1506*, ed. Enrico Celani (Città di Castello: 1906–43), 635: *Legatus, et cum eo dux et oratores quatuor supradicti equitarunt ab ecclesiam beate Marie…conventus fratrum minorum de observantia congregationis beati Amadei, extra portam Tosam, ubi celebravit missam bassam capellanus ducis, cantoribus cantantibus partem introitus, Et in terra, Patrem, Sanctus, et Agnus Dei, absque eo quod celebrans, Gloria in excelsis vel Credo, aut quid aliud cantet; sed eo dicente seu voce submissa huiusmodi incipiente, illi cantabant modus quod apud nos singule apud ducem vero Ludovicum consuetus.*

Notes

98. On this point, see the comments on this passage in Merkley and Merkley, *Music and Patronage*, 335n2.

99. Étienne Anheim, "Une controverse médiévale sur la musique: la décrétale *Docta Sanctorum* de Jean XXII et le débat sur l'*ars nova* dans les années 1320," *Revue Mabillon* 72 (2000): 221-46, esp. 233-35.

100. Lynn Halpern Ward, "The *Motetti Missales* Repertory Reconsidered," *Journal of the American Musicological Society* 39 (1986): 491-523.

101. Patrick Macey, "Galeazzo Maria Sforza and Musical Patronage in Milan: Compère, Weerbeke and Josquin," *Early Music History* 15 (1996): 147-212.

102. An eyewitness account of the duke's personal involvement can be found in a letter written to him by one of his singers, Raynero Precigney, on July 3, 1473, published in Evelyn Welch, "Sight, Sound and Ceremony in the Chapel of Galeazzo Maria Sforza," *Early Music History* 12 (1993): 151-90 (171-72 for the letter).

103. To use an expression from Merkley and Merkley, *Music and Patronage*, 218. On this imposing work, which is a mine of information for the study of musicians at the court of Milan in the second half of the fifteenth century, see the detailed assessment by Gregory Lubkin in *Journal of the American Musicology Society* 55, no. 2 (2002): 346-53.

104. See, for example, Jaap van Benthem, "*O Mater Dei, Memento Mei.* Annotations sur les structures symboliques de quatorze motets mariaux de Josquin des Prez," in *Musique, théologie et sacré, d'Oresme à Érasme*, ed. Annie Cœurdevey and Philippe Vendrix (Ambronay: Ambronay éditions, 2008), 231-89.

105. Merkley and Merkley, *Music and Patronage*, 321-57.

106. AFD, *Ordinazioni*, 1492, IV, fol. 60v, quoted by Merkley and Merkley, *Music and Patronage*, 327n12.

CHAPTER SIXTEEN:

MINISTRY OF GLORY

1. Gérard Labrot, *L'image de Rome. Une arme pour la Contre-Réforme, 1534–1677* (Seyssel: Champ Vallon, 1987), 20-21 and 29.

2. Labrot, *L'image de Rome*, 249 and 266.

3. Labrot, *L'image de Rome*, 271.

4. Labrot, *L'image de Rome*, 281.

5. Labrot, *L'image de Rome*, 282.

6. From a sizable literature, I would cite the recent summary by Danilo Zardin, *Carlo Borromeo. Cultura, santità, governo* (Milan: Vita e Pensiero, 2010); see also the essays collected in *Per ragioni di salute. San Carlo Borromeo nel quarto*

centenario della canonizzazione 1610–2010, ed. Fabiola Giancotti (Milan: Spirali, 2010). On the iconography, see Lara Maria Rosa Barbieri, "Carlo Borromeo: l'immagine di un santo. Iconografia e culto nella diocesi milanese XVII e XIX secolo," in *Norma del Clero. Speranza del gregge: l'opera riformatrice di san Carlo tra centro e periferia, atti del Convegno (Milano-Angera, 21–22 maggio 2010)* (Germignaga: Magazzeno Storico Verbanese, 2015), 143–61.

7. Michel de Certeau, "Charles Borromée (1538-1584)," in *Le lieu de l'autre. Histoire religieuse et mystique*, Hautes études (Paris: Gallimard-Seuil-EHESS, 2005), 116. This is the French-language version of the article "Carlo Borromeo" in the *Dizionario biografico degli Italiani*, published in 1977.

8. See John M. Headley and John Tomaro, eds., *San Carlo Borromeo: Catholic Reform and Ecclesiastic Politics in the Second Half of the Sixteenth Century* (Washington: Folger Shakespeare Library, 1988); Paolo Biscottini, *Carlo e Federico. La luce dei Borromeo nella Milano spagnola* (Milan: Arti Grafiche Colombo, 2005); and, for more of an overview, Claudia Di Filippo, "The Reformation and the Catholic Revival in the Borromeo's Age," in *A Companion to Late Medieval and Early Modern Milan: The Distinctive Features of an Italian State*, ed. Andrea Gamberini (Leiden-Boston: Brill, 2014), 93-117, esp. 102-13.

9. Quoted by Michel de Certeau, "Charles Borromée," 123.

10. Giovanni Pietro Giussani, *Vita di S. Carlo Borromeo, prete cardinale del titolo di Santa Prassede, arcivescovo di Milano*…(Rome: nella Stamperia della Camera Apostolica, 1610), 590–91.

11. De Certeau, "Charles Borromée," 122.

12. De Certeau, "Charles Borromée," 132.

13. Overview in Angelo Bianchi, "Sant'Ambrogio, san Carlo Borromeo e la 'carità pastorale,'" in *La città e la sua memoria. Milano e la tradizione di sant'Ambrogio* (Milan: Electa, 1997), 289-97.

14. Marie Lezowski, "L'atelier Borromée. L'archevêque de Milan et le gouvernement de l'écrit (1564-1631)," history thesis, University of Paris-Sorbonne, Denis Crouzet advisor, typescript, 2013, 1:170. A large part of what follows is owing to this author's analyses, and I thank Marie Lezowski for providing me access to her thesis in its unpublished form. Only the portion of it addressing the Ambrose library was eventually included in Marie Lezowski, *L'abrégé du monde. Une histoire sociale de la bibliothèque Ambrosienne (v. 1590–v. 1660)* (Paris: Classiques Garnier, 2015).

15. Emilio Galli, "Il sigillo episcopale ambrosiano," *Ambrosius* I (1925): 123-28.

16. Guido Cariboni, "L'iconografia ambrosiana in rapporto al sorgere e al

primo svilupparsi della signoria viscontea," in Boucheron and Gioanni, *La mémoire d'Ambroise*, 137.

17. Ambrose, *Epist.* 77 (M 22). Ambrose, Letter 22, cited in *The Letters of Saint Ambrose, Bishop of Milan*, trans. H. Walford (Aeterna Press, 2015), 146–47.

18. Marie Lezowski, "Le sceau d'Ambroise: l'exemplaire dans l'épiscopat de Charles Borromée," in Boucheron and Gioanni, *La mémoire d'Ambroise*, 523–40.

19. On these "professionals of Borromean memory," see Lezowski, *L'atelier Borromée*, 1:387–94.

20. Marco Navoni, "'Ambrosius quem sibi imitandum proposuerat': il Patrono di Milano riletto da Carlo Borromeo," in *Ambrogio a Milano e all'Ambrosiana*, ed. Raffaele Passarella, Studia ambrosiana 4 (Milan: Biblioteca ambrosiana, 2010), 118.

21. Paolo Prodi, "Riforma interiore e disciplinamento sociale in san Carlo Borromeo," *Intersezioni* 5 (1985): 273–85.

22. Quoted by Lezowski, "Le sceau d'Ambroise," 527.

23. Quoted by Lezowski, *L'atelier Borromée*, 1:171.

24. *Acta Ecclesiae Mediolanensis, a Carolo Card. S. Praxedis Archiepiscopo condita, Federici Card. Borromaei Archiepiscopi Mediolani iussu, undique diligentius collecta, & edita*... (Mediolani: Ex officina Typographica quon. Pacifici Pontij, Impressoris Archiepiscopalis, 1599), 1098. Quoted by Lezowski, *L'atelier Borromée*, 2:183.

25. Lanéry, *Ambroise de Milan hagiographe*, 426–34. The text in question is a pseudo-Ambrosian sermon on Nazarius (CPPM 1.65), included in several Milanese *libelli* of the eleventh and twelfth centuries, but perhaps going back to much earlier collections of sermons (seventh/eighth century?).

26. Lezowski, *L'atelier Borromée*, 1:146 et seq. For the text of the document, see 2:757–62.

27. Giovanni Francesco Bascapè, *Libro d'alcune chiese di Milano, fatto nell'occasione del giubileo d'ordine dell'ill. Monsig. Cardinal di Santa Prassede, Arcivescovo di Milano*... (Milan: appresso Pacifico Pontio, impressore di Monsig. Illustrissimo, 1576), fol. G5v, quoted by Lezowski, *L'atelier Borromée*, 1:176.

28. Lezowski, *L'atelier Borromée*, 1:183.

29. Lezowski, *L'atelier Borromée* 1:178.

30. Cesare Alzati, "Carlo Borromeo e la tradizione liturgica della Chiesa milanese," in *Accademia di San Carlo. Inaugurazione del III anno accademico (Milano, 8 novembre 1980)* (Milan, 1981), 83–99.

31. Introducing his version of the Ambrosian ritual (Sacramentale, 1645), Cardinal Monti, nephew of Federico Borromeo, says the following: *nonnulla*

immutari, quaedam adimi, aliqua etiam addi jussimus prout res ipsa res ipsa postulare nobis visa est; in his tamen omnibus antiquum nostrum ambrosianum ritum conservari retinerique inviolatum omnino voluimus. Quoted by Lejay, "Ambrosien (rit)" in *Dictionnaire d'archéologie chrétienne et de liturgie*, ed. R.P. dom Fernand Cabrol (Paris, 1907), 1:1375n2).

32. Enrico Cattaneo, "Carnevale e Quaresima nell'età di s. Carlo Borromeo," *Ambrosius* 34 (1958): 51–73. See also Franco Buzzi, *Religione, cultura e scienza a Milano. Secoli XVI–XVIII* (Milan: Jaca Book, 2015), 173–77.

33. Bonvesin da la Riva, *De Magnalibus urbis Mediolani* 8.5.

34. ASMi, *Registro delle Missive* 12, fol. 46r (February 25, 1452), quoted by Ludmila Nelidoff, "Le carnaval à Rome, Venise et Milan (XIVᵉ et XVᵉ siècle): un miroir de la société," *Questes* 31 (2015): 53.

35. See, for instance, Tommaso di Carpegna Falconieri, *The Militant Middle Ages: Contemporary Politics Between New Barbarians and Modern Crusaders*, trans. Andrew M. Hiltzik (Leiden: Brill, 2020), 123–27.

36. Dario Fo, *Sant'Ambrogio e l'invenzione di Milano*, ed. Franca Rame and Giselda Palombi (Turin: Einaudi, 2009).

37. Agostino Borromeo, "L'arcivescovo Carlo Borromeo, la Corona spagnola e le controversie giurisdizionali a Milano," in *Carlo Borromeo e l'opera della "grande riforma." Cultura, religione e arti del governo nella Milano del pieno Cinquecento*, ed. Franco Buzzi and Danilo Zardin (Milan: Silvana, 1997), 257–72.

38. On all this, see Marie Lezowski, "Liturgie et domination. L'abolition du dimanche de carnaval par Charles Borromée, archevêque de Milan (1576–1580)," *Siècles* 35–36 (2012), online.

39. Pierre Petitmengin, "Les éditions patristiques de la Contre-Réforme romaine," in *I padri sotto il torchio. Le edizioni dell'antichità cristiana nei secoli XV–XVI. Atti del convegno di studi promosso dalla Società Internazionale per lo Studio del Medioevo Latino, in collaborazione con l'Università di Firenze e l'Università di Pavia (Firenze 25–26 giugno 1999)*, ed. Mariarosa Cortesi (Florence: Sismel, 2002), 3–31.

40. Ambrose, *Opera sancti Ambrosii… cura Felici cardinalis de Monte Alto* (Romae, ex typographia D. Basae [ex. Typ. Vaticana], 1579–87), 6 books in 3 vols.

41. Lezowski, *L'abrégé du monde*, 58–61.

42. Francesco Costa, "Il carteggio Peretti-Borromeo per l'edizione romana delle opere di S. Ambrogio (1579–1585)," *Miscellanea francescana* 86 (1986): 821–77. On the agency of Pizzolpasso, see Enrico Cattaneo, "Un tentativo di riforma," *Ambrosius* 31 (1955).

Notes

43. Lezowski, *L'atelier Borromée*, 1:173. Carlo Borromeo read a first version of the Life of Ambrose written by Cesare Baronio in summer 1582, but we do not know his reaction or what changes he may have requested.

44. The provenance of this relic is unknown. It makes its first appearance under the designation *De dalmatica sancti Ambrosii* in an inventory of relics made on the occasion of a pastoral visit by Borromeo, February 22, 1577. See Anselme Palestra, "Le visite pastorali del Card. Carlo Borromeo al Duomo e alla veneranda fabbrica del Duomo di Milano," in *Il Duomo Cuore e Simbolo di Milano. IV centenario della Dedicazione (1577–1977)* (Milan: Veneranda Fabbrica del Duomo di Milano, 1977), 209.

45. Anna Maria Brizio, "Sant'Ambrogio in maestà nel coro ligneo del duomo fra i santi martiri e i santi vescovi della chiesa milanese," in *Sant'Ambrogio nell'arte del duomo di Milano*, ed. Angelo Paredi and Anna Maria Brizio (Milan: Veneranda fabbrica del Duomo di Milano, 1973), 59–87.

46. Arnalda Dallaj, "Carlo Borromeo e il tema iconografico dei santi arcivescovi milanesi," in *Culto dei santi, istituzioni e classi sociali in età preindustriale*, ed. Sofia Boesch Gajano and Lucia Sebastiani (L'Aquila-Rome: Japadre Editore, 1984), 649–80.

47. Quoted by Gilbert Dagron, *Emperor and Priest: The Imperial Office in Byzantium*, trans. Jean Birrell (Cambridge: Cambridge University Press, 2003), 112.

48. Ernesto Brivio and Marco Navoni, *Vita di Sant'Ambrogio narrata nell'antico coro ligneo del Duomo di Milano* (Milan: NED-Veneranda Fabbrica del Duomo di Milano, 1996), nos. 36, 38, 39, 40, and 41.

49. Quoted by Lezowski, *L'atelier Borromée*, 1:181.

50. Letter from Carlo Borromeo to Cesare Speciano, September 11, 1574, cited by Lezowski, "Le sceau d'Ambroise," 533.

51. Brivio and Navoni, *Vita di Sant'Ambrogio*, no. 56.

52. Paolo Cammarosano, "Ambrogio e Teodosio: assenze e affermazioni di temi iconografici nei conflitti tra *regnum* e *sacerdotium*," in *Scritti di storia medievale offerti a Maria Consiglia de Matteis*, ed. Berardo Pio (Spoleto: Centro italiano di studi sull'alto medioevo, 2011), 84–85.

53. *Ambrogio. L'immagine e il volto, Arte dal XIV al XVII secolo* (Venice: Marsilio, 1998), 88–89 (no. 28).

54. Analisa Albuzzi, "La barba di Ambrogio. Iconografia, erudizione agiografica e propaganda nella Milano dei due Borromeo," in Boucheron and Gioanni, *La mémoire d'Ambroise*, 186.

55. *Acta ecclesiae Mediolanensis* (Milan, 1583), 305, quoted by Jean-Marie Le Gall, *Un idéal masculin. Barbes et moustaches, XVᵉ–XVIIIᵉ siècles* (Paris: Payot, 2011), 133.

Notes

56. Le Gall, *Un idéal masculin*, 134.

57. Lezowski, *L'atelier Borromée*, 1:449.

58. *Ambrogio. L'immagine e il volto*, 82–83 (no. 24).

59. Alessandro Rovetta, "Ambrogio in Pinacoteca Ambrosiana: attestazioni iconografiche di età borromaica," in Passarella, *Ambrogio a Milano*, 179n20.

60. On the question of the resemblance of an individualized portrait, see not only the fundamental writings of Hans Belting, "Blason et portrait. Deux médiums du corps," in *Pour une anthropologie des images*, ed. Hans Belting (Paris: Gallimard, 2004), 153–81, but also the essays collected in *Le portrait: la représentation de l'individu*, ed. Agostino Paravicini Bagliani, Jean-Michel Spieser, and Jean Wirth, Micrologus Library 17 (Florence: Sismel-Edizioni del Galluzo, 2007); also Dominic Olariu, ed., *Le portrait individuel: réflexions autour d'une forme de représentation XIIIᵉ–XVᵉ siècles* (Bern: Peter Lang, 2009).

61. Rovetta, "Ambrogio in Pinacoteca Ambrosiana," 181. The image in the Roman edition was captioned thus: *Ambrosii Episcopi effigies ex antiquis eius imaginibus Mediolani olim depictis ad vivum expressa.*

62. Costa, "Il carteggio Peretti-Borromeo," 876n42.

63. Quoted by Rovetta, "Ambrogio in Pinacoteca Ambrosiana," 180.

64. Quoted by Rovetta, "Ambrogio in Pinacoteca Ambrosiana," 179.

65. Petrarch, *Rerum familiarium* 16.11.12. Francesco Petrarch, *Letters on Familiar Matters*, trans. Aldo S. Bernardo (New York: Italica Press, 2008), 2:319.

66. According to a statement by Giovanni Pietro Puricelli, *Ambrosianae Mediolani basilicae ac monasterii hodie Cistercensis monumenta* (Milan: Tip. I. P. Ramellati, 1645), 1.8.

67. Etienne Anheim, "La vérité de la représentation. L'art italien et ses récits à la fin du Moyen Âge," in *La vérité. Vérité et crédibilité: construire la vérité dans le système de communication de l'Occident (XIIIᵉ–XVIIᵉ siècle)*, ed. Jean-Philippe Genet, Le pouvoir symbolique en Occident (1300–1640) 2 (Paris–Rome: Publications de la Sorbonne–Publications de l'École française de Rome, 2015), 235.

68. Simone Piazza, "Il volto di Ambrogio. La forma del modello paleocristiano e alcune varianti altomedievali," in Boucheron and Gioanni, *La mémoire d'Ambroise*, 99–104.

69. Ivan Foletti, *Oggetti, reliquie, migranti. La basilica ambrosiana e il culto dei suoi santi (386–972)* (Rome: Viella, 2018), 53–93.

70. *Acta ecclesiae Mediolanensis ab eius initiis usque ad nostram aetatem*, ed. Achille Ratti (Milan: ex Typographia Pontificia sancti Iosephi, 1890–97) vol. 3, c. 383. See Navoni, "'Ambrosius quem sibi imitandum,'" 125 (see n. 20).

Notes

71. Gibert Dagron, *Décrire et peindre. Essai sur le portrait iconique* (Paris: Gallimard, 2007), 156.

72. Dagron, *Décrire et peindre*, 68–69.

73. Georges Didi-Huberman, "L'image-matrice. Histoire de l'art et généalogie de la ressemblance," in *Devant le temps. Histoire de l'art et anachronisme des images*, ed. Georges Didi-Huberman (Paris: Minuit, 2000), 59–83.

74. Carlo Bertelli, "La decorazione musiva a Milano dall'età paleocristiana alla carolingia," in *Pittura a Milano dall'Alto Medioevo al Tardogotico*, ed. Mina Gregori (Milan: Cassa di Risparmio delle Provincie Lombarde, 1997), 12.

75. Martin Raspe, "*Un naturale ritratto di Santo Ambrogio:* Carlo Borromeo und das Mosaikportrait in S. Vittore in Ciel d'Oro zu Mailand," in *Bild- und Formensprache der spätantiken Kunst: Hugo Brandenburg zum 65. Geburtstag*, ed. Martina Jordan-Ruwe and Ulrich Real, Boreas: Münstersche Beiträge zur Archäologie 17 (Münster: n.p., 1994), 203–15.

76. Rovetta, "Ambrogio in Pinacoteca Ambrosiana," 171–74.

77. Piazza, "Il volto di Ambrogio," 91–93.

AFTERWORD

1. Augustine, *Confessions* 6.3.3., trans. Edward Bouverie Pusey (n.p.: Cross-Reach, 2019), 35.

2. Guglielmo Cavallo, "Du *volumen* au *codex*, la lecture dans le monde romain," in *Histoire de la lecture dans le monde occidental*, ed. Guglielmo Cavallo and Roger Chartier (Paris: Seuil, 1997), 79–107.

3. Alberto Manguel, *A History of Reading* (New York: Viking, 1996), 61 et seq.

4. Jorge Luis Borges, "On the Cult of Books," in *Selected Non-Fictions*, ed. Eliot Weinberger, trans. Esther Allen, Suzanne Jill Levine, and Eliot Weinberger (New York: Penguin, 1999), 360.

5. Adriano Marchetti, ed., *Pascal Quignard: la mise au silence* (Seyssel: Champ Vallon, 2000).

6. Pascal Quignard, *Petits traités* (Paris: Gallimard, 2002), 2:60.

7. Pierre-Emmanuel Dauzat, *Les Pères de leur Mère. Essai sur l'esprit de contradiction des Pères de l'Église* (Paris: Albin Michel, 2001), 142.

8. Augustine, *Confessions* 8.12.29, trans. and ed. Albert Cook Outler, 1955. Reprinted by Dover Thrift Editions (Mineola, NY: Dover, 2002), 146.

9. Marina Tasinato, *L'œil du silence. Éloge de la lecture* (Lagrasse: Verdier, 1986), 22.

10. Tasinato, *L'œil du silence*, 27.

11. Walter Benjamin, "Theses on the Philosophy of History" [1940], *Illuminations*, ed. Hannah Arendt, trans. Harry Zohn (New York: Harcourt, Brace & World, 1968), 198 (thesis 6).

12. Walter Benjamin, *The Arcades Project*, trans. Howard Eilin and Kevin McLaughlin (Cambridge, Mass.: The Belknap Press of Harvard University Press, 1999), 447.

13. Patrick Boucheron, *Faire profession d'historien*, (Paris: Seuil, 2018), esp. 9–37. See also Patrick Boucheron, "Sauver le passé," preface to Walter Benjamin, *Sur le concept d'histoire* (Paris: Payot, 2013), 7–50; and Patrick Boucheron, "Dissiper l'aura du nom propre," in *Le roman français contemporain face à l'histoire. Thèmes et formes*, ed. Gianfranco Rubino and Dominique Viart (Rome: Quodlibet, 2014), 43–61.

14. Walter Benjamin, "Small History of Photography," in *On Photography*, ed. and trans. Esther Leslie (London: Reaktion Books, 2015).

15. Carlo Capponi, "L'altare d'oro attraverso i suoi restauri," in *L'altare d'oro di Sant'Ambrogio*, ed. Carlo Capponi (Milan: Silvana, 1996), 170.

INDEX

Index